Lord Dunmore's Folly

Treachery on the Ohio

ROBERT J. SHADE

Sunshine F

D1214194

Sunshine Hill Press, LLC

2937 Novum Road
Reva, VA 22735

Artwork with specific permission:
Front Cover: **Boundaries** by Pamela Patrick White
(www.whitehistoricart.com)

Map: **The Ohio Country 1774** by Antony Rozwadowski
(K Art and Design, Inc., www.k-artanddesign.com)

ISBN-10: 0692780750
ISBN-13: 9780692780756

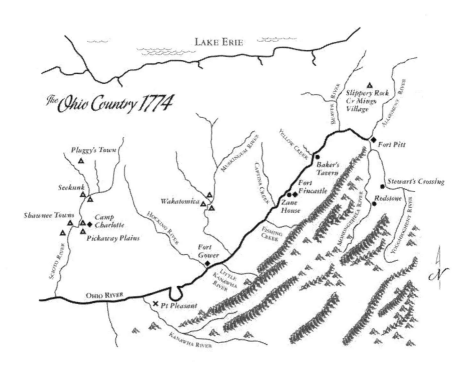

LAKE ERIE

The Ohio Country 1774

Slippery Rock
Cr Mingo
Village

Pluggy's Town

Seekunk

Shawnee Towns

Camp
Charlotte

Pickaway Plains

Wakatomica

Fort
Gower

Fort Pitt

Baker's
Tavern

Fort
Fincastle

Zane
House

Stewart's Crossing

Redstone

MUSKINGUM RIVER

CAPTINA CREEK

YELLOW CREEK

BEAVER RIVER

ALLEGHENY RIVER

HOCKING RIVER

FISHING
CREEK

MONONGEHELA RIVER

YOUGHIOGHENY RIVER

SCIOTO RIVER

LITTLE
KANAWHA
RIVER

OHIO RIVER

Pt Pleasant

KANAWHA RIVER

N

MAJOR CHARACTERS

Historical

John Murray, 4ᵗʰ Earl of Dunmore	Governor of Virginia
John Connolly	Governing Representative of Virginia in Pittsburgh
James Wood	Member of House of Burgesses from Frederick County, Virginia
Jean Moncure	Fiancée of James Wood
Angus McDonald	Master of Glengarry Manor, militia major of Frederick County
Anna McDonald	Wife of Angus
William Crawford	Militia captain/major from Stewart's Crossing
Daniel Morgan	Proprietor of freight wagon company, militia captain of Frederick County
Michael Cresap	Trader based in Redstone Old Fort, militia captain
Andrew McKee	British Government Indian Commissioner
Cornstalk	Shawnee war chief
White Eyes	Chief of Turtle Clan of Delaware Tribe
John Logan	Titular head of Mingo village near Yellow Creek in the Ohio Country
Andrew Lewis	Colonel of militia, Botetourt County
Simon Girty	Lieutenant in Pittsburgh area militia
Simon Butler	Long hunter, scout, and courier
Jonathan Zane	Scout on Wakatomica Raid

Fictional

Wend Eckert	Gunsmith of Frederick County, Virginia, Master of Eckert Ridge Farm
Peggy McCartie Eckert	Wend's wife
Joshua Baird	Militia scout of Frederick County
Alice Downy	Common-law wife of Joshua Baird
Simon Donegal	Farmer living at Eckert Ridge, former corporal of 77th Highlanders
Richard Grenough	Pennsylvania merchant and border trader
Barrett Penfold Northcutt	Advisor to Lord Dunmore
Matt Bratton	Waggoner employed by Richard Grenough
Freddie McCrae	Foreman in Richard Grenough's company
Geoffrey Caulfield	Gentleman from the Tidewater
Quinn	Caulfield's associate, former corporal of 11th Dragoons
Laughing Eyes	Mingo war captain from Yellow Creek village
Crooked Harry	English refugee wandering among Ohio tribal villages
Sally Potter	Settler widowed by war party attack near Braddock Road
Wolf Claw	War captain of the Slippery Rock Creek Mingo
Etchemin	Mingo warrior from Wolf Claw's village
Abigail Gibson/Orenda	English hostage wife of Wolf Claw
Henry Johann Eckert	Child of Wend Eckert and Abigail Gibson

Bernd Eckert   Eldest child of Wend and Peggy Eckert, junior apprentice to Wend

Andrew Horner   Senior apprentice to Wend Eckert

Evan McLeod   Family retainer to Angus McDonald

CONTENTS

PART ONE

Pittsburgh, Virginia

May – June 1774

CHAPTER ONE
Incident at Little Pebble Creek

Sally Potter had just got the baby down in his crib and was starting to chop up vegetables for the evening meal when Frank finished his drink of water. Her husband had come in from plowing the new field they had cleared over the winter and she could smell the sweat he had worked up during the long day. He stood up from the table and, glancing over to make sure that four year old Louisa wasn't watching, gave Sally a quick pat on her bottom. He smiled at his wife and then walked back out to the barn to feed the animals and milk the cow.

Sally's first indication of trouble was a sharp cry from the barnyard. She looked out the window by the door and saw Frank lying motionless on the ground next to the corn crib. Standing over his body, war club in hand, was a tall warrior in red and black war paint, rings in his ears, head shaved except for a scalp-lock. A firelock hung over his shoulder on a sling and a hatchet was stuck in his belt. She saw at least four other similarly dressed and painted warriors moving around the yard. She instantly closed and locked the shutters, slammed the door shut, and then dropped the bar in place.

She knew they must get out of the house fast. Slipping a knife from the counter into the strings of her apron, she ran to the baby's crib and picked him up, then called to Louisa. Sally lifted the little girl, who — *thank God* — was too surprised to say anything, out the back window. Then, with baby Henry in her arms, she quickly followed the girl. She pulled the shutters closed behind them, hoping that the Indian band would think she had forted up inside. Sally whispered to Louisa to be quiet and then quickly led her down the path to the creek, fearing that any second they would be confronted by a warrior. But it soon became evident that they had made it out of the house before the war party had fully surrounded the log cabin.

The banks of Little Pebble Creek were no more than fifty yards from the cabin, down a gentle, heavily wooded incline. Sally knew the trees and underbrush would make the three of them invisible from the cabin but that was scant comfort, for the Indians would soon figure out that she had run down the path. Her first goal was to reach the banks of the stream, which were several feet high and overgrown with bushes and trees. She knew the foliage would provide cover for a brief period.

They reached the creek, which was about 30 feet wide and varied in depth between a few inches and as much as three feet. Without hesitation, Sally climbed down the bank and into the cold water. She steeled herself against the shock which passed through her body. Louisa followed. Sally instinctively took a step downstream and then abruptly stopped. She suddenly realized that the war party would expect her to head down toward the wagon track — Braddock's Road — which was just under five miles away. She turned and, creeping along the overhang of the bank, took Louisa's hand and led her upstream, making as little noise as possible. They went about a hundred yards and then Sally saw the tiny island. She had forgotten it was there. It was a narrow, sandy strip of land across the creek from them and separated from the far bank by a shallow split of the stream which was only three or four feet wide. It was covered by two fallen trees and a mass of shrubs and hardly recognizable as separate from the other bank, even in broad daylight. And, thankfully, the dusk was rapidly gathering. They crossed the stream and found hiding places behind the trees. Sally prayed that they could stay hidden until full darkness arrived.

They had no sooner found hiding places than she heard voices downstream, clearly coming from the same place where they had entered the creek. The warriors shouted to each other a few times but were soon silent. Then she saw flames shooting high on the other side of the creek. The war party had torched the farmstead!

It was near a half-hour later, with thick darkness all around them, that Sally heard the noise: a quiet splashing in the stream. Someone was carefully coming upstream, searching for them in the night. Sally stared toward the sound. In a few minutes, she made out the shadowy figure of a single warrior who was moving for a few steps, then stopping and looking around at the banks of the creek. She looked at Louisa who was frozen in terror. Sally began to shake with fear and hugged Henry tight. Luckily, the one-year old seemed oblivious to the danger and merely curious about what was happening.

Sally moved her hand slowly to her waist, found the knife, and grasped the handle tightly. In a few moments the Indian was in front of their position.

And in that instant, the baby made a burping sound. It was barely audible, but enough to alert the warrior. He stopped, looked over at the little island, and Sally imagined that his eyes were boring into her. He slowly turned and crept, one cautious step at a time, toward them. She felt rising panic as he approached. Soon he must see or sense something.

In seconds he was within three feet of her face with only a bush between them. In his right hand she saw the shape of a hatchet. He cautiously reached out with his left hand and started to push aside the foliage directly in front of her face.

Instantly Sally released the hold she had on Henry with her left arm and sprang directly at the warrior, thrusting the knife forward with all the power in her right arm. The blade punctured his throat just below the chin and she drove it in up to the hilt. The man's eyes opened wide in surprise, so wide that she could see the whites even in the dark. He sank to his knees. Sally was seized with an overwhelming panic, fearing that even in his pain, the warrior would lash out at her with the tomahawk. She pulled the knife out and repeatedly slashed at his neck and face. He fell to the sand of the island and she began a frenzied stabbing of his chest which soon became a wet pulp.

Her panic subsided only when Louisa said in a calm, quiet voice, "Mama, Indian man dead."

Sally Potter stopped stabbing and knelt silently over the body, listening for any sounds. But everything was still except for the pounding of her heart and her gasping breath. Even the night insects were quiet. Then, after long moments, the sounds of the forest began to return. She listened carefully for a long time, but could hear nothing which sounded like it came from a human. She reached down and cleaned the knife in the sand and then slipped it back into her apron string. Then, shivering, she grabbed the body by an arm and dragged it over the island and into the shallow water next to the creek's bank. She quickly covered it with brush.

She picked up Henry and turned to her daughter. "Come on, Louisa," she whispered, "We need to be gettin' out o' here."

Sally knew they must to get to the road. It led westward to the little hamlet of Ransome's Tavern. If she got to the road, she could take it to the settlement and might even have the fortune of meeting travelers. She felt her only option was to follow the creek down to the ford where the road crossed. But that was where she thought the war party would be searching for her.

They started down the creek and so began the longest, most painful night of Sally's twenty-three years. She would move through the water a hundred,

5

two hundred yards, and then hole up under an overhang of the bank, often among the exposed roots of a tree, while she listened for suspicious sounds. At one point, the baby became cranky and then broke into open crying. Clearly he had gone into his clout. She took the clout off, washed his bottom with creek water, and realized that she couldn't put the dirty cloth back on or the baby would start to cry again. So she made a sling of her apron by tying the lower part around her neck and put Henry inside without anything on his bottom. It was the best she could do and at least it took most of his weight off her arms.

Right after that it began to rain. It started as a drizzle but soon became steady and drenching. The May night and the creek were cold enough, and their clothing was already soaked, but the rainfall chilled them to the bone.

Sally guessed it was near two in the morning, and they had gone maybe a couple of miles, when she heard the voices of warriors again. She figured the Indians had heard the baby crying earlier, which had put them back on her trail. Now they were up on the bank across from where she and the children huddled against some massive roots and she could tell they were discussing what to do. She hoped they had again lost her trail. After a few moments the voices stopped and all was quiet. She stayed under the overhang for what must have been another hour. Soon Louisa's teeth were chattering, even though the child made a brave effort to grit her mouth shut.

The cold forced them to start moving again just so their bodies would generate a little heat. Sally decided they would try to walk beside the creek, so that they wouldn't be quite so cold. They went perhaps half a mile that way, but it was slow, hard going. Bushes tore at their clothing and skin, and their feet were cut up by the twigs and stones even more than the pebbles of the creek had done. And they definitely made more noise. At one stop, she swore she heard something or someone moving through the undergrowth on the other side of the creek. Finally, she decided that the creek was the lesser of two evils and led Louisa back into the water.

Somehow, they finally made the ford where the wagon road crossed the creek — just as the rain-filled sky started to lighten with the promise of a gloomy dawn.

But Sally Potter was finished.

She was frozen and soaked to the bone from the rain and the creek water. The soles of her feet were torn to shreds from the sharp objects in the creek and the forest; she was exhausted from carrying the baby. She simply couldn't move her legs anymore. Sally flopped down on the muddy ground beside a fallen tree right where the road entered the creek. But she dared to hope that they had left the war party behind.

She had no idea how long the three of them sat there by the log, too tired to do anything more. The rain continued, but light was increasingly making its way through the clouds. Then Louisa tapped Sally on the shoulder and pointed upstream to the creek bank. "Mama, I see Indian men there."

Sally turned to look and realized in horror that she had failed to elude the war party. A hundred yards up the creek bank stood four warriors looking at them, talking among themselves and sometimes pointing to where they sat. Clearly they were deciding what to do with their prey.

At any moment they would come for them and it would be over.

She knew that they would kill her, for she was too exhausted to travel with them as a hostage. They might take the children or they might simply dispatch them and be done with it. She was too exhausted to feel fear for herself; she felt only shame that she hadn't been able to do more to protect Henry and Louisa. She looked up again and saw that the warriors had spread out and were cautiously approaching them from different directions. They were now only thirty or forty yards away.

But now Louisa was tugging at her sleeve again. "Mama, there's a man."

Sally said, in a resigned voice, "Yes, Louisa, I see them."

The girl tugged even more urgently. "No, Mama: Man on the hill." She pointed up the road to the top of the low ridge to the East.

Sally lifted her eyes and was startled to see that the child was right. A man sat his horse at the very crest, looking down toward the creek. The horse was jet black, long-legged, powerfully built, and stood as still as the rider. Through the drizzle, Sally could make out that the man was wearing a gray greatcoat. Slung over his right shoulder, with a strap across his chest, was a longrifle with the butt beside his head and the barrel hanging down along the left side of the horse. He wore a black, broad brimmed hat with one side turned up against the round crown. The rider was staring down at Sally and her children. Sally's heart skipped a beat and suddenly she felt hope surge within her.

With all the strength in her body, Sally screamed one word only at the rider: "Indians!" It was all she could get out. She reached out and pointed upstream.

The man turned in his saddle and his eyes followed in the direction of her arm. He sat scanning the creek and the forest for what seemed an eternity.

Then, finally, the rider moved. He reached down to pick up something which was hanging on a strap from his neck and put it to his mouth. Suddenly a shrill sound pierced the quiet of the woods. Sally realized he was blowing a whistle. Then she saw his hand go down to the front of his saddle and pull a pistol from its holster. He held the firelock over his head and swung it round in a circle. Then he pivoted the horse so it was facing down the other side of the hill and began waving the pistol as if signaling to someone back below the crest.

In a moment the man swung his horse around again and dug his heels into the animal's sides. The black horse raised its head, let out a loud whinny, and charged down the hill toward the creek at the gallop, the racing hooves splashing mud and water at every stride.

Sally turned and looked at the warriors. They had all stopped and turned to stare at the rider as he swept down the hill. Then, as she watched, they rushed to take cover.

She looked around to the road again to see the man and horse pull up in a spray of mud right beside them. The gray-coated rider threw down from the horse and was quickly at her side. She looked into his face and was surprised see it was stonily set and businesslike; only the blue eyes seemed to be alive as they scanned the woods in the direction of the hidden warriors. Then, in a calm, conversational tone, he said, "Ma'am, take the baby in your arms and shelter yourself alongside the log." He pushed her down as she cradled Henry, who was now crying loudly. "Here, little girl," the man said and then gently pressed Louisa to a prone position behind the log.

He went to his knees beside Sally, leaning over so that he covered her and the baby with his body, at the same time steadying the pistol on the top of the log as he aimed. Suddenly the pistol fired, the sharp report startling Sally.

"Well, I got a piece of that one, but not all of him." The horseman spoke quietly and evenly as if he was telling a story to someone across the dinner table. Then he put the pistol into the right pocket of the coat and pulled out a second from the left pocket. Sally heard a click as he pulled the cock back. Then she also heard something else; the sound of more horses' hooves coming down the hill. Soon she saw two more horses pull to a stop beside them and their riders dismount and take their place beside the first man.

"I've made out three or four of them, Joshua," the man crouching over Sally said to a tall, rangy man with a stubble beard who looked to be in his late forties. "And I put a ball into one of them, but not good enough to finish him."

The bearded man said, "Yeah, well, you're out of practice at this sort of thing. You spend too much time working in that shop. And you practice shootin' against wooden targets that don't move. I keep tellin' you to spend more time out hunting."

The third man spoke up in a thick accent Sally thought might be Scottish. Indeed, he wore a funny, round, blue hat like those Sally had seen on Highland soldiers back during the war with the French when she was a little girl. "Joshua, that's 'na in the cards for the lad here. Not with the tight leash Peggy's got on him these ten years. She'll 'na be allowing him to go on long hunts or to militia muster just for the fun of it."

The man called Joshua snorted, "You got that right, Donegal. Peggy's spent so much time in her father's tavern, she damn well knows what goes on at hunts and musters."

The man crouching above Sally sighed, shook his head, and said, "It might be good if you two talked a little less about my wife and made use of those rifles. So far I've done all the shooting." He reached up and unslung the rifle from his shoulder, laying it across the tree trunk.

Seconds after he spoke, the older man fired his rifle and the Highlander observed, "Damned if I don't believe you got him, Joshua. He went right down."

There was silence for a few long minutes. Then the young man in the gray coat put his hand on Sally's shoulder and said, "You can relax, ma'am. It looks like they're running away. I expect they don't like the odds."

After a few minutes, Joshua said, "I'm going out to look around for sign, particularly where that brave went down. They'll have carried him off, but I might pick something up."

The older man got up and headed into the woods. Sally noticed that he walked with a pronounced limp of his left leg. She looked up at the man who had been first to arrive, who seemed to be about thirty. "You came up just in time. I thought we was finished."

"You sure do look done in, ma'am. What happened to you?"

Sally told him her name and explained the events of the preceding night while the two men listened. She had just finished when there was the noise of horse hooves and wagon wheels and she looked up the hill to see two great Conestoga freight wagons with six horse teams coming down toward the ford, the drivers walking along beside them.

The man in the gray coat said, "It's all right, Mrs. Potter, those wagons are with us. We're going to get you and your children into one of them and warm you up. Then we'll take you up to Ransome's Tavern."

The Scotsman waved the wagons to a stop, then climbed up into the first Conestoga, to emerge with an armful of wool blankets. He carefully draped them around each of the Potters. Meanwhile, Joshua had come back from the woods, carrying a hatchet.

"Wend, Donegal, take a look at this. We was fighting Shawnee's: That's a Shawnee clan marking on the handle if I ever saw one."

Sally spoke up and couldn't hide the bitterness in her tone. "You was fighting one of Chief John Logan's war parties, that's who it was. It was Logan the Mingo who was responsible for killing my Frank, even if he wasn't there himself."

Joshua looked at Sally with deep puzzlement on his face. "Miz Potter, are you sure what you're saying? I know John Logan well. I've hunted with him and stayed with him in his home many a time. Logan is the greatest friend of the white man there is among the tribes. He didn't lift no hatchet during the French War, or even Pontiac's War when almost all the tribes was agin' us."

The younger man said, "Joshua, I thought Logan lived up north of Aughwick, near old Fort Granville. What would he be doing here in Virginia?"

"He moved westward, Wend, right after the Pontiac fight. There wasn't much sense for him to stay in Pennsylvania with all the other Mingoes gone to the Ohio. I heard he's been living with his family in a village down southwest of Fort Pitt."

Sally Potter spoke up again. "Chief Logan may be your good friend. But all I know is that everybody says John Logan is leading these raids. There was supposed to be some big hurt done to his family by settlers; I don't know the whole story. But he's got Mingoes and Shawnees working together; bands of young men anxious to take to the war trail. They hit a place ten miles away last week and now your good friend killed my husband and burned our farm."

She broke down, tears rolling over her cheeks.

Without another word, the young man in the gray coat gathered her up in his arms and helped her into the Conestoga. He fixed up a comfortable place for her and the two children to lie between blankets on top of the cargo.

Sally felt herself starting to drift off to sleep in the warmth of the wool coverings. Then she roused herself. "I'm ashamed, Mister. I ain't thanked you for saving us and I don't even know your name or where you're from."

The man smiled broadly, the first time she had seen his face with any kind of real expression. It was a handsome and kindly face, the blue eyes topped with light brown hair pulled back in a queue. There was an old, almost faded-out scar on the left side of his face just before his ear. Then he took his hat off and Sally was startled to see that there was a bald spot of scarred flesh under the queue at the back of his head, as if he had been partially scalped. He saw her staring and said, "Yes ma'am, the Mingoes took part of my scalp when I was a lad, almost fifteen years ago now. And they killed my family, just like they did your husband. So it seems we got something in common."

He looked at her for a moment. "But to answer your question, my name's Wendelmar, ma'am, Wendelmar Eckert. Most people just call me Wend. We're all from the town of Winchester and on our way to Fort Pitt with a load of muskets for the garrison. I'm a gunsmith and I've got a contract with the colony to rebuild a bunch of old long pattern muskets into the newer short version. That what's in those boxes you're lying on, Mrs. Potter."

"Beggin' your pardon, sir. *Wendelmar*? What kind of name is that? I ain't never heard of anyone with that name before. Sounds sort of Dutch to me, but you sure talk like you was Ulster, same as us."

Wend Eckert grinned broadly. "Why Mrs. Potter, I'd have to say that I'm a lot of things." He paused and she could see he was working to choose the right words. "I guess you could say that I'm German by birth, Ulster by adoption, Highlander by battle, and," he thought a moment, then laughed out loud, "I'm a Virginian by the order of a Pennsylvania sheriff!"

Sally didn't know what to say to that, but she didn't need to, for Eckert smoothed the blankets over her and the children and put his finger to his mouth for her to be quiet. He dismounted from the wagon and Sally felt a great, irresistible drowsiness sweeping over her. Then, just as she was nearly asleep, she had a vision of Frank leaning over her just like Wend Eckert had been. He was smiling and he said, "It's all right Sally: You did the best you could and you got the children away safely down to the ford."

And that was the last thing she remembered until she woke up hours later when they reached Ransome's Tavern.

CHAPTER TWO

Braddock's Road

The little caravan proceeded with great caution along Braddock's Road to Ransome's Tavern. Wend was fearful that the war party which had chased Sally Potter, or perhaps another roving band, might stage an ambush. He stationed Joshua Baird, who had years of scouting with the army and possessed an almost supernatural sense of impending danger, ahead at the point. Eckert himself rode directly ahead of the two wagons while Donegal rode rearguard. The two waggoners, Jake Cather and Elijah McCartney, walked with the reins of their six-horse teams in their hands. But they had brought out their longrifles from the wagons and placed them on specially constructed racks on the side of the Conestoga wagons which made the weapons rapidly available. Baird frequently signaled the wagons to a stop while he investigated likely attack points or stopped on the crest of hills to survey the surrounding forest.

They arrived at the little village in mid-afternoon. Besides the log-built structures of the tavern and its stable which stood on the north side of the road, there was a store of the same construction directly across from it. A few small, rude cabins stood clustered around the two commercial buildings. The land around the hamlet was cleared for fields and Wend saw a couple of farmsteads to the north beyond the tavern. Baird had ridden in minutes before and he now stood at the front door of the tavern alongside a man wiping his hands on a white apron, whom Wend took to be the tavern keeper himself. A young stable boy held Baird's horse at a watering trough. As the wagons pulled to a stop on the road, a man and woman, both wearing aprons, came out to the front porch of the store and stopped to stare at the caravan.

The tavern keeper shouted across the road, "Paul, Lizzie, come quick! They've got Sally Potter and her children in the wagons! They was burnt out by a war party!"

The storekeeper and his wife ran across the road and joined the small group in front of the tavern. Wend dismounted from his black mare and climbed up into the lead wagon. He gently roused Sally, who came only half-awake. Then he picked her up from the blankets and carried her to the front of the wagon. Jake Cather stood with one foot up on the tongue and Wend gently handed the woman down. The waggoner carefully lowered her to the ground and put her on her feet. Sally instantly came fully awake and cried out in pain.

Wend shouted, "Somebody pick her up! Her feet are torn up from running barefoot!"

Donegal had just arrived. He scooped Sally up and cradled her in his arms. "Here, I'll carry her." He looked down at Sally and said softly, "Do 'na worry, Mrs. Potter. Sure and we'll get you into a nice bed."

The woman who had run from the store asked, "Sally, what happened?"

Sally reached out to touch the woman. "Oh, Lizzie, they kil't Frank and burned us out! I had to make my way down the creek with the children to get away!" She groaned. "My feet feel like they was on fire."

Wend, still up in the wagon said, "We've got the children here in the Conestoga. They're fine, but Mrs. Potter needs care right away."

Donegal glanced around. "Are we going to take her into the tavern?"

Lizzie exclaimed, "Oh, you poor dear; we'll take care of you." She turned to Donegal. "Mister, she ain't goin' to no tavern. Bring her over to our rooms behind the store where I can tend her personal. And bring the children, too."

Wend roused Louisa and she climbed down to the ground, rubbing her eyes and staring at the people crowding around. She looked up at Lizzie. "Oh, Mrs. Kertin, I was so scared by the Indians. And Ma was so brave; she killed one with her knife, right in the creek!"

Lizzie Kertin smiled down at the girl. "Lord, it must have been terrifying, but you're safe now, Louisa. You'll be living with us for a while." She took the girl by the hand.

Wend carefully handed the sleeping baby to Jake, who passed him to Lizzie's husband. Then, with Lizzie leading, Donegal carried Sally across the road to the store and up the front steps.

Wend jumped down from the wagon. He looked at Jake, who was the head waggoner. "Check out the wagons and get the horses watered. Then you and Elijah come on in to the tavern; we all could use a drink."

Jake nodded and turned to his wagons.

Joshua smiled broadly and winked at Ransome. "Now havin' a drink; that's the most sensible thing I heard anybody say all day!"

13

Ransome, who had been watching the Kertins take Sally and her children over to the store, rubbed his hands together and smiled at Wend and Joshua. "Sure enough that's a good idea. And I got whatever you're thirsty for, gentlemen; rum, good ale, even a little whiskey if that's your pleasure."

* * *

Wend and Joshua sat at a table in Ransome's common room. There were only a few small windows, which gave the place a gloomy atmosphere. A smoky fire flickered in the hearth, spreading the acrid smell of burning wood throughout the tavern. Wend could hear the chatter of female voices from the cook room and the aroma of roasting meat wafted into the common room, mingling with the wood smoke. Ransome himself brought their drinks and lingered to talk.

Wend told the tavern keeper how they had come upon the Potters at the ford and the details of the little fight which had sent the war party on its way.

Joshua spoke up. "Miz Potter, she was pretty mixed up in her mind when we found her. I can't blame her for that, what with all that happened. But she told us something I couldn't fairly credit. No, sir, I couldn't. She said that John Logan was behind the war party which hit her place and other raids out here." Baird shook his head. "I've known John for more than twenty years and never seen him take the warpath against the whites. Not only that, he always spoke for peace at council fires. I figure she must have heard some rumor what got all twisted in the telling."

Ransome cocked his head. "Shit, Baird, that ain't no twisted tale. That's the word which came to us from up Pittsburgh way." He sat down in a vacant chair and leaned over the table. "The truth is, Logan's family — almost all of it — was murdered by a party of white men."

Joshua sat up straight in his chair. "The devil you say! For God's sake, why?"

The tavern keeper raised an eyebrow. "I've got no clue why it happened, but it was right at the end of April. A bunch of men on their way down the Ohio to Kentucky massacred most of Logan's village at a place near Yellow Creek called Baker's Tavern. Wiped out all of Logan's close family, they did."

Wend and Joshua looked at each other, aghast. Then Baird asked, "So how did Logan escape?"

"Turns out, he and some of the men of the village were away on a hunt. After the massacre, the surviving Mingoes abandoned the village and found Logan and told him what had happened. So then he pledged to avenge his family and called for war. He recruited some Shawnee warriors and Mingoes from up at Seekunk. Since then they've been raiding the border."

Wend asked, "Who were these whites? Where did they come from?"

Ransome shook his head. "Don't know any more 'bout them, except for their leader: I was told it was Michael Cresap."

Joshua exclaimed, "Did I hear you right? You say Michael Cresap, old Colonel Tom Cresap's son?"

"Yeah, that's what I hear." Ransome got up and wiped his hands on his apron again. "Anyway, Logan has promised he's going to personally hunt down Cresap and along the way kill as many white people as he can." He started back toward his counter.

Joshua started to speak, but Wend quieted him and asked, "Is there any more you've heard, Mr. Ransome?"

The tavern keeper turned and thought for a moment. "One other thing: Logan has got several war parties sweeping the border, mostly led by young Shawnee hot-heads. But the most vicious of them is a war captain they call Laughing Eyes. He's a Mingo like Logan and he's got a pretty big party of Mingoes and Shawnees with him. He moves fast and don't take no prisoners. Sometimes Logan will let women and children go, or take hostages, if it suits his fancy. But Laughing Eyes just kills them all." Ransome raised his eyebrows and looked meaningfully at them. "You better hope you don't run into him on your way up to Pittsburgh." Then he turned and went back to work at the counter.

Joshua put his hand to his chin. "Wend, this is all crazy. First we got Logan, the most peaceful of Indians, out on the warpath. Then it turns out that the leader of the attack on his family is Michael Cresap; I met him when he was a lad. But now I hear he trades with the Indians; his post is up at Redstone Old Fort."

Wend said, "So attacking a peaceful village would ruin his business."

"Sure enough, Wend. I say there's a lot more going on here than we know."

"Maybe we'll be able to sort this all out when we get up to Pittsburgh." Wend was about to say more when Jake and Elijah walked into the common room. The two waggoners flopped down in chairs at the table.

Wend waved to Ransome. "Get these men some rum!" He turned to Jake. "Are we ready to go? We've already used up most of the day. Get your rum down and we'll get a few more miles under our belt before sunset."

Jake smiled crookedly and shook his head. "Eckert, we ain't gettin' out of here this afternoon, an' that's no lie. We got work to do on the wagons; a passel of work."

Wend grimaced. "What's wrong?"

Elijah took a deep gulp of the rum which Ransome had just set in front of him. "Ain't nothing exactly wrong. But both our wagons are overdue for greasing the wheels. We ought to stop here and get the job done."

Jake said. "We normally grease the wheels 'bout every hundred miles. We ain't done the job since we started out at Winchester and that's way beyond normal. That means we got to pull every wheel off, grease the axel, and then put it back on."

"You been pushing us hard," Elijah added, "and there ain't been no chance to do the work,"

Wend was frustrated. "The way I figure, we're only about fifty miles from Pittsburgh. And this incident has put us behind schedule. Won't your wheels hold up that long? Then you could do the work in Pittsburgh before we start back."

Jake made a face. "Maybe they will, maybe they won't. But ain't none of us run wagons over this road before. We got no idea 'bout the condition of the road ahead or the number of ridges and streams we got to cross." He paused and grimaced at Wend. "You want to take a chance on having to do this somewhere out on the road when something goes wrong? There's a perfect set-up to do the wheels here at the tavern. We got a good place for the horses and solid, level ground to jack the wagons up."

Wend turned to Jake. "So how long is this going to take?"

Jake screwed up his face and thought for a moment. "Things go right, we can get it done this afternoon. We can roll out of here first light tomorrow. But if anything slows us down, we'll be lucky to leave before noon tomorrow. Either way, we got to get crackin' if we're going to get as much done as possible while there's still light today."

Wend shrugged in surrender. "All right, go ahead and get started. Joshua and I will get the horses fed and on a picket line."

Jake smirked. "Eckert, you and Baird and Donegal got to do more than that. I need your strong backs to help get some of the load out of the wagons to make jacking easier. And then we'll need some help to manhandle the wheels; that will speed things up. Gonna' take all of us if you want to be back on the road early tomorrow!"

Wend and Joshua exchanged glances of resignation. Eckert said, "Of course we'll help." Then he thought of something. "Where's Donegal? It's not like him to miss out when rum is being passed around."

Elijah grinned. "Why, he's over at that store across the road. Playin' with that little Louisa, he is; keepin' her busy while the women take care of Miz Potter."

Wend nodded. "Well, Louisa is going to have to entertain herself for a while. I'll go get him and we'll all join you at the wagons."

Jake laughed and then turned to his compatriot. "Come on, Elijah; let's go get the jacks ready."

* * *

Jake Cather, wrench in hand, worked to tighten the hub on the right front wheel of his wagon. Wend, standing behind the waggoner, looked up and realized that the evening dusk was rapidly turning into the dark of night. He scanned the sky; it was clear and the moon was rising. Clearly they wouldn't be on the road at first light, for although work on Jake's wagon was essentially finished, the two front wheels of Elijah's still had to be completed. He sighed in resignation: these things always took longer than expected.

Joshua, who had just finished helping Jake fit the wheel onto the axle, was leaning against a hitching rail near the stable. Suddenly he stood up and put a hand to his right ear. "Hey, I hear wagon wheels and horse hooves. Lots of them; coming from the west."

Wend walked out to the road from the tavern yard. Now he could also hear the sound of wagons. Then, in the waning dusk, a man on foot emerged from around a bend in the road, longrifle in the crook of his left arm. Seconds later a farm wagon appeared, followed shortly by two carts. Men, women, and children rode in the vehicles or walked alongside. All the men and some of the women had firelocks at hand. Behind the vehicles a young man and woman lead two heavily loaded packhorses. Bringing up the rear was a herd of livestock — cattle and pigs mostly — tended by three boys with sticks in their hands.

The man in the lead waved the little procession to a halt in front of the tavern. Then he walked up to Wend and said, "Howdy, Mister. What place is this?"

"It's called Ransome's Tavern, sir." The man, dressed in a linen hunting shirt above brown leggings, was tall and lean, about Joshua's age, but with hair which was turning gray. He had deep-set, piercing eyes which Wend thought conveyed a sense of extreme earnestness, maybe even zealotry. Wend asked, "Where are you bound?"

"East; east, sir, beyond the mountains. We're seeking safety from the savages." The man extended his hand. "Grayson, sir, Reverend Eltweed Grayson. These people with me are part of my flock from a little farm settlement on the Monongahela, near thirty miles south of Pittsburgh."

The man and woman from the lead wagon had come to stand beside Grayson. Wend guessed the couple was in their mid-thirties. The woman, her voice filled with emotion, said, "We're done with this country! We watched three farms go up in flames one night last week. Then we spent two days forted up in the Reverend's house and stockade."

Grayson said, "The night the war party struck, I sent off a messenger to Pittsburgh. Two days later, a detachment of militia from Fort Pitt arrived. Then we went over to see what had happened to the families at them burnt out farms."

Other people from the caravan were gathering around. The door of the tavern opened and Ransome stepped out onto the little porch to look down at the refugees. Joshua, Donegal, and Elijah had come up to hear the conversation. Only Jake remained by the wagons, working with his wrench to secure the hub on his wagon wheel before all light was lost.

The reverend said, "We found every member of the families; every man woman, and child was dead. They had been shot or clubbed. But that wasn't enough for that war party. No, sir! They had taken their scalps and chopped the bodies into pieces." He shook his head. "I been on the border near twenty-five years and I ain't seen nothing like that butchery."

The young man who had been leading a pack horse said grimly, "We spent all day burying them three families and then saying words over them. One of the families was my brother's."

Grayson looked around. "The lieutenant who was leading the militia said they saw sign of maybe fifteen warriors in the party. He said it looked like the work of a war captain called Laughing Eyes; he don't take no prisoners and he always mutilates the bodies."

Wend looked up at Ransome, who cocked his head and returned a know-ing glance.

The woman from the first wagon said to Wend, "Mister, I ain't livin' this way anymore! I don't want my young ones spendin' their life with one eye over their shoulder and worried about every noise in the night when they take to their beds."

The woman's husband added, "We was livin' near Bedford during Pontiac's War in '63 and our farm got burned out when we had run to the fort. This Logan War looks to be as bad as things were in those days. If you weren't around back then, you haven't got no idea how bad it can get."

Wend said quietly, "I was there; I scouted for Bouquet and fought at Bushy Run."

The man looked at Wend for a long moment and then nodded. "Well, if you marched with Bouquet you know what can happen." He announced to the crowd, "We've had enough. We're going to find some safe land back to the east of the mountains."

The refugees all nodded and many spoke words of agreement.

Grayson said, "I'm shepherding these families all the way to Wills Creek — to old Fort Cumberland. Then I'll be coming back to Pittsburgh. That's where the rest of the people in our settlement have gone and are camping out until the trouble is over. Then they'll go back to their farms, what's left of them, and start over. And I'll be there to help them."

Ransome looked up at the moonlit night sky. "You aren't planning to travel at night are you, Reverend?"

Grayson shook his head. "No, sir, we're not. We been pushing hard every day; traveling from first light until it was right dark. Usually we camp alongside the road." He looked around the tavern and the little village. "We'd be mighty obliged if you'd see fit to allow us to lay up here for the night."

Ransome smiled broadly. "You and your people are quite welcome. If you need provisions and supplies, between Kertin's Store and my tavern, we can pretty much accommodate your needs. That is, provided you got the wherewithal."

The reverend glanced sideways at his fellows. "Naturally we would pay for what we need." He hesitated, "We got some coin, but we prefer barter if that would be acceptable."

Ransome screwed up his face and looked at the wagon and carts jammed with personal belongings. "Barter would depend on what you got available."

Grayson nodded with a knowing expression. "Naturally, my good man."

* * *

Later, after finishing supper, Wend and Joshua warmed themselves at a table before the hearth in Ransome's common room. Each had a tumbler of rum near at hand. Wend was starting to feel the effect of the long day and was contemplating an early bed.

Suddenly his thoughts were interrupted by the sound of the tavern's front door squeaking as it swung open. Wend looked over to see a man standing there, framed in the doorway, his left hand on the latch, looking around the room as his eyes adjusted. The man was silhouetted by the bright moonlight, which flowed around him. For a second Wend thought he was from the refugee caravan, but then realized he was too well dressed to be a common settler. The man was at least six feet tall, of thin build, and wore a short jacket over a pair of breeches and calf-length boots. On his head was a broad-brimmed hat with a round crown. He carried saddlebags in his right hand and a pair of holstered horse-pistols slung by their straps over his left shoulder.

Ransome looked up from the counter and grinned broadly. "Captain Crawford! Good to see you, sir! I've been expecting you to be stopping in on your way home."

Crawford swung the door shut and walked over to the counter. "Yes, Ransome, I'll be glad to get back to my plantation. I've been hurrying; we kept to the road tonight past nightfall because I knew we could put up here at your place."

Ransome nodded. "There's always space for you, Cap'n. You can have your usual room."

"Fine, Ransome. We put the horses in the stable and my man Dick will bed down in there, if you don't mind. He'll come around to the back door for some food. I hope you've still got something warm."

"That'll be just fine, Cap'n; we'll take care of him." Without being asked, Ransome pulled out a jug and poured a drink for his visitor.

Crawford nodded, picked up the drink and asked, "Who are all those people camping around the tavern? Settlers heading for the border country?"

"Naw, Cap'n. Just the other way: They're goin' back east over the ridges, scared out by this Indian uprising."

The captain paused with his tumbler halfway to his mouth. "Uprising? Have things gotten worse out on the Ohio?"

Ransome nodded. "Plenty worse, Cap'n; Mingo and Shawnee war parties are raiding the settlements from the Ohio all the way over to here." Then he gave Crawford a quick account of the Logan family murders and the stories told by the refugees. "Last week a war party burned out the Craig family; we saw the smoke from right here. And last night they hit the Potters down on Little Pebble Creek. Killed young Frank Potter, they did." Then he pointed to Eckert and Baird. "Those two gentlemen had a sharp fight down at the ford on the Little Pebble and kept Sally Potter and her two children from bein' killed this very morning."

Crawford looked toward the two of them, then picked up his drink and walked over to their table. "Good evening, gentlemen. I'm William Crawford; my place is about 20 miles ahead on the Youghiogheny River. I've been down at Wills Creek on business." He extended his hand.

Wend stood up and shook the proffered hand. "Wend Eckert, sir, from near Winchester. And it wasn't a real fight; just a few shots and the Indians went on their way."

He was about to introduce Baird when Crawford looked down at Joshua and exclaimed, "By God, I've seen you before, sir." He thought a moment. "It was back in '58; on Forbes' expedition to take Duquesne from the French. You were Colonel Bouquet's scout — you were with him all the time." He screwed up his face. "Your name's Bird, or something like that, isn't it?"

Joshua stood up and extended his hand. "*Baird*, Cap'n. Joshua Baird. An' you got a good memory. That be more'n fifteen years ago!"

"Yes, hard to believe, isn't it? Sometimes it seems like just yesterday. I was with the Virginia troops."

Wend asked, "Were you in the Virginia Regiment?"

"Not in it, but working with Washington's battalion." Crawford reflected a moment. "Washington and I go way back. In fact, he taught me my trade — surveying. Anyway, George was commander of the First Virginia at that time and the senior officer of all the Virginia troops in that campaign. So he asked me to raise a ranging company from the border country. They were a fine group of lads and dead shots with the rifle." He sipped his drink and asked, "So where are you headed?"

Wend answered, "Pittsburgh; I'm a gunsmith and have a contract with Virginia to recondition muskets for use by the militia. In fact, they're old long land pattern muskets used by the Virginia Regiment and other units back in the French war and Pontiac's fight. We shorten them, recondition the locks and other hardware, and make any necessary repairs to the stocks. Those two Conestogas out in the yard are carrying a hundred stand of arms for Captain Connolly's garrison up at Pitt."

"Well, that's a good idea. Last time I was up there, Connolly's troops were carrying a God-awful mixture of rifles, decrepit muskets, and even fowling pieces." Then he thought of something. "How many men do you have with you? I mean, if war parties are roaming between here and Pittsburgh, are you confident you can defend yourselves?"

"We've got five people, including the two waggoners. Everyone is armed and knows how to shoot. And we've got plenty of powder and lead."

Crawford smiled. "Well, given the conditions, I'd be obliged if my man and I could travel with you until we reach my place. That would give you two additional men who can acquit themselves well with firearms."

Wend must inadvertently have given Crawford a sharp look, for he raised his hand and said, "Yes, I allow my man to handle a weapon when the need arises, despite the laws about blacks. He's been with me for more than a decade and is completely trustworthy. Of course, I'll defer to your wishes if a slave with a firelock bothers you."

"Any man who can shoot will be welcome, particularly if you vouch for him, Captain." Wend smiled. "I doubt that any magistrates will be around to enforce the law."

Crawford grinned broadly. "Actually, I *am* the magistrate, Mr. Eckert! And you and your men are welcome to rest overnight at my place."

Wend smiled, "That sounds like a fine exchange to me, sir." He waved to a chair. "We'd be honored if you'd join us here before the fire!"

Just then Jake burst through the door into the common room, looked around, and spotting Wend, strode over to the table.

Wend noticed that the waggoner seemed agitated. He asked, "What's on your mind, Jake?"

"After the day we put in, I've been trying to settle down by our fire out in the yard. But I keep gettin' bothered by that preacher and his people."

Wend was puzzled. "How are they bothering you?"

"Well, they found a problem with one of those damned carts. Got a cracked axle, it does. I went over and took a look. The split has just started, but it damn well going to get worse. Truth is, I'd lay money it ain't goin' to last another day in conditions on this rough road."

Wend shrugged. "How does that affect us?"

"Well, that damned Elijah was standing by spouting off his mouth while I crawled under that cart. He mentioned to them that we got a flat iron bar made special for the purpose of being spiked along the length of an axle. It's made just for a situation like this."

Wend thought a moment. "Have we got one in each wagon?"

"That's a fact, Eckert. We carry it for emergencies. And now that reverend has been pesterin' me to give him one for the bloody cart. Talkin' to me about charity and quotin' the scriptures about helpin' your fellow man. Fact is, that brace ain't just the right size for their cart, but they could make it work."

Wend asked, "Couldn't they shape a piece of wood to serve the same purpose?"

"They could, but I doubt it would hold up long. Once an axle starts to go, you either got to replace it or brace it with iron. I learned that long ago."

Wend tapped his fingers on the table. "If we gave them one, we'd still have another. And it's unlikely we'll need to fix both wagons between here and Pittsburgh."

Jake gritted his teeth. "Like I told you before, we ain't got no idea what kind of conditions are ahead. And, fact is, them settlers cracked that axle on the very stretch of road we're aiming to travel." He shook his head. "I ain't the least disposed to part with a brace."

Crawford cleared his throat and said, "Perhaps I could help in this situation. I know the road well. There are some rough spots, but if you've made it this far, I think your big, heavily built Conestogas will be able to handle it." He hesitated a moment, then continued, "I saw those carts out in the yard. They're dangerously overloaded. That's what led to the cracked axle."

Jake said nothing but glared at Crawford in a way which made his thoughts perfectly clear.

Wend looked up at Jake. "As I said, I think it's unlikely that we would break two axles in the last fifty miles between here and Pittsburgh." Wend made up his mind. "Cather, go ahead and give those poor people one of your braces and the spikes they'll need to do the work."

"All right, you're the boss on this trip. But you better be the one to deal with Morgan when he finds out you been giving away our tools."

"Yes, I'll explain to Daniel. And we can get a blacksmith to forge you a new brace up there in Pittsburgh. I'll cover the cost."

Jake was still visibly unhappy but said nothing further. Then he slapped his hat back on his head and stocked out of the common room.

Crawford looked at Wend closely. "Is this man Morgan a hulking giant, with big fists and a ready wit?"

Wend nodded. "True enough, sir. He runs a freight line in Winchester. Fact is, he's a friend and neighbor of mine. I hired these wagons and the drivers from him."

Crawford smiled broadly. "Well, unless I'm mistaken, your neighbor is the same Daniel Morgan who was a private in my company of rangers; a man quick to laugh and quick to anger, a brawler without equal, and a teller of amusing tales around a campfire. But above all, he's a consummate marksman with a longrifle."

Wend cocked his head. "The very man, sir. It just goes to show, Captain Crawford, this may be a big land, but it's a small world out here on the border."

"Indeed it is, sir. And by the way, as long as we're going to be traveling together, why don't you call me William?"

* * *

The two waggoners finished greasing Elijah's wagon and had the front wheels remounted by two hours after dawn. While they worked to stow their tools and jacks and hitch up the teams, Wend, accompanied by Donegal, went to check up on Sally Potter's condition.

They found the young woman seated in a chair in the Kertin's great room, covered in blankets with her bandaged feet up on a stool. Seeing her for the first time with good color in her face, cleaned up and with her blond hair washed and put up, Wend was surprised at her attractiveness. He was also surprised to see Louisa eagerly take Donegal's hand and call him "Uncle Simon." Wend exchanged a few words with Sally and the Kertins, and then the two of them left to join their compatriots in the tavern yard.

As they descended the steps from the porch of the store, Wend gave Donegal a sidewise glance and smiled wryly, "*Uncle* Simon?"

Donegal shrugged, "Do you 'na know I have a soft spot in my heart for the wee ones? Do I 'na play with your children all the time?"

"That you do. And all of them love you." He paused as a thought hit him. "But I just had an idea that maybe it's Mrs. Potter who you really want to play with."

Donegal's face turned red. "For God's sake, Wend, the thought has 'na crossed my mind. But now that you mention it, she is a pretty little lass."

Wend smirked. "Now, my old friend from the 77th Highlanders, I do seem to remember that it's an army custom for a new widow to take a husband almost immediately to keep her and her children on the ration list."

"Well, that's true enough. And the fact is, the widow Potter is safe in the hands of the Kertins for right now. But it is God's truth she's going to have to find a way to support herself pretty fast."

"Donegal, Sally Potter can't be more than twenty-three. And you're a man of thirty-seven; that's a damned unlikely pairing."

The Highlander reared up and adjusted his blue bonnet. "I'll remind you that I'm a very *youthful* thirty-seven, by God! And a man of property and some means. Such a union is 'na unheard of in this world!"

Wend laughed. "Yes, it's not; but of course, you're not actually contemplating any such thing."

Donegal screwed up his face and shrugged his shoulders. "Like I said, the thought had 'na entered my head until you brought it up!"

After they departed the tavern, Joshua took the point while Wend and Crawford rode side by side in front of the wagons. Crawford's slave Dick rode at the rear of the wagons, leading three pack horses loaded with Crawford's baggage and items purchased in Cumberland. He also balanced a rifle across his pommel.

After several hours, with the sun almost overhead, Crawford waved toward an open area in the distance on the left. He casually remarked, "Over there, that's Great Meadows," and looked at Wend as if it should mean something to him.

Wend was perplexed. He had no idea what significance the place might have.

Crawford smiled. "Doesn't mean anything to you, does it?"

Wend shook his head, "Sorry, but *no*."

The older man smiled again. "Well, you must have been in school back then. But that's where the first real fight of the French War took place; just under twenty years ago. Young Washington and a few hundred men tried to stand off a more powerful force of French. They built a mean little fortification called Fort Necessity, but they were overwhelmed. George had to surrender."

"William, when you mentioned Fort Necessity, it roused my memory. I remember my parents talking about it when I was just ten."

"Yes, the fight would have been better known under that name. Anyway, George can't shake his recollections of that defeat. He told me that he still agonizes over what more he could have done."

A short time later, Crawford said. "Right around here is where we buried General Braddock."

Wend looked around. They were on a slight downslope leading to the ford of a small creek. But he saw no sign of a grave.

Crawford laughed at Wend's bemusement. "My friend, the general's remains are probably right under our horses' hooves right now."

Wend, puzzled, said, "I don't understand."

"The general was mortally wounded at the battle which took place a few miles south of Fort Duquesne." Crawford looked at Wend. "You've heard about the massacre of his expedition, I take it?"

"Of course, sir. Everyone has heard of that."

"Well, I was an ensign with a company of Virginia provincials at the battle; just got away with my life." He shook his head and then said, "Washington wasn't in command of any troops; he was a volunteer aide to Braddock. But in the panic and demoralization in the days after the battle, he essentially made a lot of the decisions, even though the colonel of the 48th Foot, a man named Dunbar, was technically in command."

Crawford gathered his thoughts, then continued, "Braddock lingered for four days and we carried him along in a wagon as we retreated. After he finally expired, we buried the good general right in the middle of the road." He paused and grimaced. "That was George's decision. He was afraid that the Indians would dig up the body and desecrate it if they could find the grave. Then he had all the wagons of the column drive over it and the troops march across it."

Wend asked, "So there's no way to know precisely where it is?"

"No. Washington, always the good surveyor, noted some landmarks — trees and rocks and such — but weather and other things have changed the terrain. Over time, the path of the wagon track has probably shifted somewhat. It was just on this side of that stream ahead, but God knows, its banks may have moved in twenty years. George came up here a couple of years ago and we looked around together. We soon realized we'd never be sure of the exact spot."

A question occurred to Wend. "Why was Washington so concerned about Braddock?"

Crawford made a tight smile. "After the loss at Great Meadows, the British were rather displeased with George's handling of events and, quite frankly, he was shunted aside. But Braddock respected his knowledge and allowed him to volunteer for service on his staff. He treated him with great consideration during the course of the campaign. And of course, George then performed rather gallantly during the battle and afterward. He's always been extremely grateful for the chance the general gave him to renovate his reputation."

Their conversation was interrupted as the horses splashed through the creek and then the waggoners shouted at their teams as they pulled the Conestogas through the water and up the low bank on the other side.

Wend looked ahead and saw a steep ridge which started about a mile before them.

Crawford saw him staring at the mountain. "That's Laurel Ridge ahead. The road leads up along the side and then through a small gap down into a great wide valley. My place is a few miles up the valley along the Youghiogheny River, at a place called Stewart's Crossing."

Wend asked, "Is that the same Laurel Ridge which is just east of Fort Ligonier?"

"Yes, the ridge runs north and south for a long distance. Ligonier and Forbes Road are about thirty miles to the north of us now."

Wend said, "It's going to take us a long time to cross that ridge with these wagons."

Crawford nodded. "Yes, we'll spend the night up on the mountain. I know a plateau area that will make a good camp and we can reach it before full nightfall if we push hard."

Wend smiled. "That's perfect, because I'm anxious to get on to Pittsburgh." He turned around and waved for the wagons to close up with them.

Crawford, still looking up at the ridge, said, "There's something else to keep in mind: If we're going to encounter a war party between here and my place," he raised his hand and pointed to the heavily wooded mountain, "that's where it's going to happen."

* * *

Crawford's prediction proved all too correct. The caravan was well up on the narrow road which hugged the eastern side of Laurel Ridge, the horses working hard, their harness straps taking a heavy strain, when Joshua waved for Wend and Crawford to join him. The two trotted ahead of the laboring wagons and joined the scout where he sat his mount on a high spot.

Joshua announced nonchalantly, "We got some friends up there in the rocks near the crest."

Wend looked up the mountain and saw an outcropping ahead and above them. A group of Indians stood looking back at the travelers, not bothering to hide.

Crawford said. "Rather brazen, aren't they?"

Joshua said. "That's the truth. I've been watching them for a while. They been movin' along through the woods up there, matchin' our pace. An' they haven't been takin' much trouble to hide. I figure that's 'cause it's a pretty big war party — I've counted at least eleven or twelve of them."

Wend felt a spark of irritation. He asked, "Why'd you wait so long to tell us, Joshua?"

"I wanted to get a good idea how many of them was up there 'fore I talked with you. And travelin' on this road, there ain't much we can do about them 'cept keep movin'."

Wend looked back down the road at the wagons and then ahead. He glanced over at Crawford. "Joshua's right; with this narrow road and the slope of the hill, we can't pull over and fort up. And we can't turn and go back down."

Crawford smiled tightly, but there was no sign of fear in his voice when he spoke. "Indeed, the strong cards seem to be in their hands." Then he reached back into one of his saddlebags and pulled out a brass spyglass, extended it to full length, and sighted up at the outcropping. After a few seconds he said, "They're five of them standing in sight up on that rock. It looks like they're talking things over." He scanned the area around the rocks. "Mr. Baird is quite correct about the size of the war party. I can see other groups of men sitting around under trees next to the rocks."

Joshua shook his head. "They damn well know they're out of rifle range. Only a chance shot could bring one of them down."

Wend said. "All we can do is have everyone keep their firelock at hand, move on, and be ready to respond when they attack. Maybe we'll be able to find a little cove or wide spot where we can set up a better defense."

Crawford nodded. "I agree — that is the only option. But I don't know of any spot suitable for forting up until we get to the place we were planning to camp."

Wend swung his horse around. "William, I'll go back and make sure everyone understands the situation." He paused for a second and said to both men: "Wait here until the wagons and pack horses come up. We'll keep closed up as we move so we can concentrate our fire when they come at us."

* * *

The men of the caravan traveled on in a high state of tension, each with a firelock in hand, each keeping his eyes glued on the forest to detect the attack which they knew must come. It was a cool day, but Wend soon found himself perspiring and listening for the sound of a shot fired at them or the sudden outbreak of war whoops and shrieks. He wondered if the war party was running on ahead through the bush; perhaps some of the warriors preparing to fell a tree which would block the road while others got into position to fire on the stymied caravan.

They went several miles in that manner but no attack materialized. That did not relieve the tension; rather it increased because none of them could guess why the Indians were holding off. Finally, to Wend's great surprise, the caravan arrived safely at the planned campsite at early dusk. The waggoners began unhitching their teams while Donegal and Dick rigged a picket line for all of the horses. Everyone remained on strained alert, eyes scanning the surrounding bush.

Wend assessed their position: They were on a flat plateau. It was obvious the site was used frequently by travelers; there were campfire ashes and other debris. Across the wagon track from their campsite was another fairly open area which ended in a high, round hill with steep sides.

Donegal came up to Wend with a piece of discolored leather in his hand. He held it up so Wend could see it. "Look what I turned up while we were setting up the picket line: It's a cartridge pouch with the number of the 48th Foot on it!"

Crawford spoke up. "Not an unexpected find, Simon; this was the camp of Colonel Dunbar's portion of Braddock's expedition. He led the main body which was following some distance behind the advance force; that was the party of about 1,200 men which actually engaged the French and Indians. This is the camp to which all the surviving troops and waggoners retreated after the great massacre. Many men died of wounds here; you'll find their graves over there." He pointed into the bush. Crawford paused to reflect a minute, then continued, "It was here that Dunbar made the decision to retreat and burned most of his wagons – near 150 of them — and destroyed other equipment he couldn't easily carry with him."

All the men, having heard Crawford's words, looked around the site for a moment and then went back to their work. Wend, Crawford, and Joshua stood together discussing the situation.

Joshua said, "Could be the savages been trailin' us out of sight, fixin' to attack us tonight or at first light. Wouldn't put it past them."

Crawford nodded. "Indeed — I've seen that happen. We'll have to be on alert through the night. We won't get much rest."

Wend said, "Everyone will have to take watches and sleep on their arms." Then he thought of something else. "We'll have to make a cold camp — no fire to silhouette us."

Crawford agreed. "That makes sense, though we'll be damned cold up here on the mountain."

Baird made a face. "Now just be holdin' on, the both of you! I said they might have followed us, but think on it; we ain't really sure there be any Indians out there. I ain't seen no sign of them since we left that outcropping where they was spyin' on us." He looked around impatiently. "I got a hunch those devils didn't follow us at all and I damn well don't fancy spendin' the night without hot tea or decent food and freezing my ass to boot."

Wend felt a surge of impatience. "The truth is, Joshua, we don't know either way. Your hunch may be right, but we can't take any chances."

Baird snorted. "I'll tell you what: I'm going out on a little scout to see if I can turn up any sign of our friends."

Crawford asked, "Mr. Baird, it's coming on dark. How can you tell if the war party is skulking around out there?"

"There'll be a moon up soon. And after all these years I can sniff out a warrior at fifty yards by his smell and hear the sound of them if they're around."

Wend slowly nodded and said to Crawford, "That's true: Joshua's as quiet and crafty in the bush as any warrior." Then a worrisome thought came to him. "But I don't like the idea of you going out there with that left leg of yours. You can't move fast anymore."

Joshua laughed. "Shit, Wend, there ain't any movin' fast at night. You should know that as well as anyone." He laid down his rifle. "I'll go out with just my pistol and knife. And I'll be back in an hour; two at the outside." He smiled mischievously. "An' if I ain't back in two hours, you can damn well figure there *are* Indians out there."

After Joshua left, the remaining men finished setting up the camp, including laying, but not lighting, a fire. Then all took up defensive positions; the two waggoners and Dick near the picket line, Wend, Crawford, and Donegal on the other side of the campsite. They had been lying in wait for just over an hour when a voice called out from the bush, "All right, I'm back, and for God's sake put your damn firelocks down before somethin' nasty happens!"

Joshua emerged into the moonlight, brushing himself off. "There ain't no hostiles out there. Couldn't hear, smell, or see anything which moves on two legs. And all the little night critters is movin' around like normal." He pointed to the fire. "Light her up, and let's have some warm supper!"

Dick was pressed into service with a flint and steel and soon had flames crackling through the kindling. As he worked to nurture the fire, Wend, Crawford, and Joshua stood by considering the events of the day.

Wend was bemused. "I can't figure out why they didn't come for us; it was as big a raiding party as I've ever seen. Besides, with us strung out on that road, they had us at their mercy. And they must have figured that there was plenty of plunder in two big Conestogas. Yet it seems now like they didn't even follow us." Wend raised an eyebrow toward Joshua, "You have any ideas why they would act like that?"

Joshua was silent for a moment as he pondered the question.

Before he could answer, Crawford spoke up. "Here's the only thing I can figure: If what we've heard is correct, these war parties are out for revenge — they want to kill whites, not take plunder. And even though they had us in a difficult position, they could count seven well-armed men. If they had attacked, they knew we could have taken a lot of them with us. That didn't fit into their plans; so they went looking for an easier target like a sleeping farmstead."

"Could be you're right, Cap'n," Joshua answered. "Fact is, Indians don't like takin' casualties if they can help it. Push to shove, they'll fight bravely and die for the honor of their tribe or clan. But on the whole, they'd rather have an easy fight and go home to brag about their feats of valor around the village fire ring. Maybe they did just decide we was too tough a nut for them to crack without a passel of them gettin' kilt or wounded."

Wend stood thinking. Perhaps Crawford and Baird were right; indeed, it fit in logically with his own understanding of the Indian warrior ethic. But there was a knot in his stomach and he couldn't get it out of his mind that something else was behind the war party's decision not to attack. He looked at Joshua and put his doubts into words. "All you say makes sense. But I've a feeling down in my gut that something else we can't know about was in play out there today."

Joshua looked at Wend with sudden concern in his eyes. He screwed up his face. "Yeah, I know. Truth is, I got the same feelin'."

* * *

The next day they started out at first light and were off the mountain by the early afternoon. Traveling was far easier on the flatlands and the caravan arrived at Crawford's place by early dusk. It was located on a bend of the Youghiogheny near where the road crossed at a shallow ford. But Wend was surprised at the layout of the manor. It had all the normal aspects of a prosperous estate. There was a large hay barn, a spacious horse stable, and several sheds and small out-buildings. A row of small log cabins housed the slaves. A slightly larger cabin looked to be the house of an overseer. The farmstead was surrounded by exten-sive, well cleared fields and grassy pastures enclosed by rail fences. There was a herd of cattle and many horses grazing peacefully in the pastures.

What Wend found rather puzzling was Crawford's house itself. In the midst of this prosperous plantation, the family's living quarters consisted of noth-ing more than a small log cabin. In fact, the dwelling was much smaller than Wend's own house.

Crawford noticed that Wend was looking at the cabin. Wend felt embar-rassed to be caught staring but Crawford quickly spoke up.

"Everyone who comes here is surprised by the size of my house. My wife and I built that the first year we were here and then concentrated on building up the rest of the place. By the time we had the farm in good shape, we found that we had become comfortable in the cabin; it was home. My wife and I have a bedroom on the ground level and the children live up in the loft. We still talk about building a new house but just never seem to get around to it."

Crawford pointed to the cabin. "You can see that we have done some things to compensate for the small size. That log building behind the cabin serves as the cook-house. And that lean-to porch on the back serves as our dining room in good weather. Of course, in the deepest part of the winter, my wife and I, and our three children, lead a rather close life in the main cabin."

Wend said, "Well, it does look snug."

Crawford laughed. "Snug? I would say damned tight quarters, particularly when the children are restless! But you'll be surprised to know that the little place has sheltered Washington on a visit and none other than our esteemed governor, Lord Dunmore, last year on his trip up to Pittsburgh."

Wend was indeed surprised. He smiled and nodded. But before he could think of anything to say, a thin brown-haired woman came out the front door and waved.

Crawford's face broke into a grin. "There's my Hannah!" He rose up in his stirrups and enthusiastically waved back at his wife. Then he motioned at an open space by the horse pasture. "You can park the wagons right there and make camp. And feel free to let your horses loose in there with my herd. They'll enjoy the good grass and being able to move around overnight instead of standing on a picket line."

Wend turned and pointed out the location for their campsite to Joshua and Jake. He said, "We'll be very comfortable there, William. And we'll be on our way at first light."

Crawford smiled and leaned close, putting his hand on Wend's arm. "Wend, after you get your men taken care of, why don't you join my family for supper? I'm sure Hannah would love to hear any news of Winchester and lower Virginia that you could provide."

Wend was tempted; but then he realized that Crawford had been away for many days and he would undoubtedly want to spend the evening with his wife and children. His extension of the invitation was clearly a gesture of gracious hospitality. He politely declined, citing weariness and his need to be ready for an early departure.

Later, as they all sat around the fire, eating their meal in the night, Crawford appeared out of the darkness with a jug in his hand. He said, "I thought you would all enjoy a little of this; it's rum. I trust you'll find it to your taste."

Donegal rose from his seat in an instant. "Here, Mr. Crawford, let me take that, and I'll serve it out to the lads."

Crawford grinned broadly at the Highlander's enthusiasm and handed over the jug. Then he turned to Wend and pulled a piece of folded paper from his pocket. "This came for me by courier yesterday. It's from Captain John Connolly, the commandant at Fort Pitt. He wants me to come up there as soon as possible to discuss this border uprising and the question of raising the militia." He gave Wend a crooked smile. "I'd like to stay for a day or two here on the farm, but given the urgency of Connolly's summons, I should leave tomorrow. Considering the circumstances, I'd be much obliged if I could continue to ride with you."

Wend had come to enjoy Crawford's company over the last two days and welcomed the prospect. "I'd be more than delighted to have you along, sir."

Crawford reached out and touched Wend's shoulder in a companionable manner. "I'll be ready to ride at first light."

CHAPTER THREE
The Ruin of a Fortress

Wend had been surprised by many things on the long journey from Winchester, but the most startling sight came with their arrival at the Forks of the Ohio on the third day after leaving Crawford's estate. The last time Wend had been there — in 1763 during Pontiac's War — all the private buildings had been burnt to the ground by Fort Pitt's garrison at the beginning of the Indian siege to preclude their use for cover by warriors. Now he was intrigued by the size and vitality of the town of Pittsburgh which had grown up around the fort. He was also impressed by how much more of the surrounding forest had been cleared out to make way for farmsteads, fields, and pastures.

However, the biggest shock came when he caught sight of Fort Pitt itself. He abruptly pulled up his black mare and stared in astonishment. Wend remembered a proud fortress, the symbol of British power on the frontier, with its five imposing bastions, sprawling earthworks, menacing artillery, garrison of Royal Americans and Black Watch Highlanders, and its defiant Union Flag snapping in the wind from a staff on the southeast bastion.

What he saw now was a crumbling ruin. High grass and brush were growing on the earthen fortifications. Extensive segments of the brick ramparts were missing, as was the massive main gate which he remembered. Inside, entire buildings seemed to have simply disappeared from sight. The sloping eastern glacis, where Colonel Henry Bouquet's weary troops had pitched camp in August 1763 after their epic march over Forbes Road and hard-fought victory at Bushy Run, was now serving as the pasture for a herd of cattle.

Crawford pulled up beside Wend. He raised an eyebrow. "My friend, I've been riding with you for several days now; I've watched you encounter a war party, washouts, and other obstacles on the road. And you did so with almost no change in the expression on that face of yours, save perhaps a slight tightening of your lips. You have as much of a stone face as I've ever known. That is, until now."

Wend motioned toward the fortress and said simply, "The Fort Pitt I remember was a much different place."

Crawford threw back his head and laughed. "Now there's a masterful understatement if I've ever heard one!"

Meanwhile, Donegal had ridden up beside them. "God above, will you look at that? It makes me want to weep; it truly does. I canna' tell you the hours my mates and I spent buildin' up the place back in '59. Long days shoveling dirt, movin' logs, carryin' rolls of sod for the ramparts and layin' bricks." He shook his head. "It's a blessing the lads of the 77th can no see it now."

Crawford sighed. "Well, the last British garrison — two companies of the 18th Foot, The Royal Irish — pulled out in '72. General Gage ordered them up to Boston because of the troubles there. Since then, much of the fort's material has been used to build up the town. Many of the buildings you see have their origins in the fortifications and wooden structures inside the walls."

"I don't understand," Wend said. "I've been directed to deliver muskets for the garrison. But there's not much there that's fit to garrison."

"Oh, there's a garrison, all right," Crawford answered. "Since January, Captain Connolly has raised a militia company and has been struggling to restore portions of it." He thought a moment. "It's never going to be a strong fortification again, but I don't think that's necessary unless this uprising gets bigger than I expect. It's really just a headquarters and depot for operations against hostiles in the Ohio Country. But in truth, its most important function is to support Governor Dunmore's claim that the Forks of the Ohio belong to Virginia, not Pennsylvania."

* * *

Wend and Crawford, riding side by side with Baird and Donegal behind, led the two wagons through the opening of the arrowhead-shaped East Ravelin which shielded the main entrance to the fort. Dick followed, leading a packhorse with Crawford's baggage. Then the little caravan crossed over the wooden bridge which spanned the ditch that surrounded the walls and ended at the gateway itself.

A militia sentry leaned casually against the side of the entrance, with his arms crossed in front of his chest; a nondescript firelock was propped against the wall beside him. Eckert looked over the man and could detect no piece of proper military equipage or uniform about him. He wore a brown coat and waistcoat, with tan breeches. On his head was a crumpled, wide-brimmed hat.

Donegal whispered, "Good lord above, will you look at that? If I still had a corporal's knot on my shoulder I'd go down there, grab that lad by the scruff of the neck, and give him a strong kick in his ass with my own good shoe. And then I'd bang him up against the wall and learn him the regulations about standin' sentry duty in words he'd not soon forget."

Baird laughed out loud and Wend looked over to see Crawford had a crooked smile on his face.

As they approached, the sentry wearily pushed himself upright and touched the brim of his hat with his right hand in improvised salute. He called out, "Hello, there, Cap'n Crawford. Good to see you, sir!"

Crawford returned the salute and motioned toward Wend. "This gentleman has military stores for delivery to Captain Connelly. We'd like to go to headquarters."

"Sure 'nuff, Cap'n. Just go ahead on over there." Then he waved in the general direction of the village. "Hey, welcome back to Pittsburgh, Cap'n!"

Wend ordered the wagons forward and they passed under the gateway onto the parade. He looked around and saw that several of the wooden barracks which had ringed the inside of the walls had been either fully or partially dismantled. Only the long brick barracks building and the Commandant's House seemed structurally complete.

Crawford pointed toward the brick barracks. "Most of the activity is in there. Connolly keeps his headquarters in a room on the side near the house and the officers and militia men are in other sections of the building. Only a few other structures are used."

Wend looked around. "Not many of the other structures *could* be used."

They stopped the wagons in front of the headquarters. While the others waited, Crawford led Wend into the headquarters rooms. The outer office was empty save for a bespectacled young man in a dark gray coat and breeches who sat behind a desk, his face scrunched up in concentration as he worked over a stack of papers. He looked up at the sound of the visitors and his face immediately brightened. He took his glasses off, saying, "Hello, Captain Crawford. It's good you could get here so fast in response to our letter!"

Crawford nodded. "Good to see you, Mr. Westfall. Yes, I made haste, because I had just learned on my own about these Mingo and Shawnee raids." The he motioned to Wend. "Let me introduce Mr. Wendelmar Eckert, of Winchester. He's here to deliver a shipment of muskets for the garrison."

Westfall stood up and extended his hand to Wend. He was a diminutive man, coming only up to Wend's shoulder. He said, "Glad to meet you, Mr. Eckert."

Wend said, "And I, you, sir."

Westfall continued, in a self-conscious manner, "I'm an ensign in the militia and Captain Connolly's adjutant." He paused a moment. "The truth is, we've been expecting you, Mr. Eckert. Mr. Barrett Northcutt himself told us you would be arriving shortly."

Wend was surprised. "Northcutt is here in Pittsburgh?" Wend turned to Crawford. "The Honorable Mr. Barrett Penfold Northcutt is Governor Dunmore's senior aide. He's the man who I work with on my contract to modify the muskets."

Westfall nodded his head. "Yes, Mr. Northcutt rode in from Williamsburg two weeks ago. The governor sent him to look over prospective settlement land down the Ohio and help Captain Connolly properly organize the civil administration of the Pittsburgh area now that it's in Virginia's control."

The adjutant knocked on the door to Connolly's office, stepped inside for a moment, and then ushered the two visitors into the office of the commanding officer. As they entered, Wend saw a tallish, hook-nosed man of about his own age, busily writing at his desk. The captain glanced up and immediately rose to his feet, extending a hand toward Crawford.

"My dear William, welcome back to Pittsburgh! I'm gratified that you made such haste."

While the two captains were exchanging greetings, Wend looked over the commandant of Fort Pitt. Connolly had the ruddy face of a man who had spent considerable time in the open and the posture of a trained soldier. He was dark haired and blue eyed and had a slim build which showed no sign of going to corpulence. He wore a uniform which generally conformed to that which Wend had seen worn by officers in the Virginia militia, but it was not quite the same. It consisted of a blue coat and breeches with a red waistcoat. However, the blue color was a little lighter than the shade which Wend remembered and the cuffs seemed of a different cut. He assumed that Connolly had had to improvise with local materials.

Wend's observations were interrupted as Connolly finished his greeting to Crawford. He extended a hand to Wend. "I can't tell you how glad we are to see you here safely, Mr. Eckert. I've been anxious to get my men properly armed and equipped."

"Well, I think we have exactly what you've been looking for, Captain. In my wagons are 100 stand of King's Arm muskets, cut down to the short land pattern, and completely refurbished. Each stand includes bayonet and scabbard, appropriate frog, cartridge box and belt."

"Excellent, Eckert! I'm delighted." Connolly smiled and looked back and forth between his two visitors. Then he turned directly to Wend. "Barrett Northcutt told me about the good work you have been doing for the colony in rebuilding these old firelocks. He says you are indeed a master craftsman who works with great efficiency. I can promise you that we will put them to good use, particularly with this tribal uprising which is blossoming."

Wend said, "Yes, Captain, I'm sure you will. I know that you are anxious to discuss the situation with Captain Crawford. If you'll have someone show me where you want the muskets stored, I'll get about unloading them."

"Certainly, Eckert; my adjutant will work with you."

Wend nodded. "Thank you, sir. Perhaps when you've finished your discussions with Captain Crawford, you'll be able to come inspect at least one of the muskets. I'd like to have your approval of the product before we depart, simply for legal purposes."

"Of course, Eckert; I know you're eager to get your business completed. However, before you go, let me extend an invitation to both of you for supper this evening in my quarters." He smiled and looked around at the two men. "This is quite an occasion. We've finally finished most of the renovations in the Commandant's House. So this evening will be a celebration. Northcutt and a few other people will be there and my good wife will put together some of her usual fine food."

Crawford acknowledged immediately. Wend was inclined to politely decline the offer; he wanted to relax in the company of his own friends. An evening of guarded behavior in polite society was the last thing on his mind.

Connolly sensed Wend's hesitation. "You're not going to attempt to decline, are you, Eckert?" He paused, grinned, and wagged his finger back and forth. "You simply can't. My dear Susan will be devastated at losing someone with news from the lower part of the colony. And besides, Northcutt has mentioned that he wants to see you and you two can complete your business tonight. So I'll expect you." He thought a moment. "I'll send a message with the exact time — where are you staying, sir?"

Wend smiled in resignation. "Well, it seems I have no alternative but to accept your kind invitation. We're staying at Semple's Tavern."

"And a fine choice that is; the best food and rooms in the village. And right down by the river, with a marvelous view." Connolly walked to the door.

"Eckert, I'll make arrangements for Westfall to show you where to unload your muskets."

When they were momentarily alone, Crawford turned to Wend. He leaned over and spoke confidentially. "Listen, now, Eckert, Connolly was right: Semple's is the best place to stay in town. But be careful what you say in the common room. Susan Connolly is Semple's sister. Anything you discuss may be overhead and get straight back to Connolly." He smiled conspiratorially. "I don't know your political persuasion, Wend, but suffice it to say that Connolly is of the King's party."

Before Wend could answer, Connolly was back in the room, this time with his adjutant in tow. "Everything is ready, Mr. Eckert. Westfall will go with you to the armory and accept delivery of the firelocks for me. I would go with you myself, but I must discuss urgent matters with Crawford. We must get about raising a strong force to protect the local settlements!"

Wend made his courtesies and followed Westfall out of the offices and back onto the parade. All the men, who had been lounging around the wagons, came forward to meet Wend and Westfall. The young militia officer, full of official purpose, announced with great gravity, "Good afternoon, gentlemen; I am Ensign Westfall, the adjutant. Follow me; I will show you to the armory."

Donegal, standing closest to the officer and towering over him in stature, smiled conspiratorially at his companions. He winked at Wend. then casually reached out and put his hand on Westfall's right shoulder. "Oh, *Ensign*, so you'll be showin' me the way to the armory, will you now? Well, my wee fine laddie, that's passin' nice of you. But here's the great truth of it, lad: I built that damned armory with these very two hands of me own back in '59 when Cap'n Hugh Mercer was the commandant here. By the look of you, back then your sainted mother was still tucking you into bed carefully so the goblins wouldn't get you in the dark of night. So laddie, why don't you just walk along with me and on the way I'll tell you some fine stories about how the 77th Highlanders and the men of the Pennsylvania Regiment built this great hulking fort, which I might say, you don't seem to be taking very good care of these days."

* * *

Wend couldn't take his eyes from the sign which graced the large building on the north side of the town of Pittsburgh. It read:

General Store and Trading Station

Richard Grenough, Proprietor

The name of the owner brought Eckert a cold knot in his stomach and a flood of bitter memories. Richard Grenough was a man of great wealth, the head of the largest trading organization in Pennsylvania, and a charming, consummate manipulator with political influence that reached to the highest levels of government in Philadelphia. But he was also unabashedly corrupt and a heartless killer; the man who Wend held responsible for the death of his parents, brother, and sister in 1759 on Forbes Road. And he was also the man Wend knew had orchestrated the massacre of the peaceful Conestoga Indians near Wend's boyhood home of Lancaster in order to cover up his illegal trading with the Ohio tribes during Pontiac's War.

Joshua Baird, riding next to Wend, reached out and put his hand on Eckert's arm. "Calm, lad. I know how that sign disturbs you."

Donegal, on Wend's other side, said, "Damn, I had 'na thought about running into Grenough. It's been ten years since we killed his men up in the Tuscarora Mountains."

Baird responded, "Grenough operates all through the border country. He's got other stores at Bedford and Ligonier that I know about. Maybe other places by now; he's expanding all the time. More'n likely he ain't here in Pittsburgh right now; he's probably back at his manor in York."

Wend cleared his memory of thoughts of 1759 and 1764, and said, "Yes, you're right. Grenough could be at his home or anywhere within his far-flung holdings. He could be out in the Ohio Country, working on his relations with the chiefs. Or he could even be back in Philadelphia, cozying up to the Penns." Wend pointed beyond the store. "This looks like a typical Grenough operation: There's a large warehouse, stable, blacksmith shop, shed for packsaddles, and an ample pasture."

Donegal nodded, "Sure enough. There must be more than a hundred horses out in that pasture." He waved toward another building. "And look at that long wagon shed with all the rigs in it."

Baird urged his horse forward and said, "Come on Wend. Let's get down to the tavern. We've earned a night of fun. I need a mug of rum to start with."

Donegal smiled and nodded. "That's for sure. I've 'na been thinkin' of anything else all afternoon while we was movin' all those musket boxes."

Joshua laughed out loud. "All afternoon, Simon? Be honest! That's all you ever think about."

Wend refused to be distracted by the banter of his friends. "Getting back to Grenough, I'm still a little surprised by his very obvious prosperity. Joshua, you rode with Bouquet on his expedition against the Ohio Indians in '64 and told him what we knew about Grenough's perfidy."

"That's a fact, Wend. I told him about how Grenough had been trading with the tribes in the middle of the war. And laid out all your evidence about how he had spread the rumors that the Conestogas were plotting with the hostile Indians, the rumors which led to their massacre by the Paxton Rangers. And Bouquet was shaken; you know how close a friend he was to Grenough. But he said he believed what I told him. Then he immediately cut Grenough out of his job as an Indian Commissioner and sent him away from the expedition."

Wend mused, "Obviously no significant legal action was taken against Grenough or he wouldn't have been able to expand his business the way he has."

Baird shook his head. "The truth is, Bouquet *couldn't* take any action against Grenough. He didn't have no solid evidence, only our word, and we weren't around. More'n that, right after the expedition ended, he got promoted to Brigadier and then left for Florida. Takin' care of Grenough just dropped out of sight."

Donegal waved at the expanse of Grenough's property. "Well, he sure has built back up even bigger than he was back then."

Wend sighed. "It's always been very clear to me that the only thing which will stop him is death."

* * *

Samuel Semple swung open the door to the bedroom on the second floor of the tavern and then went through to hold it while Wend entered, carrying his baggage. The innkeeper was a man in his middle thirties with a receding hairline and a waistline which was beginning to bulge beneath the white apron. He said with evident pride, "Best room in the inn, Mr. Eckert; Colonel Washington used it back in '72. And Lord Dunmore himself slept in here when he visited Pittsburgh last year."

Wend looked around and saw a room which was unremarkable in appearance. It was furnished with crude but serviceable furniture: a bed with feather mattress, nightstand, dresser, two-door wardrobe, and a low chest at the bottom of the bed. A writing table stood against the wall opposite the door. The single window looked out on the Monongahela.

Wend remarked, "Well, I've been told by everyone that your establishment is the best in the village. Indeed, it certainly seems well kept."

The innkeeper clasped his hands before him. "We do what we can, given the circumstances out here. And wait until you try our table; Colonel Washington gave a supper here for the officers of the Royal Irish when he visited and he was entirely pleased with the fare." Semple fussed around the room while Wend dropped his things on the bed and then said, "I've given your men a large room just down the hall."

Wend nodded. "That's fine, sir. My two teamsters will be along after they get their wagons and teams put up at the livery stable." He paused a second, then said, "I'll be dining with Captain Connolly at the fort tonight; there should be a messenger with a note for me arriving shortly."

"Ah, yes, sir. I'll have it delivered promptly." Semple raised an eyebrow at that news, but said nothing about his relationship with the commandant. Then he said, "Well, if there's nothing else, I'll leave you to unpack."

Wend laid out his town clothes. Peggy had carefully packed them in his canvas bag which had been carried in Jake's wagon, but Wend had hoped not to use them on this trip. He had spent the entire time so far in his traveling attire: a shirt, waistcoat, and breeches. His outerwear had been either a short shell jacket or his trusty old gray army overcoat, which Corporal Robert Kirkwood of the 42nd had expertly stolen for him from military stores right here in Pittsburgh ten years ago. However, tonight would call for the suit of clothes which Alice Downy, Baird's common-law wife, had made up for him. She was an accomplished seamstress; as Eckert laid out the clothing, he remarked to himself that he would at least not feel self-conscious about his attire while mingling with the evening's company. He was pleased to see that the dark blue coat and light gray breeches had traveled with a minimum of wrinkles. The pale gold waistcoat would add a touch of color to the otherwise sober suit.

An hour later Wend went down to the common room. It was crowded and noisy; the bar was well attended by men taking their libations. He picked out Baird and Donegal relaxing, mugs in hand, at a table next to the hearth. He was surprised to see a third man seated with them.

Wend pushed his way through the room to the table. Joshua looked up, waved, and called out, "Guess who we've got here?"

Wend saw a lean man dressed in rough clothes. He had dark brown, almost black hair and brown, deep-set eyes. A pair of saddlebags lay on the floor by his chair and a longrifle leaned up against the wall beside the fireplace. Wend said, "You've put me at a disadvantage, Joshua."

Baird said, "This here is Michael Cresap hisself. He just rode in from Redstone Old Fort this very hour."

Wend looked down at Cresap, who took a gulp of rum as he watched. Wend said, "Well, Cresap, there seems to be a lot of people who hold you responsible for killing John Logan's family and causing all these war party raids in the border country."

Cresap slowly put his mug down on the table and spent a few moments eyeing Wend. Then he said in a deliberate voice, "That's a mighty pretty set of clothes you got on, mister. Who might you be?"

Before Wend could answer, Joshua said, "This here is Wend Eckert; a good friend of mine from Winchester. Don't mind them fancy clothes; he's fixin' to go over to the fort and hobnob with Connolly and some other dandy folk." Baird took a quick pull on his ale, then continued, "Most o' the time he dresses the same as the likes of you and me, Michael."

Cresap acknowledged Joshua's words with a nod. "Well, Mr. Wend Eckert, you need to know that there are a lot of people who know nothin' of what happened at Yellow Creek who are runnin' off their mouth. And John Logan is chasing the wrong man."

Wend pulled out a chair and sat down at the table. Cresap kept his eyes locked on him the whole time, a grim set to his chin. Clearly the man was wound up like a spring. Wend asked, "So why don't you explain why Logan is wrong about you?"

"Eckert, I don't need to explain anything." Cresap took another sip and then set the mug back on the table. "But I will tell you this: In late April, I was down on land I have on the Ohio with men I had hired to raise some buildings. Then along comes a courier with a circular from Connolly; it said that there had been shooting incidents between settlers and Indians and that the Shawnee were threatening war. So I took my men up to Wheeling Creek where Ebenezer Zane has built a forted house. I figured we could shelter with him."

Wend asked, "What happened when you got to Zane's house?"

"Turned out there was a bunch of travelers, hunters, and settlers there who had been mightily scared by Connolly's letter. Most of them people, 'cept Zane and me, they didn't have no experience with Indians and they was near panicked 'cause of stories they'd heard about how brutal the warriors could be in war."

Wend shrugged. "How did that lead to killing Mingoes at Baker's Tavern?"

"There was a gaggle of young hunters bein' led by a man named Daniel Greathouse. He was a Dutchman and pretty high-strung. They started talkin' about a village of Mingoes they had seen livin' where Yellow Creek joined the

Ohio, up north of Zane's place. Then a big, burly man started sayin' it was likely that those Mingoes would pick up the war hatchet to join the Shawnee. He was real loud and kept hammering at that theme, so that he got Greathouse and the other people excited. Zane and I tried to calm everyone down, but it didn't work. Soon all them pilgrims at Zane's place were convinced that those Mingoes must be hostile."

Something bothered Wend. "This burly man: was he part of Greathouse's company?"

Cresap said, "I couldn't tell; there was so many different families and travelin' parties there. But I can tell you he must have had some sort of a terrible accident in his past. He limped on one leg and somethin' had happened to his face. His nose had been smashed and the whole left side was messed up. He had grown a thick beard to cover it up, but you could see his cheekbone was pushed in and his jaw had been broken and reset, but still weren't proper. The bone over his eye on that side had been smashed bad and didn't match the right side. And there were old scars over the left side of his face; you could see some plainly above the beard."

Wend sat straight up in his chair. He, Joshua, and Donegal exchanged quick glances.

Wend asked casually, "Did you happen to get a name?"

Cresap waved a hand. "I wasn't payin' too much attention, what with all the arguing going on. But he was partnered with another man; a black-haired Irishman." He thought a second. "I'll tell you somethin' else about that big man: He wasn't right in his head. He was always laughing when no one else thought anything was funny and sometimes he would go off and hold his head in his hands like he was havin' big pain. And now you mention it, I did hear the Irishman call him 'Matt' a couple of times."

Wend felt a knot in his stomach. There could be no doubt now about the identity of the burly, disfigured man. But what he said to Cresap was: "So you did go up to Yellow Creek?"

"Greathouse and this Matt fellow was saying we ought to go up and attack the Mingoes. Someone pointed out that a man named Baker had a farm and a tavern right across the Ohio from the mouth of Yellow Creek and that he and his family would be in danger. Matt said we could go there and use Baker's place to spy out what was goin' on at the Indian village and make a plan to hit them."

Cresap took another gulp of his drink. "While they was all talkin' about the Mingo village, Zane came over and spoke to me private-like. He said, 'Michael, there ain't no stoppin' these people. Maybe if you take charge, you can keep them in check. They know you got experience with Indians and maybe they'll listen to you'." Cresap threw up his hands. "So, to make a long story short, it was agreed that I would lead about thirty men up to Yellow Creek. I made sure they understood we was goin' to scout things out and see if Baker and his family were safe and there wasn't going to be no fightin' unless the Indians showed themselves hostile."

Donegal asked, "What did you find when you got to Baker's place?"

"I didn't never get there. About half way to Yellow Creek, we stopped to rest and make plans. Then one of the men mentioned somethin' I hadn't heard before. He told me that the Mingo village at Yellow Creek was led by John Logan." He shrugged. "Right then, I knew that the whole damn expedition was all wrong. Logan weren't goin' to attack anyone."

Wend asked, "What did you do then?"

"I told all them men about Logan and said I was turning around and headin' back to Wheeling Creek. Then an argument broke out. Greathouse and that big man Matt, they was all for goin' on up to Baker's place. Matt accused me of bein' soft on the Indians 'cause of my trading business. We came near to blows over that. Anyway, the talking went on for more'n an hour. Finally, most of the men voted to go back with me. So we all returned to Wheeling."

Donegal laughed. "March up the river, then back down. It reminds me of the army."

"Yeah, the whole thing didn't make no sense." Cresap took another drink and continued, "By this time I was fed up with everything that was going on at the Zane place. And I had hands with me who I was paying wages for doin' nothin'. So I made up my mind to go home to Redstone and pay off my men."

Wend asked, "So if you didn't have anything to do with killing Mingoes at Yellow Creek, who did?"

"It was that ass Greathouse!" Cresap looked around at each of the men at the table, then said, "I was back at my place at Redstone when a pair of people who had been at Zane's house came through a few days later. They told me the story."

Donegal asked, "What happened? Did they get some sign that the Mingo were hostile after you left?"

Cresap shook his head. "Look, all I know is that Greathouse took his men back up to Baker's place. Then they set up a trick to fool the Mingo. They had Baker send over a message inviting the whole village to come across the Ohio for a day of sport and drink, which apparently had happened before. A dozen or so of the Indians came over. Greathouse and a few other men were mixing with the Indians, but the rest of them were hidden in rooms in the back of the tavern. After the Mingoes had had a lot to drink and emptied their firelocks in a shooting contest, the hidden men came out and shot the lot of them. The only Indian they didn't kill was a half-breed baby in the arms of a woman." Cresap looked down at the table, and said, "That's all I know about what happened."

Wend looked at Baird. "You were right, Joshua. Logan went to war only after an insufferable provocation."

Cresap grimaced. "Yeah, but somehow the story got out that I was in charge at that massacre. And people are blaming me for causing all these war party raids. Now tell me this: How do I clear my name?"

There was an awkward silence. Cresap's question hung in the air unanswered.

The quiet was broken when a young serving girl came up to the table. She looked at Wend. "Are you Mr. Eckert?"

Wend nodded and the girl handed him a folded paper. He opened it, read for a minute, then said, "Well, I have just enough time to make supper at Connolly's house if I leave now."

Cresap said, "Eckert, I'd be obliged if you'd give a message to Connolly for me. Tell him that I'll be over to see him directly in the morning." He continued, "I've raised the militia company he asked me to form down at Redstone, but I need powder and lead for my men. That's what I'm here to talk to him about." He picked up his saddlebags, then stood up and reached for his rifle. "Good seeing you again, Joshua. I've got to get a bed and some sleep."

Baird smiled. "You take care now, Michael."

Wend watched Cresap go; he nursed a suspicion that the man knew more about events along the Ohio than he had admitted.

After Cresap was out of earshot, Donegal slapped his hand down on the table and said, "For God's sake, Matt Bratton is out here on the border!"

Wend responded, "Yes, that big man Cresap described can't be anyone else but Bratton and he's doing the same job for Grenough that he did back east. For God's sake, what just happened to Logan's village is a copy of what was done to the Conestogas ten years ago. Bratton was right there keeping the men around him all worked up about a fake threat from peaceful Indians."

Joshua said thoughtfully, "One thing's sure: Grenough had him down there stirrin' up the settlers for some reason that's gonna benefit his company."

Donegal asked, "You figure Grenough thinks he can make some profit out of an Indian war?"

Wend said, "Of course. Cash profit and political profit; Grenough is always looking for both at the same time."

Donegal gave Wend a sharp look. "I hope you're 'na thinkin' about going after Bratton and Grenough. You ain't no twenty year old laddie on his own anymore. You got family and lots of other people counting on you."

Joshua said, "Donegal's tellin' it straight." He pursed his lips. "The best thing we can do is get the provisions we need and roll out of here fast. I ain't gonna' feel good until we're on the road back to Winchester."

Wend answered. "I'm not worried about Grenough or Bratton at this moment. Something else occurred to me while Cresap was talking. Remember this: My friend Charlie Sawak went to live with Logan's village after he escaped from the Conestoga Massacre."

A grim expression came over Baird's face.

Donegal exclaimed, "By God, I near forgot!"

Wend nodded. "Now you get it: There's a possibility that Charlie — or part of his family — was killed at Baker's Tavern." He paused and looked at each of his friends in turn. "Think of the irony: What if Charlie escaped the Conestoga Town murders only to face death in another Grenough-inspired massacre on the banks of the Ohio River?"

CHAPTER FOUR
Intense Encounters

The dinner at Captain Connolly's table was the most uncomfortable Wend Eckert had ever experienced in his life. It wasn't because he felt awkward taking a meal in the presence of a company of influential people. It wasn't because of the unaccustomed, tight-fitting town clothes he was wearing. It wasn't because everyone expected him to discuss all the news of lower Virginia, as they called the Shenandoah Valley and the Tidewater. The reason for his discomfort was the fact that he was seated directly across from, and obliged to make polite conversation with, Mr. Richard Grenough.

Wend had not seen the man for ten years. But Grenough looked essentially the same as the last time they had been face to face. That had been at Washburn's Tavern in Carlisle, when Eckert had been on his way from the village of Sherman Mill to Winchester. Grenough had put on weight but he was still dressed in his signature expensive clothing; only Northcutt, dressed by a Williamsburg tailor, wore a more elegant suit. One thing was different about the man, but that was rather startling: Grenough had a long, thin scar across the right side of his face. It started at his cheekbone even with the center of his ear and extended nearly to the corner of his lip. Clearly a surgeon had done his best to mitigate the damage, for faint stitch marks ran along the sides of the scar.

The evening itself had started with a shock. Wend had climbed the steps to the Commandant's House and been greeted cordially in the entranceway by Connolly and his wife Susan. He had just offered a polite response to their welcome when his host looked over Wend's shoulder, smiled broadly, and said in a booming voice, "Why, here's Richard! I'm damned glad you could join us tonight."

Wend looked around, to be stunned and frozen in place by the sight of Grenough.

But the trader experienced no similar reaction. Smooth as water flowing along a mill race, he exclaimed with enthusiasm, "Well what a marvelous surprise: Mr. Wend Eckert in the flesh!" He put his hand on Wend's arm in a demonstration of fellowship and continued, "Connolly, you have done me a great service. I've not seen my old friend Eckert for almost precisely ten years. Not since we last talked in Carlisle, when he was on his way to live in Virginia with his new bride." He looked at Wend with a gleam in his eye and said, "And I remember that Wend here was rather frustrated at the time, since he had to leave the colony in a hurry to take up business opportunities in our southern sister. He spoke to me of loose strings he regretted leaving behind." He turned to Wend and looked him straight in the eye, "Am I not correct, Mr. Eckert?"

Wend mustered the strength to answer, "Quite correct, Richard." He hoped that his face wasn't betraying him now by showing his internal turmoil.

Grenough smiled and looked back at his hosts. "And I can tell you, John and Susan, Pennsylvania's loss was Virginia's gain. Mr. Eckert was known throughout the border country as a man who could get things done!"

Susan Connolly beamed and said, "Why Richard, I'm so glad that we could unite such good friends. And, quite by chance, I've seated you two across the table from each other. You'll be able to catch up on old times."

Connolly waved toward the drawing room. "Most of our other guests are in there, Richard; why don't you take Mr. Eckert in and introduce him around?"

The two of them walked together toward the room where the guests were standing around talking. Wend saw that Crawford was already there with a handful of other men and two women. Grenough turned toward Wend, grinned at him devilishly, and whispered, "Well played, Eckert. And I see that you've kept that stone-faced countenance as you've aged; most useful indeed." Then, before Wend could reply, he pointed at one of the guests and exclaimed, "George Croghan! By God, I've been wanting to talk to you!" Without another word he left Wend's side and rushed over to talk with Croghan.

Wend stood awkwardly in the entranceway receiving the stares of the other guests. Crawford, seeing his dilemma, walked over, greeted him, and graciously took up the duty of introducing him to the people in the room. The process of meeting and exchanging conversation with the other guests enabled Wend to get a grip on his emotions and prepare himself for the ordeal of dinner across from Grenough.

* * *

After dinner, the ladies withdrew to what Susan Connolly called her sewing room and the men assembled in the spacious drawing room for some serious talk. Connolly had a servant charge the glasses of all the guests with brandy while several of the men used tapers to light their pipes from the fireplace amidst sociable banter. There were seven men in addition to the commandant. Eckert of course, knew Grenough and Crawford personally. George Croghan had been an Indian trader; Wend was aware that he had frequently served as an Indian Commissioner in the Ohio Country for the British colonial administration. Also, like Grenough, he was quite wealthy; during Pontiac's War he had personally financed a company of militia which had garrisoned Fort Lyttleton. Andrew McKee, who stood next to Croghan, had just taken over as Indian Commissioner for the Ohio Country. The final man was named Edward Ward, who appeared to be in his middle forties and who Wend knew nothing about save that he had overheard one of the guests mention that he had some connection with the fort. Barrett Northcutt, as the governor's representative, was the de facto guest of honor.

When everyone had a full glass, Connolly cleared his throat and said, "Gentlemen, your attention; Mr. Northcutt would like to say a few words."

Barrett Northcutt beamed and looked around at all the guests. "Let me propose a toast to our host, John Connolly, and the marvelous work he has done in reclaiming Pittsburgh and the Forks of the Ohio for Virginia!"

The men all raised their glasses with cries of "Hear, hear!" and "Aye, to John Connolly!"

Connolly nodded and smiled self-consciously at his guests.

Then Northcutt continued, "I can speak for the governor in expressing his gratitude for John's initiative. A year ago, Lord Dunmore visited Pittsburgh and saw that it was ripe for the picking." He smiled broadly, "And that John was the man to do the picking."

There were laughs throughout the room.

Wend, having politely joined in the toast, looked around at the other guests to see their reactions. He reckoned that at least Grenough and Croghan had strong, profitable ties to Pennsylvania's government. But they raised their glasses with the others in seemingly enthusiastic support of Northcutt's words and Virginia's cause.

Northcutt looked around at the assembly. "Now, my friends, we all know that Virginia's right to this area is based on royal grant, diplomacy, and the very shedding of blood! We put the French on notice when Dinwiddie sent young Washington to proclaim Virginia's rights to the Forks of the Ohio in 1753. And then it was Virginia who sent troops to fight them at Great Meadows in '54 to enforce that claim. And it is fact that in 1755 we sent the most provincial troops to support Braddock and his regulars in the advance on Duquesne."

There was another round of "Hear, hear!" from the guests.

Northcutt waved for silence. "I'll not bore you with the rest of the history of how the Forks of the Ohio were finally taken back from the French by General Forbes in 1758. You know the story as well as I. But since January, John has taken bold steps which have wrested this land back from Pennsylvania. He made a proclamation which put Pennsylvania on notice that its illegal occupation of Pittsburgh was over. Then he formed a strong militia from loyal Virginians in the territory around the forks which enabled him to turn back any attempt by Pennsylvania to respond. And he's done yeoman work in starting the reconstruction of the very fort where we stand tonight."

The man named Ward interjected, "Not to mention that he certainly put Arthur St. Clair in his place!" He turned to Connolly. "John, tell them how St. Clair tried to arrest you."

The commandant shrugged. "Yes, Arthur St. Clair, Pennsylvania's chief court officer in this area, sent men to take me into custody. I went along with them to Hannastown, near old Fort Ligonier, which the Pennsylvanians are using as their headquarters. St. Clair said I would have to face a trial for leading an insurrection against Pennsylvania. But my incarceration didn't last very long, because our militia, eighty armed men, marched for Hannastown. Faced with that threat, St. Clair released me on my promise to return in April for the trial." Connolly laughed derisively. "It was a face saving move; he knew damned well I was never coming back!"

Grenough raised his hand for attention. "Barrett, I was in Philadelphia when the word arrived from St. Clair announcing Virginia's seizure of Pittsburgh. Pennsylvania's reaction was characteristic of the colony's inability to act decisively. First, Governor Penn wrote a proclamation reasserting the colony's ownership of the Forks of the Ohio. Then he sent a message to the Assembly requesting authority and money to raise troops to take back Pittsburgh. Of course, the Assembly promptly denied the request. It was all most amusing." The trader grinned and looked around at the other men, who nodded in agreement.

Northcutt said, "Yes, *quite* amusing. So in the end, all John Penn could do was send a strong note of protest to Lord Dunmore." He paused and looked knowingly at his listeners. "Naturally, Dunmore rejected the protest out of hand." He grinned broadly at all his listeners, then continued, "*Politely*, of course."

There was laughter around the room followed by an interval of silence.

Grenough took the opportunity to change the subject. "We all agree that our host has done well in advancing Virginia's interest. But it seems there is a new challenge facing us out in the Ohio Country. It's clear that this tribal uprising is growing beyond simple vengeance raids by John Logan."

Connolly responded, "Quite correct, Richard. In fact, a few days ago we received a formal letter from Cornstalk, the most influential Shawnee chief. McKee, Croghan and I went over it carefully several times. While he wrapped his point in the usual ceremonial, confusing language, the chief ultimately made it clear that there is strong sentiment among the Shawnee to raise the war hatchet. Undoubtedly young captains are forming raiding parties right now. To put it succinctly, a full blown war is imminent."

Croghan nodded. "It is important to remember that unlike the Delaware, Mingo, and other tribes of the Ohio Country, the Shawnee never signed the Treaty of Fort Stanwix back in '68. One section of that treaty opened the land south of the Ohio, long the primary hunting grounds of the Ohio Indians, to white settlement. But the Shawnee, alone of all the tribes, adamantly refused to give up their claim to control of that area. And they have become increasingly restive as more and more settlers move into southern Ohio and Kentucky." He looked around at the listeners. "The problem is aggravated by the fact that many of the men who fought in the French war have been promised tracts of land in that very area and they are starting to take up their claims."

Grenough took a sip of brandy and then stared at Northcutt over his glass. "Barrett, mark my words: Dunmore must handle this situation with dispatch and strength. It is, in fact, an opportunity for him to clearly show the settlers of this area that Virginia will look out for their interests. It will permanently secure their support, for they know that Pennsylvania will never act militarily in their defense. Decisive action will expand and solidify your power here in Pittsburgh."

Northcutt's face hardened, his eyes narrowed, and his jaw moved as he considered Grenough's words. Then he nodded. "I believe you are quite correct, Richard. I'm going to hurry back to Williamsburg and discuss the situation with the governor. I'll advise him that we must take steps to handle this uprising promptly and to the best advantage of the colony."

Grenough responded, "That's the stuff, Barrett." Then he looked around at the other men with a conspiratorial smirk. "As I like to say, *never let a good crisis go to waste.*"

Croghan put his head back and guffawed. "Indeed, Richard, I've heard you say that many times!"

McKee looked around the gathering, concern in his eyes. He cleared his throat and said, "As His Majesty's representative, let me point out that our first resort must be diplomatic attempts to resolve this issue with the Shawnee and any allies they might have in the Ohio Country. After receiving Cornstalk's letter, I summoned him and other chiefs here for council talks. White Eyes of the Delaware has agreed to assist us in persuading the Shawnee to pursue a negotiated settlement, perhaps entailing some modification of the Fort Stanwix Treaty."

Wend saw Northcutt and Connolly exchange quick smiles. Then Northcutt said, "Of course, Andrew, we would all be most gratified if this entire situation could be resolved amicably. Our prayers will be with your efforts."

Then Connolly, ever the good host, said, "Gentlemen, I think its time we refill our glasses! He motioned to the servant, who began to make the rounds with a decanter. As he did so, general conversation and laughter sprang up around the room.

Wend stood with Crawford and Edward Ward, who had said very little during the evening. Out of curiosity, he asked Ward, "Sir, are you working for Captain Connolly here at the fort?"

Ward hesitated a moment, as if he were thinking about how to answer. Then he smirked and said, "I wouldn't say that I'm working *for* Connolly. Working *with* him might be more on the mark. Actually, I *own* the fort."

Crawford looked at Wend with a twinkle in his eyes, smiled, put his hand over his mouth, and laughed quietly.

Wend sensed that the two of them were enjoying a joke to which he was not privy. He said, with some heat in his voice, "Sir, I'm afraid I don't understand. Perhaps you would illuminate me regarding that statement."

Ward put his hand on Eckert's shoulder and grinned broadly. "I was just having a bit of fun with you. Actually, I'm the agent for a mercantile firm called Ross and Thompson. The British sold them the fort and the land around it in 1772 for the sum of fifty pounds. Since then we've been selling off lumber, bricks, metal fittings, anything of value to local settlers and the businessmen of Pittsburgh. And, I might say, turning a nice profit. So naturally it was a bit of bother to us in January when Captain Connolly marched in and declared himself the commandant and Virginia the owner of the property."

"I can see where you would find that disconcerting."

"Indeed, Eckert. But we made representations to Connolly, showed him our deed, and following some negotiations, came to a working accommodation. Connolly has sent a letter off to Lord Dunmore outlining our legal standing and requesting that the colony purchase the fort. In the meantime, it is most accurate to say that Connolly is *renting* the fort from us."

Wend shook his head, and said, "Well, excuse me if I say the whole thing seems irregular."

Ward laughed loudly. "Very droll, sir! The truth is, nothing about what is going on in Pittsburgh these days is in the least bit *regular!*"

Wend was about to respond when he noticed that Ensign Westfall was standing in the doorway looking around the room. The adjutant caught his commandant's eye, who hurried to join him in the hallway outside the room. In less than a minute, Westfall reentered and whispered a few words to Northcutt, who then followed the diminutive officer out of the room.

Wend nudged Crawford and said quietly, "William, something's going on; Westfall's got some kind of urgent news."

"Yes, Eckert, I've been watching. I fear there may be some bad news about this uprising." He paused a moment and a shadow passed over his face. "I hope everything is secure down in my part of the country."

Almost immediately, Northcutt and Connolly came back into the room, followed by Westfall. All were grim-faced. Northcutt held a piece of paper in his hand.

Connolly called out to his guests: "Gentlemen, your attention, please. We have some very sobering news which has just arrived in Pittsburgh by courier." He motioned toward Northcutt. "Barrett will explain."

Wend noted that everyone was absolutely still and quiet. He thought: *Has a war party made a major strike on some isolated settlement?* He looked at Crawford and saw grave concern written across his face.

Northcutt looked around the room slowly, dramatically, stretching out the mystery of what he was about to say. Finally, he raised the paper so all could see. "This has come directly by fast rider from Williamsburg. It is serious and concerning news of the first order." He paused and again looked around the room. "In short, gentlemen, Lord Dunmore has found it necessary to dissolve the House of Burgesses." He looked down at the paper. "This was done on the 24th of May — less than ten days ago."

From beside Wend, Crawford spoke out. "For God's sake Northcutt, don't hold us in suspense. This *is* serious business. What led to this drastic action?"

"You're absolutely right, William, it is *damned* serious. The truth is, the majority of the Burgesses voted in favor of a declaration of solidarity with Boston in that city's defiance of the His Majesty's Government and its just customs regulations. And those hotheads on the so-called Committee of Correspondence, who are of course, members of the Burgesses — men like Jefferson and that irascible Patrick Henry — have issued letters urging a boycott of English goods."

There was silence around the room as the guests digested the news.

Northcutt waved the paper. "That's all that this says, gentlemen." He paused and continued, "But it is hardly necessary for me to mention that the actions of the Burgesses and the Virginia Committee of Correspondence are causing civil unrest which cannot be tolerated. Frankly, I take this dissolution of the legislature as a clear and timely warning to these Whig radicals. Unless they begin to exert some restraint, the Lord Dunmore will have to take even more serious steps which may involve their personal freedom."

Connolly motioned with his hand to all the men. "Naturally, none of us have anything to do with these events down in the capital or the impertinence of the Burgesses. Let's have another brandy, and finish the night in cordiality."

Wend turned to Crawford, and was about to ask his thoughts on the matter, when he saw that Northcutt was coming in their direction. He stopped before the two men and put his hand on Wend's arm. "Eckert, I've been meaning to talk to you tonight. I was down to the armory this afternoon with Connolly and we inspected the muskets you delivered."

"I hope you found everything satisfactory, sir."

"Most satisfactory, Eckert. Very much up to the excellent standard of the previous deliveries you have made to the arsenal down in Williamsburg. I intend to tell the governor how well you have been carrying out this program to renovate the firelocks from the colony's stocks. You have certainly validated our decision to award you the contract."

"Sir, I'm gratified by your confidence."

"Think nothing of it, Wend. You've added to your reputation as a fine craftsman." He paused, then said, "But we need to discuss something else. In light of this incipient Indian war and the political events in Williamsburg, I must get back to the capital post-haste. I had been thinking of staying in Pittsburgh for another week or so, but that won't work now."

Wend nodded. "I can understand that."

"Let me get to the point, Eckert. I'm informed that you are leaving Pittsburgh very soon."

"Quite correct, sir. We'll depart as soon as my waggoners are satisfied with the condition of their rigs and we have restocked our provisions; in any case, not later than the day after tomorrow."

"Excellent! Here's my point: I understand that you have a strong, well-armed party. And the fact is, I'm traveling with only a single servant. So, I'm respectfully asking to accompany you until we are through the area of danger from war parties. After that, of course, my man and I will head directly for Williamsburg as fast as the horses will bear."

Wend smiled. "It would be my honor to have you join our party. We have five armed men and Crawford here will also be accompanying us as far as his home at Stewart's Crossing."

While they were talking, Connolly had come over and joined the group. Now he spoke up. "I also have favor to ask of you, Eckert. I'm sending a supply of gunpowder and lead down to the Monongahela country in support of the militia companies that we are raising. I'd be obliged if you could carry it down to Crawford's place in one of your wagons, where he will distribute it to the militia. Naturally, we'll arrange compensation for your service."

Wend smiled. "I'd be more than glad to assist you, Captain. I'm paying for the hire of those wagons and a little more money from the colony will help cut my expense for this trip."

Northcutt grinned and raised his glass. "Then it's settled. Here's to a safe and quiet journey along Braddock's Road!"

* * *

Eckert and Crawford left the Connolly house together. They lingered for a moment beside the steps, discussing arrangements for departure of the caravan.

Then Crawford furtively looked up at the entrance to the house and around the parade, checking to see that they were alone in the darkness. In fact, the only living thing around was a large dog lying quietly by the steps.

William momentarily stared at Eckert, his lips pursed, as if trying to decide what to say. Then he spoke quietly, "Wend, that was very grave news we received tonight. The political situation in Virginia is coming to a head over these events up in Boston."

Wend hesitated in order to carefully phrase his answer. He recognized that Crawford was attempting to feel him out on his political leanings. That was not unusual, given the turbulence going on in the colony and the rising resentment of the British. Wend reflected that undoubtedly such inquiries were being made all over the colonies at this very moment as men tried to determine how their acquaintances and neighbors came down on the relationship with the home government.

"William," he said, "I'm German by birth and Ulster-Scot by adoption and marriage." He grinned for a second. "Some people say I have become more Ulster than the Ulster themselves." He paused for a moment to gather his thoughts. "But in matters of politics, it has been convenient for me to remain neutral, particularly given my contracts with the colony. To be honest, they have been quite lucrative over the last few years and have helped me prosper and build up my homestead. You could say I'm favoring my German heritage, which gives me the inclination to keep my head down, tend to trade, and avoid taking sides."

"Wend, we're all doing that to some extent. But mark my words: The time is coming when every man will have to decide where he stands with regard to the Crown. And tonight's news from Williamsburg has hastened that day."

Wend hesitated a moment, then answered, "I understand what you are saying, William. The truth is, many of my friends in Winchester are deeply involved with the opposition party. The town has many Ulster people, who we both know are virtually unanimous in their agitation against the British. Fortunately, no one has yet pressed me to declare my intentions."

"Wend, every man has to walk carefully in these days. At any rate, it is clear to me that in the face of the coming Indian insurrection those of us here on the border must work with the governor for protection of our families and property. This situation is likely to defer any defiance of the British. In that respect, my position must be the same as yours."

Wend thought of something. "Well, we are going to be riding in the company of Northcutt for the next few days. Our conversation over the evening campfires is going to be interesting and undoubtedly Barrett's comments will be very informative about the lay of things in Williamsburg."

Crawford nodded. "Indeed, Eckert. And I've found that Northcutt can be quite garrulous, particularly when he's had something to drink, and," he winked at Wend, "I intend to encourage him as much as possible." Then he thought a moment. "And along the line of getting information on what's going on down in Williamsburg, I'll scratch off a letter to Colonel Washington immediately after I get back to my place. He is a member of the Burgesses and I definitely want to get his thoughts on the impact of the governor's actions."

* * *

After saying goodnight to Crawford, instead of going directly back to Semple's place, Wend walked across the parade to the ramp which led up to the southwest bastion. Then he climbed the incline to the bastion and stepped up onto a parapet looking out onto the Monongahela as it flowed past to merge with the Allegheny.

It was a moment of overpowering sentimental recollection for him.

For it was here, in 1763, that he and a young Scottish girl named Mary Fraser had spent many hours cementing the love which had blossomed during Colonel Henry Bouquet's desperate march over Forbes Road to lift the Ohio tribes' siege of Fort Pitt. They had made this spot their very own. Wend, then nineteen, would bring along a camp chair for the willowy, auburn-haired, sixteen-year-old highland girl. He would sit at her feet or on top of the parapet wall. Mary would bring a book along and they would take turns reading to each other. She was working hard to master the art of reading and Wend would help her with unfamiliar words. Part of the young girl's charm was her iron-willed determination to make a life for herself outside of the constraining pattern of a regimental camp follower. Normally that would mean an early marriage to some corporal or sergeant, a rapid succession of children, and a domestic life shaped by the nomadic, dangerous, virtually penniless existence as part of a marching regiment. Mary had been orphaned the prior year when yellow fever took her mother and stepfather, a sergeant, during the British West Indies campaign. She had thus become a child of the regiment. When not working as a nurse or laundress, she had taken the initiative to study a range of subjects under the tutelage of the chaplain of the 77th Highlanders, with the ambitious dream of gaining enough knowledge to eventually obtain a position as governess to the children of some wealthy family.

Wend would have married Mary if a fateful train of events had not intervened. She had received a grave wound in her side at the Battle of Bushy Run while tending injured soldiers. At first, it had seemed to be healing normally. But then she suddenly began to have attacks of fever and weakness. Finally, she became so sick that the doctor at Fort Pitt declared that her death was imminent. But just as she neared death, Wend was ordered away to scout for a Black Watch company on a diplomatic mission into the Ohio Country. The mission lasted nearly two months; when he returned, Mary's regiment had left Fort Pitt to return home to Scotland for disbandment. Moreover, all the medical personnel in the fort's hospital had been replaced. Wend had assumed that Mary had died. In the next year he had married Peggy McCartie, the daughter of Sherman Mill's tavern keeper. Then, just days after his marriage, while he and Peggy were traveling to their new home in Virginia, he had found out through a chance meeting with a former 77th officer that Mary had in fact survived, stayed in

America with the Black Watch, and was in the garrison at Carlisle. Wend was devastated but, in the ten years since, he had become deeply attached to his wife and the three children she had given him.

But now, as he stood on the familiar parapet, Wend felt Mary's strong presence and the years seemed to melt away. He could visualize her, as real as in life, standing or sitting beside him in one of her frayed, patched gowns or in the marching outfit she had pieced together from uniform items taken from the bodies of dead soldiers.

After long minutes, Wend reluctantly shook himself from his memories of the girl. He knew he would never see her again, for the Black Watch had finally left the colonies in 1767 and he could only assume that she had departed with it.

He turned and walked over to the western side of the bastion. From there he could look out across the Allegheny River into the dark forests of the Ohio Country. For Wend had one more act of remembrance in which to indulge himself that night. Out there to the west, less than fifty miles away, in a Mingo village on Slippery Rock Creek, lived the women who the Indians called Orenda, which meant "person with magic hands." The woman was the wife of a Mingo war captain named Wolf Claw and she was a legend among tribal villages for her abilities as a medical healer.

However, Orenda was no black-haired Mingo woman born of the forest. She was in fact the golden-haired, blue-eyed daughter of a wealthy Philadelphia family. Her English name was Abigail Gibson and she had been Wend's very first love. That had been in 1759, during the last days of the French and Indian War. Their two families had been traveling together along Forbes Road en route to Fort Pitt, then under construction. Wend's father, Johann, had been contracted to become the fort's armorer. Abigail's father, a lawyer, had been appointed as the colony's first magistrate at the growing town of Pittsburgh and the legal advisor to Colonel Bouquet. Wend had been only fifteen years old and Abigail sixteen; from their first glimpse of each other at Harris' Ferry they had felt a visceral, physical attraction. Abigail had briefly attempted to deny her feelings toward a low-born apprentice, but in less than a week she had surrendered to her desires and, at a stop at Fort Loudoun, the two had stolen away in the night to consummate their passion in an empty cabin on the banks of Conococheague Creek.

Two days later, while they were still in the all-consuming flush of first romance, Wolf Claw's war party had ambushed the caravan at the base of Sideling Hill. Wend's entire family had been killed as had Magistrate Gibson. Wend himself had been severely wounded, scalped, and left for dead lying in

Forbes Road. Abigail and her black slave Franklin had been taken as prisoners back to the Mingo village, where by dictate of the tribal elders Abigail had been made the wife of Wolf Claw. Abigail became reconciled to her fate and was partially consoled by the fact that her situation allowed her to become doctor to the Indians of her own and surrounding villages. In fact, she had learned a great deal about medicine at the hands of a neighbor doctor in Philadelphia and had become frustrated that English society would never allow her to enter the man's world of medical practice. As she lived with the Mingo, she had gained in skill by learning how to blend both European and Indian medical practices.

Wend had been found, barely alive, by Captain James Robertson's company of the 77th Highlanders which had been marching eastward along Forbes Road from Fort Pitt. They revived Wend, provided initial treatment for his wounds, and transported him back to Carlisle. Joshua Baird, who had been scouting for the Highlanders, took a liking to Wend and arranged for him to be sheltered by Reverend Paul Carnahan and his wife Patricia, who was Baird's sister. Wend lived in their home in Sherman Valley, north of Carlisle, practicing his trade until the outbreak of Pontiac's War four years later.

With the start of the uprising in 1763, Wend had volunteered, along with Baird, to scout for Colonel Bouquet on his expedition to relieve Fort Pitt from the siege by the Ohio tribes, hoping for the opportunity to find and rescue Abigail. The major conflict of his life had arisen when, during the march westward, he had succumbed to the love of Mary Fraser and his determination to find and rescue Abigail had waned. But then, just as Mary lay dying, had come the order to scout for the diplomatic mission. The company of the Black Watch had eventually come upon Abigail's village. Wend, believing Mary dead, had been able to offer Abigail the opportunity to return to Pennsylvania with him. But while asserting her love for him, Abigail made the choice of staying with the Mingoes because she had two children, and a third on the way, who she felt would never be accepted by English society. Wend had then reluctantly departed with the soldiers, learning to reconcile himself to the fact that he would never be able to make a life with either of the women he loved.

As he stood in the darkness, immersed in his memories, Wend's thoughts were suddenly interrupted by the sound of someone clearing his throat. Startled, he spun around. There, barely visible in the moonlight, stood Richard Grenough. Or rather, the trader leaned casually, arms across his chest, against the wall at the entrance to the bastion. Clearly he had been there for some time. And next to the merchant, the large dog Wend had seen resting by the stairs at

Connolly's house sat on his haunches. As he watched, Grenough pushed himself fully upright and advanced toward Wend.

Wend felt a surge of fear. His only weapon was a tiny knife in his pocket. He inadvertently stepped back until he was against the wall.

Grenough saw his movement and called out, "Oh, come, come, my dear Eckert. There's nothing to fear; I'm not armed, and I certainly have more sense than to kill you right here in the midst of a garrisoned fort. Besides, I saw you walking up here and figured that it was a good time for us to have a private discussion, one gentleman to another."

"Grenough, neither of us qualifies as a gentleman."

The trader's only reply was a laugh; then he climbed steps up to the parapet and rested his arms on the wall next to Wend, looking out across the Allegheny. "From the way you were gazing, trancelike, out there into the Ohio Country, I presume you were indulging yourself with memories of the elegant Miss Gibson."

Wend was stunned. *My God, can the man read my mind?*

Grenough didn't wait for Wend to form an answer. He smiled broadly, his white teeth showing in the dim light, and said, "Undoubtedly you are wondering how I came to that conclusion. Well, given our past history, how could I not have invested a significant amount of time delving into your background?" He cocked his head and continued, "After all, just before leaving Pennsylvania, you very clearly identified me as a 'loose string' which you intended to snip off at some later date."

"Were you so sure that I was referring to you?"

Grenough leaned his head back and laughed loudly. "Oh, Eckert, be serious. Of course you were. You had openly shot my men Kinnear and Flemming when you caught them trading with Delawares out on the Allegheny in late 1763. And by the time we talked, you had killed Mathews and Crowley in the Tuscarora Mountains on their way to the spring trading in '64. You wounded Bratton at the same place. Then you nearly finished him off with a club in that tavern brawl up at Sherman Mill." He shook his head. "Obviously, I was next."

"So you sent Price Irwin and Shane Reilly to ambush me on my way to Virginia."

"Well, clearly I had no choice. And I thought they would easily take care of my problem. Imagine my chagrin when they simply disappeared, never to be heard from again."

Now Wend looked Grenough directly in the eye. "They're spending eternity in the company of snakes like themselves. No one will ever find them."

Grenough shrugged. "Men can be replaced. But the point is, after that it became clear to me that, even in your youth, you were a very dangerous man. So I took your threat very seriously and found out everything I could about your background, including your relationship with Miss Gibson."

"All that is very interesting, Grenough, but let's come to the point. Why did you come up here to talk with me?"

"Because it's time for you and I to come to terms. We need, if I may say so, to conclude a truce or, even better, a permanent treaty of peace."

Wend struggled to keep the astonishment out of his voice. "Why should I do that, Grenough?"

"Think about it, Eckert: The world changes over time. Look at this fort: ten years ago the pride of Britain, manned by first-rate troops. Now it's a crumbling wreck in a backwater of the empire, garrisoned by a rabble of militia." He waved his arm in a sweeping gesture which took in the countryside around them. "Ten years ago this was deep wilderness. Now look at all the lights of farmsteads in the forest around us and across both the rivers. Ten years ago this very land was considered by all to be part of Pennsylvania; now it is occupied by Virginia."

Wend asked, "What is your precise point in recounting all that?"

"Just this, Eckert: Your situation in life has changed as markedly as the examples I just cited. Ten years ago you were an enraged young buck consumed by the idea of avenging the death of his family and the loss of his woman. You could discount worries about your own safety. Now, if my reports are correct, you have become a man of substantial property with a family dependent on you." He paused, and said very carefully, "Eckert, it should weigh heavily on your mind that if something fatal happens to you in your pursuit of vengeance against me, you would leave your family in dire straits."

"Grenough, I don't know how to take that except as a threat. A threat which would do nothing but make me redouble my efforts to send you to hell. Do you consider that the basis for a truce?"

"My good Eckert, not a *threat*. A simple statement of *fact;* a man with responsibilities to others isn't free to go running around the border country casually shooting people he doesn't happen to like." He held up his hand. "But there is a second, and I believe more compelling, reason for us to make peace."

"And what would that be?"

"The fact that we will both soon have the opportunity to make a lot of money."

Eckert was puzzled. "You'll have to explain that."

"Come, come, Eckert. It cannot have escaped your attention that some sort of rash insurrection against the Crown is in the offing. These despicable Committees of Correspondence throughout the colonies are inciting the rabble in support of those radicals in Boston. The Ulster people in particular don't need much encouragement to pick up their firelocks against the King's Government. Naturally, whatever uprising does occur will be put down by the army in short order."

"What you predict is by no means certain. And how will that be of benefit to anyone?"

"Men of practical vision who remain loyal and provide support to the legitimate government can expect to benefit from the gratitude of the King and his royal governors. And both of us are in a position to be of significant use to the Crown."

Wend looked at Grenough. "I can see how you could help the government. You could provide supplies, wagons, pack animals. And then there is your influence with the Ohio tribes, which might enable you to sway them to the British cause. But I'm at a loss to understand what *my* unique contribution would be to the government."

Grenough responded, "I've made sure to get close to Northcutt. The fact is, he's very high on you and impressed with your tradecraft. Once fighting breaks out, there will be a need to keep both the regulars and loyal militia armed with effective weapons. But beyond that, he's told me he has been impressed with your ability as an organizer and your efficiency in getting things done; that's always essential in military operations. But most important, he is aware of the fact that you have, as it were, one foot in each of the two largest immigrant communities — the Germans and the Ulster. That could be very useful in helping the government recruit sympathizers from among those groups."

Wend shook his head. "Northcutt is overestimating my abilities and influence."

"Nonsense, Eckert. No one is more aware of your abilities than I, and I might add that I spent some time promoting you to Barrett this very evening."

"I am *overwhelmed* by your assistance," Wend said with clear irony in his voice.

"Indeed, you should be. But be that as it may, here's what's important, Eckert: Men who stand with Lord Dunmore in the time of crisis can expect to be very well rewarded. Not only through the award of profitable contracts to support His Majesty's forces, but also in land grants after the emergency as a mark of gratitude."

Wend hesitated a moment, and answered, "I have all the land I can use now. What would I do with more?"

"Eckert, for God's sake, lift your eyes up from the narrow world of your workshop. Suppose you received a grant of 5000 acres out in the Ohio Country, which is a rather normal amount in such cases. You could break it up into 100 or 200 acre parcels and sell it off to settlers over time. It would make you a wealthy man and elevate you to the gentry. Now there's a real legacy for your children."

Wend stood silent, his mind working to absorb the array of information Grenough had imparted.

After a few seconds of quiet, Grenough spoke again. "The point is, both of us will have our hands full taking advantage of opportunities which the coming crisis will present. From time to time, we may actually find ourselves working in close proximity or even in concert. And in that situation, neither of us will want to be looking over his shoulder to see if the other is about to take revenge for events which happened many years ago."

Wend spoke with incredulity in his voice. "So you actually expect me to forget the fact that you and your men are responsible for the death of my family?"

"I think you should consider this: Ross Kinnear was the one who sent that Mingo war party to attack your caravan on Forbes Road after you stumbled onto his pack train. I gave him no orders to do so and had no knowledge of his plans. Subsequently you killed Kinnear and another five of my men. Not only that, you have cost me two fortunes in lost trade goods and the profits I would have made from them." He paused and looked directly into Wend's eyes. "Perhaps upon serious reflection you could consider that you have exacted sufficient vengeance from me, particularly given the passage of time and my lack of direct involvement."

Wend looked at the man, initially taken aback by his audacity in raising the idea of peace between them. But then it occurred to him that Grenough's consummate skill at persuasiveness and negotiation, combined with his natural affability, were the very factors which had made him so influential among government officials. He remembered Grenough's manipulation of people like Bouquet, Colonel John Armstrong, and even Benjamin Franklin during the Paxton Boys Insurrection. So instead of a sharp rebuttal of the trader's proposal, Wend simply responded, "You've thrown a lot of ideas at me tonight. I'll have to turn them over in my mind."

Grenough smiled broadly. "Naturally you will have to think things over. But I'm confident that in the end you will see the wisdom of my proposal.

However, in the interim, I intend to act as if you have accepted my offer. I'll not take any kind of action against you or your family," he paused momentarily and looked into Wends eyes, "unless I perceive that you are moving against me or my men and property."

Wend said, "I'm not making any deals, but given the circumstances, I'm not likely to take any action here in Pittsburgh."

"Precisely, Eckert. So perhaps we can discuss this further the next time we meet in a social or business arena, which, if I read Northcutt's comments about the governor's intentions correctly, could be very soon indeed."

Wend replied, "I'm sure, given your closeness to Northcutt, that you know what you are talking about."

"I try, Eckert, I do try." Grenough stepped back from the wall, adjusted his hat, and touched his hand to the brim in a casual salute. Then he said, "Take care and have a safe trip back to Winchester, sir. Braddock's Road can be very dangerous." He turned and started to walk back toward the ramp.

Those words aroused a nearly forgotten memory in Wend's mind. He called out sharply to Grenough: "Sir, the last time I heard a warning like that was fifteen years ago from your man Ross Kinnear in the forests of the Conococheague Country. And a few days later my entire family was lying dead on Forbes Road."

Grenough spun on his heel and faced Wend. He smiled broadly and his teeth again flashed in the dim light. "Why Eckert, I meant nothing by that save a cordial statement of parting. Please don't take it in any other way. I bid you goodnight, sir."

Then, followed by the dog, he walked briskly down the bastion ramp and Wend was left alone to consider all that had transpired.

* * *

The next morning, Wend pulled himself out of bed much earlier than he would have liked, given the lateness of his return from the fort. Beyond that, the memories of his encounter with Grenough had allowed him only fitful sleep. Regardless, he quickly dressed and took breakfast in Semple's common room. Then he walked in the morning sun to the livery stable where Jake had taken the wagons and their teams. The stable was on the outskirts of town where there was good pasture land. It was co-located with a combination blacksmith-wheelwright shop, which made sense considering that the stable catered to the wagon trade which brought supplies into the town and transported trader's pelts eastward to market.

The two Morgan wagons were located to one side of the large yard between the stable and the workshop, sitting next to each other on jacks with their wheels already removed to facilitate another round of greasing. Other wagons were parked randomly around the open area. Wend looked for Jake and Elijah and found them at the blacksmith shop, casually standing by while the burly smith worked over the forge.

Jake Cather saw Wend and said, "Mornin', Eckert." Then he pointed at the forge, where a white-hot iron bar was being hammered into shape by the blacksmith. "There's the new axle brace to replace the one you gave away to them pilgrims." He smiled crookedly. "Hope you brought your money, 'cause he's chargin' extra to make it for us right away."

Wend patted his pocket. "Right there, Jake; that's why I came down here, to make sure we'd be ready to leave tomorrow."

The blacksmith, an Ulsterman named Crowe, paused in his work and said, "You're damned right it will cost extra. I had to put off another important job to take on your work." He spat on the ground. "I'm not sure why you're in such a hurry, since you just got in here yesterday. But I'll get this brace ready for you this morning. Then I got to start on a new tire for a big Conestoga wheel for another customer. I got to do it fast, so the wheelwright can shrink it onto the wheel rim soon as possible." He shook his head. "Why is everyone always in such an all-fired hurry?"

Jake smiled broadly. "That's a hell of a good point. Why *are* we leavin' so soon, Eckert? We just got here and Elijah and me are going to spend all day workin' on these wagons and loading provisions. And then you want to start out tomorrow. I'll tell you, it ain't hardly fair."

"That's the truth!" Elijah said. "We din't have no time last night, what with getting the horses put up and jacking the wagons. You ain't treatin' your waggoners like you ought to, Eckert."

Wend said, "Look, Jake, we've got a commission to take a load of supplies for the militia down to the Monongahela and Youghiogheny country to help fight the uprising. That's by the orders of Captain Connolly. And we're escorting a man with urgent information for Lord Dunmore himself." Then he thought of something. "I tell you what: We'll take a break at Ransome's Tavern or Wills Creek."

Jake was about to reply when he heard the sounds of a wagon and team pulling in right behind them. He stopped to stare at something over Wend's shoulder.

The blacksmith stopped and turned to look. He nodded his head toward the wagon. "There's the Conestoga wheel I got to work on."

Wend turned and saw a small flat-bed wagon pulled by a two-horse team. A large wheel, about five feet across, was strapped to the bed. Two men were seated on the bench seat. The driver was a wiry, black-haired man. He was tying the reins onto the brake handle in preparation for dismounting. The other man had a burly chest and arms, with great, powerful hands. He had thick brown hair pulled back in a queue and a full beard covering most of his face. But no beard could fully cover the distorted left side of his face or the multitude of scars. The man sat frozen in his seat and stared down at Wend with hatred in his eyes.

Wend felt a knot in his stomach as he looked at Matt Bratton.

Bratton scowled and jumped down from the wagon seat. The big man strode quickly around the wagon, hindered only slightly by a limp in his left leg. In a few seconds he reached Wend, towering over him by at least four inches. Without a word or an instant of hesitation, Bratton grabbed Wend by his jacket collar and hoisted him onto his toes. Wend's face was within a few inches of Bratton's.

"Eckert, I've been waiting ten years for this moment! Lying awake, thinkin' about it every night! Planning what I was going to do to you." The big man took his right hand off Wend's jacket, made it into a fist, and pulled his arm back to strike.

Wend reared his head back as far as he could and tried to push himself away from his assailant. But he couldn't break free and he realized that Bratton's fist would smash into him in the next instant. He gritted his teeth for the impact.

Then suddenly a pair of hands reached up and grabbed Bratton's right arm. Another set of hands grabbed Bratton around his neck and pulled him off of Wend.

Instantly Wend jumped clear. He saw that it was Bratton's black-haired companion who had grabbed his fist and that Cather had seized Bratton's neck. Jake was shorter than Bratton, but thickly built and had the powerful arm strength of every waggoner. Together the two men held Bratton at bay.

Matt Bratton was shaking in fury. He shouted, "For God's sake, McCrae, let me free! This is the man who gave me this face and ruined my leg! Let me go, so I can give him his due!" He tried to shake himself loose and then when the two men continued to hold him tight, he shrieked in a high-pitched tone of frustration, almost like that of a woman. "Damn it; let me finish him!"

McCrae remained calm. He said, "Bratton, remember what we was told. Don't cause no stir on any account. Keep your mind on business; that was the order. Now, me darlin', don't you be gettin' me in trouble with the big man." He turned and moved his eyes up and down over Wend, as if appraising his physical characteristics and strength.

At McCrae's words, Bratton seemed to regain some control. He took a deep breath and Wend could see his body start to relax. After about a minute, he spoke in a normal tone. "Let me go; I ain't gonna hit him now."

McCrae let go of Bratton's arm and turned to Jake. "Thanks for the help, mister. You can let him loose now, he ain't gonna' do anything." He looked into Bratton's eyes and said in a demanding tone, "Ain't that true, Matt?"

Bratton looked at McCrae. He shook his shoulders as if to shed his anger. "Yes, McCrae, you're right. I won't bash him right now." Then he looked back at Wend. "But the time is coming, Dutchman, soon enough. Mark my words!"

McCrae motioned over toward the flat-bed. "Come on, Bratton, help me get that wheel off the wagon. There's a load of pelts what has got to go east as soon as possible and it ain't goin' anywhere until that wheel is fixed."

Jake hesitantly removed his arms from around Bratton. Wend quickly stepped away from the forge and strode across the yard to the pasture fence, about twenty yards away. Breathing heavily in relief, he turned and leaned back against the top rail, keeping his eyes on Bratton. He felt drops of sweat running over his face.

Jake followed him over to the fence. He stood with one hand on the top rail and looked appraisingly at Wend, just like McCrae had done earlier.

"Eckert, I know you're a hell of a marksman. Ain't nobody in Winchester can equal you. But I ain't never seen you in a fight with your fists. You never even get into a brawl just for fun. It's hard to credit what that man was sayin' — that you messed up his face like that."

"You're right, Jake. I'm not much of a brawler. So when a fight does come to me, I don't play fair. When I was with the army, I learned that there's only winning and losing." He paused and looked directly at Jake. "It is true I did that to Bratton. It was at a tavern in Pennsylvania ten years ago. He accused a woman who was close to me of being a whore. So I knocked him to the floor with a chair when he wasn't looking. He hit his head on the hearth, which stunned him, and then I beat him on the head with a long piece of firewood until he was bloody and unconscious."

Cather looked back to where Bratton and McCrae were unloading the wheel. "Well, you did one hell of a job while you was at it."

Wend shook his head. "But I made a mistake, Jake; a big one."

Jake screwed up his face. "What mistake was that, Eckert?"

Wend said simply, "The truth is, I damn well should have killed him."

CHAPTER FIVE

The Warning

Despite the grumbling of the waggoners, the caravan left Pittsburgh early the next day after making a brief stop at Fort Pitt. There they loaded several kegs of powder, a quantity of lead, and provisions for the militia. They also met Northcutt, Crawford, and their servants on the parade. Then, nine men strong, the party departed southward before the sun had risen very high in the eastern sky.

During a stop to rest and water the horses, Wend had a chance to talk with Baird and Donegal. It was the first time they had been able to speak in confidence since the first night in Pittsburgh. He took the opportunity to give them a brief outline of his encounter with Grenough, acquainting them with the trader's suggestion of a truce in their mutual war.

Donegal was indignant. "Imagine that blackguard thinking you would agree with that, after what he done to your family and them Conestogas." He thought a moment, then guffawed. "Ha! It must be that he's gettin' along in years and he's scared of you. He's afraid you'll kill him before he can settle down with his wife in that big place of his in York."

Baird shook his head. "That ain't it at all, Donegal. Grenough may be keepin' watch on Wend, but I've known him for twenty-five years and I ain't never seen him be afraid of any man. More'n likely there's some profit he's after and doesn't want to have to worry about Wend gettin' in the way."

Wend smiled to himself. He thought: *Leave it to Joshua to figure out Grenough's motives without having heard all the details.* He said, "I think you're right, Joshua. He's looking to make some big money from the government and wants to be sure that I'm out of the way while he's doing it. He'll be trying to kill me again once he's got what he wants from Virginia."

Donegal asked, "So how did you answer him?"

Wend looked at his friends. "I left him guessing, except to say I wouldn't go after him while we were in Pittsburgh. But he was smart enough to know that anyway."

Joshua looked at Wend. "But if he's going to be working in Virginia with the government, you may have the opportunity to take care of him." Then Baird shot a questioning glance at Wend. "That is, if you're *really* still of the mind to put him in the ground."

Wend set his jaw. "Don't doubt it, Joshua. I made a promise over my father's grave. And a German jaeger always keeps his promise." He thought a moment. "But there's more: After what happened yesterday, I know I'll also have to finish Matt Bratton."

Then Wend thought of something else. "Say, Joshua, Grenough must have gotten into a fight sometime in the last ten years. He's got a long scar on the right side of his face, from near the ear down to his mouth. It must have happened a while ago, 'cause all the redness has faded. Do you know anything about that? You were the last one to see him."

Baird shot a quick look at Donegal and then he looked out into the forest as if organizing his thoughts. Finally he drawled, in a casual tone, "Yeah, well, it ain't no secret that Grenough has always been one for the young ladies of the lowest class when he's away from his home. He likes to impress them with his money and power. Fact is, he got that scar during the Bouquet campaign in '64. Rumor had it that one of the girls of the camp didn't take kindly to his advances and whipped a knife across his face when he wouldn't take 'no' for an answer."

Wend furrowed his brow. "Grenough may like to bed young girls, but I'm surprised that a man who calculates his every move would take a chance like that at a time he was advising Bouquet and the other leaders of the expedition."

Donegal laughed. "I've seen many a man lose his mind over some wee young thing. If she is pretty enough they start thinking from between their legs instead of with their head. I'm 'na surprised to find that Grenough is like other men in that way."

* * *

After the evening meal, Mr. Barrett Penfold Northcutt sat next to Crawford on a log in front of the campfire, savoring the liquid refreshment he was sipping from a pewter cup. He said, "That was a good stew, Eckert. And I must say that your man Donegal makes as fine a whiskey as I've tasted out here on the frontier."

Wend sat on another log across the fire from his two guests. The other men of the party shared a second fire about thirty feet away, from which their raucous laughter frequently broke the silence of the night forest. "Barrett, I must remind you that Simon Donegal isn't 'my man.' He's my compatriot and a former companion in arms. He owns land next to mine that he earned in the King's service and he farms my land for me so that I can concentrate on my tradecraft."

Northcutt was clearly feeling the effect of several cups of libation. But he realized his gaffe. "My apologies, Wend. That was a mere slip of the tongue."

"Of course, sir," Wend responded. Then he said, "And you're quite right about the whiskey." He reached down and tapped his hand on the jug which sat beside the fire. "Simon built his distillery years ago, right after we came to Virginia. He devotes a good part of each year's crop to making whiskey and has perfected his recipe over the years. I can tell you that at first it was pretty rough stuff, but now people all over the Winchester area are eager to buy his whiskey."

Crawford said, "It is damned good, Wend. Honestly, I must admit it's better than any whiskey I've tasted up here. You don't suppose I could prevail upon Donegal to give me his recipe?"

Wend grinned. "Not a chance, William. It's his greatest secret."

Crawford shrugged. "Ah well, at least I tried. Then he reached out and picked up the jug. He glanced at Wend and winked discreetly. "Have another cup, Barrett?"

Northcutt smiled broadly. "Damn, sir! Don't mind if I do. It will keep the chill of the evening at bay!"

After Northcutt's cup had been recharged, he reached into a coat pocket and pulled out a brown tubular object the like of which Wend had never seen before. It was about an inch thick and six inches long. Wend inquired, "What's that, sir?"

Northcutt looked at his two companions. "Have you never seen a cigar before?"

Both Eckert and Crawford shook their heads.

Northcutt laughed. "Why, it's a new form of smoking tobacco, gentlemen: fine tobacco leaves rolled tightly. Our Spanish friends in Cuba invented it. You light the end and smoke it down to the stub. I can tell you it's all the style in London; it has virtually replaced the pipe in fashionable society. And it has become quite popular in New York over the last couple of years."

Northcutt reached down to the fire, picked up a stick with a burning end, and used it to light the cigar. After he had it going, he took it out of his mouth, exhaled some smoke, and said, "It stays lighted much easier than a pipe; you can talk while you've got it going. It's also cleaner since you don't have to carry around a pouch of loose tobacco."

He took another puff and then exhaled his smoke over the fire. "Making cigars has become a burgeoning business. Women all over New York are rolling them in their homes for sale in shops and production is rising around Norfolk, where I got mine." He reached into his pocket and brought out two more and offered it to his companions. "Here, give one a try."

Crawford had his pipe going, but took one to try later. Wend said, "Thanks, but I've never taken up using tobacco, Barrett."

Northcutt shrugged and took another puff on the cigar.

Crawford changed the subject. "Well, Barrett, I know that you came to Virginia with the governor when he arrived in '71. If I may be so forward as to inquire, how did you and Lord Dunmore become so closely affiliated?"

"Not at all, Crawford. glad to tell you." He took a sip of his cup. "As you know, Lord Dunmore was previously the Governor of New York and we met right after he came from England. Of course, I had arrived some years earlier."

Wend asked, "That brings up a question I've had, sir. How was it that you did come to America? I was given to believe that your family had significant land north of London."

"My dear Eckert, it's quite simple if you know the facts. I suffered the fate of being the *third* son. Naturally, my oldest brother will inherit the family estate. And father purchased a commission in a very fashionable regiment for his second son. When it was my turn, father gave me the choice of the Royal Navy — he had a friend in command of a frigate who was willing to take me on as a midshipman — or a stipend and a letter of introduction so that I could seek my own fortune, as it were. I took the money and spent a couple of years in a London counting house, bored to distraction every day. So then I decided to take my chances in the colonies, where it seemed there was growing opportunity and life offered a little more excitement."

Northcutt grinned at both his companions. "And on the trip over, I found that I had made the right choice about the navy. I was sick the entire six weeks! Hardly left my cabin the whole time and couldn't eat. Damn well looked like a wraith when I got off the ship!"

Crawford said, "So I presume your ship came to New York City?"

"Precisely, William. I arrived in '63 with a useful amount of money, still having my father's gift and a little more saved from my days in London's financial world. So I went about making investments in a range of mercantile ventures.

I became a partner in ship cargoes, trading expeditions out to the border, and land purchases. Fortunately most of these ventures paid off. Then I married a sweet girl from a Dutch family and bought a nice house."

Wend said, "I wasn't aware that you had a family; you've never mentioned your wife in our meetings."

A shadow passed over Northcutt's face. "Unfortunately, my wife — bless her soul — passed away trying to bear our first child. And I've remained a bachelor ever since."

"My condolences, sir. I'm sorry for reminding you of such a sad event."

"Think nothing of it, Wend. I've gotten over it. And coming to Virginia put me in a new setting without the reminders of family life in New York. I guess you could say I've filled my life with business and government affairs."

Wend laughed. "After negotiating with you for contracts, I can see why you've succeeded in that line."

Northcutt said, "Well, the fact is, that's actually how I became involved with Dunmore in the first place. We met during the round of welcoming parties which naturally took place after his arrival. His Lordship, upon learning of my background, asked me about the investment possibilities here in the colonies and things grew from there." He looked meaningfully at his two companions across his whiskey cup. "And I dare say my fortune has not suffered from our acquaintance."

Crawford asked, "Barrett, what do you think about the situation out here along the Ohio? Is there a way to reconcile the desires of settlers for land and the needs of the Shawnees for open hunting grounds?"

"You know, Crawford, I must say that I am very impressed with this fellow Grenough. He's close to the position of Dunmore and myself on how to handle matters here." Northcutt thought a moment. "I'll be honest with you: There are a lot of matters on the governor's plate right now. This border situation is serious, but not necessarily the most important. Frankly, the problem Dunmore wakes up worrying about every morning is the need to find some strategy which will staunch the drift of the colonists toward the anti-government Whig position. He's desperate for a way to convince Virginians that it is in their interest to work things out with the Crown and Parliament before some outright insurrection occurs."

Wend said, "We all want that."

"Eckert, I wish that were truly so, but frankly I think you're being a little naive. The governor has tried to be as conciliatory as possible. But these Whig hotheads are stirring up the people against the Crown every day. That's what is so disturbing to me about Dunmore's need to dissolve the Burgesses. Clearly friction has grown rapidly in the last few weeks, because there was no hint that such an action would be necessary when I departed for the border."

Crawford asked, "So what do you think Lord Dunmore can do to turn things around?"

"Good question, William. But, by God, I think there is an answer. The other night Grenough talked about taking decisive steps to protect the settlers around Pittsburgh and along the Ohio. In my mind we can expand that strategy to renew the loyalty of people all through the western part of Virginia. It would be a counterweight to the arguments of the Whig radicals. I think we should raise a large force of militia, not just to defend the border, but to decisively defeat the Shawnees, the hostile elements of the Mingo tribe, and any other Ohio tribes who join this festering uprising."

There was silence at the fire. After a few moments Crawford said, "Barrett, that would have to be a very large expedition, raising the militia of many counties in the west and central parts of the colony."

Northcutt leaned forward. "But don't you see? An expedition to permanently take the southern part of the Ohio Country from the Shawnee would show a broad range of people that the government had their interests at heart. Think of all the men who fought in the war with the French and are owed land grants. Think of all the Ulster and German people who are looking for fresh farmland. And such a move would greatly ease the fear settlers have of war party raids all along Virginia's border area, from here right down to Carolina. They would see clearly that their interest lay with loyalty to the Crown. By God, I see a good chance it would stop this damnable insurrection movement in its tracks, at least here in Virginia. And a loyal Virginia would split the south from the north and perhaps leave those New Englanders isolated in their treason against the Crown." He paused and looked at them, the enthusiasm clearly visible in his eyes. "So, such an expedition would solve two problems at the same time — the Indian uprising itself and the growing unrest of the of the colony's citizens."

Wend's mind was going at full speed. He shot a quick look at Crawford, then said to Northcutt, "But there's a problem there, sir. Raising a militia force of that size would take weeks; then additional time for organization and gathering of supplies. And then there's the long march out to the border. But the uprising is happening right now."

"A good point, but not totally correct, Eckert." Northcutt wagged his finger at Wend and grinned. "Keep in mind that the present war parties consist mainly of Mingoes bent on revenge and a few bands of young Shawnee warriors looking for excitement. The main force of Shawnee chiefs and warriors is still in their villages. That's why I laid some plans with Connolly before I left Pittsburgh." He leaned forward and looked at Eckert and Crawford conspiratorially. "Now listen carefully, gentlemen: The good Mr. McKee is clearly intent on negotiations with Cornstalk and any other Ohio chiefs who will agree to parley for a peace agreement. I've directed Connolly to enthusiastically support his efforts. Grenough has also agreed to help. The talks will be dragged out and it will buy us time; time to marshal our forces!"

Crawford said, "Barrett, the Indians will be doing the same thing. And they can be damned cagey."

Northcutt shrugged and waved his hand dismissively. "Frankly, I expect that. Both sides will be playing for time. I think the tribes will need just as long as we to make preparations. And there's another factor: Both McKee and Grenough say that Cornstalk is the most important leader of the Shawnee and he's not particularly enthusiastic about war. He remembers Pontiac's War and believes that a new war could be devastating for his tribe." He looked down into the fire for a moment. "Meanwhile, it's my job to get the governor's approval for the plan, muster support around the colony, and make sure that we use our time to form an effective army."

There was a silence as the three men stared into the flames and thought about Northcutt's words. Then Barrett pushed himself to his feet, momentarily unsteady as he felt the effect of the multiple cups of whiskey. He steadied himself, cleared his throat, and announced, "If you'll pardon me for a moment, I need to make a little trip into the bush!" He strode off into the woods, working to open his breeches.

Wend also got to his feet. He threw a couple of logs into the fire and then walked over to one of the wagons to stretch his legs, which had started to cramp from sitting for so long by the fire. He looked up at the words painted on the wagon's canvas cover, which were illuminated by the flickering light from the fire. It read, in large capital letters, "D. MORGAN FREIGHT" and below that "Winchester" in smaller letters. He stood thinking about what Northcutt had said.

Crawford joined him. "Northcutt is full of schemes, isn't he?"

Wend grinned and said, "And full of himself." Then he asked, "What do you think of his plan? Do you think the governor will accept it?"

Crawford was about to respond when Wend heard a zipping sound; a sound Wend had not heard since Bushy Run. Then there was a soft 'plop' and a small round hole suddenly appeared in the canvas of the wagon between the two of them, not more than a foot from Wend's face. A fraction of a second later the sound of the gunshot echoed through the forest.

An expression of shock burst across Crawford's face and he reared backward. Wend was turning toward where the shot had come from when he heard the zipping sound again and a second hole appeared in the canvas within two inches of the first, followed by the sound of the shot.

The other men jumped to their feet. They all ran for their firelocks, as did Wend and Crawford. The party took cover behind trees and under the wagons. In the midst of their scurrying for cover, Northcutt came running back from the bush, holding up his breeches.

"My God, are we under attack?" he shouted and then flung himself to the ground between Crawford and Eckert.

Crawford stared out into the darkness and said calmly, "It would seem so, Barrett."

The men lay in their positions for what seemed a long time, but was probably no more than fifteen minutes. But there were no further shots or any sounds at all from the forest. Then Joshua shouted from his position about thirty feet away. "I don't reckon that was any war party attack. They'd have been onto us a'fore this if it was."

Wend had been thinking the same thing.

Crawford looked at Wend in puzzlement. "If it's not an attack, what the devil is going on?"

Without saying anything, Wend stood up, cradling his rifle in his arm, and walked back to the wagon. Joshua came out and joined him, as did Crawford. The three stood looking at the two closely spaced holes in the canvas.

Crawford spoke up. "Will you look at that? They're both right in the center of the 'O' in the word 'Morgan'. Just like someone was using it as the target in a shooting match!"

Wend suddenly realized that Crawford was more right than he knew. The bullets had been deliberately fired into the center of the 'O' to make a point. Undoubtedly it was a message from Grenough that the balls could just as easily have been into Wend's head. Wend instinctively sensed that the message had been delivered by Matt Bratton, a man who was nearly as good a marksman as Wend and who had been his rival in matches at Sherman Valley long ago. Bratton had the skill to put two shots next to each other like that from long range. Wend thought: *Back at Fort Pitt, Grenough had offered a choice of peace or war between them and had described the benefits of peace. Now he was dramatically demonstrating the consequences of a continued war.*

Wend looked at Crawford and Joshua. "You're right, William. Somebody I knew long ago was trying to give me a warning."

Joshua smiled tightly at Wend, but said nothing. Wend knew he understood.

Suddenly Northcutt's voice came from behind Wend. "Are you saying somebody shot at you like that just to make a point?"

Wend was thinking about how to answer Northcutt when Joshua said, "Shhh! I hear something." He quickly walked around the wagon and out onto the road. Wend, Crawford, and Northcutt followed him.

Baird dropped down onto the road and cupped his hand to his right ear near the ground. He remained that way for long moments. Then he said quietly, "I hear hooves; hooves of at least two horses. Heading west, back toward Pittsburgh, at the gallop."

Wend thought, *Yes, it's Bratton. Bratton and someone else; probably that fellow McCrae.*

Northcutt asked, with clear anxiety in his voice, "Eckert, for God's sake, what is this all about?"

Crawford's face was twisted in a crooked grin. He spoke calmly. "Yes, Wend, I'm dying of curiosity."

Wend chose his words carefully. He looked at Crawford and then at Northcutt. "Gentlemen, I need to ask your forbearance in this matter. There are things I did in my youth which I am not ashamed of but which it is imprudent for me to talk about. However, let me assure you that nothing which has happened tonight puts you in any danger. And some day I will resolve the problem with honor and in my own way."

Northcutt stood staring at Wend in puzzlement for a long moment. Then a smile came over his face and he put his hand on Wend's shoulder. "As you wish, Eckert; but I must admit that I'm *damned* intrigued. You are the last man I would have expected to find involved in some dark mystery."

William Crawford smiled slyly at Wend, his eyes twinkling. "Eckert, some day when you have resolved the situation, you must tell me all about it. And I shall be *very* disappointed to find out that this doesn't have something to do with a woman!"

PART TWO
The Men of Winchester

June – July 1774

CHAPTER SIX
Visitor at Eckert Ridge

Baird and Donegal sat on benches under the lean-to roof outside Wend's workshop sharing the contents of a jug. It was late afternoon, coming on to evening, of the second day after they had arrived back home from Pittsburgh. It was Donegal who called out, "Hey, Wend, you might want to come take a look. There's a rider coming in!"

Wend, work apron over his clothes, came out under the lean-to roof and stared down the drive which led up the hill to the farmstead. He wiped his hands with a rag and stood blinking momentarily in the light. Then he saw him: A dark figure, taking his time coming up the wagon track with his horse at the walk. Watching his deliberate approach, Wend gained the distinct impression that the man was surveying the farmstead, taking in the layout and details in the manner of a scout for a military column.

Then his eyes were drawn to the rider's mount. *That man's got a nice piece of horseflesh.* The bay stallion was tall, even taller than The Mare, and with longer legs and a powerful chest. A white blaze and stockings on three legs gave the animal a striking look. *I'll bet you'd have to search all of Frederick County to find a match in speed and jumping ability.*

As the distance closed, Wend moved his attention to the rider. He was dressed in black from head to toes. A broad brimmed hat with the right side turned up, black coat, waistcoat, and breeches; a pair of gleaming black boots. And the whole outfit topped off by a cape of the same color. The only contrast was a spot of crisp white from the cravat showing above the waistcoat. For a moment Wend thought the man might be of the clergy, but that idea was soon dispelled by the style and quality of the clothing and the horse. No minister would be outfitted so well. Clearly, this was a man of some wealth.

Presently the rider reached the crest and pulled his horse up beside the lean-to. Instead of dismounting, he sat the horse, silently looking down at the trio and the workshop.

Wend returned his silent stare. In contrast to his dark clothing, the man was blonde-haired with blue eyes. The face was youthful and devilishly handsome, with fair skin bronzed by the sun. But Wend noticed a contrasting hardness in the eyes and mouth which somewhat belied the youthful countenance. The man seemed perhaps three or four years younger than Wend's twenty-nine years. After a long moment, Wend broke the silence and said, "Good afternoon, sir."

The stranger ignored Wend's greeting; instead he nodded in the direction of the rifling machine which took up much of the space under the lean-to. "I've never seen anything like that device; what is it?"

Wend put his hand on the drive shaft and shrugged. "It's a machine to cut rifle grooves in gun barrels. You'll find one in any gunmaker's shop."

"Ah, then I must be in the right place." The man smiled thinly. "Can I take it that I have arrived at Eckert Ridge, the home of the gunsmith Mr. Wend Eckert?"

Wend nodded. "I'm Eckert. Welcome to the farm."

The rider swung down from the bay in an easy motion. Watching him, Wend thought: *This is a man who does a lot of riding.* Then Wend noticed he was tall and lean; at least as tall as Joshua.

The stranger walked over to the rifling machine and inspected its layout and mechanism. Without bothering to look at Wend, he said, "You know, sir, you really should put up a sign telling travelers that this is Eckert Ridge. I guessed this must be your place from the directions given to me in Winchester, but there was nothing to note the name down on the road."

Wend, a little annoyed at his dismissive manner, thought: *He's probably the son of some wealthy planter and accustomed to people deferring to his wishes.* He answered, "We haven't really given the place a formal name. People in Winchester and the country around here have taken to calling this Eckert Ridge, but we simply call it *The Farm.*" Then he said, making sure to put a little edge in his voice, "However that may be, you have me at a disadvantage, sir. Might we know your name?"

"Ah, yes, my apologies, sir. *Caulfield,* sir. Geoffrey Caulfield." He stared into the shop. "I'm here to inquire about procuring a brace of pistols; horse pistols specifically." He turned and looked directly at Wend for the first time. "I saw some of your work displayed at a shop in Winchester — a fowling piece and a rifle — and found the craftsmanship appealing. The proprietor told me you also made pistols. So here I am."

Wend shrugged. "Well, Mr. Caulfield, you are at the right place. Come into the shop and we'll show you some examples which may please you." Wend turned and led the way inside.

The shop was a hive of activity; evening clean-up was in progress. Two apprentices were sweeping the floor while the third was cleaning the surfaces of individual workbenches. The journeyman, Wilhelm Hecht, was inspecting the work which had been performed on several muskets during the day. Wend looked with satisfaction at a row of more than twenty muskets which had already been renovated and were ready for delivery. He had been very pleased with the way that Hecht and the apprentices had kept themselves busy while he had been on the trip to Pittsburgh.

Caulfield looked around in curiosity. "Eckert, you have a very large shop and a lot of people working for you. Most gunmakers I've seen work alone or with just an apprentice."

Wend explained about the musket contract he had with the colony, which kept the extra men busy. Caulfield nodded but said nothing.

Then Wend pointed at a pair of large pistols which rested upon brackets on the wall next to his own workbench. "Mr. Caulfield, these have just been finished; I was planning to deliver them to a shop down in Alexandria which sells my wares. But I'll gladly offer them to you now, and at something of a discount, since that will spare me the cost of transport." He took one of the pistols from the brackets and handed it to his customer.

Caulfield inspected the firelock. Wend watched carefully and could tell by his confident manner that he had a good knowledge of weapons.

"Eckert, these are precisely what I was seeking."

"I'm proud to say that we've provided pistols to many gentlemen, sir."

Caulfield held the heavy pistol in his right hand, raised his left arm as a brace, and laid the pistol barrel over his forearm as if aiming at a target. As he sighted along the barrel, he said, "Yes, I do like the feel of this. They have a good heft, the lock is obviously of quality, and the finish is very good."

Then he stopped for a moment, staring at another pistol which hung on the wall. "Now that's an elegant-looking firelock, even if it is smaller than I'm accustomed to."

Wend answered, "That pistol was made by my father and myself, back in 1759. It was a gift to Colonel Henry Bouquet. He carried it at Bushy Run and during his 1764 campaign into the Ohio Country."

Caulfield raised an eyebrow. "How is it that you have it now?"

"As you may know, sir, after his promotion to general, Bouquet was ordered to Pensacola, on the Florida coast, as commander of army forces in the south.

But he died of yellow fever almost immediately upon his arrival." Wend paused and looked directly at Caulfield. "Lieutenant Welford, Bouquet's aide, forwarded the pistol to me. He sent along a note saying it was the general's wish, given on his deathbed."

"Could I handle it?"

Wordlessly, Wend passed the pistol to Caulfield, who repeated the same testing procedure he had used with the horse pistol.

"Eckert, this pistol has a superb feel to it. The curve of the grip fits my hand perfectly." He held out the pistol and aimed it. "And it's light enough to hold steady without support."

Wend smiled at Caulfield. "Your reaction is the same as many customers. The fact is my father spent years perfecting the design. His idea was to make a pistol sized so that it could function effectively either as a horse pistol or one that could be carried comfortably in a man's belt or greatcoat pocket. Thus it is lighter and shorter than a horse pistol. And after much experimentation he perfected the curve in the grip which makes the pistol virtually an extension of a man's arm and will put you on target without the need for much concentration."

Caulfield looked at the pistol for a moment, turning it over in his hands. "How long would it take you to make me a brace of these?"

Wend walked over to a shelf and picked up a case of dark wood. He set it on his workbench in front of Caulfield, then released the brass hook and lifted the case's lid. Inside, on blue felt, lay two pistols virtually identical to the one in Caulfield's hand. Their wooden frames showed a rich, well-oiled finish which highlighted the grain. The locks and brass fittings gleamed brightly. Also in the case was a charging flask of the same quality brass and a mold for balls.

"By God!" exclaimed Caulfield.

Wend smiled in satisfaction. "Yes, they're very attractive, if I do say so myself. These were also made for sale in Alexandria." He looked at Caulfield. "I'm attempting to show the tobacco gentry down in the Tidewater that guns made here in Virginia can be of the same quality as the ones they're so fond of importing from Europe." He turned and pointed to several beautifully finished long-barreled firelocks on the wall. "All those are for delivery to Alexandria. They have first rate locks from England or Germany and barrels from a fine forge near Fredericksburg."

The young man's face showed impatience. "But Eckert, you *would* sell this pair of pistols here and now, wouldn't you?"

Wend hesitated, as if reluctant. Then he said, "You came here for horse pistols. Perhaps it would be a good idea for you to test-fire both the horse pistols and then these, to see if you really find them to your taste." Wend looked directly into Caulfield's eyes. "I raise that point because, while I offered to reduce the price of the horse pistols, I won't take a penny off of my price for this pair. You can find horse pistols in many gunmakers' shops, but pistols of this design are available only here."

Wend watched the man's face carefully. Caulfield's eyes moved between the two pistol models several times. The muscles of his mouth worked repeatedly. Clearly he was trying to make a decision.

"All right, Eckert. I'll try both out."

Wend nodded, then spoke to his journeyman. "Hecht, have one of the apprentices load both sets of pistols." Then he said to Caulfield. "Let's go out to the range." He motioned to the youngest of the apprentices, who looked to be only about ten years of age. "Bernd, come with us to set up the targets."

The three walked outside to the side of the shop, where a firing range, marked out to 200 yards, had been set up. Bernd picked up a wooden target board and set it up on a stand about ten paces away from the firing mark.

Caulfield took off his cloak and then the coat, handing both to Bernd.

Meanwhile the two other apprentices carried out both sets of pistols.

Wend said, "Let's start with the horse pistols."

Caulfield shot both pistols, using the arm-brace technique. The two shots were grouped together on the upper right edge of the target. Wend commented, "Well, sir, there's no doubt you know how to shoot."

"Those pistols performed about as I would have expected," Caulfield responded. "Now let's try out the lighter ones."

Wend was glad to note a tone of eagerness in Caulfield's voice. He nodded and handed one of the smaller pistols to him. "Sir, I recommend you fix your gaze on the center of the target and then simply extend your arm and the pistol, as if pointing your finger. Don't try to sight along the barrel. Let your eye and brain work together to control your aim."

Caulfield faced the target and then quickly aimed and fired with his right hand. The ball struck within two inches of the center.

"By God!" exclaimed Caulfield.

"Repeat that, sir, with the second pistol, using the same procedure."

Caulfield complied. The second ball struck within an inch of the first. He stood staring at the result for a long moment. Then he slowly looked at Wend. "Damn, sir! You are absolutely right. These firelocks almost aim themselves."

Wend answered, "My father was a thoughtful and inventive man. If he had lived a full life, he would have been the most noted gunsmith in Pennsylvania."

He paused, seemingly lost in thought. Then he looked at Caulfield. "But now I'm the only man who knows the secret of those pistols."

Caulfield looked down at the pistol in his hand and then up at Wend. He was about to speak when the sound of a feminine voice stopped him.

"Indeed, sir. Never allow yourself to doubt that behind that stony face, my husband has the same brains as his father. And he's just as fine a gunsmith."

Caulfield and Wend turned to see Peggy McCartie Eckert standing a few feet behind the firing mark. She was wearing a work gown of her favorite color, a medium blue which complemented her raven hair and blue eyes. For contrast she had a white apron over the gown and a round white cap pinned to her hair. She was smiling broadly as she looked at the visitor.

Every time he saw Peggy, Wend found it remarkable how his wife, after ten years of marriage and three children, still had the slim-waisted figure and comely face which had made her the main attraction of her father's tavern in Sherman Mill. Few men realized that she was nearly thirty years old. And, if anything, maturity had given her face an even more alluring aura.

Wend glanced at Caulfield and saw in his face that Peggy was having the same effect on him that she had with most men. His eyes first opened wide, then focused on her as he looked at her high cheek-boned face, strong mouth, and deep-set eyes with long lashes. Then he slowly moved his eyes down her body, inspecting her ample breasts and then estimating the length of her legs.

His perusal of her body was interrupted by Peggy herself, who spoke to Wend. "I came out on the porch to call Bernd back to the house for some chores, but then I saw you had a visitor on the range, so I came over to watch the shooting and fetch Bernd directly." She looked at Caulfield and then back at her husband. "You are going to introduce me to our guest, aren't you?"

Wend made introductions. Then he watched in amusement as Peggy went into what he liked to think of as her "Tavern Girl Coquette Performance." She canted her hips, put one hand at her waist, opened her eyes wide, cocked her head slightly to the right, and gave Caulfield the broad, welcoming smile which had beguiled so many men in the common room of McCartie's Tavern.

Caulfield recovered from his initial reaction and remembered his manners. He bowed deeply to Peggy and said, "It's my pleasure to meet you, Mrs. Eckert. Clearly your husband is a most fortunate man in his marriage to such an elegant and graceful lady."

"Why Mr. Caulfield, you are *such* a flatterer." She put a hand to her hair as if to smooth her locks. "I can hardly credit your words, particularly when you see me fresh from my work and in nothing but ordinary household clothes."

As she spoke, young Bernd, still holding Caulfield's clothing, came over and stood beside her. Wend took the items from him and said, "Here, I'll take those, son."

Caulfield looked at Bernd as if really seeing him for the first time. "Ah, so the lad's your son, Eckert." He looked at Wend, and then between the boy and his mother. "I would never have guessed the relation from his appearance. But now that I look, he must take after his mother's side of the family. He certainly has his mother's eyes. And he's a fine, strapping lad." He looked at Wend again, then back at the boy. "He's already tall for his age and certainly has a powerful set of shoulders. I'd wager that he'll be taller and more burly than his father."

Caulfield didn't notice the quick look which Wend and Peggy exchanged at his words. Wend put his hand on Bernd's shoulder and said, "Indeed, he *is* a fine lad, Caulfield. And he's going to be a credit to the family trade."

Peggy gave Caulfield her most enticing smile and asked, "It's so late in the day, sir; won't you stay for the night?"

"Alas that I could, Mrs. Eckert, but I've taken rooms in the new inn at Battletown Crossroads and my man is waiting for me there."

"Well then, at least you must stay for supper. It's not often that we have a distinguished visitor." She raised her eyes. "I don't believe you're from Winchester; we should have made your acquaintance before this."

"No, Mrs. Eckert. I'm visiting Frederick County on business. And I would be enchanted to dine with your family before I ride back up to the inn."

"Wonderful, Mr. Caulfield. Then I'll see you at the house when you and my husband have finished your business." Peggy turned and walked back toward the house, which was just across the drive.

Wend watched as Caulfield's eyes followed Peggy. His wife walked in the provocative way she had when she knew men were watching her. Wend smiled, for he had seen it many times before. Then he turned to Bernd. "Son, take Mr. Caulfield's horse to the stable and give it some oats. Then join your mother in the house."

Wend turned back to Caulfield. "Well, sir, have you made up your mind?"

Caulfield smiled and, instead of answering, followed Bernd to the hunter. He removed the saddlebags and threw them over his shoulder and then reached into one and pulled out a small bag. He walked back to where Wend stood, and held up the bag, which jingled with the sound of coins. "The decision is made, Eckert. I'll take the special pair. Name your price, sir."

* * *

The evening meal was well underway in the Eckert home. Instead of the familial and somewhat raucous atmosphere which normally pervaded meals, Peggy had ratcheted up the level of formality in honor of their guest. The youngest, four-year old Ellen had been fed earlier in the cook-house and then sent to bed. Wend sat at the head of the table, with Caulfield at his right. Bernd sat beside Caulfield. Peggy sat across from Caulfield on Wend's left instead of at the foot of the table, where she would have normally held sway if there had been more guests. Seven year old Elise was placed beside her mother so Peggy could provide any assistance necessary during the meal. The girl was a miniature version of her mother.

As was customary on occasions of this nature, the cook's son Billy had been dressed appropriately and pressed into service as waiter under the guidance of his mother Wilma. Peggy liked to entertain and so Billy was practiced in his role. Since Caulfield had arrived late in the day, it had not been possible to arrange for a special menu, so the main course was simply a roasted chicken. But Wilma had been able to put together a wider variety of vegetables than normal and arrange some attractive garnishments for the chicken serving plate and decorations for the table.

After years in a tavern common room, Peggy had the skill of talking with anyone and she kept the conversation moving. She had started just as the meal began and everyone was settling in at the table and opening their napkins. "So, Mr. Caulfield, you said you were just visiting Winchester. Would it be forward of me to guess that you are up from the Tidewater? Perhaps from near Norfolk or even Williamsburg itself?" She smiled, "Is it too much to hope that you're indeed from the capital and we might be able to hear all the news from down there?"

Caulfield's brow furrowed. He hesitated noticeably and then said, "Actually, Mrs. Eckert, I'm from a little further south than that, but certainly what could be called the Tidewater area. And I have spent considerable time in Norfolk and Williamsburg."

Peggy said, "I'm so glad to hear that. And can't we be on a first name basis, Mr. Caulfield? My name is Elizabeth, but everyone calls me Peggy. And my husband's name is Wend, which is short for Wendelmar. May I presume to call you Geoffrey?"

"That would please me greatly, Peggy."

Peggy tossed her head. "Oh, good, that's so much better, don't you agree? Anyway, how *much* further south is your home, Geoffrey?"

Caulfield again hesitated for a few seconds. Wend got the distinct impression that he was trying to decide how much to reveal about himself.

"Well, Peggy, my family's holdings are actually below Norfolk, across the border into Carolina. Near a small port town called Edenton, on Albemarle Sound." He smiled at his hosts, and asked, "Have you heard of it?"

Wend nodded. "Yes, I have. I believe it is a small tobacco port, something like our Alexandria. Am I not correct?"

"Precisely, Eck..., er, Wend." He paused. "The plantation is to the east of the town, on Queen Anne Creek."

Peggy exclaimed, "How interesting! I believe that you are the first person from Carolina that I've met." Then she asked, "Now didn't you say that you were here on business?"

"Yes, uh, I'm looking for land here in the Valley; land to hold for speculation. And I'm using Winchester as my headquarters for the search, if you will." Then Caulfield cleared his throat and hurriedly changed the subject. "Speaking of homes and land, I was surprised to see the size of your place. You have many buildings on your farm and several houses."

Wend said. "What you see can be a little deceiving. This is really three establishments; three families, if you will. Almost like a small village."

Caulfield looked bemused. "I confess I don't understand."

"Well, this site and the lands to the north of here are mine; two hundred acres, of which somewhat less than half are cleared for pasture or cultivation. We bought that back in '64, when we got here from Pennsylvania." Wend paused to gather his thoughts. "The adjacent land to the south is owned by my friend Simon Donegal. He earned it for service with the 77th Highlanders during the French War."

Caulfield said, "That's interesting. But I had the understanding that land grants for military service were in Ohio or up to the north toward Canada. And I recollect hearing that the Highlanders who stayed in the colonies were granted land in northern New York or Canada."

Wend nodded. "You heard correctly, sir. But Donegal decided he liked Virginia. So we found a lawyer in Winchester who dealt in land interests. He arranged for Donegal to sell his rights to northern land for ownership of a hundred acres here. And now Simon farms both his own land and mine, which allows me to focus on my trade."

"Well, you've done quite a lot of work clearing the land and getting the farm going."

Wend laughed and shook his head. "We purchased the land from an estate and most of what you see was cleared by the previous owner. But all the buildings here on the farmstead were built since we arrived."

Peggy spoke up. "Now Geoffrey, I'll tell you a secret: The log cook-house behind the main house was originally our cabin, which Wend and Donegal built the first summer. Bernd and Elise were born there."

Wend said, "The truth is, we had a lot of help with the cabin and the barn. Our neighbor Dan Morgan, who lives a little to the north of here — actually not far from Battletown where you are staying — helped us. He organized the folks round here for a cabin raising; the main walls were built in one day. Then Donegal and I put on the roof and finished things off."

"We lived in that cabin until '69." Peggy looked at pride around the dining room. "This house was just finished five years ago."

Caulfield noted the pride on her face. "And a very charming house it is, Peggy. Two floors, the white painted siding, and a very nice central hall. I especially like the porch, the way it goes across the entire front of the house." He smiled at Peggy. "It reminds me of many of the plantation houses around Albemarle Sound."

Peggy smiled broadly at the compliment. "Oh, thank you for saying that, Geoffrey! You see, Wend and I had a bit of a difference about the design of the house. He would have built one of those square, sober looking stone German houses, like back in Pennsylvania. But I told him that we needed to have something more English looking, like our neighbors. I think the white paint and wide porch make the house look so much more welcoming." She looked at Wend. "And my dear husband, you have to admit it was much cheaper than brick would have been!"

Wend said nothing about the house. The truth was, he had come to like the look of the place, but it had become a point of humorous contention between them for him not to admit it.

Caulfield said, "Where does your friend Donegal live?"

Wend smiled. "He's a bachelor. He lives in what he calls 'The Barracks'." It's a long log building; one end contains a set of rooms which are his quarters, then there's a kitchen and eating room for all the field hands and other single men who live on the farm, and the rest of it is a long, open sleeping room for them."

Caulfield thought for a moment. "It would seem Mr. Donegal hasn't forgotten his days in the army. But you said there were three establishments here; what constitutes the third? Do you have another partner in ownership of lands here?"

Wend smiled. "The third is Joshua Baird and his woman Alice Downy. But he's not an owner."

"And what does Mr. Baird do — help run the farm?" Caulfield looked puzzled. "Is he the overseer?"

Peggy broke out into laughter. "Joshua does just what he wants and nothing more!"

Wend smiled at his wife's amusement. "Caulfield, Joshua spent most of his life roaming the border. He's been a long hunter, a trapper, a trader, and very often a scout for the army. He was the chief scout for Bouquet on Forbes' expedition to take Duquesne in '58 and then continued to work for him until the general left for the south in '65." Wend paused and then said; "Now he mainly provides us with meat from hunting."

"And Alice teaches all the children on the farm," Peggy added. She's very good at that; and she also does a lot of sewing for the people here."

Wend said, "They live in a house near a patch of woods at the back of the farmstead. We built a log schoolhouse next to their place."

Caulfield frowned, and said, with a faint hint of disdain, "I should say he sounds like one of those Ulster vagabonds one hears about, who spend their life out in the bush like some Arabic nomad, never really settling down." He thought for a moment. "Or perhaps living in some rude backwoods cabin, scratching out a living from half-cleared fields and the product of their firelock." He looked sharply at Wend. "I'm puzzled, Eckert. How is it that you, a practical and prosperous German tradesman, suffer him to live off your bounty?"

Wend felt a flash of anger. But he throttled it immediately. He recognized that Caulfield's comments reflected the attitude of the gentry toward the Ulster people, who they often simply called "The Irish." But he could not let his guest's criticism stand. After cooling for a few seconds, he said, as casually as he could manage, "Joshua helped me mightily when my parents were killed by a war party on Forbes Road. He helped me restart my life with a couple who became my second parents. Wend paused and looked directly at Caulfield. "*They* were Ulster, Geoffrey. A minister and his wife living in the backwoods of Pennsylvania. So you could say that I'm German by heritage but Ulster by upbringing."

Caulfield looked at his host and shrugged. "Well, that explains it, my dear Wend. I simply didn't quite understand the relationship. Certainly you are grateful to the man." He cleared his throat. "And quite admirable of you, sir."

Wend nodded, but decided to say nothing.

Perhaps somewhat uncomfortable at the silence, Caulfield looked around and noted that Billy was out of the room. He hastened to change the subject. "Peggy, I must say that you have trained your black man to provide excellent service. He's attended to my every want."

Peggy beamed. "Why Geoffrey, it's very nice of you to notice. I know we can't match the elegance of the Tidewater, but we do try to maintain some standards out here in the settlements."

Caulfield smiled broadly and nodded in salute to Peggy. "Never fear, ma'am, you do far more than simply maintain standards." Then he turned to Wend and said, "So, given the size of this place, it must take considerable labor. How many blacks do you have?"

"If you mean black slaves, Geoffrey, we have none."

Caulfield reared back slightly in his chair and asked Wend peremptorily, "Come now, what of the black boy who has waited upon us? Is he not a slave?"

"Geoffrey, I have a black friend who was a slave, named Franklin. He lives in Pennsylvania now with my stepparents. But his situation awakened me to the cruelty of holding a man in bondage with no hope of ever having his own future."

"So, Eckert, are you going to tell me that all your help are free men, working for wages? Come now, that would hardly be economical. Not on a tradesman's earnings and the product of a farm this size."

Wend ignored his guest's implied disparagement of a tradesman's position in society and replied, "No, you are right that using freemen exclusively would be too expensive, although we do sometimes hire day laborers for harvest. In fact, most of our permanent workers consist entirely of indentures and redemptioners, sir. And my apprentices bind themselves to me until they learn the trade. After doing some figuring, I determined that it was an affordable approach." Wend paused. "As far as Wilma, the cook, her husband Albert, her daughter Liza, and young Billy, we bought them five years ago from the estate of a deceased man, where they were household servants. Then we freed them. They work for room and board, clothing, and a small stipend. I think our approach is very fair."

Caulfield's mouth tightened and his eyebrows furrowed. "If I understand the laws of Virginia, slaves can be freed only by an act of the Burgesses. And only as the result of long and loyal service; that hardly seems to fit in this circumstance."

"Your understanding is correct, sir," said Wend. "In fact, our member of the Burgesses, James Wood, assisted us in obtaining such an act. It was based on Albert's long service to his former master."

Caulfield looked at Wend. "Quite commendable, sir; but aren't you shaving things a bit fine? It may give you a feeling of self-satisfaction, perhaps even a sense of superiority over your neighbors who maintain black slaves, but let us be honest, in using indentures and redemptioners, you are *indeed* engaging in a form of slavery."

Wend was becoming irritated. "Come now, Caulfield, there is a major, humane difference. Every person on this farm is either free or can see their way to freedom on a specific date. Many of the indentures were convicted of minor crimes in Europe and I'm simply paying for them to earn a second chance in life after seven years. The redemptioners serve only long enough to pay for their passage to the colonies, usually between two and four years. And in the meantime, we feed them, clothe them, and provide shelter. And then we make a point to give them some cash at the end." Wend slapped his hand on the table. "I strongly disagree with your assertion, sir."

"I will agree that you run a *humane* form of bondage, but *bondage* it is, Mr. Eckert."

Wend started to voice a heated reply to such a clear rebuke, but then bit his tongue as he remembered that Caulfield was his guest

Peggy was visibly dismayed at the escalating conflict. Fearing it would ruin her carefully planned evening of hospitality to a man of the gentry, she put on her most appealing smile and reached out to touch Wend's hand. "Gentlemen! We have shared such a pleasant meal. We simply cannot allow it to end in acrimony over a subject which we cannot resolve in any way here at the table."

Wend took the cue. "Yes, of course, Peggy." He turned to his guest and spoke in a calm voice. "Perhaps we can agree to cordially disagree over this matter, Geoffrey."

Caulfield sat quietly for a moment. Wend thought he saw a look of concern in the man's eyes, as if he hadn't meant for things to become so heated and suddenly realized that his comments had strayed to the verge of incivility.

"Yes, of course, Wend. You're quite correct about that." He turned to Peggy, "My apologies, ma'am, for endangering the conviviality of this evening and taking undue advantage of your hospitality."

Relief spread over Peggy's face. "Let us finish the evening in the parlor. Wend, please show Geoffrey there for a drink and I'll call Liza to put the children to bed and then join you."

Wend and Caulfield walked across the hall into the parlor where a fire crackled in the hearth. Wend asked Albert to have his son bring Caulfield's horse around to the hitching post in front of the house. Then he poured his guest a brandy and the two made polite conversation while waiting for Peggy to arrive.

Soon they heard the rustle of her petticoats as she descended the stairs and then she swept dramatically into the sitting room as both men stood up to receive her. "Oh, Geoffrey, I hope Wend has been on his good behavior and has been keeping you entertained."

Caulfield replied, "Peggy, we've been getting on famously and have been enjoying the fine brandy."

Wend poured his wife a glass. She gave him a wifely glance and squeezed his arm warmly before taking the drink.

From then on Peggy controlled the conversation in her best coquette mode, playing Caulfield like a musical instrument. She drew him out, asking him to talk about events in the Tidewater towns, laughing at his wit, and not missing any opportunity to subtly flatter him. Wend relaxed and watched with amusement as his wife completed her conquest of the younger man. And conquest it was, for it soon became clear to Wend that Geoffrey was infatuated with her. Of course, that was no surprise to Wend. Other husbands might have become jealous in watching their wife so obviously flirt with attractive men. And when they had first been married, Wend had struggled to control his irritation. Then he had realized that it was simply Peggy's nature. She was like an actor on the stage who gloried in the attention of an audience. In fact, he suspected that it satisfied an inner need she had to confirm to herself that she still had the beauty to arouse the interest of men.

After some time, Wend offered Caulfield another brandy.

Caulfield looked out the window into the night, smiled at Peggy, and said, "Regrettably, much as I would like to continue our visit, it is time for me to make my way back to the inn."

Peggy asked, "Aren't you hesitant about riding alone through the night? You know there have been reports of brigands on the roads."

"Now that is interesting news," Caulfield said, smiling broadly. "But I don't think there's much danger for me. After all, I've just purchased two very fine pistols and I do have a fast horse."

Wend called for Albert to bring Caulfield's cloak and hat.

Peggy rose and said, "I hope we see you again while you're in Winchester, Mr. Caulfield." Then a thought hit her. "Have you met Mr. Angus McDonald? He has a large farm called Glengarry just outside the town."

"Indeed, Peggy, I've had the pleasure of meeting many of the fine citizens of Winchester and Frederick County. I've been introduced to Mr. McDonald, the Reverend Thruston, and other prominent people."

Peggy smiled broadly. "Well, perhaps we'll be seeing you at Angus' place next week. He puts on what he calls his 'Glengarry Fair' every year. Did he tell you about that?"

Caulfield grinned. "As a matter of fact, he did, Peggy. And I wouldn't miss it for anything."

Peggy exclaimed, "Well, then I'll look forward to seeing you there!" She walked to the doorway. "I'll bid you goodnight, Mr. Caulfield. It's time for me to check on the children." And then she vanished into the hall, her light footsteps soon sounding on the steps.

Wend escorted Caulfield to the front porch. Caulfield thanked him for the hospitality and then descended the steps to his mount. As he unhitched the horse, the stallion tossed its head, snorted, and stamped a front hoof on the ground, obviously eager to be off.

Watching from the porch, Wend said, "I admire your horse, Caulfield. You certainly have a magnificent, spirited animal there." He paused and said, "I have a big, black mare; now almost fifteen years old. But when she was younger, she was full of spirit and restlessness like that."

Caulfield quickly put his left foot into the stirrup and then sprang into the saddle with a fluid, elegant motion. As the big hunter pranced under him, he reined him in, looked down at Wend, and touched the brim of his hat. "Well then, Eckert, strange as it seems to me, it appears that we have at least two important things in common: a love of spirited horses *and* spirited women."

Then, without a further word, he was off down the drive at a canter, disappearing rapidly into the blackness of the moonless night.

* * *

The man known as Geoffrey Caulfield pushed his stallion hard to cover the miles to Battletown, where the road from Winchester to Keys Gap in the Appalachians crossed the north-south wagon track that passed near Eckert Ridge. Less than an hour after leaving the gunsmith's farm he pulled up in the courtyard of the inn which sat at the crossroads.

A young stableboy, rubbing sleep from his eyes, came out to see who was arriving so late. "Put your horse up for the night, sir?"

"No, I'll just be here for a short while. Water him, loosen the girth, and give him some hay. I'll be riding on presently." Caulfield patted the stallion's mane, then took the pistol case from the bag he had strapped to the rear of his saddle. He tossed the boy a coin, and headed for the inn.

Caulfield pushed through the door into the common room and waited while his eyes adjusted to the light. He looked around the room. The proprietor was at the bar and a serving girl was attending to a middle-aged couple at one of the tables; obviously travelers who were breaking their journey for the night. The only other patron was a burly man relaxing at a table by the hearth with a bored look on his face. He was sprawled back in his chair, a pewter cup in his right hand, his left leg propped up on another chair. He was red-haired, had a pock-marked face, and on some violent occasion in the past the lower part of his left ear had gone missing. An observer would have guessed that it had something to do with the nasty scar on his cheek just below the remnant of the ear. When Caulfield entered, the man turned his face toward the door, revealing a nose which had clearly been on the receiving end, frequently, of other men's fists. Caulfield approached the table and the man pulled his leg from the chair and sat up.

By way of greeting the red-haired man asked, "Now, me darlin' Cap'n, did you get the new pistols you was after?"

Caulfield waved at the serving girl and called out, "Rum, if you please." Then he placed the pistol box on the table and opened the lid. "Take a look at these, Quinn."

Quinn gazed at the pistols. He furrowed up his bushy eyebrows and pursed his lips into a frown. Then he looked up at Caulfield and exclaimed, "God above, Cap'n, why didn't you get a proper pair of horse pistols, like you used to have? Bless me if these damned things don't look like toys."

Caulfield made a face and glared at the other man. "The truth is Quinn, these pistols are the best I've ever shot. Their light weight makes them easy to aim and you can carry them in your belt a lot better than big horse pistols. The gunsmith put a lot of thought into the design."

"I don't care how much thought he put into them; look at the small size of that bore. Give me my good old dragoon pistols every time. They got a ball big enough so's a man stays down once he gets hit." Quinn grinned. "And besides, in nine years riding with the old 11th Dragoons, most of the time the firing was so close that there weren't hardly no aimin' to speak of."

Caulfield snapped back, "I wish you had spent more time aiming at the sheriff you missed in that little fight we had near Culpeper last month. Maybe Swift wouldn't have taken that ball in his shoulder. He's been useless to us all these weeks. And maybe I wouldn't have had to leave my pistols behind when we ran from camp like a herd of deer chased by the dogs."

Quinn cleared his throat in lieu of an answer. Then he changed the subject. "What was it that kept you so long at the smith's place? You was there long enough for him to make those firelocks from scratch while you waited."

"The man's wife invited me to supper and I couldn't very well turn down her hospitality." Caulfield snapped the case shut. "That Eckert is a dour-faced German mechanic whose whole life is wrapped up in his trade: boring as hell. I'll wager he spends every day fiddling away at his workbench. And that Dutchman is damned self-righteous to boot. He tried to convince me what a good man he was 'cause he didn't keep any black slaves and he treated his indentures with loving care, to hear him tell it."

Quinn smiled slyly. "I'm sure you enjoyed listenin' to that, Cap'n."

"Yes, I almost lost my temper right at the table. But Eckert's wife, who has more natural grace in her little finger than her husband will ever dream of having, smoothed things over." Caulfield paused and his eyes stared into the fire for a long moment. Then he shook his head. "How a beautiful and graceful woman like that could marry such a dreary little man, I'll never understand. Dress her in a silk gown and jewelry and she would own every man's eyes in any ballroom at Williamsburg."

Quinn gave Caulfield a knowing look. "Just a guess, but could it be that it's because he's got a trade, a farm, and a comfortable house?" Then he said, "Get that rum down, Cap'n. We got a bit of a ride 'fore we can settle down in our blankets. It's gonna be a short night for us."

"Yes; where do you have the lads camped?"

"In a tight little cove well off the road, where no one will see our fire. 'Bout halfway to Keys' Ferry." The Irishman emptied his cup and said, "If we get an early start tomorrow, we'll be over the Shenandoah and through the mountain gap by mid-day."

Caulfield took a sip of his rum and cleared his throat. "We need to talk about that, Quinn. The fact is, I have changed my mind. I've decided that we're not going east toward Alexandria tomorrow. We're going to stay around Winchester a while longer so that I can go to McDonald's fair at Glengarry next week."

"Wait a minute, Cap'n. The pickings 'round here have been damned thin. The lads have been grumbling. We decided we'd find more prospects along the road down toward Alexandria. You made your excuses to that Angus McDonald when he invited you. You told him that you had to leave Winchester on business. Now what's changed your mind?"

"I heard some things at Eckert's place that made me reconsider. After talking with Mrs. Eckert, I think we may pick up some leads on wealthy travelers if I attend that affair."

Quinn gave his captain a sharp look. Then a sly grin came over his face. He put his hand to his chin. "Leads, hell! You got your eyes on that gunsmith's wife, that's what it is! You're schemin' to get her into bed."

"That will be a bonus of staying around here, not the main object. And I don't think it will take much effort, Quinn. I can tell that the woman is bored with her life, isolated on that backwoods farm, spending all her days tending to her husband and three little brats. The truth is, she's made for the life of a bustling town. I'll wager she pines every day for some excitement to come into her life." He smiled reflectively. "And I'm the man to give it to her. The fact is, she was enthralled with my masquerade as a Tidewater gentleman." He stared into the flames of the hearth and then said, almost to himself, "I have a vision of that woman smiling up at me from bed, her big blue eyes wide with pleasure, her raven hair spread out on the white of a pillow behind her, and her long legs wrapped tight around me."

"For God's sake, Geoffrey, ain't you already got enough women tucked away around Virginia? What about that young widow down in Culpeper? And how about that pretty little blond thing married to that dried up old magistrate in Fredericksburg? And probably others I don't even know about. I've said it before and I'll say it now: You're going to die at the hands of some angry husband who finds you between the covers with his wife." He pointed his finger at Caulfield. "Maybe it will be that gunsmith Eckert himself."

"Eckert? Ha! Not likely. That fatuous, small-minded mechanic makes good firelocks but he hasn't got the stuff to kill anyone." Caulfield tossed down the rest of his rum and shrugged his shoulders. "But be that as it may, my friend Quinn, we stay in Winchester. And who knows, I might indeed pick up something useful at McDonald's. Now let's ride to join the lads and get some sleep. And since we won't need to catch an early ferry to go east, we can make a late morning of it."

CHAPTER SEVEN
Glengarry Fair

On the morning after Geoffrey Caulfield's visit, Wend, who was invariably the first member of the family to arise, climbed out of bed in the predawn blackness and lit a candle from the embers of the fireplace. In the flickering light he pulled on his clothes and looked down at Peggy, still fast asleep. Her long raven hair was sprayed out over the white pillow like a flower arrangement; her countenance reflected peaceful contentment. Wend always marveled at how, when asleep, Peggy's face relaxed and looked as youthful as the day they had married.

As often happened after Peggy put on one of her social performances, she had come to bed aroused and anxious for lovemaking. And as Wend had learned over ten years of marriage, an aroused Peggy McCartie was not to be denied her satisfaction. So it had been an adventurous night.

His thoughts brought back a memory from long ago: On the their first night of marriage, Peggy had vowed that in bed she would be Wend's bad girl, so that he would never find the need to have a wandering eye. And she had enthusiastically carried out her promise. Wend had to admit that, although he had been in bed with girls on several occasions before marriage, none could compare to Peggy's enthusiasm and imaginative prowess in matters of sexual pleasure. But then, he shouldn't have been surprised. For between them there was a deep secret: In her youthful days as a tavern maid, Peggy McCartie had prostituted herself to peddlers and other traveling men who had visited the village of Sherman Mill. It had been a way for her to put aside some money because she wanted to escape the boredom of the place for a larger, more bustling town. The money had also been her hedge against the empty promises of her supposed fiancé, a waggoner who spent most of his time away from Sherman Mill and had refused to set a date for their wedding. But whatever her motivation had been, they both knew that if Peggy's past became known to the citizenry of Winchester, it would lead to their ostracism by friends, acquaintances, and Wend's customers.

There was another secret held closely between them: Wend was not Bernd's natural father. The boy was the product of Peggy's pre-marriage sexual encounters. When they had married, Peggy was newly pregnant and there had been no way of knowing who the father was, but as the lad grew, his physical attributes increasingly made it likely that the father was her erstwhile fiancé. And that man, ironically, was Matt Bratton. In fact, the fight wherein Wend had beaten Bratton's face to a pulp had stemmed from insults which the waggoner had flung at Peggy in the very public common room of her father's tavern. Wend had vowed to Peggy that he would raise Bernd as his own; since then, carrying out that promise had become one of the most important objectives of his life. In particular, he was determined to ensure that Bernd would not grow up to have the character of Bratton, the lying, self-absorbed bully who attempted to dominate every life he touched.

As he looked down at Peggy, the irony of their situation passed through his mind. *What a pair we are: A revenge killer exiled from Pennsylvania by the High Sheriff of Cumberland County and a paid tart whose first child's father would never be known for certain. Yet we are the master and mistress of an establishment that people in the area grandly call Eckert Ridge. We associate with some of the first families of Winchester and Frederick County and are counted by them as solid citizens.*

Wend cleared his head of thoughts about the past and started to focus on the day at hand. He finished dressing, descended to the first floor, and then prepared to go out to the cook-house, which was about thirty feet behind the main house. As he opened the door at the rear of the hall, his nose immediately picked up the smell of the morning's fresh-baked bread and he could hear the voices of Albert's family. There was a covered walkway connecting the house and the log building; it ran through the herb and flower garden which was Peggy's pride and joy. As he navigated the walkway, Wend looked beyond the flowers to the large vegetable garden on the other side. He noted that all the plants were coming along well.

The door to the cook-house was ajar. Wend knocked and then entered. Wilma was toasting bread at the fire, while Liza worked at a counter. Albert and Billy sat at the table over their breakfasts. Wend said, "Good morning, everyone." Then he hurried to compliment the cook. "Say, you put together a nice meal for our guest, Wilma. We didn't give you much notice, but you laid out a fine table that made us proud."

"Thankee, Mr. Wend," the cook answered, "I do like to show visitors how well we eat here on the farm."

Wend continued, "And we can all be proud of the way your Billy served the table last night. That gentleman was impressed."

Meanwhile, Liza picked up a tray which contained a pot of tea, a small pitcher of milk, and a bowl of scraps from the previous evening's meal and handed it to Wend. "Here be your mornin' things, Mr. Wend."

Wend took the tray from Liza, who then held the door for him while he left the cookhouse. He took a path which led around the side of the house toward the workshop. It lay across the drive which climbed up from the main road. The drive then led through the buildings of the farm until it ended at the log house of Joshua Baird and Alice Downy. Lights could be seen from windows along the length of the barracks and he could hear voices and laughter as the apprentices and indentures rose from bed and dressed for the day. Momentarily the farm hands would be starting out on their pre-breakfast chores in the barn and stable. Beyond the barracks and the farmyard buildings was the cabin where Hecht and his family lived. And on the other side of the wagon track, behind the main house and cookhouse, were some sheds for equipment and the cabin which sheltered Albert's family. Wend felt pride of accomplishment as he scanned the farm; ten years ago this had all been empty farmland and he and Peggy had been newlyweds from the backwoods of Pennsylvania with everything they owned, including Wend's tools, in a pair of wagons. Now the money from his trade and the product of the farm supported more than twenty people.

Wend carried the tray across the drive and then inside the shop to his workbench. He pulled out two bowls from a shelf. Then he put the table scraps into one and poured the milk into another and placed them on the workbench. He took a cup of tea and settled down at his desk next to the workbench. As dawn approached, more and more light came in through the window; Wend sipped his tea and used the time before his journeyman and apprentices arrived to plan the day's work. He realized that he would have to do his accounts for the trip to Pittsburgh, so that he could send his bill to Northcutt. That would be his afternoon's work. As for the morning, he was anxious to focus on a special project he had been working on — a new firelock of unique design.

As Wend was making his plans, he felt something brush against his legs under the desk. He looked down to see a chubby gray tomcat looking up at him. After a few seconds the feline strode toward the workbench with a proprietary air and sat before it on his haunches, staring upwards as if measuring the effort needed to jump to the surface.

Wend said, "Cat, you're getting fat and lazy. I'm telling you now, the day you can't leap to the top in one try is the day I stop feeding you and make you start hunting for all your food again."

The Cat, reacting to the tone of Wend's voice, glared defiantly at him, then gathered his strength and made a successful jump to the workbench surface. Once there, he nonchalantly walked over to the food bowl and began eating without paying attention to Wend.

Wend calculated that The Cat was at least sixteen years old. The animal was a native of Sherman Mill and had adopted Wend in 1759, when little more than a kitten. He had become Wend's companion, keeping him company as he worked alone in the tiny shop on the farm of his adoptive parents, Reverend Paul Carnahan and his wife Patricia. Then, when Wend had left Sherman Valley for Virginia in 1764, The Cat had taken the initiative to hitch a ride in the wagon carrying his gunsmithing tools. Soon after their arrival, he had spotted The Cat in with a female of mixed colors which Wend assumed he had recruited from a neighboring farm. Now Wend's gray friend was the patriarch of a tribe of cats which inhabited the farm. As head of the feline family, the tomcat also took very seriously his job of disciplining the dog population of Eckert Ridge. There were a number of hounds on the farm and all had long since learned to keep a respectful distance from The Cat.

However, over the last year, Wend had noted that his friend was showing increasing signs of aging. The animal was spending more of his time lying around the shop instead of patrolling his domain. Wend hated to think that the day when he would have to work without The Cat by his side was approaching.

While The Cat ate, Wend walked over to a rack which held firelocks under construction or repair and picked up a stubby rifle, far shorter than the others. It was in many aspects a throwback to the jaeger rifles which his German forebears had brought with them from the old country and which were still carried by many hunters. But Wend had made some changes to the standard jaeger pattern which fitted the purpose he intended for the rifle. He had been working on the rifle jointly with the oldest of his apprentices, Andrew Horner.

The young man had come to America from Germany as a redemptioner; that is, he agreed to pay back the cost of his ship fare by being indentured for several years after arrival. Wend had bought his contract through an agent in Philadelphia, intending for him to be a farm hand for a period of three years. But when the lad had arrived, Wend had interviewed him, the two talking in German, the only language Horner understood. He had quickly discovered that the boy had some basic schooling and a quick wit. It had also come out that

Andrew had started working as a wood carver before immigrating. Wend took him over to the shop and had him carve several items and was soon overjoyed to see that he had a sure hand with knives and chisels. Wend had immediately offered him an apprenticeship in the gun shop.

Wend looked over the firelock, which was essentially finished. Horner had done a lot of the work; following Wend's instructions, he had carved the stock, cut the barrel to proper length, and rifled the inside of the barrel. Before leaving on the Pittsburgh trip, Wend had installed the lock and trigger mechanism. Then, while he was on the road, Andrew had done the final smoothing of the stock and had laboriously applied the many coats of oil which provided the furniture-like finish. He had made up the brass fittings which Wend had specified and had installed them on the rifle. Now, as Wend held the weapon in his hands, the wood and brass gleamed and he knew that any prospective customer would find it appealing.

Suddenly a voice spoke from behind him. "It's ready for you to fire and check the sights, sir. I took the liberty of test firing it from the stand and setting the sights just before you came back."

Wend looked around to see Horner standing in the shop door. As usual, the young man was the second one into the shop, anxious to get to work. He nodded to his apprentice. "Yes, Andrew, we'll do it this morning. Set up the table on the range and measure out some charges of our finest gunpowder. We'll start as soon as the light is strong enough."

Two hours later, with the sun well up and the farm alive with activity around them, Wend, Horner, and Bernd stood on the firing range, ready for Wend to check the new rifle. Hecht, the journeyman, also came out to watch the proceedings. Wend reviewed Andrew's work of aligning the rifle on the test table, with the sights aimed at the center of a wooden target placed fifty yards down the range. Then he nodded to his apprentice, "Go ahead, fire three shots."

Andrew conducted the firing. The three shots overlapped each other, essentially forming one large hole, dead center in bulls-eye.

Wend was impressed, but said nothing. Then he motioned to Bernd. "Take the target out to 100 yards."

The firing group at 100 yards was a near duplicate of the first.

Horner relaxed and smiled to himself, then looked questioningly at Wend.

Wend grinned at his apprentice. "Nice work, Andrew; I couldn't have done better myself."

Horner beamed. "Thank you, sir."

"All right," Wend said, "Take it off the clamps; it's time for me to shoot."

The apprentice took the firelock off the stand, loaded it, and then handed it to Wend.

Wend dropped to his knees and braced his left elbow on the firing stand as he aimed. He started to align the top of the front sight with the notch in the rear sight. He squinted to sharpen his view of the front sight and ensure perfect alignment.

The sight picture sharpened a little, but remained somewhat fuzzy; more than ever before. Wend lifted his head, and wiped his right eye, assuming moisture or something else was in the eye. He looked around, to see Bernd and Andrew watching. Then Wend carefully aimed again, squinting harder than he had ever done.

The sight view remained fuzzy. Wend concentrated, estimating from experience where the top of the front sight was, and aligned that estimate with the top of the notch in the rear sight. Then he took deep breath and squeezed off the shot.

Bernd exclaimed, "Good shot, Father!"

Horner said, "Yes; right on the vertical with the center of the target, but a tiny amount low."

Wend handed him the firelock, and the apprentice reloaded it.

Wend again went to his knees and prepared for a second shot. The picture was as blurred as before, the top of the front sight lost in the fuzz. Considering that the last shot had been low, Wend brought the front sight up a little higher than before and fired.

Horner nodded. "That's got it sir; bulls-eye, just slightly high."

Wend stood up. He handed the rifle to Andrew. "I'm satisfied. He smiled at the apprentice and tapped him on the arm. "You did a good job on that firelock. Engrave my name and the number on the barrel."

Horner smiled and walked back to the shop. Wend turned to Bernd and said, "Son, run into the shop and bring me my best longrifle."

Soon Bernd was back with the firelock. "Do you want me to load it, sir?"

"No, I just want to check something out." Wend took the rifle, went to his knees, and carefully aimed at the target. He was relieved to see that the front sight was as clear to his eye as ever. He handed the gun back to Bernd. "Go put it back in the rack, son."

After Bernd left, Wend stood looking at the target and thinking things over. *My eyesight is beginning to go, at least for things nearby.* Clearly, he hadn't noticed it before because of the length of the longrifle barrel. But sooner or later he would find it hard to see even the sight of a longrifle clearly. He was stunned by the realization. And then another thought came over him: I'm still shy of thirty. I've never worried about my eyes before; but all the detail work at my bench must be hurting them. He wondered: *How fast will my eyes deteriorate?* It suddenly struck him: *My days as a marksman are running out.* Then an even more sobering thought came over him. Just that morning, he had been worried about The Cat's declining physical condition. *Now, by God, I'm at the very beginning of the same process.*

Wend walked into the workshop. Wilhelm Hecht, the journeyman, came over. "Are you still planning on shooting that short firelock at Glengarry?"

Wend nodded. "Yes, Wilhelm; that was the whole purpose of making sure it was ready for the fair. I want show it off in front of men who might find it to their taste."

Hecht shook his head. "I'm not sure anyone's going to take to it, sir. They're used to the longer barrel and this just won't look right, even to those who could afford it."

"Wilhelm, you may be right. But I'm convinced that there are men who will think on it the same way I did. The fact is, I get tired of carrying a longrifle in my hand on a horse. The only other thing to do is carry it on a sling across your back. That lets you have both hands free for the reins, but then the barrel rubs against the horse's side and it takes a while to get ready to shoot. This shorter gun can be carried in a sheath strapped to the saddle, so you can draw it quickly. I expect that men with money, men who travel often by horse, might find that attractive."

"Yes, but then there's the question of fouling, sir. That's one reason for going to the longer barrel, more than thirty years ago. A longer barrel uses the gunpowder more efficiently and can use a smaller bore and less powder. What you've got there is just basically a jaeger rifle." Hecht thought for a moment and then pointed to the firelock. "Except that you made the bore of the barrel even smaller than most longrifles, so it's going to foul up even faster than a regular jaeger rifle, with its big bore."

"Wilhelm, the men who can afford it will be able to buy the finest quality powder, to keep the fouling down." As he spoke, he was reminded of something. He called for Horner to come over.

Horner came, wiping his hands on a rag. "Yes sir?"

Wend handed the firelock to his apprentice. "Here, listen carefully, Andrew: Take this out to the range. Fire it, using regular gunpowder, until it is so fouled that you have to clean it before firing again. I suspect it will be not more than four or five shots. Then clean the barrel carefully and fire it again using the best grade of powder, to see how many shots you can get. I want to be able to give customers the answer to that question."

Hecht said, "A very good idea to work that out, Herr Eckert. But there's another problem: You are taking a big chance. If you don't shoot up to your usual standard, everyone will blame it on that gun."

That question brought Wend up short. *Had Hecht somehow discerned his eye problem from watching him on the range?* He asked anxiously, "Wilhelm, what do you mean by that? What makes you think I won't shoot as well as ever?"

"The length of the barrel, sir; a long barrel is better for aiming. And everyone knows you're the best shot in Winchester. If you don't win the match, they're going to say that you made the barrel too short for good accuracy."

Relieved, Wend thought: *He's not thinking about my eyesight, only the proven value of a longer barrel.* Wend looked directly at Hecht. "We've talked all this over several times, Wilhelm. When I fire the gun in the match at McDonald's place next week, I'll just have to win. If I shoot well, I wager there will be keen interest in the new firelock. And I plan to practice enough over the next few days to make sure I win."

The journeyman shrugged his shoulders and walked back to his workbench. Wend felt lucky to have Hecht working with him. He was competent and very reliable. But he lacked imagination and, to a certain extent, ambition. It was undoubtedly why a man in his thirties was still working as a journeyman instead of having his own shop.

Wend's mind went back to the shooting match in which he would show off the new rifle. Hecht was right: A lot of effort was riding on the outcome. And on the skill of a man whose eyes weren't as clear as before. Then Wend had an idea. He called out to Bernd.

"Yes, Father?"

"Now listen, lad: I want you to do two things. First, go down and see Alice Downy. Ask her if she has finished the canvas sheath she was making for the short rifle. If she has, bring it back with you. Second, go to the paint shack. Bring me a small container of white paint." He paused a second. "And keep quiet about the paint. Do you understand?"

Bernd looked puzzled and started to form a question. Wend put his finger to his lips. "Just do it, son, and don't say anything."

✳ ✳ ✳

Wend's spirits were high as he walked down to the wagon shed early in the morning of Angus McDonald's fair at Glengarry. It had turned out to be a golden day of early summer. The morning sun was warming but the atmosphere was not oppressive, as it would become later in the season. The leaves of the trees were still the fresh, bright green of spring instead of the wilted look of late summer.

The farmyard was alive with activity. Nearly every person on the farm would be attending the fair, so transportation arrangements entailed three wagons. Donegal was loading one wagon with jugs full of his whiskey to sell. Most of the farmhands were traveling with him. Joshua and Alice were driving a wagon which would carry the Eckert children, shepherded by Liza and Billy. Wilhelm Hecht, his family, and the apprentices were in the third wagon. Horner had carefully packed Wend's rifle and shooting supplies in the Hecht wagon.

Wend walked to the rightmost bay of the wagon shed and stood before the vehicle he and Peggy would drive to the fair. It was a light, two-wheeled, single horse rig which was called a "chaise," or as some styled it, a "shay." He sighed to himself, feeling a touch of irritation. Nothing in their married life had caused so much conflict as the purchase of this vehicle. Early in the year they had come across it at the sale of goods from a wealthy estate. It had been lying idle for years and was somewhat dilapidated. But Peggy had immediately become infatuated with it.

"Wend, look at its elegant lines; it's beautiful! And with a little repair to the woodwork and a coat of glossy black paint, it would be like new!"

"Peggy, why would we want to spend our money on something like that? We have several very good wagons. It's not practical: It has seats for only two people and no room to carry anything. And besides, it's too light for traveling any distance. It would be good only for around town. We wouldn't find any use for it."

"There are times when we want to drive just by ourselves, Wend. It would be perfect for when we go visiting, or when we go to Court Day in Winchester, or to the McDonald's fair! In fact, I could drive it by myself when I go to visit Anna."

As soon as she said that, Wend knew why Peggy coveted the chaise. She and McDonald's wife, Anna, were great friends. Anna had been married to Angus and come to Winchester in 1764, the same year that the Eckerts had arrived. The two had formed a friendship almost immediately, even though the McDonalds were much wealthier and had far larger land holdings. But both women came from rural, humble beginnings and thus shared a kindred wonderment at their rise in fortune. But like so many female friendships, theirs also included a strong element of competition. And Peggy had always been envious of the fact that the McDonalds had an actual carriage. Wend had realized that having the chaise would allow his wife to feel like she was on a level with Anna.

But his German practicality had made him put his foot down. And he frankly felt the damn thing looked frivolous. It was something that a Williamsburg dandy would drive. "Peggy, I'm not spending good money on that little toy cart. We don't need it!"

Peggy had looked up at him and said, "For God's sake, Wend, we're making good money with that musket contract. You said yourself it would last for a long time, because there's a whole regiment's worth of firelocks to be rebuilt. Certainly we can afford this! And besides, it's time we show people that we aren't just dirt farmers and tradesmen anymore."

Wend, getting irritated, said, "If we go around spending money on things like this, we *are* going to end up back as dirt farmers! That contract isn't going last forever and we need to save the profit for our reserve." He shook his head. "No, I won't spend our money on something like this little rig."

Peggy stamped her foot and gave Wend the tight smile which meant she fully intended not to back down. "All right, if *you* won't buy it, *I* will. I'll use *my* money."

Those words were Peggy's ultimate weapon of defiance in arguments about money. It was the equivalent of "Fix Bayonets!" on the battlefield. The money she meant was the bag of coins she had earned entertaining men in the stable of McCartie's Tavern. The day after they had married, she had offered it up to Wend to help purchase land for a farm. Wend had refused to use it; he had adequate funds derived from his parents' sale of their farm and house furnishings before the massacre. He had told her to put the coins away against some cataclysmic event which left her on her own. So now she used the threat of it to shame Wend into purchases he opposed.

Usually Wend gave in, if for no other reason than to keep peace in the family, but also because he loathed the idea of spending money earned by prostitution. Peggy had laughed at him when he had once actually said that, remarking, "There isn't any red mark on it. Money is money."

But this time, he had refused to back down. So Peggy had turned on her heel, walked up to the man conducting the sale, and told him to reserve the chaise for them, promising payment the next day. And so the "Damned Little Cart", as Wend thought of it, had come to Eckert Ridge.

This would be the first time they had used the chaise for anything except short test drives around the farm. Wend had had Horner fix the woodwork and then Specht, one of the farm hands, repainted the vehicle. Now Wend looked over the rig and had to admit that it looked quite attractive. The body was glossy black, the wheels yellow, and the traces had been varnished to show the natural grain of the wood. Peggy had prevailed upon Alice Downy to make new dark blue covers for the seats. The body was topped with a leather roof which could be folded down toward the rear on sunny days.

Wend reached down, grabbed the traces, and pulled the rig out from under the shed's roof. He turned to see Specht leading Boots, the young bay that had been trained to pull the chaise, down from the stable. Boots was a spirited three year old stallion, one of The Mare's progeny. He had a tiny white star on his face and prominent white 'boots' on his legs. Specht had harnessed the horse in the stable and now the two of them worked together to put him into the traces. The farmhand had groomed the horse's coat and it gleamed in the sunlight. There was no doubt the animal was an elegant match for the chaise.

Wend climbed into the vehicle and drove it up to the front of the house. Peggy, dressed in a gown of light green and a flat straw hat with a band which matched the gown, was loading the brood into Joshua's wagon while Albert and Wilma, who would stay at the farm, watched from the porch. The children were excited, talking and laughing about the day's event.

When the wagon was loaded and pulled away from the porch, Wend jumped down and then handed Peggy up into the chaise. He said, "You look lovely in the green. I think it does as much for you as the blue that you like so much."

"It is a lovely dress. Alice made it for me from a pattern I bought in Alexandria the last time we were there."

Wend remounted the chaise and tapped the reins on Boots' back. The young bay stepped out enthusiastically. They would be traveling faster than the three wagons, as Peggy wanted to visit with Anna McDonald before going out to the fair. As they passed Joshua's wagon, the children waved and cheered. Then they were off. Wend kept Boots reined in going down the drive, for it was fairly rough. But when they turned northward onto the main road, he brought the stallion up to a trot and they seemed to fly along, leaving a small flurry of dust in their wake.

Peggy was exhilarated. "It runs beautifully, Wend! Feel the wind on your face and in your hair!" She motioned toward the horse. "And Boots was a perfect choice. Look at the way the white of his legs flash in the sunlight as he trots." Peggy put her arm around Wend's and snuggled up against him. She flashed him her most seductive smile. "Now, aren't you glad I bought it?"

Wend had to admit to himself that driving the cart was a pleasure. It was so light that there was little burden on a powerful horse like Boots and, with just two wheels, the rig easily maneuvered around bumps and holes in the road. But he was damned if he would admit to Peggy that he liked the thing. He fixed his best stony expression on his face and said in measured tones, "There's no doubt it handles well."

Peggy looked at him shrewdly for a minute. Then she laughed heartily. "You can't fool me with that face of yours! You're enjoying it!"

Wend couldn't help smiling tightly.

She caught his smile. "I knew it!" Peggy squeezed his arm. "Now let me drive. I want to get used to handling it."

Wend slowed the horse down to a walk and handed the reins to Peggy. She didn't hesitate, but slapped the reins down on Boots' back several times, bringing him up to his fastest pace. Wend grabbed the side of the chaise as it bounced along the wagon track. He shouted, "Careful, or you'll wreck it the first time out!"

Peggy laughed again. "Not likely!"

Just then the chaise hit a high spot. Both wheels left the ground and landed with a jarring bump. The seat swayed wildly on its leather straps. Wend thought his wife would be intimidated, but it just seemed to increase her exhilaration. She smiled broadly so her teeth showed white in the bright sunlight. "Oh, I love this!" she exclaimed.

After a few minutes, Peggy slowed the horse down to a pace which he could maintain and then drove the chaise all the way to the Battletown Inn at the crossroads. They stopped there to water the horse.

Peggy jumped down from the chaise. "Wend, I'm going in to see if Mr. Caulfield is still staying here and if he has left for the fair."

Wend nodded and then tended to Boots as he drank from the trough in the courtyard.

Almost immediately, Peggy came out of the tavern with a puzzled look on her face. Wend asked, "What did you find out?"

"It's very strange. The proprietor said there's no one named Caulfield here and that he never had a room. I gave him a description and he said that a man like that was here only for a drink on the night that he visited our house. And he was with a very rough sort of man who was here for dinner and lots of rum while waiting for Caulfield."

Wend shook his head. "Well, I had my doubts about the man from the first moment I saw him. He seemed to keep everything about himself very close to his chest."

Peggy shrugged. "I'm sure he must have had his reasons for shading the truth." She thought a moment. "Perhaps he will be at Glengarry; it will be interesting to see if he has a credible explanation."

Wend smiled. "He undoubtedly had his reasons. I would say *dishonest* reasons. But at least he paid full price for those pistols in good coins."

* * *

With Boots at the trot they flew up the long drive to Glengarry House. Wagons and carts carrying goods had been pulled up on the lawn and a good many people were busy setting up sales tables along the drive. Faces turned to look at the little chaise as it swept past, trailed by a light cloud of dust. Wend heard the sound of bagpipes from the back of the house.

The timing of their arrival was fortuitous, for as they entered the circle in front of the house, Wend could see Angus McDonald and Anna standing at the steps, talking with a gaggle of newly arrived guests. He could make out Reverend Charles Thruston, Minister of the Anglican Church. He also saw James Wood, the son of the founder of Winchester, a Frederick County member of Burgesses, and master of a large estate on the western side of Winchester. With him was an elegant young woman. He asked Peggy, "Who is the lady with Wood?"

"I suspect it's his fiancée Jean Moncure, down from Stafford."

Wend kept the horse at a fast pace until they were within a few feet of the entrance and then pulled him up sharply to stop in front of the group of people.

Everyone turned to look.

Wend leaned over and whispered playfully to his wife, "Was that a dramatic enough entrance for Lady Elizabeth Eckert?"

Peggy dug him in the side sharply with her elbow. "Oh, stop it, Wend!" Then a look of concern came over her face. "You're not going to tease me about the chaise in front of everybody, are you?"

"Fear not, my lady, I promise I'll be on my best behavior."

Peggy could make no answer to that, for Angus McDonald had come to greet them, with Anna right behind him. Peggy put on her broadest tavern girl smile and gave her hand to McDonald as he handed her down from the chaise.

"Mrs. Eckert, dashed if you don't look absolutely smashing today. I think you get more lovely every time I see you!"

Peggy grinned. "Oh, Angus, you are such a gentleman to say such nice things." She gave him a quick squeeze, then moved on to hug Anna.

"Mornin', Eckert, glad to see you." McDonald looked the chaise over. "Bonnie little rig you got there."

Wend returned Angus' greeting and then climbed down. He handed the reins to the waiting post boy, then walked over to shake hands with Angus. The owner of Glengarry was a man of about Wend's own height, but had a wiry figure and boyish face which belied his forty-seven years. His youthful look was enhanced by a respectable head of hair. Wend knew that McDonald had considerable military experience. He had fought against the British in the Jacobite Rebellion of 1745 and had fled to Virginia the next year. After landing at Falmouth, McDonald had worked in commerce while getting his feet on the ground financially. He moved to Winchester three years later. He had served in the French and Indian War, most notably as the captain of a company of Virginia provincials in General Forbes' 1758 campaign against Fort Duquesne. The Scotsman currently held the rank of major in the Frederick County Militia.

McDonald gave Wend a friendly tap on the shoulder. "I hear you just got back from Pittsburgh. You know I was out in the Ohio Country just a few months ago, at the governor's request, looking at potential land for veterans. We must get together later; I found downright hostility among the tribes out there."

"You're right, Angus. I planned to talk to you about that. I spent considerable time with Connolly, and Northcutt, who was out there at the same time. There's some important news."

"We'll get together after the shooting matches." McDonald took hold of Wend's arm and leaned close. "Say, I hope Donegal is selling his whiskey here today. I've used up the entire amount I purchased from him back in the fall."

Wend laughed. "He is fully expecting to sell you a supply, Angus. He should be here shortly to set up his display."

"Now, that's capital!" McDonald looked around and whispered, "Confidently, you arrived at just the right time, Eckert. Thruston was hanging around out here making a bore of himself as usual. I was glad of the excuse to come over and talk to you. Now, thankfully, he's gone out to the back with the rest of the guests."

"Delighted I could be of service, Angus." Wend smiled; he knew that there was a long standing tension between McDonald and Thruston. Wend wasn't sure exactly what had caused it, but the rumor was that it had something to do with church finances. McDonald was a member of the vestry and apparently the two strong-willed men had clashed about some point of administration.

McDonald waved to the door of the house. "We've set up morning drinks and some food out in the garden. Take your lass back there; lots of people are there already. And Anna will be back to join you directly; she's anxious to visit with Peggy and take in the fair with her."

Meanwhile, Peggy and Anna had also been deep in conversation, smiling and laughing like young girls. Wend had kept an eye on the two of them. Anna, married to a man twenty-one years her senior, had always reminded him of Peggy's younger sister, Ellen McCartie. Anna was twenty-six, three years younger than Peggy, and the same age as Ellen. And like Ellen, Anna was fairly plain, but had a wonderful smile which could warm the heart of any man and make you forget that she wasn't a beauty. She also had an engaging personality which made everyone feel comfortable in her presence. Wend had always figured that those similarities had played a central role in Peggy's friendship with Anna.

Wend took Peggy on his arm; they walked through the central hall of Glengarry Manor to the garden at the rear. It had very extensive plantings, many of which were still in bloom, and a wide, grass-covered central area. The open space was now filled with a gaggle of Winchester's prominent citizens and landholders, all engaged in conversation while enjoying the McDonalds' spread of food and libations. They were being entertained by a curious trio of musicians. The bagpipes Wend had heard were being played by Evan McLeod, an old retainer of McDonald's family, who had followed him into exile after Culloden. Also present were a young fifer, who alternated playing with McLeod, and a drummer boy who provided accompaniment. Both were from the militia.

It was at moments like this that Wend's childhood self-consciousness reasserted itself. He hesitated, not knowing quite how to join the party. But Peggy had no such reservations.

"Look, Wend, there's Daniel and Abbey. Let's go talk to them." And without further hesitation, she pulled him toward the couple standing to one side of the courtyard.

Daniel Morgan looked as out of place and uncomfortable amidst the gathering of gentry as Wend felt. He was the tallest man present, standing head and shoulders above everyone else. He had the burly chest and powerful arms of a veteran waggoner; even though his town-going suit was not a bad fit, he seemed about to burst out of it. His face read like a book of his past history. There were several faded scars he had acquired in tavern brawls and his nose had obviously been pummeled on numerous occasions. The left side of his face was considerably different from the right, the result of a bullet which had literally passed through his mouth and broken his jaw in a long-ago Indian fight.

Abigail, or Abbey, Morgan was a pretty woman of normal height, who looked tiny only because she was standing beside her giant of a man. She smiled widely upon seeing Peggy and the two began an animated conversation.

Wend knew that Abbey was the reason that Morgan had come to prominence. In the 1750's, Morgan had been a waggoner with a proclivity for drink, carousing, and brawling. Then he had met Abbey and fallen into the love of his life. But she was the daughter of a prosperous farmer. The father had had no time for Morgan and forbade him to court her. Faced with that ultimatum, Morgan had determined to turn his life around and win over the old man. In a few years, he had expanded his single wagon and team into a prosperous freight line and used the profits to acquire a farm sited to the north of Wend's. Then he had confronted Abbey's father and won his grudging permission for her hand.

Morgan looked down at Wend and said dryly, "I hear you had some interesting times on your trip up to Pittsburgh. Jake told me you ran into Indians a couple of times and got shot at from out of the night for no good reason." He smiled. "It's a pity that I don't get to have fun like that anymore. But there's got to be an interesting story behind all that."

Wend answered, "The last part of it had something to do with the reason I'm in Virginia now instead of Pennsylvania. You know some of the story."

Morgan grinned. "Yeah, that's all right, Wend. We'll talk about it later, over some good rum or some of Donegal's whiskey." Then asked quietly, "Hey, when are you going to pay me for those wagons and drivers?"

Wend glanced at Morgan and pursed his lips. Daniel Morgan made good money from his freight company and had a prosperous farm. But like many landowners, he also had lots of debt and was always short of cash. "Daniel, I sent off the accounts to Williamsburg two days ago. You'll get paid when I get my money from the colony. You know that was the deal."

"Yeah, well I thought maybe they might have given you some sort of advance on the contract."

Wend shook his head. "You know it takes months to get anything out of them."

"I figured it wouldn't do no harm to ask." Morgan paused and changed the subject. Smiling broadly, he put his hand on Wend's shoulder and said, "However, I'm here to tell you that this is the year that I beat you at the shooting match. I've been practicing and I figure you ain't had much time to get ready."

Wend shrugged. "Daniel, you may be right. I've only been able to practice for the last couple of days. And then, I'm shooting with a new rifle."

Morgan grinned slyly. "So, you're already starting to make excuses? I must be right!"

Just then Charles Smith, the Sheriff of Frederick County, came up to the group. He touched his hat to Peggy and Abbey. Then he nodded to Wend and Morgan.

Daniel greeted Smith. "Hello, there, Charlie. Hey, listen: I just got some info on 'ole Wend here. He's shooting a new rifle today. I'm bettin' he ends up out of the money."

Wend said, "As a matter of fact, it is not just a new rifle, it is a somewhat new pattern."

Smith cocked his head. "A new pattern? Now what are you up to?"

Wend looked at both men. "You'll just have to come down to our table at the fair to see what it looks like. My apprentice Horner is setting up now."

Smith smiled at Morgan. "I'll make a point to stop by. And we'll all see how it works at the match." He raised a finger. "But listen now: I got some news that affects you both since you live out toward Battletown Inn and the river."

Morgan asked, "What news, Charlie?"

"We have a band of highwaymen operating around Winchester."

Wend said, "I heard about highwaymen working down south around Culpeper and Fredericksburg. The pickings would be pretty good for them down there; why would they come up here where settlement is much thinner?"

"Fact is, I got a letter from the Culpeper sheriff just the other day," Smith said. "He and some of his men ambushed the brigands in their camp down there. The ruffians got away, but left a lot of their stuff. And the sheriff trailed them up into the Blue Ridge. He thought they might cross over into the valley and head up here to Winchester."

Morgan said, "So, you seen any sign of them?"

"That's what I wanted to talk to you about." Smith paused and looked directly at each man in turn. "They're not only here, they robbed a family of pilgrims out past Battletown yesterday. The family was heading west to the Great Wagon Road, planning to follow it down to Carolina. They had just come off the ferry when the thieves hit them not far from Battletown. The gang took everything they had of value."

Wend looked at Morgan. "That is close to our places, Daniel."

Morgan nodded. "Damn right! What have you found out about these ruffians, Charlie?"

"Well, Dan, the family said they were all masked. But their leader is a large man with an Irish accent so thick you could cut it. Not your *Ulster* Irish, but a real Irishman. And they noticed somethin' else about him: He was missing the lower half of his left ear. They said it looked like it had been cut off with a knife, or maybe by him gettin' slashed on the side of the head by a sword."

Wend asked, "How many of them do you think there are, Charles?"

"The pilgrims said they saw five. All rough looking but well mounted. And one of them was a black man; a runaway slave, no doubt." The sheriff looked at both Daniel and Wend. "You need to be on the lookout for any sign of these men. And tell the other landholders out there to do the same. I'm going to run patrols along the roads but I need for you to get word to me if you see anything suspicious. I've only got a few men and I need to patrol all around the county, not just to the east."

Just then the piper and drummer stopped playing. Wend saw that the McDonald's had come out of the house's rear door and stood on the brick landing. The master of Glengarry raised his arms to draw attention and the hubbub of conversation subsided.

Angus stood looking at the crowd and smiled wryly. "Look at those tables! Most of the serving plates are empty. So I'd say you greedy harpies have been picking at my larder for long enough!" There was a round of laughter from the guests. "I'm told that most of our good tradesman and merchants have finished setting up their tables. The weather looks to be fair and a crowd of folk has come out from the town and in from the county for a day of happy diversion. It's time, my lads and lassies, that you go out and spend some of your ill-gotten gains on the product of their hard work over the winter. And after you've done that for a time, we'll have the athletic games and shooting match. So let's all go have a good day here at Glengarry!"

The crowd began to leave, flowing around the house out onto the front lawn. Anna McDonald came down from the porch and walked briskly over to the group. She smiled brightly. "Come on Peggy and Abbey: Let's go out to the fair together and leave these men to their own devices. There's so much I want to see."

As the three women walked away, Wend said, "Well, I'm going to find Hecht and Horner, and see how they've set up my goods." He nodded to the sheriff. "Charles, thanks for the warning on that band of highwaymen."

Morgan said, "I'll be along shortly to see this mysterious firelock you've been talking about. And then I'm going to beat you on the shooting range!"

Wend gave the big man a broad smile. "Well, we'll see about that soon enough, won't we?"

CHAPTER EIGHT
Dispatch from Williamsburg

Peggy Eckert walked out to the front of Glengarry House with her two companions. She was in high spirits. Much as she loved her three children, it was marvelous to have some time on her own with two women who she considered her closest friends. The feeling took her back to her youth when she would sometimes be allowed a few brief hours away from the never-ending work in the tavern common room and kitchen to visit with other girls.

The women descended from the front entranceway, planning to stroll down the drive to the exhibit area. They were laughing at a humorous comment Abbey had made when Peggy looked up to see Geoffrey Caulfield dismounting from his great bay stallion.

Caulfield handed the reins to the servant who came to tend his horse. Then, seeing the women, he took his hat off, swept it across his chest with a flourish, and bowed deeply. "I am truly honored to find myself in the presence of three such lovely ladies; on a fine June day like this, what more could any man desire?"

Anna said, "Why Mr. Caulfield, we weren't expecting you today. You told Angus that you had urgent business elsewhere."

"Mrs. McDonald, my arrangements changed unexpectedly. And so, still being in the county, I couldn't resist the excitement of your affair today. I do hope my presence doesn't inconvenience you in any way."

Anna flashed her widest smile. "Why, Geoffrey, you are always welcome here. Won't you come with us to the fair for a while? Our husbands have deserted us and we would be delighted if you would take their place!"

"It would be my greatest pleasure, Anna."

Anna motioned to her companions. "Geoffrey, this is Mrs. Morgan and Mrs. Eckert."

Caulfield bowed to Abbey. "My pleasure, ma'am." Then he turned to Peggy and flashed a smile. "And I have already met Mrs. Eckert. I had a most entertaining evening at Eckert Ridge after finishing some business with her husband."

Peggy smiled and said, "Yes indeed, it was *very* entertaining."

Geoffrey grinned and then bowed slightly. "I vow, I haven't been able to forget your hospitality, Mrs. Eckert." He smiled broadly and looked Peggy directly in the eye. "I hope to be able to enjoy it again very soon."

After more flirtations with traveling men than she cared to remember, Peggy was quite sure that Caulfield wasn't talking about another pleasant dinner at the family table. She thought: *He certainly is a brazen one.* Then she quickly glanced at the other two women and was certain that they hadn't detected anything other than courtesy in Caulfield's words. "Well, Geoffrey, of course you are always welcome at Eckert Ridge."

Anna asked, "Shall we go down the drive and take in all the exhibits?"

Four abreast, the group walked down the drive. Peggy asked, "Well, Geoffrey, how is your quest for land coming? Are you finding anything which pleases you?"

"Not so far, Peggy. There is considerable acreage available in Frederick County, but I've not seen anything yet that would suit my needs."

Peggy responded, "Well, I do hope you find what you want." Then she smiled at Caulfield and asked in her sweetest voice, "And how are your accommodations at Battletown Inn? It's very new."

Without missing a beat, Caulfield answered, "Oh, I'm very pleased with my rooms. The proprietor makes every effort to make one comfortable. And the fare is quite good. My only care is that I've been there so long I fear to see the accounting when I finally leave. It will be quite an assault on my purse."

Peggy smiled at Caulfield. She thought: *He lies as smoothly as any man I've known.* She said, "I'm glad you've been so comfortable. You know, we've been intending to stop by there for a meal. When we do, I'll be sure to tell the innkeeper how satisfied you are."

She watched carefully to see his reaction, but his face was as impassive as Wend's could be.

Instead of answering her, Caulfield pointed to a table they were passing and said to all of the women, "Look at those fabrics. They certainly are colorful."

Anna walked over to the table and said, "Geoffrey, you must help us here. Please show us what is in favor down at Williamsburg this season. And do give us some idea about the styles ladies are wearing."

They lingered at the table for a few minutes, Caulfield filling them in on what he said were current trends in Williamsburg and Norfolk. Then they moved on, visiting other tables. Soon they came to a woman who was selling flowers. Geoffrey quickly purchased three roses from the woman and, with a flourish, handed one to each of the ladies.

Peggy had been observing Caulfield as he solicitously attended the ladies. She had spent a lifetime dealing with men and had to admit that she had never seen a man who was so comfortable in the presence of women. It was her experience that some acted gallantly, but with a rather self-conscious stiffness. Others tried to be casual but were clearly focused on the impression they were making. A few were so cock-sure of themselves that they were insufferable. But Caulfield was self-assured and natural, as if he didn't have to put on any kind of front. Then she had a startling insight: *Geoffrey has spent much of his life in the company of women, perhaps more so than with men.*

Peggy decided to concentrate on finding out more about this man from the Tidewater. As the day progressed, she took every opportunity to tactfully query him about his background and family. But despite her best efforts, Caulfield managed to dodge every question or to answer in ways which provided little information.

Later, while Caulfield was showing Abbey something at a table, Peggy pulled Anna aside and asked how they had come to know Geoffrey.

Anna said, "Why, we just met him about ten days ago. He called at Glengarry and had a letter of introduction from a prominent merchant in Norfolk. It said that Geoffrey was from Edenton in North Carolina and was interested in buying land. It also said that the merchant had dealt with his family for years and knew that Geoffrey had access to the resources necessary for the purchases he intended."

Peggy thought a moment. "Does Angus know the merchant personally, Anna?"

Anna shrugged. "Only by reputation. Why do you ask?"

Peggy smiled at her friend. "Geoffrey is such an intriguing gentleman, I just wanted to know more about his background."

Anna giggled. "You better be careful, Peggy. Mr. Caulfield is *very* handsome. And I've been watching how much interest you've been showing in him. If you keep that up, you're going to make Wend very jealous."

"Wend jealous?" Peggy shook her head. "Not likely." Then she looked at sharply at her friend. "You know, Anna, that's an emotion I've never been able to arouse in him." She thought: *If you only knew how often I've tried.*

* * *

119

"I'm dead-on today, Eckert! And I'm gettin' better as the day goes on!" Daniel Morgan smiled devilishly at Wend as he spoke. "I'll be ready to show you some shootin' you won't forget as soon as I've finished cleaning this bore."

Wend grinned at the giant waggoner and shook his head. "Maybe I should quit right now and let them declare you the champion."

Morgan's face twisted into a look of dismay. "You damned well better not! I've been spoilin' since last year to teach you what real shootin' looks like and I'm not going to be denied that pleasure." He pointed to the short rifle in Wend's hands. "And besides, I've been waitin' all day to see you fire that little pea-shooter firelock. The only trouble is, I figure people will say that you was at a disadvantage because of that short barrel."

Wend grinned slyly. "Well, Daniel, let's get started and see if you're correct." He turned to Horner, who handed him his shooting bag.

It was late afternoon. The shooting matches had been going on for several hours. As was the custom at Glengarry Fair, Wend, the previous year's champion, would have to shoot only against the winner of all the other matches. And, as expected, Morgan had triumphed against about twenty other marksmen, thus winning the honor of going one-on-one with Wend. The athletic competitions had ended and now the entire crowd was gathering around to watch the final stage of the contest.

Wend lay the bag down by the firing mark and checked the contents. It contained sixteen pre-measured paper cartridges and the same number of balls, which had been carefully filed and shined to ensure that they were of same size and roundness. Also included were a wooden mallet, cleaning gear, a vent pick, extra flints, and a small horn of fine powder for priming the rifle.

Suddenly Wend felt a hand on his arm. He turned to see Peggy standing there smiling at him. She looked devastating in her green gown and the matching necklace. As he looked at her, Wend wondered — not for the first time — how, back in Sherman Mill, it had taken him so long to fall prey to her beauty. But now he just felt fortunate to be her husband.

Peggy put her hand on his arm. "I came to wish you luck." She looked down at the rifle. "I know that the new firelock will perform as well as you hoped."

Wend squeezed her hand and smiled at his wife. "I hope the marksman will perform as well as the rifle." Then he lay on the ground in front of the mark and Horner handed the rifle down to him. He looked over to see Morgan settling down on the ground about ten feet away.

The big man looked over at Wend. "Once again, it comes down to you and me." He winked and said, "Do your damnedest, you little Dutchman!"

Wend grinned and loaded the rifle. Then it was time to settle the question which had put him increasingly on edge as the day wore on. Would he be able to clearly see the sight on the rifle in the prevailing light conditions? He aimed at the target and looked down the barrel. Then he breathed a great sigh of relief and the tension which had been building in him flowed away. The white paint he had applied to the rear of the sight was working! The sun was reflecting off of it and he could make out the sight well enough to aim with only a little squinting!

Wend relaxed and concentrated on going into the shell he constructed when shooting in matches. He forced himself to forget about the crowd, the noise, and everything else but the target before him. He avoided looking any other person in the eyes. Now he waited only for the signal to fire.

* * *

Geoffrey Caulfield stood beside Peggy to watch the shooting, confident that the day had been productive in his pursuit of the raven-haired woman. He had been able to stay in her close company while paying enough attention to the other two women to avoid exposing his intentions. Now the other ladies had moved away; Anna McDonald to join her husband and Abbey Morgan to stand behind Daniel.

Caulfield prepared to move the conversation to a more personal level. He leaned over and said, "Your husband seems totally dedicated to his craft. Those pistols he sold me are quite ingenious and that rifle seems unique."

Peggy looked up into his eyes. "Yes, Wend is dedicated. I believe it is due to his great admiration for his father. He strives to live up to the standard set by Johann Eckert. And that short rifle is one way of doing that. His father produced guns that were known for their quality and ingenuity. Wend strives to achieve the same thing."

A thought swept through Caulfield's mind: *I would be happy if I just knew who my father was.* He looked over at Peggy and asked, "So you think that short-barreled firelock is an effort to emulate his father?"

"Of course; he wanted to make a rifle which would be as unique as his father's pistols. That's why he's put so much effort into designing it. Now he wants to win this contest to show how accurate it can be." Peggy smiled up at Caulfield. "He thinks it would be attractive for gentlemen like yourself. He's made a sheath for it which can be attached to the saddle."

Geoffrey nodded. "Yes, undoubtedly that would be convenient." Then he locked eyes with Peggy and said, "But with all that concentration on his trade, he can't have much time to pay attention to his wife. I would think it must be somewhat frustrating for you."

Peggy stared at him for a moment. "Why Geoffrey, I'm not sure what you mean."

Caulfield thought: *She knows precisely what I mean.* "Peggy, permit me to be honest. It must be lonely, on a remote farm, to be isolated in your house for long days while your husband is devoted above all to his work." He looked at her and said, "It would be natural for you or any woman to long for some diversion."

Peggy raised one eyebrow, smiled up at him and put her hand on his arm. "Why Geoffrey, you do have such a sensitive and considerate mind. But after all, I have three children and a house to keep me busy. And then there are Mrs. Hecht and Alice Downy to visit with."

Caulfield was formulating his next remark when the judge controlling the shooting match began speaking.

"Attention! It is time for the final match. It will be Captain Daniel Morgan against Mr. Wend Eckert, last year's champion!" The man turned and pointed down the range. "The targets are set at 100 yards. Each man will fire three shots at will." He turned to the competitors. "You may commence, gentlemen."

Morgan's first shot rang out almost immediately, followed by Eckert's a few seconds later. Caulfield noted that Eckert's small weapon had a sharp, high-pitched report compared to the hearty bang of Morgan's large bore rifle.

Peggy remarked, "This is the hardest part — waiting for the results. At 100 yards and beyond, we won't be sure about the placement of the shots until the boys bring back the targets after each of the men fires his three rounds."

Caulfield simply said, "Indeed." As they waited for the shooters to reload and fire their second shot, he continued the conversation. "Still, Peggy, don't you ever wish that you lived in a town where there would be more excitement on a daily basis? I think that I would become exceptionally bored living in the country all the time."

Two shots rang out in rapid succession. Peggy looked from the range to her companion. "I guess it could be, but I get into Winchester for shopping at least once a week. And then, of course, there's church." She smiled sweetly at Caulfield. "But naturally my life doesn't compare to living in one of the Tidewater towns, as you do, Geoffrey."

He nodded. "Well, let's just say that I have spent considerable time in both Norfolk and Williamsburg. And the pace of that society is quite stimulating."

There was a pause in their conversation as the third round of shots rang out. Two young boys immediately ran to bring back the wooden boards which served as targets.

While they were waiting to see the results, Peggy turned to Caulfield. "Have you been to the Governor's Palace in Williamsburg? I hear it is quite elegant."

"Why Peggy, I've been there several times for balls. They can be quite gay and entertaining, with charming music, dancing, fine food, and a brilliantly dressed company of people from the town and the plantations. There's nothing like it anywhere else in the colony."

Peggy looked wistfully in the distance. "You know, I *would* like to see that just once. We have some dancing here in Winchester, but nothing like what you describe." Then she pointed to the three judges who were hovering over the targets. "Oh, it looks like they're having trouble making a decision about the shooting."

Immediately after her words, the head judge raised his hands to quiet the crowd. Then he held up the two targets. Caulfield saw that both men had placed all three of their shots in the bulls-eye of the targets. The three large holes in Morgan's target formed a triangle which essentially obliterated the bulls-eye. Eckert's target showed three smaller holes; one was almost precisely in the very center, and the other two were just inside the bulls-eye.

The judge shouted, "We call this round a tie! I repeat, a tie at 100 yards! The next round will be at 125 yards!"

Caulfield said, "Your husband did very well, Mrs. Eckert. It seems that his little firelock is quite accurate, at least at 100 yards. And clearly your husband is a practiced marksman." He thought a moment. "But I fear that at 125 yards, his firelock will be no match for a longrifle."

Peggy looked back at him with a gleam in her eye. "You're right that Wend's a fine marksman. And he's proven that by many long distance shots, both on the range and off, Geoffrey. Some of them have been in *very* daunting conditions. I wouldn't bet against him if I were you."

Caulfield looked at Peggy. Her wifely pride was clearly visible. He thought: *How can I turn this to my favor?* Then it came to him. He said, "Well, Mrs. Eckert, based on your fine advice, I think I'll go over and place a bet on your husband."

Peggy smiled at him coyly. "You don't need to do that just on my account."

He grinned at her with every bit of charm he could muster. "Peggy, it's my *pleasure* to take your recommendation." He reached into his pocket and pulled out some coins. "Excuse me for just a moment while I place this."

He walked over to the desk where a man was arranging wagers. *I'll undoubtedly lose this money, but it will be worth it if it makes me look gallant in her eyes.* He stepped up to the table and said, "Place this on Eckert to win the match."

The short, bald-headed man looked up at him and said, "Well, there's a brave man. Most everyone else is betting against Eckert. It's hard to see how he's going to win with that little firelock."

Caulfield grinned at the tubby man. "You're probably right, sir. But sometimes, my good fellow, it is possible to *win* by *losing*."

The man looked up at Caulfield in puzzlement. Then his mouth formed a sly grin. "Sir, may I be so bold as to suggest that you desist from any more rum today?" He shook his head, took the money, and recorded the wager.

Caulfield rejoined Peggy and saw that the two men at the firing line were loaded and ready for the next round of shots. "Well, Mrs. Eckert, now we shall see if your faith in your husband is warranted."

Morgan fired his first shot followed almost instantly by Eckert. Caulfield shaded his eyes and tried to see the targets. "Well, Morgan seems to be well into the center circle, but I can't tell precisely at this distance." He shook his head. "With those little balls, it is too far to make out your husband's result."

Peggy looked at him and nodded. He could see stress in her eyes.

Soon the men reloaded and fired their second shots. Once again it was possible to just make out that Morgan's shot was near the center, but the lay of Eckert's was not discernable to the naked eye. Then Caulfield saw a well-dressed man with a small brass telescope who was looking at the targets. He called out, "Sir, what can you see?"

The man took his eye from the telescope and looked at Geoffrey. "It's damned hard to make out, sir, even with my glass. Particularly Eckert's shots. But I do believe that both men have put their balls in the bulls-eye."

Peggy was staring at her husband. She turned to Caulfield and put her hand on his arm. "Wend looks quite calm. I think he believes he's done well. Now he's concentrating on making that last shot."

Caulfield felt a thrill run through him at the touch of her hand. It was the second time she had grasped him. He reached down and put his hand on hers and was gratified that she didn't pull back. In fact, she grabbed him tightly, obviously feeling the tension of the moment as she watched the match. He nodded to her and then looked back at the firing line. Morgan was aiming and momentarily the big man fired.

Smoke flew out from the pan, but the sound of the report was flat. Something was wrong.

Then Caulfield realized that Morgan's lock had misfired. It was a classic flash in the pan and the main charge had not ignited. Meanwhile he heard the sharp crack of Eckert's gun as he fired his third and final shot of the round.

Morgan rose up on his elbows and reached for his powder horn. He raised the frizzen, recharged the pan, and snapped the frizzen back in place. Then he lowered himself fully to the ground, aimed and pulled the trigger again.

And once more the firelock misfired. There was groan from the crowd.

Caulfield heard Morgan explode in a string of loud oaths. Some men laughed; a few mothers covered their children's ears. Then the big man reached into his bag, pulled out a vent pick, and worked to clean the vent into the barrel.

Eckert, who had finished shooting, had gotten up from his mark and was looking down at Morgan. Suddenly a broad grin broke out on his face.

Caulfield thought, *So that damned horse-faced Dutchman actually knows how to smile.*

Then Eckert said, in a tone loud enough to be heard through much of the crowd, "Daniel, I've been telling you for ten years you need to buy one of my rifles so you wouldn't have problems like that."

A ripple of laughter ran through the crowd. Morgan looked up from his firelock, his face turning red, appearing like he had some choice words for Eckert. But he just glared.

At that moment Caulfield heard the sound of pounding horse hooves. So did everyone else; virtually the entire crowd turned to look. A rider was coming up the drive, keeping his horse at the gallop. Geoffrey was surprised to see that the horseman was dressed in the blue-coated uniform of a lieutenant of the Virginia Militia.

Peggy stared at the rider and asked, "Now what can that be about?"

Caulfield shook his head, but kept his eye on the lieutenant. The man pulled up his horse and looked through the crowd as if searching for someone. Then he shrugged, kicked the flanks of his horse, and continued his ride up the drive to the house.

The crowd turned back to the shooting contest. Morgan had resumed his prone position and was taking aim. Caulfield watched as he pulled the set trigger, then squeezed the firing trigger. This time the rifle fired properly.

Instantly the target boys were on their way at the run.

Shortly they were back with the targets and the three judges gathered to examine the results. Presently the chief judge emerged from the group, both targets in hand. He held up Wend's target. One hole was just a tiny fraction off of dead center. The other two were slightly to the left and down from the first, nearly touching it, and well within the bulls-eye. A buzz went through the gathered watchers.

Then the judge held up Morgan's target. A loud groan rose from the crowd. Two of his holes were positioned right around the center of the target. But the third was wide to the right, just outside of the bulls-eye.

The man with the brass glass said loudly, "That last shot was wide! I'll wager that misfire distracted him!"

Morgan vehemently agreed. He shook his head and pointed a finger at Wend. "Dammit, Eckert, you didn't beat me! That damn misfire threw me off!"

Caulfield stood frozen, surprised by the result of the contest. He had never dreamed that anyone, let alone Eckert, could shoot so well with that little firelock. He admitted to himself: *I seem to have somewhat misjudged the man.*

With the shooting over, a large number of men clustered around Eckert to examine the short rifle. Even Morgan came over, took the rifle in his hands, turning it over to see every detail, and then pointing it down toward the target area. Finally the big man slapped Eckert on the back and congratulated him on his shooting.

Then Caulfield heard a buzz run through the crowd and he looked to see Mr. Jack, the McDonalds' ancient, gray-haired butler, leading the militia lieutenant through the crowd towards where Angus stood. The two men reached McDonald and the lieutenant whispered into his ear for a few seconds. McDonald nodded several times as they younger man spoke.

Caulfield's concentration was interrupted by Peggy tugging on his arm.

She was smiling up at him with a look of amusement in her big blue eyes. "Geoffrey, aren't you going to go collect on your bet? I suspect you've won a lot of money."

A shock ran through Caulfield's body. *By God, in all the drama of the misfire situation and then the arrival of the militia officer, he'd completely forgotten the wager!* He nodded in shock to Peggy. "Yes, of course you are correct."

Peggy wrapped her arm around Geoffrey's. "Here, I'll come with you."

As they were walking to the wagering table, Angus McDonald strode to the front of the crowd. He turned toward the gathering and held up his hands. "Well, we've had a wonderful day today and finished it off with a fine shooting match. He held up a brass medallion. And this commemorative token is awarded, once again, to Mr. Wend Eckert, the winner of our shooting match." He turned and presented the medal to Wend. Then he turned back to the crowd and said, "We hope everyone enjoyed the day at Glengarry and I look forward to seeing you next year."

Then McDonald took the militia lieutenant aside and the two became engrossed in conversation.

When they arrived at the wagering table, the little bald man stared at Caulfield for a long moment, then counted out a large number of coins and handed them to him. He grinned in chagrin as he passed the money over. He raised an eyebrow. "It seems, sir, I was wrong about the effect of that rum."

Caulfield was about to make a humorous answer when he heard Peggy say, "Wend, my dear, you shot so marvelously today!" He felt her hand drop from his arm and he looked up to see Eckert standing by the table.

"I was lucky. It would have gone on longer if Dan hadn't had a clogged vent. And frankly, I might have lost if we had gone out to 150 yards."

Caulfield said, "Still, that was excellent shooting, Eckert."

Wend nodded. Then he looked at his wife and said, "Angus just got a dispatch from Williamsburg; a message from the governor about the Ohio Country. He's calling a meeting of militia leaders at the house immediately and wants me to attend."

Peggy said, "But you're not a militia leader! Why does he want you there?"

"He didn't explain. Perhaps it's because of my recent trip out to Pittsburgh." He paused and shrugged. "It shouldn't take too long."

Then Peggy did something that caught Caulfield totally off guard. She took his arm in hers and said, "That's all right, Wend. I won't be lonely. Geoffrey will keep me amused while you men are conducting your business. He's been such a gentleman escorting Anna and Abbey and me all day. I'm sure he wouldn't mind staying with me for a little while longer."

Caulfield recovered quickly and bowed his head to her. "Of course I would be delighted to keep you company, Mrs. Eckert."

Eckert nodded, his face showing absolutely no change in expression. "I appreciate that, Caulfield. And I shall be as brief as possible." He turned and was off up the drive toward Glengarry House.

Geoffrey looked down at Peggy, who was staring intensely after her husband. Her mouth was clinched tight in what looked like frustration or even anger. Caulfield smiled to himself. After this encounter, he was even more certain that his estimate of Eckert had been correct. The man was so obsessed with his trade that he was virtually ignoring the emotional needs of his wife. And Peggy's reaction during the day had convinced him that she fit the pattern of a neglected wife open to the advances of someone ready to give her the attention and sympathy she craved. Caulfield felt a surge of anticipation. *He was just the man to provide what Peggy Eckert needed.*

* * *

Angus McDonald sat at the desk in his study, looking through the two page letter which lay before him.

Besides Wend, Daniel Morgan, James Wood, Sheriff Smith, and David Rutledge, the County Lieutenant, were seated or standing. Evening dusk was settling in outside and candles had been lighted in the room.

Wend looked at the men assembled in the study. Everyone present except himself had some connection with the government or militia. He still wondered why he had been asked to the meeting. His question was soon answered.

McDonald started to speak. "Gentleman, as you might have surmised, the lieutenant who rode in here this afternoon was a courier from Lord Dunmore." He held up the dispatch. "This says that the governor is considering raising a large expedition to punish the Shawnee in the Ohio Country in response to their hostile actions and obstruction of settlement. Dunmore believes Virginia's settlement policy is entirely consistent with the terms of the Fort Stanwix Treaty and that we have every right to be in the territory that the Shawnee are disputing." He looked around at the other men. "I can tell you from personal experience that the Shawnee are increasingly hostile. As you know, I was out there in March at the governor's request to manage a surveying expedition of the lands which have been set aside for settlement by war veterans."

Wood raised his eyebrows. "Yes, Angus, and I'm quite aware that you had to pull out before you fairly got started because the Shawnee were threatening your surveyors. I understand they even shot at some of the parties."

McDonald nodded. "That's right, James. We got virtually nothing done. Well, the main point of this message is that because I was out there recently, the governor wants me to organize a battalion-sized force and make a raid into the Shawnee country. The purpose would be, as Dunmore phrases it," McDonald looked down at the letter, "to 'amuse' the Shawnee while he raises an army large enough to force them into submission."

Wood said, "Well, he's got a point. A raid like that would relieve some pressure on border settlers. The idea reminds me of Colonel John Armstrong's attack on Kittanning in '56 to punish the Delaware for their raids into Pennsylvania."

McDonald turned to Wend. "The governor's letter says that I should consult with you regarding details of the border situation, since — let me quote — 'Mr. Wendelmar Eckert was, until a few days ago, in the western country with Mr. Barrett Northcutt and Captain John Connolly and knows their sentiments with regard to dealing with the hostiles'."

Morgan frowned. "Who is this Northcutt person? I've never heard of him."

Wood laughed. "If you had spent any time in Williamsburg, or had any financial dealings with the government, you'd know about him, Daniel. He's the governor's chief advisor. They're thick as thieves. The word around the capital is that Dunmore doesn't make a move without consulting him." He grinned mischievously, "Including deciding when to call on the lovely Mrs. Blair."

There was a round of laughter from the gathered men. Rumor had it that the lady in question was the governor's mistress.

"Your right, Wood, I ain't wasted no time in Williamsburg or spent my days worrying 'bout the governor's habits."

Wend said, "Daniel, Barrett Northcutt came down from New York with Lord Dunmore. They were business associates there. And don't be so derisive, Daniel. He's the man who arranges my pay for the musket work and, of course, your charges for the wagons."

Morgan raised an eyebrow but remained silent.

McDonald motioned to Wend. "So tell us what news you have of the frontier, Eckert."

Wend nodded. He started by saying, "I spent an evening at Connolly's house and Northcutt traveled with my party for several days on the way back. As far as the conflict on the border, there are really two things going on at once. The first is Chief John Logan's campaign for revenge after the murder of his family. He's abetted by some hotheaded Shawnee who are also making raids. The second, and more threatening problem, is the desire of the entire Shawnee tribe to stop settlement in the lower Ohio Country." Wend went on to describe the massacre of the Mingoes at Baker's Tavern and the effect of both the Logan and Shawnee raiding parties. He told them about the large numbers of refugees from border settlements who were heading toward places of safety. Then he discussed how Connolly and McKee were conducting negotiations with the Shawnee and Mingoes in an attempt to delay the outbreak of widespread conflict. He finished by describing Northcutt's idea for raising a militia force from all the western counties of Virginia to overwhelm the Shawnee. But Wend made no mention of Northcutt's idea that leading the colonists in war would distract them from their growing resistance to Crown authority.

Angus nodded thoughtfully after Wend had finished. "Well, obviously things have deteriorated in even the short time since I left the frontier." He looked around the group. "To be frank, my instinct is to accept the governor's commission."

Morgan had been slouching in his chair. Now he sat straight up. "Angus, just a damn minute! It was only a few days ago that you and other men — including Wood here and Reverend Thruston — led a big meeting, right here in Winchester, to protest the British actions against Boston. There weren't hardly a person in town who wasn't there. And you signed a Statement of Resolve against the British that night." He paused and looked at Wood. "And James, you just came back home when Dunmore high-handedly dissolved the Burgesses. So now we're all going to forget about that to fight a war for Dunmore and the British?"

McDonald smiled at Morgan. "Now Daniel, hold on; it's more complicated than that."

"Hold on?" Morgan waved a hand. "For God's sake, don't you see? Taking up this commission is going to throw away what you just did to defy the British." Morgan's jaw tightened and he sprang to his feet, looking giant-like in the confines of the study. "You want to see what the British did to me?" He made as if to take off his coat.

Angus held both hands up to stop Morgan. Then he winked at the other men. "Whoa, Daniel! Whoa! We all know what that British colonel did to you during Braddock's campaign after you got in that fight with an officer. You don't need to show us the scars on your back from the lashing. I think we've all seen them at one time or another."

There was laughter around the room. Everyone knew about Morgan's hatred of the British Army and his proclivity for pulling up his shirt to show the brutal-looking, permanent scars that a sergeant had made while administering a sentence of 500 lashes.

McDonald spoke again. "So sit down, Daniel; I believe you're thinking the wrong way about this. Look, no one has more of a grudge against the British than an old Jacobite like me who fought against the King at Culloden and watched family and friends die under redcoat swords and bayonets." Angus gathered his thoughts. "But fighting this war will have some advantages for the people of Virginia and even the Whig cause." He looked around at the men and said, "And I believe if pressed, all of us would admit to Whig sympathies."

Morgan returned to his seat. "All right, McDonald, I'm listening."

McDonald said, "First, of course, it will protect Virginians living out on the border. We'd march to do that anyway, even if there were no British governor." He looked around the room again. "Second, defeating the Shawnee will secure the land which has been promised to French War veterans."

Wood, the politician, nodded. "Angus has a good point there. I'm getting appeals all the time from men who have grants and want to know when it will be safe to go out and take up their claims. They've been waiting for years. Something has to be done about that."

McDonald nodded and continued. "The third point is a little more subtle, and I should say, very confidential." He looked meaningfully at the men around the room. "None of us knows where the current political situation is leading us. Putting the militia into the field may have some important practical benefit. Our militia here in Frederick County hasn't been used much since the Pontiac War. That was ten years ago and the frontier has moved westward. We will have the opportunity to improve the organization and training of a force which we may need soon enough for purposes other than fighting Indians."

There was a profound silence in the room. Wend noted that everyone seemed to be staring into the distance as they considered the Scotsman's words.

He continued. "The Committee of Correspondence in Williamsburg has passed to the local committees information that the New England colonies — Massachusetts, New Hampshire, Rhode Island, Connecticut — are, in secrecy, drilling their militia companies hard and forming them into regiments. They're hoarding powder and lead. This war could provide us with the opportunity to do the same. So, Daniel, while we will be fighting under a British governor, we'll be training and hardening a body of troops for our own use," Angus paused and looked around the room once more, "Should, God forbid, it come to that."

There was another silence and the men nodded agreement. Then McDonald said, "I'm to send my answer back to the governor immediately by the same courier. And I intend to say that I will accept leadership of this expedition."

David Rutledge asked, "And where are the troops for this expedition supposed to come from? Are we to supply all of them from here in Frederick County?"

Wend realized that was a logical question for Rutledge to ask. As the County Lieutenant, the governor's deputy in militia matters, it was his job to raise, organize, and regulate all the militia in Frederick County and Winchester itself.

McDonald shook his head. "No, Rutledge, the governor says that Connolly is raising several companies from the settlements south of Pittsburgh, which will be available for our use. It occurs to me that we'll need a battalion of about 400 men. I think it will be adequate if we raise about 150 or 180 here in Frederick, amounting to three solid companies."

Rutledge crossed his arms and considered what Angus had said. "We have many times that amount on the rolls, in numerous companies. I would propose that we recruit your three companies by culling volunteers from the ranks of the standing companies." He thought for a moment, then said, "One company from men east of Winchester, one from the west, and one from the north." He looked at McDonald. "It would be fine with me if you picked the captains, Angus."

McDonald smiled mischievously and looked at Morgan. "Since you were so incensed about helping the British, I guess you don't want to go on this little hunting trip, Daniel?"

Morgan's face turned red and he reared forward in his chair. "Angus, stop playin' with me! If there's a war party goin' out, you know damn well I'll be there. Besides, you know I can raise a company of stout riflemen overnight just by puttin' out the word."

Angus grinned. "That's settled, then." He looked over at James Wood. "You're the captain of the largest company on the other side of town, James. But you're also one of our two county delegates to Burgesses. It occurs to me that if Dunmore does decide to go ahead with this war, he'll have to call the legislature back into session to get the money he needs. I'd be glad to have you as one of the captains, but you might want to go back to Williamsburg to be part of what's going on there. So what's your choice?"

Wend watched Wood's face, and saw him struggling with the decision. Wend thought: *Typical politician; he's working out what will be better for his future aspirations — politics or a war record.*

After long seconds, Wood said, "I'll raise a company for your expedition. Our other representative can take care of matters in Williamsburg."

"Excellent, James, I'll be glad to have you along. Now, who'll command the third company?" Angus thought a moment. "How about Harry Hoagland? He's got experience and is pretty popular up in the northern part of the county."

The other men nodded.

Rutledge said, "You're right, Angus. He's a popular enough captain. And he does keep his muster roll full of likely men."

McDonald said, "I'll talk to him and see if he's game." He looked around the room and tapped his hand on the desk. "All right, that's settled. I'll dash off a reply to Dunmore. James, Daniel: Quietly spread the word and start picking your lieutenants and sergeants. Make sure they've all put their time in during the French War or Pontiac's War. And then start looking for likely lads to fill out the ranks." He screwed up his face. "Mind you, I want no old men or young boys. It's hard country out there and we're likely to be moving fast."

The meeting broke up and the men left to collect their wives for the trip home. Wend lingered in the study until only he and McDonald remained. The Scotsman was bent over his desk, starting to compose the letter to Dunmore.

Wend cleared his throat and said, "Angus, there's more I need to tell you; it relates to this message from the governor."

McDonald looked up. "It's about this proposed expedition?"

"Yes, it's information that I learned while talking to Barrett Northcutt confidentially. Because it was gained from private conversation, I didn't want to bring it up in front of everyone, but I think you should know about it."

"Well, don't just stand there. Explain what you mean, lad." McDonald put down his quill and stared at Wend.

Wend quickly laid out what Northcutt had said at the campfire beside Braddock's Road. He explained that the governor's military expedition might be aimed more at distracting the colonists from their problems with British rule and separating the Virginians from their unity with the New England colonies than making the border safe from war parties.

Angus listened carefully and then nodded. "I'm glad you told me about this, Eckert." He shook his head. "Damn, I hate politics and politicians! They think they're so clever and there's always some hidden agenda that the bastards are pushing."

Wend said, "I can't argue with that, Angus."

McDonald was about to respond, but then a stern look came over his face and he stared at Wend for a long moment. He said, in a puzzled tone, "Now why do you suppose Northcutt told you all of that? Why would he let you in on the governor's confidential plans?"

"He had had a lot to drink. It loosened his tongue and, in fact, we had been traveling together for a while, so I think he had his guard down." Wend thought a moment. "I suspect he may regret having said so much."

"You're probably right, Wend. But thanks to you I'll know to keep my eyes and ears open when I'm talking with Dunmore or Northcutt, and to be very cautious in my correspondence with either one." Angus thought a second. Then his mouth formed into a crooked smile. "You know, Wend, the irony is that, in all his bluster, Morgan essentially was right in his suspicion of the British."

Wend joined in McDonald's smile, then said, "But don't let him know that, Angus, or we'll never hear the end of it!"

McDonald laughed and Wend made ready to leave.

Angus held up a hand. "Wait, Wend, before you go, I need a favor." He reached down and opened a drawer. He pulled out a bag of coins and counted out some onto the desk. Then he put them into another, smaller, bag and handed it to Wend. "This is for the whiskey I bought from Donegal today. Please pass it to him with my compliments."

Wend smiled. "My pleasure; he'll have it in the morning."

McDonald stood up from his chair and walked around the desk. He put his hand on Wend's shoulder. "Good, laddie. Now go take that lovely wife of yours home before it gets too late."

* * *

As they made their way home from Glengarry, Wend drove the chaise as fast as the road and intermittent moonlight permitted. The wind was picking up and sending clouds scudding across the moon. There was a decided chill in the night air. Peggy had her arm around Wend's and snuggled close to him. The other wagons from Eckert Ridge had made their way back long ago while the evening sun was still in the sky.

Peggy shivered. "I should have brought a cloak along. It is getting colder as the night goes along."

Wend looked up at the sky. "This wind is bringing in lots of clouds. I shouldn't be surprised if we had rain tomorrow." He felt his wife shiver. "Do you want my coat?"

"Thanks, Wend but we'll be home soon. We're almost at Battletown. Besides, leaning against you keeps me warm enough." Then Peggy went back to the subject they had been talking about — the governor's letter to McDonald. "There's no chance that you'll be going on this expedition, is there?"

"I can't imagine why. I haven't put much time in with the militia and I don't hold any rank. Besides, it would make more sense for me to stay here and work on the musket contract."

Peggy looked up at Wend. "Still, I can't keep from being worried. I wouldn't want to see you go out again after being home such a short time."

"Don't worry, Peggy. They want men who were in the militia before as officers and sergeants, and they plan to take volunteers for the ranks." He looked down at her. "And for sure I don't plan to volunteer. I have lots of work waiting in the shop."

Peggy squeezed his arm. She looked up at him, her white teeth visible as the moon shown through the clouds. "That makes me feel better."

Then they heard a noise on the road ahead and Wend looked up. A horseman had appeared directly in front of them and was blocking their way. Wend pulled up Boots to avoid hitting the rider and horse.

Suddenly more riders emerged from the woods around them. The horseman to their front threw down from his horse and grabbed Boots' bridle. Then Wend noticed that he had a mask covering the upper part of his face.

Wend immediately became aware that all of the other men — he counted three in addition to the man holding Boots — also wore masks and had large horse pistols leveled at he and Peggy.

Peggy grabbed Wend's arm more tightly than ever. "What's going on, Wend?"

Before Wend could answer, one of the horsemen spoke out. "Now, my good woman, that should be perfectly obvious. Do I really have to say: Stand and deliver? Or: Your purse or your life?"

Wend noticed that the man spoke with a heavy Irish brogue. As he watched, the Irishman dismounted and approached the chaise on Peggy's side. He was only a little taller than Wend but had a massive pair of shoulders.

"Now, I'll have you both out of that cart." He reached up and grabbed Peggy's arm. "Come down, my pretty little thing."

Wend said, as calmly and soothingly as he could, "Go ahead, Peggy. I'll be right behind you."

When they were both standing beside the chaise, the big Irishman smiled slyly and said to Wend, "Now, me darlin' man, the time has come for you to hand over your purse."

Wend reached into his pocket and pulled out his own purse. He left the bag containing Donegal's whiskey money in his pocket, hoping that the thieves might believe that he had given them everything he possessed. He handed the money to the Irishman and, as he did so, noticed that, visible below the edge of his mask, part of the man's left ear was missing. It removed any shadow of doubt that they had encountered the very highwaymen which Sheriff Smith had warned about.

The burly man now turned his attention to Peggy. "Now that's a fine trinket you have around your neck." He took the necklace in his fingers. "Are you going to be sensible and unhook it for me, lass, or do I have to rip it off your neck?"

Wend saw Peggy clench her teeth and immediately feared she was going to make some act of defiance. He quickly said, "Here, I'll unhook it." After fumbling in the darkness for a few seconds, he got it loose. The big man snatched it up. He held it aloft to where the moon provided a little light. "Now this little bit may make the night's work well worth the time." Then he turned to a black man and said, "Isaac, me fine lad, get on up into the cart and see if our upstanding member of the gentry here stashed anything in the cushions."

Meanwhile, a tall, lean man was staring at Peggy. He said, "This is a choice little piece, ain't she? We haven't seen one like this for quite a while." He leered at Peggy. "Maybe we could take her with us?"

The Irishman retorted, "Stop lookin' at the woman and get about your business. We don't want to spend all night here. Search the man and be quick about it."

The man started pawing through Wend's pockets. First he found the brass medallion which had been the prize from the shooting match. He held it up to the moonlight. "I don't know what this is, Corporal. It sure ain't money."

"Just give it to me. We'll look at it later."

In another second the man found the other money bag. He held up the little sack. "Now Corporal, look what we have here. He's trying to hold out on us!"

The Irishman snatched the bag from his compatriot's hand and felt the weight of it. He put the bag in a pocket, then stepped forward, grabbed Wend by his collars, and slammed him back against the side of the chaise. "You stupid swell! Do you think we don't know our own work?"

He knocked Wend against the side of the chaise again. Wend's head hit the woodwork and the world seemed to spin around in front of his eyes. His legs lost their strength and he slumped to the ground, his back against the wheel of the chaise.

The big man leaned down and put his face within inches of Wend. "Maybe that will teach you that we know what we are about. Tell your friends what you just learned; it will spare them the same treatment when it's their turn!"

Then the Irishman signaled to his compatriots; they all mounted and spurred their horses to the gallop, heading down the road toward the east.

Peggy could no longer contain her rage. She screamed after the men, "You pocked-face bastards! You assholes! You pieces of shit! Your mothers were fucked by dogs!" She continued in the same vein for some time, repeating herself only a couple times. She used several words and phrases that Wend had never heard, even in months of scouting for the British Army. The swearing was accompanied by a waving of clenched fists, a stamping of feet, and at least a couple of times she hopped right off the ground in her fury.

136

Wend reflected that it was not for nothing that his Ulster wife had grown up in a tavern common room. She could have a fiery temper, but over the years she had learned how to restrain it. Now only on the rarest of occasions did she lose control and unleash her supply of oaths.

By the time Wend had pulled himself to his feet she had expended her wrath and become quiet, turning back toward her husband.

Wend rubbed the back of his head. Undoubtedly there would be a painful bump for a few days. Then he smiled wryly at his wife. "My dear, it seems that in just a few hours you've descended from Lady Elizabeth Eckert back to Peggy McCartie the tavern maid."

"Wend, for God's sake, how can you make jokes at a time like this? How can you be so calm?" Then Peggy's face wrinkled up and she broke into tears. "That necklace was the first real piece of jewelry I ever had. I loved it so much. And now it's gone! Gone forever."

Wend took Peggy in his arms and she put her head against his shoulder and sobbed like a child. He said, "It's all right, my little vixen. The truth is, I can replace the necklace, but I could never replace you in my heart." He paused and considered his words. "At least they left us with our lives. That's what I feared about most."

Peggy looked up, her eyes round and beautiful in the moonlight. She stared at him for long seconds. "You really mean all that, don't you?" Then she hugged him again very tightly. "I really am a fortunate woman."

* * *

Both of the Eckerts had trouble getting to sleep that night. Wend lay in bed, tossing and turning, but had little luck. It didn't help that he had a throbbing pain in the back of his head from the highwayman's blow. Peggy was equally restless. Finally, after an hour or so, Wend brought two cups of whiskey upstairs, which they both downed in a couple of swallows. It was something Wend rarely did, for almost never had difficulty sleeping. But the medication helped and finally, mercifully, he drifted off.

It seemed like only a few seconds later that he came fully awake to the sounds of barking. There were at least ten dogs on the farm and it seemed like every one of them was sounding off.

Peggy asked sleepily, "What's going on, Wend?"

Wend said, "I have no idea." He got up and went to the front window and saw nothing in the darkness. But a blustery wind had come up in the night. He could hear gusts rustling tree branches and felt the house vibrate a little at the strongest blasts of air. He cursed quietly, went to a cabinet and took out the pair of pistols, powder horn, and small shooting bag he kept there. He whispered to Peggy, "I'll go take a look." Then he joked, "And if it's just the dogs barking at the wind and each other, I damn well may shoot one to teach the rest a lesson."

Wend slipped out of the house from the back door and made his way through the garden and then out along the side of the house, taking cover in case there might indeed be an intruder. The wind prevented him from hearing anything except the dogs. But Wend figured that the most likely problem was a roving animal; bears frequently came through, as did herds of deer. A fox snooping around the farm was a definite possibility. He walked out along the side wall of the house and looked over the drive between the farm buildings. He was surprised to see a slight, barely perceptible tinge of light on the eastern horizon; he realized that he had actually slept for hours and it was near dawn.

As he stood there, Wend realized that the dogs had mostly quieted down. In fact, the only dog in sight was a hound named Digger, who was standing in front of the gunsmith shop, looking down the drive toward the wagon road. The animal made a few final barks, then turned around and trotted back to Wend, wagging his tail, obviously proud of himself.

Wend reached down and patted the dog on his head. He said wryly, "Yes, Digger, I'm sure you saved the farm from grave danger."

Wend stuffed the pistol he had been holding into the waist of his breeches and made his way back to the rear door of the house. He had just climbed the steps and was reaching for the door knob when the wind died momentarily. In the sudden silence, Wend heard something; or rather, thought he might have heard something, for it was more an ephemeral, fleeting sense of a sound than the real thing. But what he *thought* he heard was the beat of horse hooves pounding at the gallop down on the main road. And then the wind resumed, obliterating his ability to hear anything. He stood listening at the door for several long minutes, waiting for the wind to stop again. But in the few times that it did, there was only the stillness of the night.

* * *

Peggy Eckert, broom in hand, stepped out onto the front porch to begin what was a key part of her morning ritual. The first piece of work she did every day after breakfast was to sweep the porch. It just took her just five or ten minutes, and usually the porch didn't even need it, but the process gave her some time to herself and let her solidify her plans for the day. Meanwhile, Liza would be cleaning up the breakfast things and doing any picking up necessary around the first floor. The two older children had already gone down to Alice Downy's place for morning school lessons. In the afternoon Bernd would come back to work in the shop with Wend and Elise would spend her time with Peggy, usually busy at their sewing.

Just as she started, she looked up to see Specht, the field hand, riding out. Peggy knew Wend had dispatched him to find Sheriff Smith and tell him about the robbery. She waved to the young man as he rode past.

After a while, she looked down at her hands; they were her greatest despair. Wend might joke about her being Lady Elizabeth, but no real lady would ever have hands like hers. She prided herself on being able to keep her weight down and preserve the looks of her youth, but the hands betrayed her age and the fact that she had worked at manual labor every day of her life. They had scars and marks from the long ago days in the tavern and more scars from working in the fields the first year they had the farm. After that, Wend had gotten help for the fields, but she still had done the kitchen work, scrubbed floors, and helped with the butchering. It had only been five years ago that Wilma, Albert, and their children had come to relieve her of the most arduous of the house and kitchen work, but by then her hands had been beyond repair. *Thank God for gloves when I go visiting,* Peggy thought.

By that time she had swept her way down to a pair of chairs which sat near the center of the porch. She had just started to sweep behind the first one when she saw something which brought her up short. Lying behind the chair was a small package, wrapped with parchment and tied with a dark blue ribbon. She picked up the packet and then saw, written across the front in an unfamiliar hand, the words "For Mrs. Eckert." Her heart skipped a beat. She stood looking at the packet for long moments and then slipped it under her apron. Leaving the broom on the porch, she went into the house and walked directly to her sewing room, which was behind the parlor and would afford her some privacy.

Peggy quickly untied the ribbon. She opened the paper and immediately froze in shock. Unbelievably, there was the necklace taken from her only a few hours before!

In a few moments, Peggy recovered from her surprise and began thinking about the implications of the package. Two things were clear: First, the delivery of the packet had been the cause of the barking dogs in the pre-dawn night.

Second, there was no doubt in her mind that Geoffrey Caulfield was behind the nocturnal delivery, probably making it himself. And then came the obvious implication: Geoffrey was tied in with the gang of highwaymen which had robbed and savaged them last night.

Undoubtedly Caulfield thought that she would consider this an act of gallantry which would further his blatant pursuit of her favors. Peggy laughed to herself. Then she froze; Caulfield was betting on the odds that she would not tell her husband about the return of the necklace. *By God, the arrogance of the man!* She stood up; her first instinct was to walk over to the workshop and show Wend the jewelry. But then she realized that he would immediately send word to the sheriff about Caulfield. Suddenly she had doubts about repaying an act of kindness, whatever the man's motivation and arrogance, with betrayal. She thought: *The fact is, I have spent a large part of my own life living a lie.* Impulsively, Peggy put the necklace back in the package and retied the ribbon. Then she hid the packet in the bottom drawer of her sewing cabinet.

Peggy Eckert decided she would have to think about the proper way to repay Geoffrey Caulfield.

CHAPTER NINE

Drumbeat of War

Wend, Sheriff Smith, and Daniel Morgan rode into Winchester on Fairfax Lane, the northernmost of the three east-west cross streets of the town. Fort Loudoun, the four-sided, stone and timber fortification which Colonel George Washington of the Virginia Regiment had built as his headquarters during the French war, sat on a low hill to the north of them. Now that the frontier had moved well beyond Winchester, it was suffering the same fate as Fort Pitt; deterioration and slow cannibalization by the townspeople. It now mainly functioned as the site for drilling militia companies.

The three men turned southward onto Market Street. A messenger from Angus McDonald had summoned them to meet with Barrett Northcutt. Along with a deputation of men from Morgan's and Eckert's places, they had been out near the Shenandoah River on a futile attempt to capture the band of highwaymen. Humphrey Keys, who operated the most popular ferry crossing, had noticed smoke rising from a normally uninhabited place along the road between Battletown and the river. The ferryman, aware that brigands were operating in the county, had become suspicious and sent a message to the sheriff. Smith, patrolling the Great Wagon Road west of Winchester, had not received the word until two days later and by the time he had organized an armed party and found the campsite, the band of thieves, if that was who had been there, had departed.

As they rode along Market Street and crossed Piccadilly Street, Wend reflected that the houses and other buildings along Market Street were a living history of the town. The oldest, built in the 1740's and 1750's, were of log construction. Recent construction featured wooden frame, stone, brick, or various combinations.

The Golden Buck Inn, about halfway down Market Street, was the largest establishment of its type in town. It was a two story building, located just across the street from the square, which was the site of the courthouse, the jail and the Anglican Church. For that reason the inn was a busy place, with men doing business in the common room and using its back rooms for more private meetings.

The three men dismounted in the courtyard and handed their horses over to a stableboy. As they strode into the common room, Smith waved to several acquaintances at tables. He inquired at the bar and then led Wend and Morgan to one of the back rooms.

As they entered, Wend saw that McDonald was seated on the far side of the table. James Wood was in a chair at the end of the table. Northcutt was standing by the hearth, a burning taper in hand, lighting one of his cigars. He got it started, blew out the taper, and looked up at the new arrivals. Wend watched as he stared at Morgan, obviously impressed by the man's imposing size.

McDonald said, "Barrett, you know Mr. Eckert. And here is our sheriff, Charles Smith. This other gentleman is Captain Daniel Morgan of the Frederick County Militia; a man with great experience in fighting on the frontier."

Northcutt nodded to Wend. "Glad to see you again, Eckert. It's my pleasure to meet you, Sheriff Smith and Captain Morgan."

When everyone was seated, Angus said, "Gentlemen, as you probably guessed, this meeting is about the border expedition we discussed last week at my house."

Northcutt nodded. "Governor Dunmore read Major McDonald's letter with great satisfaction and complete agreement with his ideas. Then, within the hour, he dispatched me to further discuss the expedition and provide final authorization. We rode at courier speed to get here. And believe me, my ass feels like it!" He looked around at his listeners, who smiled politely at the attempted humor. Then he continued, "The important point is that Dunmore wants the expedition to march as soon as possible."

Wood spoke up. "What about authorization and money for the expedition? Won't His Lordship have to get approval of the Council and the Burgesses before he raises troops?"

"What you say is generally true, Mr. Wood. And by now, the governor has undoubtedly issued a call for the assembly to come back into session for the discussion of urgent business. He was composing the missive when I rode out."

McDonald cocked his head. "So I presume what you mean is that you want me to call out my troops and make preparations to march instantly upon the governor getting approval from the legislature?"

"No, Angus. I mean *exactly* what I said at the beginning: I want you to march for the border as soon as you can manage." He looked around at the faces who were staring at him now. "The governor reckons he has authority to send out a limited number of troops to face a crisis. And a crisis is precisely what we already have on the border with these mixed Mingo–Shawnee raids. Over a thousand settlers have fled from their homes in the border settlements. We fear the raids will spread to the southern counties. Just before I left, His Lordship authorized a party of scouts, under a man named Daniel Boone, to travel immediately through the new settlements in Kentucky to give warning to the people there to either withdraw or at least fortify their houses."

Northcutt paused and looked around the table at the silent faces of the other men. Then he continued, "John Connolly has rightly called out the militia in his area to protect the settlements. Your mission, Angus, is to reinforce and support him by advancing on the Shawnee villages and thus relieve the pressure on the frontier until the governor can raise the main body of militia."

James Wood cleared his throat. "What about the money to finance this movement? Does His Lordship expect us to pay for it out of our own pockets?"

Northcutt reached down into a leather case on the floor beside his chair, pulled out a folded paper, and tossed it onto the table.

Everyone stared at the packet.

Northcutt smiled broadly at Woods. "No, Mr. Wood, the governor does *not* expect you to pay for it yourself. That's a Bill of Credit. He's put together enough funds from his government accounts and loans from patriotic citizens to get this small expedition out to the border. And of course, payment for your troops will be handled by claims from each captain in the standard manner after the campaign is over."

Wend thought: *This is all happening much faster than I expected.* He looked around at the other men and could see from their faces that they were having the same reaction.

Northcutt smiled and continued, "The main force of militia will be raised once the governor *does* have authorization from the legislature. The general plan is to have two columns of troops, each at least 1,000 strong, advance on the Shawnee territory. One, under Colonel Andrew Lewis, will advance from the southern part of the colony. The other, from the north, will be based out of Pittsburgh, and led by the governor himself." He looked at McDonald. "Angus, once your expedition has completed its mission, it will fall back and form the core of the northern column."

McDonald nodded. "All right, I think we have the picture, Barrett. And I can say that we're well along in assembling three companies from here in Frederick County."

Northcutt exclaimed, "Capital! And Dunmore has already sent off a courier to Connolly telling him to provide another three or four companies to fill out your force."

Morgan growled, "The fact is, I've already recruited the officers and most of the men for a company of about sixty men. All I need to do is call them out. I know Wood has done the same, and there's a company forming in the north of the county. We could march out in a couple of days if that's what you want."

Wood put his hand on his chin. "Morgan's right: The men are indeed ready, but we'll need to assemble enough supplies and wagons to provide for the march up to Pittsburgh. That will take some time."

Angus shook his head. "Not *wagons*, James. We need to move fast. We'll use pack horses for our provisions and supplies."

"Damned good idea, Angus." Northcutt beamed and looked around the table. "But procuring supplies for your march will take some concentrated effort if you aren't to be held up. The fact is you need a quartermaster on your staff to expedite preparations; someone who is good at planning and has a head for financial matters." He pointed at the Bill of Credit with his cigar. "And of course, I don't need to point out that the governor expects a detailed accounting of how that money is used."

Wend saw Northcutt cast a quick glance in his direction and felt a sickening lump form in his stomach. That was why he had been called to this meeting. *Dammit! Northcutt had every intention of dragooning him into this fight.*

McDonald said reflectively, "Yes, Barrett, I see what you mean. A quartermaster to look after things would be a good idea." He paused a second and then said, "I'll have to think about the proper person."

Northcutt looked at McDonald. "Angus, time is of the essence; permit me to make a suggestion. How about our friend Eckert here? I've been working with him on this musket contract. And it was my pleasure to travel with him on my return journey from Pittsburgh, where I witnessed how well he organized matters. I must say, the governor has been very pleased with his work on the muskets. And he keeps his accounts fair and accurate."

McDonald glanced at Wend and then looked back at Northcutt. "It's a good thought, Barrett. There's 'na doubt Wend's got a fine mind for business."

144

Northcutt grinned. "I'm glad you agree. And let's not forget, Eckert did march with Bouquet on the relief of Fort Pitt back in '63. So he's got some idea of the needs of an expedition."

Angus nodded, "Aye, that's true enough."

Northcutt reached down to the leather case again, shuffled through some papers, and pulled out a sheet of parchment. He slid it down the table until it was in front of McDonald. "Here's a lieutenant's commission for Eckert, signed by the governor himself, Angus. That will give him authority with merchants to get provisions and supplies." He took a long pull on his cigar and stared at the Scotsman for a long moment. Then he expelled the smoke, which wafted over the table in a long cloud. He cocked his head and said coyly, "Of course, you have the final approval, Angus."

Wend felt the eyes of Wood, Morgan, and Smith on him. He sensed his neck and face turning red and looked straight ahead, concentrating on maintaining a steely expression.

McDonald sat looking down at the commission. Wend saw a flash of anger in his eyes. Wend thought: *He doesn't like being told what to do any more than I do.* But after a few seconds, Angus looked at Northcutt, smiled broadly, and said, "It's a bonnie idea, Barrett. Wend's just the man for the job." He reached down, picked up the commission, and then handed it across the table to Wend. "You'll need to get started right away, *Lieutenant* Eckert."

Wend picked up the commission, his mind in turmoil. He thought about the promise he had made to Peggy about staying at home. He looked up at Northcutt and said, "Barrett, I need to talk with you — in private — after the meeting."

"Of course, Eckert. Actually, I want to talk to you alone about some separate business."

McDonald nodded toward Wend. "By the way, Eckert, I want Baird and Donegal on this trip. Joshua to be Chief Scout and Donegal to assume Sergeant Major; with his time in the 77th, he's just the man to train the troops and keep them in line."

Wend nodded. "You remember about Joshua's left leg — he's got to favor it while on foot."

"Yes, I understand. But he can do most of his work on horseback and there'll be other men who can scout on foot when we get out to the border." Angus made a crooked grin. "Just tell both of them they're not going to miss this little trip."

Northcutt looked around the table in a satisfied manner. "Well, gentlemen, I think we've settled a lot of matters today. And I'll be staying right here until your column marches out, to help smooth over any problems and then to take confirmation of your departure back to His Lordship."

* * *

As the other men filed out of the room, Northcutt took a final draw on his cigar and then threw the butt into the fire. When he and Wend were alone, he smiled broadly and leaned close as if they were plotting a conspiracy, and said, "Well, that all went pretty well, don't you think, Eckert?"

"You seemed to have gotten many things settled, sir. It appears that events are moving rapidly. And very much in concert with the plan that you laid out to me and Crawford back on Braddock's Road."

"Precisely, Eckert!" An enthusiastic grin came over Northcutt's face. "You know, this is exactly what I love most about both business and government service." Northcutt pointed to his head. "First you carefully conceive a plan and then you make it come alive in the real world. You watch it mature and come to fruition."

"Yes, Barrett, but sometimes things don't go exactly as planned."

"But, Eckert, don't you see? That's the real challenge; dealing with the problems that get in your way. Overcoming obstacles, by God! There's an incredible satisfaction in having successfully dealt with reversals, particularly when you can turn them in your favor."

Wend nodded. He hesitated momentarily, trying to assemble his thoughts and most tactfully tell Northcutt what was on his mind.

Northcutt impatiently drummed his fingers on the table. "So, what is it that you want to talk to me about?"

"Well, Barrett, I'm grateful for the confidence that you and His Lordship have placed in me by offering a commission."

"Think nothing of it Eckert; the fact is, you're the best man for the job. Everybody in the room came to recognize that once I explained the reasoning."

Wend wasn't so sure about that. He suspected that what they had really thought was that he was being shown a suspicious amount of favoritism. But he said, "Barrett, I believe perhaps it would be better for me to stay here rather than marching with the army. I think I should concentrate on expediting work on the latest batch of muskets. Surely you will need as many as possible for the militia companies that will be forming for the war. Many of the men you'll be recruiting won't have rifles; you'll need to provide them a suitable firelock. It's exactly for this kind of situation that we've been overhauling the muskets."

Northcutt stared at Wend for a long moment. Then he said, in an incredulous tone, "Do I understand correctly what you are saying, Eckert? You actually want to turn down a commission from the governor and the chance to play a significant role in the upcoming campaign?"

"Like I said, Barrett, I believe that I can contribute more to the effort by staying here and concentrating on my trade." Wend paused for a moment, then said, "And personally, I've promised my wife that I won't go since I just spent weeks on the trip out to Pittsburgh."

Barrett shot Wend a sharp look. Suddenly Wend realized how lame his last remark had sounded, considering all the men from the county who were about to leave their families on short notice.

Northcutt reached into his coat pocket and pulled out another cigar. He got up, took a taper from the mantle and used it to light the tobacco. Then he walked around to a position where he stood hovering over Wend's shoulder. He said, in a low voice, "Eckert, you've found that musket contract very lucrative, haven't you?"

Wend twisted his head to look up at the governor's aide, who towered over him.

Before he could answer, Northcutt said, "Of course you have. I was talking with McDonald about you earlier today. He was quite impressed with how your workshop was bustling and how you've prospered."

Northcutt took a long pull on his cigar and after a few seconds exhaled. The acrid smoke settled in a cloud around Wend's head, burning his nostrils. He fought to avoid coughing.

After a moment, Barrett asked, "Now why do you think it was that you got that contract?"

Wend waved his hand to clear the smoke from his face. "I assume it was because I offered a fair price and had the reputation for quality work."

"Are you that naïve, Eckert? Has it not occurred to you that we could have easily found an established and competent gunsmith in or near Williamsburg to carry out the work required? And that in doing so our transportation arrangements would have been easier and less costly?"

Wend had wondered about that, but hadn't spent much time questioning his good fortune.

"Now, Eckert, what does the word 'protégé' mean to you?"

Wend answered, "I'm afraid I've never heard the word, Barrett."

"Simply stated it means a person who is singled out and shown special consideration by a man of power."

"Are you saying that I am someone's protégé, Barrett? Your protégé?"

Northcutt didn't reply directly. Instead he asked, "Have you ever heard of a certain Captain Reginald Welford of the 60th Foot?"

"Of course, sir. I met him once in Carlisle when he was a lieutenant and serving as Henry Bouquet's adjutant. He was with him from 1764 until the general died in 1765, at Pensacola."

"Yes, well now Mr. Welford has been seconded from company duties in the 60th and is serving on General Gage's staff in New York. That's where he became a frequent companion of mine at the card table and a number of pleasant taverns in the city. I might add that he is a *most* gracious loser at games of chance. Along the way he told me some fascinating stories of the frontier and Bouquet's campaigns against the Ohio tribes." Northcutt put his hand on Wend's shoulder. "One of those stories was about a young German boy, orphaned by Indian attack along Forbes Road, for whom Bouquet had great sympathy and thought of almost as the son he could never have. Later, in the emergency of 1763, the young man served as a scout and helped find the path which enabled Bouquet to defeat the tribes at Bushy Run. Subsequently he performed some extraordinary feats of marksmanship which earned him the respect of the officers of both the Black Watch and Montgomery's Highlanders."

Wend said quietly, "Some of those stories are quite exaggerated."

"Perhaps, but my point is, you were, in essence, Bouquet's protégé."

"He felt responsible for the death of my family."

"Yes, but according to Welford, he came to have great respect for your intelligence and abilities."

Wend looked up at Northcutt. "How does that apply to our situation here in Virginia ten years later?"

"Just this, Eckert: What appealed to me most — and later to the governor — was the fact that you were loyal enough to the Crown to volunteer as a scout when virtually no other colonials were willing to join Bouquet's expedition."

"Barrett, I had personal reasons for marching with Bouquet."

"Be that as it may, when Lord Dunmore and I came to Virginia, one item on our agenda was to build a group of colonials, particularly in the Piedmont and the Valley, who we knew would be loyal in time of crisis. When the issue of the musket contract came up, I saw your name among the gunsmiths bidding for the work. I discussed the matter with Dunmore and pointed out that you had, as it were, a foot in two cultural camps we were interested in — the Ulster-Scots and the Germans. Both are large groups here in the Winchester area. So you qualified as a candidate for our select group by both ancestry *and* the fame of your exploits. It didn't take much thought to select you for the contract, even though we knew our costs would be higher than if we had worked with someone in Williamsburg. In essence, you became the governor's protégé. And obviously a protégé is expected to reciprocate the favors extended to him."

"I still don't understand why it is so important for me to go with the expedition, Barrett."

"I'll be quite plain. First, just like I said at the meeting, I want someone I can trust handling the money and supplies. Second, we want to ensure that the German community contributes several companies of troops to the main army the governor will be forming. I want you to help encourage that, and particularly to set the example by marching with McDonald's men. Third, it is most desirable for me to have a confidential observer along on the campaign; someone who I know has loyalty to Dunmore and me."

Wend spun around. "You want me to spy on my neighbors and friends?" He shook his head. "That's a step too far, Northcutt. I'll not do it."

"As I said, I prefer the term 'observer', Eckert. Rest easy; I just want somebody to confirm everything that we're told through official correspondence from McDonald. And of course, it would be helpful if you could comment on the loyalty of McDonald and his officers."

Wend blurted, "And what happens, Barrett, if I just refuse to join the expedition?" But even as he said the words, he knew what the answer would be.

Northcutt shrugged and waved his cigar in the air. "I should think that would be rather obvious. Lord Dunmore *giveth* and Lord Dunmore can *taketh* away. So the choice is up to you, but you certainly can imagine the consequences."

Wend felt like an animal in a trap. His family and people on the farm were dependent on the money which came from the musket work. He owed Daniel Morgan cash for the use of his wagons and men. He desperately searched his mind for some way to say no and replace the lost income if Northcutt carried out his threat. But there was no obvious way, at least in the near term.

Barrett Northcutt reached down and picked up the commission. He said in a soothing voice, "Here, Wend, I urge you to take this. It's the smart course for you and I can assure you that your loyalty will earn the gratitude of His Lordship when the time comes for new land grants."

With great reluctance, Wend reached up and took the commission.

Northcutt patted Wend on the shoulder. "Rest assured, my friend, that you have made the right choice." He went over to his chair and reached into the leather case. He handed over an envelope. "There's the Bill of Credit in the payment for the batch of muskets you delivered to Fort Pitt. As usual, your accounts were most accurate and satisfactory."

He paused and said, "And now, *Lieutenant*, I'll ask you to come with me to the rectory of the German Presbyterian Church. I've set up a meeting with the pastor and Mr. Rutherford, the County Lieutenant, to discuss the need for recruiting men from the congregation for the main body of the governor's militia force. I'm sure you know both men; your presence and support will lend credence to my arguments."

* * *

"Wend, you promised you wouldn't go with the militia! You *promised!*" Peggy Eckert sat in a chair in their sitting room, her eyes ablaze and her jaw firmly set.

It was late in the evening. Wend had arrived home after dark and after the family supper, having spent a couple of hours at Northcutt's meeting with the German minister.

Ironically, in the midst of her rage, Wend thought he had never seen Peggy look more beautiful, even when she had been dressed and groomed for some formal affair. Her cheeks were flushed by her anger and her eyes were open wide and showing a deep, smoldering blue. He pleaded, "Darling, I've told you how Northcutt has us in a bind. I had no choice. Think of what will happen if we lose the money from the contract."

"Surely we can make do! There must be some way to make up for the loss if you tell him you won't cooperate."

"Peggy, I owe money to the forge for spare parts and musket barrels. And I'd immediately have to discharge Hecht and his apprentice."

"Then discharge him, Wend."

"Peggy, that would be breaking my promise to him for least three years of work here. He moved his family up from the Hebron Valley and took on his apprentice based on that promise. No, I'll not do it." Wend gathered his thoughts, then continued, "And you know that I owed a lot of money to Morgan; money I didn't have until Northcutt paid for that last batch of muskets today." He looked into Peggy's angry eyes. "And then there are the trips to Alexandria which you enjoy so much. Think of all the fabric and notions you buy there which you can't get here in Winchester." He looked directly at her. "I couldn't have bought that necklace you loved so much if it weren't for the musket money." He shook his head. "Peggy, the truth is I had no choice but to cooperate. Northcutt had me just where he wanted me. It was the most galling moment of my life."

"Wend, there must be some way to bring in more money in from another source! You could make more guns for sale in Alexandria and Fredericksburg. People love your work."

Wend shook his head. "I could never sell enough of them. It wouldn't begin to compensate."

Peggy thought a moment and then her eyes brightened and she slapped her hand down on the arm of the chair. "Why can't we start raising tobacco like so many other farmers do? That's a good money crop."

"All we would be doing is trading one master for another. Look how all the tobacco planters are deep in debt to the buyers and bankers in London. They extend credit based on future harvests. And then the planter is never able to pay it all off. It's a cycle which can't be broken." He thought a moment. "And even if we did that, it would take at least a year to be ready. We'd have to clear more land." He shook his head. "No, that's not an answer."

Peggy was silent for a long time. The frustration was written all over her face. Then her expression changed and her jaw jutted out as she thought of a new idea. She looked up at Wend. "You know what I think? You're just using the money as an excuse. You actually *want* to go."

Wend was shocked. "For God's sake, Peggy! What are you saying? Why would I *want* to march with McDonald?"

Peggy's eyes were narrowed and piercing. "It's that girl! You think you might be able to see Abigail! This campaign will be right in the area where her village is!"

Wend was speechless. "How can you say that? This is not 1763! You know she made a conscious choice to stay with the Mingoes. Why would I want to see her now after all these years?"

"Because you've never stopped loving her. You married me because you couldn't get her."

"Peggy, that's crazy! I fell in love with you ten years ago; the night we raced my wagon over North Mountain to save your sister Ellen's life. That night, I saw — *really* saw for the first time — your beauty. And that night you earned my everlasting admiration for your determination and strength. I knew you were the one I wanted to spend my life with. I'll always have memories of Abigail, but you are my life. You must believe me."

Peggy looked up at Wend with tears in her eyes. She sat staring at him for a long time. Finally she sighed deeply. "Yes, Wend, you have been a good and loyal husband." She clasped her hands in front of her. "But it's going to be dangerous. I'm so afraid you won't come back."

Wend went around to the back of her chair, put his hands on her shoulders, and looked down into her eyes. "I will be back. I promise. And while I'm gone, I'm going to figure out a way to break our bonds to Northcutt and the governor. Please have faith in me and my love for you and our children."

Wend soothed his wife, and dried her eyes with his handkerchief. They talked for a while longer and Peggy composed herself. Then she went upstairs to check the children and prepare for bed. Wend felt relieved that she seemed to have become reconciled to the state of affairs. But he was certain of one thing: When he went upstairs to bed, he would find Peggy under the covers with her sleeping cap on, her black tresses carefully tucked inside. That was the signal she was not in the mood for loving.

Wend went to the sidebar and poured himself a measure of Donegal's whiskey. He stood there, glass in hand, looking out the window into the June night. A sense of guilt and regret came over him. The fact was, he had not been completely truthful with his wife. It was indeed true that he wasn't anticipating a meeting with Abigail, at least not of the romantic kind. But he had been living a lie for ten years; a lie of *omission*. For, unknown to Peggy, Wend had a son by Abigail Gibson. He was living with her in the Mingo village on Slippery Rock Creek. He had only seen the lad once, for less than fifteen minutes, in the brief visit of the Black Watch company to Abigail's village in 1763. The boy had been only four then, brown-haired and blue-eyed; and in the haste of the moment, he hadn't even learned his son's name. But he had never told his wife about the existence of the child. In the hectic environment which surrounded their marriage and flight from Pennsylvania, he hadn't thought to bring it up. As time passed, he realized his mistake in not telling Peggy immediately. Given her volatile nature, he feared what would happen if he suddenly broached the subject.

With the passage of time, Wend had increasingly thought about his son. As he spent more and more time with young Bernd at his side, he found his mind often drifting off to imagine what his own offspring would look like, what kind of mind he would have, how well he would do as an apprentice in the family's trade. He had also tried to picture him living in the Mingo village. He visualized him dressed in Mingo fashion, sitting at the fire or learning to hunt and fish from the men. Had he grown up to resemble Wend? Or did he more closely take after Abigail?

Over the years, his curiosity had grown into an obsession.

But now there was another problem to worry about. It had occurred to Wend on the ride back from Winchester. He had calculated that his son would be about fourteen by now. And it was not unusual for Indian boys of that age to fight as warriors. That was particularly true of the Mingoes, because of the small size of the tribe. Most villages had only a few full-grown warriors. The startling truth was, it was entirely possible that Wend's own son would be arrayed against him in battle.

* * *

Wend and Andrew Horner stood side by side in the workshop, making up packages of spare parts for rifles and muskets. The packets would then be put into canvas sacks which could be loaded onto a packsaddle. They also made ready small kegs of black powder and bags of lead which would go on a couple of other packhorses.

After some lengthy discussion between Hecht and Wend, the decision had been made for Horner to go with the militia as assistant armorer who would work under Wend. Wend, as quartermaster, was in reality contracting with his own organization for the job at the going rate. It was a necessary function, and coincidently, it was a legitimate way to get some additional money out of Northcutt.

Wend had noticed that Horner had been unusually quiet while they worked, but had assumed that he was simply concentrating on selecting the correct items and making up the packets.

Then suddenly the young man put down the package he had just finished and turned to Wend with a serious look in his eyes. "Sir, may I speak to you?"

"Of course, Andrew, what is it?"

"Must I go on this expedition? Couldn't you hire someone else for this work?"

"Why don't you want to go, Andrew? It will be good experience and you know that I'm going to set aside a reasonable amount of pay for your services. That money will serve you well when you finish your apprenticeship and are ready to go out on your own."

"The truth is that I would prefer not to be part of the army."

Wend was puzzled. "Andrew, every free man is required to be part of the militia and you'll have to participate in musters once your apprenticeship is finished. And besides, on this trip you will be considered a civilian under contract, not a militia member. You'll be in the rear areas, not involved in any fighting."

"Sir, you know that my family lived in Hesse. One of the reasons I came to the colonies was to avoid having to serve in the Landgrave of Hesse's army; Frederick is his name. My older brother was taken into the army. He lived in terrible conditions. He was beaten by sergeants. Then he died of fever he got while standing sentinel in the freezing rain. Sometimes Frederick rents out regiments to other countries to get money. I was determined not to lose my life the way my brother did, or die going into battle just to make money for Frederick." Andrew paused and looked at Wend. "Now, in this new land, it turns out that I'm being sent along with the army against my desires."

Wend didn't know what to say. The youth had always been a willing worker who never complained about any assignment. But there was no one else available for the job; particularly now that the day of departure was nearly upon them. Wend set his jaw. "Let me say again, this is not like the Landgrave's army. No one will beat you and you're not going to be asked to fight. And remember, you are my apprentice; you will be carrying out a legitimate job which can be considered part of your training. So I must insist that you come with the expedition." Wend looked directly into Horner's eyes. "Now let us hear no more about this."

The muscles of Horner's face tightened, but he simply nodded and returned to his work.

Wend thought to himself: *Now there are two of us who don't want to march on this expedition.*

* * *

With Fort Loudoun to her back, Peggy Eckert stood in the bright June sunlight watching the two Winchester companies forming into their ranks. The soldiers' women had made their goodbyes and now stood crowded together observing final preparations to leave while the children played games of tag in and around the old fort. Bernd and Elise were there, while young Ellen was back at the farm under the care of Wilma. Peggy, Jean Moncure, Anna McDonald, Abigail Morgan, and Alice Downy stood in a cluster, dressed like most of the women in attractive gowns to see their men off to war. Peggy was in her favorite color, a pale blue gown, topped with a hat with a blue band.

Evan McLeod was dressed in full highland regalia, from round bonnet to plaid kilt. He stood in front of the formation playing some unfathomable tune on the bagpipes while two drummer boys beat a martial accompaniment. Two fifers stood by, waiting for their time to play.

Peggy said to Anna McDonald, "Your husband looks very dashing today." Angus was dressed in the blue-coated uniform of the Virginia militia, but instead of the usual black tri-cornered hat, he wore a highland bonnet. McDonald and Northcutt were engaged in animated conversation. Peggy reflected that Angus was undoubtedly getting some last minute guidance.

Anna beamed. "Indeed he does. But he's got his old hunting shirt in his baggage and he'll change to that after today."

Alice Downy leaned over and said to Peggy, "Look at Donegal: He's in his glory! The man is prancing around like a rooster."

Peggy smiled back. "He certainly is taking his duty as sergeant major very seriously."

Alice laughed, "It looks like he's laying down the law now."

Donegal stood with his rifle slung over his left shoulder, his left hand grasping the sling. The other sergeants had gathered around him, nodding at his words. The Highlander had on his old regimental jacket — it was much patched and had faded over the years to a brick red — and wore his blue bonnet at a jaunty angle. Below the waist he wore breeches and leggings rather than his kilt. On his back was a military pack with the faded number "77."

The men of each company were forming into half-companies, each two ranks deep. Peggy observed that the soldiers' dress and equipment was far from "uniform." She also noted a marked difference between the two companies. Morgan's men were almost universally attired in hunting shirts and leggings while in Wood's company, which included a significant number of men from the town itself, more had on civilian coats or simply waistcoats over shirts. Morgan's men were virtually all carrying rifles. She looked at Wood's men and saw that they had a mix of rifles and muskets. All the men carried a haversack and Peggy knew that Wend had already issued each man rations for three days. Most of the men had chosen to wear broad-brimmed hats against the sun and rain, but a few were in the tri-cornered style. Then Peggy noticed another detail which aroused her curiosity: Every man had some sort of pack on his back, but while many were traditional types — with a vertical strap over each man's shoulder — there were also many which were carried by a single strap which ran horizontally across the man's chest or diagonally over one shoulder.

Her curiosity aroused, Peggy tapped Alice on the arm and asked, "I've never seen packs like that before. What's the purpose?"

Alice leaned close to her. "I once put the same question to Joshua. He uses one like that. They're called *tumpline* packs. They're Indian-style; easier and faster to get off in an emergency. Just reach up, pull the strap over your head and you're free of the pack to fight or run. The carrying strap can also be put on top of the head." She pointed to Morgan's men. "Daniel's company is filled with hunters, and a lot of them have seen service on the border. Undoubtedly that's why most of them carry their packs on tumplines."

Peggy nodded, and then thought of something else. "Wend told me there were three companies going out. Where's the third?"

Anna McDonald heard her question and leaned over. "The third company is Harry Hoagland's, Peggy, from the northern part of the county. Angus told me they would be joining the column on the march."

Peggy looked for her husband and then saw him standing with the pack train, talking to young Horner and some other quartermasters.

She had seen Wend only sparingly since the night he had broken the news to her about going with the expedition. The last four days had been extraordinarily hectic with Wend working long hours to fulfill his role as quartermaster. He had been away from the farm much of each day, arranging for supplies from merchants and rounding up horses and pack-saddles. He had also had to find willing drovers. Wend had made a deal with Morgan for most of the horses and Daniel had volunteered Jake Cather and Elijah McCartney to help handle the pack train. Wend had then hired another two sober-looking men from the town to round out the team of horse handlers.

Meanwhile, Peggy's anger had soon subsided to a simmer instead of the fury of the first evening. But for the next three nights she had continued going to bed with her cap on as a demonstration of her unhappiness. Then, on Wend's last day at home, she had come to the realization that it was time to put aside both her anger about his departure and her doubts about the depth of his love. She calculated it would be far better to send him off with a strong reminder of her affection instead of the memory of her displeasure. So that night she had prepared herself for a memorable romantic encounter.

When Wend entered the bedroom, she had been waiting in the armchair by the hearth, dressed only in a white nightgown, the top open almost to her waist to ensure that he had a tantalizing view of her breasts. She had let her hair loose, half to hang down over her left shoulder blade, the other half down her right front side, and combed it until it was smooth and shiny. Finally, she had taken out the bottle of perfume they had bought in Fredericksburg the year before — the first she had ever owned — and applied it behind her ears and to other strategic points.

Wend had worked late over the accounts of expenditures he had made from the government money. Finally, Peggy heard his weary steps on the stairway and then he swung open the door to their bedroom. When he saw her in the chair in an alluring posture, she was gratified that her preparations had had the desired effect. Wend stood frozen in the doorway, his right hand on the knob, wordlessly staring at her. Peggy rose from the chair and walked slowly, deliberately to him. She put her left hand on his, removing it from the knob, and quietly shut the door behind him. Then she wrapped both arms around him and pressed her body against his, making sure that her breasts were hard against his chest. She slid her left leg tight alongside his right and looked up into his eyes.

After a several long seconds, she said the words she had been practicing in her mind for some time. "Wend, let's put our differences behind us. I know you are doing what you think is best for our family and the people who depend on you. And despite all the things we said the other night, my love for you is still as strong as the day we married."

Wend reacted as she had hoped he would. He wrapped his arms around her and said, "My darling, I love you. The last few days have been terribly hard for me; I've had to go about my work with a sadness hanging over me because there was such a wide divide between us." He smiled down at her, for once the impassiveness gone from his face. "My greatest desire is that we can spend this last night happily in each other's arms."

Peggy had smiled up at him. "Nothing would make me happier." Then she slowly undressed him, tossing the clothes carelessly to the floor, pausing often to stroke his muscles. When he was naked, she gently guided him onto the bed, gazing for a long moment at his body and smiling down at him with her most seductive expression. She could see the desire for her well up in his eyes. Peggy moved to enhance that desire, reaching up and slowly opening the remaining fastenings on her gown until she had fully revealed her own body. She dropped the gown to the floor, then slipped into bed and pulled her body against his.

Peggy then made love to her husband in accordance with the plans she had carefully laid while waiting for him to come to bed. The night was to be all for him; her whole intent was to leave him with an unforgettable memory of her. She loved Wend's body and over the years she had taken great satisfaction from their sexual encounters. But any pleasure she obtained on this occasion would be incidental. So she had performed her role with the detached skill of an experienced tart, caressing and manipulating his body to a crescendo of excitement.

They had had sex several times and she had relented only when she could see that he was exhausted. Then they had both fallen into deep slumber, Peggy satisfied that she had achieved her purpose.

Suddenly Peggy was shaken from her remembrances by a series of shouted orders from the parade. She looked around and could see that the huddle of sergeants around Donegal had broken up and returned to their places in the formation. Morgan and Wood had positioned themselves in front of their respective companies. Meanwhile, McDonald finished his conversation with Northcutt and swung up into the saddle of his powerful chestnut hunter.

Almost instantaneously the captains called their men to attention and a quietness came over the grounds of the old fort.

In the prevailing silence, McDonald called out to his adjutant, Lieutenant Walters. "March the detachment, sir!" The drummers struck a beat and, with Donegal and the company commanders shouting orders, the men brought their firelocks to the carry and the formation wheeled into a column of fours by half companies, with the adjutant, Donegal, and the fifes and drums in the lead, followed by Morgan's company and then Wood's. The two fifers commenced a shrill, lilting tune and then the adjutant led the formation out onto the road, marching northward past Fort Loudoun. Peggy watched as Wend, mounted on his black mare, led his men and the pack train in the wake of the marching soldiers. Joshua rode beside Wend.

McDonald sat his horse beside the road, watching the column pass with the air of a general reviewing his army. As each company marched before him, McDonald acknowledged the salute of its officer. Peggy looked at Angus' face, which bore a prideful grin. She thought: *He's enjoying this to high heaven, glorying in the moment.* Peggy turned to glance at Anna beside her, and saw pride on her face. She touched her friend's arm and said, "Your husband looks very military up there on his horse, Anna."

Anna turned and beamed at Peggy. "Yes! Doesn't he now?"

After the pack train had passed him, McDonald turned his horse and rode up directly in front of the women, towering above them as the spirited animal pranced, anxious to be off. He swept his bonnet from his head and bowed. "Ladies, I pledge to bring your men back as soon as possible!"

From the very rear of the crowd a woman's voice called out, "Just see that you damn well bring *all* of them back, Angus McDonald!"

McDonald scanned the crowd, looking for the shouter, but gave it up after a moment. He smiled and bowed again, then replaced the bonnet on his head. He pulled back on his reins until the stallion reared back on its hind legs and whinnied. Then Angus dug his heels into the horse's sides and galloped along the marching column until he reached his place at its head.

Anna took Peggy's arm in her own and whispered, "I know people sometimes wonder about the age difference between Angus and me. But at moments like this he makes me especially proud to be his wife. And he does look so distinguished, doesn't he?"

Peggy smiled at her friend. "Yes, of course he does. And I think the fineness of his features makes him look youthful for his age."

"Yes, you're right about that, Peggy. I've always thought that myself."

Peggy added, "And never forget how lucky you are that he's given you the gift of so many handsome, lively children."

Anna simply nodded and then squeezed Peggy's arm even more tightly.

The women stood for a time watching as the detachment marched into the distance, the beat of the drums echoing against the walls of the old fort. Evan McCloud stood with them, his bagpipes hanging limply over his shoulder. The old highland warrior had a dour look on his face, clearly miserable that age kept him from joining the expedition. Peggy was sure she could see a glistening dampness in his eyes. She turned to look again at the departing column, but they had disappeared around a bend in the road; there was only a faint wisp of dust in the air and the barely perceptible sound of the fifes to mark their passing. Peggy suddenly felt a great emptiness in her heart. Then she glanced at the other women who stood watching silently and, from the look in their eyes, knew that they all shared the same feeling.

Soon the crowd of women and children began to break up as they left to walk to their homes in the town or to climb aboard carts and wagons for the trip back to their farmsteads. Anna, Peggy, Abigail and Alice lingered for a few moments more while making plans to visit with each other over the lonely weeks which lay ahead.

Suddenly a man's voice came from behind them. "Good morning, ladies. It pleasures my eyes to see you all on this bright June day!"

The women turned to see a smiling Geoffrey Caulfield standing there with the reins of his beautiful bay in one hand, his hat in the other. He said, "I've only just ridden into town from the southern part of the county, where I've been for the last week. Imagine my surprise to see so many of the county's men marching off." He looked at the women. "Pray tell, where are they bound, Mrs. McDonald?"

"Why, there're on their way to fight the Shawnees in the Ohio Country, Mr. Caulfield. Angus has the governor's commission to lead an expedition against the tribe." She motioned to the women beside her. "All of our husbands are marching with the column."

Caulfield turned and stared up the road after the column. Then he turned back, a devilish grin spreading across his face. "Why ladies, if there is anything I can do for you in their absence, please don't hesitate to call on me. It will be my *great* pleasure to be of service in any way that I may."

CHAPTER TEN

Fort Fincastle

Wend and Joshua sat their horses and looked over the hamlet of Ransome's Tavern which lay ahead of them. The buildings were beginning to cast long shadows in the late afternoon sunlight.

Baird pointed to the cleared area which extended to the west of the tavern and then wrapped around to the north of the building. "That's your campsite; right where that train of pilgrims parked when we was here last month, Mister *Lieutenant* Eckert. *Your Lordship* can put all three companies there easy enough. The horses can go to the east on a picket line between the tavern and the stable, where watering will be easy from the well."

Wend's duties as quartermaster included the job of selecting the nightly campsite and then placing each company in its proper spot. At the moment the main body of troops was about an hour behind them.

"You're right, Joshua, that's how we'll do it. And for *God's* sake, stop calling me lieutenant." Baird had been needling Wend about his ascension to officer status since they had left Winchester and it was getting on his nerves. "Especially when we're alone like this." He pointed toward the tavern. "Now let's ride on in and let Ransome know he's going to have lots of company tonight."

Joshua gave Wend a roguish look. "You don't want me to call you *lieutenant*? Does that mean I can start calling you *Sprout* again, like when you was young? I always did like that name for you."

"Just stop it, Joshua."

The scout grinned mischievously, but said nothing as they spurred their horses forward.

They entered the common room to find Ransome cleaning the counter. The tavern keeper stared at the two men for a few seconds and then recognition came into his eyes. "Ah, welcome back, gentlemen. Are you here with your wagons on another trip to Pittsburgh?"

Wend and Joshua smiled at each other. Joshua said, "Ain't nary a wagon with us, Ransome. But soon enough you'll see 'bout 200 men arrive, havin' worked up an all-abidin' thirst. Do you think you can handle that?"

Ransome responded, "I don't take your meaning, Baird."

Wend grinned. "Here it is in plain words, Ransome: We're the advance for a column of militia from Frederick County. We intend to encamp here for the night."

The tavern keeper's eyes opened wide as he calculated the likely revenue from this unexpected bonanza. "I can't think of a better place for you to put up, Mr. Eckert. And between my place and the Kertin's store, we can handle any needs you may have, sir."

Joshua smiled broadly. "Yes, I 'spect you can, Ransome. Now, how about dealin' with my immediate need? That would be a full cup of your rum before all those other men get here and clean you out."

Leaving Baird to his refreshment, Wend walked over to the store. He noted that a farm cart had pulled up to the front steps while he had been at the tavern. Inside, Paul Kertin, quill in hand, stood at the counter, an account book laid out before him. He was talking to the farmer, a middle-aged man dressed in homespun shirt and breeches. Lizzie Kertin was helping the farmer's wife look at some fabric from the shelves. Kertin looked up and saw Wend. "Be with you in a few minutes, sir."

Wend smiled and said, "Hello, Mr. Kertin. I'm not here to buy anything. I thought you'd recognize me from the time we came through last month."

Kertin looked up again. "Why, Mr. Eckert! I hadn't expected to see you again so soon."

Wend laughed. "Believe me, sir, I hadn't any expectation of being here now. But I'm riding ahead of a detachment of militia which will be arriving shortly." He looked around. "Is the Widow Potter still staying here with you? I thought I'd check to see how she was doing."

Kertin turned toward the open door which led to the back rooms and called, "Sally, come out! Someone's here to see you."

Sally Potter appeared at the doorway. The widow was dressed in a frayed green work gown and white apron. She held a large wooden spoon in her hand. Her faced was flushed; clearly she had been cooking. "Who'd be lookin' for me?"

"Just me, Mrs. Potter." Wend smiled, "Do you recognize me?"

"Heaven above, Mr. Eckert! Of course I do. What are you doing up here on Braddock's Road?"

Wend explained again about the militia.

Sally set her face into a serious look. With a bitter tone she declared, "Well I'm fair happy to hear that the governor is finally going after them savages. I hope there will be some vengeance for my Frank and all them other people what have been hurt out here."

Wend reflected that, like Peggy, her anger animated her face and, curiously, highlighted its prettiness. He told her, "I believe you will get your wish very soon, ma'am."

Sally cocked her head, bit her lip, and swept a strand of blond hair out of her eye. Then she asked, in a shy manner, "Does Mr. Donegal happen to be with you?"

Wend frowned as if trying hard to recall if the Scotsman was with the militia. "Simon Donegal? Oh yes; he's marching with the main column. They should be here very shortly."

As if on cue, the distant sound of a drum cadence became audible. Wend looked at the widow and grinned. "In fact, the detachment is about to arrive." He looked around and saw that everyone in the store had stopped talking and was listening to the sound of the drums. Wend said, "Shall we go out and watch them come in?"

The people in the store flowed out to the front porch. Wend stood near the steps with Sally beside him. In a few seconds little Louisa came running around the side of the building and climbed up on the porch to be with her mother. "Mommy, what's happening? What are the drums for?"

"There be soldiers coming."

Ransome and his family appeared at the front of the tavern and several more people came out of the small cabins which were clustered along the road.

The head of the column was now visible, having come over a low ridge to the east. McDonald rode at the front, his adjutant and Donegal marching just behind. Wend glanced sideways at Sally and watched her face light up as she recognized the marching Highlander.

Louisa shouted, "Look, Ma! Look! There's Mr. Donegal!"

"Yes, dear, I see him, right enough!"

"Are they going to stop, Ma? Can he visit with us?"

Wend put his hand on the girl's shoulder. "Certainly, Louisa. They'll be staying overnight. Donegal has to attend to some duties first, but I'm sure he'll be over to see you and spend as much time with you as he can."

Soon the column halted in front of the store and tavern. Donegal marched out in front of the formation and began to go through the orders for making camp.

Sally and Louisa watched in fascination. Sally turned to Wend and said, "Simon seems very important."

Wend nodded. "He is the sergeant major; that means he's the boss of all the other sergeants. You could say that he runs things for the major."

Sally beamed and bit her lip again. "I reckon he looks passing handsome in his uniform."

Wend smiled. "Yes, that's his old jacket and bonnet from the 77th Highlanders." He looked at Sally and could see in her face that her feelings went well beyond mere friendship and admiration for Simon.

Wend said, "Well, I have to report to Major McDonald and help get the troops into their camp for the night. But Simon will be over to see you as soon as he can break free."

Sally put her hand to her face and hair, then looked down at her gown and dirty apron. "Come on Louisa; I have to finish gettin' supper ready. And then we'll be seein' Mr. Donegal and I know he'll want to play with you."

Wend smiled to himself; Donegal would undoubtedly want to "play" with the mother as much as the daughter.

* * *

After the drummers had beat "lights out" and the rank and file had been sent to their blankets in preparation for the coming early morning departure, Wend walked through the camp making a last inspection; then he headed for the tavern. He found Angus and his captains gathered around the table next to the hearth. As he entered, the small group broke up and the officers headed back to their campsites.

Wend walked over to the table where McDonald was still seated and said, "Angus, I need to discuss some quartermaster matters."

"All right, Eckert, sit down. What's this about?"

"I have enough provisions to get us to Zane's place at Wheeling, but we'll need more very shortly after we've arrived. The only place I know to get them from is the merchants in Pittsburgh."

Angus was silent for a moment, and then said, "You don't need to worry about that, Eckert. Connolly is procuring the needed supplies and sending them down by boat. And your friend Northcutt also told me that Wheeling will probably be the marshalling point for the other troops of the governor's northern force. We'll fall back to there and join them after our attack."

Wend nodded, but said nothing. There was a hard edge in Angus' voice that had been there since Northcutt had announced Wend's assignment as quartermaster. Thereafter, Angus had never called Wend by his first name; only *Eckert* or *Lieutenant Eckert*. Previously they had had a cordial relationship, stemming from their wives' closeness and what Wend had considered mutual respect. Now McDonald was distant toward Wend and had limited his contact to official business.

McDonald started to rise. "I need to get some sleep, Eckert."

Wend said quietly, "I need to talk with you about something else, Angus."

McDonald looked perturbed and replied, "Is this official, Eckert? It's getting quite late. Can't it wait until tomorrow?"

"No, it's not official: It's personal but urgent, Angus."

McDonald sat down again with an air of resignation. "All right, Eckert, come out with it."

"Angus, let me be straight with you: We've been friends for ten years. But ever since that meeting at The Golden Buck, it appears that you've been treating me with distrust and disdain."

McDonald looked away for several moments and when he again looked at Wend his face was flushed with irritation. Finally he asked, "Eckert, don't you think that I might have some justification?"

"Apparently you think that I connived with Northcutt to get the governor's commission; that I knew about it in advance."

"And you didn't? It was obvious that Northcutt had it all planned out."

"Not with my cooperation. I was as surprised as you when Northcutt pulled that paper out of his case."

"Even if that's true, you could have turned it down. You saw that he was forcing me to agree in front of the others."

"Angus, I *did* try to refuse the commission. The truth is that, for personal reasons, I didn't want to go on this expedition. That's why I stayed to talk with Northcutt after the meeting."

"If you were so set against it, why did you go with Northcutt to meet with Rutledge and the German minister to encourage recruitment of German militiamen?"

Wend was surprised by Angus' question.

Before he could respond, McDonald said, "Oh, yes, Eckert, I heard about that. It seems me to that for such a *reluctant* lieutenant you were certainly eager to help Northcutt."

"Angus, Northcutt had trapped me. I was forced to accept the commission and to go to that meeting."

McDonald reared back in his chair, disbelief in his eyes. "Trapped? Forced? How in the hell could he do that?"

Wend briefly explained why the musket contract had been awarded to him and how financially binding it had left him.

Angus listened quietly, but Wend could see continued suspicion in his face.

Wend searched for some way to convince Angus that he was on his side. Finally he said, "Angus, think about this: If I was willingly allied with Northcutt, why would I have told you about his scheme for this Indian war the night of the fair? Wouldn't it have made sense for me to stay quiet about his motivation?"

McDonald nodded thoughtfully and then said hesitatingly, "Yes, that's true enough, Eckert. You didn't have to tell me about that."

"Now I'm going to tell you something else that I don't have to: Northcutt wants me to spy on you."

"The devil you say!"

"Yes, he wants me to send a separate letter on the expedition, to confirm the details of your report to him. And beyond that, he wants me to report on the loyalty of the officers of the expedition."

McDonald half rose from his chair in anger. "Dammit, Eckert, any man of honor would have refused such a request."

"Calm yourself, Angus. I tried to do just that; that's when Northcutt threatened to cut off the musket contract. If that happened, I'd be bankrupt."

"Eckert, there's more important things than money."

"Yes, there are, Angus. But be honest; what would happen to you if your financial factor in London called in all your credit?"

At first McDonald simply stared at Wend. Then he said, "After I fought at Culloden, I lost everything. *Everything*, do you hear? I had to abandon land and money. And then I started again with nothing in Virginia. But, by God, through it all I kept my honor."

"Yes, you did, and you have my admiration for that. But you were young and unencumbered. What if it happened now, when you're thirty years older and you have a young wife and children depending on you?"

Wend let Angus work through that for a moment and this time the Scotsman had no answer.

Then Wend said, "Faced with that situation, I decided to play along with Northcutt until I could figure out a way to maintain my family without the government money. But it meant that I had to accept the commission and go on the expedition. Reflect on that Angus; it was the only logical thing to do."

McDonald nodded slowly. "All right, Wend, now that you've explained it, I can see your dilemma and, to be honest, I can sympathize with what you are doing." He paused a moment, then said, "And to tell the truth, I was angered at you because I didn't like Northcutt dictating orders to me in front of all those men."

"Thanks for saying that, Angus. I'd hate to think we couldn't trust each other and continue to be friends. Now, here's something to think about: If we're going to confound Northcutt, we need to work together. After the raid, you let me know exactly what you are telling the governor in your report. I'll be certain that my report backs that up and that the governor hears that there are none but loyal officers on this expedition. I'll show you what I write."

"Damn, this is nasty business, Wend. This is what politicians always lead us to: conspiracy inside of conspiracy." Angus shook his head in frustration. "But I think we understand each other quite well." He looked into Wend's eyes. "I must admit, it's good that you forced us to talk on this, lad." McDonald raised his cup toward Wend and drained the last of its contents. "But now I think I *will* go to bed. I suddenly feel old and very weary and I don't want to be falling asleep on my horse tomorrow."

McDonald rose and trudged up the stairs to the room which he had taken for the night.

Wend walked outside into the darkness. He looked around at the camp; all of the men were in their blankets and the fires had burned down to embers. The only movement was from the few sentries which had been set to patrol around the perimeter. Wend took a long, deep breath of the night air and felt as if a heavy load had been lifted from his shoulders.

* * *

Wend and Joshua pulled up their horses at the crest of the high ridge and scanned the landscape below. Their view was dominated by the broad Ohio. At this point, it was split by a large, wooded island. A winding creek with high, bluff-like banks flowed into the river on their left hand.

Joshua pointed to a log blockhouse situated between the creek and the river. "I reckon that's Ebenezer Zane's place. But someone sure has been busy. Look at that bloody fort being raised beyond the house."

"Correction, Joshua," said Wend as he sat The Mare alongside the scout. "Lots of people *are* busy. Look at all those men felling trees over there. And there are just as many working on the fort itself." Wend looked around. "There's the military camp, down closer to the river." A thought occurred to him. "You ever been here before, Joshua?"

"Me and Paul Carnahan came down the Ohio in a canoe heading for the Scioto River. We was on a long hunt. Must have been 1740 or so; weren't hardly no white men around. This place was all forest and didn't have no name, leastways what we knew 'bout."

Wend said, "Well, we better go down and find out who's in charge."

The two rode down past Zane's house and pulled their horses up in front of a gap in the wooden stockade where Wend presumed the gate would soon be fitted. Work gangs and the sounds of saws, adzes, and axes were all around them. Wend looked over at group of men who were working on a stack of logs.

Wend called out, "Where's your commanding officer?"

A man, stripped to his waist, stopped work and looked up at the two riders. He pointed to a nearly complete blockhouse that was obviously intended to form one corner of the fort. "The major be over there; I reckon he's making out his reports. Officers always got to make out reports."

Joshua grinned broadly. "You're right 'bout that: Makes 'em feel useful!"

Wend and Joshua dismounted before the blockhouse, then walked past a rifle-carrying sentry wearing a hunting shirt who stood in a relaxed attitude at the door. They entered and stood momentarily as their eyes adjusted to the relative darkness.

A voice called out, "Well, I'll be damned; it's Eckert and Baird. If I had to wager, I'd say that the Frederick County Militia has arrived."

Wend looked around and saw a tall, lean figure standing behind a rough-hewn table. He had one hand on his hip and the other on the top of the back of his chair. In accommodation of the July heat, he had removed his coat and had unbuttoned his waistcoat.

Wend blinked again. "By God, William Crawford; I'm glad to see you, Captain."

"And I you, Wend." He nodded to Baird. "Good to see you, too, Joshua." He hesitated a moment, and said, "And by the way, it is *Major* Crawford now, by the grace of the governor."

"Congratulations, William. I take it that you are the commanding officer here?"

"Yes, welcome to *Fort Fincastle*."

Wend asked, "*Fincastle*? Where does that come from?"

Crawford answered, "It refers to our esteemed governor; Viscount Fincastle is one of his titles. Connolly picked the name. He's going around naming everything he can for Dunmore."

Joshua laughed. "Next thing you know, he'll rename Fort Pitt after the man."

Now it was Crawford's turn to laugh. "You haven't heard? He's already done that. It's now *Fort Dunmore*. And we're supposed to call the town 'Dunmore'."

"Fort *Dunmore*? Oh, for God's sake!" The words escaped Wend's mouth before he had time to check himself.

Crawford tapped Wend on his arm and smiled knowingly. "Yes, I had the same reaction. But I shouldn't say that in front of Connolly, if I were you; he's quite pleased with himself." Then his face became serious. "How many men is McDonald bringing with him?"

Wend answered, "Three companies; with pack train drovers it all adds up to nearly two hundred men." He thought a second. "And by the way, your old friend Daniel Morgan is one of the captains."

"The devil you say! That will make for some lively times around here."

Wend asked. "What about the balance of McDonald's battalion? We were told enough men would be sent here to bring us up to about 400."

"You'll get some of the men here now; I've got five companies and there are two more due to come in any day, according to Connolly. Three of these companies are yours and you get one of the new companies when they arrive. That will leave me with enough men to garrison the fort and patrol this area."

Wend nodded. "I expect that McDonald will be satisfied with that." Then he added, "I've been appointed the quartermaster of McDonald's battalion. And to move fast, we marched with just enough provisions to get us here. We were told that we would receive supplies from Pittsburgh."

Crawford picked a paper up from the table. "Yes, you did move fast. We didn't expect you for another couple of days. The provisions I have will last a few days. But we're expecting more to come by boat any day now; in fact, they should have been here a by now. But when they arrive, I expect your supply will be included."

Wend nodded. "Let us hope." Then he said, "Speaking of boats, McDonald has the idea of transporting his whole force down river to confuse the Indians about our intentions. Are that many boats available?"

"Move seven companies by boat? All at the same time?" He shook his head. "Do you imagine I'm running a shipyard?"

"Couldn't enough boats be gathered up from along the river?"

"I think McDonald is dreaming."

"He may be, but he's a stubborn Highlander. Once he gets an idea in his mind, he's not easily put off. My suggestion is that we start looking for boats."

"All right, as a mental exercise, let's think about it. A fleet of bateaux would be the ideal type, but that would take at least twenty, and I doubt if you could lay your hands on that many by the time you want to leave. We have a couple of boats here. Merchants at Pittsburgh have a number; in fact I'm sure that the supplies will arrive in a convoy of them."

Wend grinned slyly and interjected, "You do mean the merchants at *Dunmore*, don't you?"

Crawford shot Wend a look of irritation, then broke into a smile. "I don't remember you being this cheeky, Eckert. But yes, I meant the merchants of *Dunmore*." Then he continued, "But the question is getting their boats. I don't think they'll easily be persuaded to part with them, particularly given the high possibility they won't get them all back."

Wend shrugged. "Well, we could talk about the idea with the people bringing the supplies when they arrive. Do you know the contractor supplying the provisions?"

"Yes, it's your old friend Grenough. He and Connolly have become thick as thieves over the last few weeks."

Wend sighed. "I should have guessed. Do you expect he'll be coming with the supply convoy?"

"No, so far Grenough hasn't deigned to come down here. His man McCrae is in charge of transporting goods to us. We can discuss the question with him."

Wend nodded and said "Good idea; in fact, I've met the estimable Mr. McCrae." He thought to himself that undoubtedly Matt Bratton would be along. Then he pointed down toward the river. "In the meantime, William, tell me where you want the Frederick County detachment to encamp."

* * *

It was the next afternoon that a flotilla of boats carrying provisions and other supplies arrived. Wend, sitting with Baird, Donegal, and Horner at their fire, saw the first boats of the convoy pull into the landing near the fort. He looked at his companions and said, "I'd better get down there and check on provisions." He motioned to Horner. "Come along, Andrew."

The two arrived at the landing just behind Crawford and McDonald. Wend noted that three boats had already landed and immediately saw McCrae climbing out of the first boat. He quickly scanned the other two boats which had grounded at the landing, but couldn't see any sign of Bratton. But a line of other boats were still approaching and were too far away to make out the features of their crews.

McCrae walked up toward Crawford. A man Wend had never seen before jumped out of the boat and followed McCrae. The stranger was broad faced with black hair and piercing eyes. Dressed in a heavily fringed hunting shirt and leggings, he sported a worn, narrow brimmed black hat which had several feathers dangling from the left side. Wend noticed that he had pewter hoops in his ears and a ring through his nose like Indians and some Frenchmen. A long sheath knife was suspended on a strap around his neck Indian style and he carried a good quality longrifle.

The Irishman stopped in front of Crawford, smiled crookedly, and touched his hat with his right hand by way of salute. "Afternoon, Major, good to see you again, sir." Then he turned and waved at the boats. "I've brought your provisions. And right on schedule they are."

Crawford said, "On schedule, Mr. McCrae? Three or four days ago would have been on schedule. The fact is, you're late, and I've got more mouths to feed than ever before."

"Well, now sir, none of you look like you're starvin'." McCrae motioned to the man with the pewter jewelry and said, "Lieutenant Girty here will vouch that we made haste comin' down the river. Tell the major we didn't waste no time, Simon."

Girty said, "McCrae's speakin' true enough, Major. Came down with nary a delay, once them boats was loaded. The big trouble was Grenough couldn't get the supplies fast enough. We had to wait for a train 'o Conestogas from the east which came in a week late."

Crawford said, "All right, Simon." Then he turned to McDonald and Wend. "Mr. McCrae here is Grenough's agent for delivering supplies. And Lieutenant Girty is from Connolly's garrison at Fort Pitt— er, Fort Dunmore — and is responsible for providing the escort for the supplies and for carrying messages between here and Dunmore."

Angus nodded at the two men. "Glad to meet you gentlemen."

Wend had been looking out at the boats as they grounded on the river bank in sequence. He sighed to himself when he noticed that Bratton was in the last of the boats.

But at the same time the long string of boats gave Wend an idea. He stepped forward and pointed to the convoy. "Major McDonald, it seems to me that part of the answer to our transportation need is in front of our eyes. I count thirteen bateaux right there in McCrae's convoy."

Crawford looked at Wend and then McDonald. "You know, I think he's right, Angus. We could requisition them for a few days."

McCrae looked back at his boats and said, "I don't know what you gentlemen are thinkin', but Mr. Grenough had to hire those boats by the day from other merchants. We had to get practically all the bateaux in Dunmore. And I can tell you they don't come cheap. Mr. Grenough expects them back at the forks without delay."

Wend looked between Crawford and McDonald. Then he said, "McCrae, I spoke with Mr. Northcutt in Winchester before we left. He said that Grenough had been given virtually unlimited authority to provide for this expedition. I have no doubt he can submit a claim to the colony for the entire cost of the boats."

McCrae eyed Wend with suspicion and growing anxiety. He said hesitantly, "I can't let you have these boats without word from Mr. Grenough. I ain't got no authority for that."

Wend smiled slyly at McCrae. "Surely you've heard of Mr. Northcutt. He's the governor's chief aide. He's personally overseeing how things go here on the border. And I know Grenough wouldn't want to be the cause of anything which would keep this campaign against the Shawnee from moving ahead. I think your boss would be quite displeased if he found out you had hindered Major McDonald's expedition."

McCrae's eyes grew into large ovals as he contemplated the potential anger of his master whatever course he chose.

Wend felt great pleasure as he watched McCrae's discomfort. He turned to McDonald. "Angus, between Grenough's boats and the ones that Major Crawford already has here, I calculate that we have enough to transport 300 men. All we need to do is find enough boats of any kind to carry another 100."

McDonald nodded and turned to Crawford. "Damned if Eckert isn't right, William. But where to get the remaining boats?"

Girty spoke up. "Beggin' your pardon, Major Crawford. But maybe I can help. Truth is, I'd wager there's enough boats of all kinds — canoes, small rowing boats, maybe even a small bateau or two — right along the river 'tween here and the forks. Fact is, I know they got some fair-sized boats up at that tavern near Yellow Creek — Baker's place. Anyways, we could take some men and search all along the banks upstream."

Angus' face lit up. "Sounds like a good idea, Girty." He turned to Crawford. "What do you think, William?"

Crawford nodded. "It is a likely enough idea. And it seems about the only way you're going to get all the boats you need in time, Angus."

"You're right, William, I need to move fast if we're to strike the Shawnee before they guess what we're about."

Girty grinned and said, "Major, you give me a party of thirty men or so and I'll have your boats in a few days. There'll be plenty of mad people along the river, but I'll have your boats."

McDonald thought for a moment, then turned to Wend. "You go along, Eckert. As quartermaster, you can write legal requisitions."

Wend sighed. "When do you want us to start, Angus?"

"Pick your men today, and leave first light tomorrow. We can't waste any time."

Girty said, "Eckert, you might want to round up some paddles from the canoes what are already here. And one more thing: You better bring some shovels."

Wend asked, "Shovels? To find boats?"

Girty smiled slyly. "Just get the shovels, Eckert, 'less you want to do a lot of diggin' with your hands."

* * *

The boat detail landed at Baker's Tavern near dusk on the third day after leaving Wheeling. Girty had proven adept at finding the markings, usually on trees, which indicated the hiding places of Indian canoes. Some had been covered with brush, others buried. A large number had already been sent back to Wheeling and the remaining canoes of the search party were each towing strings of additional craft.

Girty said to Wend, "Since you figure we got almost enough boats, this will be our last stop; we'll camp here tonight. If we leave early in the morning, we can be back at Wheeling Creek before noon tomorrow."

Wend nodded. "That suits me." He looked at Baker's boats and canoes lined up along the water. "We'll get the rest of what we need here."

While the men pulled the canoes up on the bank and retrieved their gear for the night, Wend and Girty went to talk to Baker. Wend looked around and immediately realized that the tavern was simply a sideline of what was primarily a farming establishment. There was a log house, barn, stable, and numerous sheds, surrounded by fields and pastures. The tavern was the closest structure to the river and was a small, single level building which apparently had only a couple of rooms. There was a wide cleared area along the river.

Girty said, "Old man Baker started this farm years ago. Then he realized he had a good thing here, a place for travelers floating down the river to stop overnight. So he cleared out this space for people to camp and built the tavern. It brings him in some extra wherewithal."

Baker himself had heard the bustle of their arrival and appeared at the tavern door. He was a short, stocky man dressed in shirt, breeches and an apron which had once been white. A broom was in his right hand and a cleaning rag draped over his left shoulder. Wend looked at his thinning hair and expanded waist and judged him to be in his early forties.

Baker said, "Hello, Simon, been a while since I saw you."

Girty nodded. "Indeed, I've been busy working for Captain Connolly. Haven't had the chance to stop by, Baker." He introduced Wend to the tavern keeper.

Wend said, "Our party is from the militia force down at Wheeling Creek. We're planning to camp overnight in your open area."

Baker looked over the party of men and his eyes reflected the realization that he would have some good business that night. "Of course you're welcome, gentlemen. Very welcome indeed." He waved at all the canoes. "Are you bringing supplies down from Pittsburgh?"

Girty grinned broadly. "Nope, Baker; we're on another job." He nodded toward Wend. "Lieutenant Eckert here is the quartermaster of Major McDonald's battalion."

Baker glanced at Wend. "Oh, are you looking for provisions? I might be able to provide you with some goods." He smiled smugly. "For a fair price, of course."

Wend looked at the man, who appeared to be calculating the value of his imagined good fortune. He smiled and said, "Actually, Baker, we're not looking for supplies."

Baker screwed up his face in puzzlement. "Not looking for supplies? I'm afraid I don't understand."

Wend grinned even more broadly. "We're collecting boats to transport the troops."

Reflexively Baker looked toward the river bank to where his own boats were beached.

Wend continued, "And those two pulling boats of yours are large enough to be very useful."

Baker's countenance changed to near panic. He sputtered, "You can't take those boats. I need them to ferry people across the river and to fetch supplies from Pittsburgh!"

Girty said, "Don't make me laugh, Baker. I can't imagine that you'll be ferrying many pilgrims over to Yellow Creek in these times. Not with the Shawnee and Mingo actin' up."

"You're stealin' my livin', that's what you are. I'll not stand for it."

"Nonsense, Baker," Wend answered. "We're really just hiring the boats from you; you'll get them back sooner or later. He pulled out a piece of paper he had written up. "This is a requisition for the use of your two boats. You can make a claim to the colony through Connolly for the cost."

Baker took the paper. "I tell you, I can't live without these boats! I don't believe I'll ever see them again. And who knows when I'll get my money? You're ruining me."

Wend shook his head, then pointed to the river bank. "Look, you've got a big canoe out there; we aren't taking that. You can make do until you get your boats back."

Girty laughed. "Come on Baker, stop cryin' over spilt milk. Let's go in and have some drinks."

Later, in the full darkness of night, Wend and Girty sat beside their fire, finishing off the last of the evening meal. Girty had a jug of rum which he had been pulling on throughout the evening. The men of their detachment were at several more fires in a line along the river bank. Some were already asleep in their blankets; the combination of the day's paddling, digging, and a fair amount of Baker's rum had brought on early weariness.

Wend, curious about Girty's appearance and the source of his knowledge, decided to ask about the scout's background. In quiet moment he said, "It's clear you've spent a lot of time in the Ohio Country. Were you a long hunter or in trade with the Indians?"

"Fact is, I was captured when Fort Granville fell to the Indians back in '55 and lived with the Mingo for more'n seven years."

Wend was surprised. "You were at Fort Granville? That's just north of where I lived for a long time in Sherman Valley."

Girty responded, "Yeah, my family lived in Sherman Valley for a while. But that was before the mill was there. There were only a few scattered settlers livin' along the creek. But I hardly recollect the place, because we moved up near the Juniata in the early '50's when I was still at my Ma's skirts. That was because my Pa had died, and my Mother took a husband named Turner."

Wend said, "I've heard what happened at Granville. It was surrendered when the war party promised to let everyone go free, but then they killed most of the people inside and took the rest captive."

"Yeah, that's right. Anyway, the war party which captured and burned Granville was made up of a mixture of Frenchmen and Delawares. They took all the captives to Kittanning Town out on the Allegheny River. Turner, my stepfather, was burned at the stake there. Ma and us children was held among the Delaware. When Armstrong attacked the town in '56, my Ma, me, and two of my brothers was spirited away by the Delaware in the confusion. But my brother Tom was saved by Armstrong's men. A little later the family was broken up and I was sold to a Mingo band livin' in the Ohio Country."

Wend's ears perked up. "Did you ever visit Wolf Claw's village along Slippery Rock Creek?"

"Yeah, I been there. Never had much of a likin' for Wolf Claw; though. Thinks a might too much of himself." Girty stared inquisitively at Wend. "Why you interested in Wolf Claw?"

Wend pointed to the back of his head. "He's the one who took my scalp, back in '59 when I was just fifteen. And he killed my family. We had been traveling along Forbes Road to Fort Pitt."

Girty stared at Wend for a long time, considering what Wend had just said.

After a few long seconds, Girty said, "Well, Wolf Claw does fancy himself quite a warrior. Fact is, the only thing that keeps him from being a big war chief among the Mingo is that his village is so small; he only has a few warriors in his band."

Wend asked, "Has Wolf Claw been raiding the settlements in support of Logan?"

"Not so far as I know; it's pretty much been bands from more to the south."

Wend nodded. He felt the strong urge to ask about Abigail, but hesitated, fearing to expose too much of his background to the scout, for whom he had really not been able to develop any trust or liking.

But he was spared the necessity.

Girty shook his head and said, "Best thing about visitin' Wolf Claw's village is seein' his wife. Her name's Orenda and she's a white woman with long blond hair. Ain't no better lookin' woman in the Ohio Country, especially considering she's got children. And she does the doctorin' for all the villages in that part of the country. The Mingo think she has magic powers."

Wend looked for words which would keep Girty talking. "Well, then she obviously has adapted to life with the Indians. How many children does she have?"

"Best I can recall, there be three, including one boy who is white. She was carrying him when she was captured back in '59."

Suddenly Girty stopped talking. He stared at Wend for a long time. Then he broke into a smile. "Now that's interestin'; I just thought of somethin'. She was captured on Forbes Road the same year as you say you lost your hair. And you be about the same age as her, Eckert."

Wend played dumb. "So? What are you getting at, Simon?"

"Story goes that Orenda weren't ever married before she was captured; she was got pregnant by some white boy who was traveling with her. A German boy it was." Girty grinned slyly and pointed his finger at Wend. "And it's sure you fit the description. I'm saying Orenda was your woman and her boy, the one they call Little White Owl, is your son."

Wend sighed. "All right, Girty; you've guessed correctly. Her white name was Abigail Gibson. She wasn't my woman — I doubt she'll ever really be any man's woman — but we did make love."

"Yeah, I heard about you Eckert; I heard a lot about you. You scouted for Bouquet in '63. And right after he beat the Indians at Bushy Run, you was with a company of soldiers which visited Wolf Claw's village. While all them Mingoes were under the muskets of the Black Watch, you took five scalps from their trophy rack."

"I just took back the scalps of my family and my own scalp."

"Yeah?" Girty leaned back and laughed heartily. "Well, Eckert, that makes you the 'Scalp Stealer'. A man hated in every Mingo village as a thief and coward."

"I don't regret what I did, Simon. Or the way it happened. And it gives me immense satisfaction that I was able to bury those scalps at the gravesite of my family."

"That may be, Scalp Stealer. But you shamed Wolf Claw in front of his own people and you made his village a laughingstock around the Ohio Country. He's sworn to kill you and put your scalp up on his trophy rack."

Wend shrugged. "Wolf Claw can get in line, Simon. There are plenty of white men who want to see me dead; white men who are a lot closer than Wolf Claw. I live in danger of them every day and have for ten years."

Girty stared at Wend for a long time, as if trying to understand Wend's words, the flickering fire alternatively lighting his face and then cloaking it in darkness.

Wend broke the silence. "Now that you know that I'm the father of Orenda's son, tell me what you know of him. I only saw him once, a long time ago."

"So why do you care, Eckert? The boy's near a grown man by Indian practice."

"You don't have any sons, do you Girty?"

"Me? I never been with any woman for long enough to make babies. Least ways, not that I knew about." He took a quick sip of the rum from his jug and grinned conspiratorially at Wend. "Then again, might be a few I ain't heard about."

"Listen, Girty, if you had ever had a son, you'd understand my curiosity. So humor me, Simon. What does Little White Owl look like?"

Girty considered a moment. "I only seen him twice. Once, in the big Indian camp on the Muskingum for Bouquet's peace negotiations, when he was pretty young; then again just a couple of years ago at the village." He paused again, looking at Wend. "Now I think about it, I'd have to say he favors you. 'Bout medium height, thin face, blue eyes, and he's got that steely look like you. You can't never tell what he's thinking. And he don't say much. When other people is talkin', he just sits there takin' it all in. I 'spect that's why they call him after an owl."

A thrill ran through Wend. *By God, he does take after me.*

"And there's another thing, Eckert. Don't know if I should speak of it. But ever since you stole them scalps, Wolf Claw hasn't looked with much favor on the boy. And the other young bucks of the village take their lead from Wolf Claw. They ain't exactly hostile, but they ain't real friendly either."

"Now how would you know all that, Girty?"

"Found that out from Orenda herself. Fact is, she keeps him close, 'cause she's afraid what might happen if Wolf Claw got mad or drunk, or both. So the boy travels with her when she visits other villages to tend to sick people. That's when I talked to her about the boy, when she came to a village I was visiting."

Wend was puzzled. He remembered Abigail's aloofness. She wasn't the type to disclose her thoughts to others, particularly those to whom she was not close.

"Why would she confide something like that to you, Simon? Someone she hardly knew."

"Truth is, Eckert, I think she just wanted to talk with another white person. Comes over all of us who been adopted by Indians. They treat you nice enough, but once in a while you want to speak with your own kind."

Wend was about to ask another question when suddenly Girty raised his hand for silence. He partly rose up from the ground and stared past Wend into the bush beyond the fire. "What's that?" He called out: "Who be there?"

Wend spun around to see a large bush shaking. Then suddenly a man appeared from behind the foliage. He was a funny looking little man, bent over at the waist and tilted slightly to his left side.

The man smiled widely, his teeth showing white in the firelight as he stood by the bush. "Hello, Simon. It's me, Harry, your friend."

Girty turned to Wend and said in a calm voice, said, "Don't worry, Eckert. It just be ole' Crooked Harry." He beckoned to the man. "Hey, come on out Harry, and have a seat here with us."

Wend watched as Harry left cover and slowly walked toward their fire. It was clear why Girty called him 'Crooked', for even when he moved, he walked bent over and leaning to his left side. His left arm seemed to hang by his side and he also limped on his left leg.

Girty leaned close to Wend and whispered, "Harry was a captive at Kittanning Town with me; he had been with the Delaware for five or six years 'fore I arrived. When the Pennsylvania militia attacked, somebody took him for an Indian, put a ball in his side and smacked him hard along the head with a hatchet. It dropped him to the ground like he was dead. He came to after a while, but he's been like what you see ever since. Crippled and touched in the head. Now he wanders back and forth between the Indian towns and white settlements, beggin' and doin' light work, keepin' body and soul together any way he can." The scout shook his head. "Been better for him if he had been killed."

Wend said, "I suspect he doesn't feel quite the same."

Girty simply shrugged.

Harry came and sat down in front of the fire. He pointed to Girty's jug. "Got rum? A little rum for Harry?"

Girty winked at Wend. "Sure Harry, have some." He picked up the jug and passed it over.

Harry took a long pull, then sighed deeply and smiled. He said to Wend, "Simon and me, we always been good friends." He turned back to the scout, "Friends for a long, long, time; ain't we, Simon?"

"Sure enough, Harry," Girty said. "You been here at Baker's place for a while?"

"Long time, yes. Working for Baker and his wife. Cleanin' the tavern and feedin' the animals." He grinned and looked at the other two men. "Doin' good work, Harry is."

Wend thought of something. He asked, "Harry, were you here when the Mingoes were killed?"

"Oh, yes. Yes, Harry saw it all. He hid out an watched the killing." He wagged his finger at Wend and Simon. "Hid out because Harry didn't want to be took for no Indian when those men started to shootin'."

Wend smiled at Harry. "That was a very good idea, Harry. Can you tell us what happened?"

"Sure; Harry knows. All started when band of men came to the tavern from Zane's place. They was all worried 'bout the Shawnee an Mingo bein' hostile."

"Did you see who was leadin' the men?" Wend asked.

"Harry saw. Leader was a young man. Younger than either of you. Hardly more than a boy, he was."

Girty said, "Harry, I heard his name was Greathouse."

"Yes, yes! Greathouse — that be his name. Heard them callin' him that. Men called him *Daniel* Greathouse. He was supposed to be the leader, but Harry saw other men tellin' him what to do."

Wend's mind went on alert. "Other men were telling him what to do? Were they some of his men?"

Crooked Harry laughed and spit into the fire. "Naw, not his men. His men were just pilgrims; they was mostly boys like him and new to the river country. Didn't know nothing about the border or the tribes. Scared of Indians they was; they couldn't tell anybody nothing."

Wend leaned forward. "So who was it that was telling Greathouse what to do?"

"Two men; older than the others. One was a black-haired man, Black Irish he was. And the other was a big man with a messed-up face and a bad leg." Harry smiled. "They was doin' all the talkin' and whisperin' in Greathouse's ear."

Wend asked, "So these men told Greathouse to invite the Mingoes over here and then set up the ambush when they came over from Yellow Creek?"

Harry nodded. "Yes, yes, that's the truth. I heard it all myself."

"Harry, where did the killing happen?" Wend asked.

Crooked Harry waved his hand along the open area. "Right here — right where we sit. Harry saw it all."

Girty cocked his head and raised an eyebrow. "So tell us how it happened, Harry."

"Man with messed-up face kept giving Mingoes rum, till they all drunk. So drunk they couldn't hardly walk straight. Then they had a shooting contest. Indians so drunk their balls fly everywhere 'cept the target. Then, when Indian guns all empty, Greathouse's men came out and killed them all."

Wend looked around. "Where did Greathouse's men hide, Harry?"

"In the back room of the tavern and in the bush — where I was hiding tonight. They all came out with firelocks and shot the Indians."

"How many Mingo did they kill, Harry?" Girty asked.

Crooked Harry held up the fingers of both hands. Then he held up his right hand with three fingers showing. "That many killed. All men but one was woman. Woman who had small baby. And one boy 'bout ten years old."

Wend asked, "They killed the baby?"

Harry shook his head. "No, no. Baker stopped them from killing the baby." He looked at Girty. "Woman was John Gibson's. And baby was Gibson's son."

Girty's eyes opened wide. "The devil you say, Harry! By God, I knew John Gibson had a Mingo woman and son, but I didn't guess she was one of the people killed." He shook his head in astonishment. "For God's sake, I've held that baby in my arms. What happened to him?"

"Baker picked up baby from dead woman's arms, Simon. His wife took care of it until Captain Gibson could come get little boy."

Girty turned to Wend. "Eckert, John Gibson is in the county militia here. He's been out on the border for a long time, farming, hunting, sometimes trading. Got a place not far away. He's friends with most of the Indians 'round here; they trust him. Before all this blew up, he used to spend a lot of time in Logan's village. The woman Harry is talkin' about is Logan's sister. She was a comely one; I seen her many times myself." He shot Wend a sly look. "Truth be told, Gibson's been sharin' her blankets for a long time. Mostly in the village, but sometimes upriver at his place."

Wend nodded. Then he turned to Harry. "Were all the Indians killed by the shooting?"

Crooked Harry shook his head. "Naw, most of them boys weren't much good with firelocks. Indians was mostly wounded, not dead. So they came out and had to finish off most of the Mingoes with their hatchets." Harry thought for a moment. "Fact is they missed one boy; he was 'bout ten years old. But he was pretty smart; he fell down and played dead even though he weren't hit."

"Did he get away?" Wend asked.

Harry shook his head. "Naw, when he see'd that them men was movin' through the Indians and finishing them off, he jumped up and started running for the woods." He turned and pointed at the other end of the clearing. "Headin' for those woods, he was."

Girty asked. "How did they get him?"

"That big man with the broken face saw him running. He started laughing and then took up his rifle to shoot him. The boy started dodging as he ran, because he knew someone would try to put a ball in him. The big man, he brought rifle up and waited 'till the boy ran straight for just a second, then he fired. Hit him right in the back, he did."

"Did that kill the boy?" Wend queried.

"Naw, boy was laying on ground. He hurt bad and screaming. Boy tried to get up; pushed himself up on his hands, but legs wouldn't move. So he kept trying to pull himself away with his hands. Big man laughed and turned to the Irish one with the black hair and say, "I'm goin' to enjoy this." Then he walked up to the boy and grabbed him by his hair. "Thought you could get away, did you?" he said. Then he laid his rifle down and pulled out his knife. Took boy's scalp while he was still alive and screaming. Then he cleaned his knife off and put it away. Big man pulled his hatchet out of his belt and chopped the boy right on the head. Split his head wide open in one blow."

Crooked Harry stopped and took another pull on the jug. Then he looked at the other two men and said. "But Harry thinks it was a big mistake for them to kill that boy. Yes, big mistake."

Girty said. "Why was it a mistake? Why'd it be any more of a mistake than killing all the others?"

Harry grinned. "Big mistake because it was Laughing Eyes' son."

Wend sat straight up. "You mean the war captain who is leading one of Logan's war parties?"

Harry nodded. "Yes, Laughing Eyes was a peaceful man. But when he found out his son was dead, he was in big, big fury. He called together wildest of warriors from Mingo and Shawnee. Then he go on warpath against all whites and he kill every one he find. No captives, no white go free. Just kill."

Wend shook his head. "It's easy to understand why he's left a swath of dead settlers and burnt farmsteads through the border territory. You're right, Harry, they made a big mistake in killing that boy."

Harry nodded, silently staring into the embers of the fire. Girty looked out on the river for a long time.

Finally Wend broke the silence. He quietly asked, "Harry, what did they do with the bodies?"

Harry turned around and pointed to a spot just down from the tavern. "Bodies buried there."

Wend shuddered. *The mass grave was no more than thirty feet from their fire.*

In a little while, Girty told Crooked Harry to take the jug and go to bed. The little man smiled gratefully and limped off to a small storage shed behind the tavern where he apparently lived.

Wend looked at Girty. "Surely you realize that those two men who Harry said were telling Greathouse what to do were Richard Grenough's men McCrae and Matt Bratton."

Girty, who had been looking into the fire, slowly turned and stared blankly at Wend. He shrugged and said, "Of course; I just came down the river in the boats with them. Known them for a while."

Wend asked, "Aren't you curious about why they were down here with Greathouse's pilgrims? And why they were egging him on to kill Mingoes, including some you knew well?"

Girty's face became impassive. He ran his eyes over Wend as if he was seeing him for the first time and judging him. "You ain't really spent a lot of time on the Ohio border, have you, Eckert?"

"Obviously I spent some time here during Pontiac's War, but I haven't been much out here recently. What's your point, Girty?"

A knowing expression came over Girty's face. "Take it from me: A lot has changed since 1763. More people have come and the British Army has left. In this country, it can be unhealthy to dig into other people's business." He stared for a long moment at Wend. "Especially Mr. Richard Grenough's business; there be many things going on out here which don't bear bein' talked about."

Without saying more, Girty lay down and settled into his blanket with his back to Wend.

Wend sat looking into the fire. Now he knew that his original thoughts about the massacre here had been correct. It had been incited by Grenough in much the same way as the Conestoga murders at Lancaster a decade ago. Back then, the trader had orchestrated the Conestoga attack to distract attention from his illicit trading with the Ohio tribes. The question was: What was he trying to cover up now?

Then, suddenly, Wend understood. He remembered Northcutt's plan for a border war to distract the colonists from supporting the Whig cause. The truth was, Grenough wasn't covering up anything; he was helping to foment a conflict. And who else besides the merchant and Northcutt was in on the scheme? Certainly Connolly — his letter warning of Shawnee hostility had aroused great fear in settlers and travelers. Then Wend remembered Cresap's nervousness at Semple's; had he had more of a hand in events than he was admitting? My God, did knowledge of how the massacre was incited reach all the way up to the governor himself? The potential enormity of the treachery shocked Wend. And then a sense of shame overcame him, shame that he had allowed himself to become associated with the likes of Northcutt and Grenough.

Eckert sat staring into the flames for a long time, feeling anger and frustration. Finally, he gathered his blankets around himself and lay down. Wend had thought that, given the disturbing revelations of the evening, he would have trouble getting to sleep. But it had been a long, labor-filled day under the hot sun, and in fact drowsiness overcame him rapidly and he dropped off almost immediately.

However, after a few hours of respite, his mind served up a dream which repeated itself incessantly. It was a vision of the Indian boy's desperate attempt to escape. But there was one difference: When Bratton lifted the boy's head to scalp him, Wend had a clear look at his face. And to his horror, it was no longer the face of some ten-year-old Indian boy, but had mutated to that of Bernd. Matt Bratton was grinning as he murdered his own natural son, a virtual copy of himself. Even deep in his sleep, Wend tried to push the horrific dream out of his consciousness, tried to pull himself awake. But it was no good; sleep overwhelmed him and the nightmare continued. Then, over time, the dream changed; when Bratton raised the boy's head, Wend could see that it was no longer Bernd. It was the face of another boy; Wend strained to make out who it was. Then he realized it was a boy with a thin face, brown hair, and eyes of blue; a boy whose face looked strikingly like a youthful version of Wend himself.

Wend woke up shaking; beads of sweat were all over his forehead and the back of his neck. He tried to get back to sleep; but the images of the bloody story which Crooked Harry had told would not leave him. Nor could he shake off the knowledge that the dead Mingoes were in the ground only a few feet from where he lay. Finally, Wend stood and gathered up his blanket. He knew he would have to find another place to sleep. So he walked down to the river-bank and the line of beached boats and canoes. He found an open space in the largest of Baker's boats and climbed in, lying down on the bottom. The moon was bright above him, driving away some of the gloom of the night, and the sound of the flowing river soothed his mind. After some time, the oblivion of deep and dreamless sleep mercifully overcame him.

CHAPTER ELEVEN

The Gathering Force

After the boat detail landed at Wheeling, Wend knew that military protocol would dictate that he go directly to headquarters in Fort Fincastle to report the results of his mission to McDonald. Instead, driven by burning anger, he strode purposefully over to the military camp, looking for Joshua Baird. He found Baird, Donegal, and Horner sitting at their fire, finishing up the midday meal. Baird was in the act of raising a jug of whiskey to his mouth. Seeing Wend, he paused, the jug halfway to his mouth, and said, "Ah-ha, the prodigal lad has returned! How did your mission go, *Lieutenant* Eckert?"

Wend turned to Horner. He said curtly, "Go find something to do, Horner."

Horner's face wrinkled up in puzzlement. He wasn't used to Wend talking so peremptorily. Wend repeated to the apprentice, "I mean *right* now, Andrew."

The youth jumped to his feet and hurried off toward the fort.

Wend stepped in front of Baird, reached down and smacked the jug out of his hands with all the strength he could muster. It flew nearly fifteen feet and then smashed loudly on the ground, the whiskey making a muddy puddle around the broken shards.

Donegal stared at the broken jug with a look of horror on his face. He said, "Now there's a damned shameful waste of good whiskey. That jug was carried with great care on a packhorse all this distance from Winchester."

Baird looked at Wend. "This's a hell of a way to be greetin' your old friends. You get out of the wrong side of your blankets this morning?"

Wend said, "Old friends indeed; old friends who lied to me."

Baird looked astonished. "Lying? I haven't no idea what you be talkin' about. I've always been straight with you." He thought for a moment and shrugged. "Well, mostly straight. Maybe I exaggerated some on a few stories I told, but that ain't no sin; everyone does it."

"I'll tell you when you lied. Simon Girty and I got to talking about Richard Grenough on the trip down river this morning. I mentioned the scar on his cheek. And then Girty told me the story of how he got it." Wend stopped and glared at Joshua. "The *real* truth about how he got it. It wasn't any camp harlot who gave him that scar, some woman of easy virtue like you told me. It was Mary; Mary Fraser! And you damn well kept that from me when you told me the story in Pittsburgh!"

"I weren't lying, Wend; I just weren't spellin' things out in much detail. Didn't give you any girl's name at all."

Donegal said, "That's right, Wend, he was 'na lyin' to you; he was just bein' a wee bit short of the truth to keep you from gettin' your hackles up."

Wend turned on Donegal. "You wanted to keep me from getting excited? For God's sake, you kept this from me for ten years!"

Donegal wagged a finger at Wend. "That's right. With you bein' married and raising a family, we didn't want you worried about Mary. We figured it would have distracted your mind about matters you could 'na do anything about."

Joshua added, "Besides, tellin' you about what Grenough tried to do with Mary might have led to you acting rash up there in Pittsburgh."

Wend looked at the two men. "This is horse shit you are trying to feed me. What I want to hear now from you, Joshua, is the whole damned story."

Baird said, "I thought you said Girty just told you everything."

"He just told me that it was Mary Fraser who sliced Grenough's face. And he was talking from camp gossip. I didn't want to arouse his curiosity by asking too many questions. So you give me the details. Now!"

Joshua screwed up his face. "All right, hold on to your horses. You're snorting and pawing the ground like that mare of yours." He looked into the distance as he gathered his thoughts. "Grenough took notice of Mary at Fort Pitt when Bouquet was organizing the expedition. Just like every other man in camp, he recognized what a fine lookin' woman she was. Somehow he found out that she had book learnin' and that she wanted to become a governess to some rich family so she could leave the army."

Wend asked, "How would he find that out?"

Donegal said, "I've 'na doubt in the officer's mess; I 'spect from the chaplain. He was teachin' her and treated her almost like a daughter."

Wend nodded. "All right; that makes sense."

Baird continued. "Grenough made it his business to meet Mary. Then he got real friendly with her; you know about his slick tongue. Anyway, he bragged that he could help find a wealthy family here in the colonies that would take her on, which got Mary all excited. So, one day he told Mary if she would come over to his tent that he would give her a letter of introduction and the names of some people who might hire her. She went there and he was sittin' under a fly in front of the tent, drinkin' some whiskey. He had Mary sit down and started givin' her drinks, figurin' to dull her wits, I expect."

Donegal grinned broadly. "Old Grenough didn't have no idea that the wee lass could hold her liquor better than many a man."

Wend nodded. "Yes, that's true enough. She learned how to handle a jug early."

Joshua said, "Well, she picked it up at her mother's knee; Lizzie was right fond of the stuff." He looked knowingly at the other men. "After a while, he must have figured that Mary was feelin' the liquor. He got up and went into his tent and called out to Mary that he had the letter and list of people in there." Joshua shrugged. "So Mary went into the tent. Then, once she was in, Grenough pointed to some papers on a table. When she went to look, he dropped the flaps of the tent."

Wend interrupted. "For God's sake, Mary was gullible."

Baird shook his head. "Have a little faith, Wend. Mary grew up following a regiment; of course she was suspicious from the start. But she wanted that letter from Grenough more than anything. So when she went over to Grenough's tent, she went prepared: She took her dagger and that little Spanish pistol." He looked at Wend. "You know'd about them. And you know damn well she could use them."

Wend nodded silently.

Joshua continued. "Anyway, she tucked them under her skirts where she could reach them quick-like. Well, once Grenough had the flaps down, he walked over and put his arm around her. He said he was going to help her, but there was going to be a price for the help. Mary told me he smiled down at her and said he was sure a pretty and experienced girl like her understood that before she came over." Joshua hesitated and exchanged a quick glance with Donegal. "Then he pulled Mary close to him, laid a kiss right on her mouth, and put his hand right on her tit."

Wend said, "So Mary fought back."

Baird nodded. "You know it: She pushed him away and quick as lightnin' she had that little dagger out. Grenough reared back and tried to laugh it all off; said he liked feisty girls. Then he reached out to take the knife away from her. But Mary didn't hesitate none; she swung the dagger at his face and cut him from the ear down to his mouth. Grenough jumped back with blood drippin' down his cheek. Then Mary pulled out the pistol and cocked it; she held it on him till she backed out of the tent."

Wend felt fury welling up inside. "Why wasn't Grenough prosecuted?"

Joshua stared at Wend for a moment. "Mary never told the story to anyone except me."

Wend said, "For God's sake, why not? There was the bloody cut on Grenough's face to prove what happened!"

Donegal shook his head. "Quell your anger and think on it a moment, Wend. It would have been the word of a camp follower against that of a man with connections all the way up to the governor. Mary knew enough not to try to fight that. Besides, this happened in the Black Watch, 'na the 77th. Everybody in the 77th had watched Mary grow up from a wee lass and doted on her. In the 42nd, she wasn't so well known except by a few men who transferred from the 77th."

Joshua said, "Truth be, she was scared to death that Grenough would gin up some sort of charge against her. Maybe make up a story that she had offered him her favors for money and that things had gone bad or that he had found her in his tent trying to steal somethin'. She decided just to stay quiet and hope that he wouldn't start anythin'."

Donegal said, "Joshua's right. Think on it Wend: Back during Pontiac's War you had evidence about Grenough trading with the Indians and then being mixed up in the murder of the Conestogas. But you didn't go to the authorities because you knew they wouldn't believe you. Can ya 'na see the same thing applied to Mary in her place?"

Wend sat down on a log. "All right, I take your meaning."

Donegal said, "Besides, Mary couldn't afford to have any kind of scandalous behavior attached to her name, 'na if she was get any kind of position with a family."

A thought struck Wend. "Donegal, you seem to know a lot about this for someone who wasn't on that campaign; you were back at the farm."

Donegal exchanged a quick look with Baird.

Wend shot Donegal a sharp glance. "You've been in touch with Mary, haven't you Donegal?"

The look in Donegal's eyes confirmed Wend's suspicions.

The Highlander tossed his hands in the air and said, "And why shouldn't I be? I knew her Ma and Pa before they was even in the army. I held her on my lap when she was at Lizzie's skirts." He paused and shot a glance at Joshua. "So when we got word in '67 that the Black Watch was leaving, I had Alice write me a letter to Mary, asking what her plans might be. Just so we would know where she would be, cause we wanted to know whether she was going back to the Highlands or staying here in the colonies."

Wend asked, "Did you ever hear back from her?"

"I got a letter near a year later from her; it had been posted before she sailed, but took months to get to us. Alice read it to me; Mary said she was going back 'cause the chaplain had got her a positon with a good family. They was a Highland family with two children and another on the way. Mary would be takin' care of the children and tutoring them when they was the right age. She said she was very happy with how it had turned out."

Wend crossed his arms in front of his chest. His anger was beginning to subside; in fact, thinking things over, he admired the way that Mary had dealt with Grenough. Most of all, he was happy at Donegal's news that Mary had been able to achieve her long sought goal of serving an established family.

Suddenly Wend thought of something which gave him pause and a touch of guilt. "Donegal, you had Alice write your letter and then had her read Mary's response to you. Peggy and Alice are thick as thieves; they talk every day. Does my wife know about Mary? Before Peggy and I got married, I told her that Mary had died; I never said anything to her after we found out that Mary had survived her wounds."

Joshua shook his head. "What the hell difference does it make? We all loved Mary, but she's gone. And you're married with a family. And who's Peggy to question you about girls you knew before you got hitched, considering all the time she spent with Bratton?"

Donegal said, "Joshua's right. Mary's in Scotland. Maybe she's even married by now. I ain't heard anything after the one letter."

Wend sat thinking for a long moment, looking down into the fire. Then he looked up at the other two. "You're right, the both of you. I'll always have a special place in my heart for Mary. But after all, she's across the ocean and there's nothing which could bring her back to the colonies, is there?"

Donegal shrugged and said. "I can 'na imagine what it would be."

* * *

Wend walked over to the fort. He was impressed with the progress which had been made in just the last few days. It was a beehive of activity as the men of numerous work gangs shaped logs for the stockade itself and the blockhouses.

Crawford had pressed McDonald's Frederick County men into the workforce, cutting and hauling logs, and that had greatly accelerated progress.

McDonald and Crawford were together in the headquarters blockhouse. Wend approached the two commanding officers and made his report on the gathering of boats and canoes.

Angus congratulated Wend on the success of the mission and then changed to a new subject. He said, "Wend, I'm glad you're back. The additional militia we were expecting has arrived and William and I have just decided which companies will accompany us on the expedition."

Wend's ears perked up. He knew that he would be responsible for organizing provisions. "What companies will we have?

McDonald said, "A total of seven, and right around 360 men. That's a little less than we had planned, but it should be adequate. We'll have all three of the Frederick County companies. The other four companies will include Michael Cresap's, from the Redstone country. We'll also have his nephew, also named Michael, and his company."

Wend shook his head, "Two captains named Michael Cresap? That will be confusing."

Crawford nodded. "Yes, but you will want both of them along; they know the territory you'll be passing through." He laughed, "I call them Michael and Michael Junior, to tell them apart."

McDonald laughed. "Done; that's how we'll refer to them." He looked down at the paper. "We'll also have Abe Teagarden's and Hancock Lee's companies; both from out here in the western part of the colony and filled with good riflemen."

Crawford thought for a moment and said, "You know, there's another company coming in today, also from the western part of the colony. You can have it, too, if you think it would be helpful. And that would probably bring you up to the 400 you wanted."

Angus thought a moment. "We'll look them — and their captain — over when they arrive." He turned to Wend and said, "And of course we'll have a group of scouts. William has selected a group of six local men who know the country north of the river well."

That brought something to Wend's mind. "Speaking of scouts, Angus, you do plan to leave Baird behind, don't you?"

"Yes, of course; we'll all be on foot and moving fast. I can't take the chance of him not being able to keep up."

Crawford nodded. "Besides, these scouts have traded and hunted along the Muskingum for years."

Wend asked, "Have you told Joshua yet?"

Angus folded his arms across his chest. "No." Then he looked up at Wend. "Perhaps you could tell him after leaving here."

Wend fought a flash of irritation. "Angus, you know he needs to have it from the commanding officer. If I break it to him, he'll just walk right over here and appeal to you."

McDonald set his mouth. "For God's sake, Wend, I had to tell Evan McLeod he was too old to go with us; it nearly broke his heart." He paused a second. "And mine. The man was with me at Culloden." He sighed loudly. "Now I'm supposed to tell Joshua he's out of this campaign?"

Wend looked into McDonald's eyes. "Angus, you have the governor's appointment to lead this expedition. It's your responsibility."

"Damn it, Eckert, don't tell me my responsibilities."

Crawford said very calmly, "Angus, cool that Highland temper. You know Eckert's right. You can't avoid this job. Besides, Baird will take it better from someone nearer his own age."

McDonald took a deep breath and then nodded slowly. "You're right, the both of you. I'll have to be the one to break it to Joshua." He thought a moment and then looked up at Wend. "We're having a meeting with all the captains this evening. And I plan to have Joshua there to give us his ideas. I'll tell him in private afterwards."

* * *

Wend walked from the stockade toward the storage shed where the provisions were being kept. He intended to look over the supplies to select the right mix of items and then decide how to issue them to the men. As he neared the building, he saw something which made him pause: McCrae and Bratton were by their campfire, just a few feet from the shed. McCrae was busy packing their possessions into packs and canvas bags. Clearly they were preparing to leave Wheeling.

But what really grabbed Wend's attention was Bratton. He was lying on his blanket by the fire, his hands to his head, his body writhing in obvious pain. Sometimes he groaned loud enough for Wend to hear.

Initially, Wend had started to turn and walk away to avoid confrontation with Grenough's men. Then, observing Bratton's discomfort, he changed his mind. He turned back and strode over to the campsite.

McCrae, down on one knee as he worked, looked up at Wend curiously.

Wend said, "I take it you're getting ready to leave."

McCrae nodded, "Yeah, if it's any of your business, Eckert. Crawford has given us permission to leave for Pittsburgh in one of the canoes."

Wend waved toward Bratton and said ironically, "Does he always lie around in the middle of the day?"

McCrae looked up at Wend. "Damn your eyes, Eckert. You can see he's in pain. He gets bad aches in the head. They come on with no warnin' and there ain't nothin' he can do except lay there 'till it's over. But that shouldn't be no puzzle to you, since he says they been happenin' since you beat him near to death with a club."

Wend said, "I like to think he's paying penance for a life of transgressions against people weaker than he."

"Do you suppose you were put here by the Almighty to punish Bratton?"

Wend grinned at McCrae. "You know, I never thought of it that way; but now you mention it, I like the idea."

"Grenough told me to watch out for you, Eckert. He said you were a hard and devious man."

"Coming from Grenough, that's a high complement. But I just watch out for my interests, McCrae. And speaking of that, can I assume one of your jobs is to keep Bratton out of trouble and to restrain his desire to attack me at odd moments?"

McCrae stared at Wend with anger in his eyes and set his teeth.

Wend smiled broadly and added, "That is, aside from firing warning shots at me out of the darkness."

McCrae said, "That wasn't personal for me, Eckert; it was just a piece of work. And besides, Bratton did all the shootin'. Grenough said you'd understand what that was all about."

"Indeed," replied Wend, "tell him I understood most completely. And as for you, naturally you're just an honest workman."

Wend walked over to stand above Bratton. The man seemed to take no notice of Wend.

McCrae said, "When he has one of these attacks, he hardly knows what's goin' on around him."

Wend went over and squatted beside Bratton. "Well, I'm going to get his attention." Bratton's accoutrements were lying beside him. Wend reached down and picked up the hatchet and scalping knife. Then he lightly tapped Matt on the side of his head with the flat of the hatchet blade.

Bratton groaned in renewed agony. He turned to see his tormentor. His eyes opened wide when he recognized Eckert.

Wend held the hatchet blade just above Bratton's face. "Hello, Matt, it's just your old neighbor from Sherman Mill. I wanted to tell you that I heard about your performance at Baker's Tavern. You know, the massacre of thirteen Mingoes. I got it directly from a witness."

Bratton groaned again. His eyes were fixated on the sharp blade of the hatchet suspended above his face. "Eckert you bastard!"

"Better hold still, Matt, or I could accidently cut your face. Not that it could make your face look any worse. But as I was saying, that massacre sure reminded me of the killing of all those Conestogas in Lancaster ten years ago. It seems like murdering unsuspecting Indians is becoming your specialty."

"For God's sake, Eckert, take that blade out of my face."

"Not yet, Matt. Not till I tell you something else. You know that boy you shot in the back, then scalped with this knife and finished off with this very hatchet? Do you realize that he was the same age as your own son?"

"I ain't got no son. You can't prove I ever had any boy."

"Sure I could, Matt. All anyone would have to do is look at you standing next to him. He's your very likeness."

"I tell you he ain't mine. Don't let that whore tell you any different."

"Careful now, Bratton; that's how you got in trouble with me the last time. You know I get really mad when somebody calls Peggy names like that." Wend paused and stared at Bratton with as grim a face as he could make. "Now I'm going to tell you about your son, because with that face you're never again going to find any woman who wants to sleep with you, let alone have your children. Bernd's the only one you're ever going to have."

Wend gathered his thoughts. "That's right, Matt, the boy's got a German name. Ironic, isn't it, considering how much you hate Germans? He's tall for his age and I've raised him to be a gunsmith like me. He can even speak pretty fair German; we often use it in the workshop. He's a serious and honest boy, who knows how to honor his mother and respect all other women. In other words, he's not like you at all. And I'll make sure he never knows the name Bratton. So when you go to your grave, there won't be anyone who remembers you or knows they have your blood."

Bratton reached up and held his head with his hands. He was obviously having another attack of pain. He groaned loudly. "Oh, for God's sake Eckert, leave me be."

McCrae was standing with his arms crossed in front of his chest, watching the proceedings. He said, "Grenough was right, Eckert; you're an exceedin' hard man."

Wend looked up at the Irishman. He sighed and said, "I didn't start out that way, McCrae. I came to it because of men like Grenough and Bratton here."

Wend turned back to Matt. "Now listen Bratton. As a tradesman, I keep a ledger book where I record the accounts of all my customers and other people I have dealings with. Well, I've got an account on you; but it's in my mind instead of in a ledger. It's got a lot of entries and now I'm adding the killing up at Baker's Tavern to the account. And just like all accountings, sooner or later it has to be reconciled and closed out. You be sure to keep that in mind, because one day I'm going to come for you and make a settlement."

Wend looked up at McCrae. "Grenough knows I'm also keeping a record on him. Just tell him I'm adding Baker's Tavern to his account. He'll know what I mean."

McCrae nodded. Then he smiled and asked, "What about me, Eckert? You got me in that ledger of yours?"

Wend stood up. He tossed Bratton's hatchet and knife into the fire. "You know, McCrae, I probably should start an account on you. Maybe I'll sit down by my fire tonight and figure out what should be in it."

* * *

McDonald's meeting with the captains started in the early dusk. Wend and Joshua walked over to the fort together. Crawford had stretched a canvas fly outside the door of the blockhouse and arranged for candles and torches to provide illumination. A fire blazed to one side of the fly.

Wend saw that the captains were standing in a group, talking and joking together. Several had pipes lighted. McDonald and Crawford were looking at a map spread out on a table under the fly. When they approached, Angus looked up and saw Joshua; he immediately motioned him to join them at the table.

Wend felt like the odd man out; he hesitated to join the captains; instead he silently took a place not far from the two commanding officers' adjutants, who stood conversing beside the door to the blockhouse. He folded his arms and watched the captains. They were, as a group, sinewy, sun-darkened men who seemed relaxed and at ease with each other. Obviously they had spent a lot of time in the bush or in their fields. Wood, the politician, was a bit of an exception, for he was less tanned and dressed in a regular shirt and waistcoat, while the others wore varying designs of hunting shirt. Harry Hoagland was a robust man, but was the oldest of the lot, being nearly contemporaneous with Joshua.

Morgan, burly and scarred, towered over the others and his booming voice and rough waggoner's vernacular dominated the conversation. Dark-haired, wiry Michael Cresap stood beside Morgan. A younger man was next to Cresap; he had similar features and Wend immediately placed him as "Michael Junior." Hancock Lee looked to be three or four years older than Wend, and seemed to have little to say; like Wend, his arms were across his chest, but his eyes darted around in seeming appraisal of his comrades. Abe Teagarden had a ready laugh and was nearly as young as Michael Junior.

The final captain was visibly the youngest of the lot; but Wend found him to have a rather striking appearance; he was tall, broad-shouldered, and had a high forehead topped by a thatch of auburn hair. Wend hadn't seen him before and assumed it was his company which had come into camp that day. He would later find that his name was George Rogers Clark.

There were two other men present. Wend recognized Ebenezer Zane, the man who laid claim to the land they stood on and whose fortified house stood a short distance from the stockade. He looked to be about Wend's own age. Standing next to him was a slightly younger man who shared similar features and Wend speculated that they were related.

McDonald cleared his throat and began to speak. "Well, gentlemen, this is the first time we've all been together. But clearly we're going to spend a lot of time in company. Now, you all know the job the governor has set out for us; tonight we need to plan on how we're going to do it."

The gathered officers had all become silent, their eyes focused on Angus. The major motioned toward the riverbank. "You've all seen the bateaux and canoes lined up along the bank. They're the key to our expedition." He looked around at the faces of his captains. "The savages will undoubtedly get wind of us gathering here at Wheeling. They'll watch us and we probably can't keep them from observing our departure. But the boats will allow us to move swiftly along the river and they won't know precisely where we intend to land."

James Wood's eyes lit up. "Angus, that's quite an idea. As I recollect, there are some Shawnee and Mingo villages right along the Ohio. We could strike a village without warning, then jump back into the boats and move to another village. It would be very safe for us."

Angus stared at Wood for a moment. "Yes, James, that would be easy and safe. But that job could be done with a single company. And the fact is, it would 'na have the impact we need. Lord Dunmore didn't raise funds for an expedition of 400 men just to strike at some isolated villages along the Ohio. The governor's intent is for us to distract the Shawnee from attacking settlements or perhaps convince them to come to peace talks. To do that, we must penetrate deep into their territory and show them that their largest, most important towns are vulnerable."

Henry Hoagland grinned slyly. "All right, Angus, so where do you intend to make your attack? Are you going to take us right up the Scioto River and beard Cornstalk in his own village?"

The group of captains broke into amused smiles.

McDonald didn't see the humor. He looked at Hoagland with steely eyes. "No, Henry, you know damn well that would be too far. I'll leave that to Dunmore when he's got his full force assembled. But there's a good target for us that's closer and easier for us to strike; I propose that we strike Wakatomica on the Muskingum River."

Then he waved a hand toward Joshua. "For those who don't know him, permit me to introduce Mr. Joshua Baird. He's been traveling this country for over thirty years. He hunted in this area before the French War. He scouted for General Forbes in '58. He was the chief scout for Bouquet in the relief of Fort Pitt in '63 and the Muskingum expedition in '64." He turned to Baird. "Tell them your thoughts, Joshua."

Baird looked around the table. "For those of you ain't been there, Wakatomica is a string of villages around where a creek by that name joins the Muskingum; they are all right close to each other. They're mostly Shawnee, but there's some Mingo and Delaware mixed in. I've been there several times, the last being during Bouquet's campaign in '64. Now Wakatomica's a few long days hike inland from the Ohio. We could find a good place to land, hide the boats, and then march overland. With any kind of luck, we could do it without the Indians gettin' wind of us and surprise them, leastways at the first village. After that, they'd sure enough know we was around. But we'd be strong enough to march right up the river, hittin' each town in turn."

Wood asked, "How many warriors do you figure are in the villages?"

"I 'spect it could be near enough to 150, including the young boys just learning their business," Joshua replied.

Wood shook his head. "That's enough to give us some trouble if they get on to us early. They could stage an ambush on our stretched-out column marching through the bush. And remember, we'll be on ground familiar to them."

Morgan looked around at the other men. "But you got to figure some of them are out on war parties or hunting. That will cut their numbers down quite a bit. I'm thinkin' we'll outnumber their warriors by three or four to one."

Joshua held up his hand to quiet the captains. "Don't forget, the Shawnee must defend their women, children, and old ones. They'll have to keep a goodly number of warriors back to do that. So, all told, I'd be surprised if them Shawnees could muster more than sixty or seventy full-aged warriors to attack us, even if they discovered us early enough to arrange an ambush."

McDonald spoke up. "Well, given the likely odds, I think we can push through and destroy the villages. And that's really our mission, not just to kill warriors."

Hoagland had been sitting quietly, listening to the discussion. "I agree with Angus. We should be able to get to this Wakatomica place all right and cause a lot of damage." He looked around at the other men. "But it's getting back to the river and our boats which has me worried. Remember what happened to Rogers when he and his Rangers raided the Saint Francis tribe up near Canada? The march out went fine and they hit the savages real hard. But on the way back they ran out of food and were constantly chased and attacked by the Indians. Not many got back." He looked at McDonald. "Could be we'll face the same problem."

Concern flooded Wood's face. "Damn, Angus, Henry's right. We'll be a long way from the Ohio, with no support or reinforcements available. We could be cut off."

Angus nodded. "Give me some credit, James. I've been contemplating that prospect. Any drive into Shawnee country is going to be dangerous. We've got to recognize that. But it strikes me our situation is more like Armstrong's raid on the Delaware village at Kittanning. We've got a much shorter distance to travel than Rogers and the country is a sight less forbidding. Armstrong's battalion got back pretty much in one piece and I think we can do the same."

Baird moved to the table and pointed at the map. All the officers crowded around to see what he was indicating. "I say we land a few miles downriver from the mouth of Captina Creek. A little way past the mouth of that creek is an island; it ain't near as big as this here Wheeling Island, but it's pretty big. You go past that an' then there's the mouth of another creek, which is on the southern side of the river — if I recollect proper, people call it Fishing Creek. So we land across the Ohio from this Fishing Creek and then we head in a nearly straight line 'cross country just a little west of north, right between the Muskingum and the Captina. Our scouts will be able to bring us to strike the Muskingum just below Wakatomica."

McDonald waved his hand toward the young man who stood beside Ebenezer Zane. "Gentlemen, this is Jonathan Zane, Ebenezer's brother. Jonathan has traveled the Muskingum and visited Wakatomica itself. He's going along as one of our scouts. He turned to the youth and asked, "What do you think of Joshua's idea?"

Jonathan Zane looked down at the map, then looked up and smiled. He spoke confidently. "The fact is, I've traveled both the Muskingum and the Captina. And I've hunted in the land between." He nodded toward Joshua. "Baird's plan makes sense to me. There are a few villages between the two rivers and I know where they are. It won't be hard to avoid them on the way up."

McDonald nodded. "I agree. Joshua's plan gives us the best chance." He slapped his hand down on the table. "That's settled; we'll land across from Fishing Creek and go overland from there."

Michael Cresap spoke up. "I suggest we leave a guard detail with the boats; we'd be in real trouble if a Shawnee party came across them."

There were nods from many of the men around the table.

McDonald said, "Yes, of course we'll do that. I plan to leave a detachment of at least twenty-five men."

Wend had been standing back from the table, taking in the conversation. But a thought had sprung to his mind during the talk of what to do with the boats. He stepped closer to the table and caught McDonald's eye. "Angus, the idea of leaving a guard with the boats has given me an idea."

McDonald responded, "Go ahead, Eckert. What do you want to say?"

"We know we're going to be short on rations on the trip back from Wakatomica. Perhaps we may be totally out of rations if things last longer than expected and we can't find satisfactory food in the villages. So why don't we bring along extra rations — say two days' worth — and leave them stored in the boats? That way, we'll at least have food when we make it back to the river."

There was a nodding of approval around the table. Angus said, "A good thought, Wend. We'll do precisely that."

Morgan looked up from the map. "All right, Angus, so now we got our plan. But the big question is: *When* do we leave?" There were nods all around. "We left Winchester in an all-fired hurry to hit the Shawnee before they could get organized for raiding. Eckert rounded up all these boats soon as we got here. Now we're here sittin' on our asses building a fort. I got sixty of the best riflemen in the colony and all they're doin' is swinging axes. An' when they ain't doin' that they're drilling like damned redcoats marching around some parade ground."

James Wood nodded and added, "Morgan's right. The men are starting to grumble. They're worried about their families, farms, and tradecraft." He looked around at the other captains. "I hear that we've had some desertions already."

Crawford nodded. "That's true; a few have taken it upon themselves to leave."

Wood looked around at the other men. "I'm saying that there will be more if we continue to linger here without action. And if we don't move pretty fast, I fear that the Shawnees will figure out what we're planning, even if McDonald's boat trick works. The fact is, the longer we wait, the more chance we have of facing an ambush and less chance of success when we do make the actual attack. Either way, we could take high casualties." Wood put on what Wend had come to think of as his political face. "The fact is, I don't fancy making the rounds of Winchester to explain to wives why they've become widows."

Angus' face turned grim and Wend could see his jaw tighten. The Scotsman hesitated a moment and then pulled himself up to his full height. Then he said forcefully, "Now listen, all of you; there's 'na any man here more anxious to get started than I. Or who worries more about our boys taking musket balls. But we've been given orders to hold off while Connolly is still corresponding with the Shawnee chiefs, playing for time. He's got orders to stall the chiefs as long as possible to give the governor time to marshal the militia and march for the border."

James Wood shook his head. "I've said it before: This stalling game probably benefits the tribes more than it does us. I'd wager they're using the time to call in their hunting parties and pick war captains."

Crawford stared at Wood for a moment, a look of exasperation on his countenance. "Look, James, you're not the only one who has thoughts like that. I hadn't intended to say this, but Angus and I drafted a letter to Connolly today saying much the same thing and emphasizing that we should attack with all dispatch. We sent it off with Girty by canoe."

Angus smacked the table. "So we've done all we can. Now we wait for word from Connolly." He looked around at the captains. "So hear me out: You've all been commissioned to command companies because you have the admiration and respect of your men. It's up to you to make them understand their duty and keep their attention on the job we have ahead. Now go back to your companies, buck them up, and use the time we have to get them as ready as you can."

* * *

After the meeting ended, Wend went back to the campfire. Donegal sat there staring into the flames with great intensity. In his hands, seemingly forgotten, were his throwing knife and a whetstone. Beside him was an open whiskey jug.

Horner was away, undoubtedly visiting with other young militiamen of his own age.

Wend asked, "Simon, I figured you'd be over at the sergeant's fire with your friends, swapping lies. What's on your mind that's making you look so serious?"

"Wend, I got a problem. I'm thinkin' I want to marry Sally Potter."

Wend threw back his head and laughed. "That's a problem? She's a pretty girl. And your fixation on her has been pretty obvious since the beginning."

"You're right, I'll admit I been hankerin' for her since the day we found her." Donegal looked around as if to make sure no one was in hearing distance. "But this is like 'na other time I been around women. It's always been whores, or tavern girls, or army women. Things happened quick-like in a back room or in the hay somewhere. Fact is, I've 'na spent much time with just one woman."

Wend smiled. "Well then, you should find spending your time with Sally very rewarding."

"I do, Wend; she's a nice lassie, plenty smart, and she knows how to make a man feel comfortable in her presence. Just like Peggy and Alice do." Donegal thought a moment. "But I got a problem. I ain't got no way to be sure she's got affection for me the same way I do for her."

Wend recalled the glow on Sally Potter's face when she had watched Donegal as the militia marched into Ransome's Tavern. "Simon, I don't think you have anything to worry about from that quarter."

Donegal stared at Wend. "Now how can you know that? Has the lass said something to you?"

"In a way, Donegal; I'm a married man. I've learned to read women." Wend laughed to himself. "At least as well as it's possible for any man. But from what I've seen of Sally, she's got a great deal of affection for you."

"So you think if I asked for her hand, she'd say yes?"

There was a pathetic, pleading look in Donegal's eyes. Wend laughed again and thought: *The man is besotted.* "I said that she has great affection for you. But knowing how she'll answer your proposal is beyond the knowledge of any man and I won't pretend that I can guess." Wend sat down on the log beside the Highlander. "You're going to have to find that out on your own, just like every other man has had to do since eternity."

"I guess you are right, Wend. But I got to say, the prospect near scares me to death. I been in bayonet charges, I fought with sword and dagger, I stood up to volley fire, watching men next to me cut down, but nothing has ever scared me more than the prospect of sittin' down with Sally and asking her to marry me."

Wend said, "Simon, there's more for you to think about." He paused and glanced at his friend. "You know she's got two young children. Are you ready to deal with that?"

"I've always been good with the little ones. Why should I worry about the wee lassie and lad?"

"Being the parent of a child isn't like playing with someone else's kids on a quiet afternoon. They're in your house all the time and you often have to pay attention to them even when you'd rather be doing something else. And a baby can get on your nerves. It requires patience."

Then something else occurred to Wend. "Where are you going to live? All you've got is some rooms at the end of the barracks building."

"Sure enough, I'll have to build a house. But for the start, we'll live in my rooms. It will be tight, but it is pretty big. There's a loft and I'll fix it up for the little girl to sleep."

Wend said, "Take my word on this, Simon: Don't tell Sally about the barracks room until after she agrees to marry you."

Donegal shrugged. "It won't take long to build a house. I'll get started on that as soon as we get back to Winchester."

Wend was about to reply when he glanced up to see Baird striding toward the fire. He arrived and stood looking down at Wend, a grim expression on his face. "Angus just told me I'm not to make the trip to Wakatomica."

There was a moment of silence. Wend looked up into Joshua's eyes and saw despair.

"Joshua, it's only logical. You know how that leg bothers you on long foot trips."

Baird shook his head. "You ain't never heard me complaining 'bout my leg and nobody ever see'd me hanging back when we was on hunts. There ain't no reason I can't make the march up to the villages and back."

Wend responded, "Come on Joshua, we've only been on hunts which required walking a short distance. We mainly travel by horse. You're dreaming if you think you could keep up with the battalion on a fast march of ten days or more."

"I kept up with Captain Sterling's company back in '63 when we marched through the Beaver River Country."

Wend felt a flash of anger. "You know that we didn't have to move fast like we will on this expedition up the Muskingum. And Sterling arranged it so that you wouldn't be walking point, to spare your leg. That's why he had me do the scouting. And you know damn well your leg has gotten worse since then."

Baird stared at Wend for a long moment. Then he reached down, picked up Donegal's jug, and took a long swig of the whiskey. "This is all comin' clear to me now. You're in on this with McDonald. When you was over at headquarters earlier today, you told him I couldn't keep up with the column. You put him up to keepin' me from bein' the chief scout."

"Joshua, it's evident to everyone that your leg isn't up to the trip. It was clear to Angus without me having to tell him. It should be clear to you."

"I'll tell you why you did it. You was mad from finding out that I didn't tell you the whole truth about Mary Fraser and Grenough. So you took it on yourself to pay me back."

Wend was stunned by Baird's words. He sputtered, "My God, Joshua, my anger was over before we finished talking about Mary. How could you think that I would be so vindictive?"

Baird took another long pull on the jug. He seemed to be calming down. "Well, you'll be surprised to find that I ain't completely shut out of this expedition. Angus said I would go along in the first boat to navigate the river and to help pick out the landing spot for the boats. And then I'm to stay with the guard detail to be their scout — watching for parties of Shawnees which might try to attack the boats."

Wend nodded. "You may not believe it Joshua, but I'm glad. And you know that's an important job."

Joshua looked askance at Wend. "Yeah, right; I ain't no fool. I know damn well it's made up to console me." He looked around the campsite. "I'm goin' over to Hoagland's company to visit with some men I know who was on the Forbes campaign. I ain't in no mood to spend the evenin' with youngsters like you two."

* * *

The next evening, with dusk coming on, Wend sat at a small writing table in Crawford's headquarters blockhouse, working on the provision accounts by the light of candles. Even with the departure of the sun, it was beastly hot in the log building, which had only small loopholes to provide a flow of air. Beads of perspiration had formed on Wend's face, neck, and even on his hands. He had to wipe himself with a rag frequently to keep droplets from falling onto his paperwork. He suffered in the hot room only because he needed the table to spread out his papers.

Suddenly his thoughts were interrupted by a hubbub outside, where the canvas fly was still in place. He knew that Crawford and McDonald had been sitting there enjoying a drink in the breeze. There were voices of many people talking at once, including what sounded like a very young woman's voice. He first wondered if one of the Zane women had come over from their house, but then he realized that there was too much agitation for that to be the case. Wend stood up and decided to see what was going on; at any rate, he needed a break from the stifling heat.

Moses Louder stood before McDonald and Crawford. He was a corporal of Morgan's company who was in charge of the picket station at the wagon track from the east. Beside him were two young people; a boy of fifteen or sixteen and a girl Wend judged to be a year or so younger. Both were disheveled, their clothing torn and soiled, their faces smudged with what looked like soot.

Wend noticed Ensign Marcus Calmees, also of Morgan's company, who was standing duty in charge of the sentinels and pickets. He quietly asked, "What's going on, Mark?"

Calmees whispered, "These two youngsters just came in from a place called Hart's Store. It's a small farming village in the foothills of the mountain ridge." He pointed toward the hills to the east. "They say a war party hit the place at dawn this morning."

Wend nodded. Then he listened as the boy spoke to the two commanding officers.

"It was a big war party, sir. I 'spect there was at least fifteen of them. They hit a house first, right across from old man Hart's store. Set it on fire and then went into hiding. When the people came out and rang the fire bell, all the people ran from the other houses and started to fight the fire. That's when the savages came out of the bush and started shootin' them down."

The girl, who had been seated in a chair, looked up at Crawford, who was standing in front of her, and added, "They didn't take no care whether it were man, boy, women, or children. Just shot everyone they took in their sights." She turned to the youth. "Ain't that the truth, Georgie?"

The boy looked around at the staring men. "Emily's right. Some was still alive after they was shot, but them savages finished them with their knives and hatchets. Except for Mr. Seevers; turned out he wasn't much wounded. For some reason they made him a prisoner instead of killin' him."

McDonald said, "There's something I don't understand, son. How was it that you two were able to see everything but were spared?"

Crawford nodded. "That's a *very* good question. I'd like to know the answer."

The two young people looked at each other guiltily. Emily's face blushed and she looked down at the ground, not wanting to meet anyone's eyes.

Georgie stammered, "Well, sir, truth be told, we was sort of visiting together in the night, up on the ridge above the village. We had sneaked out of our houses after everyone was asleep. Them Indians didn't have no idea we was there."

Despite the seriousness of the moment there was a flurry of quick smiles, rapidly suppressed, among the men gathered under the fly. McDonald and Crawford exchanged knowing looks.

Wend's thoughts flew back to a night long ago when he and Abigail Gibson had stolen away in the night from their own families' wagons for a passionate tryst by the waters of Conococheague Creek. *These things never change.*

McDonald put a consoling hand on Georgie's shoulder and put the boy at ease. "Well, lad, it was a fortunate choice on the part of the both of you. I'd like to think Our Lord had a hand in it."

Crawford said, "That's the honest truth." Then he asked, "What else did you see, lad?"

Georgie said, "After they had killed everyone, they set the other houses on fire. Then they raided the store. I could see them carrying out goods, 'specially kegs of powder. Other warriors rounded up livestock and killed most of the animals. They saved one bullock, which they took with them. After they fired the store, they took Mr. Seevers and the bull and went down from the village into the valley. There be farms right close to the village. We saw heavy smoke comin' from at least two of them afore we came down from the ridge and lit out for here, sir."

McDonald turned to Crawford. "We need to send out a column to Hart's Store to clean things up and see if they can pick up the war party's trail. And maybe some people from the farms survived."

"You're right, Angus. If they leave at first light, they can be at Hart's by early afternoon. Who are you going to send?"

"I think a company should be adequate, William." Angus thought a moment. "Morgan's an old hand at this sort of thing and he's got a company of good riflemen. Besides, he's been making lots of noise about sitting around wasting time waiting for action." McDonald smiled wryly at Crawford. "So we'll give him something to do."

Crawford returned Angus' smile. "Yes, at least that will spare us from his grumbling for a day or two!"

McDonald turned to Wend. "Eckert, get Joshua. He'll go along as Morgan's chief scout. If anyone can read the Indians' trail, it will be him. And it's a job he can do mostly on horseback."

Crawford said, "I'll send young Jonathan Zane along to work with Baird. He can do the legwork and he's got a more intimate knowledge of this territory." Then he put his hand on Georgie's arm. "Now, lad, we'll get you something to eat and then bed you down for a good sleep tonight. But I must tell you, there's a grim day ahead for you tomorrow. We need to send you back to Hart's Store with the troops; you know the village and the location of farms in the area. And you know the names of the people who died. You'll have to help the soldiers identify the graves properly." He turned back to the girl. "Mistress Emily, we'll take you over to the big house to stay with Mrs. Zane. She's a good woman and she'll take care of you for now."

Angus nodded. "Good idea, sending young Zane and the lad here, William." Then he pointed to Wend. "And you're going, too, Eckert."

Wend, surprised, asked, "Why me, Angus? I've got a lot to do here writing my accounts and getting the provisions organized for the expedition."

"All that can wait. Get a detail of ten men from Wood's company. And provide them with shovels. You'll supervise the burials."

Then Angus thought of something else. He smiled broadly. "Besides, I'm a Scot, so I hate to see things go to waste. Take some packhorses and a couple of your quartermasters. Search the village for any supplies we can use. They're 'na going to need them up there." He thought a moment. "And since you'll be mounted on that big black mare, you can help Baird with the scouting if he needs you. From what I hear, you did well enough in that line working for Bouquet."

CHAPTER TWELVE
The Jaeger's Fight

The sun was just past the noon position when the three riders pulled up their horses at the edge of the tree line and stared at the remains of Hart's Store and its people. Wend's mare suddenly snorted, tossed her head into the air, and began stamping on the ground. He quickly steadied her, but then the other two horses started to mimic her actions.

Joshua said, "The animals is smellin' the stench of death and not likin' it one bit."

Jonathan Zane calmed his horse and then, looking at the scene in front of them, said, "Sure 'nuff, the war party did a complete job."

Wend was quiet, looking over the scene. There was a gust of breeze and suddenly the full smell of the bodies assaulted his nose. Working hard to ignore it, he saw that the village had indeed been tiny, consisting of only the store, which also contained living quarters for Hart and his family, and four other log cabins with their out-buildings. *Had been* was the operative phrase, for the fires had consumed virtually all the buildings. Here and there a part of a wall and stone chimney remained standing.

Baird said, "Let's dismount here. I don't want to ride right in and take the chance of messin' up some sign. So leave the horses here and walk careful-like. We got to get a good look around before the militia get here."

Zane said, "That won't be long; they ain't but a mile behind."

Joshua nodded. "Yeah, let's get to it. We'd best start by lookin' over the bodies." He walked toward the center of the hamlet, looking down at the ground and watching where he stepped.

They came to the area in front of the store, where most of the bodies lay. But Wend reflected that the term "bodies" was a misnomer, for at first glance he saw no such thing as a fully intact corpse. He looked over at Baird. "Joshua, what does this remind you of?"

Baird shrugged and looked around. In a weary tone he said, "It reminds me of all the places I've come to after a war party raid. I been doin' this since '55 and this is just the latest of the lot."

Wend motioned to the remains. "No, Joshua, this is different. Look close at the bodies."

Joshua scrunched up his face and answered, "Bodies is bodies. Sometimes the Indians leave messages by what they do to the corpses, but I don't see nothin' special so far."

Wend said, "I was thinking of the Lancaster Workhouse after the Paxton Boys murdered the Conestogas. Look at how all these bodies have been mutilated; they're all hacked to pieces."

Baird moved his eyes around the killing ground. "I guess you're right about that, Wend, now that you mention it. Fact is, I just glanced briefly into that place. You was the one who spent a lot of time in there."

Zane was walking around looking at the bodies. "I'll tell you what it looks like: it's the work of Laughing Eyes."

Baird cocked his head. "Now how can you say that just from lookin' at the bodies?"

"I seen his work twice before after raids like this." He pointed to the remains of a body. "He always has the bodies cut apart. Arms and heads chopped off, hands hacked off the arms, legs sliced off." He shook his head. "This all looks the same way. Ain't no doubt in my mind this was Laughing Eyes' work."

Then Wend was drawn to what he saw in front of the charred remains of one house, directly across from the store. It was the body of a young woman and it was the only corpse that hadn't been dismembered. The woman's body lay on its back; the legs closed, the arms at the sides, as if carefully laid out for burial. The woman had been pregnant and her abdomen had been sliced open. Laid on top of her was the dead child, a little boy, still attached by the umbilical cord. Both mother and child looked skyward with staring eyes.

Both Joshua and Jonathan joined Wend. They all stared for a long moment. Finally, Wend said, "Obviously carefully arranged as a message to whoever found the bodies. What do you think it was supposed to tell us?"

Baird shook his head. "I ain't never been good at readin' what's in a warriors mind and I don't much try."

Zane said, "Only the savage knows for sure. But to me it means that Laughing Eyes intends death to us and our children. That's all I got to know."

* * *

Wend watched as Morgan led his column into Hart's Store. It was a straggling group of men, their rifles in the crooks of their arms or carried at the trail in one hand. But they walked with the long, easy gait of woodsmen, a stride which would, with a minimum of effort, eat up the miles of a long day. Behind the main body of militiamen was the ten man squad of Wood's company led by Corporal Sam Calvert. All of Wood's men carried muskets slung over their shoulders. Behind them were Wend's quartermasters — Horner, Cather, McCartney — leading horses with packsaddles to which shovels had been lashed. Wend wondered to himself what an officer of the 42nd or 77th would had have thought while watching the approach of the company and decided the officer would have found much to criticize.

Morgan raised his arm to stop the column. The men crowded around him, staring at the grim spectacle of the destroyed village. Morgan stood still, scanning the hamlet and then the surrounding area, his jaw set grimly. He looked over to where the scouts stood and shouted, "A damned bloody slaughter, Joshua!"

Joshua nodded. "Just like in the French War or back in '63, Daniel."

After a few more moments staring at the carnage, Morgan started giving orders to his officers. "Calmees! Detail out sentries all around the village; put them out at 100 yards." He pointed up the ridge to the east. "And put two men an' a corporal as lookouts up on that outcropping." Morgan turned to his lieutenant, John Humphreys, and said, "John, find a good place to camp clear o' the stench of this place and have the men drop their packs and stack arms."

Morgan walked over and joined the group of scouts. Young Georgie came with him.

The captain waved his hand to take in the village and the bodies. "All right, Joshua, what have you found out? Can you tell me any more than I can see here with my own eyes?"

"Yeah, Daniel; Zane here is pretty sure that this was done by Laughing Eyes' war party. They been raiding the border country since Baker's Tavern."

"Yeah, I heard tell 'bout him."

Joshua said, "Based on the sign I found here, there was at least fifteen warriors; maybe more. One of the biggest parties I seen since the French War. We also found sign showin' where they came from," Joshua pointed toward the ridge with his thumb. "They headed in from the east, over the mountain." He looked at Georgie who had followed Morgan over. "You and your gal was lucky, lad. They was probably laying up on the hill for part of the night not too far from you."

Baird spit, then said, "An we also found their trail on the way out. They went a little north of the village and then down into that little valley below this flat where we're at now. Like Georgie here said down at Fincastle yesterday, they was headin' to where there be several farms."

Morgan nodded. "Like as not they hit the farms later the same day." He thought a moment. "Well, we got a lot of work to do . Makes sense for us to camp here tonight and head back to Wheeling tomorrow. Meanwhile, you follow the war party trail to see what they did to the farms."

"Yeah, Dan, I'll do that. An' I also want to see if I can figure where the war party went after they finished with the farmsteads." Baird pointed to the soldiers. "How about sending a detail of men with us — there'll be bodies to bury, and I can use one or two as messengers in case somethin' turns up."

In short order, Baird and Zane rode out, with ten riflemen following under the command of Sergeant Joe Richardson. Wend, with Corporal Calvert, searched for a satisfactory burial ground. They found a hillock just north of the store where there was a good view of the little valley and rainfall would drain off the graves. Calvert set the detail of grave diggers to work.

Then Wend started sorting through the dismembered bodies with Georgie in company. He also had Horner come with them to make a list of the names. There were nineteen people to bury; nine adults and ten children, including three very young ones. Georgie held up much better than Wend would have expected. He carried a stone-faced expression as they went about their business and spoke in a quiet monotone as he helped identify and assemble the bodies.

It was only when they found his mother's severed head that he lost his composure. He put his hands to his face and began sobbing.

Wend helped the boy to a seat on the ground under a tree and left him alone to his grief. Then he and Horner gathered together what they believed were all of the woman's parts, and two of the grave diggers carried them up to the hill.

Wend led Horner over to the pregnant woman and her baby. Looking down at the two bodies, Wend told his apprentice, "Georgie told me her name is Cora McLean. She's twenty-four years old. One of the other dead children is also hers."

He heard a gagging sound behind him and turned around to see that Horner had dropped to his knees and was struggling to keep from vomiting. Wend said, "Don't fight it, Andrew, let it come."

The youth took his hand away from his mouth and the vomit flowed out onto the ground. He said sheepishly, "I'm sorry, Mr. Eckert. I could handle the others, but this one was more than I could take."

"Don't feel ashamed, Andrew. I did the same thing the first time I saw a massacre like this. It was at Sherman Mill and it was the body of my best friend. He was burned to a crisp." He stood over the kneeling apprentice and put his hand on the boy's shoulders. He said quietly, "*Now* you understand why every man in the colony has to be a soldier. The settlement country is a brutal world and we have to make our way in it. Back in Germany, soldiers fight for pay to win a king or prince's political goals that no one really cares about. Here in America we fight for ourselves and our families." He paused and looked around at the remaining bodies. "Consider yourself lucky if this is the only time you have to see something like this."

Calvert and one of the grave diggers had joined them. The corporal exclaimed, "Oh, Good Lord above! Look at that!" Both men stared down at the woman and child with wide eyes.

Wend reflected that Calvert was a cobbler by trade. Undoubtedly he had never seen anything like this before. He said to the men, as businesslike as he could, "The name of the woman was Cora McLean. The unborn child had no name. Be sure to bury them together in the same grave."

* * *

It was near dusk by the time they had finished interring the bodies and cleaning up the village. Cather and McCartney had scoured the area around the village and found three cows grazing in thickets some distance from the village. A number of chickens had also survived the Indian raid; however, they didn't survive the soldiers' desire for fresh food and ended up on spits roasting for the evening meal. Wend's men also found some caches of grain and dried corn which they bagged in preparation for transport back to the fort. A couple of dogs which had hidden out during the attack also came in on their own accord and attached themselves to the quartermasters, undoubtedly because McCartney and Horner shared some of their rations with the animals.

Wend sat in the waning light beside the officers' fire with Morgan, Humphries, and Calmees. All were having some of the newly roasted chicken. Mark Calmees glanced up from his food and stared at something. After a long moment he pointed to the northern end of the village. "Look, Daniel, here's John Richardson and his squad back from the valley. And they got some farm people with them."

Wend looked around and saw a couple he judged to be in their middle thirties and three children, the oldest a boy he took to be about twelve. There was another boy of seven or eight. The youngest was a little girl who looked to be maybe five, holding her mother's hand. All were dirty and bedraggled.

Morgan put his food down, wiped his lips, and stood up to face Sergeant Richardson. "Let's hear your report, John."

The sergeant leaned on his rifle. "Well, Daniel, we followed Baird an' Zane down into the valley. We found two burnt out farmsteads; all the people and animals dead. We buried the people. Then Zane found a third place and we all went down there."

Richardson shook his head. "That third place was quite a sight. It was the last farm the savages hit. It was all burnt out like the other two, but it was also where they camped for the night. There was remains of several big fires which had been made right in the middle of the farmyard. Most of them was cookfires; they had butchered the bullock they took from here and roasted it for their meal. Another fire was 'bout twenty feet away from the others. And right in the middle of that fire was a high stake with a burned out corpse tied to it." The sergeant looked around at the officers. "It was the man Seevers they took from here." He paused a moment. "It wasn't no pretty sight, Daniel."

Morgan nodded, then motioned to the civilians who were with Richardson. "Who are these people, John?"

"These be Henry Flannagan and his family," Richardson answered. "They own the last farm, and they escaped 'cause they saw the fires from the other two." He turned to the farmer and said, "Here, Henry, you tell the Cap'n what all happened."

The farmer looked around at the watching officers, then said, "Well, Cap'n, I was in my barn, doin' mornin' chores and I started to walk back to the house with a pail of milk. I spied heavy smoke risin' up from the two places up the valley. With all the Indian troubles 'been goin' on, I knowed right away, sir, what was happenin'. So I dropped the pail and ran to the house; I got Martha and the children and my firelock and we ran near a half mile in the creek and then climbed up the ridge and hid in a thicket."

Morgan screwed up his face. "The war party didn't make any effort to track you?"

"If they did Cap'n, they didn't find our trail." A look of pride passed across Flannagan's face. "I was in the French War, Cap'n, in the Virginia Regiment, and I made sure we was careful to leave no sign when we came up out of the creek. We climbed out where there was a lot of rocks."

Morgan nodded. "Indeed, that may have saved you."

Flannagan continued. "We just laid low for most of the day. I was expectin' to see the farm go up in smoke. But by the middle of the afternoon, all I saw was a thin wisp of smoke from the place. So, late in the afternoon, I stole along the side of the ridge to where I could see the farmstead. I guess I was near 100 paces from the place, and high up enough so I could see pretty much what was goin' on."

Morgan asked, "Could you see how many warriors were in the party?"

"There be eighteen I could count. It looked like there was three groups, leastways that was the way they were sitting at the three fires."

Morgan's interest was roused. "Damn, that *is* a big war party. But you say three groups?"

"Yeah; and it was like they was from different villages or tribes. There be one big group of nine and then two smaller groups, one of five and the other of four Indians. I figured they was from different villages 'cause when I first spied the farmstead, it looked like the leaders were in an argument. They was shouting at each other and moving their hands like they was all excited." Flannagan paused for a moment, then continued, "Then they seemed to work it out and they all settled down at their fires and ate their meal."

Richardson said, "Henry, tell them 'bout Seevers."

"Yeah, well, they had Will Seevers tied to a post right in the middle of the farmyard. I knew it was him right away 'cause even at that distance I could see that bald head of his." He gathered his thoughts. "Anyways, after they finished with their food it was comin' on dusk and they commenced to roast poor Will. They piled up brush and firewood beside the post. Then they lit a small fire beside him and started to have their fun; they was stickin' him with knives and sticks, all the time the fire was gettin' hotter and Will was screamin'."

The officers were listening with rapt attention. Humphreys asked, "So you could see everything they were doing to him?"

"That I could, Lieutenant, but I didn't stay around to watch. I figured while they was all busy was a good time to git back to my family." Flannagan bit his lip and looked at the ground. "And to tell the truth, I didn't have no heart to watch what they was doin' to poor Will. I knew soon as they tired of tormenting him they was going to build the fire up and finish him."

Morgan reached out and put a reassuring hand on the farmer's arm. "That's all right, Henry, you were brave enough sitting up there for hours watching them. The prudent thing was to get away from there and tend to your family."

There was a long silence. Finally Richardson spoke up. "These people came down from the hill while we was buryin' Seevers' body, what was left of it. They want to go with us back to Wheeling Creek and stay there 'till the hostilities is over."

Morgan nodded. "Aye, we'll take you back with us." He motioned to Wend. "Lieutenant Eckert will see you get some victuals and get you bedded down for the night. We'll be leaving tomorrow." Then he turned back to Richardson. "Ain't you forgot to tell me somethin', John?"

"Can't think of anything, Daniel."

"For God's sake, where are Baird and Zane?"

"Oh, yeah, Cap'n. Well, they followed the Indians' trail. Joshua said he would follow them until dark, then camp for the night, and come back here tomorrow. He wanted to see where they were headin'. He figured he'd be back here by noon tomorrow or a little later."

Morgan considered things for a few seconds, then looked around at his officers. "I'll wait for them scouts until early afternoon, then we'll march back to Fincastle. We ought to be there just at dark, or a little after. If Joshua comes in after we leave, he can catch up with us or just come in on his own."

* * *

The two scouts rode into the burned-out village with the sun an hour past noon. The soldiers had broken camp, donned their packs, and were beginning to assemble for the start of the march back to Fort Fincastle.

Morgan shouted at Joshua, "What the *hell* took you so long, Baird? I damn near left without you!"

Joshua pulled his horse up in front of the captain and slid to the ground. "Daniel, you be the most impatient man I ever knew. What I was doin' was hangin' on the trail of the savages so you'll be able to tell McDonald where they went." He looked slyly at Morgan. "You *do* want to know what they're up to, don't you?"

"What I really want is to get back to Wheeling before the moon comes up." Morgan cocked his head. "But so long as you spent all this time sniffin' out that war party, you might as well tell me what you found."

"Truth is, right after they left the Flannagan place, they split into three groups."

Morgan smiled broadly. "Baird, tell me somethin' I don't know. Flannagan himself told me there was three groups making up this war party."

Joshua laughed. "Yeah? That's very good, Daniel. But I know where they went."

214

"Well, I'm waiting."

Baird waved toward the west. "I was able to follow two of the trails. They both was headin' toward the river. And they was movin' fast, not takin' much care to hide their sign. We also saw that they grabbed a lot of goods from the Flannagan place 'afore they burned it. They was takin' iron pots, clothes, and other stuff for their women." He paused and looked around at all the officers. "The plain truth is, they're goin' home." He turned to young Zane. "Ain't that the way you make it out, Jonathan?"

Zane nodded. "Laughing Eyes put together a war party made up of Shawnees and Mingoes from a couple of villages. Now think on it: They been on the warpath for many weeks, looping around the settlement country all the way east toward Laurel Ridge. I figure they decided they done enough raiding and it was time to go back across the Ohio. That's why they had the big feast at the Flannagan place; sort of a farewell get-together. Then they split up to go to their different villages." He shrugged. "Yeah, that makes the most sense to me."

Morgan considered what he had heard for a while, then asked, "What about the third group?"

Baird said, "Didn't have time to follow their trail, not if I was goin' to get back here and join this here column you're in such an all-fired hurry to march back to Fincastle. But it looked like it was leadin' the same way, at least when they split off from the others."

Morgan nodded. "That's a bit of good news we can give to McDonald and Crawford. And I was worried they might try to hit more farmsteads. Didn't want to have to try and chase them down." He turned and shouted to Humphreys, "All right, John, form the company and let's get on the road back to Fincastle. We're wasting daylight."

Wend found himself in charge of the rearguard. His motley command included Calvert's men, his quartermasters, and the Flannagan family. Wend walked because he had put Martha Flannagan and her young daughter up on The Mare. Henry Flannagan led the horse with his youngest boy walking alongside. Cather and McCartney led the packhorses with the flour and the remaining chicken carcasses loaded aboard. Much to his disgust, Horner was tasked with herding the cattle and the older Flannagan boy had been drafted to assist him. They brought up the very end, encouraging the cattle with switches they had cut from young saplings. The two dogs tagged along.

The going was slow, primarily because of the cattle, and Wend spent a lot of time calling back to Horner to keep the animals moving. But despite their best efforts, by mid-afternoon, Wend realized that they were falling well behind the main column.

As if he needed any reminder, Zane came riding back to check on them. The young scout leaned down from his horse and said, "Daniel's pushing it to get back to the fort. He don't want to have to march in the darkness. He said for you to close up, 'cause he ain't goin' to spend a lot of time waiting 'round for you."

Wend asked. "How far ahead is the company?"

Zane screwed up his face. "More'n a mile."

Wend shook his head. "Just tell Daniel to hold his horses and I'll do the best I can with these cattle."

About an hour later, Wend's little group was approaching a small creek. He was glad to see the stream, because he remembered it as being about half the distance between the village and Fincastle. Moreover, it was a good place to water the livestock.

The first shot rang out just as Wend, leading the group, reached the creek. He heard a zipping sound and then The Mare shrieked in fright and pain. He quickly turned around to see her rear legs buckle; both female riders lost their seating and fell to the ground. The little girl started crying. As he was staring, Wend felt a hot pain along the right side of his head and his hat flew off; immediately afterward he heard the report of the shot. He spun around again and was able to see from the smoke that the firing was coming from bushes on a low rise across the creek.

Wend screamed, "Ambush!" Then he pointed to the undergrowth to the left of the wagon track. "Take cover! Everyone into the bushes beside the road. Do it now!"

Suddenly a fusillade of shots rang out from a hill about forty yards from the right side of the road. Wend got a quick glance of several warriors who had risen from their hiding places to make their shots.

Wend thought, *"Lord, they've got us in a cross fire!"*

There was a scream of pain and Wend saw that Carver, one of the militiamen, had taken a ball in the right side of his chest. He had collapsed and was writhing in pain. Calvert grabbed him by his waistcoat and pulled him to cover.

Wend aimed his rifle at the area where he had seen a warrior and fired. Then he realized his mistake. Following his example, all the other militiamen fired their muskets into the area where he had fired. Wend thought, *Damn! Now we don't have a loaded gun in the squad except for a few pistols.*

By now, everyone had taken to the ground in the bushes beside the road. Only the horses and cattle were standing. There were a few seconds of quiet from the Indians and then two shots rang out from across the creek.

Wend now understood the disposition of the Indians. There were two, per-haps three warriors across the creek, acting to block their passage. The rest of the party was up on the hillock; they would make the main attack.

Wend looked along the length of his detail and realized he was wrong about one thing; there was one loaded long gun in the group. Henry Flannagan had his rifle, and was about to fire toward the hill. Wend shouted to him, "Don't fire, Flannagan; keep it ready in case there's a rush or a warrior shows himself." Wend touched the pistols in his belt. If the war party rushed them now, at least they could respond with a few shots.

Flannagan stared at Wend for a moment, and then nodded his understanding.

Wend shouted to the soldiers: "Load as fast as you can!"

Then he set about loading his own rifle. And it was while he was thus engaged that he remembered something. It was the words of Henry Bouquet cautioning young Lieutenant Campbell of the 77th Highlanders before he had sent him off through 150 miles of wilderness with a small column to reinforce Fort Ligonier. *"If you are attacked, don't act defensively, for the Indians will hide and pick you off one by one. Fix bayonets and charge! Force your way through them; they will never stand when attacked vigorously and are only dangerous to people who appear to fear them."*

Wend realized they were in precisely the situation Bouquet had envisioned. Or perhaps worse, for he had women and children to protect.

"Horner!" He called out.

The young apprentice crawled to him, a look of fright on his face. Wend handed him his rifle. "Andrew, *today* you are a soldier. There's no choice; its fight or die."

The youth looked at Wend and nodded.

Wend said, "I want you to keep the Indians across the creek occupied. Every time they fire, or you see some movement, fire at that place."

Horner nodded again, took the firelock, and crawled to a place where he could brace it while keeping the other side of the creek in sight.

Wend crawled over beside the wounded Carver and picked up his musket. Then he took the bayonet from the man's frog, slammed it onto the muzzle and turned it until it locked on the lug.

Calvert, surprised, looked at Wend. "What's that for, Eckert?"

Wend shouted to all the squad, "Fix your bayonets!"

He was met with blank stares. Finally a private named Wickham said, "What are you doing, Lieutenant?"

Wend rose to one knee so that everyone could see him. "We've got to charge the Indians on that hill."

Wend saw a couple of men shake their heads in astonishment. Wickham, a young, mouthy man, said, "Charge? Are you crazy? We'll all be killed." He pointed to the slope. "You'll never get me to go up there!"

Wend retorted with every bit of confidence he could muster. "It's the only way; if we don't charge them they'll shoot us down one by one. An hour from now we'll all be like those people we buried up at Hart's Store." He waved at Martha Flannagan and her daughter. "You men going to let that happen to them?"

They looked at the women, but Wend could still see the doubt and fear lingering in their faces.

Another private shouted, "Wickham's right! There ain't no way we're going to beat those savages in hand to hand fighting."

Wend shouted, "Now listen, all of you! We won't have to fight them close up; they'll run if we charge at them in a determined way like we mean it. I saw it happen that way at Bushy Run time after time."

Suddenly Flannagan spoke up, "Eckert's right. I saw it work like that during the French War." He reached down and grabbed Wickham's musket from his hand. "Here, give me your bayonet. And you take my rifle." As he slammed the bayonet onto the muzzle, he looked at Wend. "It may be the death of me, but I'll go with you, Lieutenant."

Flannagan turned and took his wife's hand in his, and gave it a single squeeze. Then he gave his attention to checking out the musket.

Calvert had been looking up at Eckert and Flannagan. He shook his head, gritted his teeth and slowly pulled his bayonet from its sheath. He shouted to his men, "You heard the lieutenant, fix your bayonets."

There was abject fear on the faces of all the privates, but one by one they complied.

Wend said, "Listen now, this is how we'll do it: When I give the word, everyone stand up and we'll fire a quick volley at the crest where they've been showing themselves. That'll make them keep their heads down for a few seconds. Then give as loud and fierce a shout as you can and follow me. And keep shouting at the top of your voice as we go up the hill. Sound like you can't wait to get at the savages."

Wend looked at Wickham. "Since you've vowed you won't go with us, work with Horner and shoot at any warrior you see across the creek. Can you at least do that?" He put as much disdain into his voice as he could manage.

Wickham scowled at him but picked up Flannagan's rifle.

Wend called out, "Everyone loaded?"

There were nods all along the line. Wend took a deep breath and stood up. "All right lads, stand and fire with me."

All of the squad rose to their feet. Wend shouted, "Fire!" and was answered by a ragged volley. He took another deep breath and shouted "Haaaa!" at the top of his voice and started across the road toward the hill. He dared not look back to see if any of them were following him.

Then out of the corner of his right eye he saw Flannagan come up beside him. He looked to the left and was gratified to see Calvert. He thought: *Maybe three of us will be enough to start the Indians.*

Then he heard loud shouting behind and his heart skipped a beat; he saw that they were all there, screaming like wild animals, their bayonets gleaming bright in the afternoon sun.

And then Wend noticed the two dogs.

Swept up in the excitement, they were charging along with the men and barking furiously.

Greatly reassured, Wend pushed his way upward through the bushes of the slope. He heard the others crashing along. They were about a third of the way up the hill when the Indians started to break cover and run. A couple of them paused long enough to snap off quick shots. Wend saw one warrior supporting a compatriot as they moved and thought: *One of the shots from our volley must have hit home.*

As he watched the warriors run, Wend was overcome with an uncontrollable surge of exhilaration. *By God, it was working!* He picked up his pace, suddenly obsessed with the idea of getting to the top of the hill.

In another few seconds they were all at the crest. Wend paused; he could see the last of the Indians scampering down the hill. In a few seconds they vanished into the bush. Then a measure of rationality returned. He shouted, "Halt! For God's sake, stay here; don't go after them!"

Calvert grabbed the arm of one of the privates, now infused with excitement, who looked like he aimed to start down the hill after the war party. "Eckert's right; stop right here, all of you!"

Wend stood there, looking into the bush. His heart was racing like the pounding of a galloping horse's hooves and felt like it was trying to burst out of his chest. Wend took a deep breath to calm himself, then called out, "Everyone go to ground and take cover. Reload your muskets and be ready in case the Indians rally and try to hit us back."

A sudden question formed in his mind: What would tough old Sergeant McCulloch of the 77th think of it all? A quartermaster, a middle-aged farmer, eight reluctant militiamen, and two dogs rushing up a hill screaming like banshees in no real line or formation. McCulloch would probably have laughed his head off. Maybe he would have covered his eyes in disgust and shouted a series of epithets. Then Wend smiled to himself: *But damned if it hadn't worked.*

Wend put his hand on Calvert's shoulder and said, "Take charge up here, Corporal." Then he turned to Flannagan. "Henry, come with me. There were a couple of Indians across the creek. Let's go make sure they've left with the other ones."

The two of them moved along the crest until they could see the creek below them and the small hill on the other side where the Indian shooters had been.

Flannagan said, "I can't see 'nary a sign of them."

Neither could Wend. He fired a shot into the area where the shooters had been, and all remained quiet. Turning to Flannagan, he said, "Looks like they've gone, but there's only one way to be sure."

He led off down the hill, and then the two of them splashed through the creek and up the small hill with their bayonets at the charge until they reached the position where the Indians had been.

Flannagan looked at the ground and pointed. "You can see where they was, but they're sure 'nuff gone now."

Wend looked around at the hill. Even though it was not particularly high, it had a relatively level top. He decided it would be a good place for them to fort up. He shouted down to Horner and Cather. "Get everyone across the creek and up onto this hill. Bring the animals — there's a hollow on the other side where we can hold them." He turned to Flannagan. "Go tell Calvert to leave three men up on the hill to keep watch and then you and the rest of them go on down and help get your family and the wounded man across the creek."

"That I'll do, Mr. Eckert," Flannagan pointed at Wend's head, "and in case you don't know it, you're bleedin' from that crease in the side of your head."

Wend reached up and came away with a bloody hand. He had completely forgotten about the sting he had felt in the first moments of the ambush.

Soon they had established a secure position. The militiamen crouched under cover, muskets at the ready. They had constructed a makeshift litter for Carver and Martha Flannagan was tending to his wound as best she could. The ball was still in the man's chest, and he would need the services of a surgeon back at Fincastle. She had already put an improvised dressing and bandage on Wend's head. The horses and cattle were picketed in the hollow below them.

Wend had checked on The Mare and had been relieved to find that, while the wound on her rump was serious and surely painful, she could still walk.

That's where they were when Morgan found them.

The captain came in cautiously with a half-company moving in a broad skirmish line and the other half behind in column on the road, the line of skirmishers moving quietly through the bush like the experienced woodsman they were.

Wend didn't hear them coming. It was the lookouts on the high hill that caught glimpses of the men slipping through the forest. There was a shout from one of the lookouts: "The company's coming up, Lieutenant."

Wend walked down from the hill to the wagon track and waited for their arrival.

Momentarily he was surrounded by riflemen coming out of the bush onto the road, their weapons at the ready. Lieutenant Humphreys was directing the advance, and he came up to where Wend stood. He looked around. "What's the situation, Wend?"

"It's all right, John. The Indians are gone." Wend waved at the men. "They can stand easy."

Then Morgan arrived, accompanied by Baird and Zane. Behind them Wend could see Calmees and the other half-company stopped on the road.

Daniel motioned to the bandage on Wend's head. "Well, Dutchman, you all right?"

Wend nodded. "It's not much. But one of Wood's men is up there with a serious chest wound." He waved at the riflemen standing around them. "What took you so long coming?"

"Hell, Eckert, you're lucky we came at all. There was some ridges between us and they muffled the sound of the gunfire. You got to thank young Zane here for his sharp ears. We stopped for a short rest and suddenly he says to me, 'I just heard gunfire.' So I motioned everyone to be quiet. And then we was able to hear a bunch of shots, like it was a volley. It was so faint that we would never have heard them if we was marching. Then there was some scattered shots." He shrugged. "So it was pretty clear you were in trouble back here."

Wend told them how the ambush started.

Joshua asked, "How many of them was there?"

Wend answered, "At least two on this side of the creek and seven or eight on the high hill firing down on us."

Joshua stared into the distance as he thought about Wend's words.

Wend said, "I think it was the largest group from the war party. The one you didn't trail. I think they doubled back to hit a vulnerable part of the column. They knew soldiers would be sent out from the fort to clean up things at Hart's Store."

Joshua replied, "Could just as easily been a separate war party. There's several workin' this area. Could have been John Logan himself."

Wend shook his head. "No Joshua, I don't think that's likely. I've been working this out in my head while we were waiting for the company to come back. Remember that Flannagan told us there was a big argument among the war party leaders while they were at his place? The next morning they left by separate trails. I think the argument was because the leader of the big group wanted to continue raiding and the others wanted to go home. It was that group which picked up the column and saw that the rearguard was vulnerable."

Morgan nodded slowly. "You know, Joshua, Eckert makes sense. Particularly if he's right about the number of savages that attacked."

Joshua scowled. "I still think it could have been a new war party. Ain't no real evidence it was part of Laughing Eyes' outfit."

Wend stared at the scout. *Why was Baird being so obstinate and defensive?* Then it came to him: *Joshua's miffed because he's not used to having his advice contradicted. And deep down he's still upset because he's been cut out of scouting for the expedition into the Ohio Country.*

Wend's thoughts were interrupted by Humphreys. He waved up to the hillock where they had forted up. "So you got everyone across the stream to this hill and held out until we came back." He nodded and patted Wend on the arm. "Not bad work under fire, particularly with this motley collection and a seriously wounded man."

Morgan nodded and smiled broadly and winked at Baird. "Yeah, it's not too bad for a gunsmith playin' the part of a quartermaster. I'm just sorry it took so long for us to come back and relieve you. I figure the war party took off when they heard us coming." Daniel's face wrinkled up as he thought of something. "Only thing what puzzles me is why we didn't hear much shootin' after the first few volleys."

Henry Flannagan had come up to the group. He laughed loudly at Morgan's words. "Cap'n, you didn't hear a lot of firing 'cause Mr. Eckert drove off the Indians long before you got here. He led a charge with bayonets up that hill over there." He pointed to the high ridge with his thumb. "Made the war party skedaddle as fast as their legs could carry them. It was as good a charge as I ever saw back in the old Virginia Regiment. And if Mr. Eckert hadn't got the men to go up that hill, we'd 'ave been layin' dead over there across the creek instead of waitin' for you here."

Morgan cocked his head and looked askance at Wend. "I'll be damned. Now where did you ever get the idea to do something like that, Eckert?"

Wend couldn't resist. He smiled broadly. "Why Daniel, I learned it from one of those insufferable, arrogant British officers you find so repulsive. It seems that once in a while they have a useful idea, if you listen to what they're saying."

* * *

The day after the return to Fort Fincastle from Hart's Store, Wend busied himself with treating The Mare's wound. But the fact that the black horse was at the picket line at all was the result of Wend winning a short — but intense — argument with Morgan.

After Morgan and his men had come to the relief of the afterguard, the column had made preparations to resume the march. Wend brought The Mare out from the little copse where they had picketed all the livestock; he planned to personally lead the injured horse all the way back to Wheeling. Morgan noticed the horse's wound and the limp of her right rear leg. He came over and examined the wound.

The big captain pointed to The Mare's right haunch. "Look at the gouge that ball made. It's done real damage to the leg muscles of your horse. She'll never move fast enough to keep up with the column. We'll have to slow way down for you to stay with us and we'll not get back 'till late at night."

Wend shook his head. "She'll keep up, Daniel. She's got a lot of heart."

"Not likely, Wend. And that's a hell of a deep wound; I say she ain't never going to be the same. Fact is, she may be permanently lame. You'll be kind to the animal if you take her over in the bush and shoot her, Eckert."

Wend felt himself getting hot. "Daniel, this horse and I have been together for twelve years. We've been through war and the foulest storms and she's never let me down. I'm not going to end her life over a graze in her haunch."

Morgan set his jaw. "That's more than a 'graze.' Eckert. It's torn up her flesh badly. But I can understand you bein' too close to the horse to shoot her. Give me the reins and I'll go do it."

"Dan, no one's shooting this horse today. I'm getting her back to Wheeling and treating her till she's mended."

"Look, Wend, we're going to be leaving for the Ohio Country any time now. Who's going to take care of her? That wound's liable to mortify. She'll end up with one of Crawford's men shooting her." He looked around at the men ready to resume the march. "We can't delay any longer; I got to get back to Fincastle and make my report to McDonald."

"All right, Daniel, you go ahead. Put Calmees in charge of the rearguard. I'll lead the horse back alone. But I'm telling you now, the way the rearguard will be moving, I won't be that far behind."

"Are you crazy, Eckert? You just fought off a war party. What if they're still skulkin' around? You'll be easy pickings."

Wend reached up and stroked The Mare's mane and then her muzzle. The horse nudged him in return. "I'll take that chance, Daniel. I'm determined this horse is going to finish her days in the pasture at Eckert Ridge."

Joshua and Jonathan Zane were nearby, listening. Joshua stood quietly, staring into the distance, his arms folded, obviously not willing to help Wend.

But then Zane spoke up. "Eckert's right about one thing: The rearguard's going to move pretty slow. Them women are on foot now and there's the wounded man to carry. They're going to hold you up Cap'n, even without the wounded horse. Why don't you give Eckert a few more men for protection? Then the rearguard can move at its own pace all the way back to Wheeling while your company marches fast, so you can report to Major McDonald. I'll go with them to help guide the way and be on the lookout for any sign of the war party." He looked over at Joshua. "Anyway, I don't think them Indians is coming back. Eckert here gave them enough of a thrashing."

Finally Joshua spoke up. "That's not a bad idea, Daniel. Them warriors ain't goin' to want to come back in the night."

Morgan set his jaw and stood silent for a long time. "I don't like splittin' the column and not bringin' all my men back together." He hesitated and looked at Wend and then Zane. "All right, Eckert: I'll give you another squad and you can move at your own speed. But I ain't takin' responsibility if somethin' happens."

And shortly thereafter, Morgan marched the company off at a rapid gait. Wend's rearguard moved at a slower pace, accommodating the women and the men carrying the litter. The Mare was obviously in pain as they continued the march. But the animal knew what was required of her; she moved in a determined way, fighting not to show the pain. She whimpered but a few times — only when her injured leg was jarred by stepping into a deep rut or, when in the darkness, she stumbled on the uneven road.

In the end, the rearguard finally straggled into the camp at Wheeling just after midnight. Their journey had been aided by light from the moon, but mostly they had benefitted from the knowledge and youthful eyes of Jonathan Zane, who kept them on the trail.

Now, in the brightness of the morning, after a modicum of sleep, Wend was faced with the reality of treating The Mare's wound. He had a bucket of clean water and some rags he had boiled to ensure cleanliness. He worked to wash out the wound, which was hard because the horse tried to resist and move away every time he put the damp rag into the wound.

After a half hour, he had done about as much as he could. But he was worried about The Mare's future. For Morgan had been right about one thing: Undoubtedly the expedition would depart any day now and he would have to leave the animal tied to the picket line with all the other horses. He knew she wouldn't receive the individual attention she required to heal properly. And if the wound did mortify, she would have to be destroyed.

Wend came to the realization that his animal's survival might require some sort of a miracle. He had no sooner had that thought then he heard the voice of an angel speaking to him.

"That's a beautiful horse; one of the finest I've ever seen."

Wend turned to see a pretty young girl of nine or ten standing a few feet away, looking at The Mare with admiring eyes. She had dark hair down over her shoulders which reminded him of Peggy, and had the same gleam in her eyes when she grinned.

Wend smiled. "She is indeed. And she's carried me faithfully for many years." He patted The Mare's flank. "And she's borne many a foal. She's the mother of some fine horses back at my place."

The girl smiled back. "She's big for a mare, ain't she Mister? I'll bet she can jump pretty well."

"She soars like a hawk when she goes over a fence or a small stream. And it doesn't seem like she's making any effort at all." He looked at The Mare for a few seconds. "But she's starting to feel her age. I may put her out to pasture when this trip is over."

The girl nodded, then looked up at the horse's wound. "You must be Mr. Eckert; my brother told me how you refused to shoot her after she was hit." She smiled again and said, "My name's Elizabeth Zane. But everybody calls me Betty. "

Wend grinned. "Well now, that's interesting. You see, you look a lot like my wife. And she's named Elizabeth, too. But we call her Peggy."

The little girl smiled and moved closer to The Mare. "Where did you get this horse, Mr. Eckert?"

"In a place called Sherman Valley, in Pennsylvania, just north of Carlisle."

"I'll bet you paid a lot for her."

"Actually, I didn't pay any cash. A man traded her for one of my rifles." Wend paused a second, then added, "When I'm not with the militia, I'm a gunsmith."

The girl circumnavigated The Mare, looking her over with appraising eyes, and stopped to stare at the wound. "That's pretty serious. It would be a shame to have to put a horse like this down."

"Yes, that's what I'm worried about. When we go after the Shawnees, I don't think she'll get the care she needs."

Betty Zane smiled broadly. "Well, why don't you bring her over to our barn? My aunt and I could take care of her. She's a great doctor. She treats everyone around here and the animals, too, when they need it."

Wend's heart skipped a beat. But then he realized he couldn't accept the offer of a child. "I couldn't impose on your family."

Suddenly a familiar male voice interrupted. "It's all right, Wend. It won't be a problem."

Wend looked up to see Jonathan Zane standing with his arms folded. "Fact is, I already told Ebenezer's wife, Elizabeth, about the horse. She and Betty here will take care of it. And when she's stronger, The Mare can graze in our pasture 'till you get back from the raid."

Betty Zane looked up at Wend, her eyes sparkling. "And when she's better, I can ride her."

A thrill of relief washed over Wend. "Of course you can, Betty. In fact, she'll need somebody to exercise her."

Jonathan said, "Then that's decided. Let's get her over to our stable. Elizabeth expects her."

And so, with Betty leading The Mare, Jonathan and Wend carrying her tack, they led the animal to her temporary home.

PART THREE

The Border Rifles

July – September 1774

CHAPTER THIRTEEN
The Pursuit of Peggy

The morning sun was bright and hot as Geoffrey Caulfield rode northward up the Great Wagon Road toward Winchester. He felt perspiration welling up under his shirt and coat. The big hunter had also worked up a sheen of sweat as they had traveled up from the camp, which was now several miles south of the town in a pleasant, isolated cove a half mile off the road. As horse and rider entered town, the wagon road turned into Loudoun Street, one of two principal thoroughfares in Winchester.

On his left side, beyond the houses which lined the street, Caulfield could see the vegetable gardens and orchards of the town's outlots. By law, each lot sold in the town consisted of two parts: A house site on one of the principal streets and a parcel on the outskirts to be used for agricultural purposes. In passing, he noted that the crops and even the fruit trees looked wilted from the summer heat.

By design, he was going to town on the Court Day for the month. As he rode, Caulfield could hear the hubbub from the crowd over on Market Street. As he passed the western end of the town square, which stretched between Market and Loudoun, he could see people milling about the vendor stands. But for now he paid little attention, in fact spurring his horse ahead to move rapidly past the square and arrive at his first destination of the day, which was Fort Loudoun.

Caulfield's main mission in Winchester was to scope out targets for his band of highwaymen. He knew that travelers and freight waggoners camped on the open area around the fort while staying in the town. He wanted to survey the traffic likely to be moving southward in the next few days.

Caulfield mused how different the business of a highwayman was here in the colonies than in Britain. In the home isles, the prey was generally fast post coaches and private carriages from which the purses and jewelry of the

passengers were easily taken and provided ready spending money for the robbers. He smiled to himself. When he and Quinn had first gotten started around
Williamsburg three years ago, it had been like that; they had prospered taking
purses and valuables from rich planters traveling by carriage or horse. They
had added to their crew and ranged through the Tidewater. But eventually the
local sheriffs had put together a network of patrols which made life dangerous
for them and they had moved up to the far safer Piedmont and Valley area. In
a locale of smaller, less prosperous plantations and settlers' farms, the nature of
their booty had necessarily changed. Taking purses from well-off people, such as
had occurred with the Eckerts, was rare. The amount of actual coin that fell into
their hands was limited. Instead, they most often ended up taking food, clothing, and implements which would be useful to them or could be exchanged for
barter or cash. It took more work, but, all in all, the crew lived reasonably well.

When Geoffrey reached the fort, he reined in the hunter to a walk, turned
eastward onto Fairfax Lane, and carefully observed the wagons, carts, and
freighters parked around the fortification. He was particularly pleased to see
that heavily loaded carts and farm-style wagons predominated. These bespoke
of pilgrims migrating southward toward the upper valley of Virginia and the
Carolinas. They were often more provident targets than the freighters, for they
would be carrying a wider range of provisions, household effects, and other
items the highwaymen could easily convert into money. Moreover, settlers were
likely to have a supply of cash stashed somewhere in their rig. So Caulfield and
Quinn had developed a technique of stopping likely wagons, leading them to
an isolated spot off the road, and taking their time thoroughly searching the
contents to ensure that they took the most valuable possessions and any money
which could be located. It was more dangerous than a quick stop of a coach or
carriage, but then one had to adapt to local conditions.

Having finished his reconnaissance, Caulfield turned southward onto
Market Street and pulled up momentarily to take in the busy sight. Most of the
shopkeepers had put some of their wares on display on tables in front of their
stores and numerous traveling vendors had come to place their products before
the people of Frederick County. Geoffrey could see that a fulsome crowd was
strolling up and down the street, examining the items on display. He carefully
walked the stallion forward, taking care to avoid the heavy foot traffic. When he
arrived at the square he found that most of the farmers had set up their produce
stands there. The contingent of traveling peddlers sold their wares from wagons
or had spread their products out on tables or ground cloths. The heaviest crowd
of shoppers was also in the square, for many of the goods there were often

available only once a month on court days. Caulfield pulled up his horse, taking in the different items on display. After a few moments, he dismounted and led his horse over to the Golden Buck Inn on Market Street across from the square. He tied the animal to one of the hitching posts and then turned to walk back into the square to view the activity in detail.

As he did so, he noted that the McDonald carriage was parked in the stableyard of the inn and he surmised that Anna McDonald was within; perhaps for a lunch date with friends.

Caulfield tucked that intelligence away in his mind and strolled around the square, eyeing the vendors' goods. One of the first he came to was a dealer in various paper products: writing parchment, ink, song sheets, broadsides, and large sized, rectangular papers printed with designs for table games featuring dice. He moved on and soon came to a troup of entertainers — acrobats and jugglers — who had drawn a large crowd, including many children. People were clapping and throwing coins in appreciation. Geoffrey recognized the people in the troup; he had seen them perform at Fredericksburg a few months before. Then he walked past a series of farmers' booths without paying much attention to the fruits and vegetables on display.

He also moved past a man selling cordage, another selling pottery, and the display of a harness maker.

But the next vendor was of great interest to him. It was an iron monger, working out of a large wagon. A selection of wares was displayed on the lowered tailgate and on tables. They included pots, frying pans, tools, locks, and other useful metal items. The peddler was a small, wiry man with a shock of black hair and a day's growth of scrubby facial hair, at the moment bending over a table. It was, in fact, a Welshman named Rhys and Caulfield's gang had done business with the man before.

Caulfield stopped and said, "Hello, Rhys. I might have expected to find you here."

Rhys stood up, turned around and saw Caulfield standing there. "Why bless my soul, its Mr. Caulfield! A pleasure, sir. It's a pleasure indeed!" Wymat winked. "I had no idea you were here in Frederick County."

Geoffrey shrugged. "Well, my business does take me to many places. I guess we last saw you down in Culpeper."

Rhys sidled up close to Caulfield and whispered, "You don't happen to have any goods I could use, do you? I've been on the road a while; my inventory is getting thin and I'm expecting to have good sales here. When I leave, I'll need to restock."

Caulfield shook his head. "Not at this instant, Rhys." He gave the peddler a sharp look. "Besides, why should I continue to trade with you? The price you gave us last time hardly made it worthwhile."

"Now don't get angry, Mr. Caulfield! Let's be honest, who else are you going to deal with, sir? I don't think I'm overstating the situation to suggest that local merchants might be a wee bit suspicious of the source of your goods, considering all the activity of highwaymen in this area." He shook his head. "And I might point out that there's a lot of anger about all the travelers being robbed, particularly the migrant families being relieved of their goods and life's savings."

Caulfield sighed. He knew Rhys was correct; he would have to deal with the man. Then he thought of the number of pilgrim rigs he had seen up by Fort Loudoun, likely to take road southward in the next day or two. "All right, Rhys, you're a bloody scoundrel of the first order. But you have me in a hard positon. Here's the proposition: If you could arrange to be in Stephensburg five days hence, I'll just about guarantee we can bring you a goodly quantity of items you'll be happy to purchase."

A wide smile broke out on the Welshman's face. "I'll be there, Mr. Caulfield, and ready to pay the usual price." He thought a moment. "I'd be especially keen to buy locks and keys, if you could get your hands on some. I might find it possible to give you a premium price for those items."

"Good enough," Geoffrey put his hand on the monger's shoulder. "We'll be there. But don't be anxious if we're a day or two late." He cleared his throat. "Obviously my source of supply is subject to the vagaries of an uncertain schedule."

Rhys gave Caulfield a sly smile. "Oh, now don't I understand that! I'll be there, sir, camping on the outskirts of town."

"Good, Rhys; we'll find you. But let me be plain about it: I want cash — no barter. Do you hear me?"

"Don't you worry, Mr. Caulfield. I'll pay with the King's coin."

Caulfield said, "See you don't disappoint me." Then he nodded to the iron monger and moved on.

He noted that over at the courthouse, lawyers and their clients had gathered near the front door, waiting for their cases to come up or discussing the outcome of those already tried. Caulfield knew that there were a few lawyers who resided in the town, but that a considerable number rode in for court day; some from Alexandria, others Fredericksburg. Geoffrey smiled when he spied Sheriff Smith talking with two other men. *At least today we can be sure he's not out looking for us.*

Caulfield was standing before another vendor's wagon when he looked across the square just in time to see Peggy Eckert's little black chaise pull up to the Golden Buck. The leather top was up to shade the passengers from the strong sun. Geoffrey strained to make out the occupants, who were obscured by the top. The first person to emerge was Alice Downy, whom he had met the day the militia departed. For a moment he was worried that Peggy was not along, but almost instantly he was relieved to see her climb down from the chaise and join Alice alongside. Both women were looking up the street, shading their eyes from the sun. Then Caulfield saw the object of their attention. A farm wagon pulled by a team came into view and drew up to a stop behind the chaise. It was driven by a young man, who he took to be a farmhand, and next to him was another woman, one whom he had never seen. In the back of the wagon was a black woman Caulfield recognized as the Eckert's cook.

Geoffrey easily appraised the situation: *The women of Eckert Ridge out for a shopping trip on Court Day.*

The occupants of the wagon dismounted and all the women save Peggy took shopping baskets from the bed. The farmhand took the reins of the chaise and led it into the courtyard of the inn. Then he came back to do the same with the wagon. Meanwhile, the four women spent a moment talking and Geoffrey could see Peggy motioning toward the square and then along Market Street. Soon all of them except Peggy crossed the street to the square.

As Caulfield watched, Peggy turned around and headed toward the entrance of the Golden Buck. Then she abruptly stopped and turned her head to look at something up the street; after a moment she walked toward the inn's court-yard. Suddenly he realized the object of her attention was his stallion, standing quietly at the hitching rack near the courtyard entrance. She stopped a few feet away and stared at the horse for a moment, then made a quick look around. Caulfield took a step backward to shelter behind the vendor wagon; after a few seconds he peeked out, just in time to see Peggy walk up the steps of the inn and disappear within.

Two thoughts came to Caulfield's mind: The first was that Peggy had recognized his horse and knew he was in town. The second was that she was meeting with Anna McDonald in the Golden Buck.

Geoffrey felt a surge of delight in his heart. After surveying the number of potential targets for his men, his second hoped-for objective of the day had been to find a way to engage with the beautiful Mrs. Eckert. He had dared to hope she would be in town for Court Day and now chance had delivered her to him. Clearly he was under a lucky star today!

But the question was how to find a plausible excuse to spend time with her. He pondered a moment and then an inspiration came to him. He strode off, retracing his steps back around the square to the display of the stationer. Going to the printed papers that represented table games, he paged through the stack until he found the one he wanted. He then sorted through another stack until he found the rules of the game. He carried both sheets to the stationer. He presented the gamepaper to the man and said, "I'll need dice also; do you have them available?"

"Naturally, sir," the stationer answered. "And you've selected a game which is very popular right now."

Caulfield handed him money for the items. "Yes, my good fellow; why else would I have purchased it?" He handed the papers to the stationer. "Please roll up the papers and tie it with a ribbon." He paused and looked over at the Golden Buck. "And make haste if you will, for I'm hurrying to an important engagement."

* * *

"Good morning to all of you." Caulfield rose from the deep bow he had made to the women at the table in the back corner of the inn. "I came in here to escape the beastly heat on the street and find that I have the good fortune to encounter three elegant ladies taking their leisure."

As he had expected, Anna McDonald and Peggy Eckert sat at the table. He was not particularly surprised to see that James Wood's fiancée, Jean Moncure, was with them. All three had cups of tea before them.

Anna McDonald burst out, "Why Geoffrey, it's been weeks since I've seen you. Whatever have you been doing?"

Peggy Eckert looked at him with a crooked smile on her face. "Yes, indeed; that's a very good question, Geoffrey. I thought you were here looking for land. Surely you could have finished with that by now and been on your way back to the Tidewater. Have you bought some property? Or do you have," she raised her hand in a questioning gesture, "*other* business which is keeping you riding the roads around Winchester?"

The tone of Peggy's voice put Caulfield on alert. "Actually, I haven't. Since I didn't find what I was looking for here in Frederick County, I've been riding up to the north in my search; sometimes as far as the Potomac."

Peggy raised an eyebrow, gave him an inquisitive look, and said, "Well, Geoffrey, if you are looking for property up to the north, how is it that we find you in Winchester today?"

Caulfield sought to change the subject of the conversation. "Why, I come back to Winchester every so often for the entertainment. There's nothing but farmsteads and lonely country taverns up in the north. But frankly I spend as much time in Winchester as I can because of its charming ladies."

Jean smiled up at him. "Why, that was very gallantly said, Geoffrey."

"Oh, indeed, sir; extremely gallant, as you always are," said Anna. She waved to the empty chair at the table. "You must join us, Geoffrey."

Peggy Eckert said, in a flat tone which was just one step away from boredom, "Oh yes, by all means join us. I'm sure we will find your presence," she hesitated a moment, looking directly into his eyes, "*amusing.*"

Geoffrey thought: *Damn! She's playing with me.* But he sat down and waved to a server for a cup of tea. Meanwhile, he laid the rolled up papers in his lap.

The action caught Jean's eyes and she asked, "Geoffrey, if I may be so bold, what is that roll of paper you're being so careful with? Have you had legal business over at the court?"

Caulfield looked around at the ladies with his widest smile. "Nothing so serious, Miss Moncure; I happened to stop by the stand of a stationer and perchance found a game for amusement."

Peggy laughed. "Can I assume it's a diversion for your nightly entertainment in those taverns in the rough country up north?"

Caulfield forced a broad smile and looked her right in the eye. "Why, precisely, Mrs. Eckert."

Peggy gave him a cool look. "And what game would that be, Geoffrey? Given your tastes, I expect it has something to do with dice and gambling."

Caulfield grinned. "Well, ladies, you must admit that a game must have some element of chance to be intriguing, don't you?"

Jean nodded eagerly. "Oh, you are so right, Mr. Caulfield."

Peggy asked, "So what is this exciting game you've purchased?"

Geoffrey smiled at each of the ladies in turn. Then he ostentatiously unrolled the paper, taking the instruction sheet out and laying it on the table. He held up the game board sheet so that all could see.

Jean clapped her hands and exclaimed, "Oh excellent, Geoffrey! It's the Goose Game!"

Caulfield held up his hand. "By all means, ladies, let us call it by its proper and complete name, *The Royal and Most Pleasant Game of ye Goose.*"

Jean looked around at all her compatriots. "James told me it's all the rage down in Williamsburg. Even the governor plays!"

Anna said, "I've heard people mention it, but I never knew much about it." She looked at the game board sheet. "I take it you move from square to square along the path?"

"Yes, that's right, Mrs. McDonald. Each square presents a hazard or a boon. And your movement is dictated by the roll of the dice." He held up the pair he had purchased.

Anna put her hands together in front of her chest. "Geoffrey, it does look so entertaining."

Caulfield looked around the table with his best smile. "I have just had a capital idea! We have everything we need to play, including the rules. Let me engage one of proprietor Bush's back rooms. I propose we spend a pleasant afternoon engaged in the game."

Jean Moncure shook her head. "I love the idea, Geoffrey, but I must get back to Glen Burnie for an appointment. James' mother expects me."

Peggy looked at Caulfield. "I can't play either. I'm here with all the women of our farm and our cook. I must join them to help complete their shopping."

Anna looked around the table and shook her head. "Geoffrey, all of us have things we must do today; we haven't the leisure to stay here this afternoon. But I do have an idea: Why don't we all make plans to gather at my house two days hence to play the game? Then we can have a pleasant and entertaining afternoon."

All the women nodded; Geoffrey had no choice but to agree.

After that, there was a momentary silence at the table and then Anna looked up and said, "Why, there's Sheriff Smith and he's coming toward us."

Momentarily the sheriff was standing over their table. "Good afternoon, ladies." His hat was under his arm and he touched his forehead in respect to them. Then he looked down and said, "Hello, Caulfield; haven't seen you for a goodly while."

Peggy spoke up. "Why sheriff, how is your search for that band of brigands coming?"

"I'm looking for them; can't do as much as I would like, what with so many men away with the militia." He thought a moment. "But one thing's for sure: They've moved to the Great Wagon Road and they're preying on travelers and pilgrims, the bastards."

Jean Moncure looked at Caulfield. "Why Geoffrey, you're traveling that road all the time. Aren't you afraid of being accosted by the thieves?"

Smith looked at Caulfield. "Indeed you should be worried, particularly if you travel alone."

Caulfield was formulating an answer when suddenly Peggy Eckert spoke up; she had a coy grin on her face.

"Why Sheriff, don't you know that Geoffrey has absolutely nothing to fear from the highwaymen? Nothing to fear at all, and he's quite aware of it."

Panic hit Caulfield. *My God, the woman knows about me because I sent the necklace back. Is she going to expose me? Can she be that ungrateful?* But he willed himself to answer with a steady voice. "I'm not sure what you mean, Mrs. Eckert."

The sheriff said, "Yes, what do you mean, ma'am? It's quite true that the roads are dangerous for a lone traveler. The brigands took a purse from a man riding alone north of here last week."

"Be that as it may, Sheriff, I maintain that Geoffrey Caulfield has nothing to fear from the gang. I invite you to go out and look at the tall hunter he's hitched out in front of the inn. It's the most powerful animal I've ever laid eyes on. He'll just turn and ride right away from them, flying over fences as need be. I saw their horses, the night they robbed us; their mounts are rather poor examples of the species." She smiled and then continued, "And of course he owns a brace of my husband's fine pistols. I'd say if the highwaymen encounter him, they're the ones in trouble."

The other women laughed; Smith smiled and said, "I take your point, Mrs. Eckert." He turned and looked at Caulfield. "But just the same, take care when you ride the Wagon Road."

Caulfield could feel the tension draining out of him. He asked, "So Sheriff, with Court Day complete, I take it you'll be after the highwaymen again tomorrow?"

"Wish I could, Caulfield. But instead I must be after a runaway slave. Mrs. Stephens' house maid, Brown Sarah, has gone on the run. She disappeared two days ago. She went night walking, supposedly to see relatives owned by the Barrows, and never returned in the morning. Her relatives said she never came to the Barrow estate that night. It's like she just vanished into the darkness."

Jean Moncure sighed. "I know that girl. I've seen her at the Stephens. She's light-skinned, truly nice, and very efficient. I'd never guess she'd go on the run."

Anna shook her head. "I know the girl also; but certainly this can't end well for her. What a shame."

Smith nodded. "You're right about that, Mrs. McDonald. But there's more of a mystery about her disappearance than originally meets the eye. She's been telling the Stephens that she was going over to the Barrows' at night several times a week, but she has only been there a couple of times. Clearly she's actually been going somewhere else." He shook his head. "We're going to put patrols out tomorrow. We can't let the other slaves see her make an escape." He shrugged. "But we don't have a clue where she went; nobody's seen any sign of her. I'd give a purse to know where she is at this moment."

Caulfield knew precisely where Sarah was: sitting by the fire at his camp. The truth was, she and the black man in his band, Isaac, had by chance met in town weeks ago and they had been seeing each other ever since. A week ago Isaac had convinced her to join them.

Peggy put her hand on her chin. "That is indeed a strange story, Sheriff. And I'm distressed that this will distract from your efforts to find that gang of bandits that robbed Wend and I."

Smith grimaced. "Unfortunately, Mrs. Eckert, my resources are stretched. But by God, I promise that sooner or later, we will bring justice to those scoundrels."

Peggy looked across the table at Caulfield with a devilish look on her face. "Yes, I wish you luck in that, Sheriff. By the way, do you have any information on who is leading this band of renegades?"

Smith said, "You know Mrs. Eckert, it's interesting that you should bring that up. The robbers always wear hoods or masks over their faces. But the victims report that the man who does most of the talking has a deep Irish accent."

"Indeed, Mr. Smith," Peggy said. "I remember *that* man well. He viciously knocked Wend around."

"Yes, he's a brute. However, sometimes there's a man with a cultured accent who gives instructions or talks to the unfortunate travelers. We think he's the one who actually commands the group and does the thinking."

Peggy looked back at Caulfield and gave him her sweetest smile. "Then I shall take great pleasure in seeing that gentleman get what's coming to him."

Caulfield set his jaw and stared back at Peggy.

Anna McDonald cleared her throat. "Well, I think we've engaged ourselves enough with these sordid matters. But I'm glad you're here, Sheriff, because I wanted you to know that I've just received a letter from Angus, which has news of the expedition. And you can pass the news around town."

All the women straightened in their chairs.

Smith smiled broadly. "That would be my pleasure, ma'am. I must tell you I've been getting many inquiries."

Jean Moncure said, "I haven't received any news at all. Tell us, Anna, have they been in action?"

Anna responded, "No, but I'll get to that in a second. Sheriff, I know everyone in town has been frustrated that we have no information from the men, but Angus says that's because they've been so isolated. They're at a place called Wheeling, and everything has to go through Pittsburgh. But he was finally able to get a message up to Pittsburgh by boat so it could be carried down here by someone traveling Braddock's Road."

Jean exclaimed, "Pray don't keep us waiting Anna; what did Angus write?"

Peggy said, "They were forced to leave here in a matter of days so they could quickly strike the Shawnee. That was weeks ago. Why hasn't something happened?"

Anna held up her hands. "Don't be mad at me, Peggy, I know you weren't happy that Wend had to go. But I'm just the messenger." She paused to gather her thoughts. "Angus says they've been told to wait because the governor's representative, Major Connolly, is still negotiating with the Shawnee chiefs, and particularly the main one, named Cornstalk."

Jean Moncure giggled. "Cornstalk? Where do the savages get these names? That's hardly a dignified name for the leader of a large tribe."

Anna replied, "Well, regardless, that's what they call him." Then she continued, "So meanwhile they are busy building a stockade, to be called Fort Fincastle, which will serve as a base for operations and a shelter for settlers in the area. Angus says the men aren't very happy about being forced to do labor instead of marching to the attack."

Smith grinned. "I can understand that."

Anna continued, "But Angus said, just as he was writing the letter, they learned of a war party attack on a nearby village, called Hart's Store. The Indians killed most of the people in the village and burned it to the ground. So he sent a column up to the village to bury the dead and find out what they could about the war party. Dan Morgan was the commander of the column and," she looked at Peggy, "Wend went along in his role of the battalion quartermaster with a party of men to bury the dead and gather up any provisions they could salvage. The column had just marched off when Angus finished the letter to get it on a boat up to Pittsburgh."

Jean turned to Peggy. "Poor Wend; I hate to think of him having to supervise the grim work of burying all those people."

Caulfield watched the expression on Peggy's face. She simply set her lips and he could see the muscles tightening on her face. Finally, she shrugged and said to the table in general, "Well, Wend will do his job, no matter how distasteful."

There was a short interval of silence at the table and Caulfield thought: *So Eckert is the quartermaster of the expedition.* He mentally laughed to himself. *Now there's a job which well suits the man.* It was impossible for Geoffrey to visualize the dour tradesman leading a company of soldiers in action.

Anna turned back to the sheriff. "Angus said that all the companies that were to make up his battalion had arrived at Wheeling and that they were ready to go as soon as Connolly gives them the word. And he said he would try to send me another letter just before they left, so we'll know when they've started."

Smith nodded. "Well, that's not much news, but it is better than nothing. I'll start to spread the word." He touched his forehead to the women and turned for the door.

Peggy Eckert pushed her cup and saucer away from her. "Anna, I must be going also. I promised to help Alice Downy and my cook with the shopping." She stood up. "I'm so glad for the news from Angus." She turned to Caulfield, "It's been nice seeing you again, Geoffrey. I can't wait to play the game with you."

Geoffrey stood up, as did the other women. He waved his hand over the table. "I must insist on paying for your tea, ladies; it's the least I can do after enjoying the pleasure of your company."

All three smiled and thanked him and then were off. Caulfield went up to the bar and paid Bush, then headed for the front steps.

When he opened the door, he found Peggy was standing there at the top of the steps, scanning the square and Market Street. She turned and noticed Caulfield. "I'm trying to see where Alice might be," she remarked.

Caulfield grinned. *This was the opportunity he had been waiting for.* "Mrs. Eckert, permit me to assist you through the crush of the crowd and help you find your companion."

"Why Geoffrey, that's so gentlemanly of you. But you would find it all *so* boring; I mean, walking with a woman while she shops at all these booths?" She pointed up Market Street. "In fact, I think I see Alice over there. I'll just stroll up there myself; don't put yourself out." She quickly stepped down to the ground. Then she looked up at him with a knowing smile. "Besides, I should think you might want to catch up with Sheriff Smith and find out more about his plans and what he knows about those wicked highwaymen. For a traveling man like yourself, that would be much more interesting and useful."

Then she turned and walked briskly up Market Street.

Frustrated, Caulfield stood there and crossed his arms, lost in thought. He shook his head in irony. *I came to play a game of enticement with her and she turned the tables on me.* He sighed, then came to a happy realization. *She wouldn't be toying with me this way if she wasn't interested. But one thing is sure: She is definitely a more complicated and brazen woman than I ever imagined.* A thrill of desire ran through him. *Now who would have expected to find such a lady here in the back country?*

* * *

Caulfield, smoking his pipe, sat on a log next to the creek and looked up at Quinn, who stood leaning against a tree. They were at an isolated spot more than fifty yards upstream from the gang's camp; it was a place the two often came to talk and lay plans away from the others.

Caulfield said, "Well, Quinn, you called this intimate little meeting. What's on your mind?"

Quinn looked into the distance. "I wanted to talk about that job we did yesterday. I don't mind saying it's been bothering me all day."

"Bothering you? What the hell do you mean? Damn, that was a *good* piece of work. Those people were a big family, with three generations traveling together. They had a wagon and cart, both loaded with a trove of goods we can use and others we can sell. We'll get some hard money from Rhys when we go up to Stephensburg and do our trading." Geoffrey smiled. "And that girl Sarah; she's going to be a great addition to our crew. Look at the way she sniffed out their money, like a hound going after a fox. All that time she's been in house-hold service taught her where people hide their coins when they're traveling." He paused and waved his hand, "Not to mention she's a damn good cook."

Quinn crossed his arms. "Here's the truth of it, Cap'n: I'm getting fed up with takin' goods and money from pilgrim families. These people are just look-ing to find a place where they can make a living."

Caulfield put his head back and laughed. "For God's sake, Quinn; those are damn strange words from a highwayman who escaped an English gallows by a whisker and was lucky enough to bribe his way onto a ship bound for Norfolk."

"I've no worry about lifting fat purses off swells on post coaches, or takin' jewels from perfumed women in rich gowns, like back in England or down in the Tidewater. I'll do it every day of the week, and Sunday too, with not a second thought. I don't mind sayin' I got rare enjoyment from takin' that purse and them pistols from that gentleman we robbed on the road north of Winchester last week. But taking the life savings and goods of these pilgrims, as little as it be, is sticking in me craw. They ain't rich; they're just ordinary folks like us."

"Quinn, we've been up here in the valley for months, stopping travelers like the ones yesterday; how come you're suddenly getting a conscience?"

"The truth is, it's been botherin' me for weeks. But I'll tell you what brought things to a head: It was that old woman, the grandmother of that family. She's real Irish, just like me, and she damn well reminded me of me own sainted mother: looked like her and talked like her. And then when Sarah found their money in the bottom of that keg, and I watched the way she broke down, crying and beggin' us not to take their stake, I tell you, it surely grabbed my heart."

Caulfield couldn't keep the disdain off his face or out of his voice. "You're really going soft, Quinn. She may be Irish, but she made the choice to marry an Ulster-Scot and bear his brats. And everyone knows the Ulster are ne'er-do-well farmers, always moving on to some supposedly better place, then failing there and moving again. I've no sympathy for her bad decision and for the Ulster trash that are like a plague on this colony."

Quinn's face turned red and he took a step away from the tree. "Damn you, Cap'n, what right have you to be so high and mighty? We both know you was a thief and forger in London and got sent here as a bond slave with a fourteen year sentence. The only reason they didn't hang you with the rest of the gang you was in was 'cause you was so young and sweet-lookin'. The judge took mercy on you and shipped you over here; shipped you here to be a servant in a big planter's mansion. And there you spent years learning to talk and act like a gentleman." He pointed at Caulfield. "But it don't make you no real swell, not by a long shot. You're gutter trash same as the rest of us and you had better admit you ain't much different from those Ulster people you got such disdain for."

"You can make fun of my language and manners; but my ability to mix in with the swells helps us know what's going on in the county and where the sheriff is looking for us."

"Just don't be forgettin' where you came from, Cap'n. If you hadn't run from that plantation in Edenton three years ago, you'd still be takin' trays of food to the master's wife and daughters. And bein' loaned out to wealthy families in Norfolk and Williamsburg to serve at grand dinners, standin' behind some asshole to take care of his every whim."

Caulfield controlled the anger which welled up inside him. "You can make sport of me all you want, but that's where I learned how to blend into society.

And you can say what you please, but it's keeping us safe and well-fed. And at the moment that means takin' the goods of those pilgrims."

Quinn sighed. "I always thought life had made me a hard man. I ain't shed a tear since I was at my mother's skirt. And I'll admit I've done just about everything the good book says will send you straight to hell. But Cap'n, I gotta say I've never seen anyone as heartless as you. You'll take money or goods from an old lady in a cart or a child on the street and smile sweetly while you do it."

Caulfield stared at the Irishman for a long moment, then said, "Quinn, we've been together for three years and came to understand each other long ago. This discussion is getting us nowhere. Let's get back to business. The point is, what would you have us do now? Go back down to the Tidewater, where they nearly caught us several times? Or maybe you want to go up to Philadelphia where there are so many farms and villages we'd have no place to hide? Or maybe up to New York or Boston where Redcoats are as thick as flies? I tell you, they'd be on to us in a matter of days." He shook his head. "At least here we're making a comfortable living, there are a lot of places to hide, and that Winchester sheriff is a bad jest. We can stay a couple of steps ahead of him without half thinking about it."

"Look, Cap'n, I ain't the only one who's unhappy. The lads have been complainin'. They want to make more money, instead of just gettin' a few coppers off these pilgrims once in a while." He stopped for a moment, looking directly at Geoffrey. "And they don't like the fact that you spend much of what we take on your trips into town."

"Quinn, how many times do I have to tell you those trips are helpful?"

"Yeah, particularly helpful to you in spendin' time with that gunsmith's black-haired woman. The one you can't get out of your head. And I'll tell you right now, I'm thinkin' she's the real reason we're hangin' out here instead of movin' on."

"Damn your tongue, Quinn. Keep her out of this. You know I wouldn't put the crew in danger just because of a woman."

"Well Cap'n, what I do know is you got a terrible big passion for women. Could be that comely vixen is shading your thinkin'. But be that as it may, I'm gettin' tired of keepin' the lid on the men's anger. I'm tellin' you now, we got to do something, or you're going to lose your crew."

Geoffrey took a long pull on his pipe, which gave him some time to cool down and think. "All right, Corporal, where would you have us go?"

"I'll tell you what; that Sarah has been talkin' about Charleston, down in Carolina. She was born there and then got sold up to here. She says it's a real prosperous place, with lots of planters who've gotten rich growing rice in the swampy land around the city. There be great plantations with grand mansions. Fact is, they call them the 'Rice Kings' down there. And them fat planters are always travelin' between their country places and their houses in the city. She also said there's another town down not too far south of Charleston in Georgia, called Savannah, which has more great plantations. Sounds like a spread of territory made for us and Sarah's talkin' about it has got the men all excited."

"I've heard of Charleston. But for God's sake, Quinn, do you know how far away that place is? It's hundreds of miles. And we don't know anything about the country between here and there. It would take us weeks to get there, particularly when you consider time to rest the horses along the way."

The veteran dragoon furrowed his brow, "There's no denying it would be a long journey. But I'm tellin' you, the lads want to move on or go their separate ways. You ain't got much choice or you'll be robbin' pilgrims on your own."

To buy time, Caulfield slowly knocked the ashes out of his pipe. "All right, Quinn. Tell the lads we'll start making plans. But it will take some time to get ready; we just can't mount up and head south. I'm going into Winchester tomorrow; I'll buy a map and figure out how to get there and how long it will take. But for now we'll need to keep robbing these pilgrims; we must build up a supply of provisions for the journey. That will take a few weeks."

Quinn looked at Caulfield. "Why can't we just steal food on the road?"

"Think about it, Quinn: We won't know the country along the way, or where to hide from the law if we draw attention to ourselves by holding up pilgrims or raiding farms. No, we've got to carry enough provisions so we don't have to steal. And we must have enough money to buy what additional supplies we need along the way. We must look like ordinary travelers until we get to the Charleston country."

"All right, Cap'n, now you're makin' sense. I'll tell the lads we have to build up our larder; they'll understand that."

"That's the idea, Corporal. And we'll have to get our hands on a few more horses, to carry packs. So start looking for likely candidates when we raid these pilgrims."

"Not a problem, Cap'n. And I can tell you this will make the whole crew happy."

"That's the stuff, Quinn. A few weeks and we'll be on our way south."

Quinn smiled and turned to make his way back to the camp.

Geoffrey lingered for a moment, lost in thought as he watched the big Irishman go. *This means I've got three, maybe four weeks at the outside to bed Peggy Eckert.* He gritted his teeth. *I'll just have to do whatever is necessary to make that happen.*

* * *

Caulfield dismounted before the front steps of Glengarry and turned his stallion over to the black stable attendant who came running. "Now listen, boy, don't just tie him to some hitching post and forget about him. Ease his girth and give him some hay. I pushed him pretty hard on the way over here."

"Yes sir, Massa Caulfield." The boy looked up at the tall horse and smiled. "He be a pretty one, massa," The youth moved his hand along the animal's side. "And a strong one, too. Don't you worry, sir. I'll take care of him really fine."

"See you do." Geoffrey looked around; no one else was in sight. He handed the boy a copper coin. "This might help you the next time you go night walking." He gave the young man a wink. "I'll bet you're seeing a girl somewhere."

The boy grinned broadly, his white teeth shining against his black countenance. "You bet, massa! There's a pretty house maid I'm spendin' time with over in town."

Suddenly there was the sound of a trotting horse and carriage wheels. Caulfield turned to see Peggy Eckert's chaise coming up the drive at a fast clip. She barely reined in the high-stepping horse as they entered the circle in front of the McDonald house, and then pulled up hard to stop the animal abruptly.

The boy smiled and said, "That Mrs. Eckert always drives like she was bein' chased by the devil hisself." Then he ran to hold the lively bay with white boots.

Caulfield hurried to the side of the chaise to assist Peggy. She gave him her hand and gracefully descended from the little vehicle. Caulfield looked at her and as always was taken by her natural beauty. She had a just a touch of rouge on her cheeks and appealing red paint on her lips. But there was little need for cosmetic enhancement, for her high cheekbones, blue eyes, and shiny black hair combined wondrously to give her a devastating appearance. Peggy wore a gown of her characteristic blue. A low-crowned straw hat, with narrow brim, was pinned to her carefully arranged hair; a ribbon around the crown precisely matched the material of her garment.

Peggy smiled up at Caulfield. "Why Geoffrey, thank you for the help."

Caulfield, his mind focused on the brazen, teasing treatment Peggy had shown him at the Golden Buck, had conditioned himself to deal with her jibes, ready to phrase smart repartee in response to what she might say.

Thus he was taken aback by her next words and actions.

Peggy put her arm around his, and after the stable boy had led off her horse and rig, she tightened her hold on his arm, leaned close, her eyes wide and radiating affection as she gazed up at him and said in a quiet, earnest, voice, "Oh, Geoffrey, I am so glad that you came. I've been worried for two days that business might keep you from joining us today."

The change was so startling that Caulfield was momentarily flummoxed and at a loss for words. He stood trying to think of how to respond.

Before he could answer, Peggy motioned to the front door. "My goodness, Geoffrey, why are you standing there like a lost lad? That's so *unlike* you. You *are* going to be gallant and escort me into the house, aren't you?"

Caulfield tried to regain his composure. "Well of course, Peggy; let us by all means go in."

They ascended the steps and were met at the door by Mr. Jack. He escorted them to the drawing room where they found Jean Moncure already there, talking with Anna. After pleasantries, Anna produced a square-shaped board.

"Look, Geoffrey, we can pin the game sheet to this so that it stays flat."

Caulfield nodded. "An excellent thought, Mrs. McDonald." He unrolled the paper and, using the pins Anna produced, fixed it to the board.

Anna said, "We'll need a marker for each person." She opened a small box. "I had some produced, Geoffrey." Inside were four tiny wooden blocks, each painted with a different color. "They're not very elaborate, but they should serve." She handed out a marker to each of them.

Peggy took her marker and then looked at the playing board. "You must tell us the rules now, Geoffrey."

He pointed to the board. "Well, ladies, there are 63 squares, or fields, arranged into a spiral, with the final large field in the center. Now then, you move by roll of the dice through the fields as if you were journeying along a road until you land in the center; obviously, the first player to arrive in the center wins." He looked around at the women. "But then of course, there are six special fields along the way. Five of them are hazards and one gives you an advantage."

Jean queried, "So which one gives you the advantage?"

"One of the very first;" Geoffrey pointed to space number six. "The Bridge here; if you land on it you can advance immediately to space number 12." Then he continued, "But from there on out, every special field gives you trouble.

The next special block is The Inn; land there and all the good food and drink induces sleep and you lose a turn. And worse, if another player lands on The Inn while you are resting, you must go back to the block from which that player just came." Caulfield ran his finger along the road to the end. "Now, the rest of the special blocks penalize you by losing some number of blocks or losing a turn. I'll tell you the details of each if you land there."

Anna put her finger on block fifty eight. "That one is marked 'Death'. If you land there, are you out of the game?"

"Almost," said Geoffrey. "Your goose is indeed cooked and you must go back to the beginning and start the journey all over!"

Peggy had been listening quietly and examining the game board while Caulfield explained the rules, her right elbow on the table and her hand upon her chin. "You know, ladies, we should make one of the regular blocks the sixth hazard; one which would be appropriate to Frederick County."

Jean asked, "What do you mean, Peggy? Do tell us."

Peggy said, "It should be marked 'Waylaid by the Highwaymen.' You lose a turn."

Everyone laughed.

Then Peggy continued, "But if you are a woman, you lose two turns."

Anna exclaimed, "A woman loses *two* turns? But why?"

"Because," said Peggy, "That gentleman highwayman the sheriff told us about becomes enamored by the woman's beauty and carries her off into the woods to ravish her. Then she is so pleasurably exhausted that she must rest before resuming her journey."

All of the women broke into laughter. Jean Moncure put her hand over her mouth. The indentured serving maid, who had just entered with a tray of tea and cups, could not avoid giggling. The china on her tray rattled as she laughed.

Anna exclaimed, "Peggy Eckert, you are *so* naughty. Incredibly *naughty*! I can't believe you said something like that in front of Mr. Caulfield!"

Peggy shrugged. "Oh, I do apologize. It just burst out before I could control myself." She gave Geoffrey a crooked smile. "But then, I suspect that Mr. Caulfield is not embarrassed in the least."

Caulfield was stunned and felt a touch of fear. My God, he thought, *She's taken up that taunting mode again.* He shot Peggy a glance and saw she was now looking coyly at him. Suddenly he realized: *She's not taunting me, her words are an invitation.* He felt himself flushing and hoped none of the women noticed. But he need not have worried; they were still giggling over Peggy's words and the maid was serving the tea.

Caulfield cleared his throat. "Well, ladies, the game takes some time. Shall we get started?" He laid the dice on the table. "Everyone takes a roll, and then we take turns in sequence from the highest to lowest."

They spent a pleasant two hours. Eventually, Anna McDonald pulled ahead and was first to land in the finish box. They all spent a few minutes talking about the game and congratulating Anna on her luck.

As the game went on, Peggy had contrived to give Caulfield several warm glances. He had, while making the effort to play a genial role with all the women, thought hard on how to arrange a private encounter with Peggy. He decided he must contrive to be the first to leave and then ride down the road toward Battletown and find a spot where he could intercept her as she drove the chaise home.

At the conclusion of the game, Caulfield, having had a copious amount of tea, made his excuses, and went to the privy, led by Mr. Jack. But when he arrived back at the drawing room, he was shocked by what he saw.

Peggy Eckert was gone.

He sat down at the table, barely able to hide his consternation. The maid was back, serving another round of tea and biscuits. Caulfield asked with as much disinterest as he could manage, "Where is Mrs. Eckert?"

Anna smiled. "Oh, she left. She had to get back to the Eckert Farm to check on her sick daughter."

Caulfield felt panic rising within him; his plans were demolished.

Anna said, "Geoffrey, you must have some more of the tea."

Caulfield felt a rising sense of frustration; the last thing he wanted was to have another cup of tea and a round of polite chatter. What he wanted to do was get to his horse as fast as possible and pursue the little chaise. But he felt trapped, for he knew he could not give the two women cause to think that he was leaving in haste just because of Peggy's departure. So he controlled his emotions and said, "Why Mrs. McDonald, I'd like nothing better than to have another cup of that splendid tea."

* * *

When Caulfield finally was able to escape Anna McDonald's drawing room and get to his horse, he figured that he was at least twenty-five or thirty minutes behind Peggy Eckert. He despaired of catching her, but was determined to make the try, even if he had to pursue her to the very drive of Eckert Ridge. The stableboy brought his horse, which pranced in anticipation after standing for hours. Geoffrey carefully checked, and then tightened, the cinch. Once he was sure all was in order for a hard ride, he sprang into the saddle and was off down the drive at a cantor. When they reached the road, he brought the animal to the gallop, heading east toward Battletown as rapidly as the hunter's long stride would carry them.

The stallion responded magnificently, as he always had. He seemed to run tirelessly and eat up the distance. Geoffrey had obtained the big horse on a dark night nearly three years ago, taking mount, saddle, saddlebags and other equipage from a gentleman who was imprudent enough to travel the road from Williamsburg to Hampton alone on a dark night. When confronted, the planter had been much less concerned about losing his purse than giving up the magnificent animal. Ironically, Geoffrey remembered serving the gentleman at a banquet in the Governor's Palace before making his escape from servitude. He had thus taken great pleasure in relieving the man of his prized possession.

Now, flying like the wind, Caulfield leaned forward over the animal's neck and offered him words of encouragement.

He judged they were less than a mile from the Battletown Inn and the turn southward toward the Eckert place when they rounded a curve and almost ran headlong into the chaise parked at the side of the road. The horse reared in surprise, his front hooves pawing the air and it was all Geoffrey could do to keep his seat. Once all four hooves were back on the ground, he threw down from the saddle and swiftly strode to the chaise, only to find it empty. Suddenly he heard Peggy Eckert laughing. Caulfield looked around for her, but she was invisible in the woods along the road.

"Geoffrey, I'm over here."

He turned toward the sound of her voice and saw her emerge from behind an ancient, wide-trunked oak. The raven-haired woman was giggling uncontrollably like a young girl. She leaned against the tree, her arms crossed in front of her, and asked, "What took you so long? I began to have doubts you would come."

Geoffrey did not immediately answer. Instead he slowly walked to her, and as he did so the perfect response came to mind. "Can I assume you want me to take you back into the woods and ravish you?"

Peggy put her head back and laughed heartily. "I wish you could have seen your face when I made that remark about adding the highwayman to the game. You blushed red like a bad little boy. If the other women hadn't been laughing so hard, they would have noticed your face and I fear our little game would have been discovered."

He looked into her eyes and forced a stern look onto his face. "Do you consider all of this a game?"

She was suddenly serious and her eyes looked directly into his. "No, Geoffrey, it's not *all* a game. What you said about me being lonely is true. My husband thinks only of his workshop and his tools. He has little time for me. Sometimes I feel like one of the indentured servants, valued only for the children I have borne and the work I do in the house and the garden." She paused and ran her eyes over him. "The truth is, I have been obsessed with the thought of you since we spent the day together at Glengarry Fair in June."

Caulfield put his hand on the tree beside her head. "You have a funny way of showing your affection — teasing and mocking me in front of that damned sheriff."

"Oh, Geoffrey! A girl, even a grown up one like me, must have her fun. You know I would never expose you. Not after you so chivalrously returned my necklace."

"On my honor, if I had been with the men that night, we never would have stopped you and your husband. The band was led by my second, Quinn, that night and he had no idea who you were."

"I believe you, Geoffrey, although I'm not sure how much faith I should put in the honor part."

"Now believe this, Peggy: I've seen the women of Williamsburg and Norfolk and Alexandria and most other important towns of the colony. But in all of Virginia there are none more beautiful than you; I knew that when I first saw you at Eckert Ridge."

Her face lit up with pleasure. "But Geoffrey, I'm nearly thirty. How can a young man like you find me attractive?"

"Peggy, men reach the height of their physical appearance in their early twenties. From then on, they face only decline. But I have observed that many women gain in beauty through their thirties and sometimes beyond. Believe me, you are one such lady. You must see it in your mirror when you look at your face."

"Geoffrey, you're so sweet, but you cannot be serious."

"Believe what you see in the mirror, for it is not lying; nor am I."

She reached out and touched him on the side of his face, her fingers on his cheek. He felt a surge of desire run through his body. Then she moved her finger along the cheek and finally drew it ever so lightly along his lips.

"Geoffrey, you say the most gallant things. It takes me back to when I was a young girl with dreams of romantic love."

Caulfield sighed. Instinct told him this was his moment. "But you can have that now." He paused and then, giving her his most charming smile, said, "*We* can have that now."

She was silent for a long moment, a look of inner turmoil on her face. Caulfield suddenly feared he had been too bold.

But then her face swiftly transformed into a look of desire. "Yes, yes, Geoffrey! I need that now more than anything; I long to be with you."

"Then let's make *now* the time. As you said back in Anna's drawing room; let me take you back into the trees here."

She looked back into the woods and sighed deeply, her hand over her heart. Then she turned back to him. "No, Geoffrey, not here. When I was a girl, a soft patch of grass or the straw in the corner of a stable were all that I needed for the quick passion of youth. But now I must have the comfort of a bed and the privacy of a room."

Caulfield motioned along the road. "Then let us ride post-haste to the inn at the crossroads. They have good rooms and we can consummate our passion without delay."

"Much as I would like that, I must be back at the farm soon. It is getting late in the day; there would be suspicion if I was seriously tardy."

"If not now, when can we see each other?"

"One week from now, Geoffrey, at noon. Arrange for a room at the very back of the inn. I'll wear a hooded cape and will come in discreetly through the rear entrance and stairway. Put something on the door knob to signal you are within. And then we will share our passion over a long afternoon." She put both hands on his chest and said, "Perhaps the first of many encounters, if you find I'm able to please you."

"It will be done as you say, my beautiful lady. No team of horses could keep me from this appointment."

She looked up at him. "I shall be scarcely able to control my anticipation until that day. But now I must leave if I'm to arrive back at the farm before supper."

Geoffrey put his arms around her waist and leaned forward; now was the time to for a passionate kiss. But Peggy reached up and gently put her hand over his mouth with his face only inches from hers.

"No, no, Geoffrey; we must wait until the inn or I fear I won't be able to control myself and must surrender to you right here." Then she put her hand on the back of his neck and reached up with her lips and gently touched them to his cheek. "That must suffice until we meet again."

Peggy pulled herself away from him and ran to the chaise. Caulfield followed to assist her into the vehicle, but she mounted quickly by herself and, slapping the reins on the horse's back, was off before he could arrive.

Geoffrey Caulfield stood by his horse, watching Peggy Eckert disappear down the road. Never had he been so aroused by a woman. He was a little surprised at how rapidly she had surrendered to him, but that was a passing thought, for he soon realized he had only a short time to enjoy her favors; a few brief weeks and he must ride south with his men.

CHAPTER FOURTEEN
Raid on Wakatomica

When dawn broke over the Ohio on the 26th of July, the light revealed a panorama like none Wend had ever seen. From his seat in the sternsheets of a large, flat-bottomed bateau loaded with provisions, he looked out to see a long flotilla made up of scores of canoes and boats moving down the river. There was an incessant groaning of the oarlocks in his boat as the rowers strained to keep pace with the swift canoes. A line of pulling boats of various designs formed the core of the formation, with the agile canoes arrayed around them. Wend's boat was just behind McDonald's and behind him was another loaded with provisions. Just barely visible ahead were a group of canoes carrying the battalion's scouts.

A messenger from Connolly carrying orders to proceed with the raid had arrived on the morning of the 25th, and Wend had spent the balance of the day issuing rations to the various companies. Then, working until dark, he and his quartermaster group had loaded the reserve rations into two bateaux. Exhausted, they had then tried to get a few hours of sleep before the wake-up call in the middle of the night.

Wend watched Horner pulling at one of the oars. A determined look was on his face as he struggled to keep in time with the other rowers. It was unaccustomed work for him and he was already covered in sweat. Wend reflected that the youth would undoubtedly have some blisters on his hands before they reached their destination. Jake Cather and Elijah McCartney, with their iron-like arm and chest muscles, were more at ease as they rowed. Henry Flannagan, who had volunteered to join the expedition as one of the contract quartermasters, sat across from Wend and handled the tiller. Also in the boat were men from Wood's company to provide a relay of rowers.

The distance to Captina Creek was about twenty-five miles; Fishing Creek was about five miles further. The flotilla was aided by the current and just after the noon hour Wend saw the mouth of a large creek on the Ohio side of the river.

Flannagan waved toward the creek and said, "I reckon that's the Captina. I seen it once before, years ago."

Wend nodded. "That means that Fishing Creek should be coming up on the other side of the river in just a few miles."

"That it should, Mr. Eckert." He pointed to the eastern bank. "But afore we get there, we'll see a long narrow island."

"Yes, McDonald told me we'll land just below the island."

In less than an hour, with the mouth of Fishing Creek in sight, Angus signaled for the flotilla to begin landing. The boats pulled up on the western side and the men began dragging them up the riverbank until they were out of sight in the bush. Soon the battalion was assembling in the late afternoon sun, the eight companies preparing to march northward. Scouts had already moved out to chart the path for the remainder of the day and locate the first camp.

Baird stood near Wend with a couple of men who were part of the detail staying behind with the boats. He had a grim look on his face; Wend knew he was fuming inside at being left behind. He turned to the scout and said, "Well, Joshua, we should be back in a week, or a little longer."

Baird spat. "Yeah, if'n the Shawnee let you. They're goin' to be madder'n hornets after you hit them villages. Could be you'll be fighting them all the way back."

Wend changed the subject. "Well, at least you'll be comfortable here with the boat guard."

"Comfortable, hell; I'm goin' to spend most of my time rangin' between the Captina and the Muskingum, watching for any Shawnee. If I'm supposed to be the scout for the boat guard, I'm damn well gonna do a piece of work."

Just then there was a shout and McDonald motioned the lead company to begin the advance. All the men around them donned their packs and other gear. Wend put his hand on Joshua's shoulder. "Well, good luck, Joshua."

"You're the one who's going to need luck. Just be careful and watch for ambushes."

"I'll remember that, Joshua."

Wend and his little group marched directly behind McDonald and his small staff which included the adjutant and Donegal. The group included his quartermasters, Horner carrying a pack with firelock repair supplies, and the expedition's medical representative, Howard Fleming, who had once been a Surgeon's Mate in the Royal Americans. He now was an apothecary in Pittsburgh. With him was another apothecary, named Bittock, who had volunteered to be his mate.

It was heavy going; there was no real path and the land was heavily forested with considerable underbrush. The column walked in single file and the July heat grabbed all of them like a fist. After twenty minutes, Horner asked, "Is it going to be like this all the way, Mr. Eckert?"

Wend looked at the young man. He was breathing heavily and was sweating profusely. He replied, "It's going to be this way until we cut the Captina Trail, which runs northwesterly from Captina Creek to the Muskingum. Then we'll be able to move easier and faster."

Horner sighed. "How far ahead is this trail?"

Wend replied, "Joshua told me we should reach it tomorrow. He looked up at the sun, now well toward the western horizon. "Anyway, we'll only be marching for a couple of more hours today until we make our first camp."

Jake looked at Horner, then grinned at Wend. "A couple of hours is all he looks like he's got in him, Eckert. And I'll wager we're going to march like this part of tomorrow 'fore we hit that trail."

Wend didn't reply. He glanced at Horner and was gratified to see a determined expression come over his face.

Horner scowled. "Don't you worry, Jake, I'll keep up."

Flannagan winked at Wend, then looked at Horner. "See that you do. You don't want to find out what the Indians do when they catch a man who falls behind. Think about those bodies at Hart's Store."

Horner's eyes opened wide, but he said nothing; silence prevailed and all the men concentrated on pushing through the bush.

* * *

"You say the Shawnee are expecting us?" McDonald stood looking at Jonathan Zane, who had come back to bring news.

It was late morning on the second day of August. The long column had halted, the men sinking to the ground to grab even a few minutes of rest. They were bone tired after almost a week of rapid marching through the rough Ohio terrain. McDonald and Zane were virtually the only men who stood, the major with his hands on his hips as he took the report from the scout.

Zane nodded. "That's what it looks like, Major. We've had lots of sign and we sighted a small party of Shawnees. It's obvious they were watching us."

McDonald grimaced. "Well, that put's paid to our attack being a surprise."

Zane hesitated a moment. "I think there weren't never a chance, Major. I wager they scouted us out almost since we landed."

"What makes you think that, Zane?" asked McDonald.

"Major, this morning we found a line of fighting positions. There's underbrush piled up to make it easier for them to hide and in some places they've cut down trees to provide better shelter and clear lines for shooting."

"But they've gone now?"

Zane shrugged. "Aye, Major. Perchance they saw the strength of our battalion and decided to fall back to another position, or maybe we came up faster than they expected and they weren't ready to fight. Anyway, one way or another, they pulled out."

Wend, sitting on the ground near where McDonald stood, saw that Michael Cresap, whose company formed the advance, had walked back to listen to the report.

The captain put his hands on his hips and spoke up. "I'll tell you what I think: They didn't have enough warriors gathered to take us on here in this broken land. And the fact is, we're getting close to the lowest of the villages. As I recollect, it ain't but maybe five or six miles from here."

Zane said, "That's true enough, Captain. But there's a big patch of marshland between us and that village."

McDonald scowled. "Damnation, that's going to slow us down."

Zane nodded. "I got the other scouts out looking for the best way through the marsh. Best wait here until we figure out the pathway."

Cresap waved northward. "I know that marsh; I've been through there several times on trading trips, Major. That marshland is spotty; marsh and sometimes outright swamp, mixed with firm land. But there be several ways through it. That could help us."

"Help us? What do you mean?" McDonald asked.

"Well, when you come out of the marsh, it's damned close to the first village. But the worst part of the swamp is right near the end. I'm suspecting that the reason the Shawnee pulled back is to hit us while we're in the swamp and can't move fast."

Zane nodded. "The captain might be right. And we'd be in a fix, see'in as we're marching in single file."

Cresap said, "That's why I mentioned that there are several ways through the wetland. Point is, we could form two or three columns, with a short distance between. Then if the Shawnee attacked one column, the others could come up on the war party from different directions and help break up the ambush."

McDonald stared ahead, a look of indecision on his face.

Wend, sitting on the ground, looked up and broke the quiet. "Major, when the tribes first hit our advancing column at Bushy Run, Bouquet brought in parties of rangers and a small detachment of the 60th to hit their position on the flank while the lead companies assaulted the Indians' front. It put them in a bind and they cleared out, at least for a time. What Cresap is suggesting could have the same effect."

Cresap looked sharply at Wend. "You were at Bushy Run?"

Wend nodded. "Does that surprise you? I was one of the scouts working with Baird."

Cresap shrugged. "It's just that I heard there weren't many colonials at that battle." He turned back to McDonald. "But Eckert makes my point. And remember, once the Indians make their initial attack, they always try to move around the flanks of a column and hit it on the sides and rear. It'll make it harder for them to do that if we're in a wide front of columns that could support each other."

McDonald stared ahead for a long moment, his face muscles moving as he worked through what had been said. Then he turned to Cresap and nodded. "All right, Michael. We'll reorganize right here before we resume the march." He turned to the adjutant. "Send a messenger down the column. Get all the captains up here."

Soon the captains began arriving. Wend looked them over as they came up. All were showing fatigue from the long march and their faces were covered with stubby beards. The major quickly explained the plan. The central column would be made up of the first four companies in line, with Cresap's continuing to lead. Morgan would lead two companies in the column to the right and Hoagland would head the final two companies marching on the left flank. Each column would be guided by a scout.

When he had finished giving his general instructions, McDonald spoke directly to Morgan and Hoagland. "Now, make sure you post flankers. And keep communication with the central column to ensure you remain within supporting distance." He thought a moment. "You must keep pace with the main column; if you do fall behind because of terrain, notify me by messenger." He looked at each man in turn. "Our plan will work only if we keep a proper alignment."

Both men nodded, then left to form their detachments. Meanwhile, Zane went to organize the scouts. Soon the entire force was deployed and McDonald signaled the advance of his column.

The central column pushed through the marsh for more than an hour, sometimes wading through hip-high water, sometimes walking on solid land. The sun beat down on the men; the swamp air was moist and oppressive. McDonald kept only a very short interval between Cresap's advance company and the main body and frequently sent messengers back along the line, urging the captains to keep closed up. Periodically Wend would catch sight of the other columns in the distance as they picked their way in a zig-zag path through the swampy land. But eventually he looked up and saw Cresap's men approaching a small, heavily wooded hill, maybe 150 yards ahead; the swamp gave way to solid ground in front of the ridge. He felt a wave of relief that perhaps it marked the end of the marsh.

Then he looked along the ridge and saw there was only a narrow path through the vegetation to the top. Cresap's company, which had been marching in column two or three men wide, with a small party ahead as a point, would have to ascend the hill in single file.

Suddenly an alarm sounded in Wend's mind. *My God, the perfect place for an ambush!* His eyes darted to the top of the ridge, searching for any sign of movement or the glinting of sunlight on metal.

In a second he saw what he feared: Bushes, just below the crest, moving on a windless day. Wend called out, "Angus, there's a war party on the hill!"

McDonald turned to look at Wend. "What did you say?"

Wend had kept his eyes on the ridge and now he caught a glimpse of human movement. He shouted, "There's a bloody ambush ahead! Everybody down!"

The first shots came as words of warning were still on his lips, followed by the billowing of gunsmoke along the ridge.

No further warning was needed. Almost as one man, the column took to the bush. McDonald turned and looked up to the ridge and then he too took to the ground and crawled to the cover of a dead tree.

Cresap's men had been the primary target of the initial Shawnee fusillade and they had rapidly taken cover. Wend could see one man had been hit and was on the ground; another man grabbed the soldier by a strap of his pack and dragged him behind a thicket.

Wend unslung his rifle and moved from the low bush which he had hidden behind to the cover of a tree with a low branch. He took a kneeling position and steadied the firelock on the branch. Meanwhile, he saw Cresap was rallying his men and preparing to assault the hill. It would be a hard job, given the narrow path to the top. There was no room for any kind of tactical maneuver; success would depend on the sheer guts of men climbing in single file directly into the Shawnee fire.

Wend realized that the only assistance the rest of the force could provide was a strong covering fire to prevent the Indians from shooting accurately.

McDonald had come to the same conclusion. He called back to Wood, who led the first company in line. "James, spread your men out and try to put a steady fire into the ridge! Aim is not as important as volume!"

Soon the Shawnee positions on the hill were being peppered by fire from both Wood's and Cresap's men. But Cresap's company, in position at the base of the hill, was also taking heavy return fire from the Shawnees in their elevated, well prepared positions. Wend perceived that the company must advance soon or face unacceptable losses.

Cresap realized the same thing; before another minute passed, he rose from cover and, followed by a half-company, dashed for the path that led upward. His other half-company kept up their fire from the bush.

As Cresap rushed up the slope, a warrior showed his head and upper torso above a bush just below the crest and aimed his firelock directly at the charging captain. The range was so short the Indian could not possibly miss. Wend had held fire until he could get his sights on a valid target; now he instantly aimed at the Shawnee and squeezed off his shot. The warrior's head snapped back, his eyes toward the sky, and the firelock dropped from his hands as he collapsed into the bush. Wend released his breath and went about the business of reloading.

The next time he looked up, he could see that Cresap and some of his men were nearing the hilltop. But he also saw two men laying on the ground; one near the bottom of the hill and another halfway to the top. As he looked, another militiaman on the hill dropped to the dirt, writhing in pain. Then, suddenly, Cresap and a knot of men were just below the crest, moving fast; clearly nothing could stop them now. It was also clear to the war party, for Wend could see warriors rising from their positions to retreat.

Finally, Cresap and his men were at the top of the hill; they were flush with excitement, brandishing their firelocks above their heads and cheering. The Shawnees were nowhere in sight. Cresap's second half-company had left cover and was rushing up the path to the summit. Cresap turned and looked down toward the head of the column and made a waving motion with his hand.

McDonald stood up and turned to Donegal. "Let's get moving; we'll join Cresap on the ridge."

Suddenly there was a barrage of shots from the right, also near the top of the ridge. Wend could see gunsmoke rising from the heavy foliage just below the crest. For a moment he thought the war party had staged an ambush of the right flank column. But then he glimpsed figures pushing upward through the thick foliage; men dressed in hunting shirts and broad-brimmed hats. He called out to McDonald, "Looks like Morgan is in action!"

"Aye, damned if I don't think you're right," McDonald answered, "but I don't see a path over there."

Donegal laughed. "Major, I'll wager Morgan is making his own path! He'd 'na let himself be kept out of a bonnie fight like this just by a hillside of thickets!"

McDonald nodded, then turned to Donegal and his adjutant. "It's time we were moving; let's get these men up the hill." He paused and scanned the column's left flank. Then he looked at his adjutant. "I see no sign of Hoagland's column. Send someone to make contact with him and lead his men to the path up the hill. We'll reunify the battalion on the ridge crest."

Then the major pointed at Wend. "Eckert, use your men to help the surgeon take care of the casualties. Get a squad from Wood if you need help." He looked up at the area of the skirmish and shook his head. "I saw several men fall and I fear there are some dead; bury them and get the wounded up out of this infernal swamp."

* * *

Wend could not countenance the idea of burying the two dead militiamen in the marsh; he had them carried to the crest of the ridge and found places for the graves in solid ground. Horner made up two rough crosses and planted one at the head of each grave site. Meanwhile, Surgeon Fleming treated the five wounded men; as luck would have it, all were wounded in the upper body, so that they remained mobile.

They also found two Shawnee bodies; clearly the war party had not had time to carry them away. Cresap's men had scalped the bodies before departing. Wend had the warriors' bodies buried together in a common shallow grave.

Wood had again given Wend Corporal Calvert's squad for assistance and they were taking turns digging the graves along with the quartermasters.

Wend looked around and saw that the swamp and top of the hill were within a short distance of the Muskingum; the river was in plain view just to the west. The men of the battalion were sitting in groups, resting and waiting for the march to resume.

As he was surveying the scene, Flannagan came over and tapped him on the shoulder. The veteran soldier pointed north along the river. "Look there, Mr. Eckert; smoke rising."

Wend looked where he pointed; sure enough a light cloud of smoke was visible in the sky. "Looks to be a few miles north and west," he responded.

Flannagan nodded. "Yep; I make it to be smoke from cookfires of the villages at Wakatomica."

"If they're that close, Flannagan, we may attack today."

"Can't be soon enough for me, Lieutenant; we're gettin' pretty short on rations. We need to finish our business and start back to the Ohio."

Wend nodded. The battalion had taken a zig-zag course as they worked their way northward in an effort to avoid discovery or at least confuse the Indians as to their exact objective. Consequently, it had taken days longer than expected to traverse the ninety or so miles from the Ohio to where they now stood. Most of the men's haversacks were near empty. It was imperative they find edible food in the villages following the raid or they would face a true starvation march on the way back.

While the burial party was at work, Wend went to report on the wounded to McDonald. He found all the captains sitting or standing near the battalion commander, who was talking with Zane. Wend noticed that Morgan's face and hands were covered with scratches, some still shiny with fresh blood.

"Daniel, you look like you lost a fight with a cat."

Morgan looked at his hands. "Got all this going up that damned hill; it was filled with briar bushes."

"I heard your firing. What happened; did the war party try to hit you?"

"Naw; them Shawnee tried to come down the hill, thinking to work around McDonald's flank. They picked the wrong place — right in front of us. When they saw us coming up the hill the varmints turned and started running. We just sent some lead after them to provide encouragement."

Wend grinned. "Well, Daniel, I'll bet those scratches will be burning and itching for days."

Morgan shook his head. "Already do. And all my men are the same way. Goin' to be a pain trying to sleep tonight."

Meanwhile, McDonald finished his conversation with Zane, and waved for all the captains and Wend to join him. As the men gathered around, he said, "Gentleman, Virginia can be proud of the way this skirmish was handled today. I'm entirely satisfied with the performance of the battalion and I think we can all admire the stout courage Cresap and his men showed taking this ridge."

There were nods all around; then Cresap spoke up. "It was a sharp action and I thank you, Major, for the compliment to me and my men. But, the truth is, I didn't expect to survive the day. Halfway up the hill, one of the devils stood up and aimed directly at me. Then, before he could fire, a ball took him right in the head. I'd sure like to thank the man who made that shot."

McDonald laughed. "You can do it right now. The man is standing right here." He pointed to Wend. "Eckert is the best marksman in Frederick County and he's the man who took down your Shawnee at better than 100 yards."

Cresap looked at Wend with his eyebrows raised. "Eckert made that shot?"

James Wood spoke up. "Damned right, Cresap; I was right behind and saw the whole thing. Eckert had the presence of mind to hold back while everyone else was shooting at the hill. Then he put a ball right into that savage."

Cresap made a tight smile. "I find myself obliged to you, Eckert."

Wend said, "Think nothing of it, Captain Cresap. I know you'd do the same for me."

McDonald waved toward the smoke in the distance. "Listen now, gentlemen; that smoke is from the cook fires of Wakatomica. Zane here says the villages are not more than five miles from here. I propose to march rapidly along the river until we get to the lowest of the villages."

Wood asked, "Do you plan to attack today?"

Angus shrugged. "James, our precise move depends on the Shawnee response. The Indians have two choices; come out to defend the villages, or evacuate their families and fall back westward toward the larger concentration of villages on the Scioto."

Morgan interjected, "So we'll either be in action against them or walking into their empty villages 'afore dark."

McDonald nodded. "That's my intent, Daniel."

Wood held up his hand. "Angus, there's a third choice; the Shawnee could try to negotiate."

McDonald retorted, "Negotiate? After firing on us already? That seems unlikely."

"Hear me out, Angus, it's not only possible, I think it's likely. They've seen our force now and know how strong we are." Wood turned to Zane. "How many do you estimate were in that war party?"

Zane thought for a moment. "From what I saw, couldn't have been more than fifty."

Wood held up his finger. "You see what I mean? I'd wager the size of that war party means they haven't received reinforcements from the big Shawnee towns on the Scioto. They know they can't stop us from hitting their villages."

Cresap said, "Wood has a point. When Indians know they can't win by fighting, they'll often go into talks to save their villages."

McDonald shrugged. "Fight, run, or parley; we'll see what develops. We won't find out what's going to happen until we get up to Wakatomica. So, all of you, get your companies ready to move. We'll march immediately."

Wend said, "Angus, I'm still burying the dead. The wounded can walk, but I'm not sure they can keep up with the column."

"All right, you've got your quartermasters and that squad from Wood's company. Finish your work here and follow us as fast as you can. Our trail will be pretty evident." Then he grinned and said, "And chances are you'll be able to find us by the sound of gunfire."

* * *

The quartermaster detail straggled into camp near dusk. Wend had initially followed the visible trail of the battalion's march, but for the last mile simply headed for the smoke of the militia's campfires. He found the expedition encamped in and around an abandoned village on the east bank of the Muskingum. The village was located near a shallow ford; across the river in the distance he could make out the lodges of a more sizable Shawnee town, also with smoke coming from fires.

Wend camped his detail alongside Morgan's company and then went to see the waggoner before reporting to McDonald. The big man was sitting beside a fire, smoking his pipe.

"What's going on, Daniel? We heard some brief firing earlier, then nothing more."

"It turned out that Wood was closest to being right." He waved toward the village. "We arrived here 'bout the middle of the afternoon and found the place deserted 'cept for a small war party. The lead company fired a few shots and they skedaddled. We was preparing to cross the stream and hit that big town over there when some Shawnee appeared on the other bank and called out they wanted to parley. McDonald waved them over and has been talking with them ever since." He shrugged in frustration. "Now it's so late, there ain't gonna be any move 'till mornin' no matter what happens."

Wend left Flannagan in charge of setting up camp for the detail and went to find McDonald. The Scotsman was sitting on a large log along with James Wood. A small fire had been built in front of the log. Sitting on the ground on the opposite side were three elder Indians with impassive expressions on their faces; they appeared to be sachems or chiefs. Behind the three sat a few younger men. Cresap was standing near the fire, acting in the capacity of translator.

Eckert saw Donegal standing a discreet distance behind the log and approached him. "What's going on, Simon?"

"Just a lot of words flowin', far as I can make out. They been going at it for a couple of hours now."

Just as Donegal finished talking, McDonald and Wood stood up, followed by all the Indians. The sachems turned and addressed their followers and then all the younger Indians headed for the ford and proceeded to wade across the river. The elders stood watching them, then reseated themselves at the fire.

McDonald turned to his adjutant. "Go round the camp and get all the captains and scouts here." Then he turned to Donegal. "Sergeant Major, get some tobacco and give it to the chiefs to keep them amused." He pointed to the nearest lodge of the village. "Then take the three of them over there and post a guard."

After the sachems had been led away, McDonald went back to the fire and resumed his seat on the log. He pulled out his pipe and lit it with a coal from the fire, then sat staring into the flames.

In a few minutes the company commanders and scouts had assembled. McDonald turned to face them. "Well, gentleman, Wood and I talked with those chiefs over there for more'n two hours. And believe me, they can speak for a long time without saying anything. But when you separate the grain from the chaff, here's the sense of it: They don't want to fight. They want to preserve their towns. They say the real firebrands are the Shawnees on the Scioto. They're promising to return several white hostages, including two young women captured in recent raids, as a token of their good faith, and to keep their warriors from taking the war path." He paused and looked around. For my part, I said they must join in any general peace conference which is held following hostilities, and must provide us with provisions for our return trip."

Wood spoke up. "And they are required to provide us with several chiefs or elders as hostages to ensure they won't return to hostilities after we leave."

Morgan was incredulous. "So that's it, Angus? It's all over and we just march back to the Ohio?"

McDonald shook his head. "Not quite, Daniel. These chiefs are from the village right over there." He motioned across the river. "They can't speak for the other villages northward along the Muskingum. So they sent their retainers to go round up the other village chiefs and then we'll resume talks. They promise the others will be here by dusk and they expect they'll all agree to the same terms."

Wood added, "And they'll bring in the two white women to show good faith."

There was a moment of silence, then the captains began whispering among themselves.

In a moment, young George Clark spoke up. "We came all this way to strike the Shawnee. To pay them back for all the raids along the border country. We lost two good men this morning. Now we're going to just turn around and go home having done nothing except recover a few hostages?"

There were nods of agreement from others in the group.

Cresap pointed back toward the militia camp. "McDonald, all these boys, 'specially the ones from the western settlements, left home and joined up 'cause they wanted to teach the Shawnee and Mingo a lesson. This morning we lost men we knew. I'm telling you, if we go back without hitting them Indians, there's going to be a lot of damned angry men."

Wood waved his finger in the direction of the officers. "I understand the anger of you western men. But keep in mind, most of the raids this spring have been orchestrated by Logan and his henchman, this Laughing Eyes. There have been young Shawnee hotheads with them, and a few raids by Shawnee war parties. But it all stemmed from that damned incident at Baker's Tavern." He gathered his thoughts. "If we can keep the main part of the Shawnee at peace, Logan won't be able to keep up the raids."

McDonald said, "Wood is right; if we take all these villages, and their warriors, out of the war through a parley, we will have met the objective Lord Dunmore set for us, same as if we did it by fighting them. That will enable him to march up the Scioto on Cornstalk's villages without worrying about having a force of hostiles here on the Muskingum, threatening his eastern flank."

"And," interjected Wood, "if we have to attack the villages, there's no doubt we're going to lose some more of those good men you spoke of, George. Their families will be much better off if they're back on the farm bringing in crops, instead of occupying graves here on the Muskingum."

Clark waved in the direction of the villages. "This smacks of treachery by these Shawnee. They don't have enough men to fight us, so they're using negotiations to delay our attack. Meanwhile, I'll wager they are evacuating their women, children, and elderly westward."

Cresap said, "McDonald, Clark's right; the Shawnee are just buying time to abandon all these villages. And even if they're not, and you get those hostages, there ain't no guarantee the warriors won't join up with Cornstalk when

Dunmore advances. The chiefs of these villages will just declare they can't control their young bucks." He threw up a hand in frustration. "I seen it happen like that in the French War. I tell you we'll still have to fight them."

There was a hubbub of agreement from Morgan and the western captains.

Cresap continued, "It's getting late. We can't do much before darkness, but we could burn this village and move on that village across the river before sunset. That would show them we mean business." He paused and looked around at his compatriots. "*Then* we could stop and negotiate; they'd know we're ready to move north and finish the business in the morning."

McDonald tapped the ashes out of his pipe and stood up. He swept the assembled officers with his eyes. "I gave my word to these sachems that we would wait for the other chiefs and their hostages. They've promised to get them here by dark. We'll see if they keep their word." He paused a moment and then stared directly at Clark and Cresap, who were standing together. "And if they don't arrive by then, we will make preparations to attack on the morrow."

✳ ✳ ✳

Wend and his men scoured the small village, searching for food. They found a few small caches of corn and turned it over to the companies. Otherwise the village had been stripped clean by the former occupants. Then, with dusk falling, Wend returned to McDonald's council fire to report the distribution of food and check on the status of negotiations.

He found the expedition commander impatiently walking back and forth in front of the fire. Wend looked across the river; he could see the flickering of cookfires in the village to the west of the river. He looked northward along the stream and dimly saw the distant glow of fires in the upper villages.

Wend spoke to the adjutant and learned that there had been no word from the Indians. Then he walked over to where Donegal sat beside the nearest of the lodges and settled on the ground beside the sergeant-major.

Donegal leaned close and whispered, "There's 'na doubt the old man is gettin' pretty hot. It be way past time when he expected the rest of those chiefs to show." The Highlander pointed toward the east. "Look there, Wend. The moon's showing bright near the horizon an' you can see the stars above and there're no chiefs and no white hostages."

Eckert said, "He's going to have to make a decision pretty soon."

"That's a fact. But a'fore he can make that decision, he's got to admit to himself he's been had by the Shawnee. That's the hard part for him."

Wend laughed softly. "Simon, after living with you for ten years, I know there's no one more stubborn than a Highlander. But there's no doubt he's wrestling with that right now." Wend motioned toward McDonald. "But it's hard to fault him for trying to settle things without a fight."

"If you ask me, Cresap's right, Wend. We should have burned this village right after we chased that little war party away. Then we could have crossed the river directly and hit that bigger town over there. That done, McDonald could have offered to parley."

Wend sighed. "Perhaps you're right."

Donegal said, "Now these border men are going to be sayin' that McDonald is too weak for this job."

Just then, McDonald stopped pacing and turned toward his adjutant. "Lieutenant, get the captains here!"

Donegal turned to Wend. "Well, he's finally made up his mind."

In less than ten minutes the company commanders stood in a tight group in front of the major, expectantly waiting to hear what he had to say.

Wend said quietly, "Simon, McDonald is a proud man. I wonder what words he'll use to concede that the Shawnee have out-maneuvered him." Then he stood up and joined the group of officers.

As it turned out, McDonald made no such admission. Without any preamble or explanations, he spoke in a loud voice directly to Wend, who was standing to one side of the company commanders. "Eckert, those three sachems sitting over there are our prisoners. Keep them in your custody tonight."

Then he turned back to his captains. "Cresap, find a good ford down to the south of here and move your company and your nephew's down there under cover of darkness. He pointed to the town across the Muskingum and said: "At dawn you will cross the river and attack that village from the south." He looked at Morgan. "Daniel, take your company and cross to the north of here, just below the mouth of Wakatomica Creek. You'll also cross at dawn. Your job is to move along the creek until you are north of the village and be ready to fire on the Indians if they run northward from Cresap's attack. You must also block reinforcements from the northern villages. The rest of the battalion will cross right here after Cresap's attack is underway and move on the village."

The captains stood staring at McDonald for a long moment. Wend expected a flurry of questions or outright criticism of the delay caused by talking with the chiefs.

But Angus stymied them with a steely glare. Then he said, "Gentlemen, return to your companies and carry out your orders. Reveille for the companies here in this camp will be one hour before dawn so we can be ready to move at first light."

He abruptly turned and seated himself at the fireside log and stared down at the fire, his arms crossed in front of his chest. Clearly he was not open to any conversation. The captains looked at each other for a second, then turned and returned to their campsites.

Wend took the three chiefs to the quartermaster camp and had Flannagan set up a guard for the night. Then he explained to his men the plans for the next day and sent them to their bedrolls.

As they were preparing settle in, Wend walked over to Morgan's camp. The big waggoner stood watching the quiet bustle as his men gathered up their kits and slipped into their packs. His only words were urgings to the militiamen to maintain as much silence as possible. He turned to Wend and said, "Moving upriver won't take long; it's only a short distance to where that creek empties into the river. Then we'll sleep on our arms in cold camp 'till dawn and slip quietly across the river just as its becoming light."

Wend responded, "I hope the river is shallow enough for an easy crossing. If it gets deep, it could be tricky for your men."

Morgan looked at Wend for a moment. "Now that's a thought. We'll check to make sure it's a good ford. But tricky or not, nothin's gonna stop us from gettin' across."

Wend laughed softly. "I never doubted that, Daniel."

Morgan set his jaw. "You got that exactly right. But I'm pissed. Why is Angus lettin' Cresap take the lead in all the fighting? I got all the best riflemen from Frederick County and I figure it's our turn to make the attack."

"You heard Cresap arguing with him. I suspect he's just trying to mollify him." Wend thought a moment. "And anyway, your job is critical. You could end up fighting Shawnees fleeing Cresap's attack and reinforcements from the north at the same time. That would be enough action even for you, Daniel."

A wide smile came over Morgan's face. "Damned if I don't think you're right about that. But come hell or high water, we'll be there on the north side of the village when Cresap comes stormin' in. And whether they come from the south or north, we'll take care of any of them Shawnee who get within' the range of our firelocks."

Then he patted Wend on the shoulder, waved to his men, and they were off, heading to the northward; a long single file of lean men moving silently through the forest. In just a couple of minutes they disappeared into the bush and the night.

* * *

McDonald's plan was carried out with precision. Cresap crossed the Muskingum as the sun began to rise above the eastern horizon. Then he turned north and headed for the village. Morgan's northern detachment had no problem fording and soon had taken positions along the creek which was above the village, ready to act as a blocking force. McDonald's companies torched the village on the east bank and then crossed at the main ford, fanned out into a skirmish line, and moved westward directly toward the other village.

The wind wafted the smoke from the burning village over the men as they crossed the river, blanketing them as if in a fog and hiding most from Wend's sight. Those he could see were half-visible through smoke and looked like shadowy apparitions.

As they advanced, the men of the main force heard the sound of firing from the southern edge of the village. Cresap was in action!

Near the village, the smoke cleared and McDonald waved for the companies to pick up the pace. The men cocked their firelocks and the line swept into the Indian town at the run.

And the attack landed on air.

There were no warriors ready to defend their village and no inhabitants; no women or children, no animals. There was nothing but empty lodges and an eerie silence.

Wend and his men, following behind the main line, found only a few live cook fires, most burned down to the coals. Then, minutes after entering the village, they sighted Cresap and his men approaching through the southern part of the village.

Cresap strode up to McDonald and made his report. "We crossed easily; there was a small picket of Shawnee on the west bank, but they left after a few shots. One of the men, name of Hargis, killed an Indian who stuck his head out from the bush just before we crossed. Then we headed for the village. There was a small party near the first lodges; they gave us a stiff fire while we was in the open, but then we closed on them and they lit out." He waved his arm around the expanse of lodges and other buildings. "Ain't no other living man or creature here."

McDonald set his jaw. "If the Shawnee pulled their people out, why did that small party attack you?"

Cresap laughed. "I'll tell you why, Major. Them Shawnee was a few young bucks and outright boys left behind to keep the fires burning through the night, so we'd see 'em and think all the people was still here. But the women, children, old ones and most of the warriors pulled out last evening. I'll wager they're miles west of here by now, pushing for the Scioto and Cornstalk's villages." He spat, and continued, "Them bucks couldn't resist shooting at us as an act of defiance and honor and to give the younger boys a chance at their first fight. Right now they're runnin' through the forest trails to catch up with the rest of the village people."

Wood, who had walked over from his company, said, "Well, the bright side is that at least we took the village without any cost."

Cresap stared at Wood for a long moment, a grim look on his face. "Well, *Captain* Wood, I figure the six of my men who took balls from those bucks at the river bank and in the village might look at things a bit different. They're sittin' back at the edge of the village bleeding." He turned to McDonald. "I'd be obliged if you could send that surgeon down to take a look at them."

Angus nodded. "Eckert, tell Fleming and his mate to get down there. Then let me know how bad off they are." He thought a moment and continued, "Meanwhile, have your quartermasters look through this village for any food. Wood and his company will stay with you while the rest of the battalion moves north to the other villages."

Cresap said, disdainfully, "I'll wager right now, McDonald, that you're going to find all those towns deserted. And don't forget Clark and me told you last night. The truth is, we should have hit these villages as soon as we got here yesterday."

Wend saw Angus' back stiffen. His eyes reflected burning anger. He was sure the Highlander would lash out at Cresap.

But instead McDonald stood silent for a few seconds, staring at Cresap, and working to control himself. Finally he spoke. "Perhaps you are right, Captain, but then again, other villages along the river may have decided to resist. There could be more action ahead. Go bring your men up to join us." He turned to the adjutant and said, "Tell Morgan to prepare his detachment to lead the force into the next town."

After Cresap and the adjutant had departed, McDonald looked at Wend. "Eckert, after you finish a search of this town, catch up with me as we advance."

He thought a moment and continued, "Bring the wounded with you." Then he turned to Wood. "James, place pickets to the west, on the chance that Shawnee warriors may try to hit us as we search the village. After the quartermasters are finished, burn the town and follow behind as the rearguard."

Wend returned to his quartermasters and initiated the search of the lodges. Fifteen minutes later Jake Cather found Wend standing near the central fire ring of the village. "Look what I turned up, Eckert."

The waggoner was leading and half dragging by the arm a short little man dressed in a colorful mixture of Indian and European garb, a man who straggled along with a slight limp and a bent back which made him look even shorter. It was Crooked Harry, last seen at Baker's Tavern!

Harry recognized Wend at that moment. He pulled his arm away from Jake's grasp and scrambled up to Wend. "I know you! You was with Girty at Baker's place. You stole the boats from Baker!"

Wend grinned. "Yes, I know you, Harry; surely we're friends. But what are you doing here?"

"Harry came here from Baker's. Thought to stay here for winter; know people in this village."

Jake looked askance at the little hostage. "Damn it, Eckert, I got no doubt this man's a traitor to the whites. I found him lurking in a small building beside one of the lodges. I say the Shawnee left him behind to spy on us, knowing we wouldn't hurt a white man."

"A spy? How the devil would he get word back to the Shawnee?"

"Way I see it, they figured we wouldn't guard him. He could get the lay of our strength and plans, then slip away from our camp at night and rejoin them."

Wend shook his head. "I doubt that, Jake. Harry was captured years ago and simply wanders from village to village. The Indians take care of him because they figure he's crazy." He put his hand on Harry's shoulder and asked, "So why didn't you go with the villagers to the west when they left?"

"Didn't want to go west, Mr. Wend. "Part of this village is Mingo. That's where Harry was living. They be nice people, take good care of Harry. But Harry didn't want to go west; too many Shawnee on Scioto."

"I understand, Harry. Now tell me, have all the villages along the river here been abandoned?"

"Oh yes, Mr. Wend. Yesterday all people leave, while three old men go to talk with white general across river. Chiefs leading people west to join with Cornstalk, get ready to fight Virginians. Gather up everything, load horses with goods and take all livestock." Harry pointed to north. "All villages empty! Nobody there."

"That's good to know, Harry."

"You take me with you, Mr. Wend? Take me with you so Harry can go back and stay with a Mingo village for winter? Harry wants to find a Mingo village in north."

"Why do you want to go north, Harry? There are some Mingoes not far from Wheeling."

"Don't want to be near the big fight. All the Shawnees are saying there's going to be a big fight with the Virginia men down there." The little man waved his hand to the south and west. "They say it will be much, much bigger fight than this. All Shawnee warriors are getting ready for war. And many Mingo and Delaware are going to join them. But Harry wants to go north and be away from big fight."

Wend laughed. "Yes, Harry, I don't blame you. Don't worry; we'll take you back to Wheeling with the expedition, then you can go where you want."

Suddenly Wend heard someone shouting, "Ha! Ha! Ha! Get along!" and looked up to see a black and white cow come into view from behind a lodge, followed by Horner urging the animal on with a switch in his hand.

Horner brought the cow to a halt nearby, a big smile on his face, and said, "Look what came out of the woods on her own. At least there will be some meat to distribute!"

Jake said, "Them damn Shawnee must have missed her in the hurry to get out of here."

Wend nodded. "Good job, Horner. One cow won't go far, but we could make a stew which should give everyone a little taste of meat." He thought a moment. "What else have we found in the way of provisions, Jake?"

"Nothin' but more of that old corn; most of it barely fit to eat. And one cache of grain they probably couldn't carry. That's it, Eckert."

"All right, gather it all up and put it in one place so it won't be destroyed when Wood fires the lodges and we can come back and distribute it to the men before we start back."

A couple of hours later, Wend led his motley column across Wakatomica Creek and into the next village. It included his quartermasters, the squad from Wood's company, the surgeon and his mate with nearly a dozen wounded, plus the cow herded by Horner. They caught up with McDonald, his adjutant, and Donegal at the northern edge of the village.

Wend reported to the major and provided him with the status of the wounded and the fact that, other than the cow, once again they had found little in the line of provisions. Then he told McDonald about the information Crooked Harry had provided, particularly the fact that all the villages had been abandoned and the Shawnee were talking war, and that at least some Delaware and Mingo were planning to join them.

McDonald digested Wend's report, staring into the distance, with resignation in his eyes. Then he sighed deeply and said, "All right, I've sent Zane and his men to scout all the villages. They should be back soon. Assuming that they verify what you've just told me, I'm going to burn all the towns along the Muskingum and Wakatomica Creek. Then I'll set the men to destroying the crops in the fields, which appear to be quite extensive. That will take at least until tomorrow to finish, maybe longer."

Wend responded, "I'll set my men to looking for food in this village and be ready to move on to the others."

Angus shook his head. "No, you don't need to concern yourself with that. Based on what I've seen so far, we're not going to find much more provisions. I'll appoint another officer to form work details to gather that up and distribute whatever we find. And we'll butcher that cow and give a small portion to each company."

"I don't understand," said Wend.

"I've got a more important job for you, Eckert. Take all the wounded, that hostage you found, the quartermasters, and that squad of Wood's men and head for the Ohio as fast as you can. And take Fleming's mate, Pittock, with you to care for the wounded. I'll give you one of the scouts as a guide. When you do reach the river make preparations to feed the battalion when it arrives. The men are going to be weak from hunger and they'll need to eat before we go upriver to Wheeling."

Wend nodded. "I understand. But it's going to be hard to move very fast with the wounded; it's true they can all walk, but at least one has a minor leg wound and is hobbling along. It's near a hundred miles to the river; you might catch up with us."

"Eckert, don't let that happen. You must be merciless in moving them along. Merciless, do you understand? There's no question it's in their best interest. And you've got enough men to carry that man with the leg injury if necessary."

"All right, we'll get organized and depart as soon as possible."

"Leave as soon as the scout joins you. And keep moving every day as long as there's daylight. The men need to know we'll be ready to feed them when they arrive at the Ohio, and I'm counting on you."

CHAPTER FIFTEEN
Eckert's Command

The men of Eckert's detachment sat or lay on the ground near the small pile of corn in the village, waiting to start the march south. Wend had had Flannagan measure out a share of the corn to each man, which they had put into their haversacks. The militiamen were talking among themselves, adjusting their equipment in preparation for the journey. Some were trying to rest with eyes closed. Pittock, the surgeon's mate, was fixing a sling for the arm of a wounded man.

Wend was waiting for the arrival of the scout. Meanwhile, he assessed his little command and its ability to defend itself. He had his six quartermasters, all armed with longrifles. Flannagan, Horner, Jake, and Elijah were all competent shots; he didn't know about the two contract men, Flynn and Hoffman. Then there were the ten men of Calvert's squad, who were all armed with muskets. Finally, all the wounded men carried rifles and at least half had the use of both arms and hands, so they could be of some use in a fight. Pittock carried only a pistol stuck in his belt.

Suddenly Wend was interrupted by a voice from behind him. "I'm lookin' for Lieutenant Eckert."

Wend turned around to see a young man, hardly more than a boy, standing before him, a longrifle in the crook of his right arm. He was of above average height, dark-haired, with a sharp look in his eye. The lad was dressed in a belted linen hunting shirt which reached to just above his knees, green colored leggings, and beaded moccasins. On his head was a beat-up old hat with a round crown and wide brim.

Wend took him for a messenger. "Are you carrying a message for me from Major McDonald? Is the scout he promised going to be here soon?"

The youth's mouth formed a crooked grin and his eyes twinkled. "Yes, I am here on orders from the major; but I ain't no messenger: Fact is, he told me to guide your column down to the Ohio."

Wend was shocked. He certainly hadn't expected Zane, who was serving as McDonald's chief scout. But he had anticipated that Angus would send one of the two other primary scouts, Thady Kelly or Tom Nicholson. They were veteran, experienced woodsmen who knew the Ohio Country well. Wend asked, "Well, scout, what's your name?"

The youth hesitated for the briefest instant, looked over Wend's right shoulder, and answered, "It's Simon Butler."

Wend sought to sound out the man's experience. "Well, Butler, do you know this territory?"

"Yeah, I spent some time in the Muskingum country and know where the villages are. Of course that was before I went down to Kaintuck for the hunting, but I remember the land pretty well."

Wend was astonished. "You've been out to Kentucky?"

Butler nodded. "Sure enough; I been down there for two hunts. In between, I come back up and stay at the village on Fishing Creek."

"So, you have been working with Zane on this expedition?"

"I've been ranging ahead since right after we got off the boats. Then the day before we got to Wakatomica, Zane sent me to range up along the Muskingum to check the lay of all the villages."

"He sent you by yourself?"

"Sure, like I said, I been all over this country; I know the trails. I went as far as Bouquet's old camp, which is north of all the important villages."

Wend asked, "You mean the place where he negotiated with the Indians in the '64 campaign?"

"Yeah, Mr. Eckert; the log cabins and some other buildings his men raised are still there. A band of Delawares moved into the cabins and has built some more lodges. It's turned into a fair sized village. But when I got there, they had already packed up and headed west, just like all the others." He shrugged, then continued, "So I came back to report to the major and he sent me over here to scout for your column."

"All right, Butler, we're under orders to get back to the Ohio as soon as possible. What's our route? The expedition came up through some pretty rough ground; rough even for men in good shape. We've got a dozen wounded men; if we are going to travel fast, we need an easier, more direct route."

"Yeah, Lieutenant, I thought about that while walkin' over here. Way I figure it, we go right down the eastern side of the Muskingum. There are trails most of the way. We follow the river 'till we hit the trail which runs along the Ohio, and stay on that until we get north of Fishing Creek."

Wend said, "Wait a minute; won't going along the Muskingum take us close to several villages?"

"Lieutenant, when we marched north, we were trying to avoid Shawnee scouts, much as possible. But now, all the Indians between here and the Ohio damn sure know we're here." Butler looked around at the detachment. "With this lot, if you try to go through the bush, you ain't goin' to move fast; you may find McDonald waiting for you at the boats by the time you get there."

"But you're telling me there's a good chance we'll be hit along the way," responded Wend.

Butler waved his hand at the sitting men. "Seems you got a goodly number of firelocks in this outfit and men who know how to use them; if some village puts a war party together to try to stop us while we're along the Muskingum, we'll just have to shoot our way through." He looked at Wend with a raised eyebrow. "I'll say it plain: You got to take that chance if you really want to make the best time down to the boats."

Wend nodded. *The young scout was making sense and had a confident manner.* And then a sobering realization struck him: *Damn, he's the same age I was back in '63 when I scouted for Captain Sterling on our mission through the Beaver River country. My God! What a chance Sterling took in trusting me!* He looked sharply at Butler and thought: *But I'll have to take the same chance and put my faith in him, at least until he does something which shows that he isn't up to the job.*

Wend called Flannagan, Calvert, and Cather to where he and Butler stood. First he introduced them to Butler. Then he said, "Now listen: Until we get down to the Ohio, I'm making Flannagan the sergeant of the detail, based on his time in the Virginia Regiment. Jake, you're in charge of keeping the wounded moving; I know you to be a hard man and you'll have to show little sympathy to those men, much as they're hurting. Calvert, your men will have to cover our rear." He looked around at the three men. "We'll work out other matters of routine along the way." Then he grinned at Flannagan and said: "All right, *Sergeant,* get the men up and headed for the ford. There are plenty of daylight hours left, and we need to make full use of every one."

* * *

Flannagan got the detachment moving; the men waded back across Wakatomica Creek and then crossed to the east side of the Muskingum at the same ford

Morgan had used earlier in the morning. Without pausing, Wend led them southward along the river toward the marsh where the first skirmish had taken place. Presently Flannagan motioned for Wend to look behind.

He turned to see two towering columns of heavy smoke.

"They've fired the first two villages on the west bank of the Muskingum, Mr. Eckert."

"Yes, I see. I trust we'll be seeing a lot more smoke as they move northward." Wend looked back at the column. They were straggling due to the condition of the wounded and the men turning to gape at the smoke. Wend called out to Cather, "Jake, keep the wounded closed up. Have men help them along if they need it."

Cather said, "Eckert, I already got Elijah and Horner helping McClain move, what with his leg hurtin' so much."

Then one of the wounded called out, "For God's sake, Lieutenant, we need to rest for a while. We been walkin' steady for hours, and there are men in bad shape back here. I'm tellin' you, I got pain through my arm and shoulder at every step."

Wend knew the man was right. But he spoke loudly so the men would hear. "Pittock, tend the wounded as much as you can while we're moving."

The surgeon's mate called out, "Mr. Eckert, that's easy for you to say, but it's a near impossible task to work on these men as we march. I'll do what little I can."

Wend ignored the surgeon's mate. Instead, he called back along the column, "Now listen, all of you: Butler is ahead finding the shortest, driest path through the marsh. We must get through it before dusk. If the surgeon's mate can't help you during the day, he'll tend your wounds when we make camp. Be clear about this: I'll not suffer us to stop or spend the night in middle of the swampland. So grit your teeth and keep moving."

They found Butler waiting for them at the narrow place where the path led down into the marsh near the graves which Wend's men had dug the day before. Wend relented and gave the column a brief rest while he talked with the scout about the route ahead. Then, with the wounded groaning as they got up, Butler led them down the slope into the wetlands.

It was a miserable march. The air, baked by the harsh sunlight of the August day, was steamy and fouled by the stench of the swamp water. The men's clothing was soon soaked in sweat; perspiration flowed down their faces. And despite Butler's best efforts, there were places where the men had to wade through deep, slimy water. The quartermasters made strenuous efforts, sometimes cursing, to hold McClain above the muck. They were not always successful; he had wounds both in his leg and shoulder. Despite the men's best efforts, he frequently moaned in agony as they carried him.

The column got out of the swamp with an hour remaining until dusk. Wend gave the men a few minutes rest while he sent Butler forward to find a camp they could reach by dark. Then he signaled a resumption of the advance, telling Flannagan and Calvert they would march at least for another hour. With great hesitation the men got up and struggled onward. For the first time he heard his name openly cursed from near the rear of the column. Wend ignored the words; he knew they would hate him even more, and say worse things about him, over the next few days.

Slightly more than an hour later, having followed the marks Butler had left them, they found the guide in a small clearing near a tiny creek which flowed into the Muskingum. The youth was sitting against a tree, chewing on some jerky, his rifle across his lap. In front of him was a pile of small tree branches and twigs.

Butler pointed to the pile. "There's some dry kindling I rounded up while waiting. You got fallen trees around here; I think they came down in a storm a couple of years ago. It won't be much work to get your cookfires started."

* * *

"So, Simon, how did you come to be here in the border country at such a young age?"

Wend and Butler were alone at the campfire that they would share with Flannagan, Calvert, and Pittock. Wend had just made a round of all the detachment's fires, checking on the condition of the wounded and the rest of the militiamen. The men's anger had cooled as they worked to cook their meager meal of Shawnee corn and whatever other provisions were still in their haversacks.

As the day had progressed, Wend's curiosity about the young guide had grown; his mind had seized on Butler's momentary hesitation when asked his name back at Wakatomica. Wend had puzzled on it while marching. It was just a feeling in his gut, but he suspected that Butler was hiding something. Now, under the guise of casual conversation, he was attempting to probe the youth's background.

The scout, who sat across the fire from Wend, looked off into the distance, obviously thinking about his answer. "I came from the Bull Run Mountain country back in eastern Virginia; that's where my Ma and Pa have their place."

"You seem to have been on your own since you were fifteen or sixteen. That's pretty young to leave home."

Butler stared at Wend for a moment. "Truth is, I ran away from home." He didn't say anymore by way of explanation, simply looking down into the fire and biting his lips.

Wend could see a look of unease in the boy's eyes. He laughed. "Let me guess, Simon: You didn't like being a farmer."

A quick look of relief came over the youth and he looked up at Wend. "Yeah, that's the truth of it, Mr. Eckert. I liked the idea of being a hunter out here in the Ohio Country. I'd heard plenty of stories about the border." He looked out into the darkness, then continued, "Made me want to see it and live free of all the damned chores on a farm. I knew my Pa wouldn't let me leave; so I made plans and just walked away one night."

Wend nodded. But he was suspicious of how quickly Butler had jumped on the bored farmer story. He thought to himself: *More likely he was an apprentice who had deserted his master or perhaps a runaway bond slave.* The border country was full of such men looking to avoid justice and start a new life. But he responded, "Well, that's not an unusual story out here. My friend, Joshua Baird, did about the same thing."

Butler smiled. "Yeah, you hear a lot about Baird out here. He was with Bouquet for many years. They say he knows the whole Ohio Country like the back of his hand."

"Well, that's pretty much true. Joshua taught me everything I know about the backcountry and the bush. I've known him since I was fifteen." Wend smiled and then he pointed to Butler's rifle. "Can I take a look at that?"

Butler instinctively put his hand on the firelock and cocked his head. "Why do you want to see it?"

Wend smiled. "It happens I'm a gunsmith by trade; I just like to look at other men's work when I get a chance."

Butler handed him the firelock.

Wend quickly looked the rifle over. It was the type which Wend called the "southern plain style." They were cheaply made in border settlements in southern Virginia and the Carolinas. It had a single-trigger lock of English manufacture, a sliding, wooden patch box cover, and an iron trigger guard. There was no brass ornamentation or carvings, save for simple "beavertail" pattern grooves just behind the breech, a typical mark of southern firelocks. Wend noted that this gun had been around for a while; there were numerous scratches and other signs of wear, but the wood was well oiled and the operating parts, though worn, were well functioning.

Wend asked, "Where did you get this firelock? Were you down in Carolina?"

"Naw, I picked it up from a gunsmith down below Pitt. But he said he got it in trade from a southern hunter who came north." His eyes quickly flitted over Wend's rifle, with its German double trigger lock and all its scrolling and brass fittings. "Sure enough, it ain't no decorated Pennsylvania rifle like yours."

Wend gave the youth a sincere look. "Those things don't affect its accuracy or reliability. A southern firelock can shoot just as true if it's well maintained, and I can see you do a good job." He handed the rifle back to the scout.

He took the rifle, and then motioned toward Wend's rifle. "I sure admire your piece, Mr. Eckert; I'm hopin' to use my militia pay to get one like that when this is all over."

There was a pause for a moment. Then Butler said, "Tomorrow, after we've marched for about an hour, we'll hit a pretty well-marked trail. When we get there, I'll run ahead to scout for the day, and meet you at the best location for camp. I got a place in mind, but it will be a long day's march for your crowd."

"That's fine, Butler; we'll make it."

Butler nodded. "You should be able to follow the trail pretty well on your own. I'll make marks anywhere it fades out or might be confusing."

Wend thought a minute and nodded. "That sounds reasonable; Flannagan and I know how to follow a marked trail."

Butler screwed up his face in thought for a moment, then continued, "Now, it happens there's a village across the Muskingum near the end of the day's march; I'll do my best to spy on it to see if they look like they're planning anything hostile."

"You think that's likely?"

"Naw, Mr. Eckert, most of them villages from here on down to the Ohio are pretty small; without countin' their older boys, they ain't got enough warriors to seriously take on a party this size." Then his face wrinkled up again. "Biggest thing we got to worry about is if a few of the villages along the river joined forces to come after us; then we could face a good fight."

"I pray that won't happen, Simon."

"We'll, you can't never tell, sir." Then Butler bit his lip and stayed silent for a minute. "By the way, sir, I'd like to take Crooked Harry with me tomorrow to help scout."

"Harry? Its hard to believe he'll be able to keep up with you."

"Oh, he walks sort of funny, but he can move fast enough." Butler laughed. "Leastways, he can move a sight faster than this gang you got. And I can use him to send a message to you if the need turns up."

Wend considered the idea for a moment and couldn't think of any objection. "All right, go ahead and take him."

They talked for a while longer and then the others joined them, had their rations, and before long the entire party, with the exception of the camp guards, were asleep in their blankets.

* * *

As dusk was turning into darkness on the next day, the exhausted men of the column filed into the night's camp. Butler was there to greet them and show the location of a small stream for water. Like the day before, he had piled up some kindling to help the men start their fires.

The detail went to work settling into the camp and Pittock started looking after the wounded. It was only after about a half hour that Wend suddenly realized something was wrong: Crooked Harry was missing. "Butler, where's Harry?" he asked the scout.

"Oh, I forgot to mention that, sir. I got to thinking of a way to get a better idea what the Indians of all these river villages are planning. So I sent Harry over to talk to them."

Wend was shocked. "You sent him across the river to go right into the villages?"

"Sure 'nuff, sir. Harry's known all through these parts and the Indians consider him harmless. I had him cross over and walk into the village just like he was traveling down the Muskingum Trail which runs all along the river. 'Course, he ain't goin' to tell them he's with us. He's goin' to tell them he's coming down from Wakatomica after the attack. The Indians will buy that, since he wanders through this territory all the time."

Wend, suppressing his worries, asked, "But Simon, how will he get information to us?"

Butler shrugged. "He won't contact us less he learns somethin' we need to know. He's going to keep going down the trail, spying on the villages along the way. He finds out some village plans an attack or some villages are joining together to hit us, he'll come quick to find us. And he'll meet up with us permanently when we get down to the Ohio Trail."

Wend said, "Simon, I wish you had held off on this until we had a chance to talk."

"Well, Lieutenant, I knowed there was a village across the stream from where we were and there was a ford right there. If I'd waited till now to explain, we'd of missed the opportunity."

Wend sighed. "Still, you should of . . ."

Just then the gruff voice of Jake Cather interrupted. "For God's sake, Butler, you mean you let that crazy man Harry go back among the Indians?"

Wend looked around to see that Jake and Flannagan had just arrived at the fire after seeing to their men. He explained, "Jake, Butler says he'll be able to spy on them and tell us if they plan any hostile action."

Rage spread all over the waggoner's face. "Spy for us? More like he's going to tell the Shawnee all about us; tell them where we are, how many men we got, and where we're going. Like as not, he'll help them plan an ambush."

Butler shook his head. "That ain't going to happen, Cather. I'll vouch for Harry."

Jake brushed past Wend to get right in the scout's face. He raised his hands and Wend thought he was ready to grab the youth.

Cather shouted, "Vouch for him? *You'll* vouch for him?" He turned to Wend. "Christ, that crazy man's lived among the savages since the French War; near twenty years! Now this sprout, who ain't hardly old enough to grow a proper beard, thinks he'll be more loyal to us than the people what been feedin' him for most of his life. That's just plain crazy."

Butler stood his ground calmly in front of the incensed waggoner, eying him with a steely look. Then he said in a low, firm voice, "He'll be loyal to us 'cause he wants to get out of this part of the country before the real war gets started. He wants to go north and Mr. Eckert here has promised to help him." He thought for a second, then continued, "And I've known Harry long enough to know that when he agrees to do something, he'll be true and carry it through."

Jake turned to Wend. "I told you back at Wakatomica that the Shawnee left Harry behind to spy on us. I ain't changed my mind. And now this so-called scout has helped him go back where he can tell them everything he's seen. Butler's played right into their hands and any time now we're going to pay the price."

Then Cather turned back to the scout, raising a balled fist as if to strike him.

Wend got between the two men and, putting one hand on each man's chest and slowly, carefully pushed them further apart. "Now listen, there's going to be no fighting here. Calm down, Jake; we can't change what's been done. We have no choice but to give Harry a chance."

Cather gritted his teeth and backed off. "All right, I'll not throttle this fool, but I don't like it."

That night, there was a charged atmosphere around the campfire; Jake visibly sullen, the others keeping quiet, not wanting to say anything that might cause a flare-up. Luckily, everyone was beyond exhausted and very shortly they settled in for sleep.

* * *

They marched for two more grueling days. There was no ambush and no sign of Crooked Harry. At the end of the second day, with the last of the sun, they reached the trail which followed the bank of the Ohio. They went into camp fifty yards off the trail and just east of the Muskingum.

In short order, the men had the cook fires lighted, the smoke wafting upward in the evening light. As they cooked their meager meal, there was a sense of relief among the detail; everyone knew that one more day's march would put them at the boat landing. For the first time on the journey, Wend heard men calling out to each other with jokes and jibes between different campfires and the echo of laughter around the camp.

Jake Cather had been nursing a simmering anger toward Butler for the last two days, but even he was now in a happier mood. As they were finishing up their meal, he reached into his haversack and pulled out a flask. "Well, lads, I've been saving this for a proper moment, an' I guess it's here, what with us in our last camp before we reach the Ohio." He took a long pull on the flask, and then handed it to Flannagan. "Here's a little taste of cheer to pass around."

The sergeant took a sip, then looked down at the flask and smiled. He glanced at the waggoner, "Damn, that's some good whiskey. Where did you get it?"

Jake grinned from ear to ear. "Why, from no one else than our esteemed Sergeant Major, Simon Donegal; he filled this bottle up for me himself 'afore we left Wheeling."

Wend looked around at the men at the fire, "Donegal makes the stuff himself back at his place on my farm."

Pittock took the flask and drew deeply upon it. His eyes lit up. "If Donegal's still got a supply of this back at Wheeling, I'll buy a goodly amount." He looked around, winked, and said, "For medicinal purposes, of course, back at my apothecary shop." He took another sip and passed the flask on to Butler.

Everyone laughed heartily.

But the laughter was abruptly cut off by the sound of a loud call from out in the bush.

"Hello the camp! Hello, the camp! I'm coming in! Don't shoot!"

There was a sudden, brief, silence around all the campfires, followed by the bustle of a quick reaching for weapons.

All the men at Wend's fire stood up, firelocks in hand, looking out into the forest.

Everyone, that was, except Simon Butler; he remained sitting, took a deep pull on the flask, and said calmly, "It's all right; I recognize the voice; there ain't no danger."

Wend turned to the scout. "Who is it? Harry coming back?"

"Naw, it ain't Harry."

Just then the man behind the voice came into light cast by the campfires. He was a burly man just above average height, wearing a belted, undyed linen hunting shirt with fringes around the rain flap and at the bottom hem. He had piercing eyes and several days growth of scruffy beard. He carried a long rifle casually in hand by his right side.

It was Simon Girty.

Girty smiled and said, "Hello, Eckert. You got any hot tea or coffee for a traveler who's spent a long day on the trail?"

Butler spoke up without turning around to look at the new arrival. "We got better than that, Simon." He held up the flask and said, "Try this; it's first-rate whiskey. After that, there's some tea in the pot." He shook his head. "I won't offer you any victuals, 'cause I got no doubt you're better fixed in your haversack than what we got."

Girty sat down next to Butler. He took a slug of the whiskey and made a long sigh of appreciation; then he filled his mug with the hot tea.

Wend asked, "What in the devil are you doing here? And how did you find our party?"

Girty gulped some of the tea down, then answered, "Finding you was simple. I saw the smoke from your fires and figured it must be militia; it was too large a camp for any party of Indians."

Wend repeated, "All right, but how did you happen to be here?"

"Connolly sent me down from Pittsburgh. He wanted me to find out what was happening with McDonald's force."

"And you came alone; no partner with you?"

"That's the truth. I took a canoe down to the Captina and then walked overland, making cold camp at night. Fact is, I like working on my own." He grinned and smacked Butler on the shoulder. "That is, less I got someone like Simon here with me." Then Girty looked around the camp. "Is this an advance guard for McDonald on the way back?"

Wend said, "In a way: The major sent me to get the wounded back to the boats and prepare to provide rations to the men when the main force arrived."

"So how far behind you is McDonald?"

Wend waved his hands. "That's a good question, Girty. If things worked out the way McDonald expected, no more than a day. It could be less, slow as we've been going with the wounded."

"How *did* things go at Wakatomica?"

Wend told him what had happened up to the time the detail had left, then described McDonald's plans to destroy the villages and crops.

Girty stared off into the night. "Yeah, I think you're right. They could be just behind you. I 'spect it wouldn't take more than a day to finish up with the work of destroying the place. "

"Well, that's all I can tell you," said Wend.

"That's enough; I'll take it back to Connolly." He considered a moment, then said, "I'll catch some sleep with you tonight and then leave just before dawn. I want to make fast time back to Wheeling. The Delaware chief White Eyes has come in on our side; he's brought a war party down to Fort Fincastle. Connolly and Crawford thought they might go on to catch up with McDonald if he hadn't hit Wakatomica yet, they were preparing to leave when I started out. They might be on their way by now. If they haven't left Fincastle, I'll tell Crawford they ain't needed." He thought a moment. "Anyways, Connolly is anxious as hell to get some word about the expedition, somethin' he can send down to Dunmore."

Suddenly there was the sound of shouting from one of the camp guards posted toward the trail. Everyone turned toward the sound.

"Who's that!" shouted the guard. "Stop or I'll shoot!"

Once again the men grabbed their firelocks and jumped to their feet.

"Don't shoot! It's me, Harry! Harry's coming back!"

There was a moment of silence, some crashing around in the bush, and then the voice of the guard calling, "Sergeant Flannagan: it's Harry all right. I'm sending him in."

Soon a smiling Crooked Harry appeared in the firelight.

Girty laughed, then looked at Wend. "You got Harry with you? Where did you find him?"

"He was in one of the villages at Wakatomica. We're taking him back to Wheeling."

Butler said, "Simon, I sent him over to spy on the villages across the Muskingum a couple of days ago; he's just coming back now."

Meanwhile, Harry had seen Girty sitting by the fire. "Simon's here! Hi, Simon!"

Girty stood up, then grinned at the little man. "How are you, Harry?"

Harry ran up to Girty and put his hands on his shoulders, almost embracing him. "Harry's glad to see Simon." He looked around at the men around the fire. "Harry's great friends with Girty!"

Butler, who had returned to his seat by the fire, said, "Yes, we know you like Girty. Now tell us what you found out in those villages, Harry. Is there anyone planning a war party?"

Harry responded to Butler, "No war party, Simon. No village has enough warriors to face us."

Butler looked at Jake Cather, smiled, then turned back to Harry. "Are you sure?"

Harry nodded vigorously. "Oh, yes, Simon. Harry sure. Only Angry Bear wanted to fight us. He tried to get warriors from other villages to join him, but nobody would come."

Wend asked, "Who is this Angry Bear?"

Butler answered, "He's the top warrior in the southernmost village on the Muskingum; it's almost at the mouth. He's a hothead and is lookin' to make a name for himself as a war captain."

Girty added, "But he's frustrated by the fact that his village is very small; maybe they could muster seven or eight warriors if no one's out hunting or fishing."

A thought struck Wend. "How did the Indians in the villages know our strength; how did they know we were too big for them to take on?"

Harry perked up. "Boys saw you. Two Delaware boys from village just below Wakatomica were out hunting; spied column on first day of march. Boys told their village; soon word ran down Muskingum about size of party." He shook his head. "No one wanted to fight, 'cept for Angry Bear."

Girty said, "Makes sense, Eckert. They knew you had a goodly number of men; they also were aware of the size of McDonald's force. They figured if they hit you, they might face reprisal from the main force."

Wend felt a weight removed from his shoulders. They wouldn't have any interference making it to the boat landing.

Girty looked around the men at the fire. "Well, I guess I'll settle in for the night, and I'll be on my way back to the Captina at first light; got to get the word back to Connolly."

Very shortly the entire company followed Girty's example.

* * *

Girty was up and on his way the next morning when the first sign of light was on the eastern horizon. Eckert's detail was ready to march by the first real light and in the morning gloom they made their way through the bush out to the trail. Once on the actual path, the column moved more rapidly; Wend calculated they would have a long day's march, but could make the boat landing on the Ohio by sundown. Butler went ahead to scout.

The war party hit them less than a half hour after they broke camp.

It was an elegantly designed ambush. The column was marching through rolling country and had just descended a hillock into a flat area; another small hill was in front of them. The Indians allowed the detail to pass by their positions in the bush on the top of the first hill and then took the rear of the column under fire with a volley of shots.

Wend and the head of the column were at about the midpoint between the two hills. He looked back and could see that the war party was in a broken semi-circle around the rear marchers. As he watched, one of the militiamen of Calvert's squad fell to his knees, clutching his leg. The rest of Calvert's men took to cover and began returning fire.

Wend immediately realized that the hill in front of them represented the best location for a stand. He pointed to the crest of the hill with his rifle and called out, "Cather, get the wounded up there." Then he shouted back to Calvert: "Pull back and make for the hill! We'll concentrate there!"

And in case anyone was unclear what to do, he shouted, "Everyone to the hill!"

In fact, the militiamen needed no urging. They started to run forward along the trail toward the ridge. At the rear, Calvert's men began to disengage, some of them helping their wounded squad mate.

And that's when the Indians sprang the second part of the ambush. Suddenly a burst of firing came from the top of the hill directly ahead, accompanied by a chorus of bloodcurdling war cries.

Flannagan let out a sharp yelp and went to his knees, clutching his arm. Blood began to ooze from between his fingers. The sergeant crawled off the path into the bush.

Wend screamed, "Take to the bush; everyone behind cover!" Then he found a sizable tree and flopped to the ground behind its trunk. He called out, "Flannagan, how are you?"

"It ain't hardly bad, Lieutenant," the sergeant shouted back. "I'm gettin' a cloth around it now."

Wend looked back; the detail had taken cover, bunched together at the bottom of the hill. Meanwhile, a second volley of shots rang out from the top of the hill in front of them, joined by scattering shots from the war party in their rear. There was a scream from the rear part of the column, among Calvert's squad. At almost the same moment one of the wounded in the middle cried out, "Shit, I been hit again!"

Wend counted quickly; a least four men had been hit already. Wend glanced at the men sheltering behind whatever cover they could find and saw looks of fear on many of the faces.

Then he looked up the hill to try to see the enemy. As he did so, something from the back of his mind was bothering him, but he couldn't quite figure out what it was.

It was Horner who supplied the answer. He had taken cover just a few feet away. "Mr. Eckert, I was looking up the hill when the Indians fired that last volley; I didn't see but four or five muzzle flashes!"

Instantly Wend realized the young apprentice was right. His brain had been trying to tell him that the ambushing party on the hill ahead, though strategically placed, was not large; in fact far smaller than his detail. But the problem was that the Indians didn't need a large force; he had only a few fully capable fighters.

As Wend looked up the hill, the Indians fired again. It was more a ripple of fire than a volley. But he was able to count five puffs of smoke. The attackers were in a line across the trail; two on the left side of the path, three on the right.

As he was calculating, a burst of firing came from the rear.

Jake Cather, who was near Wend, shouted, "Them savages in the rear have come up closer behind us; they got us pinched in between. We got to do something fast, or they're going to put balls into us one by one, then come in and finish it with hatchets and clubs. " He motioned toward the men of the detail, all under cover, but huddled close together. "These men are going to start panicking soon."

Wend called back, "We don't have time for panic if we're going to survive." He pointed up the hill ahead. "Flannagan, keep the quartermasters firing at the party in front of us. And get any of the wounded who can still shoot working with you." He turned, cupped his hands, and shouted to Calvert: "Have your squad shoot to the rear!"

But even as he issued the orders, he knew Jake was right; if he didn't do something soon to break the ambush, more men would be killed and wounded; panic would arise and soon enough the Indians would come in for scalps.

Wend realized that the situation called out for a quick bayonet charge up the hill ahead, as he had done on the road from Hart's Store. Then he could draw the whole column up into a strong defense position on top of the ridge. But he had no disciplined force for such an attack. Calvert's militia squad must stay at the rear. All he had at his disposal was the quartermaster group and while they were armed with rifles, knives, and hatchets, they had not been trained as a fighting unit.

Wend's mind was racing like a galloping horse; he *must* figure out a way to break the ambush. He forced himself to settle down and analyze the situation. Then, looking up the hill again, an idea came to mind. If he could put together a group of four or five men, a flank attack was possible; they could creep under cover around to one side, then up the hill to engage the Indians. It wouldn't have the impact of a charge with cold steel, but it would put the attacking warriors in a cross fire between the flankers and the men of the forward part of the column.

He turned to Cather. "Jake, you're right; we must do something, and we must do it fast. I need three men to come with me to strike the flank of the party ahead. We'll go around to our left; there's only two of the savages on that side of the trail. We can push them back to the other side of the trail, and force the entire party off the crest." He paused and gave the waggoner his fiercest glare. "And you and Elijah are elected. I know you both can use rifles and hatchets. You Conestoga drivers pride yourself on being hard men; now's the time to prove it."

"Eckert, I done plenty of fighting, mainly in taverns. But there ain't no choice now." Then Jake looked at Elijah McCartney, who was also close at hand. "You figure we can handle this?"

McCartney grimaced. "I might as well catch a ball up on that crest as down here."

Flannagan called out from across the trail, "I'll be your third man."

Wend shook his head. "No, Sergeant, somebody's got to be in charge of the column. That's you; and besides, you're already wounded."

A quiet voice spoke up from a nearby bush. "I'll go with you, Mr. Eckert. You know I can shoot true."

Wend was surprised. The voice was Horner's. "Andrew, you've never shot a man; it isn't like killing a deer."

"I guess if I'm going to live in this country, I'll have to learn." The apprentice looked around. "Besides, there's no one else to go."

Wend realized Horner was right. The other two quartermasters, the contract men he had hired, were making themselves as inconspicuous as possible behind trees. In fact, he couldn't recall having seen either of them shoot since the start of the fight.

Wend nodded to Horner. "All right, but stay close to me; we'll be fighting in the style of the warriors up there, not like soldiers on a battlefield. It may come to using your hatchet; you can't allow yourself to hesitate if it comes to that. You must lay into the Indian like he was a piece of meat on the chopping block; do you understand?"

The young man gulped and said, "I understand, Mr. Eckert. I won't falter."

"All right, you three, look up at the crest. There's already a cloud of smoke from the Indians' firing. When they shoot again, there'll be momentarily blinded by the flash and their muzzle smoke. We'll move out right after they fire; they may miss our movement."

"You hope," said Jake.

"Flannagan," Wend said, "Get together all the men who can shoot from among the wounded; when we start up the side of the hill, keep up as lively a fire as you can."

"I'll try, Mr. Eckert," said the sergeant.

"And get Flynn and Hoffman shooting! I don't care if you have to kick them in their ass or smack them with the side of your hand axe!"

"That would be the most fun I've had on this trip," yelled Flannagan.

In that moment, another round of shots came from the crest. Wend, staying close to the ground, scampered to the left of the trail; the others followed. As stealthily as possible, they worked their way around the base of the hill. When Wend judged they were approximately on the flank of the Indians, he formed the men in a line. Jake was on the left end, Elijah to the right of him. Wend put himself to the right of Elijah, and then motioned Horner to take the far right. Then they started picking their way up the hill.

As they advanced, the four men tried to maintain cover and move as quietly as possible. All of them were hunters, so they knew how to use the trees and bushes. But they weren't Indian warriors, trained from childhood to move silently and invisibly through the forest. So Wend knew that sooner rather than later the war party would detect them.

They were helped by Flannagan. Evidently he had recruited a reasonable number of men able to use their firelocks, for Wend was surprised by the volume of fire coming from the detail.

In a few minutes the flankers had managed to get about halfway up when they heard calls between the Indians, followed almost immediately by a pair of shots down toward Wend's advancing line. Wend heard a "snap" sound and then a small branch from the tree behind which Elijah was sheltering dropped on his head. The waggoner he pushed it away and called, "They seen us and got us in their sights, Eckert."

Suddenly there was a zipping sound right next to Wend's ear, followed by the crack of the gun firing. Then another two shots rang out from the top of the hill. All four militiamen hunkered down behind cover. Wend sighed, and called out, "Take them under fire as best you can!"

The fight soon devolved from an advance to a stationary shootout between the flankers and the warriors on the hill. Wend realized the Indians had shifted around so that at least three were firing down on his men, while the rest were returning the fire of Flannagan's men.

Wend thought he caught sight of a warrior, and snapped off a shot. Then he crouched down to reload. Meanwhile, Horner, on Wend's right, fired, and there was a yelp from the crest.

"Mr. Eckert, I hit one! I hit one!"

Wend looked over at his apprentice; he had partially risen in an instinctive attempt to see the effect of his shot.

"For God's sake, get down, Andrew! Get down and reload as fast as you can!"

The youth dropped to the ground. Almost immediately a shot creased the tree an inch above his head; bark spattered all over him. Horner looked up at the bullet mark, shock on his face. Then he concentrated on ramming a charge down his barrel.

The undeniable fact was that the advance had stalled. Wend realized he must try to get things moving again. He took a deep breath, pushed up into a crouch, and sprang to a tree about five feet ahead. He flopped down behind it and aimed his rifle up the hill, searching for a target. Hopefully the others would follow his example.

Suddenly a shot sounded on Wend's left. He looked over and saw that Jake had fired.

Cather looked over and called out, "I think I hit one, but I can't be sure, Eckert."

Wend sighed; that was good, but at the same time, the waggoner wasn't making any effort to advance. *Damn it, he thought, they couldn't just stay here and trade shot for shot with the war party.*

Then another shot sounded from the crest and Elijah gasped and let out a groan. Wend looked over; the waggoner had dropped his firelock and was holding his hand to the right side of his head, blood all over his fingers. There was a long cut along his head, and it appeared that the top of his ear was missing. McCartney reached down into his haversack, pulled out a rag, and pushed it up against the wound.

Cather called out, "We can't get any closer, Eckert. They'll hit us as we move. And the same if we try to move back. We're screwed either way."

"Jake, just keep firing as fast as you can. At least we're diverting their fire from the column. And they're in a crossfire; at least one of them has already been hit. They may give up the fight if they see it's not worth it."

The shootout continued for another five minutes, with neither side moving. Then, a brief lull in the firing was ended by a burst of shots. But Wend was disconcerted by the sound, for the firing was coming from a new source; it was coming from the east, from the back of the hill, putting the Indians in a three-way crossfire.

As Wend was trying to figure out what was happening, there was the sudden sound of yelling and shouting from where the new firing had emanated. But the words the new attackers were using were indecipherable. Then Wend realized they were speaking in an Indian language.

For God's sake, who could this be? Then he suddenly remembered what Girty had said the night before about friendly Delawares arriving at Wheeling. *Had Crawford decided to send them forward without waiting for Girty's report?"* Instantly he concluded that there was no other friendly force which could be coming to their aid.

Cather shouted over, "Who the hell is that shooting from the other side? Did Flannagan send some men around the hill?"

"No Jake, he hasn't got enough men to do that. It must be that Chief White Eyes who Girty told us about."

There was another round of shots from the new arrivals.

Horner, excitement in his voice, called, "Look, Mr. Eckert, the Shawnee are pulling out!"

Wend looked up the hill; he briefly sighted one scurrying warrior. Then he saw a tall Indian who was supporting a wounded comrade as they moved back.

Wend brought his rifle up, took quick aim, and put a ball into the tall warrior's left shoulder. Then man staggered, dropped his wounded compatriot, and, off balance, staggered into a tree. Wend pulled a pistol from his belt and fired. It was long range for a hand gun; Wend had aimed for the warrior's torso, but actually hit him in his right thigh. But it was good enough; the Indian slid down the tree and lay motionless on the ground.

The other wounded Indian was struggling to get to his feet. But suddenly Wend heard the crack of a shot from his right and the Indian fell to the ground.

Andrew Horner shouted triumphantly as he lowered his firelock.

Wend looked over to see a look of fierce satisfaction on the apprentice's face. Wend pulled himself to his feet and said, "Come on, Andrew, let's go up the hill. This fight's finished." He looked over and saw Cather was bending over his wounded friend.

Wend also noted there was no longer any firing from the rear of the column. Then he saw Flannagan climbing the hill, a bandage on his right arm. The sergeant called out, "Them Shawnee in the rear are gone; they skedaddled when they saw their friends up here runnin'."

As he and Horner climbed to the crest, Wend wondered how he would communicate with the Delawares. Hopefully White Eyes, or one of his party, would have some grasp of English.

They came to the warrior Horner had shot; he was clearly dead, his lifeless eyes aimed skyward. He had two wounds; one in the hip and one in the jaw, which had destroyed the lower part of his face and penetrated through his neck.

Wend looked at his apprentice. "Well, Andrew, you've killed your first man."

Horner was staring down at the body, his eyes as wide open, the muscles of his face working. He did not respond.

Wend put his hand on the youth's shoulder. "You always remember the first. Mine was a Delaware I shot with a pistol on Sideling Hill in Pennsylvania. I still wake up remembering the expression on his face as he realized he was dying." Wend looked down at the dead warrior. "The others you kill don't have the same effect."

Horner took a deep breath. "God willing, I won't have to kill another."

Wend nodded, "Yes, Andrew, God willing."

As they were talking, Jake Cather joined them at the crest. "Elijah is going to be all right, Eckert. He ain't goin' to be as pretty as before, what with half his right ear sliced off, but he'll be all right."

Wend responded, "Jake, the only human who ever thought Elijah was pretty was his mother."

Jake smiled crookedly and shrugged. "That's true enough, now you mention it." He paused then pointed down the hill. "By the way, there's a dead Indian over there. I figure either Elijah or me shot him."

"So there are at least three Shawnee down," said Wend.

"Yeah," answered Jake. "That's what I count."

Just then there was a noise of men coming up the eastern side of the hill, it was a steeper and more difficult climb. Wend braced himself to meet the Delaware Chief and his party; he turned to face the new arrivals.

From the bush emerged two men. Neither was a Delaware. In fact, neither was any other kind of Indian.

Wend was looking at Joshua Baird and Simon Butler, both breathing heavily after the climb, and using their rifles as walking sticks.

Baird's chest was heaving with the effort of climbing, but he was also grinning from ear to ear. "Hello, Sprout. Damned if it doesn't seem like I've spent half my life getting you out of trouble."

Wend, astonished, asked, "What are you doing here, Joshua? Are you with White Eyes and his Delaware party?"

Baird and Butler exchanged looks. The scout asked, "Butler, I ain't seen any Delawares; you seen any lately?"

"Not down here, Joshua. I seen White Eyes back in Pittsburgh a few months ago. I hear he's at Wheeling."

Chagrined, Wend said, "So, it was just you two who made that attack?"

Joshua shrugged. "You got it, Sprout; there ain't no one else here but us."

Wend was momentarily speechless.

But Cather, never at a loss for words, asked, "Damn, Joshua, how did you know we were here?"

"That's easy enough. I been scouting along the trail here since McDonald and his men left. I was just breaking my camp this morning when Simon here comes striding along the trail, headin' east. We was havin' tea when we heard shots bein' fired; lots of shots."

Simon added, "We knowed right away you must have been ambushed, Lieutenant Eckert. So we ran back to give you a hand."

"We heard calls in an Indian language," said Horner.

"Of course you did," Joshua answered. "That's 'cause we decided to make ourselves sound like a war party, just to amuse your friends here on the hill." Joshua made a sweeping motion to take in the three warriors on the ground.

Meanwhile, Flannagan had arrived; at his side was Crooked Harry. He said, "Mr. Eckert, we got one man in Calvert's squad dead back there and four wounded. Doc Pittock is doing the best he can with them. If this ambush hadn't been broken, there'd be a lot more. "

Cather suddenly sprang past Wend and grabbed Harry by the arm, literally shaking him like a rag doll. "Yeah, we was in a fix all right. A fix set up by this crazy bastard. He told us last night that the Shawnee weren't planning no attack on us and then we're hit soon as we get on the trail today. I tell you I've been right about him all along. I'm sayin' this guy was in cahoots with that Angry Bear fellow."

Wend shouted, "Let him go, Jake. We don't know the story yet."

"Damn it, Eckert, it's plain as day. He lied out his ass to us. I say we shoot him and put him in the ground with these dead Shawnees." Cather pulled out his pistol and pointed the muzzle at Harry.

Meanwhile, Joshua was looking down at the dead warrior at Wend's feet. "Shawnees? Well, this is Shawnee country sure enough, but that ain't one layin' there. That's a Mingo if I ever saw one."

"A Mingo?" Wend asked in shock. "Are you sure, Joshua?"

"Of course I'm sure. Look at that paint on his face and them ink tattoos on him. They're Mingo style, ain't they Simon?"

Butler nodded. "Sure enough, Joshua." He looked over at the Indian slumped down by the tree. "He looks to be Mingo, too."

Flannagan said, "Harry says he recognized some of them warriors who hit us from the rear; they was sure enough from Angry Bear's village. So looks to me like we got both Shawnee and Mingoes workin' together."

Wend turned to Cather and pushed his pistol hand down. "Jake, you just proved you're a good man in a fight and I respect you as a waggoner and a friend. But if you don't put that pistol away and let go of Harry, I'll put you on charges and see you get a lashing; do you hear me? There's a lot we don't understand about this situation and nothing's going to happen to Harry until we find out the truth."

Joshua walked over to the other warrior, about ten feet away where he had run into the tree. He was in a half sitting position, his face against the tree trunk. The scout pulled the Indian away from the tree and he fell flat on the ground.

A loud groan issued from the fallen warrior.

"Hey, this bastard's still alive," said Baird. "He's been shot in the shoulder and the hip, but he ain't finished."

Then suddenly the scout froze, looking down at the Indian. "Hey, Wend, come on over here."

Wend walked over slowly until he was beside Baird.

Joshua turned to Wend and said, "Now look closely, Sprout. This here's an old friend of yours."

Wend stared down at the Indian; his eyes were open, his visage contorted in pain. Then he recognized the face and inadvertently took a step back. "My God, it's Wolf Claw!"

Baird looked at Wend; he had a wolfish grin on his face. Then the scout pulled a pistol from his belt and handed it to Eckert. "Well, Sprout, ten years ago, back at the Slippery Rock Mingo village, you vowed you was going to kill Wolf Claw the next time you saw him." He grinned even more broadly. "So now's your chance. Besides, he's bad wounded and we might as well put him down."

Rage coursed through Wend. He took the pistol, cocked the hammer, and aimed at the Mingo's head.

Wolf Claw looked up at Wend and his eyes focused. Then recognition spread across his face. He shouted the words, "Scalp Stealer," and instinctively tried to rise, but pain exploded over his countenance; he coughed, groaned again, and fell back to the ground. Then with great effort, he spat at Wend's feet. "I know you shoot me now, but know this, Scalp Stealer: This one's spirit will chase you and curse you until the last of your days."

Then Flannagan spoke up. "Hey, Lieutenant, you might want to ask him some questions before you pull that trigger. Like, what is he doing down here in Shawnee territory ambushing us?"

Wend lowered the pistol and looked at Baird. "Ask him about that, Joshua. Ask him in the Mingo language. It will be easier for him to speak."

Baird nodded and started talking to Wolf Claw.

As he spoke, the other men crowded around. But Wend motioned them all back about twenty feet; he figured Wolf Claw might tell Joshua more if their conversation was private.

As he herded the men away, Wend noticed that Butler was looking at him with his head cocked to one side, an incredulous smile on his face. Wend said, "All right, Simon, what's on your mind?"

The youth shook his head. "*You're* the Scalp Stealer? I heard that story from Indians all over the Ohio Country. But damn, I never would have figured you to be the one they was talkin' about."

"Look, I was just taking back my family's scalps, including my own." He pointed to the back of his head.

"Lord, Mr. Eckert, that may be true, but it makes you a marked man. If you ask me, you should have stayed back in Winchester. Any warrior would give a lot to go back to his village with your scalp on his belt."

Frustrated, Wend shot back, "What makes you think I volunteered for this trip?" He turned away to speak to Flannagan.

At that moment, Joshua called out, "Hey, send Crooked Harry over here. Wolf Claw says he knows Harry and will talk only to him."

Wend motioned to Harry, who scuttled over to where the wounded Indian lay. Wolf Claw immediately began speaking.

In a few minutes, Baird and Harry walked over to where the little knot of militiamen stood. Joshua said, "Harry was right; Angry Bear didn't have enough warriors to attack. He only had eight. But last evening, after Harry left to come back to your detail, Wolf Claw's party arrived at the Shawnee village by canoe. There were five of them, and they had been on a long hunt down in the country below the Ohio. The Shawnee told them about the militia raid up at Wakatomica and asked Wolf Claw to help attack your column. So they cooked up this little ambush."

Butler looked puzzled. "But the northern Mingo haven't been on the war path. They didn't join in Logan's raids and they ain't been been talkin' with Cornstalk about raisin' the hatchet."

"You're right," answered Baird. "It's only the Mingo bands down here on the Muskingum and over on the Scioto what been sittin' at the council fire with the Shawnee."

"So why did Wolf Claw agree to join with Angry Bear?" asked Wend. "I thought the decision to make war took agreement of the elders and the women of the village."

Joshua looked back at Wolf Claw, then back to the group. "Yeah, that's true. Looks to me like Wolf Claw jumped the gun. He saw the chance for a little glory; grab a few scalps and go back to Slippery Rock Creek in triumph. So he gambled on a success which would make him an even bigger man in the village."

Butler said, "Yes, but instead he lost three men, including himself."

Wend thought a minute. "His village isn't very large. They don't have any more than ten men of fighting age."

"Yeah, and they've got three less now." Joshua looked at Wolf Claw again. "Fact is, Wolf Claw ruined his reputation today. He's going to be remembered as a fool around their council fire." Baird pointed at the pistol in Wend's hand.

"Now's the time to finish him; word will soon get back to his village that the Scalp Stealer killed him. That will add to his disgrace."

Wend checked the priming in the pistol's pan and walked toward Wolf Claw. Then abruptly he stopped. There was the hint of an idea forming in his mind; it was incomplete and lacking shape, but intriguing. He turned back, uncocked the pistol and handed it back to Joshua. "I don't think I'll kill him. He may be useful to us. We'll take him back to Wheeling with the other hostages."

Joshua stood in astonishment, his mouth open. "Are you out of your head, Sprout?" He waved his hand around the group of men. "Killin' him is the right thing to do; I *want* you to kill him. Butler here wants you to kill him."

Butler nodded. "Sure enough; put a ball in his head."

Jake Cather spat and said, "Christ, Eckert, everyone here wants you to kill him. He's a piece of shit that nearly put a bunch of us in the ground."

Baird raised his hands in frustration. "Hell, even Wolf Claw wants you to kill him. He can't go back to his village. One of the other warriors would sneak up and put a knife in him some time when he wasn't suspecting it. That's the way the Indians take care of someone in disgrace."

Wend stared at Joshua for a long moment. The idea was rapidly taking shape in his mind. He asked, "So the last thing Wolf Claw wants is to go back to his village?"

"That's the truth of it. He'd rather die right here; at least he'd have gone down in battle."

Wend turned to Flannagan. "Sergeant, get Pittock up here to see what he can do for Wolf Claw's wounds. And have the men start making litters for anyone who can't walk." He pointed to the Mingo war captain. "Including him, if the Doc says he'll survive."

Then Wend looked at Harry and asked, "How would you like to spend the winter on Slippery Rock Creek?"

Harry grinned from ear to ear. "Oh, yes! Yes, Mr. Wend! Harry loves Mingo village on Slippery Rock Creek. Harry great friends with medicine woman they call Orenda. Orenda always takes care of Harry."

Wend looked at Joshua and smiled benignly.

Baird's face wrinkled up in puzzlement. But almost immediately, realization of the meaning of Wend's words spread across his countenance. He closed his eyes and sighed. Then he grimaced and exclaimed, "Oh, shit!"

CHAPTER SIXTEEN
Slippery Rock Creek

The flickering flames reached up into the night sky and illuminated the faces of McDonald, Crawford, and Eckert as they sat by the fire in front of the headquarters blockhouse of Fort Fincastle. Wend had come by to make his proposition to the two commanders. It was three days since the expedition had returned from Wakatomica and he had had some time to work out a way to use Wolf Claw as a means to travel to Slippery Rock Creek.

McDonald took the pipe out of his mouth and looked askance at Eckert. "Why is it so important to open negotiations with the Mingoes along this Slippery Rock Creek?"

Wend was ready for that query. "Unlike the Mingoes on the Muskingum and the Scioto, they're still on the fence about joining Cornstalk's war alliance. But after our attack on Wakatomica, it's sure that the Shawnee will approach them to join. There are several villages along that creek; together they could provide sixty, seventy, or maybe more warriors. If we can dissuade them from joining, it will help weaken Cornstalk's force and lesson Connolly's need to worry about attacks emanating from the area northwest of Pittsburgh."

Crawford said, "You know, Angus, he's right about that. Those Mingoes could cross the river and have an easy time raiding into the farms and small settlements north and east of Pitt. It would mean Connolly would have to divert troops to protect them."

McDonald put his hand to his chin. "I see what you mean. Dunmore needs all the militia he can muster for his northern column."

"Exactly, sir," Wend responded. "And after raiding above Pittsburgh, these warriors could easily come south and join the forces opposing Dunmore himself."

Angus thought a moment, then asked, "But how the devil does this Wolf Claw fellow you captured play into keeping those villages out of the war?"

"We take him back to his village and turn him over to the elders there as a gesture of peace," said Wend.

McDonald responded, "So we would be giving them back their war leader to curry favor? I don't see the sense in that; he might in fact convince them to take up the hatchet."

"Angus, it's true he was their war captain, and, indeed, has distinguished himself in the past." Wend held up a finger and glanced at each of the majors in turn. "But the Mingo elders will want him back to impose justice on him, not to honor him. His impetuous participation in the attack on my detail without approval upset their diplomatic plans. In doing so, he violated Mingo customs for deciding on war."

Crawford asked, "How can you be sure about all this? Wouldn't we be just helping them if they do decide on war?"

"Joshua and I talked with White Eyes about all this; he agrees that Wolf Claw will be in high disfavor. And even more so since his attack cost them three of their warriors; two dead and himself grievously wounded and out of action for months; Baird thinks they had no more than nine or ten warriors in total."

Angus sat silently for a long moment, pulling on his pipe. Then he asked, "Why should you and Joshua be the ones to lead this expedition?"

Wend took a deep breath. "Joshua and I have both been to the valley of Slippery Rock Creek and to Wolf Claw's village; we were the guides for a diplomatic mission led by Captain Thomas Sterling of the 42nd back in 1763."

McDonald raised his eyebrows, took the pipe out of his mouth and said, "Oh, yes; I know the Sterling family. My father was friends with Thomas' father."

Wend said, "I was very impressed with Captain Sterling. But there's another reason I should go on this mission: I am personally acquainted with the medicine woman of the Slippery Rock Creek Mingo. She's a white woman, named Abigail Gibson, but known as Orenda to the tribes."

Crawford perked up. "By God, I've heard of this Orenda woman. She's a legend among the Ohio Indians for her medical work." He thought a moment. "She's fair-haired and, as the story goes, very beautiful."

Angus looked sharply at Eckert. "And just how do you happen to know this woman, Wend?"

"Her family was traveling with mine along Forbes Road on the way to Fort Pitt back in '59. Wolf Claw led a war party which attacked our caravan. My family and Abigail's father were killed; she was taken prisoner and eventually given to Wolf Claw as his hostage wife."

Crawford said, "Well, I'll be damned."

Wend hurried to make his point. "Look, it is part of Mingo culture that the woman's council must approve all major decisions; particularly in the matters of war and diplomacy. Orenda is a member and could be a significant influence on her village's decision and perhaps those of all the villages in that valley. Clearly she understands the overwhelming force that Virginia will bring to the war; I'm convinced she would argue for peace if I explain what they're up against."

There was a long silence around the fire, both majors staring into the crackling flames.

McDonald looked at Crawford. "Shouldn't we clear this with Connolly?"

Wend interrupted. "I say we undertake it on our own responsibility."

Angus asked, "Why do you say that?"

"Connolly has been conducting negotiations with Cornstalk and the other powerful chiefs of the Muskingum and Scioto area. He's working side by side with the Indian Commissioner, Andrew McKee. And that Pennsylvania trader, Richard Grenough, has been advising him unofficially. If we present this idea to him, he's going to lay it before them and let them chew it out."

McDonald shrugged, "What's so wrong with that?"

Wend responded, "Who knows how long it will take to get a decision? I say Connolly won't lift a hand without his advisors' consent. And since they're currently in negotiations with Cornstalk, it might slip out that talks with the Slippery Rock Creek Mingo are in the offing. Cornstalk could quickly send an emissary to lure them into his alliance."

Angus slowly nodded his head. "Yes, by God, you're right; it could get lost in the damned politics of it all."

Crawford sighed. "I'm afraid Eckert is making sense. You were ordered out here for a quick attack on the Shawnee, but McKee's peace negotiations kept you sitting here at Wheeling for weeks."

Wend had been saving his most potent argument for the right moment. Now he carefully laid it out. "Besides, Angus, the fact is, we wouldn't have Wolf Claw except for your raid up the Muskingum. It's an important outgrowth of the raid that we have an opportunity to separate a sizable faction of the Mingo from the main alliance." Wend looked into McDonald's eyes. "If we are successful, it will irrefutably demonstrate the overall value of your expedition."

Wend watched the Scotsman's face carefully and saw that the idea had hit the target; Angus' eyes brightened and his mouth muscles tightened.

"Damned if I don't think you're on point, Eckert," he said quietly. He looked at Crawford. "This would please the governor mightily if Wend is successful."

"Undoubtedly," said Crawford.

Angus looked up from the fire and asked, "When could you start out?"

"The surgeon says Wolf Claw will be well enough to travel by canoe in two days. We'll start then."

Crawford said, "You'll need a sizable party; who will you take besides Joshua?"

"I'd like Donegal and that young scout, Butler."

"All right," said McDonald, "anyone else?"

"Yes, two more: I'll take the former hostage the Indians call Crooked Harry. He speaks the language and knows the people in Wolf Claw's village. Finally, Joshua and I talked to White Eyes; he agrees with the plan and is making up a string of peace wampum for us to carry and present to the elders of the Mingo villages. And to verify that White Eyes and the villages he leads are joining with our forces, he's sending one of his warriors, named Little Bear, along to speak for him."

McDonald emptied his pipe ashes into the fire and stood up. "All right, Wend, you've conceived a fine plan; make your preparations for a departure. You'll be in danger, but my judgement is that the prospect of peace with these Mingoes is worth the chance." With that he turned and strode off into the darkness toward his tent.

Wend and Crawford also stood up and watched McDonald as he departed. There was a long period of silence; Crawford crossed his arms in front of his chest and finally said, "You explained everything to him except one important item. And, after the disappointing results of the Wakatomica raid, Angus was so delighted at the prospect of burnishing his reputation that he didn't think to ask about it."

Wend looked at the major. "You're right about that; Cresap and some of the other hotheads have been criticizing McDonald behind his back. He knows about the gossip and is fuming because there's no good way to respond to them. But what is this important item you think I didn't explain?"

Crawford squinted at Wend through the dim light and his mouth broke into a crooked smile. "You didn't happen to mention why you personally are so *eager* to undertake this mission."

Wend sighed. "William, I know you to be a man of honor. I'll tell you the reason if you vow to keep it between the two of us."

"Done, Eckert."

"Abigail Gibson has a white son, now about fourteen years old."

Crawford saw it instantly. "And you're the father."

"Yes, William, and I've only seen him for fifteen minutes, ten years ago, when he was at his mother's skirts. God help me, I have become obsessed with seeing him again before he reaches manhood."

Crawford took a deep breath and cocked his head. "Wend, I remember well that night somebody shot at you out of the darkness on Braddock Road. Now I find you entangled with the most famous woman hostage in the Ohio Country. Damn, man, your past seems sheathed in a web of mystery. I vow someday I'll find out the whole story. But for now, I do hope God is watching over you, for you are going to need his help to complete this journey."

* * *

The three canoes hugged the western bank of the Allegheny River, one close behind another, as they slid silently through the night, their prows making only the slightest disturbance, the paddlers taking care to avoid splashing as they dipped the blades into the water. Wend, in the leading canoe, looked over at the east bank where Pittsburgh lay sleeping in the darkness. It was nigh on midnight and only a few lights flickered from the town. None of the paddlers could miss the hulking fortress, its great bulk darkening the point where the Monongahela and the Allegheny merged to form the Ohio. Wend had arranged their transit past Pittsburgh to be in the deepest night to avoid any chance of discovery and possible interference from the garrison.

The procession of canoes continued northward for a couple of miles in silence and then from the second boat came the distinctive sound of Donegal's highland accent. "I still say we could have stopped and had a nice cup of rum at Semple's Tavern and 'na a man would have been the wiser."

From the third canoe came the high-pitched voice of Crooked Harry. "Harry likes rum."

Butler, in the rear position of the same canoe, joined in, "Harry, you like whatever you can get your hands on."

"But rum is particular fine, Simon; gives you good feeling."

Joshua Baird, paddling in the front of Wend's canoe, said, "I've said it before, this is the craziest thing you've ever done, Sprout." He shook his head and said quietly, "And this is the strangest assortment of men I ever traveled with." He took a few more strokes with his paddle and continued, "I don't know how you convinced McDonald to allow this trip but I keep thinkin' I must have been touched in the head to come along."

Wend laughed. "For years you've been telling me that I act too much on my own; that I don't trust my friends to help me. And now I ask you to help on a very special mission and you're not missing any opportunity to complain. Maybe

I should have left you at Wheeling sitting by the fire and brought Jonathan Zane instead. I'm sure he would have jumped at the chance to come on this trip."

"Zane, that callow whippersnapper? That would be the day."

"Joshua, he did fine job at Wakatomica. But you know why I asked you to come."

"Yeah, you asked me to come watch you get killed and have your scalp tied up on the Mingoes' trophy rack." He made a few more strokes of the paddle.

Wend answered, "I asked you because you know this territory better than anyone else. But most importantly, the sachems know you and respect you after all those years with Bouquet. They connect you with the British authorities. They won't dare kill me out of hand when you explain that I'm an emissary from the white chief in Williamsburg. "

"Mayhap that would work in any other village; but these be the very people you stole the scalps from. They're goin' to see red when you show up."

"They'll have to deal with me if they want peace, and I think they do. After Wolf Claw's blunder, they've got too few men to risk war. And of course, we've got him with us, back there in Donegal's canoe, to use as a bargaining chip."

"I still say you're goin' to need more than that."

"I've been thinking of some other things, Joshua. I'll just have to be light on my feet when we get there."

"That may be Sprout; you got a real gift for gettin' people to buy your ideas. But it ain't gonna be enough. They may listen to your talk about the white chief's peace and they may deal with you on that. But once that's finished, they're goin' to call the Scalp Stealer to justice. They know the rest of us can take a message back just as well as you."

Wend had no answer. But he felt a knot in his stomach at Baird's sobering words.

After a period of silence, Joshua said, "We been paddling a goodly time. I say we put Pitt a couple of miles more behind us and then pull into the bank to make camp. Then we can reach the trail which goes to the valley of Slippery Rock Creek for camp tomorrow night."

"You pick the place to stop, Joshua."

* * *

Baird's estimate was accurate. The party reached the place where the trail met the Ohio near dusk on the next night. They emptied the canoes of their kit and supplies, pulled them beyond the tree line and covered them with cut tree branches and brush. The rest of their journey would be on foot. Wend bound Wolf Claw in a sitting position to the trunk of a tree, then inspected his wounds and applied fresh dressings.

He looked down at the Mingo and said, "You better get some good rest tonight, Wolf Claw, because you're going to have to walk most of the day tomorrow. It's going to be painful for you with that leg wound." Wend looked around and continued, "But then, I expect you've figured out where we are and what's ahead of you."

The Mingo just scowled at Wend.

Meanwhile, the others had gathered wood and Crooked Harry had gotten the fire lighted. It was one of many domestic skills he had demonstrated on the trip and Wend had guessed that doing menial camp work was one of the ways that the man ingratiated himself to the people of the various villages he visited.

Soon the men were seated around the fire, the evening meal roasting over the flames. Wend's arm muscles ached from three days paddling against the current of the Ohio and the Allegheny. In fact, weariness permeated his entire body. He was ready for sleep; at first he contemplated taking to his blankets without eating, but he knew he needed the sustenance for the travails of the morrow. So he forced himself to stay awake, saying very little as the others talked and joked.

The other quiet person at the fire was Little Bear. Wend reflected that the name was an apt one; the Delaware was slightly below the average height but very burly in build. The Delaware had spoken little in the course of the trip, but had, without being asked, carried out more than his share of the camp chores and other tasks which had arisen. Wend figured that the warrior was of roughly his own age; Joshua had told him that White Eyes considered Little Bear one of his principal aides in carrying out the duties of chief of the Turtle Clan. Wend comforted himself that, as such, the man could speak with authority when they stood before the Mingo sachems.

Presently the food was ready; Harry distributed the meat and corn into the bowls of each man. Then he filled an extra bowl and carried it over to Wolf Claw and loosened his bonds so he had one hand free to eat with. As he ate, he glared continually at Wend.

Little Bear looked over at Wolf Claw. He took another bite of food and glanced at Eckert. Then he pointed at the captive and, in a quiet voice, said, "When this is over, you best kill Wolf Claw. His hate for you more hot than this fire."

Wend considered his response. After a while, he said, "I think his village will find a way to deal with him. I understand that is the custom; a knife in his side when he is least expecting it, often by another man from his family."

Little Bear remained silent for a long moment. Then he said solemnly, "Maybe yes, maybe no. His village is small; needs every man. Sachems may allow him to live, even in shame. I say again; you kill him or he will find way to kill you."

Wend shrugged. He started to answer when suddenly Little Bear froze and raised his hand. He sat silent for a few seconds, listening to the night. Then he said quietly, "Men all around us."

Simultaneously, Harry stood up and looked into the bush, fear written over his face. Wolf Claw also stared into the forest, a crooked grin on his lips.

All the men at the fire were suddenly quiet.

Baird carefully put his bowl on the ground. He looked at Wend. "He's right, there be warriors out there."

They all jumped for their firelocks.

Wend had to go over to his blanket to get his rifle; he cursed when he realized that he was perfectly illuminated by the flames.

Suddenly a voice called out from the bush, surprisingly near at hand. The words were in an Indian dialect. Little Bear, now sheltering behind a tree with his rifle in hand, responded to the hidden warrior. Then Little Bear said in English, "They're Mingoes. They have us surrounded. We must put our weapons down if we wish to live. Their leader wants to come in and talk."

Joshua said. "Sure enough, they got us in the light. We ain't got much choice."

Wend called over to Little Bear. "All right, tell him to come to the edge of the trees."

Little Bear passed the word.

Immediately they heard someone moving through the woods. Everyone stared tensely in the direction of the approaching footsteps.

In a few seconds a warrior appeared; he advanced until he stood a few feet beyond the tree line and stood looking at the group, a longrifle cradled in his left arm. The light from the fire reached out and played across his face.

Little Bear stood up and said, "This man I know; it is Mingo warrior from Wolf Claw's village. He is called Etchemin."

The Mingo said something and Little Bear explained, "He and his party were in a hunting camp when they saw our fire."

Etchemin stood silent for a long moment, staring at Wolf Claw. He said something to the Mingo war captain; the tone was sharp and angry.

Joshua whispered, "He ain't too happy to see ole' Wolf Claw. He says they thought he was dead." Baird smiled quickly, then continued, "Actually, he said Wolf Claw should be ashamed he ain't dead. There ain't much love lost there."

Etchemin looked around the scene until his gaze rested on Wend. He took a couple of steps closer; then his eyes opened wide in astonishment. He pointed to Wend, looked over at Little Bear, and spoke sharply.

Little Bear, obviously answering a question, nodded and spoke back to the Mingo. He turned to Wend. "He recognizes you are the Scalp Stealer. He ask why I would be with a coward like you."

While Little Bear was explaining, Etchemin took another step toward Wend and pulled his knife. He spoke in English for the first time. "Scalp Stealer, Etchemin kill now."

Suddenly Little Bear lunged forward, placing himself between the Mingo and Wend. "You no kill this man, Etchemin. He is on mission from white chief to your village. White Eyes, Chief of the Turtle Clan, has given him protection."

Etchemin stopped and dropped his knife down to his side, looking askance at the Delaware.

Little Bear held up the string of peace beads. "Here is wampum from White Eyes. Heed the meaning of the beads, Mingo."

Etchemin stared at the beads, then looked back at Wend with a snarl on his face. But in the end he said nothing and slowly, hesitantly, returned his knife to its sheath.

Baird interrupted, in an impatient voice, "How many men has he got out there, Little Bear? And are we going to start shooting or just spend all night talking? Or, for God's sake, can I go back to my food while it's still warm?"

Little Bear spoke a few words.

Etchemin turned his head back toward the bush and shouted something. Silently, one by one, four additional Mingoes emerged.

Three were full-grown warriors; the fourth was an adolescent boy. But all were holding firelocks on the men around the fire. Etchemin waved and they all relaxed, grounding their rifles or moving them to the crook of their arm.

Etchemin walked over to the tree where Wolf Claw was bound, pulled out his knife, and cut him free. Then he inspected the war captain's wounds.

Wend said, "Little Bear, tell him we're planning to go up to his village tomorrow. Ask him and his men to accompany us."

The Delaware spoke to Etchemin, who said something to his compatriots which caused them considerable mirth. Then Little Bear said, "He says sure enough we'll all go to the village tomorrow. But we will be under his escort. And when we get there, the sachems will decide what to do with the Scalp Stealer."

Without saying more, the Mingoes set up camp adjacent to Wend's group. And they peremptorily took custody of Wolf Claw, seating him at their fire.

But a little later, Baird, who had been watching the new arrivals closely as he ate his food, leaned over to Wend and said quietly, "They took in ole' Wolf Claw, but they ain't bein' particular warm to him."

Little Bear heard them talking and moved over to whisper, "I hear what they say. They *very* angry at Wolf Claw; say women and children cry for warriors who died. Also, village is suffering because the two men who survived could only bring part of meat back from hunting. That's why these men out hunting now."

Joshua said, "It's just like I said; he'll be answerin' to their leaders when we get up to their village."

The Delaware nodded and resumed eating.

Wend said, "Thanks, Little Bear, for letting us know what the Mingo are saying. It will help us when we have to talk with their elders."

Wend stood and walked to his blankets. Tomorrow they would take the path which led to Abigail's village. By nightfall he would see her and his son. And then a sobering thought intruded: There was also a good chance that by nightfall tomorrow he would be dead.

* * *

The combined parties left the camp with the sun just at the horizon, bringing with it the promise of heavy August heat. Etchemin led them along the narrow but hard-packed path. Wend had memories of the trail, for he had scouted it ten years before for Captain Sterling. However, then they had been traveling east from the Mingo village rather than westward, so he found it hard to recall specific landmarks.

Wolf Claw had a hard time, limping painfully as he walked. Neither party had much sympathy for him, but both groups took turns helping him, simply to expedite the journey. About mid-morning Little Bear had a short exchange with Etchemin and then fell back to where Wend walked and explained, "We make the village by dusk. Short breaks only to rest Wolf Claw."

By late afternoon Wend saw, in the distance, the hills he knew sheltered the Mingo village. Shortly thereafter Etchemin sent the Mingo youth running ahead to warn the town of their coming. Baird said, "That boy's got instructions to tell the village and the elders that Etchemin is bringing in the Scalp Stealer. It'll make him a big man in the valley."

Wend replied, "But for God's sake, Joshua, he didn't do anything to capture us. We were coming in anyway."

Joshua grinned. "Don't matter none. Etchemin's going to play this up as much as he can. Little Bear and I had a talk last night after you settled in. He figures that Etchemin is angling to be the new war captain of the Mingo village. So he has to add everything he can to his list of boasts."

Just over an hour later they rounded a bend and Wend caught sight of a woman standing by a tree at the side of the trail. She was dressed in an undyed linen shift, belted at the waist, and held a walking stick in her right hand. She was breathing heavily and beads of perspiration shone on her forehead as if she had been running or walking fast. The woman had blond hair pulled back tightly around her head with a single long braid hanging down her back, almost to her waist. And she stared at Wend with deep blue piercing eyes which seemed to penetrate into his very soul.

Wend caught his breath. Abigail Gibson was as beautiful as the day fifteen years ago that Wend had first laid eyes on her at Harris' Ferry.

As Etchemin came abreast of her, he called out in loud, impatient words and motioned vigorously with his hand. The meaning was clear; he was telling her to get back to the village.

Abigail answered him in a tone just as sharp and raised her stick as if to strike back the warrior's hand. Etchemin answered with one word, obviously an epithet, then withdrew his arm and passed her quickly.

Wend walked over to where she stood and put his hand on her arm. "You look wonderful," he said.

"For God's sake, Wend, what possessed you to come here?"

Wend smiled broadly. "Abigail, aren't you glad to see me?"

"They're going to kill you."

"Well, I have a few cards to play before that happens."

"You could have the whole deck to play, but it wouldn't do you any good. Why did you come?"

"I came to see you. But mostly I came to see our son."

"Wonderful. Your son can watch you roasted at the stake. What a memory he'll have." She looked around and spied Joshua. "I recognize you! You were the scout with that red-haired girl; the army nurse who gave me the instructions for inoculations when Bouquet was on the Muskingum."

Joshua grinned. "That's right enough, Miss Gibson. Joshua Baird is the name."

"Well, you should have had enough sense to know what they're going to do to him. Listen to me: There are enough of you to fight off the men of our village. Why don't you all turn around and run for the river right now?"

"Beggin' your pardon, ma'am, I been tryin' to tell Wend what a fool he is for better than a week. Ain't done a bit of good so far. And he ain't likely to change now."

Wend said, "I can't leave. I'm on an official mission for Virginia."

"That's not going to offer you much protection. They'll listen and then kill you."

Wend motioned to Wolf Claw. "Perhaps you should go over and take a look at your husband. He's got a couple of serious wounds and we've been pushing him hard all day." Wend gave Abigail a wink. "He would probably like a little wifely love and comfort."

"Stop that, Wend. You know the marriage is not like that. I'll treat his wounds just like I do anyone else's."

"As I recall, it's enough of a marriage that you've borne his children."

"Wend Eckert, why are you baiting me this way? You have learned some bad habits. And besides, why do you care about my marriage to Wolf Claw? That nurse, that Mary woman, said you were married and had children of your own."

"I'm not the youth who was here ten years ago, Abigail. And I've learned to be more assertive along the way."

"I can see that. And I'm not sure I like the new, sharp-tongued Wend Eckert."

Wend took her by the arm. He looked into her eyes, and she returned his gaze. "Now listen, Abigail: regardless of what we've both become, I'll always care deeply for you and respect you."

She sighed heavily, and made a visible effort to calm herself. "And I for you, Wend; don't ever doubt that."

"I'm glad to hear that, because if I'm to complete my mission and leave here alive, I'm going to need your help."

She looked puzzled, but then nodded and said, "I can't imagine what I can do, but of course I'll help in any way I can."

Just then Crooked Harry came up and joined them. He was beaming at Abigail. "Hello, Orenda; do you remember Harry?"

Abigail smiled broadly and held out her arms; Harry rushed to embrace her, his arms around her and his head against her shoulder. She said, "How could I forget my dear friend Harry?"

"Harry missed Orenda. Came to spend winter in Orenda's village. Will Orenda take care of Harry?"

Abigail grinned down at the little man. "Of course you can stay here for the winter. And I will take care of you, the same as always."

He looked up at her. "Harry will help you with cooking and sewing and with medicine. You will be glad to have Harry around."

"Surely I will, Harry. Now go with the rest of the men to the village."

Harry nodded, a wide smile on his face, and scampered like a child up the trail toward the town.

Abigail watched Harry go, then turned to Wend. She put her hand back on his arm. "I'm glad you brought Harry with you. He's part of the human debris strewn all around the border country. The normal life he would have led was destroyed by this damn conflict between the whites and the forest people."

Wend nodded. "I met him down at a place called Baker's Tavern and keep bumping into him. But I'm surprised you would be so uncharitable as to call him human debris."

"I'm not being in the least uncharitable. It's impossible not to have affection for that man. And besides, I consider myself part of that human debris."

Wend smiled ironically, "All right Abigail, now I take your meaning."

She sighed. "I must go look after Wolf Claw's wounds. You said you had cards to play, Wend. All I can say, is they better be good."

And with that she left Wend and caught up with Wolf Claw and the Mingo who was helping him walk. Wend listened closely as she talked to him in Mingo language. He couldn't understand her words, but the tone was unmistakable. Wend smiled as he remembered how imperious she could be when it suited her purpose.

Donegal came alongside Wend and grinned. He said, "I've 'na had much experience with women, but I'd say she isn't too happy with her man."

Wend smiled back at Donegal. "Simon, women have a way of making their mate's life miserable when they are displeased. But then, if you marry Sally Potter, you will find that out soon enough."

A distressed look came over Donegal. He said nothing more and resumed his way toward the village.

Little Bear came up and Wend walked alongside him. The Delaware looked at Wend and said, "You know Orenda?"

Wend smiled at the Indian. "She was my first woman, long ago when I was a youth, fifteen years ago."

The Delaware's face, usually so impassive, wrinkled in surprise.

Wend added, "This is truth, Little Bear. And here is more truth: Orenda's oldest child is my son."

The Indian walked a few steps without saying anything. Then he looked back at Wend. "Now Little Bear understands why Scalp Stealer goes to Wolf Claw's village." He shook his head. "But it is still foolish. Mingo will have your scalp."

"I have some ideas to keep that from happening. And your wampum is a big part of that. I'm counting on you to help me when the time comes."

"Little Bear will help. But like I tell you before, anger of Mingo is hot like fire." The Delaware looked at Wend. "Scalp Stealer need more help than Little Bear can give."

* * *

In a quarter of a mile they came in sight of the village. It was virtually as Wend remembered from ten years earlier; a collection of lodges and other buildings nestled in a loop of the creek. On the land side was a belt of pines which separated the village from the crop fields that extended back up against the hills which formed the northern side of the valley. The main line of the trail they had been following ran along the pine belt on its way to other villages to the west.

Etchemin led them to the center of the village where a large council fire ring had been constructed. Behind it was the trophy rack containing numerous scalps, the very one where Wend had cut down those of his family.

Wend saw that the entire population of the village had gathered to witness the arrival of the combined parties. Standing before the trophy rack were three old men, obviously the village sachems. As they approached the fire ring, Etchemin darted to the front and immediately began talking to the three elders in a tone so loud that all the onlookers could hear.

Joshua, standing next to Wend, translated. "Etchemin is tellin' the story of how he rounded us up and brought us here. Naturally, he's makin' himself look as good as he can."

One of the elders pointed to Wolf Claw and spoke at some length. Joshua said, "He's askin' how Etchemin found him and how he got up here from the Shawnee country."

There was another exchange and suddenly Etchemin motioned toward Eckert. As he did so all three sachems stiffened and glared at Wend. Simultaneously there was an angry outburst from the assembled villagers and Wend felt all eyes on him.

Etchemin resumed his speech to the elders.

"He's asking permission to have the honor of killing you. He says you deserve a coward's death."

Wend turned to Joshua and said, "This has gone on long enough. We've got to take the initiative. Come with me."

Wend touched Little Bear on the shoulder and motioned him to come along also. The three of them pushed their way past Etchemin and advanced to the edge of the fire ring. The crowd quieted as they advanced and finally even Etchemin halted his boasting.

The center sachem raised his hand and pointed at Wend. He said in English, "You are Scalp Stealer. I recognize you from long ago, when the soldiers in skirts came. You are older, but I know your face." He looked at each of his compatriots in turn, then back to Wend. "Why have you come here?"

Wend said to Joshua. "Translate for me: I want to conduct business in their language, to make sure the elders and all the people of the village understand."

Joshua nodded. "Tell me what to say."

"Ask him if I am the coward Etchemin says, why would I come to their village with only a few companions?"

Joshua spoke as the sachems listened. Then the man in the center answered.

Baird turned to Wend. "The elder in the center is Circling Hawk; he says you have shown some courage, but it's possible to be both brave and a fool."

"Tell him I am here on a mission of peace from the Great Leader of Virginia. And also tell him that Little Bear is here because White Eyes and the Turtle Clan are allied with Virginia."

While Joshua spoke, Wend had Little Bear hold up the wampum peace string.

The sachem spoke back and Baird translated, "They want to know why the leader of Virginia needs to talk peace, since the Mingo of this valley are not at war with anyone."

"Tell him we know they're aware of the war which has started between the Shawnee and Virginia and the raid on Wakatomica. Then ask them if they're not at war, why did Wolf Claw and his men attack the Virginia soldiers on the trail near the Ohio? Say the governor cannot credit their claim of peace when several of his soldiers lie dead and wounded at the hands of this village."

As Joshua translated, Wend watched the faces and eyes of the sachems. When the eyes of all three momentarily shifted to Wolf Claw and Circling Hawk's jaw muscles tightened, he knew his last words had struck home.

The sachems talked among themselves and then Circling Hawk took a step forward and spoke to Joshua.

Baird turned to Wend and whispered, "Well, sure enough they're pissed at Wolf Claw. They said the governor should know that he acted without their approval and they are grateful that we've brought him back to explain what he did."

"Tell them the governor is happy to hear that and is glad to turn Wolf Claw over to them so they can deal with him as they see fit. But the governor wants the promise of this village and all the villages in the valley that they intend to remain at peace and to observe the treaty that was signed at Fort Stanwix seven years ago."

The sachems listened carefully to Baird, then nodded and Circling Hawk answered. Joshua explained, "They say they ain't got no reason to break the treaty and they vow to remain peaceful. But they can't answer for the other villages."

"Tell them, Joshua, that we want to send Little Bear along with one of their senior warriors to summon all the sachems of the local villages to a council fire here. Tell them I will deliver the governor's words to all of them."

The elders conferred after hearing Joshua's translation and then Circling Hawk spoke for a rather long time.

Joshua said "They've agreed to your request. Etchemin and Little Bear will leave in the morning."

Wend looked at Joshua. "That's good; but he talked too long just to tell you that. What else did he say?"

"He said the Mingo respect the governor but he has insulted them by sendin' the Scalp Stealer as his representative. They will honor the governor by bringing in all the other village leaders for a council to hear his message. But the governor must understand they insist on dealing with you in their own way." He paused. "They say that they know I am Bouquet's scout, 'cause they have seen me with him at council fires. They also say that from his uniform and bonnet, they know that Donegal is one of Bouquet's skirt soldiers and that we can take back the answer of the villages as well as you."

Wend thought a moment. Then it hit him: "Joshua, don't you see what their words mean? They don't know that Bouquet is dead and that the Highland regiments left the colonies years ago."

Joshua screwed up his face. "Damned if I don't think you're right. Now you mention it, they did talk about Bouquet like he was alive." He shrugged. "But what difference does that make?"

Wend put his hand on Baird's shoulder. "I'm not sure. But I do know that after the beating at Bushy Run and then Bouquet's march to the Muskingum in '64, they fear him and the Highlanders more than anything else. There may be a way we can use that."

"Sprout, you're playin' a hell of a game here. The trouble is, the Mingo are makin' the rules."

Wend sighed. "Tell them this: The governor had no idea of their hatred for me. I will stand before them and justify my actions after we have finished with the governor's business."

"Shit, Sprout," Joshua exclaimed, "You *are* out of your mind. Offerin' yourself to their justice means you're goin' to end up dead."

"You heard their words, Joshua. They're going to deal with me one way or another. So I might as well show them I'm not afraid to face them. Go ahead and tell them what I said and then tell them I pledge not to try to leave before all the matters are settled, as long as they will guarantee my safety until then."

Baird rolled his eyes. But he went ahead and translated what Wend had said.

The sachems solemnly accepted Wend's offer and then told all the villagers to disperse. Wend's party was shown a place at the edge of the village to camp until the sachems from the other villages came in for the council fire.

* * *

They were still setting up camp along the creek when Crooked Harry came up to Wend. He had a conspiratorial glint in his eyes. "You come with me, Mr. Wend."

"Later, Harry. We're getting supper ready."

The little fellow gave Wend a sly smile. "You *want* to come with me. Orenda wants to see you now."

Wend became suspicious and frankly was a little fearful of moving through the Mingo village without any of his compatriots. "Why would she want to see me now?"

Butler had overheard the conversation and sensed Wend's suspicions. "It's all right, Lieutenant; the elders have given you their protection. No one would dare attack you, not even that bastard Etchemin."

Harry looked crestfallen. "Harry wouldn't play Mr. Wend false." He put his hand on Wend's arm. "Remember why you come to village. Now you come with me and see Orenda."

Wend nodded and Harry turned and led off.

They moved around the perimeter of the village, heading toward the valley trail and the band of pines which separated it from the fields. Soon they saw a small log building with a thatch roof, which stood not far from the trail. It was shielded from the village by a clump of trees and bush. Alongside it was a smaller building, a small, low edifice built in the style of a lodge. A small fire ring was situated in front of the door of the log cabin, within which a fire had been built.

Harry motioned toward the fire. "Wait here." Then he moved to the cabin door and knocked; almost immediately it swung open and Abigail appeared, a shadowy figure in the darkness of the interior. She reached out and put her hand on Harry's shoulder, whispered something to him, and then he turned and walked off toward the center of the village.

Abigail stepped out into the wavering light of the fire. Wend looked around. "Is this where you live?"

Abigail said, "No, our lodge is in the midst of the village. This is where I do my doctoring. The cabin is where I keep my medicines and the little lodge is where I put people who need to be isolated."

Wend turned back to Abigail. "Won't Wolf Claw be angry that you've come to see me alone like this?"

Abigail smiled. "He's exhausted from the pain of walking all day and dead asleep. And I helped him with a dose of a medicine mixed with spirits. Normally I use it to help patients who have a lot of pain. I gave him a heavy dose; he won't be awake until morning."

Wend grinned at her. "And you thought I had learned some bad habits."

"I'll do what is necessary to make patients comfortable. But I wanted him to be extra comfortable tonight."

Wend nodded. "Why did you want to see me?"

"I thought to have you meet your son. It may be the only chance you get." She turned and called back to the cabin.

Wend watched as a youth stepped out into the light cast by the fire and stood just a few feet from Wend. Wend saw the boy was nearly as tall as himself and had a wiry frame. He was dressed in a gray European-style shirt and a pair of breeches. On his feet were soft moccasins. His head was not shaved; the hair was pulled back and tied at the rear. The wavering flames intermittently lit up the youth's face. He showed no emotion as Wend stared, straining to make out the features; instead he returned the stare, his face unreadable.

Eckert inadvertently gasped; "My God!"

Abigail went over to the boy and put her arm around his shoulder. "Yes, Wend," she said quietly, "He's a precise copy of you, like a painting. Right down to your stone face."

Wend, still shaken, said to the youth, "I understand your name is Little White Owl."

It was Abigail who answered. "Who told you that?"

"A man named Simon Girty. He was a hostage with a Mingo village and said he had met you and seen our son."

"Yes, I know Girty. He's a scoundrel, but he's right; the Mingo call him Little White Owl." She turned to the boy and said something in Mingo.

The lad looked at Wend and spoke, slowly, in English, obviously taking care to properly form the words. "Good day, sir. My name is Henry Johann Eckert."

Wend said, "And good day to you, Master Eckert." Then he looked at Abigail and grinned. "He speaks English!"

"I've taught all my children. When Wolf Claw is not around, we often practice. Many hostages lose their English. I feared doing so and I also wanted the children to have it; one never knows what will happen."

"Why did you choose the name Henry for him?"

"After my father. And of course, Johann after yours."

Wend nodded and turned back to his son. "Lad, why don't we sit down on the log in front of the fire?"

Henry did as asked and Wend sat beside him. Abigail sat on the other side of the boy, the three of them shoulder to shoulder.

Suddenly the boy spoke. "Sir, why did you steal the scalps from the village? All the people are very mad at you."

Abigail laughed and said, "He's very direct, Wend."

Wend sighed. He said to Abigail, "I had hoped we could just talk for a while, but it's probably best we get this out of the way." He turned to the boy. "I took them because of a promise I made over the grave of my dead father. A promise of vengeance; and taking back the scalps was the first step."

The boy said nothing, but stared up at Wend.

Eckert continued, "Henry, I'm sure you have been told stories about your Mingo ancestors, probably by Wolf Claw around a fire on nights like this."

The lad nodded. "This is true. He told me the Mingo are great warriors sent from the north to watch the Delaware."

"Well, now I want to tell you the story of your German family and then it will be easier to explain why I took the scalps."

Henry wrinkled his brow, and asked, "What is this Ger-Man?" He stumbled trying to mouth the unfamiliar word.

Wend explained, "Germany is a land in the Old World, which we call Europe. The ancestors of both your mother and I come from Europe."

The boy was listening intently, and nodded that he understood. "Is Germany part of England, where mother comes from?"

Abigail spoke up. "No, Henry, Germany is a different land, across the water from England, which is an island."

Meanwhile, Wend was searching his brain to find a way to explain the nature of the Germanic people and land. And then it hit him how to make Henry understand. "Germans are very much like the Mingo." He paused to gather his thoughts. "Like the Mingo, there is no single chief; there are many chiefs, each with their own part of the German land. Our family came from a part of Germany called Hesse."

Henry tried to pronounce the new words and Abigail helped him.

Then Wend went on; "Our family were jaegers, or huntsman in the service of a lord."

The boy asked, "What is a lord?"

"You could think of him as a chief. Jaegers were also warriors who served as scouts in time of war, like the Kispoko clan of the Shawnee."

Henry nodded slowly. "Yes, I understand. I have heard of the Kispoko."

"Well, jaegers have a code; a tradition of beliefs and behavior, like the Kispoko and all Mingo warriors. And part of that code is to take vengeance on those who cause harm to their family. My family and your mother's father were killed by a war party from this village, a war party led by Wolf Claw."

Henry looked up at Wend, his eyes wide. He said, "So you have vowed to kill him?"

"Yes, on my father's grave I swore revenge on Wolf Claw and also the white men who helped him attack my family. Now I have killed most of those white men and it was I who wounded Wolf Claw."

Now Henry showed puzzlement. "If he was wounded, then why did you not kill him? Mingo warrior would have done that."

"I almost did; but just as I was about to do so, I realized that there was a better way to serve vengeance. I brought him to face justice here in his village for a foolish decision. Bringing him here also served the purpose of my chiefs." He thought a moment. "And I also brought him for a personal reason."

"But I still don't understand; why did you take the scalps from here? How was that vengeance?"

"The taking of the scalps was vengeance on all the people of the village for killing my family."

Henry sat looking into the fire for a long moment, then he looked up at Wend and asked, "Yes, I begin to understand. What did you do with the scalps, sir? Did you put them up on a rack in your village to shame the Mingo?"

"No; I took them back and buried them with my family, where they belong. And part of me is there, for Wolf Claw thought he had killed me with the rest of my family. He scalped me and left me lying for dead. So one of the scalps I took back and buried was part of my own." Wend leaned over and pointed to the rear of his head and pulled aside his long hair, showing the great scar.

Henry stared at the wound for a long time. Then he nodded slowly and asked, "What was the other reason you brought Wolf Claw back?"

Wend looked up at Abigail and then to the boy. "Because I wanted to see my son and I wanted my son to know me."

"Even at the chance of death?"

"Even to the point of death." Wend smiled at Henry, and put his hand on the lad's shoulder, feeling a thrill at touching him for the first time. "And now I have learned that I can be very proud of my son."

They talked for a while longer, and Wend told Henry about the farm at Winchester, his half-brothers and sisters, and about being a gunsmith. Wend was particularly gratified to see that the boy's eyes lit up as he talked about making firelocks.

After about fifteen minutes, Abigail sent Henry back to their lodge, and the two of them sat quietly watching him walk away.

Finally Abigail broke the silence. "You did that well, telling about his white heritage."

"I figured he has been steeped in the Mingo traditions and way of life. I just wanted to give him some idea about the way of a jaeger, to show him there are some similarities."

Then Abigail surprised him by changing the subject. "Tell me about your wife; what is she like?"

Wend thought for a long moment and then grinned broadly at her. "In many ways, she's the opposite of you. In fact, Franklin's wife, Ayika, said it very well at my wedding party. She told me you were a golden princess, a woman of the sun, a gift of Manitou to the Mingo, who needed the magic of your medicine. She said that since I couldn't have the golden princess,

Manitou knew I was sad and gave me a dark princess, a woman of the earth to make me happy."

"So she's dark-haired?"

"She's raven-haired. But Ayika was very perceptive; Peggy is a woman who knows how to make a man happy. She doesn't have much formal learning, but she's quick. She grew up in a tavern; she knows the most practical ways to keep a house. And the tavern taught her very well how to entertain guests, which has been most helpful in making our way in Winchester."

Abigail cocked her head, raised her eyebrows, and said, "So *you* married a *tavern maid*?"

The tone of her words reminded Wend of the privileged, haughty Philadelphia girl he had first encountered in 1759. "Yes, Abigail, but she shares an important thing with you."

"Shares something with me? I don't understand."

"She knows what she wants and will do what it takes to get it."

"Is that how you think of me?"

"That's one of the reasons I admire both of you." He thought a second. "Look at you; you wanted to be a doctor, but couldn't do it in our culture. So you realized your dream here with the Indians," He looked into her eyes. "Even to the point of staying when you had the chance to go back to your own world."

Abigail and looked at him and sighed. She opened her mouth as if to talk, but said nothing.

Wend saw a look of sadness in her eyes and on her face. He said, "What is it, Abigail?"

"Yes, Wend, when I decided to stay, I got what I wanted. I was totally absorbed by the sense of challenge and fulfillment in providing medical care to the people of this valley. I thought between that and the joy of my children, my life here in the forest with the Mingo would be full and satisfying."

"And hasn't that been the case?"

"It was at first; there was indeed joy in my life. But in recent years, as my work has become more routine to me, as the children grow older," she sighed again, "and as *I* get older, I find that something is missing. Something I have come to miss very much."

"What is that, Abigail?"

She hesitated momentarily, then said very quietly, "There is no passion in my life. Wolf Claw treats me politely, but there is no romance. And in any case I have no love for him. When he came to me in the night, it was ritualized; it was to produce children, nothing more."

"You say 'came'. Does he no longer sleep with you?"

"Not since our last child was conceived."

"I think I understand."

Abigail turned to Wend. "Do you really understand? I have come to long for, to dream for, something like those few days in our youth when we could barely control our lust. I cherish the memory of our single night together in that cabin beside the Conococheague." She turned to him, put her hands on his arms, and looked into his eyes. She leaned toward him, their bodies almost touching, and stared upward at him.

Wend saw the longing in her face and suddenly realized what she was asking of him.

"Do you understand, Wend? At night, when I'm unable to sleep, I fantasize about you coming to me in the darkness. You take me in your arms tenderly and we make romantic love like that night when we were young." She raised her chin until their mouths were only inches apart, and looked at him now with eyes half-closed.

Wend glanced around and realized how isolated the spot was. Behind them stood the cabin with its door open, almost beckoning. And in truth, he felt a longing coursing through his body. There was an overwhelming, nearly irresistible sense of temptation.

They sat there, looking at each other for a very long moment.

Wend leaned over and gave Abigail a gentle kiss on her cheek and then immediately moved back until there were several inches between their faces.

He took a deep breath. "Abigail, I can't give you what you want," he said quietly. "There was a time when I would have given all for a life with you, or even another brief interlude like our night in that cabin. And even now, I find myself greatly tempted by my love for you. But I will not break my vow to Peggy."

Abigail looked at him in that cool, direct manner he remembered from long ago. "Wend, we are here in the midst of the wilderness, in the Mingo world, not the white world. The Indians have a more understanding concept of fidelity than Europeans. What would happen here would remain in the forest; it would go no further than the trees which surround us or the walls of my cabin."

Wend shook his head. "I would that I could give you what you crave, Abigail. But I cannot. I have come to love my wife and I will not be unfaithful."

Abigail looked away and sighed, her chest heaving. Then she carefully removed her hands from his arm, stood up and adjusted her shift. She looked down at him, her mouth quivering slightly, her face red. "Wend, I respect your feelings and your decision. I'm sorry to have imposed myself on you."

Wend stood up and took her in his arms, their faces again close together. He saw the glint of tears in her eyes. "No, no, do not mistake me, Abigail, I have no regrets. My feelings toward you now are no different than fifteen years ago, and my admiration for you is undiminished. But things are different and much as I would like to lose myself in your embrace, I cannot do so in good faith to my wife and family."

Abigail broke away and stepped back. She ran her hands over her hair, took a deep breath and said, "I understand."

She stood there thinking for a moment, then said, in a businesslike voice, "Now listen: There is something you must know; perhaps it will help you in your negotiations at the council. There was an emissary from Cornstalk here just a few days ago."

Wend was suddenly very alert. "What did he want? Was he seeking an alliance?"

Abigail nodded. "Yes. He visited all the Mingo villages in the valley, requesting that they join in the coming war with the Virginians. My understanding is that some of the elders in other villages are sympathetic to Cornstalk."

"What of your elders, Abigail?"

"They are still considering his request. But they are very cautious, because of the few adult men we have, particularly after Wolf Claw's foolishness. We simply cannot stand any more losses."

Wend said, "Joshua and I thought that would be the case."

Abigail nodded. "When the time for decision comes, the question will be put to the woman's council. I will argue for peace."

Wend felt relieved. "Thank you for that."

Then Abigail pointed back toward the creek and said curtly, "Now it's time for you to go back to your camp." She looked back to the village "And I must go to my lodge and my children." She said no more; instead she abruptly turned on her heel and walked rapidly back toward the main part of the village, her back straight and rigid.

CHAPTER SEVENTEEN
The Last of the Scalp Stealer

Wend, standing before the council fire in the afternoon sun, scanned the semicircle of Mingo elders seated on the ground across the fire. There were thirteen, representing the five villages which occupied the valley of Slippery Rock Creek. Wend had just finished laying out Virginia's request for them to remain at peace during the coming war. Joshua stood on his right, performing the role of translator. Donegal, Little Bear, and Butler were seated on Wend's left. On either side of them were the people of the village, most seated. As Wend looked at the elders, he saw virtually no emotion on their countenances, no indication of their thoughts, no sign of the impact of his words.

After a long pause, Circling Hawk stood and made a long speech. Joshua listened for a while, then said, "Well, he's beatin' around the bush, but his main sentiment is that this village ain't excited about goin' to war; he says they're satisfied with the Fort Stanwix Treaty and they ain't inclined to send a war party to join Cornstalk. But they want to hear what the other villages have to say."

Tall Buck, who represented the most western and largest of the villages, came to his feet. It was easy to see how he came by his name, for he was lean as a rail, well above average height, and long-legged. He spoke for a long time and Joshua listened without translating to Wend. After a while, Tall Buck stopped talking and turned to the row of sachems, his arms opened wide to signify the end of his speech. Baird turned to Wend and said, "Here's the sense of it: He says the Shawnee and Mingoes down along the Ohio have been wronged by the whites. He talked about Baker's Tavern for a while and then about the raid on Wakatomica. He says if they don't join the Shawnee in this fight, they'll be overwhelmed by all the settlers flowing over the mountains. They must finish what they started long ago with Pontiac and Guyasuta. He says the Mingo villages down on the Muskingum and the Scioto have already pledged to join Cornstalk and the men of this valley will be thought of as women if they don't take up the hatchet to join their brothers."

The sachems had started to talk among themselves; after a few minutes, another sachem stood up. Joshua said, "That's Big Crow, from the next village up along the creek."

Big Crow spoke for several minutes in a very agitated manner. Then he turned and pointed at various elders, saying something to each.

Joshua turned to Wend. "Sprout, this ain't lookin' too good. Crow agreed with Tall Buck 'bout joining with the Shawnee. Then he went round to the sachems of each village, makin' a guess at how many warriors they could contribute. He ended up sayin' the valley could send around seventy warriors."

Wend said, "That's an army company."

"Exactly; Crow pointed out that Cornstalk and the other Shawnee leaders would be indebted to the Mingo of this valley." Joshua shook his head. "He's dead right about that. I figure Cornstalk can muster maybe 650, maybe 700 warriors. Another seventy would be a powerful reinforcement."

Wend said, "Undoubtedly Cornstalk's emissary has made promises to them."

Joshua said, "Whatever he told them, I make it out that Tall Buck and Big Crow are for war, this village is for peace, and the other two are sittin' on the fence. They could go either way."

Wend turned to Joshua. "We've got to take the initiative. Tell them this: Virginia has many men to send against the Shawnee — enough to make two powerful armies. Far more than the Shawnee can defeat. But tell them that even if they do manage to throw back the Virginians, like they did to Braddock, it won't be the end of it. The Great English Father across the sea is ready to send Bouquet and his Highlanders against all the tribes of the Ohio. There will be no victory for them."

"Sprout, are you sure about sayin' that? What if one of these sachems knows Bouquet is dead?"

"We've got no choice, Joshua. Bouquet is the one man they really fear." He turned to Donegal. "Get up, Simon, and stand beside me. And look very regimental."

The Highlander rose; then as if under discipline, marched up alongside Wend and stood rigidly at attention.

Wend whispered, "Nicely done, Simon." Then he turned to Joshua. "After you tell them about Bouquet, point to Donegal. They'll recognize his Highland jacket and his bonnet; tell them Donegal is a British officer sent by the English Father to summon Bouquet if he is needed."

Joshua sighed. "All right, Sprout. But this is like bettin' big with shitty cards in your hand." Then he held up his hands to get attention from the sachems and began the translation.

Wend watched the elders, particularly their eyes, very carefully as Baird spoke. They all remained frozen where they had been standing or sitting. Clearly they were taking his words very seriously. Undoubtedly some of them had been at Bushy Run in 1763 and had run for their lives before the bayonets of the Highlanders. And they all remembered Bouquet's march to the Muskingum with a powerful force in 1764. But Wend felt a knot in his stomach; would it be enough to dampen the sentiment for war?

Just as Joshua finished talking, a young Mingo boy of perhaps eleven or twelve came running through the village from the direction of the valley trail. He hesitated a moment before the fire, breathing hard. Then he went around the fire ring to where Circling Hawk stood and whispered excitedly in his ear.

Wend turned to Joshua. "What's happening?"

"Wish I knew; couldn't hear what the boy said."

Hawk held up his hands for attention; but he needn't have bothered, for everyone was staring at him. He spoke out in a loud voice so that everyone could hear. His words caused an instant uproar among the onlookers. All the sachems rose to their feet and Wend saw that all the villagers had also stood up and were looking toward the trail. Wend saw a look of anguish on Joshua's face. "For God's sake, what's going on?"

"It's real bad luck — our goose is cooked." Joshua shook his head. "There's a band of Mingoes coming here; men, women, children, old ones. The boy was on lookout and saw them coming up from the south. They crossed the creek at a ford a half mile west of here, then headed here on the valley trail. The boy ran and questioned them."

Wend grabbed Joshua on the arm. "I don't understand. Why is it bad news?"

"Because it's the remnants of Logan's village, that's why. "

"My God, is Logan with them?" asked Wend.

Joshua shook his head. "No, Wend, it's not Logan leading them. I wish it were; at least I know him and he sometimes listens to reason." He paused a moment, then said, "Now brace yourself, Sprout; they're being led by Laughing Eyes."

Wend felt the shock roll over him. Then he saw it all: "Oh, God, you're right; the sight of all these refugees is going to harden the resolution of these sachems. And Laughing Eyes will urge them to join Cornstalk for all-out war."

"Yeah, Sprout. We ought to get out of here now, if we could. But then, they ain't gonna let you go anywhere."

While they were speaking, the column of Mingoes came into sight. Wend could make out at least twenty-five people. At the head of the column were four warriors and a couple of youths, all armed. Behind them the women and children trudged along. At the rear were four pack horses led by a pair of very young boys, one of the horses bearing an old woman. As they watched, the column turned off the trail and came toward the center of the village.

Little Bear stood up and joined Wend and Joshua. He pointed to the man at the front of the Mingo band, a tall, lithe, handsome warrior. "That is the one they call Laughing Eyes."

As the Mingoes came closer, the villagers started to clap and cheer, many pointing toward the leader of the band.

Little Bear said, "These people know Laughing Eyes and what he has done; they honor him for his skill and bravery."

Joshua stared at the Mingo war captain, a look of astonishment on his face and finally said, "Oh, my Lord above."

Donegal glanced at Wend and then back at the newly arrived Mingo leader. "I dunna believe it can be."

But Wend was too shocked to say anything. He was desperately trying to come to grips with the fact that Laughing Eyes, the source of terror all along the border, the indiscriminate butcherer of men, women, and children, was none other than his schoolmate and best friend from long ago in Lancaster, the Conestoga Indian Charlie Sawak.

* * *

Wend watched as the man the Mingo called Laughing Eyes stopped his party of refugees and then advanced by himself to the edge of the fire circle a few feet from where Wend and his compatriots stood. He held up his right hand and said something to the three village elders in salutation. All three sachems responded; then Circling Hawk spoke for a while, his hand motioning toward the waiting band of Mingo travelers, and Laughing Eyes responded.

Joshua whispered, "They asked why these people had come to the valley."

Charlie was answering at great length. Joshua listened intently. Finally Charlie's speech ended and Joshua looked at Wend and said, "Sawak is askin' them to allow him and his people to join this village. He told them how grateful he is for the welcome the people of this town extended to him and his wife when they fled from the white man years ago. Now he's returning the favor by bringing them five full grown warriors including himself, three male youths who will soon be of fighting age, and a goodly number of women and children."

Wend shot a quick glance at Hawk. The sachem was showing a stoic face, but he was betrayed by the upturned corners of his mouth and the hint of a gleam in his eyes. Wend whispered to Joshua, "Surely they'll welcome him and his people?"

"Ain't no doubt. Eight strong males and a passel of women is a godsend to them after what Wolf Claw did. They'll say they have to consider it, and they'll make a big show of thinkin' it over, and then they'll take in Charlie and his people with open arms."

Suddenly Charlie pointed at Wend and spoke in harsh words to Hawk.

Joshua leaned over and said, "He wants to know why the Scalp Stealer, who has insulted this village, is allowed to be here."

Circling Hawk started to answer, but suddenly Tall Buck inserted himself between the village sachems and Charlie and started talking rapidly, pointing several times at Wend.

After a minute Joshua said, "He told Sawak that you are workin' for the English chief and tryin' to keep the valley Mingo from goin' to war with Virginia. Then he said the sachems of this village had weak hearts and were agreein' with you. He wants Laughing Eyes, who has suffered at the hands of the whites and who is known for great acts of war against the Virginians, to explain why all the villages must join with Cornstalk. He says that all the warriors of this valley will joyfully follow Laughing Eyes to war."

Wend's heart fell. Joshua had been right: Their goose was cooked and his doom was about to be sealed by the man who had been his closest friend. In a few days Charlie could be leading sixty or seventy warriors south to join Cornstalk.

Charlie was nodding in response to Tall Buck, but didn't say anything. Instead he turned and strode over to Eckert, a fierce scowl on his face. He came so close that it took every bit of Wend's will to conquer the urge to step backward.

Sawak stood glaring at Wend for a long moment.

Then, with their faces a few inches apart, Charlie Sawak gave Wend the briefest of winks. For a moment Wend was startled and in disbelief, but there was no denying the fast flutter of the right eye and the quick upturn of the right side of Charlie's mouth.

Then Sawak abruptly turned and faced Circling Hawk. He spoke a few words, and Wend saw Hawk nod.

Baird said, "He's asked Hawk for permission to speak in answer to Tall Buck."

Charlie walked over and stood before the seated elders of the other villages. Tall Buck remained standing a few feet from Charlie, his arms crossed and a triumphant smile on his face. Wend thought: *The bastard is certain he's going to get his way.*

Sawak stood silent for a drawn-out moment, looking toward the sky as if searching for inspiration. A pervasive quiet spread over the entire gathering. Everyone's eyes were riveted on the Mingo war captain. Finally he began to speak. He talked for several minutes, and every so often the people clapped, nodded, and cheered.

After a while, Joshua said quietly, "He started out tellin' them about the attack on Logan's people at Baker's place and how his son was murdered there. Right now he's talkin' about how many places he raided and how many settler's was killed in revenge. He's layin' it on pretty thick about bein' a great warrior and makin' the whites pay for their crime. And he's thankin' Buck for appreciatin' what he done."

Wend nodded toward Tall Buck. "Yes, Buck couldn't be happier about how things are going."

Joshua tapped Wend on his side. "Quiet now, let me listen."

After a moment Joshua said, "Now Charlie's sayin' that he and Logan have finished their raidin' to pay back the whites for Baker's Tavern. Logan has declared that he has satisfied his pledge of revenge. Charlie says he finished out his own quest for vengeance by raiding a big white village."

Wend asked, "Hart's Store?"

"Sounds like it, Sprout."

Then Joshua held up his hand for quiet. He cocked his head with an ear toward where Charlie spoke. After several long moments he looked at Wend. "Charlie said that when he was raiding, he found that there were many new settlements along the Ohio and the whites were thicker'n flies. He says all the tribes could get together and there wouldn't be enough warriors to drive the whites out."

The cheering had stopped now. All the sachems were staring at Charlie with serious faces. Buck's brow was furrowed with concern.

Baird continued, "Now Sawak's tellin' them about word he's heard from some Delawares and other Indians. He heard the whites were raisin' a big army to come punish the Shawnee for not following the treaty made at Fort Stanwix, for attacking the whites along the Ohio and in the hunting grounds below the Ohio." Joshua listened some more. "Now he's sayin' that if they think the raid on Wakatomica was big, they ain't got any idea of what's comin' when Virginia's whole army gets here."

Wend's heart began to pump; he sensed where Charlie was going.

Joshua exclaimed, "This is big, Sprout; really big! Sawak's comin' out against joining the Shawnee. He's sayin' the Mingo shouldn't get sucked into a war which is mostly over the Shawnee hunting grounds. It don't affect the Mingo, who already agreed not to hunt down into the Kentucky Country. He says the Mingo would be fools to fight the Shawnees' war."

Wend sighed. "Thank God; Charlie's coming through for us."

"Yeah, seems like; now listen: He's sayin' all he wants to do is settle down here in this village, build lodges for his people, and get ready for the winter. He won't lead no war party to join Cornstalk and none of the men from his band will take the warpath."

Wend leaned close to Baird. "Look at Tall Buck, Joshua! He's positively deflated."

"Yeah, and look at them other elders. They're listenin' close and I saw a couple that were nodding."

Charlie turned to Circling Hawk and signaled that he had finished speaking. Then he turned and walked back to join his party.

Hawk walked over to the row of seated elders and spoke for a few minutes. Wend saw them all nodding.

Joshua said, "All right, that's it, Sprout. They've agreed to go back to their villages and decide for war or peace. They'll all send word back here two suns from now."

* * *

Crooked Harry and Wend stood in the darkness before the medical cabin. The little man tapped on the door and it swung open immediately. Then he stepped back and motioned for Wend to go inside. As soon as he did so, Abigail shut the door.

Wend stood blinking, trying to adjust his eyes to the dim light of the interior. Abigail said nothing, but pointed toward the fireplace and then backed up and leaned against the wall, crossing her arms. A small fire burned in the hearth and two candles were lighted on opposite sides of the cabin. In a moment Wend made out Charlie Sawak standing beside the fireplace, the light from the flames playing across his face and glinting off of his shiny earrings.

Wend started to speak, but Charlie beat him to it.

"Eckert, what the hell possessed you to come to this village? Do you know how much trouble you caused me today?"

"Charlie," Wend began, planning to explain, but Sawak cut him off with a swift wave of his hand.

"I bring my people into the village after long days on the trail, ready to make a proposal to join this town, and what do I find? All the wrinkled old men of the valley lined up by the fire and the Scalp Stealer standing in the midst of a bunch of Mingoes who want nothing more than to roast him at the stake."

Wend replied, "Well, you certainly saved the situation. I'm very grateful for what you did today."

"Yeah, that makes two times this year that I've gotten you out of trouble."

"Two times?" asked Wend. "I don't understand."

"Oh, for God's sake, Wend. Has age drained you of all your brains? You used to be so quick. Think about last spring back on Braddock's Road: Two wagons, seven men slowly climbing a long grade on Laurel Ridge; a war party of eighteen warriors watching from a rocky outcropping. Does that sound familiar?"

"Oh my God, Charlie; that was you? That's why there was no attack."

"Yeah, and it took me every bit of persuasion I could muster. All those warriors wanted to go after the easy pickings. The Shawnees in my band were damn near ready to kill me when I wouldn't let them attack. I had to convince them that it would be too costly; pointing out that all of you had rifles. Finally I was able to sell them on going after some nearby settlers' farms instead."

There was a long silence, with Wend and Charlie looking at each other across the room.

Finally Wend said, "Charlie, I may be the most hated white man in the Ohio Country, but a certain Mingo named Laughing Eyes is despised all through the border settlements." He paused a moment and continued, "The truth is, it's hard for me to understand how you could be a vengeance murderer."

Sawak didn't answer for a long moment. Wend saw white hot anger burning in his eyes.

Then he said, "Am I hearing you properly? Am I hearing this from the man I watched shoot down three traders with cold precision in that Tuscarora mountain pass ten years ago? The man who has pledged his whole life to revenge for the killing of his family? How many men have you killed now? You bloody hypocrite!"

"Charlie, I've only killed the men who did the crimes, not innocent people just trying to make a life for themselves."

Sawak sprang from the wall and stood in the middle of the room, his fists balled, his teeth gritted, the muscles of his face working. "Damn it, Eckert, that bastard Cresap and his men killed my son!" Tears came to Charlie's eyes and ran down his cheeks. "My first born, do you understand? He was a wonderful boy: smart as a whip, brave, caring, and full of life."

"Charlie, I'm sorry about your son. Crooked Harry was at Baker's and told me how he died. I understand how you must feel."

"Do you?" Charlie gritted his teeth. "Tomorrow, go see Rose. See with your own eyes what she's become since that day. That girl used to be so full of the excitement of life, laughing all the time. Now it's like someone cut out her soul. She wanted to kill herself for letting the boy go over to the tavern that day with Logan's relatives. Now she can barely get through the day and she weeps in the night."

Wend said, "Charlie, I'm truly sorry."

Sawak pointed at Wend. "Don't you think if I could get at Cresap, I'd take it out on him? But that's not possible. Besides, twelve other people from my village died that day. There was no other way to avenge them but to attack the settlements."

"You didn't need to kill the women and children, Charlie."

"Don't be so childish, Eckert. Cresap killed women and children at Baker's place. Anyway, the Mingoes with me wouldn't have stood for letting them live." He shook his shoulders. "And we were moving too fast to take captives with us. If we left women and children alive behind us, they would have been able to put the militia on our trail. I couldn't take that chance. For God's sake, Wend, after Pontiac's War, you should understand border fighting is ugly business."

Wend took a deep breath. "There's something you've got wrong, Charlie."

"Damn it, Eckert, I can't handle any more of your sanctimonious moralizing."

"No, that's not it, Charlie. I was trying to tell you it wasn't Cresap who killed the people from your village."

"Don't be silly, Wend. Everyone knows it was Cresap. He led a band of border trash up from Zane's place and set up the ambush of our people."

"No, Charlie, Cresap started out for Baker's Tavern, but turned back when he found out it was Logan's band living at Yellow Creek, not some hostile

Shawnee. He wasn't anywhere near Baker's Tavern." Wend took a step closer to his friend and said quietly, "That's a fact, Charlie."

"So who the hell did it?"

"A bunch of young settlers led by a man named Greathouse. But they were incited, egged on by a man you well know about: Richard Grenough."

Sawak's face wrinkled in incredulity. "Grenough again? For God's sake, Wend, you've got that man stuck in your mind!"

"Whatever you may think, Charlie, he's behind it. Matt Bratton and another of Grenough's men were with Greathouse's band and pushed them to kill the Mingoes. Ask Crooked Harry; he witnessed the whole thing."

"So tell me why Grenough wanted the Mingoes massacred."

"To get a war started. He's working with Major John Connolly, who runs Pittsburgh for the Governor of Virginia. This war is about getting the Shawnee out of their hunting grounds. Grenough stands to make big money supplying provisions to the Virginia militia throughout the war and get land in Ohio afterward."

"All right, I believe you. But why are you telling me?"

"I'd thought you'd want to know this: The man who actually killed your son was Matt Bratton. Your boy wasn't killed in the general firing. He played dead, but when the men started finishing off the wounded, he jumped to his feet and ran for the bush. Bratton shot him and then scalped him while he was still alive."

Sawak stood frozen, breathing heavily.

Wend said, "If I get out of here, I'm going to find a way to kill Grenough and Bratton and finish this permanently. I'll be doing it for both of us, Charlie."

Abigail suddenly interrupted. "Which brings us to why I had you and Charlie come here tonight, Wend: to figure a way to get you out of this valley alive."

Charlie said, "Yes, that's the other headache your presence in this village has given me. Abigail told me why you're really here: to see your son. I've been trying to figure out how to achieve the tricky little matter of extracting you from this mess. I don't suppose you marched into the village with a plan that has a chance of working?"

Abigail said, "Yes, Wend, you said you had some cards to play. You better explain them now."

Wend shrugged. "I intend to tell the sachems that as a special emissary of the governor, I must take their message regarding peace back myself. If they kill me, the governor will take it as an act of war and make sure that an expedition invades the valley. That's pretty near to the truth. I'm close to the governor's personal advisor and I think they'd like an excuse to seize this land, seeing how near it is to Pittsburgh."

Charlie shook his head. "That's way too thin, Wend. They want your blood and they'll take the chance that the death of one man won't lead to a reprisal raid."

Abigail asked, "What about Bouquet? Won't they send him and the Highlanders in if they kill the governor's emissary? You talked about that and they sent that one Scotsman with you now. The Mingoes respect and fear the Highlanders."

Wend looked at her and said, "Abigail, Bouquet died of fever in Florida at a place called Pensacola, nine years ago. All the Highlanders have been back in Britain since '67. Donegal is a friend who stayed behind when his regiment left."

A look of shock came over Abigail's face. "That was all a lie?"

"Like you said, I've learned some bad habits. Deceit when it serves me is one of them."

She asked, "Well, aren't there some other army forces they would send?"

Wend shook his head. "The British abandoned Fort Pitt two years ago. Most of the British Army regiments in the colonies are up around Boston, where there's an insurrection brewing."

Abigail's face registered disbelief. "An insurrection? You mean *English* colonists against their own army?"

"There's a lot going on you won't have heard about, either of you. There's unrest from New England all the way down to Georgia. If I get the chance, I'll tell you both about what's going on back in the colonies."

Charlie said, "The way things are now, you're not going to have much more than enough time to say your prayers before they tie you to a post and light the fire. But I've been thinking about a plan which might work."

Wend asked, "What do you mean?"

"I plan to suggest that they give you a chance to fight for your life. That's not unusual."

"Fight? What kind of a fight?"

"Normally it's against their champion, using knife and hatchet." He thought a moment, "I expect the champion will be Etchemin. I gather he's been trying to take over as top warrior from Wolf Claw."

Abigail nodded, "That's quite correct."

Wend felt a chill flow over him. "Charlie, I don't know much about that kind of fighting."

Sawak laughed bitterly. "You wouldn't last a half minute with Etchemin." Charlie shook his head. "That's why I've been trying to think how to convince them to settle on another type of fight."

"Another type of fight?" Wend cocked his head. "What kind?"

"I can't explain now because it's not all straight in my mind and I'm not sure how I'm going to arrange it. But do this: When you get summoned to the council to decide your fate, don't bring your weapons. But make sure that Donegal brings the brace of pistols I saw in his belt earlier today."

Wend, puzzled, asked, "But why?"

Sawak cut him off. "Listen, Wend, there's more involved here than just your fate. I don't want Etchemin to take over as war captain." He pointed to his own chest. "I intend to be the new strong man of this village. And it's possible your situation can figure in my achieving that. So when the time comes, just play along with me."

With that, Sawak walked past Wend and put his hand on the door handle and swung it open. He turned back and said, "I've been talking long enough. It wouldn't do for someone to find us all here together and mention it to Etchemin or the elders."

"Charlie, wait a second," Wend asked. "Whatever happens tomorrow, there's something I want to request of you."

"You're already asking a lot from me. What else do you want?"

"Look out for my son, Little White Owl. He needs a man like you to show him the way, not someone like Wolf Claw. Joshua has told me that in the Mingo culture, the mother's brother takes as much of a role in raising male children as the actual father. Obviously, Abigail has no Mingo brother. I'm asking that you be the boy's uncle."

For the first time, the hard look which had been on Charlie's face softened. After a moment he said, "I will make it my duty." He reached out and touched Wend on his arm.

And then he was gone, pulling the door shut behind him.

Abigail came over and stood in front of Wend. "Do you think he can work something out for you?"

Wend sighed. "Charlie's a crafty one. When we were children, my friend Arnold Spengler used to dream up schemes which got the three of us in trouble with the adults. Charlie was always the one who figured out how to save our skins."

Abigail shook her head. "Well, he better think hard tonight."

"He'll do his best." Wend took a deep breath and looked over at Abigail. "But the truth is, that's not the Charlie I used to know. All this killing has changed him. There's a cruel look in his eyes and face that wasn't there before."

"What's happened to him would change any man. And he's right about Rose; she's just a shell of the plucky girl who came here ten years ago." She looked up into his eyes and put her hand softly on his cheek. "But then life has changed you as well; besides your sharp tongue and your ability to lie smoothly, there's a look of wariness and calculation in your eyes that the boy I knew didn't have."

Wend shrugged. "The boy trusted other people a lot more than the man does."

Abigail put her hand on Wend's arm. "But now that Charlie's left, I need to talk to you about our son."

"How do you mean?"

"Listen, Wend, I appreciate you asking for Charlie's help with him. But I pray it won't be necessary. If you survive, I want you to take Henry with you."

Wend stood transfixed, momentarily unable to respond. Finally he was able to say, "You would send him away? Perhaps, nay, *probably* never to see him again?"

She put her hands on his arms. "After I left you yesterday, I brooded about it all night. Mostly sitting in front of the fire until everyone else was long abed. The thought is devastating, but I feel it might be best for Henry."

Wend thought of something. "Is it because Wolf Claw disdains him? Do you fear he will now take his hatred for me out on Henry?"

"Yes, but how did you know about that?" she asked.

"Girty touched upon it back at Baker's Tavern," he answered.

Abigail sighed. "But Wend, there's more to it. Not only does he look like you, your blood is dominant in him. It's true he has grown up as a child of the forest; he has mastered the bow and does well in the hunt. He participates in the games with the other boys and the make believe wars they all love. But Henry's heart is not really into all that; he's a mechanic at heart, just like you."

Wend was astonished. "A mechanic? Here in the bush?"

"He is fascinated by all sorts of devices. He makes wonderful, creative snares for rabbits and other small animals. He built a machine to make it easier to lift water buckets out of the creek, using ropes, a heavy sapling over a forked branch, and large stones to counterbalance the weight of the buckets. But most of all, he is fascinated with firelocks."

"He likes to shoot?"

"Yes, but he likes studying their mechanical parts and working on them even more. It started a couple of years ago when he discovered the village's cache of broken guns; old guns that don't work. He started taking apart and studying the innards of the locks. Now he's sometimes able to fix malfunctioning rifles." Her hands tightened on his arms. "You see what I mean about him being like you?"

Wend's mind and heart were racing at the prospect of taking Henry with him.

But a new thought came to him. "Why in the world would Wolf Claw and the elders let me — the Scalp Stealer — take the boy away?"

"It depends on what happens tomorrow. If you survive, you'll have shown your courage. And Wolf Claw is discredited; he'll be worrying about his own well-being. Anyway, he doesn't really care about Henry."

"That leaves the elders. Why would they voluntarily let a healthy male leave?"

"They wouldn't have — until today. But now that Charlie and his people have arrived, the need to hold onto every male isn't as important." Abigail hesitated a moment and then continued, "And besides, the mother has the main say in these kinds of decisions."

There was a long pause, the two of them looking at each other. Then Wend said, "There's something we're forgetting. What about Henry himself? How will he respond to the idea of leaving?"

"He'll obey his mother. Moreover, he doesn't have any close friends among the boys of the village; the stigma of being your son hangs over him. And I think the idea of seeing the world beyond this village, and working with you on firelocks, will excite him. In fact, he has frequently been asking me about the white world." She shrugged and said, "I'll be able to convince him that his future is with you."

"Abigail, my God, this is selfless of you."

She looked up at Wend for a very long moment. "It's what's best for the boy; I know you will give him a life which will truly make him happy." They had been standing very near to each other; now suddenly she came into his arms and looked at him, her face close to his. "And then there's this: having him here, seeing him grow to look and act more and more like you every day, will devastate me and remind me of the man I can never have." Then slowly, gently, she slid her arms around his neck and gave him a long embrace.

Wend willingly returned her kiss; almost immediately he felt arousal coming over him. He looked around the room and saw a pallet made up next to the wall. Willpower failing, he was ready to carry her to the blankets.

And then she broke away and stood back from him, breathing heavily. "I'm sorry for giving in to my passion, Wend." She walked quickly to the door and swung it open. "It's time for you to go back to your camp," she looked at him with those deep blue, penetrating eyes, "and spend the night steeling yourself for tomorrow. Our son's future depends on you getting through the day."

* * *

In the bright sunlight of the next afternoon, the three sachems sat in solemn judgement behind the fire circle. Wend stood across the fire, with Joshua next to him. He had just finished making his case, through Joshua's translation, that the Mingo would dishonor the Governor of Virginia if they did not allow him to leave safely. Around them, the entire population of the village sat in rapt attention to the spectacle.

Joshua whispered to Wend, "Now I 'spect they'll talk with each other to make their decision."

Wend looked over at Charlie Sawak, who sat with his people in a group to the right. This would be the time for Charlie to make his move.

Instead it was Etchemin who sprang to his feet and demanded attention. Joshua said, "This can't be good news."

Etchemin had obviously prepared for this moment. He was loaded to the gills with weapons. He had a sheathed, long-bladed knife on a strap hanging down from his neck. On one side of the belt which held up his breechclout was stuck a pipe hatchet, and in his hand he held a dragoon pistol, obviously captured from a soldier in the French war.

Circling Hawk waved at the warrior and gave him permission to talk.

Etchemin began speaking in loud tones, walking along before the villagers. As he walked, he waved his pistol in the air to the accompaniment of cheers from the people. Then he pulled out his hatchet and waved it, the spectator shouts becoming even louder.

Wend tugged on Joshua's arm. "God's sake, tell me what he's saying."

"Hold your horses, Sprout. It's just the usual boasting about being a great warrior. That's going to go on for a while."

Wend forced himself to listen quietly. After a few more minutes of his harangue, Etchemin walked up to the elders and directed his words to them.

Baird stood listening closely, his head cocked. Then, after a few moments, he shot a glance at Wend and explained, "He says you shouldn't have a simple, easy death at the stake."

Wend said, "He calls burning at the stake easy?"

"Shut up. Now he's sayin' you should be forced to fight to the death with knife and hatchet. That way the people of the village would see what a coward you are when you don't have soldiers behind you." Joshua shook his head. "And of course, he's the one who should fight and kill you."

The villagers cheered and started talking excitedly among themselves. Clearly they liked the idea.

Wend shot a glance at Charlie and saw a smile flash across his face, then disappear as if it had never been there. Had Sawak somehow led Etchemin into making this challenge?

Charlie rose to his feet and signaled to Circling Hawk that he wanted to speak. Hawk motioned him permission.

Charlie walked to the front of the council fire. Then he began to talk in a low, serious tone that was in complete contrast to Etchemin's boisterous shouting. As he spoke, the villagers quieted, straining to hear his words.

"Charlie's agreein' with Etchemin that you should have to fight," said Joshua in hushed tones. "But he says that, as they know, he lived a long time in the land of the whites and learned their customs. He knows the Great Chief of Virginia would be very mad if you were killed in a fight that was unfair to you. He would send his soldiers to avenge you."

Etchemin strode over beside Charlie and said something in excited tones.

Charlie answered him in the same modulated tones he had been using.

Joshua explained, "Etchemin's pissed at Charlie for interrupting and spoilin' his big show. He told the sachems that the fight would be fair under Mingo laws. Then Charlie said the governor wouldn't understand and that soldiers would be marchin' here as soon as he heard you were dead. Charlie says the fight has to be done in a way the whites fight."

The three old men talked among themselves for a brief period, then Circling Hawk said something to Charlie. Joshua whispered, "He's askin' Charlie how the whites would fight."

Charlie spoke for several minutes. Wend looked at Baird, to see face wrinkled in puzzlement, but then it changed to an astonished grin.

Joshua looked at Wend. "Now I'll be damned! To be short, he's sayin' that when the whites settle a dispute, they do it with pistols." Baird shook his head. "He's describin' a duel like them fancy English gentlemen do when they're mad at each other. He says the whites consider it the way to settle things when someone thinks another person has dishonored them. He says the governor would sure enough understand a pistol fight to settle the Mingoes' honor for you stealin' their prize scalps."

Hawk spoke again, obviously asking a question.

"He wants to know just how the whites would do this type of gun fight," said Joshua.

Charlie spoke for several minutes, motioning with his hands. Several times one or another of the elders interrupted to ask a question.

"Charlie's givin' them the details, Joshua said. "He says they stand twenty paces apart, and on command exchange one shot. The survivor is the winner. But each man either proves his courage or shows that he's a coward by the way he faces bein' shot."

Etchemin spoke out in loud tones, gesticulating wildly with his hands. Then he pulled the hatchet from is belt and brandished it high above his head. A stir arose among the villagers at his words.

Joshua said, "Etchemin said he don't see how shootin' one shot at each other was any kind of a fight and wouldn't take any real courage. He says the only way is to fight it out with blades."

Circling Hawk motioned for Etchemin to be quiet. Then the three elders conferred for a lengthy period. Finally, they faced toward the crowd and Hawk spoke again. He paused a moment, then seemed to ask a question to all the villagers. Baird looked at Wend. "Well, they agreed to the gunfight. Now they're asking their people who should be their champion."

Suddenly Etchemin stepped out in front of the fire circle and brandished his dragoon pistol. He spoke loudly, and many in the crowd cheered him.

"Sprout, Etchemin said everyone knows he's the best pistol shot in the village and claims the right to shoot you down like a dog. But he says if he just wounds you with his pistol, he should be allowed to finish you with knife and hatchet."

Wend watched as Hawk motioned toward Etchemin and the crowd of villagers broke into another round of cheers. It was obvious he had been selected.

Then immediately Charlie spoke again. The crowd quieted down and the elders listened carefully. Then Sawak walked over to where Donegal stood. He said in English, "I need those pistols, Simon."

Donegal exclaimed, "Damned if I know what's going on, but here they are." He pulled the pair from his belt and handed them to Sawak.

Charlie stood before the fire circle and make a show of examining the pistols. Then he held them high in the air and spoke to the elders again.

"He's tellin' them that the custom is that both shooters should use matched guns, particularly guns that are strange to them. So it's only fair that both you and Etchemin use Donegal's pistols."

Wend sighed deeply and blessed Charlie. For he himself had made the pistols, tested them, and knew how they shot as well as his own pistols. They were identical to the brace he had sold Geoffrey Caulfield. Sawak had connived to give him a decided advantage.

Now Charlie led Etchemin and Wend to an open area between the village and the valley trail. The elders and the entire village followed, talking excitedly along the way. Charlie made a mark in the ground, then stepped off twenty paces and made another mark. He waved for Etchemin to take the first mark and for Wend to go to the second.

Wend watched as Charlie handed Etchemin one of the pistols and then stood talking with him for a few minutes, obviously briefing him on the procedures. Then Sawak walked over to Wend.

"Charlie, where the hell did you get this idea?"

Sawak answered, "I remember our teacher back in Lancaster, old man Dreher, talking about dueling one day in class. He didn't go into details, so I'm making up most of this little drama as I go along."

"I'm indebted to you; this gives me a chance."

"Yeah, yeah; be quiet and listen to me. If Etchemin doesn't kill you first, it would suite me very well if you could contrive to wound him instead of killing him."

"I thought you wanted to get him out of the way."

"Yes, Wend, but the elders will be far happier with me if they don't lose another grown man over this affair; the fact is he'll be out of the picture for a long time if you give him a serious wound." Charlie looked around and said, "Now pay attention: I'll ask both you and Etchemin if you're ready to shoot and after that I'll order you to cock your firelock. When that's done, hold your pistol pointed straight upward. Then I'll count to three. After that you're both free to fire."

Wend nodded, and Charlie turned and walked to a spot out of the line of fire.

Wend felt the tension building; sweat drops raised on his forehead and the back of his neck. He tried to think clearly. Then something dawned on him: Etchemin was used to shooting with the heavy dragoon pistol. He was about to fire for the first time with a significantly lighter weapon. Much would depend on the technique the Mingo used to aim.

Now Sawak was calling for attention. The loud buzz from the crowd of villagers subsided as Charlie stood with his hands outstretched. Then he dropped his hands to his side and stood still for a long moment. After all was silent, he pointed to Etchemin. "Are you ready to fire?"

Etchemin nodded.

Then Charlie pointed to Wend and asked the same thing. Wend nodded his readiness.

Charlie pointed a hand at each man and shouted, "Cock your firelocks!" in both Mingo and English.

Wend pulled the hammer of his pistol back to full cock and called out that he was ready. Then, as he spoke the words, an idea came to him.

Sawak started his count.

Wend turned sidewise, his left side facing Etchemin, to present the narrowest possible target. He held the pistol down by the side of his leg. With his heart was pumping wildly, he stared intensely at his antagonist. *The next couple of seconds would tell the story.*

Etchemin raised the pistol in his right hand to the firing position and, accustomed to shooting with the heavy dragoon pistol, raised his left arm to use as a firing rest to steady the gun. Then he tried to aim by sighting along the top of the barrel. Wend felt a sense of relief rush through his body; that was exactly what he had hoped Etchemin would do.

Now Charlie shouted the word "three."

Etchemin instantly pulled his trigger. Wend heard the zip of the ball and felt his hat spin off his head to land on the ground behind him.

As Wend had hoped, Etchemin had missed slightly too high. Wend saw a brief frown of puzzlement on the Mingo's face, then a return to a stoic countenance.

There was an outburst from the watching villagers.

Now Wend slowly raised his pistol to the firing position. Etchemin, his pistol lowered, instinctively took a step backward as he stared at the muzzle of Wend's firelock and contemplated having to stand in place for the coming shot.

The crowd of villagers went deadly silent; so quiet that Wend could hear a bird chirping in the distance.

Wend forced his mouth into the widest grin he could make. He called out, "Now, Etchemin, you see the courage it takes to make the white man's fight." He called out to Charlie: "I demand that Etchemin return to his original mark, or be declared a coward and the loser of the match."

Charlie spoke in Mingo. After he finished, Circling Hawk said something directly to Etchemin and pointed at the mark.

Etchemin glared at Charlie and then Wend, but finally stepped back up to the line in the ground.

Wend changed his countenance to a grim expression and called out to Etchemin: "I suggest it will go best for you if you stand as still as possible."

Charlie translated to make sure Etchemin understood.

Wend raised the pistol, focused his eyes intently at the spot on Etchemin's body he wanted to hit, and, resisting the momentary temptation to look down the barrel of his gun, squeezed the trigger.

There was a flash, a bang, and then Etchemin's right shoulder snapped back. A look of shock came over his face. The pistol fell from his hand and after a split second the Mingo dropped to his right knee and put his left hand up to his shoulder. Blood oozed through the fingers and ran down his chest.

Wend breathed a sigh of relief and blessed the genius of his father.

Abigail, carrying a basket of medical supplies, rushed out to Etchemin and went to her knees beside him, surveying his wound.

Wend looked over at Charlie, who gave Wend a quick nod and the barest hint of a smile. Then Wend looked at the villagers. They were silently staring at him. Moving deliberately, Wend walked over and stood before the three elders. He called out to Circling Hawk: "Have I now shown you the courage of a German jaeger? Have I earned the right to walk with honor among the Mingo?"

Baird, speaking loudly so that all could hear, repeated Wend's words in the Mingo language.

Circling Hawk stood looking at Etchemin for a long moment. Then he slowly shifted his eyes to Wend, and gave him a steely stare, his jaw set. He gave a slow nod and said something to Joshua.

"Well, Sprout, they ain't too happy 'bout it, but Hawk says you'll be allowed to leave unharmed when all the other villages give their reply to the governor's peace message. And he says you should point out to the governor how fairly the Mingo have treated his emissary."

Wend felt a surge of exhilaration rush over him. His days as the Scalp Stealer were over and, even more importantly, he would leave the village with his son beside him.

* * *

The flames of the fire illuminated the faces of the four people who sat together on a log in front of the medical cabin. Wend had brought over some of Donegal's whiskey and the four of them — Abigail, Charlie, Rose, and he — were nursing mugs of the liquid as they talked.

Abigail was explaining the condition of Etchemin. "I had a lot of trouble getting the ball out of his shoulder. It was buried deeply in his muscles and sinew and, careful as I tried to be, the removal necessarily caused more damage. It will be a long recovery and I fear the arm will never be the same."

"And how is Wolf Claw doing?" asked Wend.

"His arm wound will heal without much permanent damage. But I believe he'll always have a serious limp on his right side. The damage from the original wound was bad enough, but all the walking and other movement so soon after the injury aggravated things."

Charlie took a sip of his drink. There was a calculating look on his face. "That's all to the good as far as I'm concerned. Having both of them permanently lame clears the way for me to take over as the strong man of the village."

Abigail nodded. "Charlie, there's not much doubt of that in my mind. The people are already talking about it throughout the village. Your reputation has preceded you and there's much admiration of the way you handled things with the sachems from the other villages."

Rose, staring down into the fire, said in a low voice. "Yes, but I would that you hadn't had to acquire that reputation. And all that time you were away with the war party I lived in fear that you would never come back."

Charlie put his arm around his wife. "Now Rose, don't fret. I'm never going away again if I can help it." He looked at the others. "They may anoint me as the war captain, but in truth, I hope to be the peace captain of this village."

Wend shook his head. "You may have no choice in the matter. Many settlers are taking up land around Pittsburgh and it's only going to get worse once Lord Dunmore subjugates the Shawnee. There are thousands of men who expect to get land grants in the Ohio Country from their service in the French War and from this war the governor is making."

Charlie gritted his teeth, then said bitterly, "Yes, the English have an insatiable lust for land. I fear that settlement is soon going to overtake this valley. In a few years we may have to move the village to avoid conflict."

Abigail stiffened. "So soon? I have long worried about the press of settlement but didn't think it would affect us here for many more years." She sighed and then said, "It's so very pleasant here in this valley."

Wend asked, "Where will you go?"

Charlie stared into the distance. "I don't know; obviously westward, but how far, I can't tell. The most extreme action would be what Charlot Kaske did after Bouquet's march to the Muskingum."

Wend was puzzled. "Who the devil is this Charlot Kaske?"

"He is a half-white who became a fierce Shawnee leader. He tried to get the Shawnee and other tribes to fight when Bouquet invaded the Ohio Country in '64. When that failed, he led a band of his most loyal followers west; how far, no one knows. Some say they traveled beyond the great, wide river that runs where the sun sets."

"They call it the Mississippi, Charlie," said Wend.

"Anyway, neither Charlot Kaske nor his people have ever been seen or heard from since. He has become a legend; stories are told about him around the campfires of the young Shawnee warriors who want to fight the English. They wish their leaders had his spirit."

"Are you contemplating going that far?" Wend asked.

"I hope that won't be necessary. Perhaps we can buy enough time if we move beyond the Scioto. There must be places out there that will suffice for a village of our size."

Rose spoke out vehemently, "Wherever we go, it must be far enough to avoid any more massacres by the whites. I'll not lose another child to their lust for land."

Her words led to a long silence among the four.

Finally, Abigail said, "Wend, you were going to tell us what's going on in the colonies and explain why the people are arrayed against the army. I would like to hear about that."

Wend took a few seconds to gather his thoughts. "It really started after Pontiac's War; the English decided they needed to keep an army force here in the colonies; a force much bigger than the few independent companies that were here before the French War. Then Parliament levied taxes on the colonists to pay for the troops and the forts."

Abigail shrugged. "I don't understand; there have always been taxes. What were these new ones that caused so much trouble?"

"There were taxes on many things; a new Sugar Tax, a Tea Tax, a Stamp Tax on every legal document."

Abigail said, "Most people ignore the taxes. I remember my father saying that the Molasses Tax was a joke; the merchants just smuggled the stuff in from the West Indies."

"But Abigail, it wasn't the taxes themselves that caused the problems, it was the enforcement. The government appointed many tax collectors and they made great efforts to enforce the new revenue laws. Revenue collection vessels were commissioned to stop the merchants' ships and inspect their cargoes."

As Wend spoke, he looked at his companions; he saw puzzlement in all their faces and he suddenly realized that, isolated in the forest, it was hard for them to come to grips with the estrangement that had arisen between England and her colonies. Their understanding of the political situation, and the sentiments of the people, had been frozen in the time of their arrival in the Ohio Country. In Abigail's case that was fifteen years ago; Charlie and Rose had fled the settlements over a decade ago. He realized he must explain things in much more detail.

Wend stood up, went over to the wood pile, and threw several logs into the fire. The flames flared toward the sky. Then he turned back to his friends and grinned. "This is going to take a while; listen carefully and I will bring you up to date."

So he told them about how the colonists had increasingly resisted the taxes, about the attacks on tax collectors and on the revenue collection boats. He told them how Boston had developed as the center of resistance. Wend explained how the army had increasingly become the agent of enforcement of the English laws and thus garnered the hatred of the colonists. Then he recounted the shooting of civilians in Boston by soldiers in 1770, when they had been confronted by a mob hurling insults and stones. All of them laughed at the story of how the Bostonians dressed as Indians to throw tea into the harbor earlier that very year. Wend explained how much of the army had been concentrated in Boston to enforce the so-called Intolerable Acts which Parliament had enacted to punish the city for its defiance.

Wend finished by describing how the other colonies had come together to support Boston and strengthen their hand against the Crown. How committees of correspondence had been formed and a Continental Congress was underway in Philadelphia to discuss common actions which could be taken to resist the Crown. Finally he told them how the Massachusetts people were strengthening and training their militia for a possible confrontation with the British Army in Boston.

Charlie sprang to his feet. "You really think there might be actual fighting between the colonists and the army?"

"I don't know what to think, Charlie. But there are a good many people who think that will happen sooner or later."

Sawak became very animated, walking back and forth in front of the fire, his mug in hand. Then he turned to them. "I'm glad you told us about all this, Wend. This could change everything! If the whites are fighting among themselves, it will undoubtedly affect us." He stopped and stared into the fire for a long moment. "But how? Will a war create a pause in the spread of settlement? Who will the different tribes side with — the English or the colonists?" Charlie took a quick sip of his whiskey. "I'll have to keep my ear to the wind and perhaps rethink my plans."

Rose looked up at him. "Perhaps we won't need to leave the valley."

Charlie stared into the fire again. "Perhaps not; at the least, not as soon as I expected."

Rose stood up and put her hand on Charlie's shoulder. "I'm tired. Let's go back to our camp." She turned to Wend. "I never thought I'd see you again Wend, but I'm glad you came and kept the people of this valley out of the war with Virginia."

Wend stood up and gave her a hug. "We still haven't got an answer from Tall Buck's village. But I remain hopeful they will decide on peace."

Rose shook her head. "I don't know about these political things, but after all the trouble we had with those Paxton Men back in Pennsylvania, and then the killing at Baker's place, all I want is to raise the rest of my children in peace. Maybe you've helped make that possible."

And then the two of them headed back toward the village.

Abigail looked up at Wend and said, "Come sit with me and talk a while longer."

Wend joined her on the log. Abigail said, "You spoke for a long time about the conflict between the colonists and the Crown. But it made me wonder. All the colonists can't feel so strongly about resisting the King."

"You're right, Abigail, there are differences of opinion and many people remain totally loyal to the government. In Virginia, the Tidewater gentry are split, some supporting each side. On the other hand, most Ulster-Scots are ready to rise up against the English. The Germans mostly just want to tend their farms or shops. The colonists who come from England itself are fractured and there are bitter discussions among neighbors and within the same family."

Abigail considered that for a moment, then asked, "And which side are you on, Wend?"

Wend waited a long time to respond. In fact, he realized he didn't know the full answer. Finally he said, "I'm on the side of my family. I want to do what will keep them safe. But most of the people I associate with in Winchester are in conflict with the King's Government. I'm inclined to side with them. But here's the catch: Some men close to the governor are trying to pull me into all of this on their side. In fact, that's why I'm even out here in the Ohio Country. They pressured me to participate in this war."

Abigail pursed her lips and her brow furrowed. "This afternoon, I watched you stand calmly and let Etchemin fire at you. How could a man with that kind of courage be forced into going to war?"

"A man who is afraid to lose the kind of life he has made for himself and his family." Wend explained about how the musket contract had been steered to him and how it had led to financial obligations which made refusing the governor's commission impossible. Then he said, "But I am determined to find some way to break my dependence on government money without hurting the people who rely on my trade for their livelihood."

"How will you do that?"

Wend sighed deeply and put his hands to his head. "I don't know. I've been brooding about it for weeks and have been able to think of nothing; nothing which has a chance of success. But I must somehow resolve the problem when this war is over. If all else fails, I will be forced to discharge the journeyman gunsmith and his apprentice who work with me, send away some of our field hands, and severely restrict our other spending. The prospect has been gripping at my heart since I left Winchester."

Abigail stared at Wend. "You are so agitated Wend, I'm sorry I pried into your private life. Let us just enjoy this brief time we have together." She slid herself up against his side, took his arm, and laid her head against his shoulder. "Wend, put your arm around me and hold me tight." She looked up at him and continued, "Don't refuse me; it is such a small infidelity, and it will be all the memory of us together that I will have to see me through the years."

Wend smiled down at her imploring face and put his arm around her. They stayed there in the night, sharing their thoughts and enjoying the pleasure of their closeness, until the fire burned down to faint embers.

* * *

The three canoes grounded on the river bank at Wheeling almost simultaneously. Wend jumped out and worked with his son and Joshua to drag the craft
up far enough to be secure. As they and the rest of the party worked, several
people came to greet and assist them.

The first was Horner, who had seen them coming downstream and had run
along the bank to the landing. He said, "I'm glad to see you back, Mr. Eckert.
Everyone was worried. I'll help with your things." Then he glanced at Wend's
son, eyes moving over the boy's clothing and accoutrements. When he saw the
face he suddenly froze, stared at the youth and then looked over at Wend for
confirmation of what he was seeing.

Wend put his hand on the boy's shoulder. "Andrew, this is Johann —
Henry Johann Eckert. He is my son. Show him to our camp and help make
him comfortable."

Wend looked around and realized that the campsite adjacent to the fort
was nearly empty. He queried Horner, "I must report to McDonald. Where is
the battalion?"

The youth pointed eastward. "Back over the ridges; they're at Redstone Old
Fort."

Suddenly a voice spoke out, "Actually, Eckert, you'll report to me."

Wend looked around and saw William Crawford and his adjutant advancing toward him. He said, "Good evening, Major."

"Well, Eckert, you've gotten back alive. To be honest, speculation was ram-
pant that we'd never see you again. How did your mission go?" Then he saw
Johann standing next to Wend and stared at the boy with rapt concentration,
his brows furrowed. He broke into a broad smile and said, "By God, Eckert,
obviously the personal part of your mission succeeded far better than you could
have hoped."

"Indeed William; this is Johann. Johann Eckert."

Crawford held out his hand to the boy. "Welcome to Fort Fincastle, Johann."

Johann stared down at the proffered hand, not sure what to do. He looked
over at Wend.

Wend put his hand on the boy's shoulder. "Give him your hand, son. And
squeeze firmly. It is the white man's way of making a greeting."

Wend turned back to Crawford. "Why am I reporting to you instead of
McDonald, William? Where is Angus?"

Crawford motioned toward the stockade and said, "Come walk with me
back to headquarters. I'll explain what's going on here and you can give me the
details of your trip."

They started walking and then Crawford continued, "A day after you left, a dispatch rider came in from the governor. The dispatch said Dunmore was on his way to Lord Fairfax's place in the valley, Greenway Court, to set up his headquarters for recruiting in the northern counties. The governor ordered McDonald to join him to serve as the Brigade Major for the northern brigade. It also ordered me to send all the troops except my garrison to Redstone; they can be supported more easily there."

"Greenway Court is not far south of my farm." Wend thought a moment. "Angus could be there by now. Undoubtedly his wife Anna is happy to have him home now."

"Yes," said Crawford, "And I dare say your wife is considerably disappointed." Wend turned to look at him. "Why do you say that, William?"

"Because, my dear fellow, the governor ordered you to go back with Angus; he wanted you to help raise German recruits. If you hadn't taken your little trip to Mingo country, you'd be home by now."

"But I wouldn't have my son with me, nor would we have secured peace with the northern Mingo."

Crawford cocked his head. "So that part of your mission was also successful?"

"Yes, Little Bear is carrying peace wampum from all five of the villages in the Slippery Rock Creek Valley. Four of the villages readily decided on peace, but the fifth, led by an elder called Tall Buck, debated until the last minute. We were about to leave when a runner came in with their peace beads."

"Last minute or not, Eckert, you got their agreement not to fight. I believe Dunmore will be very grateful."

Wend thought a moment. "But what am I supposed to do now? Should I journey back to Frederick County?"

"No, McDonald and I talked it over. He'll explain your mission to the governor and you'll stay here with me. There's an important assignment for you: Our job now is to act as a base for supplies which will be brought down from Pittsburgh by boat. You're going to be in charge of organizing all that material as it comes in and getting it ready for transport by pack animals. That's why your group of contract quartermasters is still here."

"What about pack horses?" asked Wend, "There are none here at Wheeling."

"Redstone Old Fort is being used as the collection point for our herd of bullocks and packhorses. Above that, newly recruited militia companies will be sent there to join your battalion and form the core of Dunmore's northern column. When Dunmore arrives, the troops, bullock herd, and packhorses will all be marched over the ridges to here in Wheeling. This will be the starting point for the campaign."

They entered the fort and went to the blockhouse. There was a canvas fly in front of the entrance with a fire crackling before it. Crawford motioned for them to sit in two chairs and offered Wend a drink of rum, which was eagerly accepted. "Now give me the details of your adventure; I must confess my curiosity is exceeding that of the proverbial cat," he said.

Wend gave him a highly edited version of the events in the Mingo village, carefully omitting any mention of Charlie Sawak.

When he had finished, Crawford said, "Write up a report; I'll have it copied when you're done. We'll send the original to McDonald by courier and a copy to Connolly in Pittsburgh. Angus can personally take the good news to the governor and Connolly won't be able to grab any of the credit."

Wend smiled, "William, you are more devious than I ever dreamed."

"Not normally, but the more I learn about Connolly the less I like him."

"That makes two of us."

Crawford raised a finger. "This talk of correspondence reminds me of something. Excuse me for a brief moment." He went into the blockhouse and then came back with several pages of parchment in his hand. "I've just received a letter from Washington; he's representing Virginia at the Continental Congress in Philadelphia."

Wend was eager for news. "Don't keep me in suspense, William. What is happening there?"

"George says there are representatives from all the colonies save Georgia. In actuality, the discussions are just getting started, but there's already a sentiment that all the colonies should band together to support Massachusetts and to present a uniform front to press our position on taxes and the Intolerable Acts."

"It's hard to imagine all of the colonies acting in concert; there have always been sharp differences between them. Those differences will come out when the representatives get down to the specifics. I hope they can agree on something useful."

Crawford reflected and took a sip from his mug. "That's a good point, Eckert. Look at the conflict between Virginia and Pennsylvania. But I must confess I'm optimistic." He paused and said, "Aside from that, Washington writes that he hopes business in Philadelphia will be soon concluded and he can get back to affairs at his estates. He is trying to finish up some major changes he's been making in the way he manages them."

The personal plans of a member of the gentry were of little interest to Wend. But to be polite and keep the conversation going, he replied, "What changes would that be?"

"About ten years ago, George became fed up with the economics of raising and selling tobacco. He calculated it to be a losing proposition; every year he found himself deeper in debt. So he searched for another crop which would be profitable and free him from the tyranny of the London merchants and bankers."

Wend's interest was piqued. "You know, William, I had a conversation about that with my wife just before leaving for this campaign. We were looking for a way to make our farm bring in cash, not just provide food. We thought about going into tobacco, but we decided against it for the same reasons Washington mentions. And the cultivation of tobacco requires many hands; I calculated I would have had to procure a number of slaves, which is objectionable to me. I've always run my farm with redemptioners and hired men during the harvest."

"Interesting that you should say that; George was also looking for a way to reduce or eliminate his slave holdings. He thinks the cost of keeping them is the main factor making tobacco unprofitable."

Wend was all ears. "Pray tell, what crop did he decide to grow?"

"Grain, or more specifically, wheat."

"Wheat? How the devil will he turn that into a money crop?"

Crawford answered, "He sells it to other plantations and to the townspeople, shipping it throughout the Tidewater and even exporting some quantity. Now he's planning to build a mill so he can sell flour. But he is making money at it, mainly because wheat requires much less attention during the growing season than tobacco and hence much less labor."

Wend replied, "That wouldn't work around Winchester; all the local farms grow their own wheat."

But as he was speaking, Wend suddenly had an idea that set his mind racing. There was another wheat product he could sell in great quantity and for good money: whiskey! He immediately realized all the elements existed on his farm to put that idea into practice: Land to raise the grain, Donegal's distillery, and, most importantly, the Scotsman's recipe, developed over the years, for a high quality whiskey. Wend knew he would have to sit down and work out all the calculations, to see if the concept was in fact financially practical. And of course, he must convince Donegal to join into a partnership. But the idea just might provide his means of escape from Northcutt's control.

Wend raised his mug. "Well, William: a toast: A toast to Wheat!"

Crawford raised his own mug. "To Wheat!"

Then Wend responded, "Another toast: To Whiskey!"

Crawford threw back his head and laughed, "I'll always drink to that!"

PART FOUR

Exercise in Folly

September 1774 – April 1775

CHAPTER EIGHTEEN
The Battletown Inn

The chaise bounced over the road, pulled along swiftly by Boots, the spirited, high stepping bay. Peggy handled the reins and beside her sat Alice Downy, slightly intimidated by the speed of their travel. Peggy was in her black, hooded cloak, which normally would have been too warm, but luckily an early bout of cool weather had intervened and thus prevented her from looking out of place.

Alice exclaimed, "Lord, this thing flies! I swear we've been right off the ground more than once. Are you sure you can handle it at this speed?"

"Don't be silly, Alice. I've been driving this for months now. Relax and enjoy the wind in your face!"

"How can I relax when I know what you are about to do? This is all insane; I can't believe I agreed to help you."

"Just like we told everyone back at the farm, it's true that we are on our way to see Anna McDonald and nurse her in her time of sickness. It's the perfect explanation to keep anyone from being suspicious about the reason for our absence. As far as anyone knows, our stop at the Battletown Inn will be just to rest and water the horse."

"I still don't feel good about this."

"Alice, what are you so worried about? We've both entertained men on an afternoon like this." Peggy laughed and shook her head. "Although I have to say most of mine happened in the corner of a stable. At least you had a bed in your own home for the work."

"Peggy, I'll not deny that we're both like a page of parchment with smudges of spilt ink. We'll never be clean again," said Alice. "But I haven't been with another man since Joshua came back from the Ohio Country in '65 and brought me down here from Carlisle. And far as I know, you've been faithful to Wend. I can't fathom why you want to put yourself in the way of trouble now."

"Of course I've been faithful to Wend. But I love the sheer excitement of this; the excitement of being with a man who is clearly infatuated with me."

"But Peggy, you know Wend is in love with you."

Peggy sighed. "Is he? Dear God, I wish I could convince myself of that. I've played the flirt with other men in front of him and he says nothing; he just maintains that stone-faced look of his and ignores what is happening. He never shows anger or tells me he doesn't like it."

Alice looked at Peggy in astonishment. "And his calmness in the face of your flirting infuriates you?"

"Any man who sees that going on and isn't jealous can't be truly in love." Peggy's face furrowed. "It's not that I'm infuriated, it's more that I'm disappointed. The fact is, he married me because he couldn't have that Philadelphia girl and I've never made him truly mine."

"That's rubbish, Peggy. Wend understands you; he knows you love playing the coquette and he lets you enjoy yourself. But there's something else you should admit: You're pretty and smart, you've always been able to control the men in your life, and you liked that. But Wend ain't so easy to bend to your will. That makes you frustrated."

Peggy said nothing, staring straight ahead.

Alice continued, "But all that still doesn't explain why you're going to meet with Caulfield at the inn."

"If you must know, it's because he performed a certain act of kindness which he thought would win my affection. And I must return the favor in the proper way. This is my way of doing that."

"What great kindness?" asked Alice.

"I must keep it confidential for now. When this is all finished, I'll explain."

"I'm spending my time to help you in a secret and shadowy appointment and you won't trust me to know the reason? Now I feel disappointed; disappointed in your trust of me."

Peggy was silent for a long moment. Then she pulled the horse to a halt, put the reins down, and untied the fastening of her cloak. "You're right, Alice, I owe you some explanation. Look at what's around my neck."

"My God, that's the necklace that was stolen from you by the highwaymen. How did you get it back?"

"Caulfield retrieved it for me. And the circumstances are such that I can't tell anyone about it or wear it in public. Except for today, to show it to him."

"So did he buy it back from someone in that gang of highwaymen? You must tell me what he did!"

Peggy retied her cloak. She picked up the reins and slapped them on Boots' back to get him started again. She looked at Alice and after a moment of indecision, said, "All right, I'll tell you. But you must swear to secrecy — one soiled woman to another."

"Of course. You have my pledge."

"Caulfield didn't buy it back. He gave it back; Geoffrey is the leader of the highwaymen."

Alice's mouth opened in astonishment. "Peggy, how in the world did you discover that?"

Peggy sighed. "He gave himself away by returning the necklace and later essentially admitted it to me when I baited him about it."

"My God, and you're going to spend time alone with a brigand in a private room? Think of the danger!"

Peggy turned and gave Alice a tight smile. "I can manage."

Alice put a hand to her forehead and then shook her head. "Dear God, I wish I were back at the farm, tending to my sewing."

Peggy guided the chaise around a bend in the road.

Alice exclaimed, "There's the inn. This is your last chance to avoid this foolishness. We could just go on by and head for Glengarry straightaway."

"I'm determined to do this Alice."

In a few minutes they drove into the courtyard of the inn; no one was about.

Alice pointed to one of two horses tied to the hitching rack. "Look, I remember that horse. It's Caulfield's big stallion."

Peggy smiled. "I had no doubt he would be here." She pulled up by the well and then quickly dismounted. "Give the horse some water and then pull the chaise around to the back of the tavern, close by the rear door. You'll be out of sight from the courtyard and well positioned for me to jump in when I come out."

"The sooner we leave, the better I'll feel," replied Alice.

"Just be ready when I come out." And with that Peggy pulled up her hood and quickly disappeared behind the inn.

* * *

While the tavern maid changed the sheets, Geoffrey Caulfield looked around the room to ensure he had thought of everything. He'd already had her dust the furniture, sweep the floor, and place a tray with decanters of wine and whiskey and glasses on the chest near the door.

Quinn sat slumped in the one soft chair, his arms crossed, as he watched the preparations with a wry look on his face.

The maid looked back at Caulfield and said, "Now sir, it puzzles me why you've asked for clean sheets. The ones I just took off were only slept in twice, and I vow both men were both fine, clean gentlemen. You know it's going to cost you extra just for these freshly boiled sheets."

"Let's just say I'm a particular person."

The girl finished with the bed, gathered up the old sheets and her broom and walked to the door. "If that's all you want, sir, I'll be leavin' now."

Caulfield walked over and handed her a small coin. "That will be fine, miss."

After she had gone, Quinn shook his head and said, "Damn, Cap'n, I never thought to see you fuss this much over some little piece."

"This *piece*, as you call her, is very special; very special indeed. A woman such as I have never had the pleasure to pass time with before. And as we shall soon be leaving the charming town of Winchester, it will be a memorable and fitting ending to our time here."

"Well, the only time I seen her with my own eyes was that night we stopped her and that German man of hers along the Winchester road, and it was dark and windy. I didn't have no time to stand and admire her, but I do allow she seemed a fine-lookin' woman." Quinn grinned broadly and said, "But I still vow I never seen you so disturbed 'bout the prospect of spendin' time with a female."

Geoffrey felt perturbed at his compatriot. "Damn you, Quinn, I am not *disturbed;* as is my habit in these matters, I'm simply taking measures to make sure the lady is comfortable. That goes a long way toward ensuring that things go as desired."

Quinn stood up and grinned. "If you say so, Cap'n. Now the way I'm used to it, it's all much simpler: I hand the girl money and she tends to my needs."

Caulfield ignored Quinn's comment. He looked around the room again and said, "All seems ready, my friend. Now's the time for you to descend to the common room and the comfort of a mug until my encounter here is finished."

Quinn walked to the doorway. "Yes, and I'll be exceedin' glad when it be done; I don't like leavin' the lads alone all day sittin' beside that creek. There's too much chance for them to get into mischief. And anyway, we need to get back to camp and make ready for our journey."

Caulfield followed him to the door and said, "Now rest easy, Corporal; our preparations for traveling are almost complete. We'll be heading south before the week is done."

Quinn left, walking down the hall and taking the front steps down into the common room. Caulfield took a black ribbon from his pocket and draped it over the outside doorknob. He shut the door and then he quickly went over to the chest and poured himself a glass of whiskey. He downed it in a single gulp. Geoffrey had to admit to himself that he was nervous about meeting with Peggy Eckert. He was worried that she might not come, and if she did, he found himself, for the first time in his life, concerned that he might not measure up to her expectations.

He poured himself another whiskey and paced the floor, sipping at the drink as the minutes dragged by with no sign of Mrs. Eckert.

Caulfield had just finished the second glass and, standing by the chest, had poured himself a third from the decanter, when he thought he heard the sound of light steps ascending the stairs from the rear entrance of the inn. He stood frozen in place, listening hard, and was sure he heard someone approaching in the hall. He waited long moments and then his heart skipped a beat at the sound of a quiet tapping at the door.

Geoffrey put his glass down on the chest and opened the door. Peggy quickly slipped through the doorway and stood just inside. Caulfield closed the door; then his heart skipped a beat as he looked at her.

She stood smiling; her face, with its high cheekbones and deep blue eyes, was elegantly framed by the hood of her black cape. Her cheeks were highlighted by a touch of rouge and her lips were painted with a subtle shade of red. As he watched, she reached up and slipped the hood off her head. Her raven hair gleamed in the light streaming through the window.

Caulfield moved close to help her remove her cape. Standing behind her, he said softly into her ear, "I'm glad you came. You look devastating today."

Peggy untied the cape and slipped out of it. Then she looked up into his eyes and replied, "Oh, Geoffrey, you say the nicest things to a woman. I wonder how much of it is true?"

"In your case, every word; there is no need to exaggerate when the truth is so evident. And you truly look radiant." He took the cape and draped it over the chair next to the door where Quinn had been seated. He turned and saw she wore a gown of the light blue which she favored and that complemented the blue of her eyes and her hair so well.

Then his eyes went to her neck, to see the necklace he had returned to her.

She saw him staring and said, "Yes, I couldn't resist wearing it. You went to so much trouble returning it to me. And when you did so, you showed me that you were a true gentleman and gained my everlasting admiration."

"I could have done no less."

Peggy walked around the room, looking things over, seeming to stop and note every object. Then she said, "It's just a little bit stuffy in here." She walked over to the window at the rear of the room and unfastened the latch. It was the style which swung open rather than sliding up or down, and she cracked it open. "There, we'll get a little air now."

Caulfield motioned toward the chest with the tray of libations. "Would you like some wine?"

She looked at him with a gleam in her eye and then pointed at the full glass beside the whiskey decanter. "Actually, I think I'll have some of what you've been drinking."

He poured her a glass and handed it to her. "This is quite good, but also very strong. I suggest sipping it carefully."

Peggy looked down at the glass and Caulfield saw a devilish gleam appear in her eyes. Then she said, "I prefer it taken this way."

Without hesitation she put her head back and drank the whiskey straight down.

Caulfield stood staring at her, momentarily astonished. He could detect no effect on her.

"It is very good, Geoffrey. Aren't you going to drink yours?" The devilish glint was still in Peggy's eyes.

He took a deep breath and finished his glass in the same manner, steeling himself to the burning as the alcohol went down.

Peggy put her glass down on the chest and took Geoffrey's from his hand and placed it beside hers. She looked up into his eyes, then slid her arms around him and gave him a long, passionate embrace.

Geoffrey was immediately aroused. The feeling was enhanced as she moved her hands through his hair.

Peggy said, "You can't know how long I have been anticipating this moment; the moment when I would be free to show you my feelings."

Caulfield felt himself breathing heavily and worked to control his excitement and modulate his voice. He said, "I've felt the same for many weeks, my dear lady."

She broke the embrace, put her arm around his waist, and, looking toward the bedstead, said, "Let us not waste time talking of our feelings. At a moment like this, actions should do the speaking."

He took her meaning. "By all means; why spend time in meaningless chatter?"

She led him to the bed and stood him beside it. He started to say something further, but she gently put her hand over his mouth.

"Don't speak. Now it will be my pleasure to undress you, Geoffrey. I have been longing to see your body for so long that I'm all aquiver now that the moment has come."

She slipped his coat off, then proceeded to remove the rest of his clothing, one garment at a time. Caulfield noticed that, with a woman's neat touch, she was carefully stacking each item on the chair closest to the bed. Finally, when all else had been removed, he sat down on the mattress and assisted her with the tight fitting underwear.

Peggy stood looking at him, and then, starting with his face, carefully caressed him with her hands, moving downward, lightly sliding them over his neck, shoulders, and chest. Caulfield found the process exhilarating and could not stop his arousal. She looked down at his manhood as it stiffened, her eyes gleaming but showing no sign of embarrassment.

Geoffrey said "It's my turn to see you."

She kissed him again and gently guided him into a reclining positon. Then she stood back from the bed and said coyly, "Now, do what I say. Close your eyes; there are some things that women want to remain a mystery, but I promise when I tell you to open your eyes, you will be astonished."

He wasted no time in complying and thought: *Soon comes the moment I have waited for since the first time I visited Eckert Ridge.*

He was surprised to hear a clicking sound and then almost simultaneously he felt a cold pinprick on his genitals. Startled, he opened his eyes to see Peggy holding a long, thin-bladed, stiletto-like knife in her right hand, the point resting on his manhood. In shock, he looked up to see she held one of his pistols, which had been lying on the dresser near the bed, in her left hand. The lock was cocked and the barrel was pointed directly at his eyes.

"My God, Peggy, what are you doing?" Caulfield asked in fright, at the same time feeling ashamed at the high-pitched, fearful tone of his voice.

"Teaching you a lesson I hope you will carry to your grave." She pressed the point of the knife a fraction of an inch more deeply into his parts. The pain became nearly unbearable.

"No, no, please no!" pleaded Caulfield.

"Make no move, lest you lose that which is most dear to you. Do not doubt I will do it." She nodded toward the pistol. "And if you make any sudden move toward me I will not hesitate to pull the trigger."

Caulfield's entire body stiffened in fear.

"Now, Mr. Geoffrey Caulfield — or whatever your name really is — you are going to listen to me," Peggy said in a calm, serious tone. "Your bloated opinion of yourself far exceeds your attributes and your virtues. You think all women must succumb to your overtures. Perhaps the ready submission of naïve young women here in the settlements has encouraged you in this belief and led to your insufferable sense of confidence." She smiled broadly. "But understand this: I am more experienced in these matters than you could ever dream."

"No, no, Peggy, for God's sake, you misunderstand my sentiments."

"Be quiet and listen." She gave him another prick with the point of the blade. Then she made a show of looking closely at the area between his legs. "There's a trace of blood near the point, Geoffrey. Next time you interrupt I'll jab deeper."

Caulfield lay very still.

"Your ego led you to some serious misjudgments, Geoffrey. You underestimated my husband and my affection for him. Many men have misjudged Wend, thinking him a dullard. But most have done that to their great regret. Now understand this: He came to my rescue at the moment of my greatest distress and saved me from a backcountry existence I detested. Wend has provided me with a life of substance and comfort. The idea that I would betray him for a few minutes of pleasure with the likes of you is absurd." She smiled down at Caulfield. "If you were half as smart as you think you are, you would have realized that from the beginning."

Staying as still as he could manage, Caulfield asked, "But why come here at all? Why lead me on and humiliate me in this way?"

"Because of the necklace around my neck; you sought to curry favor with me by returning it. But you knew I could never wear it before my husband or anyone else who knew it had been stolen." Peggy put the pistol down momentarily on the chest and pulled at the necklace, breaking the clasp and flinging it down on the bed. It landed next to Caulfield's head. Then she picked up the pistol again.

"Keep that as a reminder of your folly."

Peggy withdrew the knife from between Caulfield's legs and threw it to the far corner of the room. Then, keeping the pistol aimed at his face, she picked up the other pistol from the chest, blew the priming from the pan, and dropped it butt-first into the chamber pot, which was nearly full.

Finally, she grabbed the stack of clothing on the chair and carried it to the window. She swung it fully open using the barrel of the pistol.

Caulfield realized her intent and cried out, "For God's sake, no! I beg of you, spare me this last indignity!"

Peggy threw back her head and laughed, then tossed the entire bundle through the open window. Without saying another word, she picked up her cloak, opened the door, and slipped through it without a backward glance. She left the door wide open behind her.

Caulfield sprang to his feet and ran for the door, pulling it closed before a patron or maid passed by. As he did so, he heard a female voice shouting at a horse and then the sound of hooves and a vehicle racing away. He ran to the window to see his clothing on the ground, now being scattered by gusts of wind. His pistol lay directly below the window.

He stood there for a long moment, struggling to think clearly amidst his rage. Then he strode over to the bed and ripped the top sheet off and wrapped himself in it. Once covered, he ran out of the room to the top of the stairs which led down to the common room.

"Quinn! Quinn! He shouted down the stairs at the top of his voice. "Quinn, get up here now!" Then he walked back to the room and seated himself on the bed to await his compatriot.

Presently he heard steps in the hall and Quinn appeared in the doorway. He leaned against the frame, a mug in his hand, and asked casually, "Now Cap'n, what's all the excitement?"

"For God's sake, Quinn, go out back of the tavern and get my clothes before they're all blown away."

Quinn's eyes lighted on Caulfield in his sheet, then swept around the room. His eyes rested on the pistol barrel sticking out of the chamber pot. "What's been goin' on in here, Cap'n?"

"Damn you, Corporal, just get down there and get my clothes. And one of my pistols is lying out on the ground."

Quinn broke into a deep fit of laughter. "By God, the bitch played you false, did she?"

"Shut up and get my things, Quinn."

The former corporal of dragoons put his mug on the chest and went down the stairs, laughing all the time.

Caulfield sat waiting on the bed, feeling his face burning. Waves of humiliation washed over him.

Presently Quinn returned with all the clothing bundled in his arms, the pistol stuck in his belt.

"Now Cap'n, here be your clothes and firelock. But you'll have to get that other pistol out of the pot and wipe it down yourself. I ain't putting my hand in that lot."

"Put the clothes on the chair, Quinn, and I'll get dressed."

"So what happened, Cap'n? Did you insult the woman?"

Caulfield was staring straight ahead, as if looking at some distant object. "The truth is, she came here planning to do this, Quinn." Caulfield sighed deeply and shook his head. "She's been playing the fool's game with me from the day of that fair at Glengarry. And I fell for it all the way." Without looking at Quinn he said, "Do me the favor of giving me a drink."

Quinn broke out into guffaws again. Then he walked over to the whiskey decanter, poured a glass, and carried it to Caulfield. "Here, Cap'n, put this down." Then he went over and poured himself a drink. "I never thought I'd see the day when a woman would put somethin' over on you."

Geoffrey, still staring at the wall, said quietly, almost to himself, "She laid it out to the last detail and then had the composure to play her role like an actor on the stage. She played it masterfully. And she made me perform, unwittingly, the very part she had written for me."

"Cap'n, damn if you don't sound like you ain't even mad at her."

"Mad? No, if anything, I have great admiration for her. She is indeed a woman like none I have ever known."

"Well, one thing's sure, Cap'n: She's finished with you." Quinn downed his drink. "Now can we get away from this cursed town and head for Carolina?"

Caulfield finally turned to look at Quinn and sighed. "Yes, it is indeed time to leave. We've got enough provisions. The sooner we go the better, as far as I'm concerned."

Quinn said, "I'll settle my bill down below, then bring the horses around back here."

"Yes, do that. I'll be ready shortly."

After Quinn left, Geoffrey went over to the bed and retrieved the necklace Peggy had thrown there. He stared at it for a long moment and rubbed his fingers over the stones in an almost reverent manner. Then he sighed deeply, went to the chest, and took his purse from the top drawer. With great care he put the jewelry into the purse.

* * *

The chaise was flying, Boots' hooves pounding on the hard-packed ground of the road as they headed westward in the direction of Glengarry. Alice Downy was turning white and holding on for dear life every time they hit a bump or hole. She kept looking back toward the inn.

Finally, they navigated a turn in the road and Peggy reined in the animal to a walk.

"Why are you so nervous?" asked Peggy.

"He might come after us."

"It will take Caulfield a while to get dressed and if he or one of his men came after us, they would think we were going back to Eckert Ridge. They won't have guessed we went this way." She smiled at Alice. "Besides, I don't think he'll follow. He's got nothing to gain by confronting us."

"If there's nothing to worry about, why were you driving so fast?"

"I just wanted to get out of sight from the inn as fast as possible so if I'm wrong, he won't see which way we went."

"All the same, Peggy, I'll feel better when we turn up the drive for Glengarry." Alice looked at her friend. "Did everything go as you planned?"

Peggy grinned broadly. "Precisely as I expected; Caulfield was like a dog performing to get his reward." She shook her head. "The truth is I haven't had this much fun since I was a young girl! The biggest problem I had was to keep from laughing while Caulfield was doing my bidding. That would have ruined everything."

"Peggy Eckert, you are a wicked, wicked woman. Now tell me the details!"

Peggy proceeded to do so, and the telling took until they turned into the long drive of the McDonald's place. Old Jack came down the steps to greet them as the groom took the reins and led Boots and the chaise back toward the stables. Peggy handed him a basket full of fruit they had brought along for Anna. Then he led them up to his mistress' sick room.

Anna McDonald was in her bed, looking miserable. Her face and nose were red, and she had a handkerchief in her hand. But a smile broke out on her face when she saw her visitors.

Peggy said, "We came over to cheer you up and help take care of you."

Alice joined in, saying, "And we'll keep the children entertained so they don't disturb you."

Peggy waved at the basket in Jack's hand. "We've got some nice fruit and there's a jar of honey in there, too, which should help with your throat. We'll have you feeling better in no time at all."

"Oh, Peggy, I was so glad to get the word that you were coming. I've had a room made up for the both of you. I shall be so happy for your company." She looked up from the bed and smiled. "It's selfless of you to drop everything and travel over here just to help me. I'm fortunate to have true, honest friends like you."

Just then there was the sound of steps in the hall and Old Jack knocked and entered, standing just inside the door. Keeping his eyes away from the bed, he said to Anna, "I beg your pardon, ma'am, but Mr. McLeod is back, with news from the sheriff."

"Oh, do send him in, Jack." Anna turned to Peggy and Alice. "Evan's been out with the sheriff and some other men. Smith got word on where that band of highwaymen might be hiding. He caught an iron monger named Rhys with goods stolen from a traveler's wagon. The sheriff threatened him with a lashing and Rhys told him where he thought the highwaymen were encamped."

The veteran Highlander stood in the doorway, his bonnet in hand, and, for delicacy, swung the door to where he was out of sight of Anna. Peggy saw that he was covered in dust and there were drops of sweat on his brow.

"Well, Miss Anna," he said, "We found those scoundrels. Caught them lying about in their den, if you will. It was just where that Welshmen said, down along a creek near Stephensburg."

Peggy and Alice exchanged looks. "Did you capture them, Mr. McLeod?" asked Peggy.

"No, damn our luck. The blackguards took to horse and foot and disappeared into the bush." Even grinned broadly. "All except the one we shot; the sheriff himself put a ball into him."

Peggy said, "Was he killed?"

"He's dead and brought to the jail tied to the back of a horse." McLeod looked around at the women. "And we found all sorts of goods in their camp: enough supplies and provisions for a long journey and several packsaddles. Sure and we took some horses, too."

Alice asked, "So you think they were preparing to leave the county?"

"Yes, ma'am. The sheriff is convinced of it."

"But now they can't, because you got their supplies," said Peggy.

"Yes, that's a fact, ma'am. We hit them in time to prevent them from preying on some other town. And now the villains are in the bush without food or any of their camp kit. Smith is going out again tomorrow with men and dogs to try to track them down." McLeod looked around at the women. "I think we can say the days of those men raiding the roads of Frederick County are over."

* * *

After leaving the inn, Caulfield and Quinn pushed their horses, intending to make the camp in time for the evening meal. They were still a mile from the place where they normally turned off the road when a black man emerged from the woods along the road fifty yards ahead and began waving frantically at them.

Quinn exclaimed, "By God, Cap'n, that's Isaac."

Caulfield said, "What the devil is he doing here?"

The two trotted up to their comrade.

Geoffrey asked, "What's toward, Isaac?"

"Mr. Geoffrey, we was attacked! We was attacked this morning after you left."

"Attacked? Who attacked you? Make yourself clear!" said Quinn.

"The sheriff and a whole party of men, that be who. They come up on us without no warning. We heared a voice call out for us to surrender; everybody jumped up and ran for their horses. And that's when they started shooting. They hit Johnny Swift with the first shot. He went down hard an' nobody could help him 'cause they was comin' so fast."

Quinn shot back: "So they took him?"

"I think he be dead where he fall, Mr. Quinn."

Caulfield felt rising panic. "What about everyone else? Did they get away? And where are they?"

"We got to the horses down by the creek. Then we rode hard right up the stream. Them sheriff's men had left their horses and couldn't follow right away. We made it to a hill a couple of miles to the west, Mr. Geoffrey. A hill all covered with trees and bush. There be a spring there where we could water the horses. They sent me down here to stop you from goin' to the old camp."

Quinn cursed. "Christ above! We should have been out of here a week ago. We should be several long days to the south of here." He turned to Caulfield, his face livid. "And we would be, too, if it hadn't been for your . . ." he paused to think of the right words, "Your *damned business at that inn*."

Caulfield looked at Quinn, then quickly away, afraid to see the rage in the veteran dragoon's eyes. He said nothing in response, instead turning to Isaac. "Where's your horse?"

"He be tied up back in the woods."

"Get mounted and lead us to the men. We must figure out what to do."

They made the journey to the refuge in dead silence. Caulfield was continually aware of Quinn's fuming; beyond that, he dreaded the reaction of the crew when they arrived. As Isaac led them deeper into the bush, Geoffrey's mind raced at breakneck pace, calculating how to deal with both the desperate situation which faced them and the anger of his men. *He would have to be very fast on his feet.*

In an hour's time they arrived, tied their horses with those of the others, and ascended to the place where the band of refugee highwaymen waited.

Isaac led them to a grove of pines with a spring in the middle. There Caulfield saw the remaining four people — Hansen, Cole, Bierly, and Sarah — clustered in a forlorn group. There was no fire. Hatchet-faced Cole stood leaning against a tree; Bierly sat on the ground, his arms around his knees; both were watching Sarah as she tended a wound in Hansen's side. Hansen sat on a log, bare to his waist. His coat lay next to him; the woman had torn up his shirt to make bandages.

Caulfield asked, "How bad is it, Sarah?"

"It be a crease on his side, Mr. Geoffrey; just a crease, but a deep one. I'm cleaning it and then I'll tie a bandage over it; that's all I can do. It gonna hurt for a while."

"Can he ride?"

It was Hansen who answered. "I can damn well ride, Caulfield. And that's what I'm goin' to do, the moment she's finished. Me and Cole is leavin'. We had enough."

Cole pushed himself away from the tree and stood with his hands on his hips. "Hansen's got it right, Caulfield. We been with you for two years, and look what it's got us." He swept his arm around. "Just what you see: nothing!"

Hansen said, "This is the second time we been raided by a sheriff; the second time we lost everything."

Bierly said, "We was all ready to go south; we had everything we needed for days now. Why the hell did we hang around here?" He looked around at the entire group, then stared beseechingly at Quinn, held his hands out toward him and said, "Can you tell me why it was so important for Caulfield and you to go off for hours today?"

Quinn didn't answer; instead he stared at Caulfield for a long moment, his jaw tight, his face reddening. The others turned and looked also; the silence was overpowering as Geoffrey stood quiet for long seconds, desperately searching for an answer. Then inspiration came upon him; he reached into his coat pocket and pulled out a folded piece of parchment. "I had some very important business in Winchester today. After looking for a long time, I finally found something we need." He slowly, carefully unfolded the paper. "This is a map of the road south through the Carolinas to Charleston. I've been looking for one and finally found it in a shop in town. We couldn't leave until we had something to guide us."

Bierly scowled. "Lot of good that will do us now; we ain't got provisions, we ain't got our camp stuff, and we lost our packsaddles and three of the horses. Me and Cole had to ride double over here."

"Now listen, I have a plan," said Caulfield. He looked at Quinn. "The corporal and I worked it out on the ride here."

Quinn straightened up and stared at Caulfield, his brow furrowed. He turned and looked at the others. Then he threw up his hands and exclaimed, "Oh, hell yes, and it is quite a plan. You'll all want to hear it. Go ahead, Cap'n, and explain."

Caulfield said, "Now listen: we're going to get out of here at dusk. We're heading north; north along the Great Wagon Road through the night. We'll hide in the daylight. We're going all the way up to Mecklenburg on the Potomac and set up a hidden camp there."

Hansen scowled. "What good is that? What's up there?" He stood up and put on his coat. "Come on, Cole, let's get going and leave this sorry lot listening to another of Caulfield's big ideas."

Caulfield walked over so that he was face to face with Hansen. "And where are you going to go? You got any money to buy food or to feed your horses?" He paused and looked around at the others. "Two strange men riding around this county; you're just what the sheriff will be searching for after today's raid. And all the local people are going to be on the lookout for strangers on the loose. I wager you'll both be in that jail in Winchester by tomorrow night."

Suddenly Quinn was in motion. He strode over, grabbed Hansen by the collar of his coat with his left hand, hit him in the face with his right, and then threw him to the ground.

Hansen groaned and put his hand to the wound on his side and then to his cheek.

Quinn's hand went to the butt of the horse pistol in his belt. He said, "Now my lad, just stay there and listen to what the Cap'n has to say."

369

Hanson lay on the ground, still gritting his teeth in pain.

The burly dragoon looked over at Cole. "And what about you? You got anything to say?"

Cole looked down at Hansen, then grinned broadly. "Me, Quinn? No; fact is, I can't hardly wait to hear what Caulfield has to say."

Bierly looked down at Hansen and shrugged. "I'm ready to listen, but the truth be we ain't got no provisions or blankets or powder for our firelocks. What good is it going to do us to travel up to this Mecklenburg place?"

Caulfield replied, "I was up there a few weeks ago on one of my scouting trips. Mecklenburg is where the Great Wagon Road crosses the Potomac. There's a ferry there and a ford. Lots of pilgrims and freighters pass through there every day coming down from the north. Some of the wagons continue south, others head west for the settlements on the border. But the point is there's lots of traffic for us to prey on."

Bierly said, "Yeah, and after a while the sheriff up there raids us and we're back where we are now, or worse, we're dead."

Caulfield looked at Bierly for a long moment, then said, "No, he won't have the chance. Because we're not going to stay there for a long time. Just long enough to replace our lost horses and get an adequate amount of provisions; then we're heading east; east to Fairfax County and the river country around Alexandria. That's a richer area, with a goodly number of tobacco plantations along the Potomac. We can take enough money and goods from planters there to prepare for our journey south. We'll move around a lot to keep the local sheriff guessing. Once we've taken what we need," he brandished the map, "We'll come back to the Great Road and head for Carolina, just like we've planned."

Bierly retorted, "That's all fine and good, but at this moment, just like you said, we ain't got food for us or the horses. We need that just to make it to Mecklenburg. And the way I see it, takin' from pilgrims along the road will bring the sheriff down on us."

Caulfield nodded. "That's a very good point, Bierly. But I look like an upstanding traveler; I'll buy what we need along the way; there are taverns and stores on the road."

Bierly cocked his head. "And just where are we goin' to get the money for that?"

Geoffrey reached into his coat pocket and pulled out his purse, and jingled the coins. "Right here. That's why I've always carried our money with me. So it wouldn't be lost if we got raided."

Quinn put his hands on his hips and said belligerently, "All right. You heard the plan. Now is there anyone who's got more questions? Is there any one of you figurin' on pulling out on your own now?" He glared at each of them in turn. No one spoke up.

Then Quinn walked over in front of Hansen and stared down at him. "What about you? You got any more questions?"

Hansen shook his head.

Cole spoke up. "Give it a rest, Quinn. We'll not be leavin' now. We're in, long as this here plan works out the way Caulfield said."

Geoffrey breathed a sigh of relief. He said, "All right then, that's settled." He looked up at the sun, now low in the west. "Dusk will be coming on in about an hour. We'll pull out then. So get some rest." He motioned to the big Irishman. "Quinn and I will go down and check the condition of the horses."

The two men walked down to where the animals were picketed. When they got there, Geoffrey turned to Quinn and said, "I'm obliged to you for backing me up, Corporal."

Quinn said nothing. Instead he grabbed Caulfield by the lapels of his coat and slammed him up against the trunk of the nearest tree.

Caulfield's head snapped back painfully with the force of it.

"Now, you listen," said Quinn through gritted teeth, "that's the last fuckin' time I'm standin' by you. This all happened 'cause you wanted to hang around here to poke that Eckert woman. Now we lost everything and poor Johnny Swift lies dead." He stopped for a moment, then continued, "You better keep that fine mind you're so proud of on our work, or I'll be gone with the rest of them. In fact, I'm givin' you a month. If things ain't workin' out by then, I'm leavin'. You understand?" He slammed Caulfield against the tree again, then released him and stepped back.

Geoffrey sighed and adjusted his coat. He looked into Quinn's eyes and saw smoldering anger there. He said, in as calm a tone as he could manage. "Yes, I understand." He rubbed the back of his head. "You didn't need to emphasize your point so . . ." he hesitated, "so *forcefully*."

"I wanted to make sure you remembered what I said."

"Now listen, Quinn, I pledge to you that all my energy will be aimed at restoring our fortunes and preparing for the journey south."

"It better be." Then he looked quizzically at Caulfield and asked, "When the hell did you get that map? We didn't stop in town today."

"Days ago, corporal; on one of my trips to Winchester."

"And what about this money you said would pay for us to travel over the next couple of days? I calculated we was low after buying liquor for the men two days ago and payin' for things at the inn today."

Caulfield reached down and pulled out the purse, opened it, and held out the necklace.

"Damn, where did you get that?"

"Mrs. Eckert saw fit to return it to me as part of her performance at the inn. I figure we can trade the stones for much of what we need, at least to get up to Mecklenburg."

"It damned well better work, after what you told the lads." Quinn thought a moment, then looked up the hill. "And now I'm going back up there and make sure Cole and Hansen don't cause any more mischief. Meanwhile, you had best start figurin' out how we're going to get this forlorn lot past Winchester without being seen by some citizen ready to run to the sheriff."

With that, Quinn turned and strode back to the gang's lair.

Caulfield stood shivering in the evening, but not from the chill. He was relieved that he and Quinn had been able to keep the band from dissolving, but was well aware how close a call it had been. And the Irishman was right; it would take every bit of Geoffrey's attention and forethought to recoup their fortunes and guide them through the next few weeks or months. But he was even more aware of something else: The partnership between Quinn and himself had shifted, with the balance swinging more toward Quinn. Caulfield knew he would have to walk carefully, *very* carefully, in the future and make sure that their plans led to success.

CHAPTER NINETEEN
Dunmore on the Ohio

T he garrison stood to attention, drawn up before Fort Fincastle. The formation faced the landing where Lord Dunmore would disembark from the bateau carrying him down from Pittsburgh. Crawford and his adjutant stood watching the string of boats approaching, ready to greet the Commander in Chief of Virginia's forces. Wend and his quartermasters stood behind the garrison. His men were civilians, not susceptible to full military discipline, but Flannagan had gotten them into a line and Eckert reckoned they looked presentable.

Crawford's fifers and drummers stood behind him and now, as the governor's boats neared the riverbank, they broke into a slightly ragged rendition of *The British Grenadiers*. As Dunmore stepped ashore the garrison presented arms, albeit with a lack of precision which would have driven any sergeant of regulars to tears.

Wend looked over the party and saw that McDonald, Northcutt, Grenough, and indeed even Connolly, were with Dunmore. There was a round of greetings and then Crawford led the group to a spot near one end of the stockade where several tents had been set up to serve as the governor's headquarters. Once the official party departed, the captain in charge of the formation dismissed the men. Then, just as Wend was about to go back to his own camp, he saw the adjutant coming toward him and waving.

"Eckert," called out the adjutant, "You're wanted at headquarters."

"Now why would they want me?"

"There's going to be a meeting to discuss the campaign. Mr. Northcutt told Crawford to ensure you were there."

Wend thought: *What does Northcutt want now?* He looked himself over and decided he was as presentable as the situation allowed. Then he headed for the governor's tents.

He arrived to find the Lord Dunmore lounging in a camp chair at the end of a table with Northcutt and Grenough seated on his right and left hand. Crawford, McDonald, and Connolly were ranged around the lower end. Crawford had provided some rum and all were sipping at mugs. Two other officers, a captain and lieutenant, stood behind the Earl's chair. The governor was carrying on a conversation with Crawford about the status of provisions while the others listened attentively.

Wend felt awkward and was unsure what to do, so he stood quietly about ten feet from the table. It was the first time he had ever seen the governor. John Murray, the Fourth Earl of Dunmore, was in his forties and had a pale complexion contrasted by ruddy cheeks. His red hair tended toward the auburn, but still a shade or two lighter than Eckert remembered Mary Fraser's was. Dunmore was dressed in the blue uniform of the Virginia Militia; his midsection was showing the inevitable thickening of middle age, bulging out against the buttons of the red waistcoat as he sat at the table.

Northcutt, also in uniform, glanced over at Wend. He smiled and turned to the governor. "My Lord, here is Lieutenant Eckert."

Dunmore turned and swept his eyes over Wend.

Wend stiffened, cleared his throat and said, "Good afternoon, Your Lordship. The adjutant told me to come here, sir."

"Quite, Mr. Eckert; I'm glad to meet you, sir. Northcutt and McDonald have told me much about you. Clearly you have done us valuable service on this campaign. We were impressed with your leadership during the ambush near Hart's Store and the way you gallantly managed that fight on the withdrawal from Wakatomica. By God, sir, your maneuver saved those wounded men."

Wend said, "You are very kind, Your Lordship."

"Not at all, Eckert. And then there's the matter of this diplomatic initiative with the Mingo along that creek north of the Ohio Forks."

McDonald prompted, "Slippery Rock Creek, My Lord."

"Ah yes, Angus; *Slippery Rock Creek*. See here, Eckert, I read your report; most dramatic and damned gratifying, sir. We are grateful that you were able to take as many as seventy warriors out of the picture. That fits well, *very* well, with our plans for this campaign."

"Thank you, sir."

"You volunteered to put your life on the line for Virginia. That is the kind of loyalty we need from our officers if we are to prevail in this endeavor."

Wend felt his face flushing. "Your words are indeed kind, My Lord."

"Well, I intend more than words of gratitude. With the esteemed advice of Major Northcutt and Major McDonald, it is my pleasure to appoint you to my staff as an Aide de Camp, joining these other two gentlemen." He motioned toward the two officers standing behind his chair.

Wend was shocked and dismayed. "Sir, I'm extremely grateful for your confidence. But I don't feel qualified to serve in such a role."

"Nonsense, Mr. Eckert." Dunmore smiled and looked around the table. "Northcutt, McDonald, and I discussed this appointment on the way here. We all are convinced that having a representative of the Valley and the western border country on my personal staff would be of inestimable value. And your knowledge and experience would seem to fit the requirement precisely." The governor put his left hand on Grenough's shoulder. "And Mr. Grenough here, with all his experience on the frontier, enthusiastically concurred. That fixed my mind on the matter."

Grenough beamed at Wend.

Eckert realized further protestation would be futile and unseemly. "It will be my great pleasure to join your staff, sir."

"Excellent, Mr. Eckert," The governor motioned to two officers behind him. "My other aides are from the Tidewater and I think your association with them will greatly add to their education and understanding of the western part of the colony."

Wend glanced over at the officers and saw no evidence in their eyes that they shared the enthusiasm of their commander.

Then the governor announced, "Gentlemen, let us now discuss the forthcoming campaign." He turned to the captain standing behind his chair and said, "Marsh, your map, if you please."

The aide stepped over to the table and spread out a map of the Ohio Country.

Then Dunmore resumed, "Before leaving Fort Dunmore, we ordered the forces at Redstone to begin their march to this place. And Major Connolly's battalion will come down from the forks by boat tomorrow." He glanced at McDonald. "Our Brigade Major will explain the organization of our force."

McDonald said, "We will have three battalions in our brigade. As His Lordship said, Connolly will command the men raised around the Forks of the Ohio, to the number of 200, to be known as the West Augusta Battalion. Crawford will assume command of my former force, to be called the Frederick County Battalion, which has been augmented by another 100 men recruited from the county. And Colonel Adam Stephen will lead the Berkeley County Battalion. He has also raised about 500 men. Altogether, our brigade will have over twelve hundred men."

Dunmore said, "Colonel Andrew Lewis, of Greenbrier County, has raised a force of similar size from the southwestern counties. We sent orders for him to march to the Ohio along the Kanawha Trail and wait for us to join him at the mouth of the Kanawha River."

Northcutt said, "With that many men, it should be clear to the Shawnee that we can readily defeat them and whatever allies they have gathered and then drive them in retreat before us all the way to Cornstalk's town on the Pickaway Plains."

Marsh nodded. "A most accurate observation, sir."

Crawford said, "Yes, Northcutt, but in my opinion, the key is to quickly mass our full force. I assume we will march as rapidly as possible for the Kanawha to confront the Indians with a unified army."

Northcutt shrugged. "Crawford, I don't see that as so urgent. The important factor is the overall size of our force. I believe that alone will intimidate the savages and permit us to force them to treat with us." He looked around the table and grinned. "Frankly, I think we can contemplate a bloodless campaign."

Crawford leaned forward and spoke very calmly. "Barrett, I would it were so. However, our scouts universally believe the Shawnee will fight. And I know from my own experiences out here in the border country how belligerent the young Shawnee warriors have become over the last year. I believe, even in the face of our great strength, they will attempt some offensive action against this army."

Northcutt quickly cut in, "And precisely what kind of action do you contemplate they would take? Our information is that they have no more than 700 warriors."

Crawford shrugged. "I have no crystal ball, Northcutt, but I know Cornstalk is a wily warrior. I believe he will attempt to attack before we can unite the two forces. With 700 warriors, their fighting skills and knowledge of the forest will make them a match for either one of our brigades."

Northcutt frowned. "Each or our brigades has a decided advantage in size over the entire Indian force. You seem to have little regard for the fighting ability of our militia."

Crawford set his jaw, then said, "It might be helpful, Barrett, to remember that at the Monongahela in '55, there were no more than 200 French and 600

Indians present against Braddock's 1300 and we later learned that their casualties were minimal after killing hundreds of our men."

Northcutt's face reddened. He shot back, "And you, Major, might remember that this isn't 1755 and our force is composed of border-hardened riflemen, not Irish foot regiments filled with raw recruits."

Crawford said, in a heated tone, "Northcutt, I maintain the Shawnee warriors are to be reckoned with, even against the best of our riflemen."

Dunmore spread his hands palm down in a calming motion. "Now, now, gentlemen, let us not argue amongst ourselves." He looked down at the table, reflected for a long moment, and then smiled at Crawford. "Major, let me explain something of which you have not yet been apprised: While at Fort Dunmore, we took the step of dispatching the Delaware Chiefs White Eyes of the Turtle Clan and Captain Pipe of the Wolf Clan to meet with Cornstalk and his subordinate leaders. White Eyes believes, as I do, that once the Shawnee fully appreciate our numbers, they will come to peace talks. In any case, it is known that Cornstalk dreads this war and is looking for an excuse not to fight. Thus it remains only for us to demonstrate our determination and readiness for combat and, if necessary, begin an advance toward the Indian towns along the Scioto. I am convinced that we will not find it necessary to actually engage the Shawnee in the field. I intend to emulate the achievement of Bouquet a decade ago when he marched to the Muskingum and dictated terms to the Ohio tribes with virtually no loss of life."

Lord Dunmore looked around the table as if challenging anyone to contradict his assertions. All was silent. After long seconds he turned to the captain aide and said, "Please enumerate our planned movements, Captain Marsh."

"Certainly, sir," said the aide. "Once the troops from Redstone and Fort Dunmore arrive, we will begin our movement to the south." He moved his finger along the map. "We intend to march southward until opposite the Hocking River. Major Crawford and his battalion will escort the pack train and bullock herd down to the Hocking. Crawford will find a good location to pasture the livestock, and be ready to send them across the Ohio if that becomes necessary."

Crawford leaned forward and pointed to a spot on the map. "My Lord, Colonel Washington and I camped near the Hocking back in '71 on a surveying expedition. There are sites there which are relatively open and will well serve our purpose."

The governor said quickly, "That's excellent, Crawford." Then he looked over at Northcutt and his face broke into a crooked smile. "The esteemed Mr. Washington does seem to get about, doesn't he, Barrett?"

Northcutt smiled and said, "Indeed he does, including joining this rebellious assemblage in Philadelphia, this *Congress* as they call it; a meeting which could represent a bit of jeopardy for him."

Dunmore nodded. "That it could, sir; and for all the other men involved." Then he waved for Marsh to continue.

"It was our original intent to continue southward to the Kanawha and unite with Lewis. Now, however, we will stop at the Hocking and prepare a site there for negotiations. We have directed White Eyes to bring Cornstalk and his allied chiefs to that point." Marsh then put his finger on the mouth of the Kanawha and said, "When, in our estimate, Lewis' brigade should have arrived at the original rendezvous point, we will send a courier directing him to move up the Ohio and join our force at the Hocking. Then, when all the elements of the expedition have assembled, we should have more than adequate force for any eventuality."

Lord Dunmore said, "Thank you, Marsh." He turned back to the men at the table with a self-satisfied smile and said, "There you have it gentlemen, a simple but effective plan which promises to bring complete attainment of our objectives. I commend you to Major McDonald to assist him in working out the details and timing of our movement. Our brigade will be assembled here in a matter of days, and we shall march at the earliest opportunity."

Then he rose, signaling the end of the meeting.

* * *

The fire in front of Grenough's tent blazed strongly, illuminating the faces of Grenough and Northcutt as they lounged in camp chairs. Wend sat with them, having been summoned by Barrett. In addition to the three men, the large, brown, non-descript dog belonging to Grenough lay beside his chair.

Grenough looked down at the cup in his hand and said, "This whiskey is indeed fine. I've rarely tasted the like of it."

Northcutt raised his own cup and looked over at Grenough. "I thought you'd like it, Richard; I was introduced to it when traveling with Eckert on the way south from Pittsburg last spring. His compatriot McGonagall distills the stuff. Now I savor the rare occasions when it is available." He waved his cup toward Wend. "Eckert here was kindly enough to bring some over for us."

Wend said, "My friend's name is *Donegal,* Barrett."

"Ah, yes, *Donegal.*"

"I'll admit it is a nice change from rum, Barrett," said Grenough. "And quite superior to the normal border whiskey one encounters." He reached down and rubbed the head and ears of his dog.

Barrett winked at Wend. Then he said to Grenough, "Richard, you favor that dog almost like he was part of your family. You keep him with you every step you take."

"Indeed I do. I've trained him to serve many purposes for me. I never go into the bush without him."

Northcutt said dismissively, "I've never been particularly fond of dogs myself. But that could be because my brother's pet cur bit my hand when I was very young."

Grenough laughed. "Barrett, knowing you, I'll wager you were baiting the animal when he did it."

Northcutt frowned and looked sharply at Grenough. "Now that I recollect, it's possible you're right, Richard." Then he motioned toward Wend. "Let me add my congratulations to you on the way you have dealt with things here on the border, Eckert. You've justified my faith in you, by God. That mission to the Mingo was brilliant."

Wend shook his head. "I just took advantage of a stroke of fortune when we captured Wolf Claw. And I must confess this to you, Barrett: I had personal reasons for going to Slippery Rock Creek."

Northcutt cocked his head. "Personal reasons? Pray tell what reasons?"

"I wanted to see my son."

Both Northcutt and Grenough stared at Wend. Then Northcutt said, "Your son, Eckert? In a Mingo village? I admit to being profoundly confused."

But Grenough got it right away. A crooked smile broke over his face and he turned toward Northcutt. "Let me enlighten you, Barrett, about some of my old friend Eckert's history. He and a young lady named Abigail Gibson, a beauty from a good family in Philadelphia, had a youthful romance fifteen years ago when traveling along Forbes Road. But immediately afterward the young lady was captured by a Mingo war party. She subsequently became the hostage wife of none other than Wolf Claw himself."

Northcutt shot a look at Wend, then quickly back at Grenough. "The devil, you say, Richard!"

"It's true, Barrett, but I confess ignorance, until now, about the child." Grenough looked at Wend. "Eckert, I am, of course, assuming the child in question is the result of your dalliance with Miss Gibson?"

Wend glared at the trader. "Dalliance is not the word I would use, Grenough."

"Forgive my objectionable choice of words, my dear Wend."

Northcutt took a quick sip of his drink and then grinned at Wend. "By God, you have had an enviable record with regard to the ladies, Wend. The governor and I met your wife during our stay at Greenway Court, when the McDonalds had a reception for His Lordship up at Glengarry. I must say that he was quite enchanted with her beauty. He mentioned to me on the way back to our quarters that she would rival any of the ladies he'd met in Williamsburg."

Grenough broke into a knowing smile and put his hand on Northcutt's shoulder. "Let me assure you, Barrett, that Peggy Eckert has had that effect on many men. Those in Cumberland County eagerly sought her company when she was a," he paused, looked at Wend with a knowing glint in his eyes, coughed delicately and said, "shall we say, young *maiden*. Is that not so, Eckert?"

You bastard, thought Wend. But he forced a smile and replied, "She was indeed the object of many men's attentions, Richard. I am most fortunate that she accepted my proposal."

"I'll drink to that," said Northcutt. He took another sip of the whiskey. "You know, Eckert, were I married to her, I should be most jealous when other men even looked at her."

"I am confident in my wife's love and respect her enjoyment of social moments, Barrett."

Grenough laughed and said, "Come now, Barrett, you've watched Eckert's face. You know he is a man in control of his emotions."

"True, Richard," replied Northcutt. "But Wend, you should be happy to know that Dunmore commended you to her in most glowing terms. Then he explained why you had not come back with McDonald, describing your mission to the Mingo and how indebted to you he would be, assuming its success."

Wend's heart sank. He had counted on being the first to tell Peggy about the trip to Slippery Rock Creek. Now she would be nursing anger about his contact with Abigail. And things would be further inflamed by the unexpected arrival of Johann at Eckert Ridge. But he kept his face impassive and said, "I'm sure she was gratified by the governor's comments."

"Oh, indeed, Eckert; she told him that she couldn't wait until your return so she could hear all about your adventures among the Mingo. She said she was sure your story would arouse her blood." Northcutt smiled, "Lord Dunmore was only too happy to enhance your esteem with your wife."

Wend said, "I am obliged to him. But to pursue my original point, while the governor has showered me with praise, I must repeat that I had my own interest in mind for traveling to the Mingo villages. And you should be aware that my son has returned with me and is now at this camp."

Northcutt shrugged. "For God's sake, don't be so contrite, Eckert. His Lordship has no objection to a man combining government business with his own. It can't have escaped you that many of the men in our army are here to cement their land rights in Ohio." He looked around at his companions. "The governor himself plans to reserve a very large parcel of land for himself, just as he did in New York. Confidentially, gentlemen, he sees his future here in America after his term is complete and these difficulties with the colonists have been resolved." He hesitated, smiling to himself. "He fancies the title of *Lord Scioto*, or perhaps *Lord Pickaway*. They do have a unique American sound, don't they?"

Northcutt paused and then changed the direction of the conversation. "Now, Eckert," he said, "let's get serious. I'm greatly interested in what the officers and men are saying about this Boston business and, indeed, the government in London. And anything they are saying about Dunmore and the conduct of the campaign. You have been in a position to hear much."

"Barrett, most have been too busy to think much about it. Of course everyone is interested in events taking place in Boston, but there has been little recent news. Most of the men know about this Congress which is underway, but they don't have any firm idea of what it will produce." Wend had no intention of disclosing what Washington had written to Crawford. He concentrated a minute to find words which would satisfy Northcutt but protect the actual conversations he had heard around the militia campfires. Finally he said, "Most of the men are content that Dunmore is doing everything he can to keep the Shawnee away from the border settlements." It was essentially true and what he knew Barrett wanted to hear.

Northcutt put his hand to his chin and nodded slowly. "Good, good; that is what we had hoped. Now I commission you to keep your ear to the ground, Eckert. I expect you to make regular reports on the sentiments of these militiamen." Then he rose from his chair. "Dunmore expects me back at his table for cards. I must bid you both a good night."

As Barrett walked off, Wend also got up to leave.

Grenough waved him back into his seat. "Don't be in such a hurry, Eckert. I think it's time we enjoyed another personal discussion."

"What do we need to talk about? We came to understand each other back at Pitt."

"For a start, I wanted to complement you on the *mature* way you have conducted yourself since our little talk back in May. I flatter myself that our peace treaty has worked out well for both of us."

"Well, since you bring all this up," said Wend, "It's hard to ignore the fact that you did feel the need to reinforce it with a few shots out of the darkness that night on Braddock's Road."

Grenough took out a cigar and carefully lighted it from a candle on the table beside his chair. Then he looked into Wend's eyes and said, "I have always maintained that diplomacy, between people as well as between nations, works much better with some demonstration of force behind it." Grenough grinned. "In any case, you managed to return the favor by shaking up Bratton right here at Wheeling. And I might say, my man McCrae found your technique very impressive."

"I hope so, Richard. And speaking of technique, we are both aware that you instigated the murder of the Mingoes at Baker's Tavern to get this war started. The same way you orchestrated the massacre of the Conestoga in Lancaster."

"A tried and true tactic which served the needs of both myself and the governor. Northcutt and Connolly were very appreciative of how I managed that."

Wend asked, "So they were aware of the plan to kill the Mingo?"

"Of course, Eckert; don't be naïve."

"I suspect John Logan and Laughing Eyes were somewhat less appreciative of your work, as were the settlers who have faced their ire."

Grenough smiled over his cup. "Come, Wend, one must learn to keep these things in proportion. Actually, I consider it a rather meager loss of life when you consider the benefits to Dunmore's cause."

Wend gritted his teeth and took a sip of his whiskey. "Can I presume that you are serving your own cause by having your men leading pack trains out to the west with powder and lead for the Indians, just like you did in the Pontiac War?"

"My dear Eckert, you should *not* presume that at all. In fact, I've discontinued trading into the Ohio Country until hostilities are over. My contract to provision these Virginia forces is hugely profitable, far more profitable than dealing with the savages and obviously much less hazardous. I supplied all these provisions and other supplies you've been organizing here at Wheeling and I acquired all the packhorses and bullocks assembled at Redstone. Beyond that, I'm already in preliminary, and highly confidential, discussions with Northcutt to provide supplies to the governor's forces when the Whigs inevitably start their foolish insurrection. After that is swiftly dealt with, I should have sufficient wealth to withdraw to my estate in York and spend the rest of my life in a gentleman's pursuits."

"That's a nice future to contemplate, Richard."

"I dare say, Eckert. But then, you have a lucrative future to contemplate yourself."

"Enlighten me, Richard."

Grenough smiled slyly. "I've been making the case to Northcutt and Dunmore for you to receive a large grant of land when this is all over. We've discussed thousands of acres; a parcel sufficient to make you independently wealthy. I can say the governor is quite amenable to the idea."

"Why are you working so diligently to help me?"

"Shouldn't that be clear to you, Eckert? I want to make our little agreement work and put the unpleasantness of the past behind us. As I said at Fort Pitt, it gives me peace of mind to keep you on friendly terms. Surely you can appreciate that?"

Wend nodded slowly, realizing that Grenough held all the cards. For the present, he had to go along with the merchant. "All right, Richard, the truth is, I'm beginning to see more clearly the advantages of working with you on these matters."

"Marvelous, my dear Eckert. I recall you were somewhat hesitant about all this when we talked back at Fort Pitt, but I'm delighted that you've now had time to reconsider the situaton." He raised his cup. "Let us toast to the success of the campaign and our increasing prosperity."

Wend raised his cup and smiled at Grenough. Inside he felt a gut-wrenching loathing of both Barrett Northcutt and the man sitting before him. But most of all he loathed himself and the game he was being forced to play.

* * *

The northern brigade of Virginia's army departed from Wheeling a few days after Dunmore's arrival. Crawford and his battalion struggled southward along the eastern bank of the river in their thankless task of tending the pack train and bullock herd. Most of the other two battalions were ferried down river in stages, while a detachment marched along the western bank of the Ohio to provide a flanking force and scouting information. Wend had an easy journey, riding in a bateau with the governor and his staff. As per the plan, by the seventh day of October, the entirety of the force had congregated on the eastern side of the Ohio, just across from the mouth of the Hocking River.

On the morning after their arrival at the Hocking, the governor assembled his staff to discuss the status of preparations for meeting with the Ohio Indians.

Captain Marsh, the senior aide, spoke up. "My Lord, Lieutenant Girty, who we sent by canoe down to the Kanawha with a dispatch telling Lewis to bring his brigade here, returned minutes ago."

Dunmore, in a jovial mood, grinned broadly. "Excellent, Marsh! Can I assume Lewis is on the way? When can he arrive here?"

"My Lord, the fact is, Girty found no sign of Lewis' force at the Kanawha."

"What? Are you sure, Marsh?" Dunmore's grin disappeared.

Northcutt exclaimed, "By God, back at Greenway Court we charted, with great care, his expected progress along the Kanawha Trail."

Dunmore said, "Quite right. We have allowed them ample time to make the journey. I should have expected, at the very least, an advance party to be encamped there."

Marsh looked around the table. "Gentleman, I can only repeat what Girty reports."

Grenough glanced over at Wend and gave him a knowing wink. Then he turned to Dunmore and said, "My Lord, perhaps I can supply some perspective. I have traveled the Kanawha trail, albeit some time ago. But I can say that it is quite rugged, crossing many ridges and streams. I am not particularly surprised to find that Lewis, marching with a thousand men and a long pack train, is behind schedule."

Marsh said, "My Lord, Girty contrived to leave a message for Lewis. He cut a mark on the trunk of a large tree and placed your dispatch within a hole in the trunk where it would be protected from the weather. Girty assures me that this is a customary procedure here on the border and that Lewis would instinctively look for such a notification when he arrived."

Dunmore nodded. "Well, that at least is reassuring. But it appears that we will have to be patient with Colonel Lewis." Then he turned back to Marsh and said, "Captain, I anticipate that we will soon be in receipt of communication from White Eyes. And I believe that we will witness the arrival of Cornstalk and his allied chiefs shortly after that. It is imperative we be ready to receive them in the proper style and then have ready a proper venue to conduct negotiations."

"Yes, My Lord, I've taken the initiative to begin preparations for the council meeting. Before we left Williamsburg, I studied reports of General Bouquet's meetings with the tribal leaders on the Muskingum back in '64 and have taken steps to emulate his approach. I have directed Major Connolly to build a bower at the site of the council fire. We'll place a camp chair in the bower for you, sir. The chiefs, on the other hand, will sit on the ground across the fire from the bower."

Dunmore put his hand to his chin, considering what he had been told and then he beamed, "Rather like the King giving an audience to his subjects."

Marsh responded, "I thought that would please you, sir. And it will put the chiefs at a subtle disadvantage as negotiations proceed."

"Capital, Marsh," responded Dunmore. Then he raised a finger. "But I caution you, sir; be sure to provide blankets for the chiefs to sit on; it will give the appearance that we are showing some consideration for them."

Northcutt agreed, "An excellent idea, Your Lordship; we must be magnanimous toward them in their moment of submission."

"Yes," said Dunmore, "Clearly it behooves us to spare them any embarrassment beyond which they already feel."

At that moment, Wend heard shouts and calls emanating from the edge of the camp and realized they were coming from the camp guards. He stepped out from under the tent fly and looked in the direction of the sounds. Soon he saw three figures striding toward them. One was a lieutenant of the guard. The second was Simon Butler, who he knew had been on out on a long scout into Ohio. Walking beside Simon was Little Bear, who had rejoined White Eyes after the trip to Slippery Rock Creek. Wend stepped back under the tent fly, where the staff was still busy discussing the details of forthcoming negotiations.

Wend cleared his throat and said, "Beg your pardon, Lord Dunmore: I believe you will have your answer from the Shawnee shortly. The warrior known as Little Bear, from White Eyes' clan, is approaching with one of our scouts."

All heads turned just as the lieutenant stopped in front of the headquarters tent with the scout and warrior standing behind him.

The guard officer reported to McDonald that the two men had come into camp through one of the guard posts. Meanwhile, Wend walked out to where Butler and the warrior stood waiting.

"Hello, Mr. Eckert. Glad to see you sir," said the scout.

"Welcome back, Simon. I expect there's news from White Eyes?"

Butler waved at Little Bear. "That there is, sir. Last night I was in camp 'bout fifteen miles to the west when Little Bear comes out of the bush and asks if he could camp with me. Then he told me he was on his way to find the governor with a message from his chief. So the pair of us came back here as fast as we could."

Wend nodded and then said to Little Bear, "Greetings, my friend. I understand you have come to see the governor."

"This is true, Eckert. I come from the Pickaway with important message from White Eyes. Will give word only to the Virginia Chief."

Meanwhile McDonald had explained the situation to the governor and he summoned Butler and the warrior to the table.

Northcutt looked over at Dunmore and grinned broadly. "Well, Your Lordship, things have developed more expeditiously than we expected. Cornstalk must have convinced his people to face reality."

Dunmore returned Northcutt's smile. "Indeed, sir, but let us hear from White Eyes' courier."

Wend said, "Excuse me, My Lord, but you should be aware that Little Bear is more than a simple messenger. He is White Eyes' right hand man in diplomatic affairs and a sub-chief in his own right. He was with my party at Slippery Rock Creek and assisted us greatly."

Dunmore looked at Little Bear with renewed interest. Then he said, with more solemnity in his voice, "Welcome, Little Bear. We are glad your journey has been safe and swift. And we are ready to hear your tidings."

Little Bear drew himself up to his full height. "I bear word from White Eyes, Chief of the Turtle Clan of the Delaware. He sends you greetings."

An impatient Northcutt interrupted, "Can we assume he and his party is coming in behind you with Cornstalk and the other Shawnee chiefs?"

Little Bear stared at Northcutt for a moment, his face impassive. Then he looked back at the governor. "Chief and Captain Pipe are on way back to own towns. Has completed what Virginia Chief asked them to do. Talk with Cornstalk is finished."

The smile left Dunmore's face, replaced by a look of concern. "White Eyes returned to his village? I don't understand; the plan was to come here. Then what is the message you have for me?"

Little Bear stood silently for a long moment, slowly looking around the faces at the table. Then with great solemnity he said, "Cornstalk no come here. Shawnee are for *war* against Virginia. Some Delaware from along Scioto and Muskingum will join Shawnee. Southern Mingo will also fight."

There was a stunned silence around the table. Wend looked at the faces; all reflected profound dismay.

Northcutt slapped his hand on the table. "I don't believe it; I'll wager this is a ploy by Cornstalk to improve his negotiating position."

Dunmore exclaimed, "Yes, for God's sake. All our indications were that Cornstalk wanted an opportunity for peace talks."

Little Bear scowled briefly at Northcutt. Then, with great dignity, he said, "War parties coming into Cornstalk village all time White Eyes was there. Great number of warriors gather. Shawnee high shaman bring ancient war charms from lodge to present to captains for luck in battle."

Butler, who had stood silently leaning on his grounded rifle, spoke up for the first time. "They don't bring out those relics unless they mean to fight, sir. I talked with Bear along the way. From what he said about the numbers, I figure they got more than 700 warriors from all three tribes. Ask me, sir, they're gonna' fight, sure as sin."

Little Bear fixed his eyes on Dunmore and repeated solemnly, "Virginia Chief need to know there will be war."

A murmur rose from the officers around the table. Dunmore quieted them with a wave of his hand. "We thank you for bringing the word, Little Bear. Give White Eyes my appreciation for his help in these matters."

As the scout and Delaware withdrew, the silence persisted and Wend looked around the table. Dunmore appeared shaken and was staring down at his hands. Northcutt was looking grimly into the distance. Grenough was eyeing the governor, his hand to his chin, the hint of a smile on his face.

Northcutt was the first to react. He held up his hand. "Let us not be precipitous about this development. While we obviously will have to change our immediate plans, I believe our overall strategy remains sound. Once we're united with Lewis, we will have sufficient strength to force the Shawnee into a defensive campaign. As we march westward, they will soon realize they must submit. Our objective remains a relatively bloodless war; it just seems that the enemy must be exposed to a little more persuasion then we originally anticipated."

McDonald said, "Lord Dunmore, in my opinion, we must move the entire brigade and the pack train to the west side of the river immediately. We must be over the river before the Shawnee can advance and possibly contest our crossing. Then we need to establish secure defensive positions while we wait for Lewis' brigade to join."

Grenough said, "That makes great sense, Governor. That way the boats will be free to ferry Lewis to the west bank when he arrives."

Dunmore sighed. "Yes, order it at once. If indeed Cornstalk intends to fight, we are the obvious target."

Grenough spoke up again. "Let me point out that regardless of what develops, this campaign will be longer and more arduous than we expected. I submit that we'll need additional provisions." He looked at the governor and then Northcutt. "With your permission, I'll send my associate McCrae back to arrange delivery of more goods from the Forks by boat."

Dunmore nodded and said, "Excellent idea, Richard. Please do it at once."

"Thank you, My Lord," replied Grenough. "And one further suggestion: I recommend the immediate construction of a stockade on the west bank of the Ohio, to be garrisoned by a small force. It will serve to secure the supplies as they arrive. Our friends the Shawnee are quite capable of raiding in the rear of an advancing army."

Dunmore slowly nodded. "By God, he's right. Our supplies would be a tempting target for them." He turned to McDonald. "We'll have Crawford construct the fort, just as he did Fincastle at Wheeling."

There was a pause and Wend took the opportunity to speak up. "My Lord, the biggest vulnerability is while our two brigades are separated. I believe we must take action to get Lewis' force here as soon as possible."

Marsh scowled and shot back, "Weren't you listening, Eckert? He's not at the Kanawha; we've just gotten word of that from Girty."

Wend held his temper and said, as calmly as he could, "Yes, but his column must be getting close to the Ohio. I suggest we send Girty and Butler back down the river. And if they find Lewis' force still has not arrived, they should proceed eastward along the Kanawha Trail until they meet Lewis' vanguard."

Marsh retorted, "Girty left the governor's dispatch where Lewis will find it. I don't see the need to send someone to tell him the same thing."

Wend shook his head. "Much has changed since that message was written. We now know the Indians are at war and that either of our brigades could be hit any time now. Lewis must be warned so that he is alert and understands the urgency of uniting with us."

Northcutt's jaw was working. He said slowly, "Much of that is true, Eckert, but I maintain there is not much hazard to Lewis' force; they're protected by being on the east side of the Ohio. It would be much easier for the Indian force to engage us, particularly since we're moving to the west side of the river."

Dunmore held up his hand. "Barrett, I share your opinion that there's little danger to Lewis. But I do agree with Eckert that we should have scouts find Lewis and spur him to move more rapidly." He turned to Marsh. "Once Girty has had adequate rest, send Butler and him back down to find Lewis. And draft a dispatch with the most recent information."

* * *

It took two days to get the brigade over the Ohio. The first day was taken up by the complex task of swimming the pack horses and then the bullock herd across the broad river. On the second day, boats shuttled both the men of the battalion and the loaded packsaddles over. Once across, Crawford learned he had the thankless task of building another fort. He soon set his men to work felling trees while he laid out the shape of the stockade near the banks of the Ohio. In this case, Dunmore broke with his practice of naming things after himself; instead he named it after his brother. The new edifice was to be known as Fort Gower.

Meanwhile, Girty and Butler returned with the word that Lewis and elements of his brigade had finally arrived at the juncture of the Ohio and the Kanawha. Wend happened to be at headquarters when the pair came in. Dunmore, Northcutt, and Grenough were nearby and quickly gathered to hear the courier's report.

Dunmore was buoyed by the news of the scouts' arrival. He quickly asked Girty, "Lieutenant, when will Lewis be ready to march northward to join us? How soon does he think he can be here?"

Girty bit his lip and hesitated for a few seconds. "The truth is, My Lord, he won't be ready to move for several days at the earliest."

Dunmore's face changed from excitement to dismay. "*Several* days? Did you tell him the Shawnee were on the move and that we needed to unite in time for a possible engagement?"

"Yes, sir," replied Girty. "But, truth be told, not all of his brigade has arrived. The Fincastle County Battalion got started late and is still days away. And Lewis says his packhorses are exhausted from crossing the ridges. They need to be pastured for a few days to recover their strength." Girty looked around at the men, then said, "Colonel Lewis believes it might be better for the northern brigade to move south and join his force on the Kanawha, just like the original plan."

There was a long silence. Finally, Wend asked Girty, "Is that all that was said?"

"Yes, they was busy settin' up camp and Lewis wanted to explain to his colonels the new information. Then he told me he would send a courier up here when his whole column had assembled and he could say when they would be ready to move."

Wend nodded to the scouts. "Thanks, Simon, I know you're tired. Both of you get some rest; it's possible you'll be needed to take another message down to Colonel Lewis."

Girty touched his hand to his hat in salute and then the pair departed.

When they were out of earshot, Dunmore exploded. "Damn Lewis! Damn his impertinence! For God's sake, *we* should march to him?" The governor's hands balled up into fists. "Barrett, I've half a mind to relieve him and put someone in command down there who understands orders and the urgency of our situation."

Northcutt screwed up his face. "Unfortunately, My Lord, that would cause more trouble than advantage for us. I fear it would raise the ire of his men." He pulled a cigar from his pocket, walked over to the fire, and lit it.

Dunmore joined him and asked, "Have you got another of those, Barrett? I prefer my pipe, but in this moment your rolled tobacco will suffice."

Northcutt handed the governor a cigar and helped him to light it. Soon both were puffing furiously as they looked into the fire and contemplated the situation which Lewis had handed them.

Then Grenough spoke up. "Perhaps I can throw some light on this development, Your Lordship."

Dunmore took the cigar from his mouth and said, "Right now, Richard, I would appreciate anything you can say."

"We must understand," responded Grenough, "that we are dealing with militia here, not regulars."

"For God's sake, Richard," said a petulant Dunmore, "of course I know they're militia!"

"My Lord, the point is, these men were glad to hear that you were ready to confront the Shawnee and were quite eager to join you in a drive into the Ohio Country. That's why they turned out in such numbers."

Northcutt interjected, "Richard, that's still what we are about. The question is: Why is Lewis suddenly so hesitant?"

"Because, Barrett, they now have been informed that a powerful force of Shawnee is on the move, not just waiting to protect their villages. If Lewis' brigade comes north to join us, there will be nothing to keep war parties from flowing eastward down the Kanawha Trail to attack the settlements in the southwestern part of the colony. And gentlemen, the militia who would normally protect those settlements are virtually all in Lewis' force. They're thinking about their wives, children, and property."

Dunmore nodded slowly, considering what Grenough had laid out. "I take your meaning, Richard. But we still must initiate some action to compel the Shawnee to come to terms."

"Yes, My Lord, that is the crux of the problem," said Grenough. "I believe our only option is to immediately advance toward the Pickaway Plains."

Northcutt looked at Grenough sharply. "What? With just the force we have here? Without Lewis' brigade in company? And missing the men forming the garrison of Fort Gower? That would vastly reduce the odds in our favor."

Grenough shrugged. "If we do that, Cornstalk will have to direct his full attention to us in defense of his home territory. He won't be able to diminish his force by sending raiding parties to the east. But we would have to move fast, before Cornstalk can attack us or even Lewis."

While they had been talking, McDonald and Marsh had joined them at the table. Dunmore turned to his senior aide. "Marsh, get that map of yours and spread it out here. We have some serious planning to do."

When the map was in place, Marsh pointed to a spot on the Pickaway Plains and said, "Our information is that Cornstalk's village is approximately at this point. Other villages are spaced out along the Scioto. The hostile Mingo are concentrated further north along the river in at least five villages at an area called Seekunk. Pluggy's Town, with more hostile Mingo, is somewhat further upstream."

Dunmore said, "We had plotted our way to Pickaway from the mouth of the Kanawha; now we must plan a line of march overland from along the Hocking."

Grenough said, "The way is plain, My Lord. Look at the course of the Hocking itself; it is an arrow pointed at the heart of the Shawnee villages. It has been over ten years since I traveled along the Hocking, but I recall trails that closely parallel the river which will expedite the journey. Undoubtedly our scouts are aware of them."

Dunmore turned to McDonald. "How soon could we depart, Angus? Is tomorrow possible?"

McDonald shook his head. "It is near evening; too late to make many preparations. We must get marching orders out to the battalions. Crawford must tell off enough men to garrison Fort Gower." He said, "I say we can be ready early the day after tomorrow."

"Make it so, Angus," responded Dunmore, "and get the scouts out instantly to mark the way."

Northcutt put his finger on the mouth of the Kanawha. "What about Lewis? Are we going to simply let half our force sit on the Kanawha?"

Grenough said, "As I said, the main concern of Lewis and his men is to prevent war parties from hitting their homes. I suggest we have Lewis leave an adequate force behind, say a couple of companies, to block the passes just to the east of their position. That should assuage their worries. Then, when his packhorses are rested, he can cross the Ohio and march up the western part of the Kanawha Trail directly toward the Scioto, just as we originally planned for the entire force."

Dunmore smiled. "I like that, Richard. The Shawnee will have to confront two advancing forces, each of which is superior to their entire army."

Grenough waved his hand. "Precisely, My Lord; or, may we dare hope, they will reach the decision to come to terms."

Northcutt nodded. "I can't fault the strategy, but we must spur Lewis to move as rapidly as possible; our two columns must move in concert." Then he looked at Dunmore. "We must send a courier back to the Kanawha with peremptory orders for him to advance with all dispatch."

Dunmore motioned to Marsh with his cigar. "Draft such an order, Captain, leaving no room for Lewis to procrastinate, and send Girty back down by canoe today." He looked around at the gathered officers. "Gentlemen, the morrow is Monday and we will have a busy day making preparations. And then on Tuesday we will march to beard Cornstalk in his lair."

* * *

The next day was indeed hectic. Wend was busy in the early morning, passing orders to various units. Then, in mid-morning, he snatched a bit of time to drop by the Frederick County Battalion to see his son. Crawford's men were encamped along the river, near where the lines of the new fort had been laid out. Stacks of logs were already piled up and work on the stockade had begun.

He found Horner on his knees, bent over the parts of a rifle lock spread out on a piece of canvas next to his campfire. Beside him were bags of gunsmithing supplies. The apprentice was beginning reassembly of the lock. Johann was kneeling next to him, watching intently.

Wend stopped and stood about ten yards away, unnoticed by the pair as they worked. In the weeks since Wend had brought his son back from Slippery Rock Creek, the two youths had bonded. Johann had essentially become an apprentice to the apprentice, following him around and assisting with gun repairs. Horner had verified what Abigail had said about the boy; he was indeed a quick study on mechanical subjects. Horner had also found that Johann had a good basic understanding of the functions of all the parts of a lock, but had had to teach him the correct nomenclature for each item.

Wend stepped over where he could see their work. "Andrew, that looks like more than a simple part replacement."

Horner and Johann looked up, noticing him for the first time. "Yes, Mr. Eckert," responded Horner. "A man from Wood's company brought this rifle in; it had a broken spring. But when I checked it out, I found the lock was old and had many worn parts. Even before the spring broke, it couldn't have been working well. So I'm replacing the most worn items." He pursed his lips. "The man should have had this looked at long ago, but he's from the town and doesn't do much shooting."

"Yes, so now that it suddenly looks like there may be actual fighting, he brings it to you at the last moment before we march." Wend studied the rifle a moment. "Can you get it done before tomorrow morning?"

Horner nodded. "Yes, I've got everything I need."

Wend replied, "That's good, because you and Johann are going to stay here as part of the garrison of Fort Gower."

Wend had arranged for the two of them to remain behind. There was no telling if combat would ensue and he wanted Johann safe. So he had arranged the matter with Crawford.

Horner looked up. "Won't the Frederick County Battalion need a gunsmith?"

"There are gunsmiths with the other two battalions; they can take care of any problem which might arise during the campaign. And there needs to be someone to tend the firelocks here at the fort." He looked at the two of them. "That's why you're staying."

Horner looked like he was about to question the situation, when suddenly Johann stood up, a look of concentration on his face. Without saying anything, he walked over to the bank of the Ohio, looking downstream. Then he kneeled, leaning over and putting his hands to his ears.

Wend and Horner followed and stood beside the youth.

"What is it?" asked Wend.

Johann motioned him to be quiet and leaned forward as if straining to hear. Then he dropped his hands and looked up at the two of them. "Guns firing to the south; many guns firing all at once. Long way distant."

Horner's face wrinkled up. "I can't hear anything."

"Neither can I," said Wend, "but Johann has grown up in the bush. His ears may be more sensitive than ours."

Now Johann put his hands to his ears again, a frown on his face. "Firing all the time."

Wend looked up in the sky. It was a very hot, muggy day for October. "Johann, maybe it's a storm far in the distance with rolling thunder."

Johann concentrated even more, closing his eyes for long seconds. "No, Father, not thunder; firelocks."

Wend stood looking downriver, thinking hard. The mouth of the Kanawha was more than fifty miles distant overland. With the curves in the river, it was considerable further by water. Even if Lewis were engaged with Cornstalk's force, it was unthinkable that the sound of gunfire would carry that distance. He thought of other possibilities. They had scouting parties out looking for any sign of the Shawnee. Maybe scouts, ranging to the south, had encountered a war party and were engaged. Or possibly it actually was distant thunder that Johann was hearing.

"Well," he said, "whatever it may be, you've got to get that lock reassembled. So I'll leave you both to your work." He put his hand to Johann's shoulder. "I'll be back to say farewell before we march, son."

The youth, still distracted by whatever he was hearing, nodded. Then he got up and joined Horner back by the fire.

Wend walked back to the headquarters tents, still mulling over what it could have been that Johann had heard. When he arrived, he was surprised to see something of a commotion. Northcutt, Grenough, and the governor were talking and laughing with a stranger. He was dressed in a well-cut shell jacket, breeches, and leather riding boots. There was something familiar about the man, but Wend couldn't recollect a name or place.

Northcutt looked up and spied Wend. "Eckert, come here and greet an old friend. Captain Reginald Welford of the 60th Foot! He's currently seconded to General Gage's staff in Boston and has come down here to spy on us for the general. He just this moment arrived by canoe."

Welford looked at Wend for a long moment; then recognition spread over his face. "Ah yes, Eckert; I remember we met briefly at Washburn's Tavern in Carlisle, back in early '64 when I had just become Bouquet's adjutant."

"Yes, I recall that day very well, Captain. You said I wasn't suitably dressed to see Bouquet. You tried to send me away until he happened to come out of his office and invited me to lunch."

A look of displeasure came over the captain's face. "Yes, now that you mention it, I seem to recollect something about that. But of course I later learned much about General Bouquet's fondness for you during our days campaigning."

"I've always been grateful for his consideration of me."

Welford nodded. "Yes, he often said he wished you'd been along on the expedition to the Muskingum." Then he thought of something else and continued, "I say, did you get that pistol I sent to you? It was one of Bouquet's last bequests as he lay dying."

"It's on the wall of my workshop, Welford. One of my most cherished possessions."

Dunmore had been standing by impatiently. Finally he interrupted, "Now see here, Reginald, I'm glad to see you again and I hope we can spend some time together at the card table as we did in New York. But I don't think General Gage sent you down here simply to renew old acquaintances."

"I'm here unofficially, Your Lordship; technically on leave of absence so there's no direct connection to the army. The general knew he couldn't show official support for this expedition since it is a Virginia initiative." He looked around and glanced briefly at Wend. "But frankly, I have a message for you, sir. Perhaps we could speak privately."

"Nonsense, my dear Reggie; there's just the five of us, all part of my military family. Please go ahead."

"It is sensitive, sir."

Northcutt waved dismissively. "It's all right, Welford. Mr. Grenough and Lieutenant Eckert are of our party and both have demonstrated commendable acts of loyalty to Virginia and the Crown during this campaign. You can speak freely."

The governor motioned to the table. "Gentlemen, let us sit down so we can talk in comfort."

Once they were seated, Welford said, "I'm ostensibly here to observe progress of the expedition and report the outcome to General Gage. But more importantly, he wanted me to confide to you the situation in Boston and explain how events there might figure in your conduct of the campaign."

The governor straightened. "There are new developments up there which will somehow impact us?"

"Exactly, sir," continued Welford. "The truth is, the situation has become extraordinarily grave over the last few months. Boston has the feeling of a city under siege. The colonists are surly and exhibiting hostility every time we send a column outside of the city."

Northcutt asked, "Damn, Reggie, has there been any outright conflict?"

"Not yet, Barrett, but understand this: The colonists have purged the Massachusetts militia of officers and men loyal to the Crown. And they've organized special units which they call 'Minutemen' ready to be called out on short notice. Our informers tell us they're drilling and practicing firing at marks on a frequent basis." Welford looked around the table. "Beyond that, we know they're acquiring supplies of powder and lead. And most disturbing of all, they have put their hands on at least a few cannon."

Northcutt looked over at Dunmore, a confident look on his face. "Thank god things haven't gotten that far out of hand down here."

Dunmore nodded. "Quite right, Barrett; not by a long shot."

Welford looked askance at the two and sighed. "Let me offer words of caution: You may not see the visible signs of insurgency, but Gage is convinced that the rot is spreading throughout all the colonies. Witness the existence of these Committees of Correspondence and that blasted Congress in Philadelphia." He looked at Dunmore. "And, speaking frankly, we are well aware that you had to dismiss your legislature just a few months ago when they drafted resolutions in support of Boston."

Dunmore shot Welford a look of irritation. "Yes, there have been a few incidents like that. But see here, Welford, you can't imply that things here in Virginia are anywhere near what you are facing in Massachusetts."

Welford's face took on a grim visage. "Perhaps, sir, but we are getting very serious reports from up and down the coast of increasingly defiant acts by colonists. Moreover, the general considers that incidents of armed conflict in Massachusetts are only a matter of time and the right spark to set things off."

Northcutt said in an incredulous tone, "You sound like Gage expects outright war."

"General Gage hopes to avoid such a development. He has cautioned all troop commanders to act with great forbearance when on the march outside the city and dealing with the populace. But he cannot discount the likelihood that some incident could ignite a sustained uprising; an uprising which might spread through all of the colonies. We would be hard pressed in that case, for there are less than 6,000 regulars on the continent, the majority clustered in Boston. And in fact, we have sent an urgent request for troop reinforcements from Britain."

Northcutt said impatiently, "All right, Reggie, we can all agree that the Whigs have gotten more aggressive over the last year. But you said you had a specific message for us here in Virginia. What might that be?"

Dunmore nodded. "Yes, by all means, Welford, get to it."

"All right, gentlemen. If this insurgency should flare into actual rebellion and the perpetrators were able to put significant bodies of organized troops in the field, we may need all the allies we can arrange, even those we might normally consider less than desirable."

Northcutt asked, "Allies? Who precisely do you mean?"

"General Gage believes we might make use of the tribes. As your need to be present here on the Ohio demonstrates, they are already upset with the spread of westward settlement. He feels that if war actually breaks out, we might induce the leaders of certain tribes to raid into the border settlements and thus distract our adversaries."

Dunmore said thoughtfully, "I see what you mean; the insurgents would have to fight on two fronts."

"Precisely, My Lord," responded Welford. "Now we are confident that, through the efforts of the late Sir William Johnson in New York, the tribes of the Iroquois Confederation will be inclined to make common cause with our efforts. But we need the Indians of the Ohio Country to also take our side."

Grenough asked, "Reggie, are you suggesting that this war is counterproductive to the Crown's cause? Are you trying to tell us to give up the expedition?"

Dunmore became agitated and half-rose from his seat. "By God, the very purpose of this campaign is to win the support of the colonists and head off the insurrection you fear. I'll not entertain any assertion that we are working contrary to Crown interests."

Northcutt was equally disturbed. "Welford, you must understand that this expedition has energized the western people of the colony. Look at how many volunteers we have in the field; the equivalent of two army brigades. I dare say we are earning the gratitude of the people, a fact which will pay off here in Virginia even if the uprising you fear does come about in the northern colonies."

Welford made a calming motion with his hands. "Gentlemen, don't take me wrong. General Gage has no intent, nor does he feel he has the provenance, to inject himself in the business of Virginia. The conduct of the campaign is entirely under your control. We merely wish to consult with you on the terms of the eventual treaty."

Dunmore cocked his head. "And what is it that Gage wishes us to consider?"

Welford looked conspiratorially at the other men. "The general suggests that once you have defeated the Indians, you extend generous terms to the Shawnee and their allies, so that they will remain amenable to our diplomatic advances if a rebellion does arise."

Grenough coughed. "Gage is asking a lot, Welford. You can't understand the depth of anger here on the border. There have been bloody raids by both Mingo and Shawnee war parties since the beginning of May. Considerable numbers of men, women, and children are dead. There has been a flood of families fleeing eastward, their lives disrupted. Many of our militiamen have volunteered because they seek retribution against war party leaders such as Logan and Laughing Eyes."

Northcutt nodded. "Grenough is correct. We have made a list of demands to present to Cornstalk and his allied chiefs. These include giving up the lands south of the Ohio, free passage on the Ohio, surrendering the most blood thirsty war captains for the imposition of justice, and the giving over of high level hostages to us to guarantee good behavior of their tribes. Now you are asking us to moderate those demands."

There was a long silence as Dunmore sat mulling what Welford had explained. Finally, he said, "Welford, I must admit that the conditions which you describe in the north are far worse than I had known and, frankly, quite shocking. Obviously, as the Crown's representative, I must defer to the general's request. We shall have to walk an extremely fine line in negotiations with the Indians." He looked around the table. "Gentlemen, it is evident we must craft a treaty which will provide a modicum of satisfaction to our citizens, but not so severe as to preclude establishing cooperation with the tribes if a rebellion materializes."

Grenough raised an eyelid. "My Lord, I sympathize with Gage's positon and your responsibility to him, but I can assure you there will be an uproar among our officers and men when they learn of mild peace terms."

Dunmore gave Grenough and then Northcutt hard looks. "Now hear me: You both have been my agents in dealing with these border people. So it will be up to you to put the best light on the eventual peace terms and justify our actions to the militia." Then Dunmore shifted his gaze to Wend. "And I will be counting on you also, Lieutenant Eckert. I'm told you have influence among the German population and respect among the Ulster-Scots from your work with Bouquet during the Pontiac War. You must help put a positive light on the outcome of this negotiation."

Wend felt a sinking feeling in his gut. Once again he was being backed into a distasteful corner.

Welford smiled broadly. "Governor, General Gage will be most gratified that you have been so gracious in accommodating our position."

Dunmore responded, "Let the record show that I am always ready to support the Crown while pursuing the interests of Virginia." Then he pointed at Welford. "And you, Reggie, will, of course, accompany us on the campaign so that you can carry the outcome back to Gage."

"My Lord, nothing would give me greater pleasure."

Northcutt grinned broadly and said, "For my part, nothing will give greater pleasure than taking more of your money at the card table, Reggie."

Dunmore rose to leave. "I've some letters to deal with in my tent. See to Reggie's comfort, Barrett."

Northcutt led Welford off to his own tent.

Momentarily Wend and Grenough stood alone under the canvas fly. The merchant pulled out a cigar and stepped over to the fire to light it. Then he stood up, exhaled a cloud of smoke, and looked over at Wend. He winked and said, "Well my friend, I would say the game is about to get vastly more entertaining. Dunmore and Northcutt have made some grand plans. But they seem to have overlooked one singular fact."

Wend asked, "What would that be?"

Grenough raised an eyebrow and said, "The fact that Cornstalk undoubtedly has some plans of his own." He laughed, and asked, "And just what do you think about all this, Eckert?"

Wend said, "I think the next time you and Northcutt cook up a little war like this you should leave me out of it." Then he turned to leave and said, "I'm heading for the picket line. I need to see to my mare before we march tomorrow morning."

He walked off to the sound of Grenough's laughter echoing behind him.

CHAPTER TWENTY
The Governor's March

The bustling sounds of the brigade going into camp enveloped Eckert as he walked back to headquarters from picketing The Mare. Dusk was coming on rapidly. Men, weary from a long day marching over rough forest trails, were hurrying to light cook fires, perform evening chores, and spread their bedrolls before nightfall. Wend looked eastward along the trail which bordered the Hocking and saw that the train of packhorses was just arriving in camp. An officer who assisted MacDonald was directing the leader of the train to the location for their campsite. After three days and forty miles on the trail from the Ohio, the brigade was becoming accustomed to the routine of the march.

As he approached the headquarters, Wend saw Dunmore, Northcutt, and Grenough clustered around the newly lighted headquarters fire as a group of men erected the tents which would shelter the staff. Marsh stood to one side talking with a small group of officers.

Suddenly there was a call from the headquarters sentry, "Riders coming in! Riders coming down the trail from the east!"

Everyone turned to look. Wend saw two horsemen riding at the gallop. As they approached, Wend recognized the lead rider as an ensign who was a member of the garrison of Fort Gower. The other man was a stranger.

Marsh walked over to the group by the fire and said, "Your Lordship, that's Ensign Cobb from Gower, sir. There must be some news; I'll go see what's toward." He strode quickly to where the horsemen were dismounting. Wend watched as a few words were exchanged and then Marsh, a shocked look on his face, led the strange rider back to the campfire. He said, "Your Lordship, there's been a battle; a battle down at the Kanawha. The bloody Indians attacked Lewis!"

The governor froze. "The devil, you say!"

"It's true, sir. This is a courier from Colonel Lewis; he came up river by canoe."

The courier stepped forward. "Yes, sir, my name be Fowler, Your Lordship. Colonel Lewis told me to get to you soon as I could with the word 'bout the big fight we had with them Shawnee; Shawnee and Mingo and Delaware they was."

Northcutt spoke up. "Just when did this happen, Fowler?"

"Monday, sir. They hit us first thing in the morning."

Wend's heart skipped a beat; Monday was the day Johann had sworn he'd heard gunfire.

Northcutt asked, "Had Lewis' force crossed the Ohio?"

"No, sir," answered Fowler. "We was still there in camp at the mouth of the Kanawha. Point Pleasant we was callin' it."

Dunmore looked astonished. "You were still east of the river? How did the Indians get across the Ohio?"

"Them crafty savages built a mess of rafts, sir. We found them abandoned the day after the battle. Rough things they were, but they served. Surely they did." Fowler reached into his shirt and pulled out a folded piece of parchment. "Here be a letter from Colonel Lewis tellin' you what happened, sir. But I can tell you what be in it; I was standin' there as the colonel wrote it."

Dunmore opened the letter and began reading.

Northcutt said, "Continue, Mr. Fowler. We all want to hear."

"They had us boxed in with our backs to the Kanawha and a high bluff to the east. An' of course, the Ohio was to the west." Fowler shook his head. "There weren't hardly no room to maneuver. It was just a shoot-out. Bloody as hell. Men bein' hit everywhere."

"And what were your casualties, sir?" asked Grenough.

"Well, it be right there in that letter from the colonel. But I heard say there was seventy-five dead and more'n 150 wounded, sir." Fowler bit his lip. "And, I'll tell you straight, many of them wounded boys was in pretty bad shape; a goodly number was shot two or three times."

Dunmore looked up from Lewis' letter. His face had gone white. He looked around at the gathered officers. "The casualties Fowler cites are quite correct. And the dead include the colonels of two of the regiments and many of the company captains. One of the dead colonels is Charles Lewis."

There was a shocked silence among the group. Then Fowler spoke up. "Yes, sir, that all be true. Colonel Lewis lost his own brother. And Colonel Field, who was leadin' the men from Culpeper County, he was killed stoppin' them Indians from hittin' on the flank."

Welford spoke up. "Colonel John Field? Of Culpeper?" He shook his head. "He was the leader of the Virginia Rifle Corps which led Bouquet's advance during the march to the Muskingum in '64; a very good man, Governor."

Dunmore looked up from the letter again. "Lewis says there were six or seven hundred of the Indians. They fought all day and only retreated in the late afternoon when it became apparent they couldn't fully destroy our force."

Grenough asked, "Fowler, what were the Indian casualties?"

"That be hard to tell, sir. You know them savages carry off their dead when they can. Truth is, we only found about twenty Indian bodies on the battlefield. But it's damn sure we killed more. And we did see bodies floatin' down the Ohio. So they must have thrown a lot of their dead into the river to keep us from findin' them."

Northcutt pulled out a cigar and put it unlit into his mouth, chewing on it. Wend could see he was thinking rapidly. Then he took the cigar from his mouth and said. "My Lord, the important thing is that Lewis' brigade beat the savages off. Obviously Cornstalk's objective was to destroy Lewis and put his force out of the campaign. He failed in that."

Dunmore nodded slowly, then looked at Northcutt. "So what are you getting at, Barrett?"

"It's simple, sir: Lewis won a *victory*. He was attacked by a large force of warriors and defeated them. By all measures, the force which holds the battlefield is the victor."

Dunmore looked at Northcutt. "Yes, Barrett, but at what cost? Well over 200 casualties!"

Northcutt shrugged. "Casualties are an expense of any war. But My Lord, it is a victory by any measure. And now we need to capitalize on it. We must send a messenger up to Fort Dunmore so they can forward the good tidings to Williamsburg. The people must know about the successful progress of your campaign."

Grenough grinned. "And its best if they get the word in a message written by us, if you take my meaning."

Dunmore stared at Northcutt for a long moment, and then over at Grenough, considering his words. He said, "You're both absolutely right. We'll prepare a dispatch so that all of Virginia shall celebrate and take comfort in the success of our arms!"

Wend had a thought. "Fowler, what are Colonel Lewis' intentions? Will he have to remain at the Kanawha to attend to his wounded and reorganize his force?"

Fowler shook his head vigorously. "Sir, Colonel Lewis and all the men are mad as hornets at what them Indians did. They want to get at the devils and finish them. The Colonel said he would leave a small garrison at the Kanawha to tend the wounded, cross the Ohio, and march for Pickaway as soon as possible." He pursed his lips. "Ask me, they'll be across the river soon."

Northcutt looked at the governor. "Sir, this is very favorable for the campaign. If Fowler is correct, we will soon have two forces advancing toward the Shawnee villages, just as we desired. Cornstalk has achieved what all our urging couldn't get Lewis to do."

Dunmore's face brightened. "Damned if I don't think you're right, Barrett. We'll carry on with our advance and see how Cornstalk reacts."

Northcutt nodded. "Quite correct, Your Lordship. Let us go to your tent and compose the announcement of this great victory; we'll get the courier off at first light."

After they had left, Grenough leaned close to Wend, a crooked smile on his face. He said in low tones, "Well, Eckert, a victory of sorts down at the Kanawha." Then he winked, "But so much for Dunmore's much touted *bloodless* campaign."

* * *

Angus McDonald, in his capacity as Brigade Major, had the duty of orchestrating the order of march for the force. He had assigned a group of experienced scouts to range far in advance of the column. But McDonald also perceived the need to have an inner line of scouts, ranging just ahead of the advance guard to provide warning if any war party slipped in behind the first group. He selected Joshua Baird, with his intimate knowledge of the Ohio Country and the web of trails which crisscrossed the territory, to recruit and lead this second group. The veteran scout, mounted on horseback, worked with the captain of the vanguard.

So it was that Wend, at headquarters on the evening of the sixteenth of October, was not particularly surprised to see Baird and another man riding in from the west. They pulled up and dismounted directly in front of him. Wend walked out to greet the pair. "Hello, Joshua. Have you got a message for Angus?"

Baird and the other man tied the reins of their horses to a tree. "Not me, it's this fellow here. His name is Elliott; Matthew Elliott. He's a trader with a place on the Pickaway Plains, close by Cornstalk's village. He's married to a Shawnee woman; that's why he's still around here and in one piece."

Elliott touched his hat to Wend. "That's the truth, Lieutenant; I've always been fair with the Shawnee and they treat me the same way. Didn't see no need to leave when the troubles started."

Wend nodded. "I'm the governor's aide. Do you have some news?"

"Got a message he'll want to hear. Direct from Cornstalk himself."

"From Cornstalk?" Wend was all ears. "What does he say?"

"He wants to talk peace. All them Shawnee, Delaware, and Mingo warriors came back to Pickaway after the fight down on the Kanawha and had a big council fire. They decided they had no choice but to negotiate and they sent me here to fix things for a meeting with the governor. I'd be obliged if you could take me to him."

A voice came from behind Wend. "That won't be necessary. Lord Dunmore is here."

Wend turned to see it was Northcutt who had spoken, but Dunmore and Grenough were with him.

Wend told them who Elliott was and why he had been sent.

Dunmore said, "We are certainly ready to discuss peace terms with Cornstalk. But how do we know this isn't a ploy; perhaps to lure us into an ambush?"

Northcutt interjected, "Or maybe simply a stratagem to buy time for them to send their women and children away to clear things for battle. Look what happened at Wakatomica. So, Elliott, how do we know they are sincere?"

"Beggin' your pardon, sir, but I'll swear on the Bible they're dead serious. My wife heard what happened at the council fire they held last night. Them chiefs argued for hours, but Cornstalk clinched things, as it were. He pointed out that they threw everything they had at the militia down on the Kanawha and couldn't beat them. So he asked: 'If we can't destroy one force, how are we going to beat two forces coming at us at the same time?' And nobody had a good answer to that. No, sir, they didn't have no answer. So then Cornstalk stands up and gives them a choice. He said, 'We can kill our women and children and then go fight to the death. Or we can go ask for peace. Which shall it be?' Well, sir, nobody answered him. All them chiefs and sachems just sat there staring into the fire. So then Cornstalk sent for me an' asked me to go arrange for talks. And here I am, sir, after nearly gettin' shot by one of your scouts, I might add." Elliott looked around at all the officers. "That's the absolute truth, sir, all of it."

Dunmore and Northcutt looked at each other for a long moment. Then Dunmore called for Marsh. "Captain, get the map and let us lay out a route which will take us to Cornstalk's village."

Marsh came quickly and spread the map out as all the officers crowded around. "We're pretty close, My Lord. One day's hard march will do it."

Dunmore smiled and looked around. "Well, it took longer than expected, and regrettably the blood of some unfortunate men, but our strategy has finally paid off. I would say that we can look forward to achieving complete success within a few days."

Northcutt smiled broadly. "You are to be congratulated, Your Lordship. I dare say this expedition will go down in history beside those of Forbes and Bouquet."

Welford said, "As Bouquet's former adjutant, I can second that, sir. Your campaign has been most impressive."

Grenough cleared his throat; everyone turned to look at him. The merchant said, "Let me join in the congratulations, Your Lordship. But I must point out one small difficulty."

"Difficulty? What could that be?" asked Welford.

Grenough put his finger on the map on a point south of the Hocking River. "We have a column of more than a thousand men, pushing along the Kanawha Trail toward the Shawnee villages, with their blood up and revenge on their minds and in their hearts." He looked around the table. "I submit that we must take immediate action to stop Lewis' brigade where they are now."

Northcutt sucked in his breath. "My God, Grenough is right! We can't let Lewis' men get near the villages or things may get out of hand. We may not be able to restrain them."

Dunmore shrugged. "Well, that's simple enough. We'll send a courier down to locate Lewis' column with a dispatch ordering him to cease his advance." He motioned to Marsh. "Draft the appropriate message and send it by one of the scouts."

Grenough held up his hand. "My Lord, I submit that may not be adequate."

"Not adequate? What the devil do you mean, Richard?"

"With all respect, sir, I believe we should send someone from your staff who will have more impact than a simple scout; someone who can answer questions with your authority behind him."

"Grenough, are you suggesting that Lewis would not obey my written order?"

"I think we're dealing with militia; men who are enraged and not as well-disciplined as regulars."

All the officers mulled the import of Grenough's words. Then Dunmore nodded slowly. "I understand what you're saying, Richard. We need to send someone who whose words will carry weight."

"Yes, My Lord, and I suggest that it should be someone from the border country, to whom they can relate." Grenough looked at Wend and smiled.

Dunmore's eyes settled on Wend. He exclaimed, "Eckert, you are the one choice. Not only are you from the settlements, you are my aide. Pick yourself a party and be prepared to ride."

Wend sighed and said, "Yes, sir."

Dunmore said, "Come with me, Marsh. I'll personally dictate the message." Then he led the way back to his tent with Northcutt and Welford on his heels.

Wend looked at Grenough, who still had a sly smile on his face. He said, "Richard, I told you to stop doing me favors. You knew I would be the choice."

"Think of the opportunity." He chuckled, then continued, "The governor will be indebted to you and will admire your diligence and courage."

"I'm thinking more about the opportunity of being shot off my horse by a Shawnee. There are plenty of tribal scouting parties between here and the Kanawha Trail. And I believe I've had enough of Dunmore's admiration and support to last me a lifetime." Then he motioned to Baird. The scout walked over to join them.

Joshua looked at Grenough, a sardonic smile on his face. "Well, Richard, it's been a long time; I ain't seen you since Bouquet's campaign in '64."

The merchant's body tensed and his face hardened. He said warily, "Indeed, that's correct, Joshua."

"Yeah, Richard, and there weren't no chance to say goodbye, since you left in such an all-fired hurry right in the middle of the campaign."

Grenough's hand reflexively went to his right cheek, touching the long scar. "Yes, I had, uh, *urgent* business back east. And in any case, matters with the Indians were pretty much settled. Henry said he could get along without my services."

Now Baird broke into a broad smile. "Yes, and then there was that wound on your cheek. Doc Highsmith, of the Pennsylvania Regiment, told me that you somehow cut yourself while shaving."

The two men glared at each other wordlessly.

Wend was gratified to see that Grenough's face was turning bright red. He said, "Well, Richard, as a matter of politeness, I had not intended to ever remark on that scar. But now that it's come up, I thought perhaps someone had attacked you with a knife. But *shaving*? My God, how careless of you."

Anger flared in Grenough's eyes. But he controlled his words. "Yes, Eckert, the scar is the result of my being careless about a matter that should have gone very smoothly." He gritted his teeth and said, "Now if I were you, I would take great care on your journey through the bush." Then he turned on his heel and strode off.

Joshua broke into a broad grin. "Well, we got to him on that, didn't we?"

Wend shook his head. "Joshua, you are a devil. But I enjoyed watching you bait him. He knew you were talking about Mary."

Joshua nodded. Then he said, "I heard what the governor told you to do. That could be a dangerous trip."

"Yes, and obviously I need someone familiar with the ground to lead the way. So you're coming along."

"The Lord knows I been leadin' you and keepin' you out of trouble for fifteen years." He thought a moment, then asked, "Just the two of us?"

"No, we need more rifles. I was thinking of Flannagan; he's a good man."

"I'll agree with that. And how about Butler? He knows this country, and he's in camp right now. He just came back with a message from Girty."

"Yes, that's good. And make sure all of you are well mounted." Wend looked over at the governor's tent. "We'll leave as soon as the dispatch is written; we can make a few miles before full dark."

* * *

The four of them forded the Hocking, pushed southward overland until dusk turned to night, then made a cold camp beside a narrow creek which ran in the lee of a small hillock. They picketed the horses and fed them from bags of grain they had brought along. The men's repast consisted only of some dried beef.

After the meal, Joshua laid out his bedroll, then stood up with his rifle in the crook of his arm. He pointed to the top of the hill. "I'll take the first watch; up there, just below the crest; it'll give me a good view of the countryside. I may be able to see the fire of a war party if they feel confident enough to light one."

When he was gone, Wend, Flannagan, and Butler settled in for a long night in the chilly October air. Flannagan asked, in a quiet voice, "Mr. Eckert, how serious do you think the Shawnee are about peace?"

"Hard to tell, Flannagan, you know as well as I do how they often use negotiations to cover what they really plan to do."

"Well, I do hope they're serious this here time. I'm anxious to get back to my farm."

Wend was surprised. "You're going back to Hart's Store? After all that happened? Why, the war party burned your farmstead and killed a man right in front of your house. Everybody in the village is dead. I'm not sure I could live with all those memories surrounding me."

"There ain't no choice, Mr. Eckert. We put too much time in clearing all that acreage and puttin' up fences to leave it now. We'll salvage what we can and rebuild the rest. I just want to get back in time to put shelter over our head and save any crops we can." He sighed and continued, "Any way you figure it, we're goin' to have a hard winter."

"That's an understatement, Flannagan, with only your wife and oldest son to help with the real work."

"We won't be alone. We'll have extra hands to help."

"I don't understand," said Wend, "everyone else up there is dead."

"Them young ones, Georgie and Emily, are coming with us. They'll help us rebuild and live with us at the farm. In the spring, they'll help with the planting. Once things are fixed up at our place, we'll help them set themselves up in one of the abandoned farms."

"I'm glad you're helping them, Flannagan. They deserve a chance for a good start."

There was a long moment of silence. Then the farmer said, bitterness in his voice, "There's one other thing that would make me happy. When the governor makes peace with the savages, I hope he punishes them good. And I sure enough hope they make them give up Logan and that Laughing Eyes, the one they say led the war party what hit Hart's Store and our place. I want them two to see justice. Be a good thing if they just strung the both of them up soon as they're handed over."

Wend thought of the peace settlement being planned by Dunmore, with its lenient terms for the warring tribes. Flannagan and many others were going to feel betrayed when they learned of the outcome. Then Wend's mind went to Charlie, thankful that he was secure in Abigail's village, far away from the danger of retribution.

Flannagan said no more and presently Wend heard the measured breathing which meant that he had dropped off to sleep. Butler had been asleep almost from the time he had settled into his blankets. And in a few minutes Wend joined them in slumber.

They were on their way in the morning twilight, picking through the bush, often leading the horses when footing was uncertain. Wend reflected it was the first really hard work that his mare had faced since her injury and he was gratified that she was handling it well. He mentally thanked the Zane women, and particularly young Betty, for the tender care they had given the animal. On the day Wend had reclaimed the big black, the girl had led the horse out, her eyes gleaming with a mixture of pride and tears; pride at the job she had done in nursing The Mare, tears at having to give up the animal which had become her pet.

Just after noon they cut the Kanawha Trial and turned eastward. The men were able to push the horses faster on the hard-packed ground, and late in the afternoon they sighted the advance of Lewis' brigade. It was a company of riflemen and several scouts led by a rough looking Ulster-Scot captain.

Wend turned to Joshua in surprise. "They're further west than I would have expected. I didn't think we'd meet them until tomorrow."

Joshua laughed. "They be all border people. I 'spect they're travelin' light and movin' a far sight faster than Dunmore's column."

Once they had identified themselves and their mission, the captain assigned a man to lead them back to the main body.

They found the brigade just going into camp for the night. Wend looked back along the trail and could see the dust from the pack train, still on the march to catch up with the main part of the force. Lewis and his small staff were near the head of the column. The commander of the brigade was sitting on a log beside the path, drinking from a wooden water bottle. Wend saw a lean-framed man in his fifties. He had a face with deep-set eyes, heavy brows, a high forehead, and a Black Irishman's hair. Dressed in a knee-length linen hunting shirt belted at the waist and a broad-brimmed black hat, Andrew Lewis could have been taken for any one of his rifleman.

Wend had been carefully formulating his first words to the colonel, but in the event, he didn't get a chance to say them. As they approached Lewis, the colonel looked up and laid eyes on Baird. He motioned toward the scout with the water bottle and said, "I recognize you; you're Bouquet's scout, Joshua Baird."

"Yes, sir, Colonel. You got a passable good memory, after all these years."

"Last time I saw you was in '58, you was sitting your horse next to Bouquet just as we marched off to Fort Duquesne with that British bastard Grant. I spent over a year as a prisoner with the French because of that fool." He looked more closely at Baird. "I'll say this, you ain't changed much in fifteen years."

"I'm glad you said that, Colonel, 'cause there be lots of people who think I'm gettin' old and decrepit." Joshua grinned at Wend and then put his hand his shoulder. "But puttin' that aside, this here is Lord Dunmore's aide, Lieutenant Eckert. He be here with a dispatch for you."

Lewis looked at Wend sharply. "Eckert? Seems I know that name." He stood thinking for a moment. "Haven't I seen firelocks with that name on them? "

"Sir, I am a gunsmith. As was my father before me."

Joshua interjected, "His Pa marched with us in '58."

"Well, I'm glad to meet you, Eckert. But I'm a little surprised to see you as aide to Dunmore. I would have figured he would have had some dandy from Williamsburg."

Wend said, "The governor brought me onto his staff because I have some experience in the border country, sir."

Lewis grinned. "Sometimes that man surprises me." He looked up at Wend. "So what does Lord Dunmore's dispatch say?"

Wend reached into his pouch and passed the message to Lewis. "It's all in there; but in summary, it says that Cornstalk is ready to talk peace. So the governor is advancing with his column to the Pickaway Plains for a council. And your column is to go into camp, remaining here until peace negotiations are completed."

Lewis stood staring at Wend, a stunned look on his face, the written message still in his hand unopened. His jaw tightened until his face reddened and the muscles stood out. Finally, through clenched teeth, he asked, "Has our esteemed governor lost his senses?"

"I don't believe so, Colonel. My perception is that he wants to bring this war to a swift conclusion."

"This is bloody rubbish! *Rubbish,* do you understand? The only reason Cornstalk wants to talk is because we whipped him down at the Kanawha. He's sure to be low on powder and lead and knows he can't keep us from sweeping to the Scioto and destroying his villages. So now he's going to try and best us by talking. That's what always happens as soon as we're in position to punish the Indians."

Wend said, "Colonel, perhaps we can get what we want by talking without more bloodshed."

"Look, Eckert, I got a more than a thousand militia here. And every one of them lost friends or relatives back at the Kanawha. For God's sake, I lost my own brother, Charles, shot dead almost before my eyes. We built a whole damn stockade just to hold the wounded. I tell you, every man in this column wants vengeance. They ain't going to be satisfied until they see dead Shawnee warriors, lodges in flames, and crops wasted. They want to see some of the chiefs hangin' from tree limbs." He stood for a moment shaking in anger. "Now I'm supposed to tell them to sit here and wait while Dunmore gives away the fruits of our victory?"

Wend was about to reply when Lewis held up his hand. "You don't need to answer." The colonel opened the dispatch and quickly read through it. Then he looked up and said, "All right Eckert, you've done your duty. You can go back to His Lordship and tell him I've received his message." He paused, looking down at the paper again, then back up at Wend. "Can we offer you anything before you start back?"

"I'd be grateful if you could supply us with oats for our horses. We only carried enough for one day."

Lewis waved to an aide. "Gifford here, will arrange what you need, Eckert."

They followed the aide to a place where they could wait, then Gifford went off to find the needed grain. Wend looked back to see Lewis in a heated discussion with other officers.

In about fifteen minutes a man appeared, carrying a canvas sack. "Are you the ones who need the oats?"

Wend nodded, and all four of them took their own feed bags from their saddles. The man poured oats into each bag in turn. When he came to Butler, he suddenly stopped and stared at the young scout. Then he exclaimed, "Hey, ain't I seen you before?"

Wend saw Butler's face go white underneath his weathered countenance.

The scout stood looking at the man. "I don't believe so. I can't recall you."

"Well," said the man, "You sure look like a young boy I remember from back in the Bull Run Mountain country, years ago."

"I never been there, mister," retorted Butler. "Anyway, all boys look alike when they're young. You got me confused with someone else."

The man shrugged. "Well, mayhap you're right about that. Sorry for the mistake."

The little party headed back east after getting the feed for their mounts. It was nearly two hours later, when they were leading their horses just before going into camp that Wend found himself walking beside Butler. He said quietly, "Simon, why did you deny that you were from the Bull Run Mountains? Back at Wakatomica you told me that's where you came from."

"I got my reasons, Mr. Eckert. And anyway, I really didn't remember seeing that man before. I was real young when we lived back there and didn't take much notice of older people."

"It would have been easier to just say that to him, rather than deny you had been there. It certainly sounds like you've got something to hide."

Butler sighed. "It ain't nothin' important; but I made a mistake years ago. It be somethin' I don't want to talk about."

Wend smiled at the youth. "All right Simon, I won't push you on it. But if you ever want to tell me, I'll be ready to listen. And if I can help you with anything, I'll be willing to do what I can."

Their journey back to the northern column was uneventful; they spent a short night, then had a long hard day following the trail of the brigade. In the last of the light they found their compatriots in camp along a small creek which Joshua said fed into the Scioto, not far distant. To the south they could see the smoke rising from a Shawnee village.

Just after they passed a picket of camp guards, Wend saw a crudely lettered wooden sign affixed to a tree; it read, "Camp Charlotte."

As they rode by, Joshua pointed to the sign and said, "Well, at least this is one place Dunmore didn't name for himself."

Wend grinned and replied, "No, he didn't. He named it for the Queen."

* * *

Wend looked around at the council site. Dunmore's staff was gathered and an honor guard drawn from all three battalions of the brigade was formed up. The men were fidgeting as they stood in their ranks. Instead of an open bower, as had originally been planned, the peace talks were being held in an enclosed lodge built specifically for the purpose.

Over several days of negotiations, the treaty with the Indians had been finalized. Today would see the ceremonial completion of the council. The Shawnees, their Delaware allies, and most of the Mingoes had agreed to the treaty. But there was one fly in the ointment: The Mingoes of the northern part of the Scioto, the area called Seekunk, had refused to join in the treaty and their chiefs had withdrawn to travel back to their villages.

Northcutt was getting impatient. "Where the devil is Cornstalk? He and his cronies should have been here by now."

Grenough smiled. "Barrett, be patient. You should know by now that they will arrive in their own good time. Cornstalk is undoubtedly being intentionally late, just to show defiance."

While they waited, Wend pulled Northcutt aside and said, "We need to talk privately."

Northcutt was impatient. "What's this about, Eckert? Dunmore is about to arrive."

"You asked me to give you information on the sentiment of the militia. I have something you and the governor might find interesting."

Now Northcutt was all ears. "Yes? What might that be?"

"It's the way negotiations have been conducted. Many of the militia officers are angry that none of them have been included in the council discussions; in fact, not even allowed inside the lodge to witness the talks."

"Eckert, you were there when Welford briefed us on the conditions in Boston and the constraints Gage suggested for the treaty. Do I have to explain why confidentiality is required?"

"Barrett, the secrecy has inevitably aroused suspicions. There are bitter discussions around the campfires at night."

Northcutt snapped, "I don't agree with their sentiment. It's not like there aren't Virginians present at the negotiations. Marsh is there and so am I. We're certainly Virginia militia officers."

"Barrett, you know these border officers don't see it that way. You asked for unvarnished truth from me and now I'm passing it on. Understand this: There's boiling unrest out there about the way the governor has conducted these peace talks."

"All right, Eckert, you've told me." There was a dismissive tone in Northcutt's voice. "It's too late to do anything about it. And frankly, I think it's of little consequence. The militia will soon be on their way home and they'll be occupied with thoughts of their families and farms. And they'll be happy about the outbreak of peace on the border."

"Barrett, they may be happy to go home, but this will add to distrust of the Crown and Dunmore."

"All right, I'll mention it to His Lordship. But there's something you don't know, Eckert. And I think it will go a long way toward mollifying the militia, if you are right about this dissension."

"Do you care to enlighten me?"

"Yes, my dear Eckert; the governor has decided to punish those Mingoes who have refused to accept the treaty. He's planning to send Crawford and his battalion up to Seekunk to destroy the villages there. They'll depart, in secrecy, as soon as the treaty is finalized and the rest of the army is on the way back to the Ohio. It will demonstrate to the Ohio Indians the consequences of refusing the governor's leniency. And it will show settlers on the border that the governor has their interests at heart. "

Wend was considering Northcutt's words when he heard a faint crackling noise in the distance to the south. For a moment he couldn't place it. Then it dawned on him: gunfire! He was hearing the reports of weapons being discharged. He saw that Grenough had put his hand to his ear.

Wend asked, "Do you hear that?"

The merchant exclaimed, "Yes, by God. It's firing!"

Now everyone was straining to hear.

Marsh asked, "Could it be some hunters out after game?"

Wend looked at the aide. "If it is hunters, Captain, the prey are firing back. Listen to the pattern of the shooting. It's a fight of some kind."

Northcutt spoke up sharply. "Marsh, do we have any scouting parties out in that direction?"

"No, sir. Only pickets, but they're much closer than that."

Dunmore had also heard the noise; he came out of his tent, dressed in his blue and red militia uniform, and stared in the direction of the firing. Northcutt and Marsh strode quickly over to join him.

Wend glanced over at Grenough, who was smiling, his head cocked slightly to the right. He asked, "Richard, what are you thinking?"

The merchant grinned broadly. "Lewis."

Wend was shocked. "Lewis? But for God's sake, he and his men are supposed to be camped far back on the Kanawha Trail. He was ordered to stop!"

"Precisely."

Wend was about to say more, when suddenly he saw an officer of the camp guards approaching at a fast walk. Behind him was the trader Elliott, anxiety written all over his face. The officer looked around, then saw the governor over at the tent. He led Elliott in that direction.

There was another burst of firing in the distance.

Grenough said, "Let us join the governor, my dear Eckert. Light is about to be shed on this intriguing complication."

They followed Elliott to Dunmore's tent.

Dunmore laid eyes on the trader and said, "Mr. Elliott, can I assume the tribal chiefs dispatched you?"

The trader took off his hat. "Yes, Your Lordship; they're mad as hell. You told Cornstalk that Colonel Lewis' column had been stopped. But early this morning a Shawnee scout ran into Cornstalk's village saying a group of militia was comin' up the Kanawha Trail, not far from Grenadier Squaw Town, the eastern village."

Northcutt asked quickly, "What about this firing we just heard to the south?"

Elliott shook his head. "I don't know nothin' about that, unless them militia laid into the villages."

Dunmore called out to Angus McDonald. "Major, have you sent any patrols ranging to the southwest that could be near Shawnee villages?"

"Not a one, sir, I pulled them all in when negotiations started."

Dunmore stood staring southward. He muttered, "What the devil could it be?" Then enlightenment spread across his face. "Oh, my God! Lewis!"

Northcutt said grimly, "It can be no one else."

Welford scowled and exclaimed, "You can't trust militia! They have no discipline. They do what they damn well please."

Northcutt grabbed Welford's arm and said quietly, "Reggie, remember yourself."

Welford looked around, suddenly realizing he was surrounded by militia officers. He closed his mouth and crossed his arms.

Dunmore turned and looked at Wend. "Eckert, you carried the orders to Lewis. Did you ensure he understood the intent?"

Wend answered, "Sir, I told him precisely what was in the orders and then he read them in front of me."

McDonald spoke up. "Governor, there hasn't been any firing for a while now."

Everyone listened closely for a long moment. No gunfire could be heard.

Dunmore gritted his teeth. "We must send someone immediately to ensure Lewis advances no further."

"My Lord, I don't believe that will be good enough," said Grenough.

The governor snapped, "What precisely do you mean, sir?" Anger was rising in his voice.

"It won't be sufficient to send a messenger or even an aide, sir. I submit you must go yourself."

Northcutt spoke up. "I'm afraid Richard is right, Your Lordship. I think that damned Irishman will only listen to you."

Dunmore sighed deeply. "It seems I have no choice." He turned to Elliott. "Sir, how far is it to this Grenadier Squaw Town?"

The trader pointed with his hat. "Sir, I reckon it be six or seven miles to the south of here."

415

Dunmore turned to McDonald. "Major, form me an escort guard. I will march there as soon as you can do so."

Grenough held up his hand. "Sir, I don't think a guard of infantry will be timely enough. And the sight of a column marching through the bush could provoke warriors already stirred up. I recommend you take to horse with a small party and get down there as soon as possible."

Dunmore glared at Grenough for a second, then bit his lip and seemed to calm down. "Richard, I'm damned tired of you being right all the time."

"I apologize for my lack of consideration, sir."

The governor motioned to Marsh. "Captain, get both my horse and yours saddled." Then he turned to Wend. "Eckert, you're coming too. And get that party of men who rode with you on the last trip. That will make six of us; that should be adequate."

In half an hour the six of them were riding south through the bush as fast as the terrain would permit. Joshua led, followed by the governor on his own horse, a long-legged, muscular hunter. Marsh followed immediately behind and then came Wend, Butler and Flannagan. Wend watched Dunmore ride and had to admit that, whatever his other talents, he was an accomplished horseman, going over fallen tree trunks and other obstructions with grace. Joshua pushed the pace, picking out the most advantageous course through the trees and bushes. Butler and Flannagan, who were much less experienced riders, lagged behind but kept the others in sight.

After an hour, they saw a village to the west, which Wend took to be Grenadier Squaw Town, and a few minutes later came to a pathway. Joshua called back to the governor, "This is the Kanawha Trail; we'll head east until we come to the column."

Soon they climbed a ridge and in the distance saw the smoke from many fires.

Joshua pulled up and pointed toward the fires. "There's Lewis' camp!"

Dunmore stared at the sight, dismay spreading across his face. Then Wend heard him mutter, "My God, he really did come this far west."

Wend realized that despite the events of the morning, the governor had been mentally denying the fact that Lewis had disobeyed orders.

"All right, Mr. Baird," said Dunmore in an angry voice, "let's ride; we can waste not a minute."

In less than a mile the party met the first outpost. Once the young ensign in charge recovered from his astonishment at encountering the governor, he wasted no time in sending a runner to headquarters and then personally conducting them to meet Lewis.

Lewis stood in front of his tent, arms crossed in a defiant posture. Colonel Christian, the second in command, was at his side and a group of officers behind him. The greetings between the governor and the leaders of the brigade could most charitably be described as frigid.

Dunmore glared at all the officers standing by and said, very formally, "Colonel Lewis, we must talk privately."

Lewis waved to the officers, "Gentlemen, I would request that you withdraw." As everyone made haste to move a discreet distance away, Lewis took Christian by the arm and whispered something in his ear. Then he conducted the governor into his tent.

The others gathered into a group about fifteen yards away. Christian turned to an aide and ordered, "Get the camp guard here quickly. And then go recruit an additional guard detachment from companies which weren't at the battle and march them here

post-haste. Select older men; if possible get men who were in the Virginia Regiment and understand discipline. Now move and get the guard here fast."

The aide scurried away.

Wend asked Christian, "Why all the urgency? Does the Governor of Virginia need protection among his own men? "

The colonel pointed behind him; Wend turned and realized there were already more than a hundred men standing around and he could see that many others were rapidly streaming toward the headquarters.

Christian said, "You're about to see what real anger looks like. They're mad as hell at the governor. Lewis fears there could be violence."

Wend eyed the growing crowd of militiamen. Then he asked, "Colonel, what was the firing about this morning? Did Lewis order an assault?"

Christian shook his head. "Lewis did no such thing. It was merely a chance affair of detachments. One of our scouting parties came into contact with a party of Shawnees, obviously keeping watch on us. Both sides fired at each other for a few minutes and then withdrew. Our scouts then realized we were close to that village up ahead and Lewis gave orders to stop the advance."

"Well, Colonel, that chance affair has stalled the conclusion of negotiations with the chiefs. That's why the governor came down here."

"Now look, Eckert, I told you it wasn't intentional."

Suddenly they were distracted by a loud voice from the headquarters tent; it was the governor. There was a sharp reply from Lewis. Both men were obviously angry; the words themselves were not quite intelligible.

Wend continued, "Was it unintentional that you advanced right up to the Pickaway Plains after the governor's order to halt?"

Now anger showed on Christian's face. "Look, Eckert, how would you have liked the job of trying to stop these men after what they went through at the mouth of the Kanawha?"

"But brazenly disobeying orders?"

"Eckert, the men have lost respect for Dunmore. They're convinced Cornstalk wouldn't have dared attack if the northern column had been at the mouth of the Kanawha to meet us on schedule. And after the fighting they did, Lewis couldn't deny them the chance to be in at the finish of the campaign."

Just as he finished, the guard of the day came marching to headquarters. Their officer positioned them to form a line between the still growing and now very loud mob of militia soldiers.

Shortly thereafter, the flap of Lewis' tent opened and the two men emerged, both with red faces.

As the governor came into view, there was an angry hubbub from the crowd and a few shouted epithets. Dunmore ignored the mob and called out to Marsh, "Captain, my mount; we're riding back to Camp Charlotte." Then he turned to Wend. "Eckert, you stay here and keep Baird with you. After an appropriate period of rest, this brigade is going back to the Ohio. When they have departed, you will report the fact to me." He looked over at Lewis. "I trust that we understand each other?"

Flannagan came up leading the governor's horse, and after a terse farewell to Lewis, Dunmore mounted. Then, without further ceremony, he rode off, followed by the rest of his party.

The officer in charge of the camp guard had his men start to break up the crowd of soldiers and order them back to their fires.

Meanwhile Lewis walked over and stood before his staff. Wend noticed he was breathing heavily and his face was still redder than normal. He said to the officers, "Well, gentlemen, some bitter news: The war is over. For better or worse, the governor has settled the terms of peace with Cornstalk and his allies."

Christian asked, "What are those terms? What is to be required of the Indians?"

Lewis broke into a mirthless smile and looked over at Wend. "Why don't we ask the governor's aide, Lieutenant Eckert, who is here to spy on us? I'm sure he can explain better than I."

Wend felt all eyes turn toward him. He said, "There are several provisions. One, the Shawnee will give up their hunting grounds below the Ohio. Two, they will allow safe passage of all traffic on the Ohio. Three, they will provide high level hostages to guarantee the peace. Four, our traders will go into the Shawnee territory above the river only by license granted by the colony."

Christian blurted out, "Why, those are the provisions of the Fort Stanwix treaty, nothing more."

Lewis said, "Exactly right, Colonel. Exactly! After abandoning our farms and crops during the harvest season, marching hundreds of miles through the deepest wilderness, fighting a bloody battle, burying scores of our friends and relatives, and seeing many more suffer grievous wounds, all that has been achieved are the terms of a seven year old treaty. The Shawnee and Mingo have raided our farmsteads from Pittsburg down to Carolina, killing men, women, and children, and they will suffer no punishment for their actions. Their villages are to remain untouched and their war captains receive no justice."

An aide said, "Why sir, this is nothing short of folly. Nothing has been achieved."

Lewis pointed at the aide. "Folly is a good word indeed! Folly at the hands of Lord Dunmore to be precise and we have all been made to participate in it."

Christian asked, "Eckert, what about the most vicious of the war captains: Logan and Laughing Eyes? Where are they? Will not those two be made to answer for their crimes?"

Wend said, "Logan is hiding out in an isolated cabin to the west of the Shawnee villages. The governor sent an emissary to have him come in to the peace council, but he refused. Instead he sent a message laying out his grievances and saying he had finished his revenge war." Wend looked around at the men who were staring at him, then lied as convincingly as he could manage, "Laughing Eyes has gone to ground. No one knows where he is hiding."

There was a long silence as the officers absorbed the information. Then Lewis said, "Gentlemen, there is no sense in us remaining here for long. We march back east tomorrow morning. So let us prepare the orders."

The officers began to disperse. When they were alone, Lewis turned to Eckert. Wend could see fierce anger still burning in his eyes and when he spoke, his words were heated. "Eckert, I charge you to tell this to Dunmore: He has had his way and I had no choice but to obey. But by God, things are changing; changing fast. Unrest is running through the land like fire and the outcome of this campaign will do nothing but add fuel to the flames. There will come a day when I will face Dunmore and not be constrained to follow his bidding. And then I vow there will be a reckoning for all of this."

Wend shook his head. "No, sir, I'll not accept that charge. I understand your sentiment, but I will not repeat those words to Lord Dunmore."

Lewis stared at Wend for a very long moment and then his chest heaved. Eckert could see the anger began to flow out of him. After a long minute his shoulders relaxed. "Yes, you are probably right." Then he looked at Wend. "Eckert, permit me to offer some advice: You need to watch yourself. You have become identified with the governor and the King's faction. That soon may be an uncomfortable reputation for a man of the border."

"Colonel, I did not volunteer for duty on Dunmore's staff. I was pressed into the service."

"That may be true, Eckert; but how many of the men in this army, and how many of your neighbors are aware of that?" Lewis waved his finger at Wend. "If I were you, I would find a way to put some distance between myself and Lord Dunmore."

* * *

Wend stood beside Crawford within the stockade of Fort Gower. Around them were many of the militia officers of the northern brigade. After the Treaty of Camp Charlotte had been finalized, Lord Dunmore wasted no time ordering the militiamen back to their homes. With great enthusiasm the entire brigade rapidly marched back to Gower.

Upon reaching the fort, Dunmore himself had soon embarked in a bateau bound for Pittsburgh. He and Northcutt wanted to get back to Williamsburg as early as possible. Grenough had departed with them to tend to his affairs in Pittsburgh.

The meeting in the fort was directly related to the copy of the Virginia Gazette which Wend held in his hand. When they arrived at Gower, the militiamen had found that copies of the newspaper had been brought down from Pittsburgh and contained important, and what many found stirring, news of developments from the Continental Congress in Philadelphia. The delegates had voted in favor of the association of colonies that Washington had written Crawford about, had made a declaration demanding the repeal of the Intolerable Acts, and had declared a boycott on British goods until the acts were rescinded. Ominously, they had also advised all the colonies to organize, fully arm, and train their militias against any contingency. Finally, the delegates declared the intent for Congress to meet again in the next year to assess London's response to the actions of the colonies.

Colonel Adam Stephen, commandant of the Berkeley County Battalion, had led a group of officers in composing a resolution in support of Congress' actions. Now he stood in front of the gathering, ready to read their statement.

Stephen banged a long stick against a log and then mounted the log. "Gentlemen! Gentlemen, I beg your attention!" Slowly the raucous gathering quieted down. When all was silent, he began an oration. "Gentlemen, having now concluded the campaign with honor and advantage to the colony and ourselves, it only remains that we should give our country the strongest assurance that we are ready, at all times, to the utmost of our power, to maintain and defend her just rights and privileges. That we are a respectable body is certain, when it is considered that we can live weeks without bread or salt; that we can sleep in the open air without any covering but the canopy of heaven; and that our men can march and shoot with any in the known world. Blessed with these talents, let us solemnly engage to one another and our country in particular, that we will use them to no purpose but for the honor and advantage of America in general and of Virginia in particular. It behooves us then, for the satisfaction of our country, that we should give them our real sentiments, by way of resolves, at this very alarming crisis."

A loud voice shouted out "For God's sake, Adam, stop all the jabbering and get to the point!"

Wend looked at Crawford. "That could be no one else but Morgan."

Crawford winked and nodded. "He's rough and he's loud, but I tell you, Eckert, you should have seen him leading the charge of his company of wild riflemen into the first village at Seekunk. I think he terrified the Mingo all by himself!"

Wend laughed, "I can see that, William. He was frustrated by Cresap having all the action on McDonald's raid at Wakatomica."

Meanwhile, Stephen resumed talking. "All right, here is what we propose to send to the Gazette for publication to the good citizens of the colony. This first part reminds the King we are loyal subjects:

Resolved, that we will bear the most faithful allegiance to his Majesty King George the Third, while his Majesty delights to reign over a brave and free people; that we will, at the expense of life and everything dear and valuable, exert ourselves in support of the honor of his Crown and dignity of the British Empire.

Stephens paused, then said, "Now the next paragraph is the meat of our resolve; pray listen close now:

But as the love of Liberty and attachment to the real interests and just rights of America outweigh every other consideration, we resolve that we will exert every power within us for the defense of American liberty and for the support of her just rights and privileges; not in any precipitate, riotous, or tumultuous manner, but when regularly called forth by the unanimous voice of our countrymen."

Stephens looked around, and said, "I take it you can all agree with that sentiment?"

Heads nodded and there were universal shouts of approval. Then Stephens continued, "Now the following words are a polite conclusion so that we do not offend the governor:

Resolved, that we entertain the greatest respect for his Excellency the Right Honorable Lord Dunmore, who commanded the expedition against the Shawanese; and who, we are confident, underwent the great fatigue of this singular campaign from no other motive than true interest of this country."

There were catcalls and one voice shouted, "Damn, Colonel, do we need that?"

The colonel motioned with his hand to calm the men. "Yes, I repeat this is not the time to show any disrespect to Dunmore or the Crown. I say that the second paragraph makes it clear beyond doubt that we are ready to fight if necessary." He paused, looking down at the officers. "Now, do we all agree to the sense of this document?"

There was a chorus of agreement.

Stephen said, "All right, I'll have my clerk Ben Ashby send this to the Gazette so the citizens understand how we feel and can be assured that their militia is ready to confront the government if that should become necessary." He paused and smiled, then said, "I guess we can all go home now!"

There was a cheer and the officers began to disperse and return to their companies.

Crawford turned to Wend. "As Stephen was reading that, I had a thought. Do you remember the night Northcutt explained his plan for this war to us? The same night someone shot at you from the woods? He was convinced that conducting a war against the Indians would solidify the loyalty of the colonists."

"It would be hard to forget that night, William."

"Well, think of the irony: Here we are, at the conclusion of that war, warning the King that we're ready to fight in an insurrection; the very thing Northcutt sought to head off." Crawford shook his head. "It would seem that the business has been a bit of folly."

Wend laughed. "Strange you should say that, William. Lewis and his officers used the same word. They called the war Lord Dunmore's Folly because in their eyes it achieved nothing."

"Actually, Eckert, it did achieve something." Crawford smiled mischievously. "Virginia now has a seasoned, trained militia ready to take the field against anyone who would attempt to restrict our rights, just as the Continental Congress has requested. And the real irony is that Lord Dunmore caused it to happen and paid the expense."

Wend smiled at Crawford. "A very good point, William." Wend looked around at the interior of the stockade, now nearly empty. "Well, I must get back to my camp, and make preparations for leaving." He extended his hand to Crawford. "I hope I have the pleasure of your company again in the future, sir."

"And I the same to you, Wend Eckert. Take care on your way home."

* * *

As Wend walked back to his fire, he encountered a gang of men hauling supplies from the stockade to a picket line of packhorses. Directing the work was the Irishman McCrae. And then Wend saw that Girty and Butler were moving among the horses, apparently inspecting their condition.

Wend approached and asked, "What's happening, McCrae?"

The Irishman turned and looked at Wend. Then he waved at the growing pile of kegs and canvas bags. "We're getting ready for a tradin' trip up to the Pickaway Plains, Eckert. Grenough bought all this stuff back from the colony."

Wend looked closely at the supplies, "That's mostly gunpowder and lead."

"Exactly, Eckert; them Shawnee and Mingo up on the Scioto used up most of their ammunition in the fight with Lewis down on the Kanawha. So Grenough wants to be the first trader into the Ohio Country. He figures the savages will be desperate to give him all the pelts they got and anything else of value they can dig up for the powder and lead they need for winter hunting. I'm leading a big string of packhorses up the Hocking trails at first light tomorrow."

Wend quickly realized McCrae was right. Then he thought of something else. "But under the Treaty of Camp Charlotte, traders can only go into the Ohio Country with a permit from the colony."

McCrae grinned broadly. "That's right, and Grenough has got the very first permit issued by Virginia. It was written up and signed before the governor and his party left for Pittsburgh. I got it right in my saddlebag. There ain't no other trader who has the right to deal with the Indians."

Wend gave a sigh of resignation. "Naturally Grenough got the first permit. As they say, 'To the victor goes the spoils'."

"You know, Eckert, that's the damnedest thing. Mr. Grenough remarked almost the same thing to me about that license."

"I find myself unsurprised." Then Wend motioned toward the picket line. "What are Girty and Butler doing?"

"Mr. Grenough signed them up as guides. I ain't no expert on this part of the country."

Wend thought a moment. "Where's Bratton? Is he going along with you?"

McCrae smiled and shook his head. "Naw, he be up in Pittsburgh. Grenough didn't want him down here near you. He said there would be too much chance he couldn't resist layin' into you and Grenough didn't want no unpleasantness."

Wend laughed. "Unpleasantness might as well be Bratton's first name." Then he nodded to McCrae and headed over to the picket line to speak with Butler.

Butler saw him coming. He waved and said, "Hello, Lieutenant Eckert."

Wend greeted the scout and then said, "How did you get hooked up with Grenough's company, Simon?"

"I'm tryin' to get some money together to buy that rifle I told you about. Girty convinced Mr. Grenough to hire me on for this trip."

Wend looked around at all the men hauling supplies and the string of horses. "Well, I wish you a safe journey, Simon. But a word of admonishment:

Watch out for yourself while you're working for Grenough. And I would not make it a long term arrangement."

Butler shook his head. "I figure to just make this one trip. And then I'll go get my rifle made and be off on a long hunt. I ain't the kind to be no trader."

Wend walked on, thinking about Grenough. He welcomed the fact that the merchant obviously still considered their truce to still be in effect. Then another thought hit him: The biggest winner in the war wouldn't be the governor or the border militia which had fought it. The winner would be none other than Richard Grenough. The man always came out on top. Wend gritted his teeth at the idea. But then he felt a surge of determination. The time was coming when Grenough wouldn't be the winner, and when he lost, he would pay with his life.

CHAPTER TWENTY-ONE
The Chill at Eckert Ridge

Wend was bent over his desk in the workshop on a morning in late March. He was absorbed in financial calculations regarding the production and sale of whiskey. On the march back from the Ohio Country, Wend had convinced Donegal to form a partnership with him in the whiskey business. Since returning in November, the two had been very busy preparing for expanded distilling. They had enlarged the distillery and renewed all the components. They had also kept the hands busy at preparing the additional fields for growing the required grain supply. That included clearing the brush growth from a couple of fields on Eckert Ridge which had been laying fallow and locating fields on nearby farms which could be rented. Now, Wend's computations convinced him that he could indeed replace the income from musket repairs with whiskey sale revenue and thus break free from the hold Northcutt had on him.

Then, amidst his thoughts, Wend noticed that Bernd was standing beside him.

"Father, there's a man here to see you."

Without looking up, Wend asked, "Who is it, son? Does he need to see me or can Hecht deal with him?"

"He asked for you by name, father. He said he knows you from the war and his name is Kenton."

"Kenton? I don't know anyone by that name."

"He looks like a hunter, Pa."

Wend put his work down and stood up. "All right, Bernd. I'll go see him." Wend turned and walked toward the door. The morning was cold, but the shop was a busy and cheery place. A fire crackled in the hearth. Horner was at his bench, shaping the stock of a rifle. Hecht and the other apprentices, including Johann, were working on the latest batch of muskets.

Wend looked at the man who stood just inside the door. He was heavily bundled against the cold, wearing a threadbare wool overcoat, a broad-brimmed hat, and an improvised scarf around his neck. He wore breeches with leggings and a pair of leather shoes. Beside him lay a tumpline pack. He held a rifle in his left hand; a powder horn and pouch hung on their slings over his shoulders. A large knife was strapped on his left side. Wend looked more closely at his face, which was burned red by the winter wind, and suddenly recognized him: It was Simon Butler.

"Come on in, Simon, and sit beside the fire! I didn't know who you were at first; my son called you Kenton. He must have misheard you."

Simon picked up his pack and walked to the chairs in front of the fireplace. "No, Mr. Eckert, he heard me right. I'm going by my real name now."

Wend sat down beside the woodsman. "Your real name?"

"The truth is, I been on the run since I was fifteen. I got into a fight near my home back in the Bull Run Mountains." He looked at Wend and then continued, "It were over a girl."

Wend laughed, "Of course it was."

"Anyway, I hit the man and he went down hard and didn't move. I checked him and he was limp and I didn't think he was breathing. I reckoned he was dead." Kenton shrugged. "So that very moment I lit out for the border. And I took the name Butler from a man who gave me some work. Then just after Girty and I got back to Pittsburgh from the Ohio Country on that trading trip for Mr. Grenough, we ran into a man from back home who recognized me. He told us the man I fought with didn't die; he was just knocked out. Truth is, there ain't no charges on me at all."

Wend nodded. "It must be a relief for you, Simon. But, if I may ask, why have you come here?"

"I'm goin' to Kentucky. Man named Boone is organizin' pilgrims to settle there now the war is over. I figure to go out there, get enough land for a cabin, and maybe do some hunting for farmers."

"Simon, Kentucky is in the other direction."

"I came here to buy a rifle from you. I need a good firelock." He patted his pack. "I got money in here to buy it; got my militia money and what I made workin' for Grenough."

"You came all this distance just to buy one of my rifles?"

"I want the best, Mr. Eckert."

Wend said, "It will be my pleasure to make one for you, Simon. And if you are going out to Kentucky, you'll need to keep as much money as you can. I'll make you the firelock for just what it costs me."

Kenton beamed. "I'll be obliged to you, sir."

Wend said, "This will take some time. What will you do in the meantime?"

"I guess go back to Winchester and find work."

Wend shook his head. "No you won't. There's plenty of work here for you. We're starting the spring planting."

"I was a farmer before I started hunting."

"Come with me. Let's go see Donegal."

After dropping off Kenton's pack at the barracks, they walked to the distilling building where they found Donegal inspecting his equipment. The Scotsman recognized Kenton at once.

Wend said, "Donegal, I've got another farm hand for you. I know you're looking for help in planting."

"Sure'n that's the truth; we've got to get Widow Callow's big field sown with wheat."

Marian Callow, a woman near sixty, had lost her husband in December, leaving her unable to farm her land. Wend had acted rapidly, arranging to rent most of her fields, which pleased the woman mightily. Now he and Donegal planned to plant them in wheat, barley, and corn.

Wend pointed to Donegal. "He's got to get the planting done in the next couple of weeks. When he's done, he's heading up to Ransome's Tavern to get married to a pretty, golden-haired widow named Sally Potter. She gave him her hand on the way back from the Ohio Country."

Donegal smiled broadly, but then a worried look passed over his face. "Sure enough, if she's 'na changed her mind by the time I get back there."

Wend winked at Kenton. "The woman just turned twenty-four and is quite comely. Donegal's worried she's going to have second thoughts about marrying an old man of thirty-seven and some young buck is going to steal her away from him."

Kenton put on a long face, his hand to his chin. "You know, Mr. Eckert, I'd say he could be right to worry. There be a lot of lusty young fellows around that country who would jump for a likely woman that could give them lots of children."

Donegal looked at each of them, concern all over his face; then he caught on to the joke and said, "Just stop it, the both of you."

Wend laughed and said, "Anyway, he and Joshua and some of the hands are taking a couple of wagons up Braddocks Road. After the wedding, they're going to go to her old place on Little Pebble Creek which was burned out by a war party last spring. They'll bring back anything left that's useful."

Kenton said, "That's on my way, Mr. Donegal. If my firelock is done by then, I'll travel along with you and help out."

"I like that idea. Extra hands are welcome travelin' that road," answered Donegal. "You get settled in the barracks. You can sleep right next to Johann; there's an empty bed there."

Kenton looked at Donegal, then at Eckert, puzzlement on his face. He blurted out, "Your son doesn't sleep in the house?"

A hand clutched at Wend's heart. "Yes, Simon, my wife has had a hard time accepting him into the family. She is a strong-willed lady."

"But she knows he is your flesh and blood? And doesn't have the heart to welcome him?"

Wend closed his eyes and controlled the mixture of regret and frustration which rose inside him. "The fault is partially mine, Simon. I failed to tell her about Johann all the years of our marriage and therefore she was greatly shocked when he arrived with me after the war. I'm hoping the passage of time will soften her heart toward the youth and toward her husband." Then Wend turned to leave.

Kenton reached out and touched Wend's arm. "Mr. Eckert, forgive me for raising the matter. I was too surprised to consider my words."

"It's all right, Simon. I have consoled myself to the situation." He sighed, then said, "When you finish with Donegal, come back to the workshop and we'll measure you for your new firelock."

As Wend walked back to the shop, he could not keep his mind from going over the day of their return to Winchester and the uncomfortable situation which persisted in the Eckert family.

In the shadow of Fort Loudoun, the two returning companies had been dismissed, the men breaking up to be greeted by their families and friends. Johann, intimidated by the crush of people dressed in ways he had never seen before, stayed close by Wend's side. Eckert had been going over in his mind the proper words to explain things to Peggy, but he never had the opportunity to express them. She had simply looked at the boy standing beside him and her face instantly flushed with anger. But she restrained her rage and, speaking very slowly in controlled words, asked, "Well, Wend, what is your son's name?"

It was on the way home that Peggy allowed herself to give voice to her anger. The two of them rode in the chaise with The Mare tied behind. The other members of the Eckert Ridge contingent rode in a wagon. Wend began by apologizing for not telling her about the boy and then tried to explain the events which took him to Abigail's village. But Peggy was having none of it and accused Wend of betrayal and worse, repeatedly and in vehement terms. Finally, having verbally lashed him in every way she could think of, she had subsided into frigid silence, refusing even to respond to his words. The rest of the journey home had seemed like an eternity to Wend.

When they turned up the drive to the farm itself she had suddenly burst out, saying, "I'll not have him within my house, Wend Eckert. He can live in the barracks with the hands. I'll be polite to him, but I'll not suffer to make him part of the family."

Wend had tried to argue, but soon saw it was futile. He had then personally escorted Johann down to the barracks, finding him a bed and place to stow his meager belongings. He had started into a long, detailed explanation of why Peggy would not accept him, but Johann put his hand on Wend's arm and gently cut him off. "I understand, Father. She must get used to my presence."

And so the long, cold winter had begun. Peggy had been civil to Wend in family matters and to all appearances, life returned to normal in the house. But every night the sleeping cap was on her head and she took to bed with her back to Wend.

For his part, Wend began spending even longer hours in the workshop than normal, which allowed him to avoid the chill of Peggy's presence. It also allowed him to spend time with Johann. Wend took satisfaction in teaching the boy about his tradecraft and helping him to improve his English. A bright spot was that Bernd and Johann soon bonded, working side by side in the shop and going off to Alice's school together.

In those long hours, Wend also had time to make his plans and calculations regarding the production of whiskey and he soon felt assured it could be a profitable business. The figures convinced Donegal beyond any doubt, who looked forward to using the money to build his house and support the family he was about to gain. The two of them set to work enthusiastically and spent the winter making their preparations. Wend had dug into his limited coffers to fund the improvement of the distillery and rent additional fields. He knew it was a gamble, but also realized that he must take the risk to free himself from Northcutt's grasp.

* * *

On a bright morning in early April, Donegal's caravan of two wagons departed for Ransome's Tavern. Joshua and Donegal rode their horses while Specht and another farmhand drove the wagons. Simon Kenton, his new rifle cradled in his arm, rode with Specht in the lead wagon. Despite the early hour, virtually all the residents of Eckert Ridge had turned out to see them off and bid them luck on their journey.

Peggy came out and stood on the porch, Ellen and Elise standing beside her. She saw that Bernd, Johann, and Horner were with Wend in front of the workshop. Alice Downy lingered with Joshua beside his horse, sharing some final words with her man. Then Baird swung up onto the saddle and Alice walked over to join Peggy.

As the wagons rolled past and started down the drive, Elise asked, "Mother, how long will they be gone?"

Peggy answered, "Three, maybe four weeks, if everything goes well. And they have to spend some time at Mrs. Potter's old farm, salvaging what they can. She says the barn didn't burn all the way down and there's a plow, harness, and some good farm tools that they can bring back."

Alice added, "And the rains are going to start soon. That will make the wagon track difficult. So it might take longer than that."

Peggy nodded. "Alice is right. We just won't expect them until we see them." She turned to Elise. "Now take your sister and go in for breakfast. Wilma and Liza have the table ready for you."

After the girls had left, the two woman stood watching as the wagons rolled down the drive and turned northward on the road.

Alice said, "Things will be quiet here until they all get back. Then it will be interesting with a new family on the ridge."

Peggy nodded. "I'm looking forward to meeting the woman who finally tamed Donegal."

Alice didn't answer at once. After a long pause, she said, "Why don't you take this time to finally reconcile your argument with Wend? Surely the heat of your anger has been gone for a long time and, in truth, the situation is unsettling everybody on the farm. There's embarrassment at seeing Johann exiled to the barracks. It would be nice if harmony were restored by the time Donegal and his wife get here."

Peggy set her jaw. "I'm not ready to take Abigail's half-savage boy into my house. Or forgive Wend for lying to me for ten years. It's more proof he never loved me." She stamped her foot. "Besides, he slept with that woman while he was in the Mingo village."

"You don't know that."

"Why else would he go there?"

"You're letting your jealously and hatred of the woman blind you. For God's sake, Joshua and Donegal say he went there expressly to see his son. And he put his life on the line to do it."

"No one doubts Wend is brave. I just wish he'd have the courage to show his love for me."

"So you're back to worrying about him not being jealous when you flaunt yourself at other men?" Alice shook her head. "I've told you before, he understands you so well that he puts up with it."

"Do we have to go through all this again? I'm going inside to breakfast."

"Wait, Peggy, and listen: You have enough experience to know that no two people love each other equally or in the same way. You probably love Wend more intensely than he does, but that doesn't mean he doesn't truly care for you. You must adjust your feelings to that and stop tearing yourself apart."

"Is the speech over now, Mother Alice?"

"There's one more thing. I've had a chance to observe Johann during lessons. He's a good boy and he's smart. All the other children love to hear his stories of life in the Mingo village. And Bernd admires him greatly. Think about this: After years of murderous antagonism between Wend and Matt Bratton, wouldn't it be good to see their sons living in brotherhood?"

Peggy turned white. "For God's sake! You think Bernd is Bratton's son? How can you possibly believe that?"

"Don't be silly. I can count to nine. And anyone who's ever seen Matt knows who Bernd looks like. There's nothing of Wend in Bernd, except what he's put there by being a good father."

Peggy's face was red. "All right, there is much to what you say. But I need time."

"You've had nearly five months. If this goes on much longer the damage may be permanent. I wager, even in your stubbornness, that's not what you want."

With that, Alice went down the stairs and walked briskly toward her house. Peggy watched her go, her face still burning from her friend's lecture. Then she looked over at the workshop. Wend had gone inside, but Horner was instructing Bernd and Johann on the rifling machine. She had to acknowledge that the boys got along well. And she had to admit to herself she was becoming increasingly lonely in withholding herself from Wend's company.

Peggy sighed. *Alice is right: I must end this conflict.* But Peggy immediately realized she was in a trap of her own making. How could she reconcile with Wend and bring Johann into the family without admitting she had over-reacted in November? She thought: *I'll go to the sewing room after breakfast and put my mind to it. There must be a way to work this out before Donegal gets back with his wife.*

* * *

Angus McDonald, James Wood, and Sheriff Smith took their seats in the Eckert parlor. It was early afternoon in the last week of April. The three men had ridden up the drive, dismounted in front of the workshop, and, with an air of mystery, asked to see Wend in private. So he had led them over to the house.

Wend stepped to the side cabinet and asked, "Shall I pour some libation before we address whatever grave business has brought you to the farm?"

All three readily accepted and Wend dispensed whiskey to each of them. Then he sat down with his own cup. "Well, gentlemen, it has occurred to me that you didn't ride out here simply for a social call."

The three exchanged glances and Angus cleared his throat. "Indeed, Eckert, we have come on business; very confidential, and I might add, delicate, business."

Wood nodded. "The truth is, we were asked to come here by the Committee of Correspondence. And we must ask you a serious question: To wit, do you consider yourself a supporter of the Whig movement?"

Wend said nothing for a long moment, looking into the eyes of each of the men in turn. Then he countered, "Why am I being asked this question?"

Angus answered, "There those who are concerned that you have appeared to be very close to the government."

Wood said, "Yes, everyone knows you have been favored with a lucrative musket contract. Then there was the militia commission presented by Northcutt, your assistance in recruiting German volunteers for the militia, and finally the appointment as the governor's aide."

Wend fought rising anger. He looked at McDonald. "Angus, you know I didn't want to go to the war and protested the commission when it was offered to me. You know I supported you throughout the campaign and informed you of things that were said about you by the governor and his staff."

"That's true, gentlemen," said Angus. I'm indebted to him for that."

Then Wend said, "And Angus also knows I protested being made an aide to the governor."

"Yes, that's correct. I was there at the time."

"Thank you, Angus." Wend turned on the other two. "As for being part of the Whig movement, I can tell you that I don't like what's happening in Boston and in fact I'm opposed to some of the high-handed things Dunmore has done here in Virginia. And I'm convinced there is going to be some sort of uprising, if for no other purpose than to show the King and Parliament that the American colonies must be allowed, in large measure, to govern themselves. So I suppose if I must be involved in politics, I lean toward sympathy with the Whigs. But what I really want is to be left in peace to pursue my craft and the well-being of my family."

Smith looked at the other men. "I think that is about as positive a response as we can expect. No one expects Eckert to be a firebrand."

Wend said, "Excuse me, gentlemen, but you didn't travel all the way out here just to ask me if I was a Whig. There's something more you want of me, which obviously depends on my support of the Whig cause. Why don't you just get to the point?"

Wood nodded. "It's about your musket contract."

"I suppose the members of the Committee are not happy about it?"

Smith said, "Actually, we consider it quite fortunate."

Wend shook his head. "I don't understand what you are getting at."

Smith asked, "How many muskets do you have on hand now?"

"There are two lots: One lot of fifty is almost finished being repaired. A second lot of fifty has just come in and we haven't started work yet."

Wood's face lighted up. "That is excellent, Eckert."

Wend thought a minute and then realized where they were heading. "I take it the committee wants me to slow down the work?"

Wood grinned. "Precisely, Eckert. Listen: Every message we get from the north carries grim news. Mobs form every time British soldiers march out of Boston. There was nearly an armed fight in November when a British column advanced into the countryside to search for hidden arms. Things have been quiet since then with the troops tucked into Boston for the winter. But with the spring, matters may come to a head."

Angus interrupted, "Everyone expects Gage to start sweeps back into the countryside with the end of winter. That could happen any time now. The Committee believes that could touch off the insurrection you spoke of, Wend."

Wood cleared his throat. "More to the point, we just received news of great concern here in Virginia. A few days ago Lord Dunmore had the commander of a Royal Navy warship send a landing party ashore and seize all the powder in the Williamsburg magazine."

Smith said, "Clearly, Dunmore fears his own people."

Wend now understood the three men's visit. "I take it you want me to delay delivery of the muskets to Williamsburg."

Wood nodded. "Quite right, Eckert. Find some way to delay shipment of the ones nearing completion, and slow your work on the second lot."

Smith said, "One hundred muskets would provide for two companies of militia."

Wend laughed. "It would also deprive me of payment for those muskets. That money feeds a lot of mouths. Is the Committee going to pay for them if I turn them over?"

"Consider this, Eckert," said Wood. "If no uprising occurs, you eventually send the muskets on to Williamsburg and get your money. If it does happen, I submit the last thing the governor will be thinking about is paying your account."

Wend said nothing but realized that Wood could very well be right.

Smith spoke up. "This may be useful to you, Eckert: Barrett Northcutt arrived in Winchester yesterday. I saw him at the Golden Buck. He said he was riding down to see you tomorrow to settle up with some work on your contract."

"Yes, he does owe me payment for the last batch we shipped back in the fall."

The three men looked at each other again. Then McDonald said, "There's something else we wanted to talk to you about."

"It's a longer range matter," added Wood. "But it also has to do with muskets."

Wend shrugged. "Pray, don't keep me in the dark."

McDonald said, "The Committee sees the possible need to have a source of manufacture for new muskets. You are the logical choice, since you've been repairing and rebuilding them for years now. How hard would it be for you to engage in production of new firelocks?"

The idea took Wend by surprise. He asked, "I assume you mean making copies of the muskets we have been working on?"

McDonald nodded. "Yes; that is what you are familiar with."

Wend made some quick calculations, conscious that the others were staring at him. Then he said, "Building new muskets is a different proposition then repairing existing ones. Numerous parts will have to be manufactured elsewhere. A forge will have to be found to make the barrels and parts for the lock mechanism. But I do have a small foundry and can cast parts made of brass, such as the side plates and butt plate. And of course we can carve the stocks."

Smith asked, "But the overall answer is yes?"

"It could be done; it will take time to organize matters before work starts. But the real question is: Where would the money come from?"

Wood laughed. "That's a question for the future; the committee just wanted to understand the feasibility of the idea."

McDonald spoke up in a serious tone, "But the final question is: Will you do it if the need arises? You must understand that if conditions develop which force us to equip an army for the field, the person supplying weapons would be considered treasonous if the cause failed."

Now they were all staring at him. He thought: *This is the real question which they have come to ask me and now I must finally make the decision about where I stand.* Wend smiled. "You know, I have the men, I have the tools, and most of all, I have the knowledge. And beyond that, I have developed a strong dislike for Lord Dunmore and his minion Northcutt. It would be a shame to allow all that to go to waste if war does spread across Virginia."

Smith said, "And you'll find a way to delay sending back the muskets you have now?"

"I regret to say it is hard to get my lazy apprentices to work as fast as they should. And soon the rains will make the roads impassable for wagons until later in the spring."

Wood and Smith smiled. Angus straightened in his chair and exclaimed, "Good for you, laddie. I knew count on you being on the right side."

Wend stood up and poured each of them another round of Donegal's whiskey. "Well, gentlemen, here's to the future, whatever it may bring."

* * *

In mid-morning the next day Wend carefully inspected the work on the muskets, wanting to ensure that everything was in order for Northcutt's first-ever visit to Eckert Ridge. Then he spent some time at his desk, going over his records on the contract. As he did so, he remembered he had taken a ledger over to the house to review the previous evening and had forgotten to bring it back. He walked over to the house to retrieve it.

Wend was standing in the parlor, looking at the last page in the ledger, when he noticed Peggy in the doorway. She was leaning against the frame, her arms crossed in front of her.

"I was just wondering when you thought Mr. Northcutt would be here. Should I be ready to serve him the midday meal?"

"I don't think so; Smith thought he would probably come in the afternoon. But it wouldn't hurt to have enough to serve him if necessary."

Peggy nodded, but instead of leaving, she remained in the doorway. After a moment of silence, she asked, "Why do you think Northcutt is coming?"

"As I told you last night, he wants to settle up for the latest delivery of muskets."

"I've been thinking about that. Surely it could have been done by a courier, as has happened in the past. It has occurred to me that he's here to involve you more deeply in the governor's affairs."

Wend closed the ledger and looked at her in surprise, for that very prospect had been bothering him. "You could be right. The man is always scheming."

Peggy walked into the room and stood with her hand on the back of a chair. She spoke again in a quiet, warm tone: "Wend, you've done a lot of work to get ready to increase the distilling of whiskey. I've admired what you have accomplished."

Wend was startled. It was the first time she had spoken to him beyond what was necessary to manage the house or family affairs. And always there had been a sharp tone in her voice. He looked into her eyes and said, "I'm glad you've noticed. We haven't talked much about it."

She responded, "Yes, I've noticed. You said you would find a way to be free of Northcutt's hold on us and you've kept your promise. Is this the time to make a break with him?"

Wend considered her words. "Perhaps; it will depend on what transpires in the meeting. I'll not be forced to compromise myself any further. However, the Committee of Correspondence would probably desire that I not make any breach with Northcutt and the governor due to the matter of the muskets. So I must walk a thin line."

Peggy smiled at him. Wend realized that it was the warmest smile she had shown him since his return from the Ohio Country.

She said, "My thoughts will be with you as you meet with Northcutt, in the hope that we can finally be shed of him. Perhaps we can return to the state of harmony we shared before you met that man." Then she turned and left the room.

As he stood there with the ledger in hand, it occurred to him that Peggy was trying to end their feud. He sighed deeply and prayed that was the case.

* * *

Barrett Northcutt arrived in mid-afternoon, having ridden down alone from Winchester. Wend showed him around the workshop, introducing him to Hecht and the apprentices, explaining all the equipment. Northcutt was visibly impressed with the rifling machine and the foundry. Then, with the preliminaries finished, they walked over to the house where Peggy met them in the hall and exchanged pleasantries, then left them to their business.

Northcutt settled into a chair in the drawing room. Wend offered his guest a choice of rum or whiskey.

Northcutt smiled, "Whiskey, if it's some of that fine stuff that Donegal makes."

Wend poured him a drink.

Barrett pulled out one of his cigars and lit it from the hearth. "Well, Eckert, I'm quite impressed with what I've seen today. I've been to many tobacco plantations and I've heard of furnaces being called iron plantations, so I guess what you have here could be a firelock plantation."

"I'd say that would be apt, Barrett."

"Indeed, sir." Then Northcutt reached into his leather case and pulled out an envelope. "Speaking of firelocks, here is a Bill of Credit in payment for the last batch of muskets you sent down to Williamsburg."

Wend took the note and placed it in a chest.

"Now, Eckert, here's an important question: How soon can you have the batch of muskets you are nearly finished with down to Williamsburg?"

Wend looked into the fire as if he were seriously considering the question. "It depends on two things: First, the availability of freight wagons, and second, the condition of the roads. We're overdue for the spring rains."

Northcutt pulled on his cigar, considering what Wend had said. "All right, Eckert; just get them to us as soon as you can. And I admonish you to accelerate as much as possible the work on the second batch of fifty muskets."

"Barrett, you know it normally takes months to finish the overhaul of each lot. And we can't get started until we finish the first group."

"Eckert, these aren't normal times. We may soon need every musket we can put in hand."

"Does this have something to do with the conditions in Boston?"

"Listen, Eckert, you heard what Welford said when he joined us last fall. Things have only gotten worse in Massachusetts and frankly we are seeing more signs of resistance to the Crown here in Virginia. And then there are those treasonous resolutions coming from the Congress in Philadelphia."

"Are you saying that the people have not rallied to the governor, even after the Ohio campaign? Wasn't that the reason for the expedition?"

Northcutt grimaced and took a quick puff on his cigar. "No, damnation! The war did not have the desired effect. And that cursed Fort Gower Resolve, published in the Gazette, made things worse. Do you know that it has even been read before the House of Commons? Those damned officers played us false."

"So now you may need these muskets to use against an actual uprising of the colonists?"

"Yes, Eckert, the fear of such conflict is palpable in Williamsburg."

"Barrett, I've heard about the governor's seizure of the powder at the Williamsburg magazine. Actions like that will just put fuel on the fire."

"Eckert, there's no doubt that things are rapidly coming to a head. And that brings us to the real reason I've come to see you." Northcutt reached down into his case and pulled out several papers. He laid one on the table. "Here is your grant of 10,000 acres in the southern Ohio Country. The governor was most insistent that you receive a generous amount for your valiant services during the late war."

Wend picked up the document and skimmed it quickly. "I must tell you, Barrett; I have never been much interested in land on the border. The amount I have here has always seemed adequate to my needs."

"You would be a fool not to take it, Eckert. Consider it an investment for future sale."

"I can't argue with that, Barrett."

Northcutt handed Wend another paper. "Here is your commission as a captain in the King's Loyal Virginia Regiment."

"I've never heard of that regiment. And why am I receiving another commission?"

"The regiment will be raised if the Whigs start an armed insurgency. By the grace of Lord Dunmore, I will be its Lieutenant Colonel Commandant and Reggie Welford will be the senior major. Your captaincy, as is the custom in these matters, is contingent upon you raising a company of men." Northcutt handed Wend the last paper. "This is a second grant of ten thousand acres, valid when you report with your company to the regimental rendezvous."

"I'm not a soldier, Barrett. I just acted like one during the last war."

"Don't be silly, Eckert. You led two sharp actions and showed a good head for independent duty. Many people have heard of your role. We expect you'll have an easy time recruiting among the German people here in Frederick County."

Wend found himself speechless, looking down at the parchment in his hands.

Northcutt smiled broadly at Wend. "Now, Eckert, here is the best news of all for you: Lord Dunmore has just sent out letters to this rogue Washington and many other large landowners who we know are among the ringleaders of this unrest. He's giving them due warning that their property will be forfeit if they participate in this insanity. Once we have put down the uprising, officers such as you who have been loyal to the Crown and the governor will be the beneficiaries of their confiscated land, among the choicest properties in the colony. You will be a rich man."

Wend rose from his chair. He dropped the commission and contingent grant into Northcutt's lap. "I'll not do it, Northcutt. I'll not go to war against my neighbors and friends. Take these back to the governor and tell him I'm not one of his men."

"You can't be serious, Eckert. Think of the financial implications of losing the balance of this musket work. You can be certain the payment you just received will be the last."

"The governor can have his contract, Barrett. I've taken measures to replace the income."

Northcutt's face contorted into a scowl. "Then think of your safety and that of your family. This incipient rebellion, this treason, is doomed to failure. The King's forces will put it down ruthlessly, just like the Highland rebellion thirty years ago. Ask your friend McDonald what it was like after Culloden."

"I'm through being compelled by threats, Barrett. Now you listen to this: I'm German by birth, Ulster by adoption, ..."

Northcutt cut him off scornfully. "What is this? I damn well know your lineage, Eckert."

"Stop interrupting, Barrett, and hear me out: "I'm a Highlander by battle, and a Virginian by the order of a Pennsylvania sheriff. But by God, I'll choose sides in this uprising by my own free will! Do you understand, Barrett? My own free will! You're through controlling me!"

Northcutt's response was not as Wend had expected.

Instead of reacting with anger, a great calmness came over him. He sat silently for a long moment. Then he sighed and said in a sad tone, "I'm sorry you have taken this position. But I can understand your passion in this moment.

Perhaps if you think things over, you will change your mind." He carefully put the commission and land grant papers on the side table. "I will leave these with you, Wend. If you do come to your senses, simply send a letter to me saying you have accepted the commission and all will be as before."

Barrett stood up, picked up his leather case and took his hat in hand. Wend escorted him to the hall and then the front door.

As they reached the entrance, Northcutt turned and said, almost wistfully, "You know, Eckert, this is rather inconvenient. I was traveling down to Williamsburg from Pittsburgh with Welford, Grenough, and one of his men. We stopped in Winchester for business, with others as well as you. But in fact, Grenough and his man left today to go on to Fredericksburg for some business of his own. Welford and I stayed on at the Golden Buck so I could see you. If I'd known the outcome, we could have traveled with Grenough. He planned to camp near the Shenandoah tonight and take Ashby's Ferry first thing in the morning."

"Barrett, I'm sorry to be the cause of your inconvenience."

Northcutt sighed, "Well, there's nothing for it now. We'll leave tomorrow and catch up with him in Fredericksburg."

"I bid you a safe journey, Barrett."

"Well, Eckert, we've been friends and associates in some important matters. I'd like to think you'll change your mind when you have time to reconsider." He smiled and held out his hand. "Who knows what the future will bring in these troubled times, but at least we can part amicably."

Wend shook his hand and then Northcutt descended the steps and mounted. Wend watched as he rode down the drive.

In a moment Peggy was beside him. "What happened, Wend? What did he want?"

Wend turned to his wife. "Well, for better or worse, I've made my break with him and Governor Dunmore. They wanted me to lead troops for the King if rebellion breaks out. So I told him I'd never fight against other Virginians and the musket contract be damned."

Peggy put her arms on Wend's. "Oh, Wend, you stood up to him! I've never been so proud of you. I know we'll have to be careful with money for a while, but I'm sure we will make it and all will be well in the end."

"Yes, I'm glad that it is settled. But I have something I must do now. I'm riding out immediately for Ashby's Ferry."

"To Ashby's? My God, that's hours away. Why on earth are you going there?"

"Richard Grenough is camping on this side of the Shenandoah tonight and I'm riding to finish things with him. I'm sending him to hell this very night."

Peggy Eckert's face changed from happiness to horror. And with full understanding of what Wend intended came instant anger. She gritted her teeth, the muscles in her face standing out. "You can't be serious!"

But Wend was already down the steps and striding rapidly toward the stable.

CHAPTER TWENTY-TWO
Ride to Retribution

Peggy stamped her foot. Her eyes were burning with anger, her teeth gritted together, her face flushing as she glared at Wend. "This is insane! Insane, do you hear me? You're abandoning your family for the sake of some fifteen-year-old pledge no one cares about."

They were standing in front of the workshop in the growing dusk as Wend prepared to depart. Wend was beside The Mare, adjusting the girth. The horse had been in the pasture for many weeks and was excited by the prospect of doing some work. She pawed the ground restlessly and snorted her impatience to be off.

Wend turned to look at his wife. "This is about a pledge I made to my father over his grave. I mean to keep it."

Johann came out of the shop with Wend's pistols and holsters. "I've loaded them, Father."

Wend nodded and placed them in front of the saddle and lashed them in place. He turned to Johann. "Lad, bring me the new firelock — the short rifle and its sheath."

Johann nodded and scurried back into the shop.

Peggy waited until Johann had disappeared, then said, "You're going to be killed. Don't you care what will happen to your family? What will become of us without you?

"I have no intention of being killed. Grenough has no idea I'm coming; I'll take him by surprise. Peggy, listen to me: I *will* be back."

The boy arrived with the rifle, a powder horn, and a pouch containing balls. Wend attached the rifle sheath on the right side below the saddle, then slipped the straps of the accoutrements over his shoulders. He looked at Johann. "There's a short-handled axe on the wall by my desk. Please fetch it."

Peggy stamped her foot again. "If you go, I'll leave you. I swear I will. I'll take the children and go to my parents back in Sherman Valley."

Wend stared at her for a long moment with his stone face. Peggy felt his eyes boring into her. Then he shook his head slowly, made the slightest smile, and said, "No, you won't; you won't leave. Your greatest desire as a young girl was to get out of Sherman Mill. Winchester and this farm are your home now; they've become part of who you are and you'll not leave the life you've made to return to the backwoods of Sherman Valley." He mounted and looked down at her. "We both know there's been a wall of ice between us since I brought the boy back; we'll work this out when I return."

Johann came back with the hatchet and handed it up to Wend, who slipped it into his belt. He smiled at the youth then reached down and squeezed him on the shoulder. He looked over at Peggy and said in a calm tone. "Grenough is not far down the road. I'll finish the business and be back in the morning."

Peggy watched as Wend touched his heels to The Mare's sides, took her down the drive at the trot, and then turned southward on the wagon road. He did not look back. Peggy knew his mind was already focused on the grim things he must do that night. She and Johann stood silently watching until he disappeared behind the trees along the road. For a few seconds longer Peggy could hear the sound of hooves and then all was silent.

Johann walked over to her and, reading the dismay on her face, put his hand on her arm. It was the first time he had ever touched her. Then he said in a solemn tone, "Do not worry, Mrs. Eckert. Father is a great and crafty warrior. He will defeat his enemy and come back to us."

* * *

Wend headed south, The Mare's hooves pounding on the hard-packed surface of the wagon track. He took thanks that the heavy spring rains had held off, or they would have been struggling through deep muck. He looked up; clouds moved across the sky, propelled by a gusty wind. But there was still enough moonlight for him to see the way. Meanwhile, he noted the power of The Mare's stride. It was clear that in her long convalescence she had recovered her strength. Wend listened carefully for a few minutes and was soon satisfied that the animal had enough wind to maintain the pace he had set.

Once sure of the horse, he started thinking of his quarry. The road ahead ran southward for several miles; then it angled southeastwardly toward the

Shenandoah and the ferry. Northcutt had said that Grenough would camp just short of Ashby's Ferry and then make an early morning crossing. That meant Wend had around two hours ride ahead of him until he would be in the proximity of the campsite. Given the April chill in the night air, he was confident that the merchant would keep a fire going; little did he know it would serve as a beacon for Wend. Barrett had also said that Grenough was traveling with a single retainer. Wend wondered if it was McCrae or Bratton, or someone else. Either way, that man would have to forfeit his life alongside his leader. There was no other choice but to eliminate any witnesses if Wend was to accomplish his task without finding himself facing trial. Given their complicity, Wend felt no hesitation at the thought of dealing with any of Grenough's henchmen.

At first the country was relatively open, with fields, pastures, and farmsteads along the road. Candlelight glowed in the windows of dwellings. But after the first hour, there were no more lights and the number of fields bordering the road diminished. Finally the forest closed in around Wend and The Mare, the tree branches overhanging the road to form a dark, unbroken tunnel. The wind picked up, producing a steady rustling of the tree branches.

Perhaps it was the gloominess of the forest, or maybe it was simply weariness catching up with him after a long day filled with work and contentious events. But Wend's spirits, which had been high upon leaving Eckert Ridge, began to flag as he rode on, his mind increasingly occupied with depressing thoughts.

First, he could not stop thinking about Peggy and their marriage. For ten years he had felt secure and happy living with her. Their marriage had seemed strong. But ever since the day he had told her that he must leave for the governor's war, the palpable strain between them had been like a constant cloud over him. And then there was the problem of young Johann's presence. Wend had anticipated some difficulty about bringing him to Eckert Ridge, but he had been shocked at the depth of Peggy's antipathy and her angry refusal to accept him into the family. He was at wit's end to find some way to make her understand his need to have the boy in his life. Wend felt a lump form in his stomach at the thought of a disintegration of his family; he tried to shake off the problem and concentrate on the desperate job ahead, but his mind kept coming back to the threat Peggy had made just before he left. He knew she would not carry out the vow to leave him, but the fact that she had even thought to say such a thing weighed heavily on his mind. They had argued in the past, but never had she even come close to making the threat of leaving.

Then his mind returned to what he was about this night. As The Mare bore him through the dense darkness of the forest, he began to worry. Doubts grew in his mind about his abilities and chances against the odds of two to one. He knew that his success depended on surprise, but what if something gave him away? What if he found himself against an alerted Grenough and his retainer? His mind began to run through all the things which could go wrong. In earlier years, thoughts of failure had never entered his mind, or if they did, he immediately banished them. But he had last embarked on a mission of this nature a decade ago; then he had been full of the strength and immortality of a twenty year old. Moreover, he had been single and poor, with no one depending on him. The only thing he had to lose was his own life.

But now things were different. His mind flashed to his family. He thought of the children: Bernd, Johann, Elise, and Ellen. He thought of the farm and the shop. Suddenly, for the first time since he had determined to go after Grenough, he began contemplate actual consequences of his failing tonight. The truth was, if he died, the family would indeed be in dire straits. Peggy would have to sell the farm for whatever she could get. The money would last for a while, but she would soon be unable to support the family. Then she would have two choices: Remarriage or return to her parents in the tavern at Sherman Mill.

These thoughts kept running through Wend's mind, like a horse doomed to endlessly gallop around a racetrack.

Presently he pulled up at a creek which crossed the road. It was swift flowing, and undoubtedly ran down to the Shenandoah, which he realized could not be far ahead. Clearly they were getting close to Grenough's camp. Wend dismounted and led The Mare down the steep bank to the water.

He gave the horse her head to drink. Because of the high banks, it was deathly quiet in the stream bed, the sounds of the forest muffled; the only noise was the running of the water. The cloud cover had increased so that the sky above was only intermittently illuminated by the moon. Wend guessed it was about an hour before midnight. As he stood there, isolated in the vast forest, his fears and self-doubt reached a crescendo. His mind formed the words which until then he had not dared recognize: *For God's sake, what am I doing out here by myself riding to commit murder? In the end, what will it achieve, whether I triumph or am defeated and lose my life? Will it benefit my family in any way if I succeed? Who will rejoice at Grenough's death besides myself?* Suddenly he was convinced of one thing above all others: *Being here was an act of his own selfishness. Peggy had been right all the time.*

At that moment Wend Eckert resolved to abandon the quest, turn around, and ride back to Eckert Ridge. If he did that now, nothing would be lost. He and his family would be secure.

Wend looked at The Mare; she had finished drinking and was staring straight ahead, waiting for whatever came next. Wend led the horse back up the bank to the road and put his left foot into the stirrup to mount. "Come on, old girl, we're going home."

Then, as he swung up into the saddle, he suddenly caught sight, in the corner of his eye, of a brief glimmer of light. He turned and looked harder; it was toward the east in the direction of the Shenandoah. Then it disappeared.

He froze, staring toward the place where he had seen the light. But all was darkness. Had he imagined it? Then suddenly the light reappeared and shone brightly, like flames fed by a gust of wind or because of wood thrown onto the coals.

By God, it had to be Grenough's camp.

Wend held The Mare still as he watched the distant fire for several minutes; it alternately flared up and then faded to a mere point of light.

The brain is a strange and mischievous thing. The sight of the fire triggered a near forgotten memory in Wend's mind. It transported him back through time to another fire; the fire at their campsite on Forbes Road in front of Fort Lyttleton in 1759, on the night before the massacre. Magistrate Gibson had discovered Wend and Abigail in passionate embrace and had exploded in anger. Then he had castigated Johann Eckert for letting his son impose himself on his daughter, obviously of a social status far above a simple mechanic's son. Wend had expected to be dressed down by his father, but surprisingly Johann had vociferously defended him to the Magistrate. The two men had all but come to blows. Later, Johann had shared a draught with Wend in front of the fire, man to man, explaining with pride about their family's German heritage and particularly about their descent from the jaeger class. And most importantly for the business at hand, he had explained how a jaeger, once set upon his prey, never wavered until he had hunted it to destruction.

Wend looked at the fire in the distance and knew in his bones that his prey was there. The prey he had sworn to pursue and destroy. And suddenly the doubts and fear he had felt down in the creek bed were banished. Wend Eckert, jaeger of Hesse-Cassel, with single minded purpose, turned The Mare toward the Shenandoah. Then he kicked her in the side, swiftly rode down the bank, splashed through the little stream, and drove the animal up the other bank to the road.

Whatever it took, he would complete his pledge to his father before the sun rose.

* * *

Peggy stood still in front of the workshop for a few moments after Wend had departed. An all-pervasive silence seemed to settle around her and Johann. Then, after a few moments she began to feel the chill of the night. Shivering, she turned and returned to the house. Entering the parlor, she went to the liquor cabinet, took out a jug of Donegal's whiskey, and poured herself a full pewter cup's worth. Then she lighted a candle lantern from the hearth. Finally, she went to her sewing room, grabbed her black cloak from a peg on the wall and, whiskey and lantern in hand, went back to the porch. She placed the lantern on a hook by the door and settled herself into one of the chairs; she would wait here until Wend came back or it became evident that he would never return.

Then Peggy saw that Johann was still there in the drive. He was right across from the porch, crouched down on his haunches, his arms around his knees, sitting absolutely still, staring down the drive.

"Johann," Peggy called out, "There's no need for you to wait here. Go to bed."

The boy sat still for a long moment, showing no sign that he had heard. Then he slowly turned to look at her, but with no change in the position of the rest of his body. He displayed the blank, expressionless face she had seen so often on Wend. Then he said, "I will wait here until my father returns from battle."

Peggy didn't respond at first. Instead she took a deep gulp of the whiskey. She welcomed the burning feeling as it went down and almost immediately began to feel the warming sensation of the alcohol. She savored the taste for a moment, then said to the boy, "All right, Johann; suit yourself."

Her thoughts returned to the words that had passed between herself and Wend before his departure. She sighed; already Peggy regretted the threat she had made to leave her husband. Of course she would not leave Wend. The threat had been born of her anxiety and anger, which had exploded to the point of total emotion rather than rationality. His response, delivered with an impassive face and assurance that her words were empty, had infuriated her even more.

Peggy glanced at Johann. He remained frozen in place, his eyes staring down the drive as if they could penetrate the darkness. She marveled at his still-ness and patience. Obviously it was a trait he had learned in the Mingo village. She had been quietly observing the boy over the months since he had arrived at Eckert Ridge. He was undeniably a physical copy of Wend. Even more, despite the Indian upbringing, his manner was also a near duplicate of his father.

The two of them, distant companions, waited wordlessly for perhaps a half-hour more. Then suddenly Johann raised his head ever so slightly and became even stiffer than before, if that was possible. He remained that way for perhaps a minute. Then he looked over at Peggy. "Wagons coming, Mrs. Eckert; coming down the road from the north. They're almost at our drive now."

Peggy thought for a moment, then said, "That's strange; who could be traveling this late at night?"

Johann shook his head slightly by way of answer, still listening closely. Then he suddenly rose to his feet and quickly walked down the drive until he was in front of the workshop.

"What's happening, Johann?"

"Wagons are turning into the drive, Mrs. Eckert."

Peggy put her drink down, pulled her cloak tightly around her shoulders, and went to join the boy. She stood quietly beside him and now she could hear the noise of wagons climbing the drive, getting louder as they came. "You're right, Johann."

"I expect it's Mr. Baird and Mr. Donegal, Mrs. Eckert; back from Ransome's Tavern."

"This late at night?" Then she realized he must be right. Other travelers would have stopped for the night by now.

Suddenly something was moving in the darkness and then she saw a horse and rider. She squinted to make him out. It was Joshua! Joshua riding with his rifle slung over his shoulder, mounted on his great hunter. Then, in the moonlight, she could see a wagon with Donegal driving, a young blond woman beside him, holding a child in her arms. A few seconds later she made out another wagon behind and soon was able to recognize Joe Specht driving it, with a little girl on the seat beside him.

Joshua pulled up the horse in front of the shop and dismounted stiffly. "Hello, Peggy, my lass. We was so close to home when dusk settled that we just figured to keep goin' through the darkness."

Peggy ran to him. "Joshua, I'm so glad to see you! You've got to help. Wend is in great danger!"

Joshua smiled and said, "Whoa, girl! Slow down. How is Wend in danger?"

"He's gone after Grenough to kill him! Grenough is camping on the Ashby Ferry Road and Wend rode out just at darkness to find him. Oh, for God's sake, you've got to ride after him!"

Joshua put his hands on Peggy's shoulders. "Settle down, girl. You're beside yourself. Give me the whole story."

Peggy took a deep breath. Then, calming somewhat, she gave him the details.

As she was talking, Donegal came up beside them and listened. Then he put his hand on Peggy's arm. "Now, lass, sounds to me like its 'na Wend who's in danger, it be Grenough, that filthy bastard!"

Peggy shook her head. "Who knows what could happen? Joshua, you've got to ride after him in case he needs help."

Baird and Donegal looked at each other. Then Baird said, "I've been gettin' the Sprout out of trouble since back in '59. So of course I'll go. And so will Donegal."

"That's the truth," answered the Highlander.

Joshua turned to Johann. "But we'll be needin' fresh horses, lad. These have been goin' all day and they're plain wore out. Take them down to the stable." He handed the reins to the boy. "Get us a pair of strong horses saddled. I'd say Boots and Whiteface. They both got good strides and good wind."

Donegal turned back to the lead wagon. "Meanwhile, I got to get Mrs. Donegal and the children down to my place. Come and meet my lassie, Peggy. Then we'll be out of here before you know it."

And indeed they were. Twenty minutes later Peggy watched as the two men spurred their mounts down the drive into the darkness.

* * *

Wend found himself appreciating the gusty wind. It had been unsettling as he rode through the dark forest, but now as he approached the flickering fire ahead, he realized that the rustling sound of the trees would cover the noise of The Mare's hooves and allow him to leave her in a hiding place close to Grenough's campsite. The gusts were also causing the flames to flare up frequently, making it easier for him to keep his bearings as he moved along the road.

Wend found a little open space in the woods which he judged to be about fifty yards short of the fire and secured The Mare out of sight from the road. He pulled the pistols from the holsters and stuck them into his belt, then withdrew the rifle from its sheath. He made ready to enter the bush and make a slow, stealthy approach to the campsite. He took a single step and then stopped abruptly as a thought struck him: *Feeling his way through the woods was not necessary.* There was a better strategy, one which would take less time and would minimize the chance of causing an inadvertent noise in the underbrush. He turned around and carefully walked out to the edge of the road. He looked eastward, making sure all was clear, then crouched and crossed the wagon track to the far side. Once there, he began walking slowly, carefully along the edge toward a point opposite the fire. He would be hard to see along the side, and he could perhaps get a clear view of the campsite from the road.

He inched along the side of the wagon track, ready to drop to the ground or take cover in the bush if the necessity arose. After what seemed an eternity he reached a position where he could see into the camp. It was in a small, cleared, grassy area which Wend thought had probably often been used by travelers on the way to the ferry. He could see the fire and on the opposite side sat Richard Grenough himself. He was facing Wend and for an instant Wend had the unnerving feeling that the merchant was looking directly at him. But then Wend saw that the Irishman McCrae, who was sitting across the fire from Grenough, was the actual recipient of his stare. The two were engaged in conversation. Grenough's dog was lying beside the fire. Obviously the two were not aware of his presence.

Wend quickly formed his plan. He would take McCrae with a quick head shot from the rifle and then rapidly move in and cover Grenough with his pistols. He wished that Grenough's companion had been Bratton, for he had no real desire to kill the Irishman, but there was no other choice. In any case, he would then finish Grenough with a pistol shot, but only after he was sure that the man knew who was killing him.

Wend looked down and carefully, silently, cocked the rifle.

Suddenly he heard a pounding of footsteps on the hard ground of the road and looked up to see the terrifying vision of Matt Bratton, looking gigantic in the moonlight, coming toward him at full tilt, arms outstretched. Before he could react, Bratton smashed into him, knocking him to the ground and landing on top. The breath was literally knocked out of Wend and he gasped for air.

"Now I've got you, you bastard. Got you after ten years, Dutchman, and Grenough's given me free rein to finish you." As he spoke, Bratton's hands closed around Wend's neck. Wend had not been able to get his wind back and now the encircling hands were pressing in on his throat. His lungs began to burn. Then Wend felt Bratton's right thumb feel its way up the side of his face until it touched his left eye.

"That's right Dutchman, I'm going to pop your eyes right out of your head before I finish you, just for the pleasure of it. Take your last look around, 'cause you'll die a blind man."

Wend's arms were pinned beneath Bratton's chest. But he was somehow able to yank his right arm free. Then he grabbed one of the pistols in his belt. Instantly he pulled it back, cocked the hammer, put the muzzle against Bratton's side, and squeezed the trigger. The pistol fired with a crack which reverberated through the night.

Bratton's eyes opened wide and he expelled a burst of rancid breath which smelled of meat and rum. But more importantly, his hands instantly loosened and Wend was able to push him away and to the ground. Wend sprang to his knees and pulled his knife from its sheath and, without hesitation, drove it deep into Bratton's ribs just below the heart.

Matt Bratton's face formed into an expression of bewilderment, then he looked up to the sky and said three words only: *Mother! Oh, Mother!*

Then Wend heard a gurgle from Bratton's mouth, felt the big man's body go all limp, and knew he was gone. *My God, thought Wend. This hard, villainous man cries out like an innocent child for his mother at the moment of his death!*

Then there was the sound of running steps coming toward Wend. He looked around just in time to see McCrae right in front of him. He had a horse pistol in his hand and was swinging it. Before Wend could react the barrel smashed into his face and the world went blurry. Wend was conscious, but stunned, unable to control his limbs.

McCrae grabbed Wend by the collar and pulled him toward the fire. Wend half-walked, half-stumbled along, dizzy and unable to fully control his legs. Several times he fell to the ground and the big Irishman yanked him up. Finally they were at the fire and McCrae let Wend collapse onto the ground. He shook his head, trying to rid himself of the dizziness.

McCrae quickly tied Wend's hands behind him with a leather strap. Wend's head cleared somewhat and he looked up into the smiling face of Richard Grenough, who was sitting in the same position as when Wend had first seen him. As he watched, Grenough reached down and grasped a bottle of whiskey. He poured himself a pewter cup full of the liquor.

"Well, Eckert, we've been waiting for you. You certainly took your time getting here."

Wend tried to speak, but found his mouth hard to work. He felt blood running all over his face and could tell his lips were beginning to swell.

Meanwhile, McCrae spoke up. "Sure and he finished Bratton before I could get there, Mr. Grenough."

Grenough looked out into the dark in the direction of the road and sighed. "Pity." Then he reflected a moment, looking down at his cup. "But actually, McCrae, I believe Eckert here did our companion a favor. He's been a tortured soul ever since that fight ten years ago."

McCrae nodded. "I'd say you're right, sir. God knows, Bratton's been fighting demons in his head and had those attacks of pain as long as I've known him."

"Yes, he's been a shattered man because of Eckert here."

Wend finally was able to speak. He asked through the swollen lips, "How did you know I was coming?"

Grenough shook his head. "Eckert, I'm embarrassed by how bemused you look. Of course, it was all by plan. If you had accepted Barrett Northcutt's offer of a commission, you'd still be up at your farm, in bed with your wife. He wouldn't have told you where I was traveling. But when you turned it down, and essentially declared for the Whig cause, you recall that he carefully told you about my location. Then when he left, McCrae here was waiting on the road close to your home to meet with him and carry the word to me post-haste. We were quite certain you would leap at the opportunity to finish me."

Grenough pointed to the big dog which lay at his side. "And of course, my dog here has been trained to quietly signal the approach of strangers. That's one of the reasons I've always felt safe traveling the roads. He alerted us and then we stationed Bratton in the woods to intercept you."

Wend asked, "I don't understand why Northcutt would connive with you to get me killed."

"Oh don't be obtuse, Eckert. You knew too much about the details of how the recent war was instigated; you had been at confidential meetings of Dunmore's inner circle, and Northcutt had told you about the military plans for holding Virginia. So if you didn't commit to the loyal side, it was imperative that you be taken out of the picture, permanently."

Wend made an effort to smile, but it proved extraordinarily painful and he was not sure if his lips were doing what he desired. "And it was also very convenient for you."

"Ah yes, there was a remarkable convergence of interest. And of course, I achieve the peace of mind I've long desired. No more looking over my shoulder to see if you are about to fulfill your pledge of vengeance." Grenough took a long sip of his whiskey.

Wend sighed. "I guess I was a fool not to think of a trap."

"Oh, I wouldn't feel too remorseful, Eckert. It was all rather skillfully laid out, if I do say so myself." He paused and sipped again. "There weren't any obvious clues. So you can go to eternity without any real regrets. And, of course, you have the consolation of having sent Bratton to glory ahead of yourself."

"I'm sure you'll feel great satisfaction shooting me, Grenough. Why don't you get on with it?"

"Oh, my dear Eckert, indeed I will take immeasurable pleasure at your demise. But I'm not going to do the sordid deed myself. By now you should know that's not my style." He motioned toward McCrae with his cup. "That was going to be Bratton's job, but now I'll let the loyal Mr. McCrae perform the actual execution." He paused and smiled at Wend. "And speaking of that, there's no sense in delaying any longer. The night is wearing on and we must dispose of two bodies before we take the ferry in the morning. Please proceed, McCrae."

The Irishman raised the pistol to Eckert's temple. Then he said, "Mind now, Eckert, I am not taking any pleasure at this. It's just a job of work."

Wend took a deep breath and tensed his body.

And then a voice with a deep Irish brogue said, "Now, me fine lad, let's see you lower that pistol. Nobody's doing any shooting at just this moment, unless it be myself."

Wend, Grenough, and McCrae all turned their heads simultaneously toward the sound of the voice, which came from the direction of the road. Standing there was a man holding two cocked horse pistols aimed at the group by the fire. He had a nose which had been broken many times, a scar on the left side of his face, and half of his left ear missing.

In astonishment, Wend realized it was the Irish highwayman who had led the band which robbed him and Peggy.

There was a noise in the bush and then several other rough looking men came out of the forest at intervals around the camp, all pointing either pistols or rifles.

The dog took one look at all the strangers and firelocks and took off into the bush.

Grenough looked after the fleeing animal and shook his head. "He always was skittish around guns."

A brief silence persisted, then an elegantly attired, golden-haired young man walked past the scarred Irishman and into the light of the fire. He was dressed all in black and was holding a brace of finely finished, small-bored pistols in his hands.

My God, thought Wend: Geoffrey Caulfield!

Caulfield, a broad grin on his face, stood surveying the scene. Then he said, "We were camping in a little cove just up the road, when we heard the sharp report of a firelock. A shot fired so late at night obviously aroused our interest and we thought it appropriate to join the party, as it were."

Suddenly the Irish highwayman exclaimed, "Mother of Mary! Is that you, Freddie McCrae? After all these years?"

McCrae squinted at the other Irishman. "Lord above, its Corporal Quinn! I've not laid eyes on you since I left the 11th Dragoons back in '62."

Quinn turned to Caulfield. "Cap'n, this be one of my mates from Lieutenant Sullivan's troop of the old 11th! He's a good man."

Without saying anything, Caulfield walked over to McCrae. While holding his right pistol on the Irishman, he put his left pistol in his belt and cautiously reached out and put his left hand on the barrel of McCrae's horse pistol and said, "I'm gratified to see such a fond reunion. But be that as it may, regretfully I must insist on taking charge of this firelock for the present, sir. I fear it might go off at an inopportune moment."

McCrae shrugged and smiled thinly. "As you please, Your Lordship."

Caulfield took the pistol and handed it to a black man. Then he walked over to Grenough. "I beg your pardon, sir. But I would be negligent if I didn't relieve you of the weapons I'm confident that you have in your possession."

Grenough sighed. "Naturally, sir." Then he reached down beside the tail of his coat, produced a pistol, and handed it to Caulfield.

Caulfield smiled thinly. "And the other, sir? A gentleman of your stature would undoubtedly carry a brace."

Grenough shook his head in resignation. "Sir, you are quite perceptive." Then he produced another pistol from his left side. "One does have to be prepared."

Caulfield nodded and said, "I understand completely, sir. One always faces the danger of encountering blackguards while on the road."

Grenough looked around at the gunmen surrounding the campsite, and said ironically, "Precisely, sir."

Then Caulfield turned to Wend. He looked him over and then shook his head. "Bless my soul if it's not the Dutchman Eckert. My dear sir, you are certainly looking the worse for wear." He reached under his coat and, producing a small knife, bent down and sliced through the strap binding Wend's hands. Then he retrieved a handkerchief and offered it to Wend. "Perhaps you would like to take a moment to wipe your face before we proceed with business."

Wend used the cloth to clean his face, while Caulfield surveyed the campsite. Then he turned back to Wend. "I confess to being extremely puzzled by this little vignette; perhaps you would care to enlighten me as to what you are doing here in the middle of the night, with the esteemed Trooper McCrae, late of His Majesty's 11th Dragoons, holding a pistol to your head."

Wend gathered his thoughts and opened his mouth to explain when Caulfield suddenly held up his hand. "Oh, wait." He turned and pointed toward the road. "Eckert, am I to believe that you have something to do with the rather large corpse laying out on the wagon track?"

Grenough interjected, "Of course he does. He was attempting to kill me and my men."

Caulfield looked at Grenough, then back at Wend. "Judging from the situation we found when we arrived, he didn't seem to be doing very well." He shook his head. "In any case, it's hard for me to credit that Mr. Wend Eckert, gunsmith of Winchester, rode out into the night by himself to kill three men; hardly attractive odds for a simple mechanic."

Grenough's face reflected puzzlement. "Might I ask how you know Eckert?"

"Why sir, I've patronized his gun shop," He held up one of his pistols, "And enjoyed the hospitality of his table."

A look of concern swept over the merchant's face, then disappeared. He said, "The fact is, Eckert is much more than a simple mechanic. In truth, I know him to be a remorseless murderer." He paused a moment, then said, "Might I know who you are?"

Caulfield shrugged. "I should think it would be rather obvious that we are gentlemen of the road and our business quite evident. The precise names are quite irrelevant." He paused and looked around the camp. "And it is time we are about our business."

Wend saw Caulfield motion toward one of his men. And then he noticed it wasn't a man at all, but a woman in man's clothing, wearing a coat, breeches, and a black, wide-brimmed hat. He looked at her face, and realized she was a high mulatto, with near-white features. The woman nodded to Caulfield, put the pistol she had been holding into a pocket, and began going through all the baggage and other items in the campsite.

Caulfield motioned toward the woman and smiled at Grenough. "Sarah is very efficient at finding valuables. She was a maid for many years and knows all the places the wealthy use in hiding their possessions while traveling." He stepped up to the merchant. "Meanwhile, it would be easier for us all if you expeditiously handed over the purse and any valuables you have on your person."

Grenough grimaced, then reached into a coat pocket and pulled out a small bag. "Here is my money, sir. There is a considerable amount there. And you are quite welcome to it if you leave me to my journey and my business with Eckert."

"My dear sir, your generosity is gratifying. But the plain truth is that we are going to have the purse in any case and we're going to have anything else of value." He looked back at Wend, then said to Grenough, "Meanwhile, I would be obliged if you would continue your explanation of why you consider Mr. Eckert such a disreputable fellow."

Wend had finished wiping his face, and took the opportunity to speak up. He said through his swollen lips, "It's true I'm here to send this man to his rewards; he is a scoundrel who deserves to die."

Caulfield turned back to Wend and cocked his head. "This is very intriguing. We have two men who each claim the other is a villain. But, proceed, Eckert."

"This man is Richard Grenough, a Pennsylvania merchant and schemer who has caused much misery to me and the people of that colony and Virginia. He's arranged many conspiracies and caused scores of deaths."

The highwayman looked at Grenough and then back at Wend. "This man? He looks like an aging swell to me, not an arch-villain. You're going to have to do better than that, Eckert."

"In '59, his men led Indians to kill my entire family and caused a beautiful English girl from Philadelphia to spend her life as a prisoner of the Mingo. After the massacre, I found that he was leading a conspiracy to provide war supplies to the Indians during the French war and Pontiac's War. I caught him and his men at it several times. In '63 he instigated the murder of the Conestoga Indians near Lancaster to cover up his dealing with the hostile tribes. Then he helped stir up the Ulster-Scots in the Susquehanna Valley to rebel against Pennsylvania in 1764."

Caulfield held up his hand and looked at his compatriots. "I heard about that." He broke into a wide grin. "However, I never thought that arousing the border men against all those fat, arrogant Quakers in Philadelphia was a crime!"

The band of highwaymen all broke into laughter.

Frustrated, Wend continued, "And just last April, he engineered the massacre of a peaceful band of Indians out on the Ohio. The ten year old son of a great friend of mine was killed there and it started the recent war with the Shawnees."

From behind, Wend heard Quinn laughing. "That war drew all the men away in the militia; it sure made life easier for us around here!"

There were nods of agreement from the band of highwaymen.

Caulfield said, "So you see, Eckert, it is all a matter of perspective. What seems despicable to you is looked at rather differently by others."

Wend looked around at the grinning, laughing men. He sighed, despairing about his ability to convince Caulfield. He felt sweat rolling down his face as he desperately tried to think of something which would make it clear why Grenough had to die.

Just then Grenough took advantage of the pause. He pointed at Wend and said, "Look, the fact is that Eckert is making this up out of whole cloth. I'm a legitimate merchant. I trade with border settlers at my stores in Bedford, Ligonier, and Pittsburgh. I've been providing supplies to the militia for the war in Ohio. In fact, I'm on my way to Williamsburg now to settle accounts with the government." He paused and looked up at Caulfield. "The truth is, Eckert is a cold-blooded murderer, just like I said before. In 1764 he killed two of my men by rifle fire and then burned a wagonload of goods they were taking to Fort Bedford. He's wanted by the High Sheriff of Cumberland County in Pennsylvania for that crime; that's why he had to flee that colony ten years ago."

Caulfield put his hands on his hips and looked down at Wend. "Eckert, now damned if I'm not impressed by that more than anything else I've heard tonight; if this gentleman is correct, you're a first rate criminal masquerading as a respectable gunsmith."

Quinn said, "Damned if he ain't a man after our own hearts, Cap'n."

The band of highwaymen laughed and clapped at Quinn's wit.

Grenough continued. "Now listen to me! The fact is, Eckert's whole life is based on lies. Not only is he a murderer posing as an honest tradesman, his wife is a well-known tart. Men from all over the Cumberland Valley used to travel to Sherman Mill to partake of her services. In fact, Eckert's oldest son isn't even his own; he's the spawn of her whoring! The pair of them are not fit to keep company with respectable society."

The smile on Caulfield's face instantly disappeared. He gritted his teeth and Wend could see the muscles in his face standing out. The highwayman's back stiffened and his hands closed into fists. He slowly turned to face Grenough. "Sir, say that again, for I want to be sure I've heard you correctly."

Grenough winked conspiratorially. "It's the simple truth, sir. Peggy McCartie, now Peggy Eckert, was a well-known whore who worked out of her father's tavern. All over the county, men used to talk about her captivating eyes, seductive smile, raven hair, long legs, and striking bosom. Peddlers would go out of their way to visit her and then brag about how good it was."

Caulfield stood quietly staring at the merchant for a long time, his jaw working, his face reddening. As the silence lengthened, his men also quieted and it became deathly silent around the campfire. The smile on Grenough's face slowly disappeared as he began to comprehend that his last words had somehow changed the situation.

Geoffrey Caulfield turned to Wend, anger smoldering in his eyes like the hot coals of a campfire. The highwayman reached down to his belt and pulled out a pistol, reversed it, and offered it to Wend. "Eckert, if you have the stuff to shoot a man when you are looking directly into his eyes, I'll not stand in your way."

Wend stood up and took the pistol in hand. He looked down at Grenough and saw, for the first time ever, abject fear in the man's eyes.

The merchant screamed at Caulfield, "For God's sake, you can't let him do this!"

Caulfield simply stared at Grenough, his face grimly set.

Wend cocked the pistol. Then he had a sudden thought. He reached down and touched the tip of the pistol's barrel to Grenough's cheek, right where the long scar ran from his ear to the edge of his mouth.

"Grenough, you know why I'm going to kill you. But there's one more thing you need to add to the list before I pull the trigger: I know it was an auburn-haired camp girl named Mary Fraser who gave you this scar. I've added her anguish to your debt."

Grenough's eyes and mouth opened wide at the sound of Mary's name. His face turned red. He exclaimed, "Oh my God! What is she to you?"

"I made her a woman long before you tried to take advantage of her."

Wend raised the pistol and aimed between Grenough's eyes, which now seemed to be bulging out of their sockets.

Then Wend had an idea. He lowered the pistol's barrel until it pointed at the center of Grenough's chest and squeezed the trigger. The sound of the shot echoed around the camp. A small hole appeared in the merchant's chest and almost instantly blood began to ooze from the wound.

Caulfield stared at the wound for a moment and asked, "Eckert, why in God's name did you shoot him there instead of the head?"

But it was Grenough who answered. With great effort he shook his head, as if trying to throw off the pain. "Don't you understand? He wanted me to suffer, to feel the death spreading over me."

Wend spoke through gritted teeth. "That's right, Grenough; I wanted you to know it was happening. Just like my mother and father and brother and sister did. Just like those poor Indians at Conestoga and Baker's Tavern who were hacked to death for your profit. Just like my friend Charlie Sawak's son did when Bratton shot him in the back and then scalped him while he still lived."

Grenough opened his lips to speak again, but instead of words, blood erupted from his mouth and flowed down his chin. With great effort he spit out a copious amount and, in halting words, said to Caulfield, "Now do you believe me? You see I was right. Eckert is a stone-hearted man who kills without the slightest hesitation or regret." He gasped for breath, and said almost to himself, "I should have had Bratton kill him when he was still a callow youth."

And with that, Richard Grenough fell over on his side, his face on the ground right in front of the fire, his eyes wide open and staring into the fire.

Wend looked at the corpse and said to no one in particular. "I hope the last thing he saw was the flames, for its certain he'll spend eternity in the fires of hell."

Caulfield reached over and carefully took the pistol from Wend's hand. Then his eyes met Wend's, a grim look on his face. "Damned if I didn't misjudge you, Eckert. You are a far harder man than I could ever have imagined. Few men can kill as easily and coldly as you did."

Wend returned Caulfield's stare. Then he said, "I came by that hardness because of Grenough. It was living with the knowledge of his evil for fifteen years which changed a naïve boy into a stone-hearted man." Wend thought for a moment. "Now perhaps I can go back to my family and learn to soften my heart."

The two men stood there in silence for a long moment.

Then Quinn broke the quiet. "What about McCrae, Cap'n? I say we let him throw in with us. He'd be a useful man."

Caulfield looked at McCrae. "Do you want to ride with us, Trooper McCrae? It's a hard life, one step ahead of the gallows, but it does have its rewards."

McCrae didn't answer Caulfield immediately. Instead he turned to Wend. "Eckert, have you been keeping that ledger on me we talked about back at Wheeling? Is there anything you're holding against me? I don't want to spend my life in fear of you like Grenough."

Wend walked slowly over to McCrae. He tried to smile through his swollen lips, but he wasn't sure the effort was successful. He said, "There's only one minor thing." Then, without warning, he hit the former trooper square in the face with every bit of strength he could muster.

McCrae fell over backwards. Blood flowed from his nose and lips.

Wend said, "Now I'd say your ledger is clear."

Caulfield grinned and helped McCrae to his feet. "Trooper, Eckert seems to have taken payment in kind."

McCrae nodded to Caulfield. "Aye, and now that's done, I'm with you, Cap'n."

Caulfield smiled. "All right, McCrae: Your first job is to strip the bodies bare and then get them lashed onto their horses. We'll dump them into the Shenandoah before dawn. He turned to the black man and said, "Here, Isaac, give McCrae a hand."

Meanwhile, the rest of the band had joined Sarah in going through the camp baggage, collecting everything useful.

Sarah herself came up to Caulfield, several small bags in her hands. "I found all this coin around the baggage, Cap'n. I ain't never seen so much money in one place; no sir I haven't, even at my old master's house, and that's no lie." She handed the bags to Caulfield.

The highwayman turned to Wend. "We owe thanks to you, Eckert. If we hadn't heard your shot, we might never have come upon this bounty. It's just what we needed for a comfortable journey."

"Journey? May I ask where you're going?"

Caulfield smiled. "I think it's safe to confide in you since it's unlikely you'll tell the local sheriff about this night's work." He looked around at his men, now busy carrying their booty to horses. "We seem to have exhausted all of our opportunities here and in Fairfax. So we're heading south, Eckert; *far* to the south — indeed, all the way to Carolina. We hear the rice planters around Charleston are rich and ripe for the plucking." He thought a moment and winked at Wend. "And it's also said that the southern ladies are unmatched in their beauty." Caulfield waved his hand around the campsite. "But we need all the capital we can get for expenses along the way and your friend Grenough has provided it. We'll cross the river tomorrow and be on our way."

Wend nodded and said sincerely, "I never thought I'd say this, but I wish you luck, Caulfield."

"Yes, we'll need it to go that far without running into trouble along the road." Then he thought a moment. "But, the fact is, you'll be clear of suspicion for this night's work. When the sheriff finds this site, he's going to immediately blame it all on us. It's the logical conclusion for him. And it will be days until those bodies wash up somewhere, if they're ever found. In any case, the sheriff will be hunting us, but we'll be long gone."

Wend posed the question which had been bothering him. "I'm indebted to you, Caulfield. But I'm puzzled about one thing: Why did you take my part against Grenough? You would have been just as well off if he had killed me."

A sly smile came across the highwayman's face. "You flatter yourself, Eckert. It wasn't about you at all."

"Not about me?"

"For God's sake, Eckert, it's about your wife."

"My wife? I don't understand."

Caulfield looked off into the night for a long moment, then sighed and locked his eyes with Wend's. "No, Dutchman, I expect you don't. And I'll not stand here trying to explain. Let's just say that I don't want so elegant a lady to face the hardships of life without a husband to provide for her." Then he broke into a wide grin. "Besides, Eckert, I've found that your wife has a finely honed sense of humor with which to entertain a man."

While they were talking, Quinn had approached and stood beside Caulfield. He laughed out loud at his boss's last comment. "Fine sense of humor? Hell, Cap'n, I'd say it was pointed; pointed as a knife!"

Caulfield's head snapped around to look at Quinn. For a brief second Wend saw a flash of anger in his eyes and thought for a moment that Caulfield would lash out at his henchman. But then he took a deep breath and regained his composure. He turned back to Wend.

"Eckert, I'll leave it at that. Perhaps if you want further explanation you should talk to your wife."

"Talk to Peggy?"

Caulfield stared at Wend for a short moment, then said, "Yes. Now look, I don't have the time or inclination to continue this conversation. We have much to do before dawn. And you need to get home to your warm bed. It would not do for you to be seen on the road tonight." He paused, then continued, "So gather up your weapons and your horse and leave us to our work."

A quarter of an hour later Wend stood in the road, holding The Mare's reins. He had found his rifle, which he had dropped in the fight with Bratton, and had walked back to where he had left the horse. Now as he prepared to mount, he looked back toward Grenough's campsite. The fire had been put out and all was dark. As he watched, the band of highwaymen began to emerge from the woods to the road, mounted on their horses. They were shadowy figures in the night, barely discernable with the moon temporarily behind a cloud. But Wend could make out two led packhorses carrying supplies salvaged from Grenough's baggage. Another two led horses carried the bodies of Grenough and Bratton strapped over their saddles. As he watched, the gang headed eastward toward the river.

Then a lone figure, mounted on a tall horse, emerged from the bush. From his stature and riding posture Wend could tell that it was Caulfield. Suddenly the moon reappeared, bathing the highwayman and his magnificent animal in light. He had pulled up the horse in the middle of the road and sat there looking toward Wend. Even at that distance the moonlight reflected off of his blond hair and fair-skinned face, making them stand out against the blackness of his clothing. Suddenly a gust of wind blew Caulfield's cape out like a streaming flag from the staff of a ship at sea. The vision lasted for a brief second, then Caulfield reached up and swept his hat into the air and waved it toward Wend. In a second he returned it to his head and immediately touched the stallion with his spurs, turned the horse toward the river, and then, bringing him to the gallop, followed in the wake of his compatriots. Horse and rider were visible for a few seconds, then the moon slipped behind a cloud momentarily and, when it reemerged, Caulfield had disappeared around a bend in the road.

* * *

Wend mounted and turned The Mare homeward. His face still ached from McCrae's blow. But his mind was preoccupied with Caulfield's last words.

"Perhaps if you want further explanation, you should talk to your wife."

He was at a loss to understand what that could mean. Then suddenly it dawned on him: *Had Caulfield and Peggy had a dalliance while he had been away with the militia?* The thought hit him so hard that he pulled up The Mare in astonishment, to work through the idea. In all their years of marriage, he had never thought for a minute of Peggy with another man. *But was a new love the reason for Peggy's distance in recent months? Was that a factor in her refusal to accept Johann into the family?*

While they were stopped, The Mare suddenly became skittish and snorted, tossing her head; she pranced in the road, turning sideways in the wagon track. It brought Wend out of his reverie and he pulled her around and touched the animal with his heels to get her started again. But as they rode, she bobbed her head and snorted several more times and then tried to turn her head to look back.

Wend knew the horse was trying to tell him something.

Were they being followed? Wend pulled her up again and looked back, scanning the darkness; but nothing was to be seen.

They went another quarter mile with the animal still nervous. Wend kept looking back, and then, as they started around a turn, he saw a shape in the darkness behind. It was indistinct and in a split second blended into the bush alongside the road. But it had definitely been there.

There was no longer any doubt that they were being followed.

Wend looked around and made out a fallen tree trunk along the road. He stopped The Mare and dismounted, then led her into the bush and tied her to a tree about ten yards off the road. He pulled out his pistols and rifle and took cover behind the fallen tree. He steadied the rifle on the log and sighted down the road.

As he waited, he tried to fathom who might be following them. Had Grenough had another companion who had hidden out in the bush and was now attempting to take revenge? It seemed most improbable. Had Caulfield changed his mind and decided to eliminate the only witness who might tell the sheriff what had happened at Grenough's camp? That was even more unlikely. No explanation he could think of made any sense.

As he lay in wait, searching his brain, he suddenly heard a noise in the distance. He froze, concentrating to identify the sound. Then he realized it was horse hooves pounding at the gallop. There was more than one horse and they were coming down the road toward the ferry landing; coming from the opposite direction of his pursuer. *God, what riders could possibly have business on the road at this hour?*

Wend gritted his teeth. *Lord, would this night ever be over?* Would there be no end to surprises and new dangers? He was tired and his face throbbed in pain. He found himself shaking in frustration and, he admitted to himself, in plain fear. Wend sighed and willed himself to be calm and think what to do. First, he must deal with the shadowy stalker following him. Then he would turn and face the horsemen coming from the north, ready to receive them, be they hostile or friendly.

Wend forced himself to concentrate on the sights of the rifle and scan the road. And as he did so, his pursuer came into view, still a shapeless form in the night. Wend cocked the firelock and gently wrapped his finger around the trigger. He would hold fire until the follower was close enough to be identified and he could not miss.

As he waited for the stalker to close the distance, Wend steeled himself to ignore the sound of the relentlessly approaching hooves as they echoed through the forest.

CHAPTER TWENTY-THREE
All Quiet on Eckert Ridge

Peggy came awake in her chair at the clanging of the pewter cup dropping from her hand to the planking of the porch. After helping Sally and her children settle down in Donegal's rooms in the barracks, Peggy had come back to the house, gotten herself another drink, and then returned to her porch chair. Now, after rubbing sleep from her eyes, she looked over and saw that Johann was still at watch in front of the house.

Peggy picked up the cup. Johann, hearing her move, looked over and she asked, "How long was I asleep?"

"I'd say nearly an hour, Mrs. Eckert." He looked up into the sky and said, "It's at least three hours since Joshua and Donegal left; still maybe four hours to dawn." Then he pointed his hand down the drive. "Wind has died; mist starting to form."

She looked over toward the shop and saw he was right; there was still some moonlight, but the shop was already partially obscured, looking ethereal in the night. It would be one of those mornings when the ridge and the lowlands around it would be blanketed in ground fog.

Then suddenly Johann rose and cupped his hands to his ears. Peggy tensed in the chair. "What is it?" she asked.

"Horses to the south! Coming at the gallop!"

Peggy stood up and put the cup in her chair. "How many horses?"

"More than one." He continued listening, then took a few hesitant steps forward. "Horses have stopped at bottom of the drive." Then he surrendered to curiosity and broke into a run down the hill.

Peggy grabbed the lantern, descended the stairs, and hurried over to the shop where it would be easier to look down the sloping drive. One hand grasping a post of the lean-to, she strained to see through the mist. For a few minutes there was nothing at all and anxiety swelled within her. Then she saw two figures emerge, ghostlike, leading horses: Joshua and Donegal, walking wearily. She took a few steps toward them then called out, "What happened?"

Joshua said, "What happened is that I got stiff as hell, riding all the way down to Ashby's and back, right after travelin' all day with those wagons. And my damn left leg has commenced to be hurtin' like the devil."

Simon said, "And I left my bride to settle in alone in her new home. What's she going to think of me?"

Peggy said, "For God's sake, stop playing with me: What about Wend? Where is Wend?"

Baird and Donegal exchanged glances and then Joshua casually raised his left hand over his shoulder with the thumb pointing behind him. "You'll be findin' him back there."

Peggy could stand it no longer; she hitched up her skirts and walked rapidly down the drive, the damp mists swirling around her. After a few steps she sighted Johann leading the black mare. And slightly behind, Wend walked stiffly. He had the holsters of his pistols draped over his right shoulder and carried the short rifle in his left hand. Then, in the light of the lantern, she saw his face; his lips and cheek on the left were swollen, giving him a lopsided look.

She held the lantern high and saw dried blood all over the swollen side of his face. "My God, what happened to you?"

Wend just smiled and the mouth looking even more lopsided. Then, ignoring her question, he said, "See, I told you I would come back. You should learn not to doubt me."

"For God's sake, tell me what happened to your face!"

"A very large Irishman hit me with a horse pistol."

She turned and walked alongside him. Soon they came up to Joshua and Donegal, who had stopped in front of the shop and were loosening their girths.

Wend turned to Johann. "Son, take all the horses down to the stable. Give them grain and then let Boots and Whiteface loose in the pasture. But leave The Mare in her stall."

Peggy turned to Joshua and pleaded, "Will you please tell me what happened? Wend is playing riddles with me."

Baird shrugged and said, "Damned if I know the whole of it. We rode down towards the ferry and a couple of miles short of the river we found Wend crouched behind a log, fixin' to shoot that dog."

"Dog? What dog?"

Baird pointed past The Mare. Peggy looked and saw a large, brown-coated dog sitting quietly on its haunches in the drive.

Wend said, "Its Grenough's dog. He's dead and the dog followed me. In the darkness, I thought it was a man stalking me. Just before I pulled the trigger, I realized what it was."

She said, "That's the ugliest dog I've ever seen."

"Yes, but he grows on you. And he can do some very useful things."

"What's his name?"

"Never heard it." Then Wend looked at her for a long moment and said, "You might be interested to know that Matt Bratton is dead. He jumped me in the darkness while I was creeping up on Grenough. I shot him with a pistol and finished him with my knife."

Peggy shrugged. "I have no regret for him. He forfeited any feelings I had long ago." Then she asked, "But you were still able to kill Grenough?"

Wend looked at her for a long time. Then his injured face contorted into a tight smile. "Yes; yes I did. He is burning in hell. But it was only by the good grace of your friend Caulfield."

Peggy was thunderstruck. "Caulfield? Geoffrey Caulfield? He was there? I thought he and his men were chased out of the county by Sheriff Smith."

"They were passing through the county on their way south to Carolina. They heard the shot which hit Bratton and then when I had been captured by Grenough and his man McCrae, they intervened just in time to save me from being shot."

Peggy was at a loss for words. She looked at him and saw that his face had turned deadly grim. "But I don't understand. Why would he save your life?"

"Perhaps you should tell me why. He said it was in admiration of you."

"He said that about me?"

"Yes, and the way he said it made me extraordinarily jealous. It made me think that something had occurred between you and he while I was gone."

"Wend Eckert, are you *jealous*?"

"Perhaps you would care to explain why I should think differently."

"My God, you *are* jealous!"

"Can you give me reason why I shouldn't be?"

Peggy looked at Wend and saw genuine anger burning in his eyes. But Peggy felt tears of joy welling up in her own. Wend *really* was mad and jealous at the vision of her and Geoffrey together! Suddenly the love of him surged through her and for the first time in her life she was convinced that he felt the same. She moved close to him and took both his hands in hers. Looking up into his eyes, she said, "My love, my *dear, dear* husband, please listen: It's true that Geoffrey tried to proposition me, but I showed him, in a way that he could not possibly misunderstand, that his advances were completely unwelcome. You must believe me!"

Wend looked at her for a long time with hard eyes. Then he said sternly, "I'm not sure what to think. It seems we should discuss this tomorrow, after we've all rested." He took his hands from hers and continued, "I must see to The Mare. She behaved magnificently tonight and I want to care for her myself." Then he turned and walked toward the stable. The brown dog rose from its haunches and trailed after him.

Peggy Eckert smiled warmly at her man as he strode toward the stable. Then she thought about what he had said and concluded she had absolutely no intention of spending any more time discussing Geoffrey Caulfield with Wend. She stood thinking a moment and then smiled to herself. She knew exactly the way to banish all thought of the highwayman and infidelity from her husband's mind.

* * *

Wend arrived at the stable just as Johann was letting Boots and Whiteface out into the pasture. He put his hand on the boy's shoulder. "That was a fine thing you did, keeping Peggy company all night, lad, and I'm grateful. But now it's time for you to get some sleep. Despite everything that's gone on tonight, we'll still have to get some work done tomorrow."

Johann smiled and said "Good night, Father," and walked off toward the barracks. Wend thought to himself: *This is the last night my son sleeps with the hands and apprentices. When I talk with Peggy, I'll insist that he move into the house.*

Johann had brought a lighted candle lantern and Wend moved it to where The Mare stood in her stall. He fed her some more oats and then gave her a quick brushing. The dog sat watching as Wend worked.

Then The Cat walked into the stable. He spied the dog and froze; his back arched and his tail went straight up in the air and puffed out. He hunkered down and hissed at the canine. In response, the dog went into a crouch, his tail straight down, ears back, his mouth formed into a teeth-bared snarl. Then he lowered his head, emitted a low growl, and took a step toward the hissing feline.

Wend watched as the standoff persisted for a few seconds. He expected the cat to lash out and mercilessly claw the dog's eyes and snout, as he had seen him do often enough. Instead, he was mightily surprised when The Cat simply turned and, with a show of great casualness, walked off into the dark recesses of the stable. For his part, the dog let out another growl, watched The Cat depart, and then curled up on the ground. Wend said to himself: *It seems there may be a new order in the animal world of Eckert Ridge.*

He finished grooming The Mare and then led her out through the yard to the pasture gate. Standing next to her head, he said quietly, "We've been through a lot together in the last thirteen years and you've always done your best for me. But now I've finished Grenough and I'll saddle you no more. You're the queen of the herd and you can spend the rest of your days bossing all the other horses around to your content."

He unbuckled her halter and The Mare snorted and shook her head as if acknowledging his words. Then, without hesitation, she trotted off, intent on finding out where the herd was grazing. The big black disappeared into the darkness and mist in just a few seconds.

Then Wend heard Peggy's voice behind him. "With those long legs, she moves with an elegance possessed by few horses."

Wend turned around and saw his wife standing with a bucket in her right hand and a bundle under her left arm. He said, "Yes she does and we're lucky to have her as a brood mare. She has borne us some fine foals." Then he said, "I had expected you would be abed by now."

Peggy walked into the stable, pulled a stool away from the wall and put the bucket down beside it. She tossed the bundle onto a pile of hay in the corner. "Here, sit on the stool; I'm going to wash all the blood off your face."

"Wouldn't it be better to do that in the house?"

"Be quiet and sit down."

Wend sat and she began to carefully, gently wipe his face. Then she said, "I met Johann on my way down here. I told him to bring his things to the house in the morning and move in with Bernd."

Surprised, Wend looked into her eyes for a moment and said, "I'm very grateful for that."

Peggy said, "He earned my respect tonight. And Alice tells me all the children love him."

She finished cleaning Wend, then walked over to the hay pile and unrolled the bundle. Wend saw that it was a pair of blankets. Peggy spread one out over the hay. Then she turned and looked at Wend in a way he hadn't seen since he left for the war. She smiled and said softly, enticingly, "You know I always do my best work in stables."

Then she settled herself on the blanket and motioned for Wend to come to her.

Wend didn't hesitate. He blew out the lantern, then joined Peggy in the hay and put his arms around her. Their lips met in a long embrace. In a few moments they had undressed and Peggy had wrapped the second blanket around them.

* * *

Much later, Peggy snuggled against Wend, both of them warm and drowsy and about to succumb to sleep. Then suddenly she lifted her head, coming wide awake. "Wend, there's something I forgot to tell you!"

Wend said sleepily, "Why don't you tell me in the morning?"

"It's important. Listen now: Evan McLeod rode in while you were talking with Northcutt. He was carrying news to all the farms along our road; news that was brought down from the north by relay riders. Angus sent him to spread the word the moment they got it in Winchester." She paused and gathered her thoughts. "There's been a riot up near Boston; it was in a place called Lexington, back on the nineteenth. A column of Redcoats marching from Boston fired on militia mustered on the town's common."

Wend shook the drowsiness out of his mind. "You say they *fired* on the militia?"

"Yes, and the militia fired back. Some people were killed. And then the British soldiers marched on to a town named Concord and there was another fight with the militia there."

Wend was totally alert now. "What else did he tell you?"

"Not much, except the militia from all around Massachusetts rose up and chased the British back into Boston, killing many of them along the way." She reached up and pulled some hay from her raven hair. "What do you think it means?"

"You're right, it could be very serious."

"Well, do you think it will affect us in Virginia?"

"You know how many people are upset with the Crown and Parliament. Remember, that's what Northcutt was here to see me about. The governor is worried that the Whigs are ready to defy the government. This disturbance in Boston could be the spark which sets off violence here in Virginia."

Peggy sighed. "Well, we're sure to hear more news from Boston in the next few days. Maybe now that blood has been shed, people will think hard about all this and calm down before worse happens."

Wend nodded and simply said, "Perhaps," although he didn't think that was at all likely.

Peggy said, "Anyway, we can't do anything about it. And it's time to get some sleep." She put her head on Wend's chest and closed her eyes.

Wend said, "Maybe we should get up and go into the house. We wouldn't want to sleep too late and have everybody see us walking to the house in broad daylight."

Peggy opened her eyes and looked up at Wend, a coy smile on her face. "That wouldn't be all bad; at least then everyone here on the farm would know the feud between the Eckerts was finally and completely settled." She closed her eyes and snuggled more closely.

Almost immediately Wend heard her begin the regular breathing of deep sleep. He continued to think about the events in Boston, trying to guess their import and how they might affect Virginia; but he soon gave up as the weariness of the long day finally overcame him. In a few minutes he joined his wife in the sleep of exhaustion.

AUTHOR'S NOTES

AND ACKNOWLEDGMENTS

Lord Dunmore's Folly was originally planned to be completed and published in late 2014 to bring the adventures of Wend Eckert up to the end of the colonial period. Historically, it was intended to tell the story of the little-known border conflict that occupied the attention of Virginians for most of 1774, at the same time events in Massachusetts were building to the outbreak of rebellion. At first blush, the historical events seemed limited in scope and rather straightforward. It also seemed fairly simple to weave an intriguing fictional story about Wend Eckert, Richard Grenough, and the other characters of the Forbes Road Series around the war's key action. Alas, researching and writing this novel was somewhat like the home improvement project you expect to whip out in a weekend and, with complications and interruptions, ends up taking months to complete. The more deeply I delved into the history, the more nuance and complexity showed up. It didn't help that most published accounts of Dunmore's War dated from the 1800's and early 1900's and were contradictory in many details. Also, as I developed the plot and subplots and dealt with the numerous "loose ends" hanging out from Forbes Road and Conestoga Winter, it became clear that telling the tale would mean a longer and more involved story than originally envisioned. Accordingly, the project stretched out and it became evident that the original deadline could not be met. In view of the delay, the novella *The Camp Follower Affair* was researched and written to tell the story of Bouquet's campaign of 1764 which ended Pontiac's War. Thus Lord Dunmore's Folly, finally completed, becomes the fourth and concluding volume of the series, and carries Wend et al to the very outbreak of the Revolution.

The following are notes and comments on certain aspects of the novel and the associated history. As usual, I point out where significant deviations from actual events and timeline were made to facilitate flow of the story.

<u>McDonald's Raid</u>. In the course of doing the research, it became clear there are many ambiguities and conflicts in accounts of the expedition which constituted the first military operation of the war.

Location of McDonald's landing. The historical accounts are divided; several simply say that the landing was at the mouth of Captina Creek. Others indicate it was opposite the mouth of Fishing Creek (Now called Fish Creek), which is several miles downstream of the Captina. I chose the latter because boats beached along Captina would be more subject to discovery by hunting parties or other Indian travelers, particularly since a major trail passed through the area. Pulling the boats up into heavy bush along a more remote part of the Ohio itself would present a greater chance of preserving surprise while the battalion advanced toward Wakatomica.

Company commanders. There is also ambiguity about the number of companies and their commanders on the raid. Looking at the different accounts, it appears likely that there were eight companies, with commanders as follows: Daniel Morgan, James Wood, Henry Hoagland, Michael Cresap, Senior, Michael Cresap, Junior, Hancock Lee, Abraham Teagarden, and George Rogers Clark. The real question is about Clark: While it seems clear that he was along on the raid, it is uncertain whether he was a company commander or was fulfilling a role such as guide or scout. The book *Lord Dunmore's Little War of 1774* (See reference list below), shows the muster lists of each company in Dunmore's army, and attempts to identify which were associated with the different operations. One muster role shows Clark in command of a company and states it was along on the raid. Accordingly, I've included him as a likely company leader.

Results of the raid. The objective of the expedition was a damaging strike against the Shawnee which would cause them to restrict war party raids and possibly convince tribal leaders to accept peace terms rather than face a major invasion. Instead McDonald got bogged down in negotiations. Although contemporary newspaper reports of the expedition were positive, the historical judgement has been that it was essentially a failure; in fact, after the raid, Shawnee war party raids increased and the chiefs became resigned to full scale war. However, the fact is that McDonald did destroy several towns, the associated crops, and his advance forced the inhabitants to flee, which undoubtedly caused some disruption of the overall Shawnee war effort. This writer had a discussion with Glenn F. Williams, Senior Historian at the U.S. Army Center of Military History, whose forthcoming book, *Dunmore's War, The Last Conflict of America's Colonial Period*, is likely to become the authoritative narrative of the war. During that conversation, Mr. Williams stated that he felt the raid was a tactical success but a strategic failure. That assessment generally matches my own conclusions.

Historical Characters. During the period of Dunmore's War, the border area of Virginia and Pennsylvania was richly populated with individuals who would later play noteworthy roles in the Revolution and early United States history.

William Crawford. Crawford was an influential figure on the border throughout the colonial period and the Revolution, in part because of his relationship with Washington. During the Revolutionary War, he reached the rank of colonel in the Continental Army, raising and commanding a regiment of the Virginia Line. Stewart's Crossing is now Connellsville, PA; the town maintains a replica of Crawford's cabin as described in Chapter Two. For this narrative, Crawford's activities during Dunmore's War have been altered in a couple of aspects. First, his trip to Wills Creek (Cumberland, MD) is fictional; at the time he was at his home or surveying in the Ohio Country. However, this deviation facilitated his introduction to readers and to Wend, and permitted his use as a narrator of past events along Braddock Road. A second deviation regards his connection with the construction of Fort Fincastle. In this case I changed the timeline somewhat: Historically, McDonald's force, not Crawford's, arrived first at Wheeling and laid out what would become Fort Fincastle. Crawford's detachment arrived somewhat later but performed the major construction of the fort. This reversal was made simply to streamline flow of the narrative. Crawford's punitive raid on Seekunk, while touched on lightly in the narrative, was a much harder hitting affair than McDonald's attack on Wakatomica, with more Indian casualties and quite significant destruction. The raid earned Crawford abiding hatred among the tribes of the Ohio Country and would ultimately lead to fatal retribution when a border raid he led late in the Revolutionary War went bad and he was captured and burned at the stake.

Simon Girty. Readers of the Forbes Road Series will remember Girty from a brief appearance in *The Camp Follower Affair*. Little known or discussed today outside the circle of history enthusiasts, he once had a major place in the pantheon of American villains, only slightly below Benedict Arnold. When the Revolutionary War broke out, he initially sided with the Whig cause and performed well. But, perceiving that his efforts weren't receiving due credit, he switched to the British side and was accused, rightly or wrongly, of many dastardly acts against settlers along the border. Most grievously, he was alleged to have had been in a position to save Crawford from the stake, but desisted from taking action. In recent years, historians have treated him more evenhandedly. My use of him in the story is generally consistent with his participation in Dunmore's War. He did play an important function as a scout and courier and was particularly important in carrying communications between Dunmore and Lewis. One account mentions that he was sent down into the Ohio Country by Connolly to ascertain the progress of McDonald's Raid, where he encountered a small group of militia returning from Wakatomica. That story is the genesis of Girty's fictional meeting with Wend and his ragtag detachment in Chapter Fifteen.

Simon Butler/Kenton. Kenton became one of the most notable figures in Western Virginia/ Kentucky/Ohio history, ultimately settling in Ohio. He was with Boone for a period in Kentucky and at one point he was captured by the Shawnee. Surviving ritual torture, Kenton was adopted into the tribe. He subsequently escaped and participated as a scout in George Rogers Clark's 1778 expedition against the British in Illinois. Kenton fought in most of the border Indian wars subsequent to the Revolution, including Anthony Wayne's 1794 campaign which climaxed with the Battle of Fallen Timbers. He was later appointed a brigadier general in the Ohio militia. The fictional relationship with Wend generally highlights the essence of Kenton's service in Dunmore's War, including the fact that he and Girty were friends and often worked together in scouting and courier assignments.

The Zane Family. Ebenezer Zane, born 1747, first laid claim to the area near the mouth of Wheeling Creek in 1769, and by 1773 had settled his family there in a fortified house. He was accompanied by younger brothers Jonathan, Silas, Andrew and their families. By 1774, other settlers had moved nearby; the Zanes are thus credited with founding Wheeling, WV. At the time of our story, Ebenezer was around twenty-seven and Jonathan was twenty-five.

"Kid sister" Betty Zane was born in 1765 and thus was nine at the time of the Dunmore conflict. She became a legend of the Revolutionary War by her actions when Fort Henry (the renamed Fort Fincastle) was under siege in 1782 by Indians supporting the British cause. When the garrison ran low on gunpowder, she reputedly made a heroic dash from the fort to a house where a supply of powder had been left behind and fetched the powder back to the fort in her apron, thus enabling the militia and settlers to outlast their besiegers. Betty was the subject of writer Zane Grey, best known for his western novels (*Riders of the Purple Sage*), who published the historical novel *Betty Zane* in 1903. Grey was Betty's great-grandnephew. Although I credit her with nursing Wend's wounded mare, it's likely that the girl was away at school in Philadelphia during Dunmore's War.

After independence, the Zane family played a significant role in advancing settlement of Ohio, including founding the town of Martins Ferry and cutting a wilderness road into the interior. Zanesville, OH commemorates their activities.

<u>Highwaymen in Colonial America</u>. Highwaymen on the model of those prevalent in England were rare in the colonies. As illustrated by the discussions between Caulfield and his henchman Quinn, the number of well-off travelers and coach lines was too low to make the profession lucrative. However, there were indeed a few. The most famous was a scoundrel named William Parsons, who served as the inspiration for Caulfield. The son of an English baronet, he was transported to Virginia for gambling debts and the crimes of theft and forgery. Based on his well-born background and cultured manners, he was able to elicit the sympathy of Lord Fairfax, who extended him the hospitality of his household and the use of a well-bred horse. Parsons repaid his benefactor by skipping out with the mount and engaging in thievery along the roads of Virginia. Eventually he accumulated sufficient funds to buy passage back to England, where his further and more serious misdeeds led to his death on the gallows at the age of thirty-four. As opposed to Parsons, Caulfield was, of course, born in the gutter, trained as a thief on the streets of London, and learned to practice the manners of the gentry as a house servant after being sentenced to bond slavery in America.

<u>References for Further Reading</u>. The following publications, among others, were useful in preparing this novel and are recommended for readers interested in the period of Dunmore's War.

Dunmore's War, The Last Conflict of America's Colonial Period, (Westholme Publishing, Scheduled Publication 2017), Glenn F. Williams.

Dunmore's New World: The Extraordinary Life of a Royal Governor in Revolutionary America, with Jacobites, Counterfeiters, Land Schemes, Shipwrecks, Scalping, Indian Politics, Runaway Slaves, and Two Illegal Royal Weddings, (University of Virginia Press, 2013), James Corbett David.

Documentary History of Dunmore's War, 1774 (Wisconsin Historical Society, 1905) Edited by Reuben Gold Thwaites and Louise Phelps Kellogg.

History of the Battle of Point Pleasant Fought Between White Men and Indians at the Mouth of the Great Kanawha River (Forgotten Books, 2012, Reprint of 1909 book), Virgil A. Lewis

A Colony Sprung from Hell: Pittsburgh and the Struggle for Authority on the Western Pennsylvania Frontier, 1744-1794 (The Kent State University Press, 2014) Daniel P. Barr

Point Pleasant 1774: Prelude to the American Revolution (Osprey Publishing, Ltd, 2014), John F. Winkler

Lord Dunmore's Little War of 1774: His Captains and Their Men Who Opened Up Kentucky & the West to American Settlement (Heritage Books, Inc. 2002) Warren Skidmore with Donna Kaminsky

Chronicles of Border Warfare (McClain Printing Company, 1998, Reprint of 1895 book), Alexander Scott Withers, Ed. Reuben Gold Thwaites

Notes on the Settlement and Indian Wars of the Western Parts of Virginia and Pennsylvania From 1763 to 1783 (Heritage Books, 2006, Reprint of 1912 book), Rev. Dr. Joseph Doddridge, Ed. John S. Ritenour and William T. Lindsay

The Shawnees and the War for America (Viking, 2007), Colin G. Calloway

Simon Girty Turncoat Hero: The Most Hated Man on the Early American Frontier (Flying Camp Press, 2008) Phillip W. Hoffman

Simon Kenton: His Life and Period 1755-1836 (Kessinger Publishing, Reprint of author published book, 1935), Edna Kenton

Stand and Deliver: A History of Highway Robbery (The History Press, 2001), David Brandon

Winchester, Virginia and Its Beginnings, (Heritage Books, 2007), Katherine Glass Greene.

Acknowledgements. I'm grateful to many individuals for their assistance in producing this concluding volume in Wend Eckert's colonial period adventures. Pamela Patrick White extended permission for the use of her painting, *Boundaries,* for the cover and promotional activity. Tony Rozwadowski of K Art and Design, Inc. took on the tough job of converting my sketch to the map of the Ohio Country which is displayed in the front section. Major John Chapman, USMC (Ret) provided support and a much appreciated first outside reading of the draft manuscript. Christine Charboneau performed a much needed and appreciated line edit of the text. My loving appreciation goes to my wife Cathy, who read and critiqued every chapter as they came off the keyboard and then dedicated herself, despite some challenging medical issues, to reading the full manuscript in two days in order to evaluate the impact of the complete story. Finally, I want to thank all the readers who have followed Wend and his friends through the first three books, contacted us through the website to express their appreciation for the stories, and advance their ideas for the future of the characters.

Robert J. Shade
Sunshine Hill Farm
Madison County, Virginia
August 2016

87913533R00272

Made in the USA
Middletown, DE
06 September 2018